10855177

THE COLLECTED EDITION

THE GREAT WORLD

The Great World

DAVID MALOUF

Chatto & Windus
LONDON

First published 1990 by Chatto & Windus

1 3 5 7 9 10 8 6 4 2

Copyright © David Malouf 1990

David Malouf has asserted his right under
the Copyright, Designs and Patents Act, 1988
to be identified as the author of this work

This collected edition published in
the United Kingdom in 1993 by
Chatto & Windus Limited
Random House, 20 Vauxhall Bridge Road, London SW1V 2SA

Random House Australia (Pty) Limited
20 Alfred Street, Milsons Point, Sydney,
New South Wales 2061, Australia

Random House New Zealand Limited
18 Poland Road, Glenfield,
Auckland 10, New Zealand

Random House South Africa (Pty) Limited
PO Box 337, Bergvlei, South Africa

Random House UK Limited Reg. No. 954009

A CIP catalogue record for this book
is available from the British Library

ISBN 0 7011 6122 1

Printed and bound in Great Britain by
Mackays of Chatham PLC, Chatham, Kent

I

1

People are not always kind, but the kind thing to say of Jenny was that she was simple.

Children whose mothers were cooking and found they were short of something, breadcrumbs or a kilo of flour, would set up a wail at the thought of having to go down to Keen's and fetch it. 'Aw no, mum! Why me? It's Brett's turn. Make Brett do it!'

It wasn't the walk they objected to, though it was far enough, down the hill and off the main road to the river, or even the interruption to their favourite programme on TV. It was the odd feeling you got when you stood on the doorstep with the bead curtain still clattering behind you and saw the old woman half-sprawled on the counter there, breathing like a big fish that had just been hauled out of the river and stranded. Sometimes she was asleep. You would have to poke a finger into the wool of her cardigan and she would start up and look around in a wild sort of way, then, when she saw that she knew you, give a wet smile.

But simple was the wrong word for her, or so smaller kids thought, because the real thing about Jenny, as she flopped about with her thick arms and shuffly slippers, was that she was likely to say things, and do things too, that you weren't expecting and could make neither head nor tail of.

They felt too a kind of doubt she raised about the order of things. She was ancient, over sixty, but grown-ups treated her as if she was six. You could tell that from the way they spoke to her.

Real children looked at Jenny Keen and she was neither a nice old lady nor a stranded fish, neither a grown-up nor another bigger kid. So what was simple about her?

She was slumped now with one elbow on the flaking sill, looking out across the yard, past the clothesline and the rotting pepper tree, to where her brother was sitting at the edge of the river, just where the bank shelved to the stream.

3

The river was wide, this side of it sunlit, the other in shadow. Digger had a line out and every now and then he jiggled it, but he wasn't fishing. When Digger does something he gets absorbed. The whole of him under the old felt hat is drawn to such a pitch of concentration you can feel it, *she* can, even at a distance; it can be frightening. What he was concentrating on now was the other feller's talk. The line was a bluff to make the talk or the listening easier.

She made a face. She pushed her tongue up under her lip and squinted. She rubbed the back of her head where the hair was hacked off short as a man's. 'C'mon Dig,' she said out loud. 'Givvus a break.'

The two men sat apart but had their heads together, you could see that: Digger in an old sweater that was loose at the elbows and had a couple of good-sized holes in it that she meant to mend; the other feller, Vic, in a smart-looking overcoat. He was the same age as Digger but looked younger because he took care of himself. He was always very well turned out. He sat now with his shoes, which were new and well polished, set down very carefully in the dirt. She noticed the shoes because each time he came they were different, he must have a dozen pairs.

She narrowed her eyes, trying to get the gist of what they were talking about – it was the third time he had been here this week. She couldn't actually hear anything, not at this distance, but if she really put her mind to it she could sometimes pick something up. Not always. But after a minute or two, with nothing coming through, she made a huffing sound, got up, went in behind the shelves of the store into the kitchen, and took a peek at the oven.

This was more like it. Scones. Scones were her long suit. They were coming on nicely.

She went back, leaned her elbows on the linoleum of the counter, and was just beginning to get comfortable when she saw that two magpies had flapped down and were perched now on the clothesline, shifting their heads from side to side in an abrupt, interested way and keeping watch. It was the end of any consolation she might have got out of the scones.

She had a war on with the magpies. She had lots of wars, but this was her fiercest and most continuous.

Big black-and-white brutes with sharp little eyes and even sharper beaks, she hated them, and wondered really what they had been put in the world for except to be a torment to smaller creatures. They strutted

4

about as if they owned the place and were just waiting to take over. As if they had been given control of it; to spy and patrol up and down and peck and punish. Black and white, like bloody nuns.

If she put out the baking-dish, for instance, where she'd just cut up the last of a bread pudding, they would all swoop down, a dozen or more, all jostling, and the little birds, the wrens and finches, would be too scared to come near. 'Get away,' she'd yell, and kick out with her boots. 'This isn't for you.'

But she couldn't be there all the time. She had housework to do and the shop to watch. They'd parade about then as if the yard was theirs, yodelling, muttering their magpie rosary. They'd sit on one of the clothesline stumps and shift their heads, following her every move. If she went out with a basketful of washing they'd go for her head, swoop and dive-bomb her the way they came down flapping and took the eyes out of baby lambs.

It was a war that had been going on for years. It was on a daily basis. Sometimes she won, sometimes they did. But there was only one of her and heaps of them, and they kept coming.

Occasionally an old feller would fall victim to one of the feral cats; or he'd choke on a lump of bread, or a kid with a slingshot would get him. But before you knew it September would be round and there would be babies again, except that these babies were as big as adults and just as fierce, but black, they were born black. So there was no way in the world that you could win.

She had a war on with cats as well, the ferals, but she had inherited that one. It wasn't personal. She kept it on out of loyalty to her mother, to stop the lazy buggers from lying down and sunning themselves in the flowerbeds and flattening the plants, though there were no plants much any more, just a few straggly gerbera, a rosebush or two and a patch of mint. It was partly to make up to her mother for letting the garden go that she kept after the cats.

They were huge. When they stretched out in their matted black or grey fur they were like old felt rugs with just the red of an eye in them, that could suddenly come alive and snarl or show a claw. 'Garn,' she'd tell them, 'don't try that on me!' Every now and then, out of habit, she would slosh a bucket of mop-water at them.

These were her open wars. The others she had to be cunning about.

The young fellers and their girls, for instance, who came into the shop just to tease and make a nuisance of themselves, picking things up

and putting them down again just to aggravate. She had to stop herself
from yelling at them, telling them off. 'Look youse, if yer gunna buy
that tinna jam just buy it, don't stand there chuckin' it about.' But if
you did that there would be trouble. For one thing, they were
customers, and for another they were dangerous. They had spiked
hair, green some of them, and the girls were all in black like widows,
and they had earrings, even the boys did, and tattoos. 'How much
is this?' one of them would ask while another one got off with a
Picnic bar or a packet of crisps. 'See ya,' they'd call, letting the door
slam, and she would shout after them 'Drop dead!' – but under her
breath.

Her fourth war, which she also had to wage in silence, was with this
feller Vic. It went back years.

'So waddazee want?' she had demanded when he first turned up.
'Who *is* 'e?'

Dumb, that was. She knew no better in those days. That wasn't the
way to find out.

'A bit of a chat.' That's all Digger would tell her. ''E's a mate.'

A mate! Men had mates. She had never even had a friend. All she had
ever had was Digger, and that's just what she had against *him*, this Vic.
He butted in. He got between them. He took Digger off.

The first time he turned up she thought he was a ghost, he was that
washed-out looking. As pale as potatoes.

'Who are you?' she challenged.

He was standing there in an old army coat that fell to his ankles, all
chapped and unshaven, with a short back and sides and his blondy hair
sticking up in peaks. You could have blown him over with just a puff.
She was younger then. Pity she hadn't done it and got him out of the
way once and for all, and saved herself the next forty years. He would
have gone over like ninepins.

'I'm Vic,' he said, as if he expected her to know.

If he wasn't a ghost she didn't know him from Adam.

She looked at him hard and saw that for all his being such a tuppence
worth of God-help-us he was pretty keen on himself. 'Digger about?'
he asked, casting little looks around and ignoring her.

'Of course 'e's about,' she snapped. ''E's off somewhere.' She jerked
her head towards the river, not to be too specific (let him do his own
finding), and stood with her hands shoved down into the pockets of
her cardigan and watched him trudge off with his ears sticking out and

6

the coat hanging from his thin shoulders. She knew where Digger was, all right. He was out the back.

'So waddazee want?' she demanded when Digger appeared at last and saw him mooching about there under the she-oaks. She wasn't going to be fobbed off with this business about mates. 'What's 'e after?'

Digger's face clouded and he was a long time replying. 'Nothing much,' he said, his eyes away there. He didn't seem all that anxious to go down and meet him.

'Listen, Dig,' she had said, lowering her voice, 'I could get ridduv 'im.'

'No,' Digger said after a minute. 'He's all right. He's a mate.'

He went down across the yard, ducking under the line, that was low on its props, to where the fellow in the coat had turned and could see him. He looked so forlorn there, for all his tallness, that she might have felt sorry for him; but she had sensed something in him, first thing at the door, that made her wary. He was stronger than he let on.

She watched them face one another.

They stood a long way apart. Digger was nodding his head and she could tell from the pitch of his shoulders what his eyes would be like; he was an open book, Digger. Then he moved, touched this Vic very lightly on the shoulder and they turned away together under the she-oaks.

She couldn't tell at that distance whether they were talking or just sitting in silence.

If it was talk it had the tense, quivering quality of long silence.

She was a pretty good judge of silence. If you lived with Digger you had to be.

Since then he had been turning up on a regular basis every three or four months – till these last weeks.

It was always the same. Digger afterwards would be as silent as the grave; he couldn't be reached, you couldn't get through to him. She'd flop about like a wounded bird, not knowing what to say or do that would bring him back to the table or into the house even, he'd got so far off. She would try to be quiet with the dishes, but each time her hands let her down and they would clash and bang. When he laid his knife and fork down and went out, she would watch him wandering about there in the moonlight, walking up and down under the clothesline, lost in himself.

7

Digger had other visitors, also mates, but they didn't affect him the way Vic did, and they didn't come so often. That's what she had against him.

Ern, one was called. Another was a jolly, one-armed fellow called Douggy Bramson. He was the one she felt easiest with. For one thing, he had a bit of conversation and wasn't afraid to share it with you, he enjoyed a joke. Then there was the sleeve tucked up neatly with a pin; it aroused a soft feeling in her. Something missing. She tried not to look at it but couldn't help herself. Douggy understood that and didn't mind. Once, when he caught her at it, he winked.

Douggy kept poultry out at Regent's Park, near Parramatta. He always turned up with a dressed chook.

They were Digger's mates from away back. She knew that much because old times was what they talked about while they downed a pot of tea and a couple of pikelets. Hovering about behind them, fetching butter or strawberry jam, she would pick up snatches of what they had to say: names, odd bits of stories. She tried to keep the names in her head in case one day the men who owned them turned up, but they never did.

Mac was one name. Jack Gard was another. Jack Gard had eaten forty-two boiled eggs once at a show up near Tenterfield, and Ern told this story pretty well every time he came. He laughed each time as if the story was new and the others hadn't heard it, and said, 'Can you credit that? Forty-two bloody hard-boiled eggs at a single go. Waddaya think a' that, eh Missus?'

He was noisy, Ern, but Douggy was the one who asked for more pikelets and told her how good they were.

Once or twice what they talked of was the great world.

Occasionally, too, the name that came up was Vic's. She pricked her ears up then, eager to hear some bit of information about him that Digger hadn't told; but they had none, or only what she knew already: that he was a big noise out there.

'Seen Vic lately?' they'd say, 'Vic Curran? – Oh, 'e's been down again, has 'e, t' see ya? Good.'

They knew nothing more than she did. They were fishing for information. They waited, so did she, for Digger to come across with something, but he never did.

He could drive you wild, Digger, with his secrets and his silences. She had learned to live with it. Sitting quietly together over a cup of tea, around nine say with the table cleared and Digger working on some bit of a thing he was fixing, leaning close up to it with his glasses on the end of his nose while she got on with her knitting, she would find his voice in her head, and so clear that she automatically answered it. But when she looked up he was lost in his work. He hadn't spoken. Or if he had it was without thinking.

Still, there were times when he did speak up, and abruptly enough to startle her. 'You and me and Billy –' he would say with the hint of a laugh in his voice, and she would jump right out of her skin.

'What?' she'd say. 'What Billy?'

There *was* a Billy, only she didn't think Digger knew about him. Billy the Rigger. Once, years back, she had gone off to Brisbane with him.

'*You* know.'

'Do I?'

'I told you. Our brother Billy.'

'Oh. *Him*.'

He would have a story then, one of the little incidents of their childhood that he recalled and she did not, though she was three years older. Involving a tyre their father had rigged up under the pepper tree as a swing – he would have been two years old then, could he really remember these things? – or a shoebox full of silkworms, and as he described it she would begin to hear again the rustling of them and see the fat little creatures, all silvery but with darker feet, lifting their heads as they munched and moved about among the leaves; feel the breath too of a smaller kid on the back of her neck. Was that Billy?

She could have turned her head then and seen him, but she had to protect herself; she didn't want him to become too real. If he did she would only miss him when he was gone again or he'd start growing up and become a nuisance. If she let that snuffling little kid with the stream of snot in his nose (which she would not turn and wipe) start growing, he'd end up being sixty years old and right here with them. Then she'd be in a pickle. More sheets to wash, another couple of potatoes to peel, another smelly towel beside the tub, more snores and sniffles. He'd butt in.

'What'd *he* die of?' she would ask, to get it over and done with. It was kinder in the long run. 'Was Billy diftheria?'

9

Kind and quick. She wished she'd done that with Vic, ages ago, but Billy was easy, he was dead.

The trouble with Digger was, he remembered too much. Give him long enough and he'd remember *everything*.

2

Newcomers to the Crossing, calling on Digger to discuss a bit of work they needed doing, a sundeck extended or a new roof, took it for granted that he had got his name from the war. He was lean-jawed and leathery, said little, was never without a fag in the corner of his mouth and a spare one, newly rolled, behind his ear.

In fact he had been Digger from birth, or very nearly. They had called him that, with no special foresight, before there was any hint of a new war he might be growing up for.

Albert was the name his mother had picked out for him, meaning to call him Bert. But to the father, from the very first, he was another man about the house, a little offsider and mate.

'Right, dig,' he would tell the boy when he was barely old enough to understand, 'we're gunna take a look at this greasetrap. Are ya with me? Geez! Not so sweet, eh?' Or: 'C'mon, digger, we better be makin' tracks or the ol' lady'll rouse on us. We wouldn' wanna be in 'er bad books.' The name became Digger and stuck. After a time even the mother used it, since that was what he answered to, but she regretted Albert.

She had thought of him as Albert, Bert, all the months she was carrying him; had had conversations with him under that name, and believed later, he was such a knowing little thing, that he must remember this and the secrets she had confided to him. But once he was born the father's needs prevailed. He became Digger and that was that.

Their first little girl, Jenny, was slow. The second, May, was already gone before Digger was born. So was the third, Pearl, who survived just long enough to become another absence to tug the mother's heart. She had been banking on Bert.

Back home in England, in the orphanage where she grew up, she had had a brother called Bert. He was the only thing she had that was in any way her own. A stocky, dark little fellow, two years younger than herself, she had fussed over him and come to believe he couldn't get on without her.

Because he had no memory of their real home, or of their mother, she had set out to give him one, to impress upon him by constant telling and retelling all she could remember of their dark little room and the life they had lived there. There wasn't much, but some detail, she hoped, a yellow dress their mother had worn, a picture she recalled of two long-haired cows in a mist, might take life in him and become memories of his own. She owed it to him. To their Ma as well.

But when she sat him down on a form opposite, their knees touching, she could recall very little and he was too young to listen. What she found herself doing was searching his face for some resemblance that would link them and make solid a vision of their mother's pale, pinched features that had already gone ghostly for her. She was assuring herself that she was not alone in the world. Her intensity at these moments scared him. He would hide to avoid her.

Her last sight of him was in a line of other boys, all big-eyed and bony-kneed, shuffling about in the cold, on the stone steps that led up to the schoolroom. She stood below in a made-over dress and with a little bundle they had given her. She was eleven and was going out to begin her working life. In service.

His dark face above the curve of the banister rail was the last she would ever see of him. He was on tiptoe, frowning. Then he raised his hand and waved. When she went back three years later he had gone to be apprenticed in Liverpool.

So when what she knew was proved at last and she had a boy, she had fought for him, from the first day searching his face for some likeness to his namesake, Albert, Bert, and for some hint that her own family, about whom she knew nothing, had come through. But in the end she had given in. Her heart got the better of her. She knew what loneliness was, and how this man she had married, this boy, longed for a form of companionship that she could not give him or which he was not able to accept. Digger, she told herself, wasn't so much a name as an assurance that he would have it at last. She could not deny him that. But before she knew it Digger *was* a name. The child answered to no other. Albert, Bert, the gesture she had made to a past that was beyond recall, was just the name in a register that he would never use.

He wasn't the last. A year later there was Bill, then James, then Leslie, but by then Albert was used up. And they didn't survive anyway, these boys, any more than the girls had. In the end there were just the two children, Digger and Jenny.

Billy Keen had run off to France when he was fifteen. By the time he got home again, a survivor of Pozières and Villers Bretonneux, he had already, at just eighteen, had the one great adventure of his life. Though married and more or less settled as chief ferryman at the Crossing, he continued to live in spirit, since he was barely out of his lively boyhood, at that intensified pitch of daring, terror and pure high-jinks that would forever be his measure of what a man's life should be when he is at full stretch. Anything else was a tameness he could not endure.

History had conspired, for a time, to set him in a world where risk, up to the very edge of extinction, was a point of honour, and animal energy had scope. It was his natural element. After that, life at the Crossing seemed to him like daily punishment. He hated the regularity of it, the timetable the ferry ran on, the six-minute crossing, then the same time back, his having to be home, and already washed and brushed up, for dinner at twelve and for tea at six, the fuss about knives and forks and the state of his socks. It meant nothing to him that Keens had been at the Crossing for a hundred years and that the place bore his name. He was too young, he felt, for the responsibilities that were put upon him by a household that had arrived from nowhere, had simply crept up on him (that's how he saw it) while he was dreaming at the wheel. *She* was the trouble, the girl he'd got.

He had met her the first week he was back. She was a barmaid in a city pub. He had taken one look at her and told himself: 'She'll do.'

He said this thoughtlessly, because he was eighteen, wanted a girl of his own and didn't know any better. He was home now, and the next thing to do was get married. It was what blokes *did*. What else was there? He knew nothing about her except that she was lively, had newly arrived in the place and had a soft mouth with just a touch of colour to it. He had spent three years dreaming of that colour. She ruled the rough clientele of the pub, which was a waterside pub at The Rocks, in an easy, no-nonsense way that impressed him. You could play up to her but there was a line, and she soon let you know if you tried to cross it. He was amused by that.

She knew what he was after. He was no different in that from the rest. But there was something in him that appealed to her. He was like a cricket, very chirpy and always on the dare. His military bravado took the civilian form of impudence, especially where girls were concerned. He would look you straight in the eye with so much confidence in his own attractions that she was tempted to laugh outright. 'Yes, it's me,' the look said. 'I'm a bit of all right, eh?' He would wink then and you could see the utter satisfaction he felt in himself. 'Well, that oughta do it.'

In fact he was wrong. It wasn't that that did it. She could take with a good deal of salt the sort of swagger, of inexperience too, that made him feel she could be caught (girls are easy) just like that. 'Not me, m'lad,' she told him with a look of her own, and set her jaw.

But she too was eager to get out of her present life and be settled. It was what she had come all these miles for. And something he had said, just in passing, had caught her ear. The place he came from bore his name. Back home in England that meant something, an ancestral house or manor, or a sizeable farm at least. Family names on a map were solid; they rooted you in things that could be measured, so many acres. So what, she wondered, was Keen's Crossing? It wouldn't be a manor of course. She knew what country she was in; she wasn't quite a fool. But it must be *something*. She was a practical girl and added it to the immediate and more touching fact of his ears.

It would have surprised Billy Keen, and might have reduced him a little, if he had realised that what had fetched her was not the line he ran, not at all, but the giveaway reddening of his ears. What he had awakened in her, though she didn't know it yet, was the mother she would be in less than a year if she took him. His ears made such perfect shells.

In fact they were deceived, both of them. What she took for boyishness in him was a lightness he would not outgrow. He was strong-willed and stubborn, in fact. He would not be led. As for what amused him so much, her competence – the ease with which she managed men and change and glasses and all sorts of daring backchat – he did not like it much when it was applied daily to *him*. She was competent all right. Ambitious too. And when she got hold of a thing she hung on to it.

She would remember the journey to Keen's Crossing for the rest of her life, perhaps because she was to make it just the once. Every detail of it remained new for her.

Years later, towards the end, on a windy day in August, she would climb the bluff behind the Crossing and be astonished to see that

Sydney, a place she thought of as worlds away, further even in some ways than England, had all the time been visible, just thirty miles from where she was. She could have gone up there and looked at it any day of her life. Its outer suburbs by then were already climbing the far side of the ridge.

But it wasn't in fact the same city she had come to and left more than thirty years ago. That had been a big country town with arms of the harbour breaking into it at every turn, open trams bucketing about and sparking on their poles, wagons with heavy carthorses loaded with barrels and barefoot boys shouting headlines at every corner; a shabby place, all steep hills and with ships of one sort or another, or masts at least, at the bottom of every street. What she saw now, from a distance of half a lifetime, was skyscrapers.

The thirty-mile journey by train, and then sulky, had taken all day. At first through suburbs that were all new brick bungalows and gardens dense with pin oaks and rhododendron; then, with the last of the streetlamps, market gardens tended by Chinese. At last they had come out on to a plateau under a scud of clouds. Stretches of low flowering scrub lay on either side, broken by platforms of rock. When they left the little isolated station and made their way down to the river, the Hawkesbury, the road (a highway they called it) took bend after bend, and the trees, which were both above and below them, were of a kind she had never seen before, giants with feathery tops in bunches, and trunks and limbs of a naked pink or white, incredibly twisted and deeply creased at the joints with folds like fat. Ridged outcropping ledges tilted and thrust out at angles, and there was a smell of animal droppings, dark and heavy, mixed with the crush of ferns. She soon saw how different it was from England, and how wrong, how romantic, her expectations had been.

They turned off the highway, took a less frequented road which was also a highway, and came down to where the store occupied its elbow of dust in an arc of the river. The ferry was idling at the bank.

'Well,' he said, 'this is it. Waddaya think?'

She didn't. She had given up thinking miles back and had sworn then that she would never come this way again. Whatever it was, she would accept and make the most of. Thirteen thousand miles, plus thirty, was enough.

The road they were on came to a halt at the ferry, then took up again on the other side, where it went all the way, he told her, to Gosford,

Woy Woy, Maitland: he spoke these names as if they offered the possibility of escape. But she had never heard of any of them, and told herself she could do without them. Sydney, too. She would stick to what she had got.

It wasn't much. Whatever modest grandeur or continuity she had imagined, and had hoped in her ignorance to find in a settled-looking house and garden, had to be taken up from the landscape. It was wild, but once she stopped thinking in the old terms and opened her eyes and let it work on her, she was struck by the stillness of it, the space it gave you to breathe.

It wasn't what she had wanted – how could it be when she hadn't even known such a place could exist? – and she wasn't sure, either, that she had the qualities to deal with it, since she had been preparing most of her life for something else. But *something* in her wanted it, now that it was here. Something new in her, that the place itself would deal with.

She committed herself immediately, come what might, to *that*, and made a mission of it.

Newly come home and not too happy about it, Billy watched her closely, seated on a log and sweating, knocking away flies. 'You're not disappointed?' he asked.

She was the one who had wanted to come here. If only to take a look. He had banked on her being put off by the dreariness of the place. They would look and go back to town. Sydney was what he wanted.

Her look of fierce resignation was the first indication he got that she might not be what he had taken her for. She strode about looking, asking questions. He fell deeper into gloom. She *liked* it. She was making plans.

The river was wide between granite bluffs that were all yellow-orange in the sunset and forested with the same weird, fleshy trees they had come down through. But there was a pepper tree in front of the store and, behind, Scotch firs. Very gloomy they looked too, compared with the lightness and airiness of the bush trees; familiar, yes, but that was just what she didn't like about them. Still, it was through them that she saw what the others might be.

No sign of a garden. Not even a geranium in a tub.

Not much of a house either. Just the gabled store, all weatherboard, unpainted for ages she thought and a lot of it gone to ruin, with, at the back, three pokey rooms.

What Billy couldn't know, following behind her and feeling more and more uneasy, was that it was more than she had ever had in her life before. It was all to be *made*, and what she made would be hers.

The store was boarded up. 'Well,' she thought, 'we can reopen it.' The house was filled with rubbish except for one room. Billy's brother Pete lived there, or rather, camped in a space he had made by pushing the rubbish it contained into the corners of it. He immediately offered to give the place up to them, and his job at the ferry to Billy if he wanted it. He couldn't wait to get away.

She had looked forward to this brother, hoping to learn from him some of the things that Billy didn't know or couldn't be bothered to tell. Having got a relation at last she was determined to make the most of him. She had seen herself making meals, looking after his clothes, in exchange for which there would be confidences.

But one look at Pete was enough. He and Billy might have been strangers for all they had to say to one another; and when she followed him to the woodpile, and tried to draw him out, he was scared out of his wits. He leaned on the axe and muttered, so awkward and shy she thought he might choke. He had none of Billy's lightness. Billy stood at the door of the shack and laughed.

Pete had been living in the house as if he had come upon it by chance, and Billy came back to it, she saw, in the same spirit. The house, all this, meant nothing to them. For the remainder of the week, which he endured only to collect his wages, Pete avoided her, then was gone and they heard no more of him.

This carelessness about things she held sacred astonished her. The place after all bore their name; the house was the one they had grown up in, even if it was given over now to the bush rats whose nests were everywhere, and to big spiders with egg-sacks under their bellies, and woodlice and centipedes. Rolling her sleeves up she got the three rooms cleared and clean again, but Billy scarcely noticed and did nothing to help. He was happiest camping in one room like Pete, wearing the same filthy shirt he had worn all week and splashing his face with two fingers of water from a pail. He was, she saw now, a kind of savage, as resentful as a ten-year-old of any suggestion that he should wash his neck, or his feet at least, before he came to bed.

There were few relics in the place of any former habitation, but rummaging about one day in the bottom of a cupboard she found a stack of photographs, dusted them off, set them on the rickety sideboard and spent the rest of the morning studying them for some clue to this family she had married into – what it was that might go into her children, when she had them – and for some clue to *him*. When he came in she questioned him.

'Oh, that's Merle,' he said lightly of a big girl, lumpish and worn-looking, whom she had taken at first for the mother. He stood easing his braces over his shoulder and peering.

'Yair. That's Merle. She lives up Lismore way. Or Casino. *I* dunno.' Prompted, he named the others.

'That's Jess. Geez, what a tartar!'

'Where's *she*?' she demanded.

'*I* dunno. Married. Out west somewhere, I dunno. She's no loss.'

Eric had gone to work on the railways. 'Funny feller, Eric,' he laughed. 'A bit touched.'

Leslie?

'Went ta Queensland, oh, ages ago. Just ran off. You shoulda heard dad roar! I was on'y a nipper.'

He told all this with only the most casual interest and with none of the little details that might have made any of it real. They had gone. He didn't expect to see them again and didn't care, one way or the other. Should he?

Her parents-in-law, the mother and father of this scattered brood, appeared on their wedding day; he in a tight-looking suit with a stiff collar, a grim-faced working man who didn't know where to put his hands; she in a cup-shaped chair in front of him, her skirt spread and at her elbow a pedestal and urn.

She tried to find something in them, stunned to immobility as they were by the occasion, that would explain why every one of their children had gone off without a backward glance, or, so far as she could see, a twinge of regret. What brutality was it in the father? What empty-headedness or ignorance or dull indifference in the mother? What failure to hang on to things, or even to see, if Pete and Billy were an example, that there was anything to be held.

'Yairs,' he said. 'That's dad.'

He frowned, rubbed his chin with the heel of his hand, sounding resentful.

He took the photograph and peered at it. 'Yairs,' he said, 'that's me *mother*,' as if what she had been demanding of him was the identity of the woman at his father's side, rather than some living detail of her. 'When she was young.'

It was all he had to say, and she looked at him now and wondered what it was that had bruised all feeling out of him. Or had he never had any?

She had thought at first that he was simply lackadaisical, unwilling to be bothered, and had put this down to his youth. But the truth was that he did not care and wondered why *she* did. He looked at her in genuine puzzlement and was hurt, then irritated, but a moment later was all brightness and affection, whisking her about on the scrubbing boards, full of fun and boyish roughness and urging her to go to bed when it was still daylight.

'What is it?' he asked when they did lie down together. 'You're the one who wanted to come. I thought you liked it here.'

'That's your father's family,' she would tell Digger and Jenny. There was a vehemence to her voice that amounted to savagery, though she tried to hide it.

'This is your grandma. And this is your father's dad, your grandpa,' and so on for each of the uncles and aunts. She was determined that they should have a family and was giving them all she had to show. It infuriated her that she had never seen any one of these people except Pete.

They might have dropped out of the world the moment their likeness was taken, for all the evidence they had left in the house, or anywhere else for that matter. No toys ever turned up. Not even a peg-doll or a home-made top. Even in the yard when she broke the soil for her garden. Not one of them had ever carved his name on a bit of furniture, or scribbled drawings on a wall, or left height marks on a door. Billy, unless urged, never mentioned any one of them, and had no tales of his childhood to tell. He might never have had one. He was born with the war.

Her own family, she was convinced, would not have given in so easily to extinction. She sent letter after letter to the orphanage in an attempt to find Bert.

It was in defiance of this almost criminal indifference in their father's people that she began to inculcate in Digger, and in Jenny too so far as she was capable of it, her own view of things, which was fanatical. She had been famished all her life for what these people, these Keens – Billy among them – tossed away like the merest trash. She wouldn't let *her* kids grow up like that.

The Crossing first: *Keen's* Crossing.

They belonged here for all time now, it was marked with their name. They could see it on a map if they liked: a dotted line leading away from the highway; at the end of it a dot marking the store; beside that, in italics, *Keen's Crossing*. To turn your back and walk away from it was a crime. Against yourself first of all. Then against what had been trusted to you. Then against the place itself, and if you didn't know what *that* was, then just open your eyes and look around you.

Family next. That too was a kind of place, a place in time. Turn your back and walk away from that and you lost all hold on the line of things. The line was blood. Turn your back on your family and you drained the blood from your heart.

She painted a fierce picture, and Digger at least was terrified of her. It was a religion she was preaching, her own, and she was its implacable embodiment.

One more thing. At the orphanage they had got a good dose of preaching. She had been unimpressed by most of it, but one thing struck her and she had incorporated it into her own system. It was this: what you got in the next life was neither more nor less than what you had gathered and made something of in this one. So if you went through life with nothing, nothing was what you got in the next life as well. It was a harsh law but it chimed with something in her nature and she had taken it literally.

Her vision was of a room with curtains, furniture, the smiling faces of children round a table piled high with food (including pineapples), and with good cutlery laid out and glass and plates such as she had seen in the houses she worked in. A German roller in a cage would be trilling away and ducking its head in a bath and shaking off brilliant drops. In drawers, if you opened them, would be aprons, teatowels, napkins, all neatly folded, and silver serviette rings with initials; plus sugar tongs and grape scissors, embossed.

She saw all this very clearly, though as yet she possessed not a single one of these things. She had nothing at all. Every least bit of it however was already there, just waiting to be gathered, and would go to the making of her life; and when she was dead she would sit grandly content and justified in the midst of it, her children and grandchildren about her and each item at last in its place, even the meanest redeemed out of ordinariness and alive again in the eternal, yet recognisably and tangibly itself.

She tried to pass this vision on to Digger and Jenny as a way of explaining to them why it was that she hung on to things. She did succeed with Digger, but he took the idea and interpreted it in his own way. His vision too was literal, and it was a good while before she saw that it was not at all like her own. She had made him a priest all right, but of his own religion.

It was in this spirit of making and gathering, this dedication to the religion of *getting*, that she set about reviving the store.

She had a head for figures, orders, invoices and such, and took no more nonsense from the travellers who turned up with samples than she had from the drinkers at the pub she had worked in. When the store was ready she got to work on the house. From the David Jones catalogue she chose curtains and wallpaper; then later, a utility set for them to eat off, Wood's Ware, not cheap Japanese, and a set of celluloid serviette rings with initials.

Billy watched all this with suspicion. Her orderliness made him uneasy, and her tendency, as he thought of it, to put on the dog – maintaining a bit of decency was how she would have put it – enraged him. He had married a plump little girl with blonde curls and a bit of colour to her mouth, and had ended up with a woman who could run things. She tried to run him.

He submitted at first. Anything for a quiet life, that was his motto; women were odd, you had to humour them. But when she tried to rule him he rebelled. He didn't want to be cleaned up and made respectable, it didn't suit him. He hated the neat little curtains she hung, the amount of washing she put out and the new poles he had to cut for her lines, the floors he couldn't walk on in his hobnailed boots, and all the other evidence of what hampered and restricted him, this domestication she expected him to be *grateful* for.

Wasn't she making a home for *him*? That was the song she sang. Well, he could do without, he didn't want it. He resented all these little wants she had, that were in fact criticisms of the way *he* preferred to live. He even resented, at last, the success she made of the store, because of the strength it gave her. It put him in the shade. *He* could support them. He didn't need her to do it, and to show him up with how clever she was, and with manners she had picked up from people who were not their kind and that he had no time for and no wish to imitate, and all the palaver as well that went with them. Like serviette rings! She cast a gloom over him with the life she was making. So did the Crossing. He hated it, always had. Her passion for it was exaggerated. He took it as another form of rebuke to him, another criticism. Everything he wanted, everything that gave his spirit scope and made his blood beat, she forbade or cast scorn on.

He set himself against her. He wouldn't have done; he was easy-going by nature, and at the start he had been genuinely fond of her, had wanted her to have whatever it was that made her happy. But she had set herself against *him*.

He would sit out on a stump and curse when he was supposed to be chopping firewood for her copper, deliberately dawdled over jobs he could have finished with one hand tied behind his back, not to give her the satisfaction of having him always on call. He stayed out with the boys when she was expecting him on the dot for tea, and complained bitterly to his mates, when he had had a drink or two, of the haste with which he had put himself in harness. What a fool! At twenty-one his life was finished.

Back there in the trenches, even if you ran the risk of extinction, and maybe most of all then, you were alive. He had known the full power of his own presence, breath and balls and fingers and the small hairs at the back of his neck. It had spoiled him, that glimpse of what a man might be. The life he was living now was nothing. Maybe it would be different if he had someone who knew what he was on about when he wanted to talk.

Then Digger came along, and he had someone at last that he could be himself with, a mate; an ally too against the world that she was mistress of, that took no account of a man's world because it had no use for it, only for the dumb, animal side of a man, work, and the bit of pleasure he would be allowed in the getting of a kid. All they wanted beyond that was to make a dummy of you, with a lot of rubbish about clean collars and toenails that didn't do damage to the sheets, and serviette rings and God knows what other useless lah-de-dah lady's business.

These were some of the things he raved about when he had Digger alone. But when the anger left him at last he had other things to pass on to the boy.

They were inseparable from the start. As a toddler with his nappy sagging and their dog Ralphie at his heels, he trotted in the father's footsteps or squatted beside him with a toy hammer in his hand, imitating the father's muttered curses and his way of holding his head to one side and sucking in his cheeks as he got set to belt a nail.

He was good with his hands, Billy Keen. Everyone knew that. He could knock up anything you liked, a table or a medicine chest, dovetails and all; or hang a door or fix a roof. He was good with machines, too. Machines, people said, would talk to him, start purring and singing the moment he laid a hand on them. It was a gift. Digger had it too, or by intuition had picked it up from him.

Machines were alive to Digger in the same way Ralphie was; and he was so close to Ralphie that it had taken him ages, when he was little, to see that they were of different species. The mother, who could not always be on the watch – she had Jenny as well as the shop and house to care for – was forever having to snatch Ralphie's feeding dish from him. 'Leave that, you little grub,' she would tell him, 'that's Ralphie's. Here, spit that out right now.' In a storm once he had crawled into Ralphie's kennel, out under the pepper tree, while thunder rolled, lightning blasted and the whole yard turned to mud. He had never felt so safe or warm. In dreams sometimes he found himself back in the dark, animal smell of the kennel, with Ralphie's warmth against him, and felt he had arrived at a place where he knew at last where he really was, had rediscovered, in the individual grains of dirt he was pushing into his mouth, what it meant to be on the earth. It was the same way with machines. He understood the workings of them as if they were continuous in some way with his own nature. They purred for him, they sang, as they did for his father. There were no words for this.

At barely ten, a scrawny kid, tough and hard-heeled, with a skin so pale you could see sunlight through it, he would relieve his father at the wheel of the ferry, feeling the huge power in his arms as the barge, with its load of vehicles, swung out into midstream. His father, leaning back against the machinery and blowing smoke, would direct him.

'One day,' he told himself, 'this job will be mine.' He had no thought but to follow in his father's footsteps.

He watched his father, picking up from him mannerisms he thought of as being essential to the man, and acquiring thus a set of gestures that were not individual to the father at all. Billy Keen, as a lad of fifteen, unsure of himself and eager to be recognised as a man, had picked them up from older fellows in the army in France. So at seven Digger had already the loose slouch that is the soldier's stance when he is off-duty or between moves. He would sit on one heel and narrow his eyes at the distance before there was any distance much to be seen.

The mother saw all this and began to regret the mistake she had made in letting go of him. She had thought then that she could afford to; there would be others. But the others all died on her, and though Jenny was a soft-mouthed, good-natured little thing, you couldn't depend on her. Digger, in fact, had been her only chance.

And the miracle was that for all his loyalty to the father she hadn't lost him after all; that was the sweetness of him. He stuck to the father, but he stuck to her as well. They were bonded. They had their own codes and passwords, that others did not recognise, even when they were at the same table. They talked in silence. And one of the things they talked about was the others, the ones who were gone now, all but Jenny, but whose invisible presence she still clung to because they clung to her. They hung on to her skirts when she was out at the clothesline wrestling with sheets. They moaned and whimpered from corners, spat out mouthfuls of porridge and chewed crusts, sat in the sooty stove-alcove and banged on saucepans with spoons. And Digger, who had barely known them you might have thought, not only saw them there but could speak to them and give you details out of their brief existence that even she had forgotten. He was extraordinary, Digger, in what he saw.

It was his ability to call up these little ghosts, and so clearly and in such detail that it broke your heart, that constituted the bond between them and made her believe that his memory might go back further still: to the time when, in her loneliness, she had talked to him in the womb.

So she too had her triumph. Let them be mates, or whatever it is these men are together! Let them! He is bound to *me*.

She was hard on him, she had to be. She couldn't be certain to what extent he had inherited his father's weakness. She believed he would see this one day and be grateful to her.

Given the choice (but who has a *choice*?) she might have let him off. There was a part of her nature in which nothing would have pleased her more than to be one of the serene mothers you read about in books. But what good would that do him, or her either?

The rages she got into scared her. She did not know at times, when she struck out at him, cuffing his ear or sending a stinging blow across his cheek, what it was in him that made her so angry, except that there were occasions when his simply being there was enough to do it, the soft look he wore, the vagueness of him. She was afraid he would go his father's way. But she was equally afraid of his brightness, his curiosity. These too might draw him away.

For all the skill he had with his hands, it was his mind he lived in, and there was no way of fathoming *that*. There were too many things in there, even if they were facts, that had no weight in the world; that's what she saw and had to warn him of. If he clung to them he would drift.

The father wasn't blind.

'You mustn' let yer mother put you off, Digger. I mean, women don't know everything, you know, though they reckon they do. It's a different world, their world. A hard one, I admit. Yer mother's got a hard life. That's me, partly.' He gave a laugh as if he were in the end quite proud of it. 'On'y we don't tell 'em everything we do, you know what I mean? All the bits of fun we have, or what we're thinkin' sometimes. They wouldn't understand. Yer mother now. I don't want t' speak badly of 'er, she's a good woman in most ways. But she's a worrier. Yer better off – you know – keeping some things t' yerself, you know what I mean? I mean they got *their* world, son, and we got *ours*, an' the two are chalk an' cheese, you can't trade 'em. Yer mother wants to hang on t' you. She wants to spare you from life. I don't blame 'er fer that. It's understandable. She doesn't want to lose you. On'y you can't go on tryin' to live her way forever, Dig – it's just not possible. One day, one way 'r another, you'll have to go out into a man's world. Believe me, son, yer mother won't help you then. I seen all that. Fellers cryin' out fer their mothers in no man's land, with half their head shot away or their guts spillin' out. They could cry as long as they liked but I never seen no mother turn up. It was a man's world you was in. It was other men you had to rely on. Stretcher-bearers, if you were lucky, otherwise just yer mates. That's the truth, Digger. That's what yer mother won't tell yer.'

These conversations took place on Sunday mornings when Digger and his father, with Ralphie trotting behind, went out with a 202 to get something for the pot.

Not far from the Crossing was a bit of a branch line that had once served a mining village back in the hills. It ran for twelve miles through cuttings, round sheer hillsides, and was little more now than a playground for kids who liked to walk its rails like a tightrope with outstretched arms, and a scavenging place where men would come with a crowbar to tear up sleepers or gather coals.

Digger loved the line, as they called it. So did Ralphie, who would leap off down the bank on the scent of something, a feral cat, maybe a rabbit, while they called after him 'Skitchum, Ralphie. You skitchum!' The walk, the stopping and starting, the intervals given over to getting a bird and bagging it, imposed a rhythm on these outings that was good for storytelling but also for talk. They were not always so chatty as they were out here. They could work side by side for hours sometimes without exchanging a single word.

The stories were the same ones over and over, and Digger never tired of them. In their daring close-shaves and feats of bravado he got glimpses, quick ones, into his father's other nature, the one that was under restraint here, the necessary restraint of the family man. In that other dimension, he was a boy not much older than Digger himself, light-footed, eager for the world, full of energy and pluck. They were of an age there, and here too once the stories got going.

'It wasn't all bad, Digger. There was a good bitta fun to be had if you looked out fer it. Always is. But a lotta the time it *was* bad, and some of it was hell. The cold fer instance. Wicked it was, you can't imagine. But you'd be surprised what blokes c'n put up with. When you really get down to it. Well, I was one a' the lucky ones.' He said this fiercely and went silent, and his mouth was so grim that Digger, watching him, wondered if he really believed it.

His stories always involved the same characters and Digger got to know the men's names as if he had known *them*. They were the men, he guessed, that his father was closest to, even now; closer certainly than to any of his drinking cronies at the pub, or fellows they exchanged a word with here and there at the ferry – regulars – or when they went into town to find some machine part they needed.

Wally Barnes was one. Digger saw him, for maybe the hundredth time, go sideways off the duckboards. Saw his eyes turned up white, filling with mud; his mouth already full as the weight of his boots, his pack – his own weight too, he was a big fellow – took him down. Felt at the end of his arms the tug of the fifteen stone, and would close his eyes and with a jerk, as his father had, for the hundredth time, break his grip.

Billy Keen told these horror stories in a voice that scared even himself, as if no amount of telling would ever get him used to the fact that they had happened, and he had once been part of them. He lifted his head and looked about the still place they were in, which was all sunspikes and glitters, almost soundless except for the flutter of a grasshopper's wings, as if it was this that he needed to be convinced was present and real.

Digger too felt a chill go over him; and the father, seeing it, would feel sorry for the boy, for having dragged him so deep into things.

'Well,' he would say, 'at least you won't have to face that, Dig, not that. It won't happen again. Can't. We finished it once 'n fer all. It can't happen twice – not that sort a' thing.'

'Can't it?' Digger asked himself. 'Is there a rule?'

He looked at his father's youthful shoulders, the jaunty way he stepped over the sleepers, and thought: 'Well anyway, he come through it. I reckon I will.'

He did not think this in a superior way. For all his mother's criticisms, which she did not hesitate to present the moment she had him alone, he knew his father's qualities and admired them. He took no part in their war.

'I'd watch out if I was you,' she warned him. They would be out under the pepper tree where he was helping her hang out, shifting the props, or it might be Friday nights in the back of the shop where she was making up deliveries, weighing out salt, flour, rice, tea in brown paper packets, while he read to her from the order book and packed each thing as she handed them to him in a butter-box. 'You'll catch *his* disease if you don't watch out. You'll be a dreamer like him.'

'Is Dad a dreamer?'

He wouldn't have said so. Action was what his father was in love with.

'What else would you call it?'

She plonked another bag on the scales, settled the half-pound weight, and poured in another dozen grains. She was precise about these things.

He took the bag from her, folded the top down and settled it in the box.

What she was really warning him of was the difference between what she called reality, or duty, or fate – she had different names for it on different occasions – and a hunger he had, and which his father had too, for something that began where her reality, however clear and

27

graspable it was, left off. Something he knew existed because he had already got glimpses of it, from his father; from fellows too who talked to him at the open doors of their cars during the six-minute ferry crossing; from books; from the pictures he had been to; and from some physical stirring as well in his own belly.

What it had to do with was the sheer size of the world, and the infinite number of events and facts and objects it was filled with. Things you could touch and smell, but other things too that were just thoughts; which were real enough, and could even be put into words and turned this way and that, but you couldn't see them.

There was no set of scales in existence that could measure all that, and no number of little paper bags would be enough to contain it, but your head could. That's what he had seen. Your head. Which was the same shape as the world, and really was the world, only on an infinitely small scale; an inch to a million as on the globe he loved to look at, where the tip of your finger could cover an area of thousands of square miles, and whole cities with millions of people in them, but only because in your head you could *see* this. Didn't she know these things? Didn't she want to know them or want him to? He saw the scared look on her face.

'Don't worry, Mum,' he could have assured her. 'I'll be all right.'

But that wasn't really the point, and he knew it. So what he said, putting his arm round her waist and hugging her, was, 'Don't worry, Mum, I won't leave you.'

'It's not me I was thinking of,' she told him, and pushed him off. 'You know that.'

'Who then?'

'You know.'

He did, too. She meant Jenny. But more than that, the Crossing. But what she really meant you couldn't put a name to. It was so powerful that when she summoned it up he could accept and bow his whole life before it, yet at the same time he wanted to break and run.

Jenny.

There was no moment he could recall when this sister of his, this big soft girl who was three years older, with her milky breath and bubbly lips, had not been at his side.

When he was very little she liked to look after him.

'Now you watch Digger,' the mother would tell her, 'there's a good girl,' and just to be safe, so as not to lose sight of him, she would haul him on to her knee and hold him so tight he would go breathless.

'No, love, I said *watch* baby, don't squeeze him like that. He's a baby. He won't go away.'

But she had seen others and *they* had gone away. She kept hold of him, and if she didn't, and he began to crawl off, she would go running on her stumpy legs to their mother: 'Digger! Digger's under the dunny! Digger's eating dirt! Digger's getting *away!*'

But by the time he could talk Digger knew that he was the younger only in years. Whatever they pretended, he had on all occasions to look after *her*. To be an interpreter between her and a world that would always go too fast for her or come to her in forms she could not comprehend.

The fact that there had been others, and that in one way or another they had failed to live on, was a warning, and accounted, he saw, for the fear with which their mother guarded them, and for her intense possessiveness.

He resented these others. She would never let him forget them; never a day went by without her evoking one or other of them, May or Pearl or James or Leslie.

Pearl was just a name to him, a small dissatisfied spirit that each time he went to his mother's breast was already there, fighting him off. May, just weeks before he was born, had pulled a kerosene tin of boiling water off the stove. Her howls, he suspected, were often in their mother's ears, even when she was trying to keep her temper and talk quietly to him. She was their mother's favourite, the daughter whose company she had longed for, since Jenny was not able to provide it. She had never trusted herself after what happened to May. She had become over-cautious, terrified of the capacity of even the most ordinary objects to turn murderous on you, and the house was full of them.

Of the others, the three boys, only Billy had been round long enough to be quite real. Digger had nursed and petted the others, but Billy had been old enough to follow him round the yard, and they had played together, all three. Billy had had time to develop features and his own smell in the room where they slept, all in the one bed; a voice, demands, little oddnesses that took your heart or raised in you an antagonism that reinforced your separateness and for that reason stuck.

Billy had wandered off into the river. The river after that had a new meaning to them, the sound of it at night, the cold touch of it when you reached a hand in. It was no longer just a boundary that let you say which side you were on, or the broad stretch of sunlight in motion that their father, and later Digger too at times, sent the ferry out on. Even dropping a line into it became a different act.

'Watcha doin'?' Jenny had asked him once when she saw the line trailing. 'Are you gunna find Billy?'

She often said things you had thought of but never quite come up with, and when you did, bit off.

These deaths made the house more crowded than it might otherwise have been, but also emptier, exerting a pressure all round that forced him and Jenny, who, as his mother told him over and over had only one another, into a space that was too narrow and which he felt at times was another sort of coffin. Their having survived imposed a heavy responsibility on them: of living not just for themselves but for the others as well, and in this way letting them get another go at the world, a second breath. Since Jenny was limited, and always would be, the main weight was on him.

'It's not me, Digger,' his mother would insist when he bucked at the unfairness of it. 'How many times do I have to tell you? Do you think I would want to put a thing like that on you? It's not me. It's life!'

'C'mon, Dig, Digger, tell us somefing.'

In the beginning he told her everything he knew. His voice, velvety in the dark of their little room, was what made the world real to her. A lot of what he told was made up. She could not tell the difference.

'For God's sake, Digger!'

Hearing his voice rise as it often did to a point of dangerous excitement, their mother had come from her sewing, stopped a moment in the shade of the door, and heard him. The moment he saw her he knew how angry she would be. But he couldn't help himself. Coming to the edge of some extraordinary possibility, he would let himself claim it, put it into words; if he didn't, the force of it, huge and expanding in his head, might make him go flying off from the centre of himself. What he did now, shamefaced at being caught, was explode in giggles.

'Jenny, love,' she said, 'be a good girl and see if the postman's been.'

'He hasn't,' Jenny said. 'I been listnin'.'

'Don't you answer me, Miss,' the mother spat. 'If I say go, you do it. Quick smart!'

'You little bugger,' she said when Jenny was out of earshot, but her anger had died before the shamefaced look of him. 'How can you do that, Digger? Scaring the poor kid. What gets into you? You know what she's like. I should box your ears.'

Instead she reached out and touched the corner of his mouth with her thumb as if there were a crumb there. Sobered, he looked up at her. He never knew what she was after. She was so unpredictable.

She drew her hand away. She had been reassuring herself yet again that he wasn't simply a child of her wishing. She could not imagine sometimes where he had sprung from. He wasn't like her, or like his father either, not really. He was like no one she had ever known. Tell him something once and it was there forever. He remembered things she didn't even know she knew till he recalled them to her. 'You remember, Mum. You remember,' he would insist, and he was right, she did. Talk, facts, happenings from away back, the names of things, whole pages of any book he had read. Where did it all go in the skinny arms and legs (she thought of it as other mothers might think of food), all this knowledge he picked up and swallowed.

One night, hearing him reading aloud to his sister long after they had been told to go to bed, she had burst in in a fury.

'Digger, I've told you a thousand –'

But there was no lamp alight, no book. He was reciting the pages off, sentence by sentence, out of his head. He looked up at her, all innocence. He was nine years old.

She had known then that it was too late, that she could not hold him. It was already *in* there, the world she wanted to keep away from him, and expanding at a rate she could not control. She did not know enough to keep up with him.

He came at times like a small child, hugging her waist and hanging on. 'None of that,' she would tell him. 'You're all kidstakes. That's all that is.'

She believed he would leave her, but she never said it outright. She was protecting herself against loss.

'No I won't,' he would have assured her, 'how could I leave? Ever?'

He meant it and he did not.

*

'Tellus somefing, Digger,' Jenny would whisper in the dark of their little room. 'They're asleep, they won't hear.'

He no longer told her everything, but he did tell her some things.

People he saw on his deliveries, for instance, like the Breens: Mrs Breen in her old felt slippers, who always gave him ginger ale in a peanut-butter glass, sitting him down at the kitchen table, then sitting down herself, right opposite, and watching him drink.

Mrs Breen had Eddie, a big fellow nearly twenty who was a mongol. All the time he was there Eddie would be hanging about in the hallway outside. Sometimes he would poke his head round the corner and grin. 'Hullo Digger,' he'd call, too loud. Other times he would be scowling, as if he begrudged Digger his mother's attention and the mouthful of sweet soft-drink he was getting. Once, when Digger looked up, Eddie had his dick out and was playing with it. He looked quickly at Mrs Breen and she pretended not to notice, or she really didn't notice, she was too intent on *him*. As if there was something miraculous in his just being able to drink a glass of ginger ale without spilling it.

Then there were fellers he met at the ferry, commercial travellers some of them, and the stories they had to tell, including jokes; and things he got from older boys down at the river, where there was a deep pool and you could swing out over the swirling blackness on a rope. Later, when he ventured to the pictures at the School of Arts, and to dances where he hung around outside with the older blokes, smoking, swapping yarns, there was news of visits some of these fellows had made to Sydney or to the Riverina to pick fruit.

He would slip away to these dances, or to the picture shows, in secret. Not much more than fourteen, he would wait till he thought the others were asleep, then, getting up softly in the dark, pull his pants on, and with his shirt and boots in his hand creep away to finish dressing in the yard.

'Where y' off to, Digger?' she would whisper, sometimes, in her sleep.

'Sshh. I'll tellya t'morrer.'

Beginning softly in the dark, he would tell her things. He would start in a whisper, but quite soon he would get excited, break into giggles, or his voice would crack in squeaky shouts.

'Shuddup in there, get ta sleep,' their father would shout through the wall, 'or I'll bloody come in an' make yer.'

Then, after a moment, their mother's voice:

'Go t' sleep now, Digger, you can tell that t'morrow. It'll keep.'

3

'So,' Digger said, 'how'm I doin'? Still on top?'

Vic grinned. 'You're doing OK. Want a statement?'

'Nah! I'll trust ya.'

Exchanges of this sort between them had become ritual in these last weeks. They were jest. There were subjects still that they steered clear of, where they would have felt shy and constrained with one another, but there was no lack of trust between them.

Vic, elbows on knees, looked past Digger to the river and its dancing swarm, bits of winged life in millions whose bodies at moments caught the light and made a second river up there, as if the first had thrown off a lighter variant of itself, all living particles, with the freedom to hover, prop, dance on the spot, while the other, earthbound, could do nothing but flow on. Occasionally the oily surface broke. A pair of jaws rose up and snapped down a dozen of those lives, or a hundred – whatever it could get. He watched Digger jiggle the handline.

'Waddabout you?' Digger asked.

'I don't know, I think I'm winning. But they're crafty buggers. I can't be sure.'

'They still after you then?'

'Yes,' Vic said. He had caught the hint of scepticism in Digger's tone. 'They're still after me.'

Digger pretended to be occupied with the line. After a moment, falling back on an older game between them, he said: 'I don't know why you don't pull out while the going's good. I would. I don't know how you put up with it.'

There was at times, Vic thought, something prim and old-womanish about Digger. 'These are just the sort of things,' he thought, 'that mothers must say. Looking just like that, too. Half-horrified, half-impressed.' This side of Digger was a source of amusement to him.

'And young Alex?'

Young Alex, as they called him, was Vic's nephew, though in fact he was no longer young. He was forty-three.

Vic frowned. 'Oh, he's against me, I think.' He made it sound a matter of no concern. 'Only I can't be sure of that, either. He doesn't give much away.'

No, Digger thought, I bet he doesn't.

'If they get me this time,' Vic said, and Digger looked up, caught out by something he hadn't heard before, 'I'll chuck the towel in. Do you believe that?'

Is he serious? Digger thought. But Vic had already covered himself.

'Maybe I should just do that anyway,' he said. 'Chuck it in and come up here.'

He laughed at that, and after a moment Digger did too. It was so improbable.

Their lives were as different as any two lives could be that still touched and crossed and could at moments like this move quietly as one.

'You've left us f' dead,' Digger used to tease him in the early days. The mockery was of the gentlest sort, but Vic was sensitive on the point of loyalty and would look hurt.

'What do you mean? Because I'm makin' a bit of money? That doesn't make any difference.'

But as time went on he stopped protesting. It did make a difference; not so much the money as the level he moved at, the moves he made there, and the amount of interest people took in him.

'I see you've been in the papers again,' Digger would say, and Vic, though he was pleased Digger had seen it – he was still hungry for admiration, he could never have enough of it – would make a face. 'Oh, the papers,' he'd say. 'You can't take any notice of the papers.' And to make up a little for the gap between them, he began to tell Digger stories, frank, light-hearted ones, of his activities out there among the cannibals, laying it on pretty thick at times and delighting in Digger's expressions of disbelief, of disapproval too, often enough, and playing when he could for sympathy.

'Well, I'm glad it's you and not me,' Digger would tell him, letting them both off the hook. 'I dunno how you stand it. I couldn't do it. Not for quids.'

Digger in fact was being disingenuous. He knew Vic. You could trust him with your life. On the other hand, you couldn't trust him with tuppence. He had been surprised at first that some fellow he knew, and knew well, should be getting on in the world. But he saw

35

after a time that this was naive. The very qualities he knew in Vic, both sides, took another form out there and were just what was needed. That told you something about the world, and Digger, in his own way, took note of it, but he didn't let on to Vic what he had seen.

'I stand it,' Vic would say, 'because I've got to. I've got no option.' What he meant was that change, risk, action, were essential to him.

He was inclined to look about, when he came up here, and ask how Digger stood it. It was a world, up here, that had no need of you. Everything you looked at or touched, the long strips of bark that peeled back to show glossy colours, the squiggles on a trunk that were little lives, birdcalls that came out of the scrub, ker-*whip*, ker-*whip* – all these gave you the same message. Come on in if you like, but you might as well not for all the difference it will make.

It could be a comfort, that, for an hour or two. It took you out of yourself. But any more and he felt ghostly.

What he needed was things that told him he *was* here. Lucky for him the world was full of them.

But three weeks ago he had changed all this. He had come to Digger and asked a favour of him.

For a day or two after the idea first struck him he had held back. Not because he was afraid Digger would refuse him. He knew he wouldn't. But because by asking it he was disturbing a balance that had existed between them, sometimes shakily, for more than forty years. He hesitated. Then, just as he knew he would, he went ahead and did it just the same.

'Listen, mate,' he had begun, a little shy now that he had come to the point, 'you know I wouldn't involve you in anything that wasn't strictly above board. But the fact is, Digger, I've got a favour to ask you. I wouldn't if there was anyone else.'

'What is it?' Digger said straight out. He was surprised. They didn't ask favours of one another. He wondered what it could be that was not covered already by the friendship between them.

The note of distress in his voice unnerved Vic, but he was in now and what he had said was true: there was no one else. Quickly he laid the thing out, sticking to the plainest terms. Digger heard him through.

'But what use would I be?' he said at last. 'I don't know anything about *shares*.'

'You wouldn't have to. You wouldn't even know it was happening.

All we'd be using, Digger,' and he paused a moment before he could get it out, 'is your name.' He went on quickly to cover the embarrassment of it. Digger was looking more and more uneasy. He was actually wringing his hands.

'You see, we need someone who isn't known, who couldn't be traced – or not easily. It's a matter of timing – to get it all done before it turns up in the records. Oh, there's nothing illegal to it. It's a bit *clever*, that's all. You know what these business fellers are like. You see, the law says I can only buy one and a half per cent of the shares every six months, even if it *is* my company. It's a silly law, but there you are, it's the law. So I need someone else to do it. *I* put up the money – well, not money exactly, collateral, you know what that is, other companies that I can borrow against. All *you* would have to do is sign a few papers. Albert, isn't it?'

'Yes,' Digger said bleakly, 'Albert.' The unfamiliarity of it was at this moment a relief.

'You see, mate, someone's after me, I don't know who. It could be anyone. Alex, even. All I know is, they've started to move. So what I've got to do is get in before them. Get the cash together, wait for the right moment, then before the others can do it, zap! we go in and make a bid for the whole show. Or as much of it, anyway, as will give me the whip hand.'

He was sweating. The boldness and danger of it excited him, but there were things too that he needed to keep back. It might scare Digger if he knew the scale of what he had in mind. For instance, the sums that would be involved.

'The thing is, to get it all over and done with in the shortest possible time. Forty days, that's the maximum. So you see, Digger, it won't be for long.' He could see how pinched Digger looked. He was sorry for that. 'I'm up against it,' he said simply. 'I wouldn't ask if I had the option. You're the only one.'

Digger worked his Adam's apple. The trouble was, he had no point from which he could judge all this, no knowledge, no experience, and there was no one he could ask. Was there an element of madness in it that anyone who *knew* about these things would see straight off?

'I'm not imagining things,' Vic said in an aggrieved tone, 'if that's what you're thinking. I know it sounds dramatic. Paranoia, is that what you're thinking? Honestly, Digger, this is the way these things are *done*. It may seem mad to you, but don't you think I know what I'm doing? This is a game I play every day of the week. Believe me, I'm good at it.'

So Digger had been drawn in, and in the weeks that followed several prime targets, companies, that is, that were vulnerable to take-over, began to pass through his hands, all as Vic had promised, with no trouble on his part; without his even knowing for the most part what had occurred. It was a phantom existence he was living out there.

The companies – Morton Holdings, Cathedral Steel and Concrete, J. & R. Randall were the largest, but there were smaller ones as well – consisted of warehouses in three states, factories, offices with desks and filing cabinets and typewriters and computers, cafeterias, fleets of vans, stacks of cardboard boxes or steel girders; but all Digger saw were papers. And even the papers, it seemed, were just promises, negotiable items of trust, no more to be associated with actual notes or coins than the name Albert Keen was with the man who was signing for him.

Digger was astonished by what was revealed to him, the glimpse he got behind the scenes into a world he had thought till now was unshakeably solid.

'But I told you it was a game,' Vic told him. 'Didn't you believe me?'

The magic for him lay in the very thing that Digger found so unsettling, the extent to which the structure he was erecting, for all its being underwritten out there by so much that was real and touchable, was a secret one, visible only to himself, Digger, his advisers and a few collaborators who were in the know. But it was solid enough. 'There's banks in this, Digger,' he would whisper, when he saw that Digger had doubts, and he would name them. But Digger, instead of being consoled, was terrified. Men drew their wages, their families put clothes on their backs and bread into their mouths, bought TV sets and video recorders; buildings went up; produce was shifted; a whole society breathed and ate and slept – but the basis of it all was no more than air, no more than promises, trust.

Vic laughed. 'But what else could it be?' he asked, as if Digger were a child. And Digger was scared by that, too. By common agreement they fell into the habit of talking as little as possible of all this, and then only in the lightest terms.

'Agh,' he said now, hauling his tackle in, 'this is a mug's game. Let's see if Jenny's got a cuppa tea,' and he made to move, but Vic stopped him.

'Not yet, eh? Let's wait a bit. It's early enough.'

Digger was surprised but made no objection. He stowed his line, leaned back, and they settled and sat in silence. There was nothing unusual in it – they could spend long periods just sitting; but he was uneasy just the same. It was the third time in a week that Vic had just turned up like this.

'I'm on tenterhooks,' he had confessed the first time, 'about this bit of business we've got on. This last bit. You don't mind, do you?' He was worried about the market. 'I want t' get all this finalised,' he said, 'a bit sooner than we thought. The market's too high. In fact that's good for us, it's what we need. Only I don't trust it.'

But they had none of that sort of talk today. It was something else.

Vic, his boots set down carefully in the dirt, his back hard against a she-oak, felt the silence swell; out over the swarming river, but back too into the clearing where the store was and beyond into the trackless scrub. But the real expansion was in him. Sitting quietly now with his head back, he saw from outside him, above and at a distance, these two old blokes sitting at ease beside a river, and it seemed miraculous to him that one of them, against all the odds, should be himself. Miraculous, too – there was no other word for it – that this breath should be here for him to catch hold of, and that this moment, just after four on an autumn afternoon in 1987, should have been waiting up ahead for them to reach it; like the leaves here that threw shadows on his hands, and had also been growing slowly towards it, and having arrived now, were turning over with a sound that was just perceptible if you listened, a little shush and scratch against the stillness.

'Listen, Digger,' and Digger was disturbed for the second time by something new in his voice, 'do you remember a cove called Anson?'

Digger sucked his cheeks in and looked out at the river. After a little he said: 'Anson, yes. John Archibald.'

Vic let out a long breath. 'Yes,' he said, 'that'd be him,' though in fact he had never till now heard these other names. He could not have explained, even to Digger, the ease he felt at having them spoken.

He was a jackaroo from up Singleton way, twenty, maybe twenty-one or -two. Claimed to have played half-back for one of the state teams but was almost certainly lying. 'What year was that, mate?' one of the others had challenged. Vic remembered the lie.

One day early on, sitting in the sun in just their shorts, they had played a game of draughts. They were seated on either side of an upturned drum, he couldn't remember where, but the heat was intense and the sunlight blinding. Changi. Or it might have been earlier, on the ship going up.

Blue eyes. Hair bleached to unruly straw. Rough, very cocky, and dead sure when they sat down that he would win.

'Only I was surer,' Vic thought, and could feel even at this distance the little spurt of triumph, the joy in his own good fortune and skill, as the move came up and he took it, 'Ha, I've got ya!'

The look of utter astonishment on Anson's face – that too had been such a pleasure to him. The feller couldn't believe it. Couldn't hide his irritation either. He had been so certain he would win.

They were in different mobs and had nothing to do with one another after that, even when they found themselves in the same camp up on the line. Then one day, in a period when they were working sixteen hours at a stretch and were half dead on their feet, in a trance most of them, so sick and brutalised they hardly knew where they were, he had been sitting over his bit of midday rice, and in glancing up for some reason – no reason, in fact – had seen Anson squatting just yards away at the side of the track.

There was no modesty among them, they were past all that; but he looked away, and then, after a moment, looked back again, just as Anson, with a worried frown half-turned to glance behind him (they all did that) and inspect what he had done. Vic saw it too, and their eyes met.

They were mostly indifferent to one another by now, too preoccupied with their own terrors to care how the next man felt. But they all knew what a white turd signified. Cholera. It was a sentence of death.

He meant nothing to him, that fellow; but he had thought he would never forget his look – or the stab of panic he felt in his own bowels – as that bit of intelligence passed between them.

He had forgotten it, of course, in time. As he had forgotten so many other things. Till just this week it had come back to him as if no time at all had gone by, just seconds. The man, moving back into himself, got to his feet and stood there, his fingers working clumsily to adjust his shorts.

The man, the *man* – but what was he called? It seemed shameful to Vic that he could not remember, though in fact they had only spoken the once. He worried his way through the alphabet, finding other names that he had also forgotten, but not that one. Then he took his mind off it and it was there.

What he had been struck by, after that first glance of panicky recognition, was the mildness with which Anson stood watching his own fingers deal with his shorts; with the ordinary but quite tricky business of hooking them up so they wouldn't fall. He had felt a kind of awe at the futility of it, as if a cold hand had been laid on him, too. He was amazed (but there was horror in it too) at the distance Anson had come since their draughts game. There was no truculence in him, none at all. With a kind of dumb patience he stood tying the rag-ends together, then turned and moved away.

But what he thought now was something different: that it had taken him forty years to accept the hard facts of existence, whereas that fellow Anson had got there in just months.

Digger sat quiet.

Anson. He came early on the list. After Amos, Reginald James. He could have gone on if Vic had required it. To Aspie, Ball, Barclay, Baynes, Beeston . . .

There were nine more after that. Then Curran.

4

Great events do not always cast a shadow before them. In Malaya in 1941 the Japanese Imperial Army arrived on rickety bikes. It didn't look like the first part of a triumph or a moment from history.

You saw them pedalling up the track between the rubber trees, rifles slung across their backs, glasses ablaze, rubber boots and leggings working up and down. Very spindly, the bikes looked. The riders sweated in their heavy gear. You took aim, squeezed gently, and the whole enterprise went haywire, the rider waving his arms about as if he believed there was something up there, the hem of a garment or the big toe of one of his ancestors, that he could grab hold of to hoist himself aloft. He scrabbled for it. Meanwhile the wheels went spinning, gravity insisted, and rider and machine slewed off into the ditch. It was comic.

But their own men died and they pulled back. Big guns lifted, rained down shells. The heat and the noise grew terrific. The narrow streets of Chinatown hurled themselves skyward. Walls ripped, flew upward and came down again as lumps of plaster and dust. Locals, Chinese mostly, ran this way and that in the oily darkness with cashboxes or rolled carpets or children in their arms, or chickens or sewing-machines or little screaming piglets. Or they trotted by with half a household on their shoulders, all the chair legs pointing upward, and fell down with fire running along their backs and the load smashed and scattered, or got up and hobbled on again among the armoured cars and the field ambulances and the walking wounded that were streaming in over the causeway to the island fortress.

That was Sunday. On the Sunday night, fellows who had been fighting hard the day before in rubber plantations on the island, or hand-to-hand on factory sites, Digger among them, were at ease at last, preparing themselves for the next stage of proceedings by darning their socks, rolling them neatly, and pushing them down the side of their packs. When all was shipshape, they counted their coins, cleaned their fingernails, and jabbing into a tin of condensed milk, sucked comfort from a metal tit.

All around, at campfires and in places off in the dark, trading had started up again: a packet of cigarette papers and two frenchies for a fountain-pen; an ounce of tobacco for a tin of the best gramophone needles, steel, with a record of Paderewski's Minuet in G thrown in.

It was as if the whole division had been constituted and shipped north for no other purpose than to ensure the movement, from one continent to another, of a million articles of no great worth or use that might otherwise have sat gathering dust in a country store, or mouldering away in a suitcase under a bed. An underground economy unknown to statistics, it was in progress at every instant here, between fights, between mouthfuls of coconut milk or bully beef, through fences, across the space between bunks. It went on even at the borehole, while the two men were engaged on that other unofficial business of easing their bowels.

Transactions. Deals. They took up so much energy, engendered so much feeling, you might have thought they were the one true essential of a fighting man's life, of tenacious, disorderly *civilian* life inside the official military one, exposing in pocket form the real motives of all this international activity, compared with which all talk of freedom and honour and patriotic pride and the saving of civilisation was the merest mind-fogging gibberish.

It was a hot night thick with cloud and the pall of rubber godowns that were blazing along the docks. Firelit shadows were in play as men went about the tasks of settling and making camp. The voices in the stillness were of fellows stirring pots, playing mah-jong or blackjack, or swapping lazy obscenities.

Others, newcomers mostly but some old hands as well, were still talking about the big fight they would be in, tomorrow or the day after, that would finish the little buggers off.

Such talk was bullshit. Those who had really done any fighting – Digger, for instance, and Mac and Doug – would have nothing to do with it. The heaviness that hung over the island was not just weather, or smoke from the storehouse of the Empire going up in flames. The rumour was (it was only a whisper as yet, men were afraid to let it out) that the commanders were already negotiating.

By eleven o'clock it was official. In a meeting with the Japanese

43

commander, General Yamashita, the commander of the Allied Forces, General Percival, had signed an unconditional surrender, to be effective from 10 p.m. Japanese time.

So all their watches were wrong – that too. They were on Jap time now, and would be for as long as it lasted. They had, without knowing it, lost their status as soldiers, and some other qualifications as well, and been prisoners of war for the last two hours.

On the Monday they began marching, fifty thousand of them it was said, into captivity, though all it meant as yet was to move twelve miles to the other end of the island; a mass of men so huge that you couldn't conceive of it, Digger couldn't, till you came to a slope and looked back and saw the dense massed columns passing away into ghostliness in the haze.

They took everything they could carry. The army had taught them that much. What you had you hung on to: rations, equipment, an old tobacco tin, spare sweaters and socks. But also cheap watches traded or knocked off from the Chinese, propelling pencils, fly-swats, bronze Buddhas, copies of *Gone with the Wind* and *Moby Dick* and Edgar Wallace, bolts of shantung and Thai silk, inkwells, packs of cards, flasks of Johnny Walker Red Label whisky. Each man was weighed down with twenty to forty pounds of it and staggering; his shirt pockets stuffed, and such lighter articles as bottle-openers, pen-knives, screwdrivers, metal cups and water-bottles dangling from the straps of his pack or his belt-loops or from a thong round his neck. They looked less like the remnants of a military enterprise, even a failed one, than the medicine men of an advanced cargo cult, or a horde of Syrian pedlars about to be unleashed on all the country towns of New South Wales. They tottered, they clanked with relics, the accumulated paraphernalia (anything that could be upended and slung across a shoulder, or unscrewed or wrenched off) of a world that had exploded in fragments around them, and would have now, in the spirit of improvisation, to be reconstructed elsewhere – on the move if that's what it came to. But they were experts at that. They were Australians. A good many of them had been training for it all their lives.

These miscellaneous oddments, the detachable parts and symbols of civilised life, were all they had now to reassure themselves of where they had come from and what they were. What was contained in a set of surgeons' knives or a pair of pliers and a coil of wire – and in a way that was very nearly mystical – was the superior status, guaranteed, of those who had invented them and knew their use. Civilisation? That's *us*. Look at this.

But as the day wore on, and the twelve miles became a martyrdom of raw feet, raw shoulders, thighs chafed with sweat, and the sun beat down shadeless and blinding, the weight would not balance, not even against an unknown future. By nightfall even the dullest and most stubborn of them had learned something, and what he had learned could be picked up, weighed, turned over and a price put upon it, by the thousands of scavengers who moved along with them, snapping up whatever they cast aside or dropped, and would be laid out that night under lamps in shanty shops – as proof of what till now had been barely graspable: an extraordinary surrender of power, made once on paper and once in a form you could actually see and lay your hands on; in the world of commodities. What a break-up! Idlers surveying this windfall were bug-eyed with amazement at the sheer scope of it. A quartz inkwell, look, without a single chip!

It was a general stripping. In it, whether they knew it or not, they had been making decisions on which their lives would depend. Everything a man had grasped about human nature (including his own), and the unpredictability of things, was in the choice between a six-bob alarm clock and a pair of scuffed but serviceable boots.

At a point back there they had stepped, each one of them, across a line where the weight of each thing in the world, even the smallest, had been added to; but they themselves were lighter.

Sitting among so many in the sweltering dark, Digger rested against his pack, boots off at last, socks peeled painfully from the blistered flesh.

They were in an open encampment at the eastern end of the island. Changi, the place was called.

The unit was scattered. They had started off in good order, but men had kept falling behind, some to bargain with one another or with the natives who ran alongside, grinning, pointing to things that had caught their eye and shouting offers, others because they had gone sick or lame, or been poleaxed by the sun. Many of them were still straggling in, and on all sides the company sergeants were at work, shouting roll calls of their men.

Twelve days ago Mac had been wounded, not too badly, in the

thigh. For most of the march, Digger on one side, Doug on the other, they had half-carried him. He lay now with one arm across his eyes, as white as chalk. Digger worried and fussed.

Doug, who could never sit still for more than two minutes at a time, was out scavenging. That was the excuse. What he was really doing was walking up and down in jubilation at the scene.

He was in his element. The sanctified irregularity and disorder of it, the mixing in of Australians and British and Dutch and native troops, the great braying noise they made far off into the night, all this was tonic to him. He danced up and down among the various groups – he was a big fellow but very light on his feet – chiacking, greeting acquaintances, dipping down every now and again to share a word or two with this one or that, and to draw out the bullshit artists among them who were already sketching glorious futures for themselves among the guerrillas, or boasting of what they would have done if they'd been given the chance. He came back with a packet of Ardaths and a swag of gleeful tales to tell.

'I tellya,' he told them, 'this is gunna be a little Chicago, you mark my word. You'll see now what human nature is.'

This last was a crack at Mac. Human nature was a term Mac was strong on; he and Doug did not see eye to eye on it, or on much else, really. Their affection was based on passionate difference. He threw it out now in the hope that it might stir Mac up.

Like most men who have never had a day off work, Doug was uncomfortable with illness. His belief was that if he could only stir Mac up a bit, and lift his spirits, he would be himself again.

'Word is,' he told them, 'that we're gunna give in our gear. Wouldn' you know? So that the bloody officers can be turned out like gentlemen and impress the Nips. Walkin' shoes for all officers, two pairs apiece. Commandeered if fellers aren't willing to give 'em up. Shoes are goin' pretty cheap out there. Blokes are gettin' rid of 'em fer anything they can get, smokes, watches, silk stockin's. Silk stockin's are pretty safe.' He laughed. 'I'd settle fer smokes, meself. You watch. Smokes, bully, condensed milk, that'll be the currency. A good pair a' boots. It always comes down to the same things in the long run, belly, dick or feet. There won't be too much dick in it this time, I reckon. It'll be bellies, you watch, an' feet.'

He shook out the pack of Ardaths, offered one to Digger, then passed it across to Mac. He raised his head and looked out over the great mob of them that was scattered over the flat ground. All the nonsense had gone out of him.

'They're mugs, most a' these blokes,' he said sorrowfully. 'Wouldn' know their arseholes from the back end of a rabbit warren. It's pathetic. Half of 'em are still puking up their mother's milk.'

Mac had lighted up and had his head back, drawing in smoke.

'How's it going, chief?' Doug said, settling beside him. 'A bit rugged, eh?' He looked quickly at Digger, then away.

They were spread out over a low area without definition, except that somewhere, away in the darkness, you could smell the sea. No fences, no wire, no sign of Nips. There was movement, a kind of restlessness as of a huge animal stretched out on the ground there, the sound of its breathing, a muffled roar. But everything, their movements, their voices when they spoke, had a subdued air, as if they were under surveillance and the Nips were there after all, but out of sight.

They were in the open, without protection, contained only by the gentlemen's agreement some Englishman had made in their name. It was eerie, that.

'What's up, Dig?'

Mac, who often knew what Digger was thinking, looked back over his shoulder. His expression was quizzical.

'Nothin',' Digger said. 'Just thinkin'.'

'Farewell the plumed troop, eh? And the big wars that make ambition virtue.' Mac's voice was hoarse and full of weariness, but there was some of his old humour in it. He could see they were concerned about him and was making an effort.

Doug, who got embarrassed when things took a literary turn, drew on the last of his fag and sent it in a fiery arc across the dark.

'Farewell the neighing steed,' Digger recited, taking up where Mac had left off, and in a voice that had none of the roughness of his ordinary speech, 'and the shrill trump, the spirit-stirring drum, the ear-piercing fife, the royal banner, and all quality, pride, pomp, and circumstance of glorious war.'

He came to an end, and looked up, a little shy but not at all self-conscious. They often played this game.

Mac was grinning, genuinely delighted.

He was an older fellow, thirty-eight. Back home he was on the trams. He lived at Bondi Junction with his sister-in-law, Iris, who worked in a cake shop (he had told Digger all this), and was what

47

Doug called a black-stump philosopher, full of all sorts of wild arguments and theories and extravagant optimisms that wouldn't have worked in Paradise, let alone where they were now. His pack was crammed with books, and every week at home he bought at least a dozen of them from barrows or second-hand bookshops down George Street. His room at home was stacked to the ceiling with them.

'He never fails, this boy,' he said now, inviting Doug to admire the phenomenon. 'Amazing, eh?'

Digger shook his head. It was nothing, a trick, that's all.

Doug was about to offer his own ironical comment when another voice broke in: 'Hey, I know that.'

It was Doug's mate, if you could call him that, Vic.

'Good fer you, son,' Doug said drily. The others, Digger and Mac, exchanged glances.

He was a big, solidly-built fellow, not yet twenty, who had recently attached himself to them and was proving hard to shake off. Originally, like Doug, from a mining village up Newcastle way, he saw this as a bond between them and made a good deal of it. He was just out of school and had, so far as Digger could see, no experience of any kind. He tried to hide it by speaking rough and making a big man of himself. Digger couldn't stand him. Mac didn't think much of him either.

It was Doug he had set his sights on, but for some reason it was the others he played up to, and this made them like him even less. But when they complained about him, Doug, who was all generosity, would shrug his shoulders and say: 'Oh, Vic's all right.' Still, this didn't prevent him from teasing the fellow.

'Go on,' he'd say with mock astonishment when Vic came out with some bit of self-promotion by which he hoped they might be impressed.

He did, too, regularly, and sank himself.

'Here,' he said now, 'I brought you something.' It was a little tin of Ideal milk.

Doug took it and turned it over in his hand. 'What's this for?' he said. 'Somebody got a birthday?'

Vic's neck burned. It wasn't *for* anything. It was something he had picked up for them, that's all. He waited for Doug to accept the thing and get it out of the way.

'Ta,' Doug said at last, and set the tin down, a bit too prominently, on his pack. Vic took this as an invitation to settle on the grass among them.

'So,' he said, 'here we are, eh? How long d'ya reckon this'll last?'

'I dunno.' Doug offered him the pack of Ardaths. 'Long as the war, could be. How long d'you reckon?'

'Well,' Vic said, 'I heard they want to exchange us. Right away, one bloke says.'

'Go on! – You hear that, Mac? – What would they exchange us for?'

'Wool, I heard. They want wool.'

Doug laughed outright. 'They'll need a lotta bloody sheep in exchange fer this lot,' he said, looking out over the mob of them. 'So howdaya reckon they'll do it – by weight? I'll be oright, they'll do pretty well outa me. You too. But waddabout Digger? Hardly be worth tradin' a mingy little bugger like that. Waddaya weigh, Digger?'

'Eight eight,' Digger laughed.

'I can just see it,' Doug said. 'It'd be like the bloody day a' judgement. I don't know whether I could be in *that*.'

'Well,' Vic said uncomfortably, 'it's on'y a rumour anyway. You know, ya hear all sorts a' things. I don't suppose it'll happen.'

'No,' Doug said, 'I don't think so either. You can breathe again, Dig, we've scrapped that plan.'

Vic watched the exchange of smiles between them. He wasn't a fool. He caught Digger's eye on him. Scornful. Digger was the one he would have trouble with. He looked like nothing, there was nothing you would notice about him; but of the three he was the one who considered longest, said least, and would be the hardest to win.

'I wish he'd bugger off,' Digger was thinking. 'Can't he see we don't want him? He spoils things.'

He was one of a large number of replacements who had only recently arrived on the island.

Three weeks before, they were still being seasick on the way up from Perth, or, in baggy shorts and boots, their shoulders blistering, had been leaning far out over the rails to sight flying fish. They had been recruited and shipped straight here, it being the intention of the service chiefs to train them on the spot. Their kit and a week's rifle practice on the range at Bukit Timar was the sum total of what made them soldiers.

49

The voyage, the adventure of leaving Australia, the tales they brought with them, heard from old-timers in country pubs and on the job in timberyards and sales rooms, or from uncles while the women were washing up after Sunday dinner, had raised them to a pitch of heroic impatience, a keenness untempered by any contact with army regulations or the rigours of drill. All fired up and ready for conflict, they had walked down the gang plank into *this*. Captivity.

Vic had taken the turn of events as a personal affront. Since ten o'clock on Sunday night, all the qualities he knew to be in him were out of fashion. He was among men here who had already been toughened by experience, even those of them, like Digger, who were no older than himself. They might think they had the right to despise him, for no other reason than that he was young, raw, and had had no chance to show himself. But he couldn't put up with that. He knew what he was.

He squatted on his heels looking easy – he was a pleasant-looking fellow, his hands hanging loosely over his thighs, his slouch hat across his back. But he was never easy. There was always some little irritation that pricked at him. Very aware of slights, he stayed alert and watchful.

Doug, meanwhile, had found a new topic to rave over.

'They reckon Gordon Bennett's missing,' he said. 'Have you heard that? Pissed off home in his own little rowboat and left the rest of us up the creek. Be just like 'im, eh?'

He had a poor view of anyone in authority; officers, bosses, little jumped-up clerks behind a desk who hum and ha and make you feel like shit before they'll stamp anything for you; all of them eager to lick an arse or kick one according to whether it's above or below them; all of them determined, like the bloody second lieutenants here who would soon be strutting about in their shoes, to hang on to every last little sign of privilege.

'Typical,' Doug said, and spat.

'Well, I don't know,' Vic said. He had always to be saying something. 'D'ya reckon one of our blokes would? I mean, I know 'e's a general and that, but would 'e?'

Doug said nothing, just sat there with his eyebrows raised and looked at him. The silence was too much for Vic.

'Well, would you?'

Doug laughed. 'Are you barmy? Of course I wouldn't. But I'm a bloody footslogger, I can't just piss off home. Haven't got a bloody rowboat for one thing. Neither can Mac here, or Digger. Neither can you. But who's t' say what I might do if I was a general? Or you either – well, not *you* maybe, but I wouldn't like to swear what I mightn't do if I had half the chance.'

Vic frowned. He didn't care much for the line the talk was taking. 'Anyway,' he said, 'it's just a rumour, really. Like that wool business, eh? The place is full of 'em.' There was a beat of silence. 'So,' he said, 'here we are, eh?'

Doug looked about, and the sigh he gave was theatrical. 'I dunno,' he said. 'How did I get inta this? I was always such a careful bloke. Never put me foot down on cracks – not even when I was a grown-up. Changed me socks twice a week, never went out with fast women or stepped under ladders or broke mirrors, or let 'em give me a ticket with a thirteen in it. Ya can't be more careful than that. If I saw a Chinaman I'd rush right up, you know, and jus' tip 'im, like, then duck away, fer luck. An' after all that I was mug enough to join up. I ask you, what makes us do it? Are we rational beings or aren't we? Oh Gawd, I thought, they'll send me to the *real* war. Greece maybe, Egypt, I don't want that. But they sent me up here. I 'ad Digger 'n Mac with me. I thought, "This is all right. Tropic nights. Taxi dancers ten cents a go. Chinamen all over. You'll be all right here, Douggy. This'll do." An' now look what's happened. I ask you, honestly, is there any logic to it? Do any of us know what we're doing, even when we're bloody doin' it? Is anyone weighin' it all up in a pan? – and I don't jus' mean so they can trade me for my bloody weight in wool!' He laughed. 'Still, if it does come t' that – we oughta start buildin' you up, Digger –'

'I'm all right,' Digger said, laughing.

'Here, mate.' He scooped his big hand down, swept up the tin of Ideal milk and flipped it to Digger in a quick pass. 'You get that down ya,' he said. 'You don't mind, do ya Vic? Digger's our local flyweight –'

'Feather,' Digger put in, to be accurate.

'No one in this mob can touch him.'

'Oh?' said Vic. You could see the little flicker of challenge and interest. He was surprised. Digger was such a mild fellow.

'On'y 'e wouldn't be worth a ball a' nine-ply if they took up that wool business. Wouldn' hardly make a cover for a coat-hanger or the left side of a kiddie's cardigan. Sorry, mate,' he told Digger, 'but you're in trouble. Here, gimme that!'

He took the can, spiked it twice with his jack-knife and flipped it back. 'Ta, Vic,' he said, on Digger's behalf.

Digger took a good swig.

5

Digger's reputation as a fighter had been established their first week in camp. He had gone three rounds with a state amateur champion, then fought for the unit in the battalion titles. It was Doug who put him up to it. He didn't let on to them, or not at first, that he was a professional.

For eighteen months before he joined up he had been working the country shows with a boxing troupe, in a street of gaudy sideshows and circus freaks that included a pin-headed Chinaman, a strong man who also ate swords and swallowed fire, a couple of daredevil motorbike riders (a husband and wife team who three times nightly faced the Ring of Death), a fat lady and the Human Torso, a fellow who was just a head and shoulders on a mobile tray. Digger's job had been to stand among the crowd and, if no other mug did it, offer himself up to go a round or two with one of the troupe.

He had always been a follower of fairs. The sound of a merry-go-round and the wheezy music it pumped out, the sight of a dozen men in shorts and blue singlets with sledgehammers and guy-ropes raising a tent, turning a bit of waste ground into a carnival site, was enough to draw him away from any message he was on. More than once he had got a good box on the ears for slipping under the canvas and getting in late for tea, or for hanging around outside to hear the spruikers and coming home with a mouthful of nonsense (he could learn off the most intricate patter in just minutes) that filled Jenny with a wailing desire to experience these wonders for herself.

He loved the lights strung from pole to pole, red and blue and orange, casting weird shadows where the warm breeze struck them, the smell of animal shit, the satin and spangles the showies wore, which could be grimy when you got up close, but under the lights, and in the glow that was created by the spruikers' empowering descriptions, took you right out of yourself.

Toddlers swung up high on their fathers' shoulders would be dazed or crowing. Noisy youths with slicked-down hair and a fag in their mouth would be lining up to fire at a row of ducks or to swing a hammer and ring a bell, their girls, all permed and lipsticked, looking on and pretending they weren't bored. Only later, with a kewpie doll or alarm clock or plaster dog under their arm, would these girls find something at last that really touched them. Looking out from the vantage point of a rough normality they would feel a pricking fear run up their arms at the sight of the pin-headed Chinaman drinking tea from a dolly's cup, or a poddy-calf sad-eyed and huggable on its six legs.

Digger, who had been haunting such places since he was ten years old, would move about in an excited trance, taking in the noise, the sweat, the colour, the cruelties. And always at the centre of it all, not quite a freak-show but drawing to itself some of the loose emotion the freak-shows generated, was the tent with the boxers; half a dozen fellows, not all of them young, but all dark – half-castes or Islanders – lined up on a board in front of a painted flap.

The flap showed two boxers, taller than the real ones, shaping up. On a separate platform to one side was a spruiker to stir the mob. Already gloved and booted, in silk shorts and dressing-gowns that proclaimed their fighting names in letters of gold, the coons would be dancing about just at head level, jabbing the air, hissing through their nostrils, looking terrible.

They were there as a challenge. To question the toughness and assumed manhood of the farmhands and counter-jumpers who stood about with a girl on their arm and a stick of sugarcane or a cornet of fairy-floss in their fist, asking themselves, but secretly, if they measured up. Mugs, they were.

Telling it over later to Mac and Doug, Digger would laugh, a little shamefaced before these new friends of the role he had played, but carried away by the sheer fun of it. He would do a take-off of one of those muscle-bound farm-boys standing with his arms bared and his mouth open, breathing through his nose; or the others who cat-called and chiacked, too fly themselves to step into a pounding, but quite willing to urge on their mates.

There was, after all, something very stark and simple in it that appealed to fellows whose fathers and grandfathers had cleared the country, fought off blacks, made themselves a reputation in a war. It was over, all that. Life now was a tame affair of scrounging for a living and worrying always how to pay the rent and feed the kids, or, worse still, of lining up for a hand-out; and with the vague suspicion always that you had been let down and betrayed – only who by? – and a gnawing resentment in you that needed something out there you could nail and take a poke at.

What was on offer here was a real fight: amateur against professional, white against black, an ordinary man's muscle and skill, a dairyman's or meat worker's, against forces that had to be pushed back every now and then, flattened and shown their place, or you wouldn't know what you were worth. Those were the terms.

Partly it was what the spruiker put into their heads with his quickfire clever patter. But mostly, and especially after a few beers, it was the sight of the coons themselves looking so flash up there in their leather gloves and their maroon or green silk gowns with the stitched-on lettering. You could smell them. For all the showy material of their get-up they were just abos, coons.

It was a put-up job. That's what the mugs didn't realise. But once it got going there was enough bitterness on both sides to make it real. Blood, that's what the mob wanted. To see one of the coons get laid out with a cut lip, or, if the mood took them, to see some swaggering lair, a local bully, get done over by a black. The crowd was unpredictable. It could switch sides just like that.

Most of the challengers in fact were no match for the fast-footed members of the troupe, even those of them who had seen better days and were soft-headed with grog or from the beatings they had taken in real fights. They were professionals and knew all the dodges. They had been in this game, most of them, since they first learned to shape up, and were wily and tough. All the challenger had was brute strength, his hatred of flash niggers, and the wish to impress the girl he was with or his mates.

Digger's job, standing in his shirt-sleeves in the warm night air, while the music of the merry-go-round rose and fell and beetles hurled themselves at raw bulbs, was to make himself one of the crowd, a country kid like the rest (which he was of course), and to appeal to the spirit of emulation or savagery in them.

'That big bloke don't look so tough,' he would remark to one of his neighbours, 'waddaya reckon?' and he would begin to urge this or that man on. Only if no one else would be in it would he step forward himself.

'You sure about this?' the spruiker would ask as he climbed the stairs to the platform. 'Yer mother knows about it, does she? You *are* sixteen? – Nice lookin' bloke, isn't 'e girls? Shame about that nose. Well then, son, yer on! The rest is *your* lookout.'

The first time, carried away by the noise and excitement and the certainty of his own skill, he had just gone up like any other mug and got floored. But he went two rounds and was good. The crowd liked his clean looks, his keenness, and the manager, seeing the possibilities in him – he was slight and boyish but surprisingly tough – had come out while he was washing up and offered him a job. He was to do, for three pounds a week, what he had just done for the heck of it; only from now on it would be play-acting. He would live with the troupe, travel with them from town to town, and be part of the show. What did he think of it? He jumped at the offer.

It wasn't just the three pounds, though that too was a consideration when so many thousands were out of work, or the chance to be one of the show folk, or the prospect at last of seeing the world. It was the chance it offered (he touched on this very lightly, hardly confessing it even to himself) of stepping aside from what fate, or his mother, who claimed to be its agent, had set up for him. Of getting *away*.

He kept the news to himself for a day or two and made his plans. Then he told his father.

'Good on yer, mate,' his father said, delighted to see Digger show a bit of fight and to be part of a conspiracy. 'Don't you worry, I'll cover for ya. You get away while the going's good. Wish it was me!'

He was young and took things lightly, including the bruises. It was an education. He had eighteen months of it and saw every town from Albury right through the west and up the coast as far as Bundaberg. Bought himself boots, a kangaroo-hide belt, a couple of flash shirts, and soon got to know the other showies on a neighbourly basis.

The fat lady had started off in a pet shop in Vienna, selling larks: they put their eyes out, she told Digger, to make them sing. The Human Torso was an accountant. But there was a market out there whose values prevailed, so they had decided, with only a little urging on the part of a manager, to cash in on their advantages and put themselves on show.

The fat lady read cheap romances, in French, and had a little gramophone in her wagon on which she played gypsy music. She gave a lot of attention to her nails. She did in fact have very pretty hands, which were the most diminutive part of her, except for her ears. She kept a black velvet glove on her dressing table that was stuffed up to the size of a real hand and covered with rings; but she had too much refinement herself to wear more than two at any one time. Her favourite film star was Edward G. Robinson, whose features, heavy with menace and the promise of soft violence, looked down in a dozen poses from her dressing mirror. Her only female pin-up was Hedy Lamarr. 'She's from Vienna,' she told Digger. 'Like me.'

The Human Torso was a gambler. He spent all day, wherever they were, poring over the racing sheets and drinking Beenleigh rum. He had a system. The rumour was that he had thousands of pounds stashed away in banks all over the country in different names. An American by birth, he was a loud-mouthed coarse fellow, but when you caught him sober he wasn't. He lent Digger a book by Theodore Dreiser, told him Europe was finished and that all the world's troubles were the fault of the Jews.

They were happy days in spite of the misery of the times. He did not mind living as he did.

The war came and his father went to it, changing his age again but putting it down this time. They had a drink together in Sydney.

'You should be in this, Dig,' his father told him, looking smart in the uniform of the Light Horse.

But Digger did not think so. Living with the blacks had made him see things in another way: from the side and a bit skew, but with a humorous scepticism, as they did. He wasn't one of them, he knew that; but after a time they were as open with him as if he was. 'You're all right, Digger,' his mate Slinger told him, but you could never be sure with Slinger that he wasn't having you on. 'Maybe yer a blackfeller on the *other* side a' yer skin.'

Then one day in Newcastle, when he was just hanging about looking at shop windows and considering the picture ads, he came upon a mob of fellows who were in a line to join up. A recruiting platform had been set up right in the street, flags and all, English and Australian. Men in their shirt-sleeves, and in suits too, some of them, were moving one behind another towards it. At the back of the line a fellow was putting on a turn to keep the others amused, and Digger stopped a moment to listen to him. The other men laughed, but self-consciously, and looked at one another, a bit leery of the line he was taking. He talked like a Communist.

He was a big fellow in a woollen shirt, a blusterer, but for all that there was a kind of lightness to him. If he danced you felt he would be very light on his feet, and his talk was a kind of dancing. He played up to his audience, keeping them always in tow, and after a time his play began to take in Digger as well. When Digger laughed outright once the fellow turned to him and said, as if they had known one another all their lives, 'Givvus a fag, mate, willya?' Digger stepped from the wall where he had been leaning, gave him the fag he had been rolling and rolled another. 'Ta,' the man said, dipping his head, when Digger was ready, to take a light. 'Bramson's the name. Doug.'

The others stood watching, not knowing what to make of it and hanging still on his words. He knew it and held off.

After that Digger too stood openly listening. It was all nonsense really – Digger was reminded of Farrah, the spruiker; just the sort of thing to pass the time while the line shuffled on. 'This feller could talk right through a world war,' Digger thought. 'The time'd pass pretty easy, too.'

At last he turned to Digger and said: 'You in this line, mate?'

'What?'

'Are you joinin' up or just considerin'?'

Digger was nonplussed. He hadn't been doing either, in fact, just passing the time. He looked at the pavement, ground the butt in with his heel, then glanced up under his brows, but Doug had already turned away. The question had been put, that's all, offhand. It wasn't a test.

But, standing in line with these men, he felt something. The warmth of being, in the easiest way, one of a mob, as on nights back home when he had stood round a burning log outside a dance-hall, smoking, yarning, listening to bits of local gossip, or to jokes that might have needed explaining if you didn't know the lingo. That's what he'd missed these last months. Suddenly he felt homesick. There was an easy pitch to it that was different from the one he had been living at.

The coons were touchy. He was in their world and they accepted him, but only provisionally; and there were times when he felt he would never really understand them, not even Slinger. He had never faced the indignities they had, the humiliations. He had no idea in the end what kept them going.

These fellows he did know. They were the same ones he stood among each night playing his part. He could join them now and they wouldn't see any difference in him – he *hoped* they wouldn't; unless he had picked something up from Slinger and the others that he didn't know about; a way of leaning maybe, or holding his shoulders, a smell, but he didn't *think* he had. He felt a need suddenly to be taken back, to share whatever it was these men were letting themselves in for, to be relieved of putting on an act. He turned himself inside out again and came out white.

The others hadn't noticed anything. Their attention was all on Doug. He was the star here.

As Doug went on with his patter new chaps kept coming and falling in behind, till at last it was Doug's turn to step up and sign on, and after that, Digger's.

'Listen,' Digger told Slinger that night, 'you won't believe this. I joined up.'

It was after the show. They were pouring scoops of cold water over one another's shoulders, dousing down in a rigged-up showering place behind the camp.

Slinger was an Islander, a big shy fellow, over six feet, a heavyweight. He paused now with the scoop of water, then slowly let it pour over his head.

'Done it this arvo,' Digger said. 'I was a mug, eh?' He took the scoop and dipped it.

'Shit, Digger.' Slinger looked genuinely upset. Digger was pleased by that. 'Whatt'd ya do *that* for?'

Something in Slinger's voice made him think of his mother, but it was only when he sat down later to drop her a line that he saw how she would see it: that what he was doing was taking himself further away.

He sobered. The water running over his chest was cold.

'Must of been a mug all along,' he offered.

'Yair,' Slinger said, 'you must of. An' I thought we'd learned you something.'

6

'Chilly, eh? Once the sun's gone.'

Digger looked up, startled. He had been miles away, years; feeling the shock of cold water as it poured over his head, plastering his hair down over his eyes, all his white skin goosepimpling, his cock and balls shrivelling up as he danced on the boards of their rough and ready washing place and reached for a bit of towel they were sharing.

Vic shifted his gaze to the river. 'What about that cup of tea you mentioned?'

Watching them come up the path towards the store Jenny began to fluster. This was the third time he'd been in here in not much more than a week. He'd never done that before. He was after Digger for something and Digger was worried. She'd heard him at night through the wall, tossing and turning, but he wouldn't let on to her what it was.

That last time, Thursday, he'd turned up with a present. He was always bringing her presents. It was his way of getting round her. He'd been trying it for years. He never learned.

In the early days it had been little things. A plastic hair-clip in the shape of a bow, it was once. Pink. Another time scent, 'Evening in Paris'. 'Ta,' she'd say, and put the thing aside. She wouldn't even look at it. She didn't want anything from *him*. He'd put some sort of a spell on the thing, that's what she thought, and if she used it, put it on, the hair-clip for instance, he'd have her just where he wanted.

Later the presents got bigger and came with a lot of packaging. 'Here,' he'd say, offering to help. 'I can *do* it,' she'd tell him fiercely, shoving him off. She was only opening the thing to be polite.

A jaffle-iron, that one was. Useless! Then a pressure cooker that scared the wits out of her and which he was probably hoping would blow her to buggery. Then a special pan for doing poached eggs, which Digger never ate anyway. Then a tin-opener you stuck to the wall. He came in all ready with a screwdriver and in two minutes flat had it fixed to the wall beside her sink. 'Here, I'll show you how it works,' he said, and opened a half-tin of apricots – what a waste! – when she'd already made a bread-and-butter pudding.

They were always things that were no bloody use, or that *she* couldn't use anyway without a lot of showing.

'Honest,' he complained once, 'you're a hard woman to please.'

Yair, mister, you bet I am.

But once her heart almost stopped. He turned up with a little kid, a little blond fellow of maybe five or six, in jeans and a coat with buttons on it in the shape of wooden barrels. He had blue eyes and his front teeth were missing. She held her breath. What was *he* for?

He sat very quiet, swinging his legs, which did not quite reach the ground, and every minute or so would lean forward and peer down over his knees, as if he expected, since he last looked, that he might have grown a bit. Or maybe he was just fond of his boots. He was very pleased with himself.

And why shouldn't he be? Someone, his mother probably, had got him up for a proper outing. Everything about him was neatly buttoned and tied, his hair combed, nails clean. He was perfect except for his teeth. She could have whipped him up in her arms and half squeezed the breath out of him. But little kids scare easily, she knew that from experience. She didn't want to put him off. At last she got round him with a lolly.

She offered it and he looked sideways at Vic, who was busy talking, to see if he should accept, and when Vic nodded, put his hand out, undid the wrapper and popped it into his mouth. Then looked in dismay at his sticky hands. He was a very neat little fellow.

She took the wrapper from him and ran off into the house to get a flannel, but when she got back he was licking his fingers like a cat. What amazed her was the pinkness of his tongue. She laughed, just to see it, and squeezing up to him on the bench, said, 'Hey, what's your best colour? Mine's yellow. What's your best cartoon?'

He looked at her then, a little crease appeared on his brow, and he shifted on the seat, closer to his father. She'd lost him.

So all the years he'd been coming it was something different, the present he brought, and he was different too. Meatier.

Digger was the one he was after, but she was the one he tried to get around. She knew that and kept an eye on him. She wasn't that much of a dill.

And each time the car he came in was different too. Bigger, a new one each time. He would drive up to where the track turned down sharp towards the store, park it there under the firs, then walk.

Sometimes, after they had had a bit of a talk, he and Digger would go back to the car and look it over. Walk round and round it, opening the bonnet, putting their heads in. Then Digger would get into the driver's seat behind the wheel, the engine would turn over, and she would hold her breath, expecting them to take off. But all they did was let it run a little. They never went anywhere. They would sit in the car then and talk.

When they got out and were down the river again, she'd go and have a bit of a look for herself. She didn't open the bonnet. Just stuck her head in the front window on the driver's side and smelled the leather, and looked at the numbers and that on the dashboard.

There was a mystery about cars – they were men's business, cars – that she had never fathomed. It had to do with going places.

Men didn't like to stay put. She knew that from her father. From Digger too. You could see it in the way they got their hands round that wheel. Some power came right up through them when the motor started and they used their foot to make it roar. They were already on the way.

That's why Vic let Digger do it. He was letting him in on the mystery. When they looked under the bonnet they were examining the source of it. When he got Digger into the driver's seat and let him start the engine up he was offering him the chance to get away.

Unhappily she walked round the thing, looked at the tyres and kicked the back one hard. It had air in it, but if it hit a nail for instance it could go flat. She considered using a pin, only they'd know who did it.

The big shiny machine, always well polished and each time bigger, parked there at the entrance to the track, was a warning he set. It was meant to show her the power he had: what it was, out there, that he was in touch with, and that Digger might have too if he went away. Big, it was. All metal and shining. With an engine in it that roared and could take you off fast. Anywhere.

Once they came up on her when she was still looking.

'Let me take you for a spin,' Vic offered, but she was too smart to fall for that one.

He was grinning at her. Crafty bugger!

'No thanks,' she told him, and stomped off.

She did think she had him once. Just this once he arrived in a car driven by a chauffeur and was in a real state – she had never seen that before. She watched him and Digger walk up and down, then went off quickly to see what the chauffeur was up to.

He was sitting in the front seat with his cap off and his eyes shut, a good-looking young feller, sleeping.

But when she got up close he wasn't sleeping at all. He had like little buttons in his ears and was tapping his fingers, with their bitten-down nails, on the steering-wheel.

Well, she knew what that was. Digger had one. Vic had given it to him. Only Digger's had a metal band that went over his head, under his hat. He would sit out on the porch and be there for hours sometimes while she raged up and down looking for excuses to break in.

He had an old genoa-velvet lounge out there and a mulga-wood smoker's stand with a tray, and he would sit for hours with that *thing*, that Walkman in his lap, plugged in. You had to shout to get him to come in for tea, and even then he didn't always hear; he was too absorbed. She would have to go out and signal, do a slow dance, and he would look up puzzled, as if he was so far off that he couldn't make out who it was galumping about on the horizon there and signalling to him.

He wore the phones to spare her the dirges he listened to, she knew that, but she resented them just the same, and suspected Vic of giving Digger the thing as another way of taking him off. Digger was a walkover. Anything mechanical he couldn't resist.

She would have liked to listen in one time, just to see if the music *told* you anything, gave you a clue. It was classical, of course, but who knows? – she might have got something out of it. But all she caught when she got close was a high tinny sound, like some animal, a calf or a nanny-goat wearing a bell, that had strayed off and was wandering along a boundary fence somewhere trying to get through.

What she did know was that once Digger was plugged in to the thing all communication between them was cut. He was off in a world of his own, like the kids that turned up in the store on Sunday afternoons, shuffling about to the noise in their heads, and when she spoke to them shouting as if *she* was the one that had deafened herself. So she knew that far-off look on the chauffeur's face.

She lowered her head to the back window and he didn't even see her. He was smiling, his head on the back of the seat, his eyes closed. His cap, which was black with a shiny peak, was on the shelf above the dashboard. He was tapping his fingers on the wheel. She could smell the leather in there.

Suddenly he jerked upright, his eyes open just a foot from hers. 'Jesus!' he said. She had scared the pants off him.

Later, watching from the house, she saw him get out of the car and take off his jacket. All he had on underneath was braces. He walked down to the river and sat. He picked up bits of bark and tossed them into the stream, watching them whirl and slip away. Over and over he did it. At last she went down to him.

'I bet you could do with a cuppa,' she said, as lightly as she could manage. She wasn't used to young fellers. She scared them.

He looked up at her. He was so bored with waiting.

'I don't mind,' he said, and gave a bit of a grin.

'An' a pikelet, eh?'

'I don't mind,' he said.

'And jam.'

He looked at her again and there was a flicker of doubt in him. She always went too far. 'Come on then,' she said quickly.

She sat him at the kitchen table and recalled vaguely that she had planned this a long time ago, only on that occasion it had been a little kid. Could this be him grown up?

'Hey,' she said, as she set a plate in front of him. 'You oughta put bitter allers on 'em.' She was referring to his nails, which were bitten to the quick.

'What?' he said.

'Bitter allers. It's 'orrible – but then you wouldn't bite 'em.'

He flushed and put his hands away under the table. He was a good-looking feller but with eyes that kept darting about. He was unsure of her, or maybe it was of himself.

She tried a few questions. 'Hey,' he said to show how clever he was, 'you're on the pump!' He laughed. But once he'd shown that he knew what she was up to, he was quite happy to rattle away.

Brad, he was called. He had been Mr Curran's driver for two years. Before that he'd been a courier and before that worked in a motorbike shop. He'd struck it lucky this time. Vic Curran was a good sort of bloke to work for, very strict mind you, but fair, and he had stacks. 'Stacks,' the fellow said, taking another dob of cream, and his eyes lit up in a way she found unpleasant. He was greedy.

'Got a terrific house out Turramurra,' he said, 'I wouldn' mind livin' in it. I got this nice little flat now, North Sydney, two rooms. Costs me ninety-eight dollars a week – that's cheap! But I wouldn' mind livin' in a place like that. I will too, one day . . .'

He would have gone on like this, but she got impatient. This wasn't the sort of thing she was after.

'You're stupid,' she said viciously, and the young man, his mouth half-open and full of pikelet, looked as if she had leaned across and bitten his nose. He was that astonished. Serve him right.

'What about Digger?' she demanded.

He drew back and looked at her. 'Who's Digger?' he asked.

That did it. She gave him a shove then with the heel of her hand against his shoulder, and for all the heftiness of him he very nearly went over backwards out of his chair.

'All right,' he said. He got up, very flushed and foolish looking.

He didn't know how to deal with her. If it was a man he would have flattened him.

'F' Christ's sake!' he said under his breath. He got into his uniform jacket and tugged it down hard, making himself stiff and formal. He was on his dignity now. He strode out.

'I buggered it up,' she told herself miserably. 'It was me best chance and I buggered it up.'

She never saw that driver again, as she had never seen the little boy either. The next time Vic came he drove himself.

When she was very little and Digger just a baby she had been set sometimes to look after him. 'You watch Digger now,' her mother had told her, 'there's a good girl. I'm depending on you.' She had believed always that the time might come when she would have to do it again.

Digger thought he was protecting her, and he was too, she was dependent on him. But he was too trusting, Digger. He knew a lot, he knew heaps, he could *do* things. But he didn't know about the world, and she did. She knew how cruel it was. It didn't matter what you knew or where you'd been – Digger had been overseas even, to the war even, she'd never been anywhere. To Brisbane. That wasn't anywhere. But she did know what the world was. It could come at you, all the evil and cruelty of it, in a single blow: a big hand wet as a mackerel coming slam at the side of your head, knocking you sideways, and in just a fraction of a second you'd got all there was to know of how wicked it could be. Sister Francis of the Wash, that was. All six foot of her, looming up in a cloud of steam just as you were hoiking a stickful of sheets out of the copper, and knocking you sideways without a word. Wuthering Heights, that was. Or to give it its proper name, All Hallows Convent, The Valley, Brisbane, Queensland, Australia, The World. *Hell*.

Some girls, all lined up in buff-coloured uniforms and pale stockings, got a good education there, or so they said. They paid for it. Others, who had fallen like her and had nowhere else to go, worked in the laundry. Except she hadn't fallen at all – or not till Sister Francis got going. All she had done, once or twice, was lay down.

While she was still carrying her baby she scrubbed floors, and after she'd had it and they took it away without letting her see it even, to see if it had all its right parts, she worked in the wash. Bloody terrified she was most of the time of that Sister Francis, but even more of having to leave.

'Please, please, Sister,' she'd jabber, ducking under the fat palms, 'it wasn' me. Honest, Sister, I swear t' God!' But they kept coming down just the same, all suds, over your left ear or across your face, with all the weight of a six-foot Irish virgin behind them, her temper got up by the fact that you had fallen, and been picked up again, and were *still* no good. The weight of the whole Catholic Church as well – and she wasn't even a Mick!

She had run away, oh, heaps of times, heaps! On trams. But that didn't get you anywhere.

'Sorry, girlie, this is the terminus.'

A feller in a blue uniform and a little round white cap told her that, a conductor bloke with a leather pouch at his waist and a punch for clipping tickets.

It was Dutton Park that time. She got off the tram, which went on sitting at the end of the line, and climbed up to a bandstand all painted but peeling. From there you could see the whole city, not too far away: the three bridges, the river switching back and forth, even Wuthering Heights with its steep black roofs on a cliff above the water.

The tram, all silver, went on sitting on the line and you could see right through it except for the driver and the conductor bloke who put their feet up on the seat and smoked.

At last the conductor got down. He stood for a moment looking up at her, then swung the pole, and the tram moved off.

It began to get dark. A couple of sailors came, Yanks, with girls, and she got scared.

She ended up walking all the way back. Hours it took. In the blackout, with men and women barging about the pavements and searchlights swinging overhead and crossing, catching stars.

Another time it was a different terminus: New Farm Park. She sat on a bench this time among the rosebushes and a feller come up and started talking to her very fast and with a lot of spit, but kind really. He put his arm round her. He was a bit smelly. Grog. Then he put his wet mouth to her ear, which wasn't as bad as Sister Francis's fist, and whispered something dirty; then shoved his hand up her skirt. It was no good her saying anything. But when some people come past she got up quickly and followed them, but turned after a minute to look back.

He was still sitting on the bench. He looked at her like he was ready to cry – he was that disappointed – and she thought, 'Well, I might as well let him have what he wants, poor bugger, why not?' He looked that hopeless. Wanting something and seeing you take it away.

She walked back, sat beside him, and they spent a while sleeping in tram-sheds and that. It wasn't too bad. But when he got on the grog he bashed her about, just like Sister Francis, and called her a dummy, so she went back.

It wasn't the fear of being alone out there that took her back each time. It was all the hands, even in a crowd of strangers, that kept reaching out to grab or squeeze or pinch or turn themselves into fists and go smash at you. Some of those hands, she knew, might be gentle, but you couldn't take the risk. Even if they started off gentle, you never knew when they were going to switch. So she went back.

She could have tried a different tram (there were lots), to some other terminus. But she'd already seen two and two was sufficient. She didn't reckon Ashgrove or Enoggera would have been any better. Or Kalinga or The Grange. So she stuck, and then one day Digger appeared and said, 'I've talked to the boss here, the Mother, and you c'n come back home,' and that was it. Digger too had been shut up somewhere and had got out – she didn't know where.

So that was all she had actually *seen*.

But it was so astounding that it stopped her breath even now just to think of it. The terror of what was possible out there, the cruelty of some people, and how helpless you were once they got stuck into you. You don't need all that much *experience*. Two seconds flat and she'd got to the end of her own power to bear it, that was the point. There's nothing more.

The difference between her and Digger was that Digger had *not*. He'd never come up against whatever it was, out there, that could utterly flatten him.

'That sister of yours is a hard nut to crack,' Vic had said once in the early days, when he still had some hope of winning her over.

'Yairs, well – she's got a mind of her own,' Digger told him. 'I wouldn' worry about Jenny.'

But he did.

Today, as she bashed the crockery about – 'There, that's yours, mister!' – she kept fixing her eye on him. She had something on her mind.

They sipped their tea and she was still looking. At last, in her abrupt way, she came out with it.

'Hey,' she said, cutting right across something Digger was saying, 'what've you done with that little kiddie?'

When they failed to catch on she got furious and shouted.

'The one you *come* with!'

It was Digger who saw what she meant.

'Jenny love,' he told her, trying to pass it off, 'that was ages ago, you know that. That was Greg.' He shot a glance at Vic. 'He's grown up. Ages ago.'

That little feller with the sticky fingers that she'd given a lolly to? She couldn't believe it. How could he? She felt a real dill. Ages, Digger said.

It was true she hadn't seen him, or even thought of him, for a bit. But ages! And in just that little while he'd grown up into someone. 'Who?' she wondered, and was about to ask but thought better of it.

But she felt sad. Something in the news put a real damper on her. Something she had been looking forward to she knew now she would never have.

She glanced up. And that Vic had the oddest look on his face, like there was suddenly nothing to him. Like something, some*one*, some Sister Francis, had loomed up out of nowhere and king-hit him. She saw right through him to that feller in the long overcoat who had come looking for Digger the first time, nothing to him, thin, pale as potatoes, and she found herself thinking, in spite of herself, 'You poor bugger! Now what's gone wrong with *you*?'

II

1

The basin was enamel, white, chipped black at the rim. In the year his mother died Vic brought it to her three and sometimes four times a day. When he was at school or out playing one of their neighbours did it.

He held it close and in the early days had had to turn away not to be sick himself. But there was no escaping the smell of it or the sounds she made as the last strength was torn from her. 'I'm sorry, love, I'm sorry,' she would murmur over and over.

When he had cleaned up some of the mess he would carry the basin out and empty it in a place in the yard that was all rusty cans, chop-bones and bleached pippies and crab-shells, then kick sand over it, turning his head away in disgust and taking quick gulps of air that had a taste of coal-dust in it.

The yard backed on to barren dunes. The rise behind was always on the move. There was a time, not so long ago, when he had had a rabbit cage out here, but it was gone now, yards back under the dune. There had even, further back, been a couple of trees. He remembered climbing them. He wondered sometimes how long it would be till their whole house was covered. He would lie at night hearing the wind and the individual grains rolling. The great white slope of a wave would rise up and break in his sleep, come trickling first through the cracks in the walls, then press hard against the windows till they fell with a crash and sand came pouring over their table and chairs and the rafters caved in and the whole hill went over them. He would be fighting to get above it.

The shack they lived in was just one room knocked up out of timber, old packing cases mostly, and patched with fibro and corrugated iron – anything his father had been able to scavenge.

There was a dunny behind, and for privacy a curtain his mother had sewn out of bags.

Their neighbours down here were all squatters like them, families that in one way or another had got into trouble and been evicted. It

71

was four years since they had lived in a proper house, in a street with fences between the yards and a number on the gate. Number 6, Marlin Street.

He swilled the basin with water from their tank, once, twice, then went in and sponged her brow with a damp cloth; then poured water so she could clean her mouth.

'You're a good kid, Vic,' she would whisper as he settled her pillow. It was grey and stiff with dirt. 'You're all a mother could wish for.'

He did all he could for her. Sitting beside her on a butter-box, he read the books that one of their neighbours, Mrs Webb, got from the library behind Williams' store. At nine he was an excellent reader. He hardly ever stumbled over the words.

When he slipped away to play cricket with the other kids in the hour before dark, he would pause a moment and bury his nose in the sleeve of his jumper.

That smell – ingrained dirt, coal-dust, salt from the sea, mutton-fat, sour milk – he loathed it! Stripped to the waist in their outhouse, with a cake of Sunlight soap and a scrubbing-brush, he would punish his flesh till it was raw, but the smell persisted. It was a condition, like a disease, and went so deep you couldn't get at it; or like character, or family features. It was *their* smell, *them*. Whatever the ads said, it was beyond the power of Sunlight.

The other kids at school held their noses when he appeared. Pooh! they went, even the ones he was mates with. He flashed out but his spirit squirmed. He loved his mother and hated to feel ashamed of her. His father was another matter. There was nothing anyone could do about *him*.

All this he bore in silence, he was proud; and they were all outcasts, more or less, the kids like him who lived along the railway and down the dunes.

He wasn't by nature morose. The brightness of his blue eyes and their steady gaze, his quickness and sturdiness of limb, belonged to a disposition that was meant to be sunny. He should have moved easily in the world. But circumstances had taught him to hold back. Indirectness, an intense secretiveness about all that mattered most, had become second nature to him, the first surviving in an assurance, which belonged to his physical side, that the world must some day lay itself at his feet, though he was pretty certain now he would have to force it to.

As for the ready smile and liveliness of manner that came so easily to him, they could leave you vulnerable, he had discovered, unless used as a mask. They disarmed people. That was their use.

He ought to have been without hope. But his body was hopeful and he trusted it. Everything he did he looked forward to with an eager impatience. As a little lad he would come rushing in from play and suddenly stop dead on the doorstep, wondering, now he had arrived, why he had been in such a hurry to get back; as if he had expected the house to have changed while he was away. His mother saw the look on his face and it went right through her.

When he examined the world he was in he could only assume that an error had been made in the true workings of things. He was harmed by this. It would make life hard for him. But he intended to rectify the situation any way he could and would have no mercy on whatever it was that had sought to rob him of his due.

Standing still out there in the fading light and knowing that the moment he went in his eyes would lose their capacity to follow the flight of a ball or catch a disturbance in the grass, he would try to keep contact with the animal part of him, trusting to *that*, and would feel his whole body come to the edge of something – something he could have too, if he could only grasp what it was.

Here, at the smoky edge of darkness, even stones lost their sharp edge and their heaviness a moment and seemed ready for flight. He felt his body leave the earth. That was the animal in him, which was sure-footed and had perfect timing. It took off in a long leap and he held his breath.

The land breeze had fallen, just on the turn. Everything was suspended, hanging for one last moment between daytime and night, between its day life and that other darker life of the night hours. His body too was suspended.

But after a moment of almost miraculous lightness in which he felt he had actually done it, and worked the change, he came back to earth. The weight of his body, light as it was, reclaimed him. It was too heavy to shake off.

The sea breeze quickened and in kitchens all down the shore they would be feeling its coolness now. His eyes had adjusted. The lights were hard window-squares.

'Maybe,' he thought grimly, 'there *is* no other life to be broken through to. It's all continuous, and you just keep getting thicker and thicker and heavier and heavier as it builds up in you, and that's *it*.'

He thought this but could not believe it. That sort of fatality was not in his nature. He would sigh and go home disappointed, but not hopeless, never entirely without hope.

Mornings, out early to fetch the milk, he would see the local men gathering at bus stops on their way to the mine. Other fellows from villages down the coast would be on bikes and would call to them as they passed. Happy enough they seemed, with their little lunch-boxes. They were the lucky ones who still had work. The rest, unshaven, in pyjamas some of them, would be pottering about behind fences, digging a bit, keeping busy. Later, still unshaven but dressed now in collarless shirts and braces, they would be hanging about in groups outside the pub, quiet enough till they got going. Horses were what they were passionate about, or greyhound races or football teams.

At the weekends you could see them, in the same groups, walking to matches with their hands in their pockets. Younger blokes in flash suits, their girls in stockings and high heels, would be stepping along beside them, occasionally calling across to a fellow they knew, or the girl would call to a neighbour she recognised. They would have a fifth share in a lottery in their pocket, these youngsters, maybe a frenchie just on the off-chance.

'Doin' all right, are yer?'

That question from an older man, with just a touch of envy in it, would satisfy in most of them the need for recognition.

'Can't complain,' was the conventional, understated response.

A raw, scrubbed look, hair cut short around the ears and palmed down with California Poppy, a suit. Kids like Vic, still barefoot, in an old knitted jumper with a hole at the elbow from leaning on a desk, were supposed to be impressed by that and to catch in it a hint of what they too might step into, if they did what they were told, stayed on the right side of the law, and the Depression ended.

Vic considered this and didn't think much of it. He would make his own life, not just pick up what was passed on to him. He would. He knew it.

His father was a miner, or had been till an old war wound asserted itself – 'came good', as the cynics put it. He had a pension and spent his days now, winter and summer, down at the jetty where the coal-loaders put in and there was always a little crowd of men lounging about or casting a line for whiting. There or in one of the town's three pubs.

He was a well-set-up dark fellow with the same blue eyes Vic had (Vic resented this, whatever value they might have in the way of foxing people), and a natural slovenliness in all he did that affronted the boy. It was to assure himself of the impossibility of there being any link between them that Vic tormented his spirit into hardness and punished his skin with the scrubbing brush.

Easy-going – that was the word for him. They had both been easy-going, Dan and Till Curran, in the days when he was still in work and she was a big woman who liked a beer or two and a hand of poker. They had friends all over. Vic was little then, but he remembered Marlin Street and the rowdy nights.

His father now was a byword in the town. A drunk and a scrounger, he was always dancing about on the edge of whatever crowd there was at the Pacific or the Prince of Wales, and there was a point in his booze-sodden day – Vic had been witness to it more than once, and could not, young as he was, wipe out the horror of it – when he would, with a show of clownish good humour, easy-going as ever, do whatever was demanded of him so long as there was a beer at the end of it: run messages for people, tell tales, swallow insults – always with a silly smile on his face and a fawning eagerness to make himself agreeable.

He had no shame, and it amused some of the smart-alecs of the town, a good many of whom had no shame themselves, to see how far he would go. With a mixture of low pleasure and fascinated disgust, a touch of fear too at what they might have in common with him, they would taunt him with insults, amazed that he should just stand there smiling, blinking, and make no effort to defend himself.

He would do anything, Dan Curran, if he was far gone enough. Lick up your spit and thank you for it, laughing. Then swallow his schooner at a gulp.

There were others, decent men who had worked in the pit with him or been in the same class at school, who felt humiliated themselves to see a man with so little regard for himself.

'That's all right, Danno,' one of them would say stiffly, 'have this one on me.' A couple of coins on the linoleum would save him then from his own weakness. But after a minute or two he would have an empty glass in front of him and start making up again to his tormentors, since they were more reliable in the long run than the occasional benefactor.

When he got home he would be in a shouting mood. Then suddenly he would break down and weep.

Every stage of this daily drama disgusted Vic and confirmed him in the view that this vicious crybaby who claimed to be his father had nothing to do with him.

The shame of it was that in the early days, when things had not yet come to their worst, when his father was just newly out of work and had time, since he was home all day, to take Vic fishing and tell him stories of the war, they had been mates, and Vic had been inveigled on more than one occasion into going round to the back door of the pub, just on closing time, to fetch a couple of bottles. Jimmy, the Pacific's barman, would slip them to him and he would get back fast to hear the end of whatever it was his father had been telling. It was a secret between them – Jimmy, his father and himself. The bottles came in loose straw jackets and they went out and burned them quickly in a corner of the yard so that his mother wouldn't find them, a real blaze. The empty bottles they sent sailing into the dunes.

But Jim Hardy the publican got to hear of it and told his wife, and when she told Vic's mother, she cried and was angry with him. Didn't he know, couldn't he see what was happening?

He did see then. His mother and father, who had always been so lively together, began to have brawls, and in no time at all, or so it seemed, were forever clawing at one another.

'You're a bloody wowser,' he complained when she refused to drink with him. 'I din' expect that. I din' expect you t' turn into a bloody wowser. If there's one thing I can't stand it's a bloody whingein' woman an' a wowser!'

He would come home belligerent now, ready, on a point of honour, to take offence at everything.

'You shoudn' be sewin' for bloody Sam Goddard's bloody wife,' he bellowed. '*That* bitch! Here, gimmee that,' and he would wrench the bit of work, whatever it was, a skirt to be let down or a new blouse, right out of her hands. If she resisted he would hit her.

Now, when his father tried to get around him, Vic used his elbows to push him off.

'You git away from me,' he would hiss, quite prepared to fight if he had to. 'I won't do yer scroungin' for yer.'

He would go out in the dark and sit on the woodpile and look at the axe swung down hard into the block. There would be a breeze from the sea, cooling the sweat on his upper lip, and he would sit there letting it cleanse him.

But when he went back in his mother would say: 'You oughtn'ta speak to 'im like that, Vic. Don't think you're doin' it for me.' She would have a cut on her lip or a puffy eye, and still she said it.

He hated that. The way she found excuses and put up with things. He was a fighter. He wanted her to be.

'Vic, love,' she told him, 'you don't understand these things. Don't be too hard on me.'

Later, when they thought he was asleep, he would hear them in the double bed. She would be saying his father's name over and over, gasping it, and with her cut lip kissing and petting him.

He loved her, but her weakness enraged him. When his father flung about with his fists and they were all in a savage moil, shouting and using their shoulders and elbows, he would have given his last breath for her, and was in a frenzy of such rage and blind impotence that he thought he might die of it; of being caught up with them – between them at one moment, at the next outside and beating with his fists to get in, and of shame at being so big for his age and so helpless to do anything.

In the closeness of such moments, when they were all three struggling and shouting, they were like creatures trying to give birth to something, some monster, that's what he thought, and he saw at last what it was: a murder, that's what it was. One day soon, as soon as he was strong enough to keep hold of the axe, he would kill this man.

Then his mother took sick. In just weeks she fell away from being a big soft woman to skin and bone. He brought her the basin, and watched her, one hand clutching her side, drag herself from chair to table to doorknob, then across the sandy yard to their dunny. His father was nowhere in sight. Never home now. He had stayed sober for a day or so, right at the start, but now he was drunk from morning to night, though he stayed quiet enough. There was no more shouting. He slunk home after midnight and went to bed in his boots.

Too young to see beyond the immediate horrors, it did not occur to Vic that his father was a man in panic: that what subdued him, drove him deeper into himself, but also kept him away, was an animal terror of what was happening here, the wasting of the big body he had clung to, so that he barely knew it any more, her pain that was like a wild thing in the bed between them, all teeth and claws. He never came near her, that's all Vic saw. When he did, he couldn't wait to get away again.

His mother knew what he was thinking. 'You're wrong about yer father, Vic,' she told him, but her voice was no more than a whisper. She was too weak to elaborate.

She died at last. Vic was ten. His father wept and tried to cuddle him. 'There's just the two of us now, Vic,' he said. But Vic was not deceived and offered no sympathy. When his father held on he pulled away.

His own sorrow was overwhelming. He dealt with it. But what feelings he had left over were for himself. He had none for this drunken bully who whined and snivelled and laid claim to him but did nothing but bring them shame.

'You're a hard man, Vic,' the father said bitterly. 'I wouldn' wanna be in a world where you was God. God help me if I was. There's no softness in yer. Not like yer mother.'

He was trying to get around him again. Vic shut his ears.

So long as his mother was there to see it, for her sake, and to set himself at a distance from his father's slovenliness, since *he* would do nothing, Vic had tried to keep things in order, wiping the oil-cloth after they ate, rinsing the galvanised iron tub they washed up in, sweeping the floors.

It was hard enough. No matter how often you used the broom there was always a grist of sand under your feet. It settled on the skirting boards and along the windowsills, got between the sheets and scratched when you climbed in. There were always a few grains of it in a teacup when you took it down from its hook.

He had been concerned, in those last weeks, when his mother lay all day in a coma, with her mouth open, that he might come home and find her choked with it, and had nightmares of having to use his fingers to scoop sand out of her throat.

Once she was gone he did nothing. To spite his father he let the dirt accumulate as a witness to all he was responsible for. Food lay about the table, a mess of bread-crusts, open jam tins, knives smeared with fat. Flies gathered and big cockroaches swarmed and scuttled. The beds were unmade, their sheets growing filthier from one week to the next. Milk soured in the jug. Dirty socks and shirts piled up. The whole place stank of fish and sour milk and sweat, and when the windows grew thick with coal dust and salt they stayed that way. He wouldn't lift a finger. He too stank, he knew that, worse than ever, and was itchy.

He loathed filth of every kind, but he let it accumulate, and lived with it out of spite, to torment himself and as a witness against his father.

The one thing he kept clean was the edge of the axe. He would stand stripped before the bit of broken mirror in the outhouse wall and make a muscle with his arm, the right one. A hundred times, in fantasy, he went through with it. Without these acts of assertion he might never have been able to tolerate it, the muck they lived in, and the look on his father's face when he sat in his singlet on the bed with one dirty foot across his knee, sore-headed and sorry for himself.

'Givvus a hand, son. Git yer dad 'is boots, eh? There's a good lad.'

'Fetchem yerself,' the boy would tell him, pulling on his shirt for school and jerking in the belt of his hand-me-down trousers.

'Yer a callous bugger,' the father whined, while Vic stood at the window chewing a bit of crust and taking a good swig of tea, and the whine was enough to close the boy's ears if he had been inclined to respond. 'You don't give a bloke a chance, do you?'

The roof of the house had no lining. You could look up at night and see, under the corrugated iron peak of it, the bare rafters with mice skipping along them. It was, Vic had thought when he was younger, like living inside a huge tree, all branches. An owl lived in this tree, and sometimes, in his childhood sleep, it flew right into his head, and quietly, very quietly for all its heaviness, flopped about there among the rafters woo-hoo-ing and blinking its yellow eyes. He would feel its warm droppings come down. He would wake sometimes with his arms flailing to keep the big bird off.

He had not had that dream for ages. Now the big bird reappeared. It flew about, its wings beat, warm droppings fell. But when he woke in his dream and looked, the owl had a mouse in its beak. The droppings were blood. He woke with warm blood in his mouth and was too choked to cry out.

*

79

A night came when his father brought a woman home, a big girl of seventeen called Josie.

Vic had seen her round often enough, with three or four littlies, her brothers and sisters in tow, and had heard stories about her from the older boys. *She roots.*

At breakfast, which she had ready by the time he got up, she looked at Vic without hostility but without attempting to win him over either, as if she already owned the place and he came with it. She had, it seems, laid her hand on everything she needed, the right teapot, the only one with a decent spout, and had solved their curious way with labels – tea in the cannister marked sago, sugar in the one marked rice. She had chopped her own wood, too, and laid a proper table. She was the sort who got on with things and knew how to make do.

Vic resented the ease with which she had discovered the oddnesses of their male housekeeping. He was embarrassed – as usual he had woken up with a horn – at having to dress in front of her, though she paid no heed. When he came in at lunchtime she was still there and was cleaning the house. He was furious, but realised, when he saw the windowpanes clear again and the floorboards scrubbed, how important it was to him, this orderliness and the smell of suds.

His father did not change and Josie did not demand it. She took things as they came. Vic could hear them at night, and the fury of it tormented him. He was nearly twelve.

She was soft with him, but expected nothing in return. She was a person, it seemed, who had no expectations of any sort, and this touched him but he held back. He was wary of her. He resented the way she took over things his mother had treasured and changed their use.

She kept the house clean, did their washing and sang a bit as she shifted the clothes-props and hung it out. In the afternoons when he came in she would be reading a magazine, *Photoplay* or *Pix*, with her bare feet up on a chair, and was glad to have someone to talk to at last. Putting the magazine aside she would ask him about school, and despite himself he was drawn into talking things over with her.

'No,' she admitted, 'I never was much good at parsing. Algebra I am – that was my long suit.'

Occasionally she read things out to him: 'Myrna Loy and William Powell,' she read, 'are close friends, both on and off the set. Since appearing together in *The Thin Man* . . .'

Sometimes they played Ludo, which was the only game she seemed to know.

When boys at school, or outside the pictures, taunted him, he found himself standing up for her. This was just what they wanted. 'Gettin' a root now, are ya Curran?' the older boys jeered. He reddened and went for them.

He continued to exercise at the woodpile. She thought he was doing it for her, a boyish gallantry, and his fantasies became more complicated: she kept getting in the way of what had been a simple act of violence. What it was now he could not quite determine. The fantasy was its own satisfaction. He did not want to give it up.

In the end it was taken out of his hands. One night his father, who had lately become combative, got into a brawl. A man came to the door to call Josie, and she and Vic went running. For once, it seems, he had stood up for himself, refused some piece of self-abasement no worse than others he had complied with (but who can tell how he saw it?), struck out with an empty glass, and the other fellow, one of his persistent tormentors, infuriated that he should be challenged, and by a fellow for whom everyone had contempt, struck the top off a bottle and took his guard.

No one could say what happened then. The man's account was that Dan Curran had thrown himself at the jagged edge and cut his throat. When Josie burst in, with Vic behind, though rough hands tried to hold him back, he was dying. There was a six-inch gash in his throat and blood all over.

Vic was astonished. The blood in his own throat thundered. He looked at his hands.

The men were standing back in a ring, their boots making a cordon round the head with the long open wound across its throat, the cheeks and brows grey as mutton-fat, and the sawdust floor like a butcher's shop all pooled with blood.

People were kind to him. They took him aside and gave him a nip of something that burned and brought tears to his eyes, but it was this unexpected kindness, not grief, that made him weep.

Josie was inconsolable. They sat at the table together under the branching rafters and he looked up for the owl. He had shown no grief.

'You're a real shit, Vic – you know that?' she told him fiercely.

She was white-faced and looked childlike in her big-girl clothes. They had the house to themselves.

'Don't you worry, mister high-and-mighty virtuous – you'll find out, one day.' She saw the look on his face and laughed. 'What's that?' she asked, though he had not spoken. 'Well, there's a *lot* you don't know.' She leaned close and for a moment he thought from the scornful look of her that she might hit him. If she did, he would not defend himself.

He was shaking. Her face was very close now. Two inches closer and he could have kissed her.

They sat like that for a full minute, then she burst into tears and he put his arms round her till she cried herself out.

Later, when she had crawled into bed, he went out to the woodpile and sat. The axe was where he had put it, with a good swing, when he had chopped the wood for her at teatime. In the block.

His father's blood. It had stunned him, that, the thickness of it, the liveliness. He had had a vision of his own blood rushing with a thump to his heart, swirling through him, pushing out into the roots of his hair, swelling the veins in his wrists.

He felt obscurely, and not for the first time, some limit to his imagination, his grasp on the complexity of things, that sent a wave of depression over him. You could be so wrong! His mother had warned him of that. He felt himself butting against something, some wall that would not yield. He might never discover now what was on the other side of it, though he knew there was a wall and that his failure to penetrate it was important. Without thinking, he smelled his hand.

Sweat. His sweat, with the grime in it of things he had touched. He rubbed hard at his shorts. Guilt moved in him but he did not know what it was for since he had done nothing.

Maybe (and a shadow cast itself across his heart) it was for something that was still to come.

And the anger he had hoped to relieve himself of? To throw off forever with one swing of the axe? It would have no relief now, ever. He would be left with it.

He rubbed his hands again on the rough of his shorts. So his father had got the better of him after all.

He sat in the dark of the woodpile with the wall of the house behind him and the moonlit slope of the dunes in front and saw the great wall of it shift and begin to move. It rolled towards him. He did not move. It covered the pile of rubbish in the corner where he had so often emptied the basin, covered the smell of it and the old rags and papers there, and the burned ash of the straw jackets off beer-bottles, and the rusty tins and fishbones, then the woodpile till only the axe-handle poked out above it; then it covered that too and rolled on to push against the windows of the shack and break in and cover the chairs and table and the stiff grey sheets on the beds, and climbed into the teacups high on their hooks, till the whole room was filled to the ceiling and the rafters and roof were covered and there was no sign any more of them or of the life they had lived except in his head.

2

His life changed abruptly, and in ways so like his own secret wishing that he wondered later if he hadn't, by some power he only half guessed at, brought it about, and that *that* was the guilt.

His father, though he had nothing to leave, had made a will. Vic was the sole beneficiary. But more important, he had named an executor, a Captain Warrender of Strathfield, Sydney. For three years during the war Dan Curran had been Captain Warrender's batman, and the officer had agreed, in the event of Curran's death, to act as guardian to any children he might leave. He appeared now, nearly twenty years later, to make good his word.

He was a large shy man in a three-piece suit. He patted Vic on the shoulder, then shook his hand, and Vic saw immediately that of the two of them it was Mr Warrender who was the more ill at ease.

He had come up from Sydney by train. The dirty little town, scattered at the edge of the sea, all unpainted timber and rusty iron, the sandy yards full of rubbish, the coal dust which that day was blowing all about in a stiff south-easterly making the sea air sharp with smuts – all this was unfamiliar to him. So was the barefoot boy with his raw haircut. At home he had only girls.

But for all his shyness he had eyes that looked right at you, not unkindly but with perfect frankness about what they were up to that showed you frankly, as well, what they saw.

Vic, who had put on a clean shirt and wet-combed his hair, stared straight back. He knew his best qualities and was confident they would show. He trusted this man to see them.

Mr Warrender looked for a long time, then patted Vic's shoulder again and nodded.

Vic did not relax, not quite yet, but he saw that Mr Warrender did, and that was a good sign.

What he had grasped by instinct was that Mr Warrender was innocent and had better remain so, whatever glimpses he might have got into the truth of things from the squalor of their shack. He could have no idea how much Vic really knew, and Vic saw that he would need to be careful about this, hide it, bury it deep inside him and be a kid again. He would learn about life (or pretend to) all over again, on Mr Warrender's terms. He could see, just from looking at him, that this was what he would expect.

When Mr Warrender explained that he was taking him to Sydney, Vic said nothing. He let him go on.

Mrs Warrender and the girls (there were two of them) had been told about him and were looking forward to his arrival, to having another man in the house. Vic still said nothing, but smiled to himself as Mr Warrender, in order to set him at his ease – which wasn't necessary really, he *was* at ease, it was Mr Warrender who was nervous – made this acknowledgement of their shared masculinity.

He would have a room of his own of course and would go to high school. Only first, perhaps, they ought to go into town and get him some shoes.

Out of a fear of upsetting him, or out of embarrassment at the whole business of 'grief', Mr Warrender said nothing at all about his father, and Vic wondered at this. He wondered, too, what Mr Warrender had been looking for when at first he stood there studying him. Not what he had found – he was confident of that – but what, knowing only his father, he had expected.

Sitting beside him on the train, impressed by the smell of damp wool he gave off, which was oddly comforting, and watching the landscape fly through his own ghostly face in the glass, in a new pair of shorts, a sweater and boots that they had bought a size too large, Vic felt his body draw into itself, compact and sturdy, as solid on the velvet seat as the man's, and got hold at last of the consequences of the thing. 'I'll never see this place again,' he told himself as stretches of flat beach flew behind. It was a promise. There was only one thing he regretted, his mother's grave.

He stayed quiet and would continue to be until he knew where he stood. He saw that Mr Warrender, who was observant, was impressed by this, and by the pride he showed in not feeling he had to be saying 'thank you' all the time, though he was very polite. He squared his shoulders, and when Mr Warrender spoke to him looked up very frank and steady, so that what Mr Warrender saw was a reflection of his own lack of guile. He was grateful for this chance to show himself in the best possible light, and to be looked at as if frankness and steadiness could be taken for granted in him. He felt a wave of affection for this shy man.

'You'd better call me Pa, Vic,' Mr Warrender said, 'if that's all right. It's what the girls call me.'

Vic relaxed and smiled. By now he had done some observing of his own.

When Mr Warrender smoked he held the cigarette between thumb and finger like a pencil, and sucked, like a kid taking his first puff, which was odd in so bulky a figure. But he did it voluptuously. Vic thought that very strange, and after a time he decided that Mr Warrender, for all his air of solid assurance, *was* strange. That lack of ease he had felt in him hadn't had to do only with the uncomfortable nature of the occasion. It was part of the man. He wasn't intimidating at all, Vic decided, not at all. I needn't have worried.

It occurred to him then that his father must have found Mr Warrender easy to fool, and this brought him up sharp. All the more reason, he decided, why I should be open and honest with him.

They were coming in to Sydney now, and as street after street flashed by, little backyards with chook-houses and rows of vegetables, and off in the distance smoke pouring up out of giant chimney stacks, he felt some wider vision open in him as well, an apprehension of just how large the world was that he was being carried towards, and the opportunity it offered of scope and space.

Strathfield, when they came to it, was an older suburb not too far from the centre, with avenues of big detached houses that had once been fashionable and were now in a state of elegant disrepair. Along the railway line there were some meaner streets, workmen's houses in terraces that were quite scabbed and shabby, the alleys behind them piled with filth. Still, it was Sydney at last, the big smoke, and Vic had never seen anything like it.

Mrs Warrender, Ma, accepted him with open arms.

The girls, Lucille and Ellie, were sceptical at first, he saw that; but he knew just how to deal with them.

There was also an old lady, an aunt of Mrs Warrender's, who wasn't in her right mind and thought he was someone else.

*

Mrs Warrender showed him his room and they stood for a moment, the two of them, not knowing what to say to one another. Mrs Warrender was plainly embarrassed.

'Well, Vic,' she said at last, 'I'll leave you to get used to things.' She thought he might want to be alone with his grief. 'The bathroom, when you want it,' (maybe it's only that, she thought, she wasn't used to boys) 'is first down the hall.'

She stood at the door, looking at him as he stood with his boots on the carpet in the middle of the room, and his look said, Don't go, I don't need to be alone. But she fiddled with her hands a little, then went.

He sat on the edge of the bed, which was rather high, and looked at his boots. They were heavy. His shoulders slumped and he heard himself sigh. A wave passed over him. Not grief, but desolation, a feeling of utter loneliness that surprised him after the confidence he had felt downstairs. Maybe it was the largeness and whiteness of the room, which he was afraid he would betray himself by dirtying with the grime off his hands; its emptiness, too, since he hardly thought of himself as occupying it – it was so big.

He looked at the case he had brought. It was a little cardboard one with a leather strap. His mother, in the days when she had taken in sewing, had kept buttons and snips of ribbon in it, and off-cuts she could use for patches. What it contained now were the new shirts Mr Warrender had fitted him out with, underpants, even socks. He had brought nothing out of his old life but what was all the heavier for being invisible, and he would have left that too if he could, or shoved it down the windy lav in the train; only there was no way you could get your hands on it. It came along in the roots of his hair, in the mark his fingers left on everything he touched.

Another boy, with his sour miseries and anger deep hidden, had come along with him, and would push his feet each morning into the new shoes, leave dirt marks round the collar of his shirts, soil the bed, these clean sheets, with the sweat of his dreams.

He felt the despair of that boy flow into his heart and sicken him. Getting up quickly, he went to the long mirror of the lowboy, and in an attempt to drive him off stood very straight and square, as he believed Mr Warrender had seen him, in his new clothes.

He turned sideways, and as far as he could, rolling his eyes, looked at himself from that angle too. Then he put his face close to the glass, breathed, and his features vanished in fog.

After a moment, when they came back again, he went to the door along the hall and found the bathroom. It had green tiles. Unbuttoning his shorts, he lifted the seat of the lavatory, pissed, and when he was finished stood for a time and played with his dick till it was stiff. Then he pulled the chain and watched the bowl flush.

In a china shell above the basin was a fresh little cake of soap, very smooth and white. He smelled it, then carefully washed his hands. The smell was allspice.

He looked at his nails, took a little brush, and scrubbed them. They didn't come clean, not quite, but with soap like this they would eventually, he was sure of it.

When he dried his hands the soap smell was still on them. It was still on them when he came downstairs. He checked, in a new rush of confidence, just before he went into the room where Mr Warrender, Pa, was waiting to show him about.

The Warrenders' was a big old-fashioned house, dilapidated in parts and modern in others, with a cast-iron verandah in front, another wooden verandah at the back that had been closed in with pink and green glass to make a sleep-out, and on either side a squat, steep-roofed tower. It stood in a garden of firs and bunyah-pines, and to the left, with no fence between, was a factory, a square brick building with bars on the windows and a paved yard behind that was flagged and full of carboys and barrels. The barrels were brought in on trucks with 'Needham's' painted on the side in a flourish of gilt. When Vic and Mr Warrender came up, one of these trucks was parked at the loading bay. Two men in leather aprons were rolling a barrel down a plank.

'Hullo, Alf,' Mr Warrender said to the older of them. 'How's it going?'

Alf set his boot against the side of the barrel to steady it and said: 'She's right, Mr Warrender. Got a good load on today.' He drew the back of his hand across his nose, which was running, and looked at Vic.

'This is Vic,' Mr Warrender said. 'Vic, this is Alf Lees – and Felix.'

Felix was a dark youth with muscles and a smirk. He said nothing. He stood with his hands under his leather apron and flapped. Vic thought at first that this was some sort of insult. He reddened and looked about to see if Mr Warrender had noticed. But Felix was rolling his eyes up, bored, his big hands under the apron, which flapped and flapped.

'Vic's come to stay with us,' Mr Warrender explained, as if these men needed to know, and Alf, with his boot against the side of the barrel, nodded.

'I thought I'd show him round.'

There was a long pause.

'We won't get in the way.'

Mr Warrender's shyness suddenly overcame him, and Alf, his boot against the barrel, steadying it, also looked uncomfortable.

Vic saw for the first time now another of Mr Warrender's oddnesses. He had difficulty in bringing things to a conclusion. He started off well enough but didn't know how to go on. He stood looking down at the pavement, lifting his huge bulk up and down, very rhythmically, on the toes of his shoes. After a moment, to Vic's surprise, he began to hum.

'Well,' Alf said abruptly, 'no rest for the wicked. C'mon, Felix. Don't just stand there,' and, ignoring Mr Warrender, he took his foot away and allowed the barrel to move on to the bottom of the plank.

Mr Warrender, relieved of his difficulty, said genially, 'So long, boys.'

Vic, glancing back, saw that Felix, under his flop of black hair, was smirking after them. Alf made a gesture to him to get on.

The moment you went through into the dark, high-raftered gloom of the factory itself you were aware of activity; not visible activity, there was very little of that, but a brewing and bubbling that made the air tremble and produced a perceptible heat. It was like crossing the line into a new climate. The atmosphere was thicker. You began immediately to sweat.

A great vat was the source of all this. Mr Warrender led Vic up to it, and for a moment he stood regarding the thing with a kind of awe that struck Vic as surprising; the continuous low hum of it seemed to put a spell on him. He bent his head to the metal surface as if he were listening for a message there that would provide the clue to something that had long puzzled him. Only the message, it seemed, was in a language he had failed to learn.

The bulk of the thing under the high rafters, and Mr Warrender's respectful silence, made Vic think of an altar. It was, little as he knew about churches, the only thing that would explain the sense Mr Warrender gave of being in the presence of something that was both grand and invisible.

Two men wearing white coats appeared round the side of the vat, and one of them, after a brief nod, went back again. The other, looking none too pleased, Vic thought, came on.

'What is it?' Vic was asking. 'What are they making?'

The man in the white coat had come right up to them now, and Mr Warrender made a little gesture in his direction, as if the right to answer, perhaps, were his. But when the man said nothing, he was forced to go on.

'Soap, Vic. It's soap. In this vat here we've got fats – tallow mostly – that's what Alf and Felix were bringing in – and caustic soda. That's right, isn't it, Hicks?'

'That's right,' the man in the white coat said.

'This is Vic,' Mr Warrender told him. 'Vic, this is Mr Hicks. He's our manager. Then,' he went on, 'when it's all been boiled by the steam that's going in there – you can feel the steam, eh? – the soap separates out from the glycerines,' (he sounded like a boy repeating a lesson) 'and when we've boiled it again, only with brine this time, we get soap.

'Well,' he said, after a pause, 'that's a very superficial version of what happens, eh Hicks?'

Vic could see that Mr Hicks, in his white coat and round gold-rimmed glasses, thought it was very superficial, and that Mr Warrender had not explained it very well, but Vic's sympathy was with Mr Warrender.

Mr Hicks moved round now and stood between them and the vat, as if he had to protect the thing, and what was mysteriously happening there, from the sort of superficial interest that might actually prevent it from taking place. Vic felt the hostility he projected. Impatience, too. No doubt he wanted to get back to his own part in the process. Mr Warrender might be the owner, but they were on *his* ground.

Vic, who had a strong sense of these things, of territory, saw that and found himself feeling protective of Mr Warrender and a little injured on his behalf. He seemed out of place here, yet the factory was his.

'Further along,' he was saying, 'we have what we call pitching and settling.' Vic looked for the curl of Hicks's lip. 'One day, Mr Hicks will take you through the whole thing – eh Hicks? – and you can see it all from whoa to go.'

He was running out of steam. In a moment they would come again to one of his awkward silences. But this wasn't quite the end.

'All these processes,' he said, and you could see that it was the first thing so far that really interested him, 'are called "the changes".' He reddened a little as he said this. The word, for him, was charged. 'Pretty poetic, eh, for just soap?'

Mr Hicks was scowling, he couldn't hide it. He was affronted. Maybe he felt something proprietorial about this word, and did not care, since it had a precise scientific meaning, to have Mr Warrender use it in his own way; or maybe he objected to his even telling it at all. Mr Warrender, he guessed, from Hicks's point of view, was not being respectful enough, or his respectfulness was of the wrong kind. The look was dismissive.

'Well, thank you, Hicks, for letting us into your sanctum. Mr Hicks is pretty strict about visitors, Vic. We're privileged.'

Mr Warrender was talking of Hicks the way you talk about a child, humouring him, but in a way that Hicks, you could see, did not care for. He shook hands with Vic, nodded briefly to Mr Warrender, and stepped back behind the vat. Mr Warrender visibly relaxed.

'Times are a bit rough, you know,' he explained to Vic as they turned and went out under the lintel into the blinding sunlight of the yard. 'The big companies have got us by the short hairs, if you'll pardon the expression, we're all men here. The makers, you know,' and his voice took on the fruity tones of an ad on the wireless, 'of Lux toilet soap. We're out of our depth.' But even this he said as if he were repeating a lesson. 'So, young feller,' he said, 'what do you think?'

'I liked it.'

'Good,' said Mr Warrender, 'so do I. But I didn't grow up with it, you know. That was Mrs Warrender. Her father. And liking, old fellow, isn't quite good enough.'

He paused, looked at Vic, and, after considering a moment, decided not to go on.

'Now,' he said, 'we'd better go and take a look at the girls. Otherwise they'll feel neglected. You'll like the girls.'

Some of the girls, it turned out, were over sixty. They were packers and they worked in an overwhelming scent of that allspice Vic had been so delighted by upstairs. Mr Warrender was very gallant with them, and they made a fuss of him and of Vic too.

'So,' Mr Warrender said, 'now you've seen the whole show. We'll just slip round to the kitchen and see if Meggsie can find us a nice cup of tea.'

3

He grew fond of the Warrenders, especially of Mr Warrender, Pa. He was delighted at last to give his softer instincts scope. He had wanted, always, to be the perfect son, and this was easy because the Warrenders were so nearly what he might have conceived of as the perfect parents. He put the past behind him, rediscovered a kind of innocence, and let his spirit loose, slipping back into his heavier nature only when he had shut a door behind him. He could look grim then, and Mrs Warrender, if she had seen it, would have been stricken. A nervous woman, always on the lookout for what was about to go wrong, she might have had to ask herself what they had done to the boy to make him so miserable.

The Warrenders were a source of endless astonishment to him. He had known a life till now that was too harsh to allow for playfulness. The poker games his parents had gone in for, all cigarette smoke and beer, had been rough affairs.

A spirit of boisterous exuberance prevailed in the Warrender house. The games they preferred were childish ones, played at night with all the lights off and a lot of noise. Even Ma, rushing about in her stockinged feet and with her hair flying, would give herself up to easy recklessness, shrieking louder than either of the girls. The girls were wild enough – they were encouraged to be – but Ma outdid them.

Aunt James, who was too old for what she called 'high-jinks', would sit in the dark of the dining room and laugh under her breath, while Ellie or Lucille or Ma tiptoed in and hid behind her chair, and lights flashed on and off in the hallway, and there were rushes, stumblings, evasions that took no heed at all of chairs or vases, then shrieks of childish laughter as the seeker shouted: 'I've got Pa' – or Lucille or Ellie or Vic.

These night games were not the only ones they indulged in, and Vic, who was prudish, found he was often tested, and not at all in the ways he had expected. He had thought he might be too rough for them, so he was surprised when Pa, with no sign of embarrassment, talked about

93

farting, and the girls took it up and elaborated, and even Ma had a laughing fit.

There was a carelessness about the Warrenders, an indifference to what he had imagined was good behaviour and propriety, that would always be foreign to him. They had a passion, all of them, for practical jokes, physical ones, the rougher the better; even Aunt James was not spared. It was a test of character here to take these raw dealings with equanimity and a show of sporting humour. He was delighted when he was at last included and became the butt of one, but never got used to being caught out and mocked. He thought too, after a time, that there was something false in it. What they pretended was that they were all very thick-skinned and impervious to hurts; whereas in fact, as he soon discovered, they were always protecting one another from truths that really wounded, and this rough-and-tumble was a way of disguising it.

Lucille, for instance. He realised after a little that all these eccentricities and raw jokes her parents went in for were a mortification to her. She hated them. She was very proud, and he had thought her hostility to him had to do with that. But he saw at last that what she really had against him was the extent to which they had exposed themselves to him. She was afraid he might take it upon himself to judge Ma and Pa and despise them. She did herself sometimes and was ashamed of it, but her pride would not allow him to.

In the beginning he was flattered by this, but saw that he would have to sacrifice his vanity if he was to make her see he could be trusted. And he could be, too. His loyalty to Pa and Ma was beyond question. It had to be, and especially this matter of loyalty to Pa. The whole household was based on it. Pa's moods, his whims, had at every moment to be respected and allowed for. Ma saw to this, and the girls and Aunt James, even Meggsie, for all her grumbling, complied. Mr Warrender tyrannised over his house of women. They spoiled him and made a great show of it; but the spoiling was a substitute for something he wanted more and which they thought he might never get. The fuss they made was to conceal from him that he had no real authority. But Pa was too intelligent to be deceived. If the household was shaky, and it was at times, it was because of this.

He was an odd fellow, Pa. For all his generosity of flesh he was not expansive. People who thought that all large men should be jolly and lovers of life were disappointed in him. He was not jolly at all, and the roughness of the games he liked to play, the practical jokes, far from expressing a crude vitality, belonged to a version of himself that he reached out for but could not catch. He was often despondent, and sometimes downright gloomy. On nights when he did not happen to be in the mood for noise he would sit with his eyes closed, his brow lowered, while Ma or one of the girls rubbed his shoulders to soothe the ache he felt in being all locked up in himself.

He was a man who had spent a day in heavy traffic with the world, which had buffeted and exhausted him. He needed to be restored now with the ministering of soft hands. The fact that all this had been *mental* traffic made no difference. The results were the same.

He had spent his day getting under everyone's feet, as Meggsie put it, poking about the house looking for things that he or other people had mislaid, making angry phonecalls to lawyers in town, to the council or the newspapers, enervating himself with trivialities to the point where he was quite incapable of settling to any work.

What this work might be, if he did settle, remained unclear. Sometimes it was the regimental history he was writing, in which, Vic supposed, his father might figure – he would be interested in that. More often it was 'something literary'. He had an office and a desk, all leather, that had belonged to Mrs Warrender's father; but he had no sooner got himself in there than he was out again, calling for a pencil-sharpener or his tobacco pouch or the paper, or the volume of Gibbon he had been reading that morning in the lav, or his glasses or his old boots.

On the day each month, 'our dreadful Fridays', Ma called them, when he had to appear at the Needham's board meeting, he would be exhausted, utterly drained, a mere shadow of himself. He would sit through these meetings in a state of maddened irritability, listening to gloomy reports from auditors that he could make nothing of, and angry ones from travellers that he kept rewriting in his head, illiterate accounts, full of irrelevant details or diversions, of encounters with the managers of department stores and chemist shops and beauty parlours, and all the while, under the eye of the chairman, he would be filling the margins of the page with doodles, little half-imaginary animal figures or scornful caricatures.

He would laugh at these meetings the day after, finding in them a source for extravagant mimickry, but the occasions themselves were painful to him. He knew he was of no use there, a straw man, invited only to make up the numbers and have a member of the family on show. He was ashamed of the frivolous manner he assumed but could find no other. He felt humiliated.

Vic was surprised, and sometimes in a painful way, by the differences between this baffled household figure and the one he had sat beside in the train, in whom he had found so much manly steadiness, and warmth and ease. But he continued to honour without qualification the understanding that had been struck between them. What he would remember always was that on that occasion of their first being alone together, and at leisure to observe, Pa, out of an innate generosity, had seen only his best qualities, and accorded him, even if he was just a kid, the full measure of his possibilities. It was for Vic a matter of feeling. The affection it evoked in him, and the loyalty, endured.

Of course he had been presenting himself in the best possible light. It was an opportunity and he had taken it. If Pa had been deceived in some ways, what he had seen was also the truth; it was what Vic, in his deepest nature, aspired to be.

Perhaps Pa too had recognised an opportunity to show the better side of himself. What he had shown, as Vic soon discovered, was the mere externals of his nature, but Vic understood that and would not allow it to make a difference.

He did not reason these things out. He could, with Pa, move back into a state of feeling where those first moments on the train extended themselves and covered all the years to come. The understanding between them, once achieved, was undiminished.

And there was a further dimension to all this. Pa's difficulties offered him an opportunity, or so Vic felt, to step in and show that the qualities that had been accorded him were actual and could be put to use. One day he would do for them what a son might do, and that perhaps was just what had all along been intended.

It was under this aspect of a larger and as yet undeclared purpose that he considered Aunt James's refusal to see him as a stranger. She had simply assumed, from the first day, that he was a member of the family, but, in the weird view she took of these things, a secret one. The fact that she had got the details wrong was neither here nor there.

'I kept all your letters,' she told him in a whisper the first time they were alone. 'I knew you'd be back. They told me you were dead, Stevie, but I knew *that* couldn't be true. And it isn't, is it, sweetie?' She laughed and poked him in the ribs, as if it were a good joke between them that he was not a ghost. 'Well, I would have thought your own sister might have known you.'

Stevie was Mrs Warrender's brother. Years back, at a time when Ma and Pa's marriage was being settled, he had got into some sort of trouble, been despatched to New Zealand, and died there by taking his own life.

Vic felt uncomfortable. It was crazy, and spooky too. She was herself a kind of spook. When they played their games he would keep away from the dining room where Aunt James was sitting, her eyes, her ears too, made sharper by the dark. 'Ah, Stevie,' she would whisper as he tried to tiptoe past the door, 'is that you? You come and hide by me. I won't let *him* get you.'

It did not trouble him in the daylight. He could treat it as a joke. But here in the dark, seeing her grey hair lit up in points where the light from the garden touched it, and hearing the passion in her voice, which was so low and croaky, he would feel a coldness on the back of his neck, and stop still sometimes, unable to move.

For all Mr Warrender's generosity to her, Aunt James was still loyal to the scapegrace Stevie, and for more than twenty years had looked forward to his return. Mr Warrender knew this. No doubt it upset him. But he accepted it as another of Aunt James's disconcerting eccentricities.

So when she saw in Vic's appearance among them the return of the prodigal, the banished brother-in-law, she was making mischief. She was enlisting him in an alliance against Pa.

Vic decided (they were all so open about it) that he could take this side of the thing lightly, presenting himself as a victim, as Mr Warrender himself was, of the old girl's crazy fits. But it worried him a little and made him more determined than ever to do nothing, whatever turn things might take, that could be construed as disloyalty to Pa.

He was helped in this by Aunt James's inconsistency. There were occasions when her mind skipped sixty years rather than twenty and he became her own brother Bob, a spoiled and sickly child who had been killed in a riding accident when he was just the age that Vic was now. In this guise she would poke her tongue out and, snatching the bread off his plate, shout, 'Let him go without, the little bugger!' being pretty well certain that no one else could see him; or she would lean out and pinch him hard, daring him to cry out and show her up.

He did not know how to react. He felt a fool just sitting there and letting an old lady pinch him. He could hardly pinch her back. But the girls, who had put up with Aunt James's tricks for as long as they could remember, were delighted, they thought it hilarious. Even Pa was amused, but did give him a look as if to say, 'Well, you see how it is, old man. It's the same with me. But what can we *do*?'

But he saw now why the girls asked their friends to the house only when Ma could guarantee that Aunt James would be out of the way, and why they had been so uneasy at first even with him.

Ellie wasn't – or not for long. But Ellie was just a little girl, rather wild and tomboyish, glad to have someone new to play with and a boy in the house. Lucille he had to win.

He did it by not trying to, by letting her discover for herself how solid, how utterly loyal he was.

They were the same age, and she too was glad at last to have a boy in the house, though for other reasons than Ellie's. At thirteen she was quite grown-up, or thought she was, and very aware of the power she had over people, only a little scared as yet of the consequences of it.

She did not set out to make a worshipper of him, but he became one. The little game he had been led into, of getting around the difficulties of her character, of impressing and pleasing her, became a habit, then a pleasure and a misery. Before long he was, he told himself, in love with Lucille, and in his usual way began to include her in the visions he gave himself up to of what his life would be.

She accepted this at first. She was just the age for it, for talking dreamily of ever afters and for being in love. But she grew up faster than Vic did; he could not keep up with her. He found himself, more often than he would have wanted, turning to Ellie for the rough-and-tumble games that the boyish part of him still hungered for, and he was hurt when Lucille drew her mouth down and mocked at him.

By the time she was fifteen Lucille Warrender had become a young woman, very demanding and wilful and with a tribe of followers. He did not despair when she began to go about with older boys. He knew he had a year or two yet in which to grow up. But he agonised, and wore such a long face that Ma, who saw all this and was increasingly fond of him, was at a loss. For all his stolidity he was easily hurt. And he had a romantic streak. Other people might miss it, but Ma didn't. She didn't know how to help him.

The fact was that she was scared of Lucille, who seemed to her too grown-up altogether. She thought too highly of herself. For days on end she would be all moods and little female fads and whims that Ma had no time for. Then suddenly there would be floods of tears and she would want to be cuddled and forgiven. She was neither one thing nor the other. She was proud and critical and unthinkingly cruel; not so much by nature as from inexperience. She did not know herself or how to act in a way that would spare either her own feelings or other people's. It was Vic who bore the brunt of it.

'After all, Vic, you're not a stranger, are you, so it doesn't matter.' These were the words Ma used when she came up to his room, as in time she often did, to consult with him. 'I can talk to you, Vic. Goodness knows, I can't talk to the girls or Pa.' She meant she did not want to alarm them with her fears.

She believed, young as he was, that Vic was tough and practical. Practical was one of her favourite words, and a great compliment. He would sit feeling pleased with himself, tough, compact, and yes, practical, while she gave herself up to visions of disaster. That was the word she kept flying to.

She was a worrier, Ma. With a magazine in one hand, *The Bulletin* or the *London Illustrated News*, which she would snatch up as a guarantee that she had something to do, and in the other a cigarette that she mostly forgot to smoke, she would prowl the house like an unhappy ghost, peering into rooms that her mother, in the days when they had five maids, had filled with whatnots and the souvenirs of travel – Venetian glass and little boxes and figurines in porcelain or Parian or bronze, that they could afford to keep dusted then but were impractical now. On Pa's urging, and for reasons of common sense, she had cleared it all out, all the gloomy mahogany and velvet and bric-à-brac, and furnished the place in modern veneer.

The trouble was, she missed the old things. She would put her hand out for a bit of familiar furniture and be shocked that it wasn't there. Or she and Meggsie would spend half a morning going through drawer after drawer looking for some old newspaper cutting she wanted to consult, or a bunch of artificial violets she thought she could use on a hat, or an earring to match one that had turned up again after seven years, and she would realise with a pang that she had left it in one of the sideboard drawers when it went off to Lawson's to be sold.

This was her parents' house, the one she had grown up in. What she had done, she felt, for all her talk of what was sensible, had been an attempt to drive their spirits from the place. She felt ashamed now. She ought never to have done it. And anyway, she had failed.

Standing at the long drawing-room window and looking across to the factory, she would feel her father there in the room behind her. He would be wearing a savage look and waiting, not too patiently (he had been a rough, uneducated fellow), for her to explain herself. What had she done with his splendid enterprise?

She thought of the answer she might give him. 'For heaven's sake, Pop, this is 1936!' (As if this improvement on 1919, when he died, could stand against the other figures she would have had to give him, which these days were always down.) 'I mean, there's a depression on.'

All this was nonsense, of course. 'I ought to have been a boy,' she would tell herself, and she would tell Vic this too. 'Then they would have taught me how to *do* something about it.' But Stevie was the boy, and her father, in a fit of self-righteousness that was to be fatal, had destroyed that possibility by driving him away. So who was to blame? And why did *she* feel guilty?

Wandering about the house in her stockinged feet, elegant but careless, she could be there, as Meggsie complained, before you knew it – unless you smelled the smoke.

'Lord bless the Irish!' Meggsie would exclaim when Mrs Warrender appeared, anxious to have a sit-down at the kitchen table and go over some problem about the girls, 'You scared the daylights outa me!'

Meggsie had girls of her own: two of them unhappily married and settled, the other still getting her glory-box together. She had known Lucille and Ellie since they were babies. She spoiled them, always took their part and could see no problem with either of them.

But Mrs Warrender was in no mind to be convinced. As if by habit, and ignoring Meggsie's clear displeasure, she would go to the dresser, find a sharp little knife and set herself to help Meggsie peel and core apples while she went over the thing.

Meggsie fumed. She had her own way of doing things, and Mrs Warrender's did not suit her. As Ma got more and more excited, a good half of the apple she was working on would disappear as scrap. If it was peas she was shelling she would pop at least one from every shell into her mouth. Finally Meggsie would stand no more of it. Ten years older than Ma, she took the line that Ma was not much more than a girl herself. Taking the knife out of her hand, or pulling the bag of unshelled peas to her own side of the table, she would say: 'Now you listen to me, dear. You should stop stirrin' yourself up like this and just let things go their own way. Let *nature* take its course.'

Mrs Warrender was appalled. She had seen nature take its course. That was precisely what terrified her.

'They're good girls, both. Let me tell you, you don't know how lucky you are. Now *trust* me. Did I ever serve you up a brumm p'tata?'

Mrs Warrender would sit a moment. In fact she did feel easier. Maybe it was the few minutes of working with her hands and actually doing something. More likely it was the light in Meggsie's kitchen, which she had loved since she was just a little thing and would come to make patty cakes in the stove. Or Meggsie herself and the rhythm she imposed on things. It was different from the rhythms of the rest of the house, which were either too hectic or too lax – she should do something about that, but what? Just being in this cool, back part of the house was refreshing and she found herself wishing that Meggsie, who was proprietorial, had not made it so exclusively her own. She would have been happy to work here if Meggsie would have her: peeling potatoes, chopping vegetables, putting her hands into greasy water, acting as a slavey in her own home. But Meggsie, polite but insistent, couldn't wait to get rid of her.

'Now you go and putcher feet up on the verandah, dear, and I'll bring you a nice cuppa tea. I'm busy. I got the pudding ta think of. If I don't, pretty soon, there won't be any.'

Mrs Warrender went, feeling quieter, but dismissed.

'I wish,' she was fond of saying, 'that my father had let me learn typing or something – or serve in a shop even. At least then I would *know* something and people wouldn't talk to me as if I was some sort of dimwit. I mean, we aren't *born* impractical.'

Quite soon after Vic arrived in the house she took to waylaying him in the hallway as he came in from school, and later, when she began to see in his sturdy and sometimes grave figure a kind of equilibrium that came, she thought, from 'experience' (and how in the world, at his age, had he come by *that*?), she would at the oddest hours wander right into his room and, settling herself on the edge of the bed, start in on whatever it was that was fretting her.

Sometimes, abstractedly, as she talked, she would pick his dirty socks up off the floor and begin to roll them, or a shirt or a pair of underpants. Once she held one of his socks up to her nose and smelled it, and did not look at all offended – in fact, rather pleased. Or she would open and close the drawers of his dressing table, moving things about and seeing they were properly folded. She wasn't spying, he knew that, because she wasn't actually looking at things. Just touching them and reassuring herself that one article was cotton, another wool, so many pairs. It helped her order her thoughts and re-established, in a motherly way – socks and shirts and underpants were a mother's business – her intimacy with him.

'Mr Warrender, Pa,' she would tell him, 'is a wonderful man. He's the kindest, most generous – . People don't realise. Look how he is with Aunt James! But like the rest of us he has his limits. He can't do wonders. They keep asking too much of him.'

Vic would sit silent and follow her restless pacing about the room, wondering at this way she had of putting a case for the defence as if she were a lawyer addressing an unseen jury, and Pa always the man in the dock.

He was too young at first, and too unused to being confided in, to do more than take it all in and hold his tongue. But he did wonder who *they* could be. Ma's parents? Aunt James, Meggsie, Mr Hicks? He decided then that Ma was rather queer in the head, or overwrought, hysterical. For a time he took an amused attitude and regarded her, secretly, with a kind of affectionate contempt.

But as he got to know the household better he saw at last that she was the only one here who really thought about things. He did too, and she saw that and was grateful. As he got to be older and more responsible, their little 'confabs', as she called them, became serious discussions about family affairs, that took up the whole business of the factory and its running, loans, interest rates, finances. She knew more than you might expect, Ma, about loans and such things. What she knew she shared with him. They were in a bad way: that was the heart of the matter. That's what she was trying to face up to.

They did not give themselves airs, the Warrenders – they had too much style for that. They would have been ashamed to appear opulent when around them so many others were being crushed. The car they drove, a grey Hup, was the same one they had been careering about in for fifteen years. You still had to crank it. The house was large enough, but a lot of it was in poor repair and half the rooms they never went in to except when they played games. There was only Meggsie to do anything. The girls had been brought up to think of themselves as poverty-stricken, and might have been ragged if Meggsie hadn't taken a hand.

All that was a kind of insurance, a sop to the fates. They were *not* poor, not by most people's standards, but they soon might be. Poverty these days could hit you just like that. Ma had seen it happen to others, and she was scared. What scared her was that she did not know what it was, or how, when it came, she would meet it.

Vic knew and could have told her, but what would she have learned from that? He would have had to bare at last what he was determined to keep hidden, even from her.

Occasionally, when he came in from school, there would be a man in the yard, often, as he grew, a boy not much older than himself, chopping wood for Meggsie's stove. Normally this was his job.

Resting on the axe a moment, his shirt dark at the armpits and sticking to the small of his back, the man would draw a wrist across his brow, which was dripping, and nod under the greasy hat. Some of these fellows were not used to it, you could see that. They were making a mess of the job.

They were men out of work, battlers who came to the back door looking for any employment they could get: chopping wood, cleaning out gutters or drains. Meggsie had authority, or had assumed it, to give them something, usually bread and dripping or a bowl of soup. The work was an acknowledgement that what they got they had earned, a gesture towards masculine pride and the insistence that what they were after was work, not charity. Meggsie knew them like her own. They might have been her sons or brothers. Just the same, she kept an eye on them.

They haunted Vic, these men or half-grown boys who a few months back had been storemen or clerks in shipping offices or drillers in mines. He felt his shoulders slump a little at the sight of them. He felt humbled. When he had taken his school jacket off and rolled his sleeves, he would go out sometimes and have a word with them – nothing much, but he knew the language.

They were embarrassed. He didn't talk like a boss, but he was at home here. So what was he? What did he want? They wished after a while that he would leave them alone to get on with it. He felt the hardening in them of something he had touched and offended, and knew what it was but could not help himself. He found excuses for hanging about the factory yard with his hands in his pockets, kicking stones under the firs.

Worst of all were the times when he came on one of them hunched over the soup Meggsie had given him, apart and feeding.

They scared him, these men. Not physically – there was very little that scared him that way. It was his spirit that shivered and got into a sweat. They were everywhere you went: hanging about with no change in their pockets outside the picture shows, the boldest of them still flash enough to whistle at girls; in lines on the pavement. You would have had to tag on to the end of one of these straggling, endlessly shuffling lines to find out what it was, up ahead, that had drawn them. He didn't really want to know, but felt there was something wrong. He had got off too easily. He was in the wrong dream.

He went out for a time with a girl, not one of Ellie and Lucille's friends, but a girl he had met at a dance. She lived at Granville and worked as a salesgirl in the city. She had two older brothers who were out of work, her father too, and could type a hundred words a minute and take shorthand, but the only job she could get was selling paint in a hardware shop. He was getting nowhere with her but he didn't mind, he liked her so much; she was so lively and certain of her own competence, and so pleased with herself because she had a job. Her whole family depended on her.

But one hot night when he went out to meet her, as he sometimes did, at the tram, she was in tears and would not speak to him, just went rushing past in her neat high heels, sobbing, and when he caught up with her she pushed him off.

She had been sacked. They'd sacked her for coming in three minutes late from lunch. It had been so hot that she and another girl had stopped off a minute in the park, sitting on the edge of a fountain to bathe their feet and let the spray blow over them. Three minutes! In a mood of over-confidence set off by their moment at the fountain, which was still bubbling away in her, she had stood up for herself and the manager had sacked them, both of them – and the other girl hadn't said a word! She was inconsolable. She just looked at him. Didn't he see what it meant? Was he too stupid even to see that?

What angered her was the vanity of his assumption that he could soothe an outrage in her that he had not even understood.

She had lost the one little bit of ground she stood on that gave her a choice. It was that, and the shame of what she had let them do to her, that had beaten the spark out of her.

They were in a world in which forces were at work that took no account of ordinary lives, and as things everywhere got tougher he saw that Ma's fears, which he had thought exaggerated at first, were real. All around them people were being swept into the gutter and could not save themselves.

Friends of the Warrenders, a family that had seemed quite safe and prosperous, were revealed overnight to have been living on nothing but show. The father, a solicitor, went to prison. The mother, and the boy and girl, moved to Melbourne.

Things were closing in. It was for Ma's sake now, as well as Pa's, that he set to work, but in a practical way, to save them. Pa was too high-strung and sensitive to be a businessman. 'Well,' Vic told himself, 'I'm not sensitive, I can't afford to be. Business will do fine for me. I'm not so particular.'

He had thought at first that he ought to be; that his readiness to muck in and dirty his hands with money-making was an indication that even his finest instincts might be coarse. But when he got to see things more clearly he began to ask himself what the value was of so much fineness if all it did was spoil you for action – and it was in action that he meant to prove himself.

He took a second look at his coarseness. What it amounted to was a wish to get on in the world, and a view, a hard-headed one, of what you might have to be to do it.

For one thing you had to see things the way they were. No good giving people credit for virtues they did not have. Most people were selfish. They had low motives rather than noble ones. You had to start from *that*. You ought to act nobly yourself (he always would), but you couldn't expect others to.

He could live with that, he wasn't squeamish. The times had revealed pretty clearly what sort of world they were in. Lack of fastidiousness might be an advantage when things got rough.

He kept faith with the glimpse Pa had given him that first day of 'the changes'; he had been moved by all that, and if it was a term he had any use for he too might have called them poetic. He was not without idealism, or imagination either. But this did not prevent him from seeing these processes, in their real physical form, as what they were:

natural occurrences accountable to strict chemical laws, and also, if need be, to the balance of costs.

He had been fascinated by the vat from the moment he saw it sitting there so cool and mysterious, the great rounded girth of it with its rows of darker rivets, the pipes climbing away at all angles, the activity it set up in the air around you, which throbbed with an added heat. Twenty-four hours a day it sat there, quietly humming to itself, and it wasn't just soap it manufactured, the pure white cakes that moved up and down on conveyor belts, went out at last to be wrapped and packed by the girls in the work room, and from there, in trucks, to the department stores and chemist shops and beauty salons where it was handled by sales ladies, and came back at last in the form of the ready cash that Pa jingled in his pockets and doled out on Saturday mornings as pocket money, and which Ma used to run the house. No, it made something else as well, and they lived on that, too. It was a dynamo pouring out energy that when it crossed the yard was translated into the little actions and reactions that made up their daily lives. (Not literally, of course. He was thinking now in terms that in Pa's mind would have been 'poetic'.)

Standing at his bedroom window he would look across the dark of the yard and be reassured by the faint glow of it there, still humming away. He saw it in his sleep as well. Awesome and huge it looked, but comfortably familiar. The energy from it fired his dreams.

In the afternoons after school he would slip across to the factory to 'bother' Mr Hicks. But the manager, once he saw the seriousness of him, and that his interest was not just boyish curiosity in the nuts and bolts of things, was happy to show him all he knew. The boy was bright, that's what he saw. And he had imagination, too. He saw things large.

'That's a good question,' he told Vic once, chewing on his moustache. 'If we knew the answer to that one, young feller, we'd be on the way to millions.'

'Would we? Really?'

Hicks paused a moment. Vic, he saw, had taken him literally. The word millions meant something definite to him.

'Well, millions is an exaggeration,' he said. 'Let's say: to setting ourselves pretty firmly on our feet.'

But that wasn't enough for Vic. It might do for a start. But millions!

He put this bit of information, which was still a question, at the back of his mind. He'd work on it.

What Hicks had failed to see was that millions, even if you took it literally, wasn't simply, as Vic saw it, cash. It was an evocation of scale rather than an accountable sum. In an action of that size, Vic thought, coarseness would blur into insignificance.

He still smarted over the presence of this negative quality in himself, but was determined not to deny it; to find instead a means of using it in an action that would be fine. At least his *motives* were fine. He would be doing it for *them*; anything that might accrue to himself would be sheer profit. He would be repaying his debt a thousandfold. Wasn't that noble enough? In millions! Even Meggsie might be impressed.

He had an irritant, Vic, a grain of scepticism about his own nature that would not let him rest. He could never quite prevent himself from looking, on each occasion, for the little giveaway flicker in another's eye that would warn him he had failed to get away with it; that for all his swagger, he had been sniffed out. It gave him a dark pleasure, that, which he could not account for. It was always the one person in any company who had not been taken in, who had not succumbed to the tricks he used to win people, that he was drawn to.

He went on trying to, of course. That was only natural. But with half of him he wanted them to resist.

What he was after was a truth that could not be mocked.

He had seen at once, when Mr Warrender first took him round to the kitchen to be introduced, that Meggsie was the one here that he would have to be on guard against.

'Vic is it, eh?' she had said, looking once and weighing him up. 'Well, you just watch them boots, young feller, on my floor. I jest mopped it.'

These were her first words to him. He looked at the floor. It was lino in big black and white squares like a draughts board.

'Oh, Vic's all right,' Pa assured her, but lost confidence under her glare.

He knew what she really meant because they spoke the same language.

'Never seen a floor like that, have you, son?' That's what she meant. 'Floor and boots both, I dare say. Well, the floor's mine, I'm the boss here. As for the boots, don't you get too big for 'em, that's all. You may fool some people but you won't fool me.'

It wasn't hostile, but it was a warning. The look of amusement on her face suggested that she would be watching with interest but he could expect no quarter. She had her girls to think of. She didn't care for boys.

He went easy with her. No good trying to get around Meggsie. She'd see through that right off. She knew the world he had come out of and she knew, because she had scrubbed them, the grime he got on the cuffs and collars of his shirts and the state of his sheets. A kind of game developed between them. It wasn't the sort of game the Warrenders would have understood. It was a joking game, watchful on her part and contentious, but not without affection. 'I know you, young feller, I've known lots a' fellers like you. Believe me, I can read you like a book.'

So far as Meggsie was concerned, he would always be on probation. That was the nub of the thing.

Apart from Mr Warrender, to whom she was fiercely loyal, there was only one man Meggsie had any time for. This was the actor Sessue Hayakawa. Vic knew him because he had been one of his mother's favourites too.

'He's a dream,' Meggsie would tell Vic and the girls when they came bustling into the kitchen to scrape bowls.

'I thought he was a Jap,' Vic would say cheekily.

'Well, 'e's a gentleman. Which is more than can be said fer you, young feller, with them *hands*.' She meant his nails weren't clean, but he was ashamed of his big hands and hid them. 'Yer not in the race.'

'The Jap race,' he said under his breath (this was for the girls), and giggled. But the girls were not amused. A year back they would have been, but only Ellie laughed now, out of loyalty, and he felt oafish.

'He's *suaaave*,' Meggsie told them, and Vic had a vision of the sleek, cruel, broodingly attentive lover she must dream of, who stood at the furthest possible distance from what she had known in the flesh. From 'fellers', as she would have put it, 'round here'.

'Well,' he thought, 'yes, but she's never had to change *his* sheets.'

'What does Meggsie think of her dreamboat now?' he wrote home after the Japs hit Pearl Harbor, still smarting, long after, from the snub he had felt and the disadvantage she had put him at in front of Lucille. But it would be four years before he got his answer.

1

The early days at Changi were all idleness and neglect. The Japs, caught out by the suddenness of the collapse and the falling into their hands of so many thousands, had no idea as yet what to do with them. Left to their own devices, they did nothing. Even Doug, after his first picnic vision of it, fell quiet and was depressed.

To Digger it was terrible. The daily hanging about in irregular groups, the looseness, the disorder: sudden outbreaks of rebellious anger, then periods when the whole place seemed ghostly and they were struck, all of them, with the sleeping sickness.

The time they were in, like the unenclosed space of the camp, was limitless. Without boundaries it had no meaning. Young fellows who only weeks before had been full of fight and spirit, setting up races with one another, or boxing, or riding out on bicycles to the Happy World to have their fortunes told and play rough and find girls, shuffled about now like old men in a hospital yard, sucking fags, swapping rumours, feeding petty grievances. They neglected everything: let a grain of rice fall for the flies to swarm over; at the latrines were too lazy to cover their shit. Their insides went liquid. Everything they ate turned to slime.

This was despondency in its physical form, so childish and shameful that grown men wept at it. 'I hate this,' Digger told himself. 'It's worse than anything.' It was the sun scrambling their brains. It was lack of activity. It was the shame and desperation they felt at being sold out by the higher-ups. It was the failure of the officers to impose order. It was their native slackness and refusal to accept authority – those were the theories.

But slowly, as the days went by, a kind of order began to emerge. It was rudimentary enough, a simpler version of the old one, but it grew in such fits and starts and bits and pieces that you could make nothing of it.

Makeshift shelters began to appear, flimsy affairs knocked up from whatever the men could scrounge. Cook-houses were established.

Three times a day food was doled out, rice and a few vegetables with maybe a lump of fish in it, and you spent a good hour sometimes hanging about in lines. A few of the officers, who still had faith in the civilising power of education and saw in the enforced idleness and boredom of the lower ranks an opportunity that might never recur, set up a school. They had textbooks, and a blackboard and chalk. They called themselves a university and gave lectures on all sorts of things. Digger went along once and heard a talk on Ancient Rome – the monetary reforms of the emperor Diocletian. Another time it was the Soviet Union, but that occasion ended in a ding-dong battle over Stalin's pact with Hitler, and the anger on both sides was murderous.

Mac tried to talk Digger into doing French. They sweated over a lesson or two, but learning a language would take years, even Mac saw that, and they had no idea what they would be doing next week.

'You'd be better off learnin' bloody Japanese,' Doug told them. 'On'y I don't s'pose they're bloody offerin' that. Bad for morale.'

Standing in line one day, waiting for his issue of rice, Digger found himself addressed by a fellow he had never seen before. He was muttering. All Digger had done was turn his head a little to see who it was.

'They're all bloody thieves in this camp,' the boy told him passionately. 'I lost a fucken good fountain-pen. Some bastard swiped it straight outa me pack!'

Another fellow, half behind the other, half beside, gave a scornful laugh. 'You could'a done worse,' he said. He turned to Digger. 'He don't even know how to write.'

'Yair? Well what's that gotta do with it?' the first boy shouted. 'Eh? Eh?' and he began to jab the heel of his hand into the other's shoulder. 'I traded that pen fer a fucken good pair a' socks. A man oughten'a steal from 'is mates.'

Faced with this fiercely honourable proposition the other fellow shrugged and turned away.

'Me name's Harris,' the boy told Digger, 'Wally' – as if he had seen that Digger was the one man in all this throng who might remember it for the rest of his life. He waited for Digger to respond but Digger drew away. He had nothing to do with these men. He had been late lining up, that's all. He had his own mob. But the boy would not be put off.

'I oughten'a be here by rights,' he confided. 'I'm on'y sixteen. I lied to 'em. Me mum didn' mind.'

Standing with his dixie and spoon in hand and the hat far back on his curls, his expression was a mixture of cocky satisfaction at his own cleverness and dismay at where it had got him. He was trying to interest Digger. He was one of those fellows that no one notices and he was eager now to pick up with someone, anyone, having grasped by instinct that you could only survive here if you had mates.

'I could'a done a good swap for that pen,' he said, 'it was a real goodun. Listen,' he said, dropping his voice so that the other fellow could not hear, 'waddaya reckon I oughta do? I don't feel so good. I got the shits all the time, I'm crook. What can I do?'

But Digger was at the head of the line now. He took his rice and moved away. He saw the boy turn and look after him, but there were dozens of fellows like that, who once the ranks were open were helplessly adrift.

'I don't eat it,' another man told him, another stranger, when he was once more in the line. 'I don't eat the shit.' Digger wondered then why he was lining up for it. He was a big, heavy-shouldered fellow, blond, red-faced, pustular.

'If they keep feedin' us this muck, and we keep eatin' it, our eyes'll go slanty. Dja know that? This professor tol' me. It's what the bastards want! T' make fucken coolies of us. They hate white men.'

Digger frowned. Was he crazy? He was dancing about behind Digger with his dixie all washed and ready in his hand. Half crazy with hunger, he looked.

'On'y I don't eat it, see? They can't make yer, can they? They won't get me! I'd rather bloody starve! All it does anyway is give yer the shits.'

But a moment later Digger saw him, big-eyed and wild-looking, shovelling the stuff into his mouth. Their eyes met and Digger looked quickly away.

More than ever now he clung to Mac and Doug. Only in those who were close to you was there any continuation of cleanness and sanity. But now they had Vic as well and were an uneasy foursome, unbalanced, as they never had been when they were three. Forever looking about to see what you might be thinking of him, Vic was all little burrs and catches, always uneasy with himself yet at the same time cocky, and anxious at every opportunity to put himself forward or to get the better of you. Digger couldn't stand him.

'Oh, Vic's all right,' Doug would say. 'Take no notice of 'im.' But the foursome began to split into unequal twos.

Digger missed Doug. He missed his lightness and good humour. He was civil enough to Vic but resented his butting in. He and Mac thought alike on this. They thought alike on lots of things.

He was an odd bloke, Mac. When he was in the mood for it he could talk the leg off an iron pot. Not like Doug, who loved an audience and to joke and pull people in, but in a quieter, more reflective way.

He was full of stories, odd anecdotes and theories he had picked up from meetings or lectures he had attended or fellows he had heard on Sundays in the Domain; or from books, or from conversations he had had up at the Cross.

For a time he had had a flat there and known all sorts of people: radicals, poets, fellows who wrote for the *Herald* and *Smith's Weekly*. It was an education. 'Sydney wouldn't be Sydney without the Cross,' he told Digger. 'That's where you oughta head for when you get outa this. The Cross. No place like it.'

It seemed to Digger he had seen nothing really, for all the places he had been. Not after what you heard from other men. Mac's tales of life round the city and on the trams, the different depots, and the runs he went on out to Bondi, Bronte, Clovelly, Watson's Bay, the best pubs and pie shops, and Sargents, where his sister-in-law worked, which made the best cakes – all this brought Sydney to life for Digger and fed his hunger for a world of ideas and talk and action that he thought he would never get enough of, not if he lived till he was a hundred and three. He took in every detail, and each one was sharper for his having to picture it in his own head.

The walk up the long gully at Cooper Park, for instance. Could any place be greener on a nice Sunday afternoon? Mac and Iris and the boys would go for picnics there, and after an hour or so, when their meal had gone down, Mac would coach the younger boy, Jack, in the high jump.

'I dare say he'll be out of the juniors,' Mac would say a bit regretfully, 'by the time we get back. Grows like a beanpole, that kid. No stopping 'im. He'll be five three or four by now, I reckon. You should see 'im take off – the spring he's got!' Digger could see it: the boy's legs scissoring as he went over the bar, Iris seated on the grass with a chequered cloth spread out in front of her, and the scraps from their tea, with maybe a bottle of pickles. In time, out of Mac's bits and pieces of description, and stories and instances, the whole household came into view.

The house itself, in Bon Accord Avenue, Digger could see as if he had lived his whole life there.

Mac slept on the side verandah in a room he had closed in himself with the help of a mate, another trammie. It was floor to ceiling books and there were more books in stacks under the wire frame of the bed and along both sides of the hall. Mac had not read these books, or not all of them; they were for his retirement. But the majority of them he had at least dipped into. How could you resist? On the way home, last thing Friday nights, when he had just picked up a new lot, he would take a good long look and be content then to have the rest of it stored up and waiting for him.

Technical manuals on everything from book-binding to telegraphy, novels, journals, books of travel, psychology, history – that's what he liked. He'd been reading since he was a kid, like Digger – anything he could lay his hands on: Shakespeare, Shaw, Dickens, Jack London, Victor Hugo. They swapped favourite characters, told over incidents, laughing, and Digger, a bit shyly at first, recited out of his head from *Hamlet* or *Henry the Fifth*. They were Mac's favourites.

'Amazing, that is,' Mac would say. 'Ruddy amazing. Honest, Digger, you oughta be in a sideshow. What I wouldn' do with *your* gift!'

'What?' Digger wondered.

It had become clear to him, even before any of *this* happened, that his 'gift', as Mac called it, even if it turned out to be the one thing that was special to him, was not to be the source of any fame or fortune. It would never be useful in that way. It had some other significance, or so he thought, that was related to the image his mother had put into his head, that room where all the things were gathered that made up your life. He was a collector, as she was. He hung on to things. But his room was of another kind, and so were the things he stored there.

Mac had been married – still was, in fact. Two years it lasted. The girl left him; not for another bloke, as it happened, but to live her own life and run a nursery in the Blue Mountains.

'She got fed up with me,' Mac told him, and put on a humorous look; but Mac's humour, Digger knew by now, was a way of protecting himself, and you too sometimes, from the pain of things. 'I never understood what she wanted, really. I reckoned I did, like most blokes, on'y I never had a clue really. She had a bad time, poor girl. Me too.' When his brother died in a shipping accident in the Islands he had moved in with his sister-in-law, who was glad of the extra money and to have a man's help with the boys. Mac got letters from her and had a pile, five in all, that he read over almost every night.

'If anything happens to me, Digger,' he said once. 'I'd like you to have 'em.'

It was a solemn offer, and Digger, who felt the weight of it, was moved. 'OK,' he said.

He had had only one letter himself, from his mother, an angry one. His father had got himself wounded in Crete.

But more important to Digger in the end than Mac's yarns, and the passionate and sometimes pedantic flights that put him pretty firmly, as Doug said, in 'the ratbag brigade', were the times when they just sat cleaning their gear or doing a bit of mending; saying nothing much, just quietly enjoying the company.

Self-possession. That was the quality in Mac that drew Digger. It was rare, and seemed, the more he thought about it, to be the one true ground of manliness. It was a quality he had never attained himself, and he wondered sometimes if he ever would. He had ants in his pants. That's what his mother would have told him. Everything grabbed his attention and led him away from himself. He was always in a turmoil, never steady or still. The world was too full of interest. He got lost in it.

One of the things Mac introduced him to was music. It stood, for Mac, in some sort of middle position between talk and silence, with similarities, if you could imagine such a contradiction, to both, and it was this, Digger thought, that explained the link he felt between music and Mac's particular brand of self-possession. If you understood the one, perhaps you would get a clear sight of the other.

He encouraged Mac to talk about the pieces he liked. Mac, who was a born teacher, was only too pleased to introduce him to bits of opera and things by Chopin and Fritz Kreisler.

'*Nessun dorma*', 'none shall sleep'; that was a good one. They heard that one night during their first week in Malaya, in the early days before the Japs landed. Digger was amazed. It was in the open, under the stars, and almost a thousand of them had been sprawled there on the grass. But there was a lot of music to be heard at Changi, too. Fellows who had carried their records with them would bring their favourites along, and dozens of men, hundreds sometimes, would come in out of the dark to listen. Digger would sit back a little and take his cue from Mac.

Mac's characteristic expression was a long-faced, half-woeful, half-comic look that went with his being, as Doug said, a 'black-stump philosopher'.

'The big trouble with you, mate,' Doug would tell him, 'is that you know too much fer yer own good. All it does is make ya mournful. Now, I ask you, what's the use a' *that*?'

'I'm not mournful,' Mac would insist.

'A' course you are. You're about the mournfullest bloke I ever laid eyes on. Honest, Mac, you oughta take a dekko at yerself. I tell ya, mate, you look as if the world ended last Mondee and you just got news of it.'

These sallies were pure affection. They took in a side of Mac that in Doug's opinion was excessive. He needed to be jollied out of it. It was his ratbag side, the side of all those failed, unforgotten utopias that blokes like Mac, dyed-in-the-wool idealists, would give their lives for – and other people's lives as well if they could get them, all in the name of some future that most fellers didn't want and couldn't use and weren't fit for, and couldn't be *made* fit for either, unless you wrenched them this way and that till there was nothing left that was human in them.

Mac defended himself, lost his temper, became just the sort of angelic storm-trooper Doug accused him of being, then laughed and put on his self-deprecating, comic-suffering look, but refused to admit defeat.

Doug's rough cynicism beat him every time, but somehow, when it was over, he was not beaten. He was self-possessed, Mac, but he was also passionate, and contradictory too. Only when he was leaning forward into the music and utterly absorbed by it were the different sides of him resolved. What you saw then – what Digger saw – was the absolute purity of him.

'I'll never be like that,' Digger thought. 'Not in a million years.'

Then Mac would catch him looking and wink, and what you saw then was the odd humour of the man.

When the chance came to move out of the camp and do some real work they leapt at it. The work was coolies' work, hard labour at the docks, but they wanted the exercise. There was nothing dishonourable in it, if you didn't see it that way. Besides, there would be good pickings among the piled-up stores in the godowns. Best of all, they would be on their own again, away from the sickness of spirit and irregular violence and filth of the camp. Nearly three hundred strong, they were to set up quarters in the abandoned booths and tea-gardens of the Great World, an amusement park where in the early days they had gone to drink Chinese beer, dance with taxi-dancers and have their pictures taken. From there they would march, each morning, in parties to the docks.

'This is all right, eh?' Digger said when he saw it. A fairground. It was like coming home.

They spent the first night cleaning the place up a bit and fixing showers. There was plenty of running water. Then, all washed and spruced up, they went for a walk through the alleys and lanes between the stalls. A real maze, it was, of lathe and crumbling plaster, with sketchy paintings, half-faded, of horses and misty-looking mountains and clouds, and avenues of bulls with bulging eyes and miniature pagodas. It seemed unreal with no crowd to fill it, none of the noise and sweat and cooking smells from food stalls or the smell of charcoal from smoky stoves.

They wandered in groups and kept meeting other groups at the end of alleys. Very odd they looked too, in their boots and baggy shorts and nothing else. Like kids, Digger thought, who'd got locked in after the store keepers had shut up shop and the taxi-dancers, the actors in the Chinese theatre and the sellers of potency pills and balms had all gone home.

They greeted one another shyly and had to make themselves small to get past in the narrow lanes, their skylarking self-conscious in so quiet a place. There was a moon. Everything looked blue. The walls were mostly blue anyway, 'celestial' blue. The reflections from them gave men's faces, from a distance, a luminous, rather ghostly look. It was weird though not scary.

It was an interlude of pure play, but they were so subdued by the emptiness of the place, its peeling vistas and derelict squares, that it became dreamlike. At last they went whispering through the alleys like quiet drunks, still full of high spirits but afraid to wake someone.

Ourselves, Digger thought, as their boots echoed on the gravel and laughter came through the walls.

2

They had been working all morning, a small party inside a larger, mixed contingent of Australians, British and Dutch, in one of the biggest godowns on the docks. It was an immense place like a cathedral, a hundred and fifty yards long and sixty wide, all slatted walls where the light that beat in was dazzling, and, high up in the gloom under the rafters, sunshafts swarming with dust.

The dust was from the chaff bags they were lumping, or that others had lumped before them. They were choking with it. Their eyes were raw, their hair thick with it, they were powdered to the navel with a layer of fine dust that streaked where the sweat ran and where it got into their shorts, and went sodden round their balls, painfully itched and rubbed. It was a kind of madness they moved in. Half-naked, and barefoot mostly, they stumbled through a storm in which they were shadows bent low and tottering under the hundredweight sacks.

The guards too suffered. They had swathed their mouths and nostrils in knotted scarves, but the dust got in under the collars of their uniforms, clogged their lashes, and hung on their brows with an eerie whiteness. They wore heavy boots and leggings, the sign that they were masters here, but sweated for it.

Generations of coolies, Chinese for the most part, but Tamils too, had worked to unload ships and stock these godowns with bales of rubber, wool and cotton; sacks of flour, salt, sugar, rice; and cartons of corned meat, condensed milk, apricot halves and pineapple chunks in cans. A new sort of coolie, they were clearing it now to be shipped as spoils of war to the new masters of this corner of the earth.

Vic humped his sack with the rest. It was an animal's work though a man could do it, and the dust was a torment, but none of that worried him. Neither did the weight, the two hundred pounds laid on his neck, which he had to trot a hundred yards with. He could do it. He was strong enough. And there was something in him that these things could not touch. He was lit up with the assurance of his own invulnerability. Had been all morning. There was no reason for it.

He knew the danger of such moods. They had dogged him all his life. In the drunkenness of his own power and youth he would lose track of things, grow reckless, and out of sheer physical exuberance say something sooner or later that he did not mean to say, or blindly strike out. That was the danger. He knew this. He was watching himself.

What hurt him, and in the most sensitive part of himself, was that somewhere not so very far away, fiery battles must be taking place, fought by fellows no older than himself, and no more daring either – part of a war that would be talked of for all the rest of his life, and which he would have no share in; no campaign ribbons, no medals, no stories to tell except this shameful one. He would live through this stretch of history and be denied even the smallest role in it.

He was sufficiently certain of his own courage to believe that in the ordinary circumstances of the soldier's life he would, given the chance, have acquitted himself in a quite superlative way. He had spent his youth studying to be noble. But the world he was in now was a mystery to him. You do not prepare yourself for shame.

The guards were edgy. All this dust and the heat of the place maddened them. They too were young. They resented having to stand guard over coolies. To restore their own sense of honour they would suddenly strike out, and there was no way of knowing when the blow was coming or where from. Out of the storm of dust, that's all, whack! and you took it.

But for all that, he could not convince himself that the conditions he was under held force. All morning his spirit was light and he swaggered. In brute fact his back was bent and he was tottering like the others in a dense haze, choking, streaming with sweat, feeling every ounce of the two-hundred-pound sack on his neck, but his spirit was coltish. Nothing could touch him.

After a time a rage of frustrated power began to build in him. If there was a girl here his energy might have been taken up in some other way; but there wasn't. Each time he straightened he felt a surge of exultation and the bitterness of having to rein it in. This was one of his moments – every nerve in his body told him that – and he would miss it for no other reason than that the timing was wrong. That's what hurt him. The moment, and with it the event – whatever it was – that belonged to it, would be lost and would not recur. The unfairness of it maddened him.

He could never be sure what happened next. As he passed, the most bad-tempered of the guards, a smart young corporal, out of boredom it might have been, or the idle spite of those who have been given power for a moment but no scope to use it, or more likely because, in his own youthfulness, he had caught from the mere look of him the state of rebellious excitement Vic was in – this guard, idly, almost indifferently, leaned out and jabbed at him very lightly with a cane. There was no contact. But Vic, with the load still on his back, stopped, turned, and his spirit acted in spite of him.

Even when he saw it happen he was not dismayed. Some part of him was, and he went cold at the enormity of it; but in the other part, in a kind of triumph, he was exultant. Time stopped dead while he hovered with the two-hundred-pound sack on his back and he and the guard faced one another across a distance of perhaps two feet. He was aware of the hair on his scalp as a dense forest, of his body soaring up from where his feet touched the earth. The moment released itself from the flow of things, expanded and was absolute. He spat in the guard's face.

He ought to have been a dead man then. That was the logic of the thing. But as the guard hurled himself forward, Mac, who was next in line, stumbled against him, was knocked off balance, and his sack went. There was a soft explosion and they were immediately, all three, swallowed up in a storm of white.

In a moment Japs had rushed in from all directions, and when the others in the party swung round to see what it was, they were using their rifle-butts, their bayonets too, all screaming and out of control.

Vic, his own sack still heavy on his neck, stood at the centre of an absolute fury in which boots and heads and rifle-butts and steel went everywhere. The bayonet blows were synchronised grunts and screams. He too had his mouth open screaming, but it was Mac they were going for.

For Digger it was a moment that for as long as he lived would remain apart and absolute, its real seconds swelling till he felt as if his body had been suspended over a gap where the sun was stopped and chronology had ceased to operate. Duration was measured now only by the mind's capacity to grasp all that was taking place in it.

He had turned at the first hint of trouble (Vic, that would be, it had to be), slewing on one foot. Heard shouts. Saw the rush of guards, and then, in a storm of dust, saw that someone had gone down. He was thirty feet away and still had the sack on his shoulders. He could see nothing clearly.

Madness was loose, that's all he knew. From a time, just seconds back, when they were in a world, however harsh their lot in it, that was familiar and human, they were hurled into a place where anything could be done and was done, in animal fury and darkness, in blood, din and a thick-throated roaring before words. They were all in it, all shouting.

It would pass. It had to. But until it did, for what seemed an age, they were outside all order and rule, in a place of primal savagery.

Digger had risen on one foot. He did not come to earth. That's how he saw it. He hung there as from hooks in his shoulder blades, weighed down by the blood that was being pumped into his hands and the big-veined muscles in his neck; by the weight of the sack he was carrying too. But his limbs, no longer attached or subject to gravity, were flinging about in a passion like nothing he had ever known, that took him right out of himself, over horizons he had never conceived of.

It was a kind of dance, in which he shouted ecstatic syllables that passed right through him, lungs, mouth, consciousness, as if he were no more than the dumb agency of the rhythm he was pounding out in the dust of the godown, beyond smashed bones and the gushing of blood. The cries that came heaving out of him belonged to a tongue he did not recognise, and for all his gift (he who knew whole plays by heart), when his foot came back to earth at last, and the seconds linked, he could not recall a single one of them. They were in a language that his mind, once the moment was gone, no longer had the shape to receive.

His foot came down; he took the full weight of the sack again, and found himself gasping for breath. Like a man who had run miles bearing a message he was too breathless now to deliver – and anyway, it had gone clean out of his head.

Still in a panic, shouting and slapping now even at one another in their recriminations over what had occurred, the guards forced them into a mass, drove them with canes, battens, a wall of rifles, till they were huddled in a close heap on the floor of the godown, hands locked behind their heads, heads hard down between their kneecaps.

They kept their eyes lowered, not daring to look up. To show the guards something as alive and jelly-like as an eyeball might be to set them off again. They were still shouting and shoving at one another, entirely out of control.

Digger forced his head down, his fingers so tightly knuckled that he felt he might never get them unstuck. His heart hammered. He was rigid but quaking. The guards were all round them, kicking up dust, dancing about in a rage at one another, uttering gutturals and shrill howls.

On one side incomprehensible crazy activity. On the other this heart-pounding, frozen immobility in which they sat squeezed into a single mass just where they had fallen.

Digger had Vic's mouth at his ear. He could smell the foulness – terror was it? – of his breath. The sweat was pouring off him, off all of them. What he had thought at first must be Vic's arm twisted and caught between them was another man's altogether. It hardly mattered.

He saw very clearly then what they were at this moment: meat, very nearly meat. One flash second this side of it.

'There is a line,' he thought. 'On one side of it you're what we are, all nerve and sweat. On the other, you're meat.'

All herded together and with the breath knocked out of them, they were right on the line. Things could go either way with them. Only when the Japs stopped yelling at one another, and rushing about in a panic, and began to move again at a human pace, and they were allowed to unlock themselves from one another and lift their heads, would they be back again on the right side of things.

For Mac it was too late. He had already been pitched across, and was lying over there somewhere – even Digger did not dare shift his head to see where it might be, but it was unnervingly close. Back in the half-dark of the godown, in a scrabble of wet dust; but further than that too, in a dimension, close as they all were to it, that was already beyond reach.

Vic too sat hunched and painfully twisted, in a silence he thought must be a kind of deafness – one of the guards must have deafened him – since all round he could see them shouting. There was an invisible membrane between him and the world. Inside it he was choking for breath.

They were jam-packed together in a heap, no space between them, hard bone against bone; but he felt himself entirely cut off; at an immense distance from the shouting, the panic, the hot presence of the others as they pressed against him. It was as if space now had developed the capacity to expand that just a moment back had belonged to time. He tried to make the laws of time and space operative again in his body, to get himself back into the world the others were in. If there was a price to pay for that he would pay it. He had no illusions about what they must think of him.

Everything that came to his senses had a ghostly quality, yet he had never been so aware of his own physical presence, the sensitivity of his lips which when he ran his dry tongue over them were all puffed with blood, the lightness of his belly, the terrible flexibility of his wrists.

Whenever, in flashes, his mind worked, all that had happened came back to him, and he was flooded with shame. But always it was his body that had the final word, and his body thought differently. It lived for itself and did not care.

'How could I let it happen?' he asked himself, 'how could I?' When the moment for action came and he should have moved into the gap he had opened, he had hung back and done nothing. He had stood there, too slow to move, too astonished that the moment he had been waiting for had actually come. Or this body he was lumbered with, always slower than the spirit, or cannier, or more cowardly, had acted in its own interests, and while it hovered there – it could only have been a second or two – the world had moved on, pushing him away to one side. The blades had come down and missed him. His body saved itself, *and* him, but shamefully, leaving him with a lifetime to face of the life it had bought for him. And the most shameful thing of all was that he could live with it. He was breathing hard. All his blood was pumping. He was full of the smell of himself.

His body was driving it home to him. You won't die, son. Not of this.

The guards, themselves shocked to silence now at what had been done, began to get them to their feet, urging them gently, like children. No one among them, guard or prisoner, was ready yet to meet another man's eye.

Vic too got to his feet. No one looked at him, and he felt a little rush of defiance come over him, like a child who has been unjustly accused. He began to find arguments in his own defence. He hadn't asked Mac to step in between him and whatever fatality he had provoked. 'I didn't ask him to!'

They formed a line again and went quietly to their work, and when they came back through the godown with their load Mac's body was no longer there.

They moved quietly, scarcely daring to breathe. As if sound, any sound at all, might set something off again. When one man jostled a chain and a length of it fell and rattled, they jumped like frogs, all of them, as if even the clank of iron against iron could send out ripples and break a head.

When he got his meal Vic did not know how to act, whether or not he could sit with them. He was still tense and close to tears, but determined now to tough it out. He took his dixie and sat a little way away from where Digger and another fellow, Ernie Webber, were already eating.

But when Doug came in he saw immediately how things were and came without fuss and sat at Vic's side, but did not look at him.

Digger did. He looked up, noted what had happened, then looked away and went on chewing.

Seeing it, Vic put his head down, animal-like, and plunged his spoon into the mush. He ate. He was ravenous – that was the body again. He was ashamed but he couldn't get enough of the sticky mess he was shoving into his mouth. He could have eaten pounds of the stuff, and still it wouldn't have satisfied the craving he felt. He ate fast, with his head down like an animal, and the tears that welled up in him were tears of rage.

Slowly in the days that followed his life came back and began once again to be ordinary and his own.

His wound was still raw in him, and when his mind moved back to that fraction of a second before Mac went down, his blood quickened, he stepped forward, and his youthful spirit did what it had to do to save his honour. He died happy.

The awakening from this dream sent a wave of new shame over him. He would flush to the roots of his hair and look about quickly to see if any of the others had seen it.

He went out on the usual work parties and in the same group; taking the weight of the sack on his bent back and trotting with it to the place where it could be dumped, welcoming the opportunity it offered to lose himself in the exhaustion that extinguished thought. The young guard was there each day and acted as if nothing had happened. They ate their meal in a group just as before, shared what they scavenged, and Vic got his share. When he scavenged something he offered it round and even Digger took it. The lump in his throat began to melt.

'I am nineteen,' he told himself. He did not offer this as an excuse. His youth, if anything, was an affliction. It made things hard for him. What he meant was, 'Nineteen is all I've got.' It seemed, as the sum of what he had experienced, a large thing. But what he was thinking of was the future. 'All this,' he thought, 'can be made good in time, if I get it. All I need now is time.' Putting his head down in an animal way and getting on with it was the first step.

It wasn't simply a matter of outliving his shame and the blood on his hands; but of proving to them, whoever *they* might be, that this life of his that had got itself saved, by whatever means, had been worth saving.

Meanwhile he dealt with the others as they dealt with him. He was prepared for the hostility Digger showed him.

They had never been close, but there was in Digger's avoidance of him now a harder quality, a kind of contempt. What it said was: for me you are not there, you're dead; you died back there where you ought to have done, instead of *him*. And in his old way, while deeply resenting this, he also, in another part of his nature, accepted it. Digger became the one among them whose good opinion he most cared for – because he knew Digger would not give it.

He deliberately put out of his mind the Warrenders and his old life, feeling that in betraying himself he had betrayed them, too. It hurt him to look at what he had done through their eyes, even more through Lucille's. He set himself to live in the present. That is where he would remake his life. But once, in a dream, his father came to him. It was something he had dreaded. He shrank into himself.

He was drunk, of course, and there was a smirk on his face. 'Well,' he said, 'fancy meetin' you here. Fancy you an' me bein' in the same boat, eh?' He was delighted that Vic had been brought so low. 'We're the same kind after all.'

'No we're not,' Vic told him. '*You* might think we are.'

'Oh? Why don't we ask yer mates?'

He laughed at that, a dribbling laugh, and Vic thought again of all those hours he had sat out in the dark of the woodpile in a trance of blood.

'So how does it feel, eh? Still think yer better'n the rest 'v us? I s'pose you'll be askin' now fer a second chance.' He paused, and Vic quaked. 'Well, good luck t' ya! – But did you ever give me one?'

It haunted him, that, but he put it out of his mind with all the other things he had decided to turn his back on. He had his life to save.

3

Digger too was in turmoil. It shook him that he could feel so much hostility, and to one of their own blokes too, not even a Jap. The thoughts that came to him, the wish to see Vic pay or for the events in the godown to take a different turn and for *him* to be the one, scared Digger. He wouldn't have believed he was capable of that sort of vindictiveness. But the loss he had suffered was too raw in him to be amenable to reason. There were things, he decided, that you couldn't be reasonable about – and oughtn't to be, either. But then he thought: 'Where was I when Mac needed me? What did *I* do?'

He and Mac had crossed for the last time at the loading point. Mac had been next in line behind Vic, and as he took the load on his neck and tottered past he had caught the look Mac flashed him, just the tail of it, through the sweat and his lank hair which was streaming.

It was nothing special. One of those little gestures of easy, affectionate contact that keep you going, that's all: that make the ground firmer, that's all. But in that moment they had been just twenty, maybe thirty seconds away from it. Would he have seen something if he had been more alert? That's what stumped him. Mac was just thirty seconds from death. They had been looking straight into one another's eyes.

Fifty feet further on, trotting now with his neck bowed under the weight of the sack, he had heard a ruckus and turned awkwardly on one foot to see what it was.

It was Vic. He had known that immediately. Who else would it be? A sack had burst, and figures were struggling in a storm of white, one of them, from the bulky shape of him, a guard.

Could he have glimpsed Mac's face then, in the confusion of the moment, through the cloud of floury dust? He thought he had; the image of it was so clear in his head.

A face wiped of all expression is what he saw. Or maybe that was just the flour Mac had been showered with in the exploding storm. But what Digger *thought* he saw was the look that might come over a man who is on the brink of extinction, and knows it, and has already let the knowledge of it possess and change him. An impersonal look of neither panic nor despair; which was the certainty of his own death passing physically from head to foot through him, a kind of pallor, and changing him as it went.

It was Mac's sad-faced mournful look, as Doug would have put it, which they had seen him wear on a thousand occasions, only raised now to the highest pitch, so that everything that was personal in it was gone, and yet it was utterly his own look that you would have known anywhere.

Had he really seen that, or was it what his mind had pictured to fill some need of its own? He could never be certain now. But as time went on the image stayed clear, if anything, grew sharper. So in the end it was what he might never have seen at all that meant most to him.

He also had the pile of letters Mac had left him. When, months later, they were organised into forces and sent to Thailand, the letters went with him.

4

They were at a place called Hintock River Camp, one of dozens of such work-camps that stretched for three hundred miles between the Malay and the Burmese borders. The map of it was not clear to them, because their knowledge of these countries was limited to the patch of jungle that shut them in, and because the line they were on was as yet an imaginary one.

It ran in a provisional fashion from Bangkok to Rangoon, and their job, under the direction of a Japanese engineer and several thousand Japanese and Korean guards, was to make it real: to bring it into existence by laying it down, in the form of rails and sleepers, through mountain passes, across rivers, and even, when the line met them, through walls of rock. Eventually all the bits of it would link up. Till then, they were concerned only with their own section, with bamboo, rock, rain and the rivers of mud it created, the individual temperament of their guards, the hours of work the Japs demanded of them (which kept increasing), the length of rail the authorities decided should be laid each day or the length of tunnel completed, and their own dwindling strength. The limits of their world were the twenty or so attap huts that made each encampment – one of which was set apart as a hospital, or rather, a place for the dying – and the site, off in the jungle, where their daily torment took place.

They had come up here from the railhead at the Malayan border in a series of night marches, since it was too hot to move by day, and had passed many such camps, some better than the one they were in, one or two of them a lot worse. These camps either had native names like Nakam Patam, Kanburi, Nan Tok, or they had been given the sort of name you might have used for a creek or a camping spot at home: Rin Tin Tin Camp, Whalemeat Camp. One, however, was called Cholera Camp.

The work was killing. So was the heat. So, once they started, were the rains.

Back where they came from they had belonged, even the slowest country boy among them, to a world of machines. Learning to drive was the second goal of manhood – the first for some. Fooling about under trucks and cars, tinkering with motorbikes and boat engines, rigging up crystal sets – all this had become second nature to them, a form of dream-work in which they recognised (or their hands did) an extension of their own brains. It had created between them and the machines they cared for a kind of communion that was different from the one they shared with cattle and horses, but not significantly so. For most of them machines were as essential to the world they moved in as rocks or trees. Tractors, combine harvesters, steamrollers, cranes – even the tamest pen-pusher among them had dawdled at a street corner to look over the wire in front of a building site to see the big steamhammers at work driving piles. It had changed their vision of themselves. Once you have learned certain skills, and taken them into yourself, you are a new species. There's no way back.

Well, that was the theory.

Only they found themselves now in a place, and with a job in hand, that made nothing of all that. It might never have been. They had fallen out of that world. Muscle and bone, that was all they had to work with now. An eight-pound hammer, a length of steel, and whatever innovative technology they could come up with on the spot for breaking stone.

Some of these men had been storemen and book-keepers. Others were shearers, lawyers' clerks, wine-tasters, bootmakers, plumbers' mates, or had travelled in kitchenware or ladies' lingerie. They had had spelling drummed into them, the thirteen-times table, avoirdupois and troy weight. 'You'll need this one day, son. That's why I'm caning you,' a lady teacher had told more than one of them, when, after getting up at four-thirty to milk a herd, they had dozed off at their desk. They were all labourers now. Someone else would do the calculations. So much for Mental! The number of inches a pair of drillers, working closely together with hammer and steel, could drive through sheer rock in ten or twelve hours a day. The amount of rubble, so many cubic feet, that could be loaded, lifted and borne by a man who had once weighed thirteen stone, now weighed eight and was two days out of a bout of malaria. All this to be balanced precisely against the smallest amount of rice a man could work on before he was no longer worth feeding and could be scrapped.

The work was killing. So was the heat. So, once they started, were the rains. But they also suffered from amoebic dysentery, malaria, including the cardiac variety, typhoid, beriberi, pellagra and cholera.

The doctors among them diagnosed these diseases, but that didn't help because they had none of the medicines they needed to cure them, and it didn't help a man to know that the disease he was dying of was pellagra, any more than it helped to know that the place he was dying *in* was called Sonkurai. The name, however exotic, in no way matched the extraordinary world his body had now entered, or the things it got up to, as if what *it* had discovered up here was a freedom to go crazy in any way it pleased.

Only one thing set them apart from the other coolies who for centuries had done this sort of work for one empire and then the next. They knew what it was they were constructing because it belonged to the world they came from: the future.

It was as if someone, in a visionary moment, had seen a machine out of the distant time to come, a steam engine, and had set out with only the most primitive tools and a hundred thousand slaves to build the line it would need to move on if it were to appear. If you could only get the line down, then the machine would follow – that was the logic. It was true, too. In this case it would happen.

So, if they could only finish the line and link up all the sectional bits of it, they would have made a way back out of here to where they had come from: the future. When the engine came steaming round the bend, its heavy wheels perfectly fitted to the track, the sleepers taking its weight, its funnels pouring out soot, they would know that time too had been linked up and was one again, and that the world they had been at home with was real, not an unattainable dream.

5

The fevers came on every ten days.

The first time he was hit Digger looked up out of his delirium and saw Vic was there; squatting on his heels like a child and with a quick, animal look in his eyes. He was spooning rice up from a dixie, shovelling it fast into his wet mouth. Between his feet was a second dixie. Empty. When he saw Digger was watching he stopped feeding a moment and just sat, his eyes very wide in the broad face. Then, without looking away, he began to feed again, only faster.

'That's my rice he's eating,' Digger thought. 'The bastard is eating *my rice.*' But his stomach revolted at the thought of it. 'Well, let him!'

When he woke again, Vic, a little crease between his brows, was sponging him with a smelly rag. He wore a look of childish concern, and Digger thought: 'That's just like him. Steals the food out'v a man's mouth, an' the next minute he's trying to make up to him by playin' nurse. Typical!' But the dampness was so good, so cooling, and the hands so gentle, that Digger closed his eyes again and drifted.

What puzzled him was the utter candour of Vic's look when he had caught him like that with the second dixie. He didn't try to cover up. He wasn't ashamed. There was something in that look Digger did not want to let go of. Some truth he needed to hold on to. He worried at it.

It was so different from the look he wore when he was offering you some bit of a thing as a gift. He would look sly then, calculating; but when he was stealing the food out of your mouth you saw right through into the man. It was an innocence of a purely animal kind, that took what it needed and made no apology, acting on *that*, not on principle.

Digger saw there was something to be learned from it: a hard-headed wisdom that would save Vic, and might, when the time came, save him as well.

The time came almost as soon as Digger was on his feet again and could go out to work. The fever took Vic now, and it was Digger's turn to eat the second dixie, hold Vic when he raved, and use the cloth.

There was an affinity between them that was almost comical. When the one went down with it the other was well, time and about, ten days at a stretch. Vic accepted it as a fact of nature, a utilitarian arrangement that was good for both of them. Digger resisted at first – he had something against this cove that was fundamental – but when the fever struck him he had no option.

Their natures, though wildly out of order in other ways, were matched in this. They were made for one another. Digger was struck by the irony of it, but they were in a place now where ironies were commonplace.

Under the influence of this arrangement – the close physical unit they formed, the right on occasion to eat the other man's rice, the unpleasant and sometimes revolting duties they had to perform for one another, and which Vic especially carried out with a plain practical tenderness and concern you would not have suspected in him – under the influence of all this, there grew up between them a relationship that was so full of intimate and no longer shameful revelations that they lost all sense of difference.

It wasn't a friendship exactly – you choose your friends. This was different; more or less, who could say? There was no name for it.

The old bitterness died hard in Digger. Vic knew that and accepted it. It seemed to Digger at times that Vic sought him out just because of it. But that was *his* business.

There were days when they couldn't stand the sight of one another. That was inevitable up here. They were always on edge. The petty irritations and suspicions they were subject to in their intense pre-occupations with themselves made them spiteful and they would lash out in vicious argument. Digger was sickened by the hatefulness he was capable of. And not just to Vic either, but to poor old Doug as well. He would crawl away, humiliated and ashamed.

But there was something cleansing in it too. What came out in these senseless flayings of one another was the contempt they had for themselves and the filth they lived in; the degradation they accepted at the hands of the guards: and what was especially shameful to men who had thought the spirit of generosity was inviolable in them, the peevish grudging they felt for every grain of rice that went into another man's mouth. It was a relief at last to get rid of the poison in you.

'It's amazing,' Digger thought after a time. 'I never meant to be, but I'm closer to this cove than to anyone, ever. Even Slinger. Even Doug.'

Then another thought would hit him: even Mac. Mac wouldn't be as practical as this bloke is.

He hated himself for letting that thought through. It would just be there, a thought like that, because he was at his lowest. His resentment of Vic would be strong then, fed by guilt. He would draw off in revulsion from him, which was really a revulsion from himself, and was surprised each time at the way Vic bore it and put up with him.

It went back to that animal-innocent, candidly guilty look he had seen on his face when he was finishing off the second dixie. It was a look that risked judgement, even invited it, then revealed, through its utter transparency, that there was none to be made.

6

In his fever bouts, Digger found himself passing in and out of his lives.

There were, to begin with, the conversations with his mother. They took place outside time as clocks or calendars measure it, neither before nor after.

He would be floating. He had a mouth and ears. He had his sex. But they were far off; further anyway than his fists, if he unclenched them, could have reached. She was talking to him in their old way, without words.

Digger? she was saying, Digger? You come on now. I will *not* let you die on me. You hear me, boy? You get breathing now, get feeding. I've given you this, Digger, and I'm determined you're goin' t' have it. You know how I am if I set my heart on a thing. There are stars, Digger, there are gerberas, I planted 'em. There's a whole lot more as well that I haven't got time to go into. So you just buck up now and come on.

You see this? This is earth, boy, dirt. You'll eat a whole peck of that before you're through, before you die, I mean, an' you haven' had more than a few grains of it yet, you've got a whole lot more eating to do. So you just start to get it down, you hear me, Digger?

This is your mother talking. Oh, you know me, boy, don't pretend you don't. Don't pretend you're not awake, I won't let you off *that* easy, you don't fool me. I've got a whole lot more to say, Digger, and I won't let you go deaf on me. I can be a terror, you know that. You're always running out on me, or trying to – you an' your father both! But believe me, Digger, I'm coming after you, there's no running away from fate. You know that. I've got enough ghosts on my hands already, without you trying to be another one. I won't have it, hear? Now you get breathing, boy, you *breathe*! You come back into the real world and give up this dreaming. Here, take this.

She passed him something. It was a thread and he saw now that she was unravelling the sleeve of an old grey jumper he had worn holes in. Beginning at the shoulder, he watched the stitches hop back over invisible needles as the rows ran backwards from shoulder to cuff and the sleeve passed through an invisible wall into non-existence. He had to wind faster and faster to keep the wool running over his fist.

It was another version of her talk, this, and he couldn't resist it. The thread ran between them, dark and fast, till the whole jumper, which he had worn through four winters and slept in, and which had his smell on it – sleeves, front, back – was gone, and there were nine balls of clean knitting-wool in her lap.

He began to fear almost more than the physical racking this having to face up to her each time the fever took him.

She never let up. He would thrash about, drowning in sweat, but she wouldn't let him off the hook.

He made himself an eel, eels are slippery. He reduced himself to just a mouth and eyes – no ears, no sex, no fingers; but she got furious, hauled him out and thumped him into shape.

He tried going on all fours. Digger, she yelled, are you out there, you little grub? That's Ralphie's. Now you come in.

He stayed out. There were stars, there were gerberas. It was thundering and Ralphie was tonguing his neck, he could feel the thickness of Ralphie's tongue rasping.

He knew he was out of his body. Well, good, he thought, that's *one* way! It was the lightness of his head and his sex that told him that.

He got down in the dirt. He was swallowing it, getting down his peck. When he found Ralphie's water-tin, the water he lapped up was the water of life – cool, sweet, slaking this thirst he had been tormented by, which was not the thirst of his body but of what his body had left when it shook him off.

He lapped and lapped – Ralphie didn't mind, didn't begrudge him the water he got from the dried-up bowl; or the bone either, which was alive with maggots. He got his teeth into it, defying the flies. It filled the hunger in him, fed some earlier body than the one he had abandoned, and did him good. Some animal part of him, which he loved as he had loved Ralphie, and which *was* Ralphie, wolfed it down, maggots and all, took the strength from it and was enlightened. He felt the strength gather in him; and lightly, on all fours, began to run light-footed over the earth. Under the moon, past bushes that lay low before him so that he could leap over them, across plains that burned but did not blister. He ran and ran and had breath for it, and came in the early morning down the track to Keen's Crossing.

He woke feeling refreshed and fed. His dreaming body had fed his thin, racked frame, slaked its thirst, licked him into life again.

'I'll live,' he thought, 'this time. I'll live.'

7

Coming in from the line they would be so exhausted sometimes that a man might nod off with his bowl in his hand before he had taken a single mouthful.

'That horse is done for,' he would shout, right out of his sleep. 'Better shoot the poor brute.' Or: 'Don't you move, Marge. I'll get it.'

The others would stare in wonder at his having got so quickly away, and would be reluctant to call him back.

That was one of the things the body could do.

Once they were sitting over their bit of a meal when Ernie Webber, one of the fellows who had been with them since the Great World, made one of his 'remarks'.

He was a likeable fellow, Ern, but very poorly educated, a windbag, inclined, with great assurance and whether you asked for it or not, to give you the benefit of his thoughts. 'I was perusing the papers once,' he would say – it was one of his typical openings – and go on then with some rigmarole of a thing, half-heard and largely misunderstood, that was so plain foolish it was hard to keep a straight face sometimes. Newcomers took it for a subtle brand of humour and might offend Ern by laughing outright. What he said on this occasion was no more foolish than usual. 'I knew there was gunna be trouble,' he said. 'I said we're gunna have trouble with this feller Musso. Soon as I seen he was linkin' up with them niggers, them Abbysiniums.'

'Them who?' This was Clem Carwardine, a fellow who generally said very little. His tone now was so scathing that they sat up shocked. Ernie was a joke and his ignorance under protection. He sat blinking now.

'My God,' Clem said with a savagery he had never shown them before, 'I thought a chook was about the most brainless object in the universe, but compared with some of you blokes a chook is Einstein.'

'That your last word on relativity, is it Clem?' Doug put in. He was trying to turn the thing into a joke, but Clem's look was murderous.

'A half-witted six-year-old knows more than you,' he told Ern. 'You brainless article!'

Ern was too confused to be indignant. He couldn't believe that Clem Carwardine, who was such a nice bloke, could turn on him, and so savagely. Older than the rest of them, and very well spoken, he had never acted superior. He was looking at them now with such utter contempt and fury that they felt embarrassed for him; but there was a kind of puzzlement in his look too, as if he was as surprised as they were at what had just come out of his mouth. The puzzlement increased, then, without another word, he jerked his head back, shot his feet out and keeled over backwards.

He was dead. Cardiac malaria. Just like that. It seemed wicked to Digger, who liked the man, that his last moments should be so uncharacteristic, and that it was this they would remember of him. Ernie was especially upset. He kept harking back to it as if there was something in the event that he had failed to grasp and for which he was to blame.

The body could do that too.

They had never given them much thought, these rough and ready bodies of theirs. You got that drummed into you early: not to look at it, not to touch. A half-dozen schooners got down fast before closing time, and if it was too fast you puked. A run at football on Saturday arvo. A bit of love-making, easy exercise. Nothing fancy or too passionate. Nothing out of the ordinary. If you got a scratch you dobbed a drop of Solyptol on it if you were particular and waited for the scab to form. Warts maybe, whitlows. Chilblains in winter if it was cold enough. Measles, mumps, chickenpox. That was about the limit of it. The body went its own way. It was serviceable. You could forget it was there.

Up here the body ruled. You watched it night and day, you got obsessed with it as you saw the flesh fall away and the ribs and the big knuckle-joints come through.

They wouldn't have believed, if anyone had told them, how fast it could go, the meat they carried, all that their grandfathers and great-grandfathers had shoved into their mouths to build the big frames they had brought up here and the muscle to stock them with. They needn't have bothered, those black pudding and porridge eaters, those kids tucking into the dripping, spreading it thick and wiping a crust round the bowl. It could fall away overnight under the right circumstances, till you looked like someone who had never, in all of time going back and back, known more than the few mouthfuls of pap they were getting now, that were as thin as slime and went right through you, and when you squatted, ran down as slime.

They had had no idea that the equality they claimed and thought they had already achieved would be like this. For each man the same scoopful of thin gruel morning and night.

The big blokes were the first to go, and took hardest the indignity their bodies heaped upon them of needing more than their fair share and of being the weaker for it. They went quickly, some of them. It was pathetic. They hadn't known (and might have expected, in the normal way of things, never to have brought home to them), how much of what they were was dependent only on the meat.

It was all you had, all they had left you. You kept feeding it and it kept falling away. Up here only the tools you carried, the picks and shovels, had the power to keep their true weight in the world. Just getting a fist around them, feeling the solidity of wood and steel, was a guarantee of something, as in straggling lines you picked your way towards the beginning of a path, stepping gingerly, always on the lookout, however hardened your feet had got, for a hidden stump or thorn, since the merest scratch could cost you a leg if the flesh broke and an ulcer formed. An ulcer could cover half a man's leg, eating it away till there was more bone to be seen than flesh. The doctors would use a hot spoon then to jelly it out. If you were lucky you kept the leg. If you were less lucky you lost it. Being unlucky meant it lost you.

You got to be an expert at last on the tricks it could play, this body that was so crude and filthy a thing but was also precious and had to be handled now with so much delicacy. You watched for the smallest change in it, fixing your attention on every square inch of yourself, even the skin under your balls, and what normal man among them had ever done *that*? It had an imagination of its own, and fellows who had none at all, or not of that sort, looked on astonished at the horrors it could produce, stared in amazement as the first brown patch appeared, then spread, and they began to go black.

Digger remembered a joke that Slinger had made. 'Maybe yer a blackfeller, Digger, on the *inside*.'

He saw fellows now turn inside out. He saw the skin of a man's face grow thick as elephant hide. He saw thin boys blow up till they were the size of the fat lady, though no one would have paid to look at them – there was no market for it, not up here. They got so big at last that they couldn't move, even to turn on their pallets. Two of their mates would have to roll them; but gently, like a two-hundred-pound drum full of some dangerous fluid. Their balls would be the size of footballs, their dick eight inches round; but no one laughed, it wasn't a joke. Only the skull with its familiar features stayed normal; but they were pin-headed now and the eyes in the tiny head were lost in terror at the dimension of what was happening all round them – ankles thick as tree-trunks, feet like balloons, but *heavy*, weights they couldn't even think to lift.

'If they keep on feedin' us this rice our eyes'll go slanty.'

Digger had laughed at the man who told him that – or might have done if he hadn't seen the fury in the fellow's eyes. He had felt superior to that sort of dirt ignorance.

But what was happening now made slanty eyes the mildest of changes. Their bodies had gone berserk and were dragging them back to a time before they had organised themselves into human form and come in from chaos.

There were occasions now when he thought Mac might have drawn the best bet after all. He was scared of these thoughts, which came without his will. They were dangerous. If you gave in to the least bit of despair the body would be onto it; it was on the watch for that sort of thing every minute, and you had to watch *it*. They watched one another. He would catch Doug's eye on him, or Vic's, or one of the others, and think, God, what is it? What can he see? Has it started?

When it did start, in Doug's case, they pretended not to notice, not to see, either, the terror he was in, because he had discovered it even sooner of course, felt the little worry of it growing, beginning to swell.

They rolled him like a drum when the time came and carried him out on work-parties to make up the numbers as the Nips demanded. It was, all the time, a question of numbers. The Nips were fanatical about it.

'Watch it, fellers,' he joked as they lay him beside the track, 'I spill easy.'

He lay there all day, patient and uncomplaining, every now and then shouting across to them just to keep himself in the swing of things and one of their number – the living. Then at nightfall they carried him back.

It was the jokes, Digger thought later, that kept Doug going. That little bit of health in him, a stubborn refusal to give in to the sheer weight of things, a belief in lightness. He emerged again out of the huge bulk of himself in the old form, rangy, tough, and more certain than ever now that he could survive whatever they put up to him.

Vic too felt he had passed through the monstrous stage and emerged in something like his old form; but in his case it was mental. The work was what saved him, or so he felt. Even the weight of a basket full of rubble cutting into the rawness of your shoulder could be a reminder that the body was still with you, still in the same line of gravity as stones.

If you accepted that, you could begin to live. If you couldn't, you were done.

There was a way in which absolute deprivation confirmed him in a thing he had known from the start. Basically, when you get right down to it, we've got nothing.

He thought, and there was bitter humour in it, of the times Aunt James had snatched the bread off his plate and shouted 'Let him do without!' There had been so much malice in the old girl. Or maybe in her crazy way she had seen through into the future and was warning him.

He thought of those fellows under the tree outside Meggsie's kitchen, wolfing soup from a bowl, and how he had felt then that he was on the wrong side of things, that he had got out of some shame and humiliation that had been meant for him too. Well, he had it now. Did that balance things?

'I'm at rock bottom,' he told himself. 'I can face that. I didn't get into the world on the promise of three meals a day and a silver spoon to bite on. There was no promise at all – not for my lot. If I have to live like this, right through to the finish, on nothing but will, I can do it. I know what *real* is. I'm not like Digger. I don't need dreams.'

There were times when Digger's way of seeing things maddened him. 'This time next month,' Digger would tell them – or next year, or by Christmas – 'we'll be outa this. The line'll be joined up an' they'll take us back.'

There were plenty of fellows who thought like that. They were dreamers. Always on about the future.

He denied himself that luxury as he denied himself the luxury of the past. There was only one place where you existed with any certainty. That was here. The only *line* was the one that went downward, straight down through you into the earth. He clung to that with a dumb tenacity.

He reckoned this way because he was of a reasoning nature, taking pleasure in the hardness, the harshness of it, stripping himself of all illusion.

But in relying only on the body, he reckoned without its power, which he had already seen in other circumstances, to go its own way and think for itself. One day, in one of those moments when he had fallen out of space into mere time, when his mind lapsed in him and the moment he was in lay open to the flow of things, he raised his head and saw just ahead of him, coming from the opposite direction but in the same line, so that they must inevitably collide if one or the other did not leap aside, a figure he recognised, or thought he did – a big-shouldered, white-haired fellow for whom he felt a flicker of inexplicable warmth and interest. The feeling surprised him; and it was because he was diverted by it that he failed at first to see who it was.

It was himself: far off in a moment that was years ahead and which he was, it seemed, inevitably making for. He had no sooner realised this than the figure was on him and he felt his body open and let it through.

He did not look back. It was forbidden, he knew that. If he looked back they would both be lost.

Still in a state of astonishment, he kept his eyes dead ahead, and when the next breath came, he took it. But a little of the warmth and affection he had felt still glowed in him.

'Well,' he told himself, 'if that's how it's to be I've got no option, have I, but to stick it out?'

8

Digger's most precious possessions, since he had only the one short note of his own, were the letters he had inherited from Mac. Folded small, he had carried them from camp to camp and got them safe through all searches.

He knew them by heart, of course. No trouble about that when he knew so many plays off and had in his head the names and numbers of the whole unit. The letters were just a few hundred words. But the words themselves were only part of it.

Reading took time. That was the important thing. Constant folding and refolding had split the pages, and in the continuous damp up here the ink had run and was hard to read. Each time he took them out, especially if his hands were shaking and wet, he ran the risk of damaging them. But he liked the look of the unfolded pages, their weight – very light they were – on his palm. Even the stains were important. So was the colour of the ink, which differed from letter to letter, even from page to page of the same letter, so that you could see, or guess, where Iris had put the pen down in mid-sentence to go off and do something. So what you were reading was not just words.

He would close his eyes and imagine her being called to the door. The baker's lad, that would be, with a basket on his arm and the warm loaves covered with a cloth. (He would tear the corner off a loaf while they weren't looking and pop it warm into his mouth. Lovely, it was.) Or one of the boys would be calling. Ewen looking for his football socks – weren't they dry yet? – or Jack nagging for a coconut ice-block. Digger let his mind rove. He knew enough from what Mac had told him at one time or another to find his way about the house. It was one of the ways, just one, of getting back.

He did not gorge himself. He read one letter only and took his time. But there were days when he *needed* to gorge himself, and then he would read all five at once, then over again.

It was a strange business. Since the letters already existed in his head before he even started on them, it had to be a process, almost simultaneous but not quite, of letting each word fall out of his mind just before he came to it, so that he could discover it anew.

Playing music must be like that. Even if you had played a piece a thousand times over, and your fingers knew it on their own, you would have to clear your head of all knowledge of the next note so that your fingers, when they found it, could surprise themselves.

'I've planted sweet-peas,' she wrote on St Patrick's Day.

That was over two years ago. The sweet-peas would have sprouted, climbed the trellis, come out, filling the yard with their sweet smell, then died again; but he could still smell them where they had gone back into the earth, and still see them as well in the colours she named, pink, mauve, white. He could see the whole wall of them, pale green, with leaves that were scratchy to the fingertips, like the legs of a praying mantis, and the light shining through; the trellis repeating itself in shadow on the sun-blasted weatherboard; the poles tall as a row of men, but sweet-smelling, opening their buds that were set flaglike at a stiff right-angle to the stalk, white, mauve, pink.

Cut, in a tight little bunch, they would sit in a glass in the front room. He saw the room empty, with the curtains drawn against the sun, which could be strong, even in winter, and the glass with its two kinds of light, one air, one water, and the pale stalks and paler blossoms on a table in the centre of it. He would stand in the hallway and breathe the smell of sweet-peas and it revived him.

When the sun went down and the room grew dark, the glass was still there, the water still central and a source of light. He would lower himself into its coolness, its clearness, at the centre of the dark, quiet room. In the rooms on the other side of the hallway opposite, the breath of sleepers: in one room Iris, in the other the boys, Ewen and Jack, still safe in their boyish dreams, and out the back in a third room, the closed-in sleep-out, Mac's records and his piles of books.

Back and back he went to that house he had never been in. He let Mac show it to him again, room by room. They were shining, both; all cleaned up, their hair combed wet, their feet washed.

There was a wooden rack over the sink with plates in it, thick white ones. They leaned there, drying, and had been washed a thousand times with a block of Sunlight soap in a little wire cage-like contraption, and rinsed, lifted out of the water and left. Beautiful, they were. He could have sat at the table and just looked at them forever, over and over. Because it happened that way, over and over.

Regularly, three times a day, the plates were taken down, set on the cloth, used and washed again. That was the beauty of it. Order, repetition.

But how boring! The same thing, day in day out, over and over! For him that was just the beauty of it. The cloth shaken out in the yard and the sparrows flying down. Light on the lovely glazed and crazed smoothness of the plates in the rack. The calendar on the wall turned to the right month, and the days, black or red, coming up in their numbers, workdays, weekends, the next page already there, and the next and the next all the way to Christmas.

In the dark, while the house slept, he waited quietly in the kitchen, his spirit touched by the light off those plates, in his hands the dryness of a bit of stale bread. There was a whole bowl of it, set out for the morning, to feed the chooks. His spirit broke off a bit and swallowed it – the chooks won't mind, he thought, though he could hear them shifting their claws on their perches in the dark.

Once, standing there, he heard a movement behind him and Iris came in in her nightgown. She didn't see him, of course. She walked right past him to the sink, took a glass, filled it with water from the tap, and drank, very slowly, gazing out into the dark yard.

He watched her as if the ordinary act was miraculous.

It *was* miraculous. It slaked his thirst.

9

Memory was a gift, when they really set themselves to it.

Lists. You started one and it could be extended forever, back and back, and gone over endlessly, and what you called up became a magic formula for keeping yourself in the world or for wiping yourself, temporarily, out of it.

For some it was a numbers game. What they went back to was the number-plates of the various cars they had owned or had driven at times for the firms they worked for. These numbers were *it*. Got into the right order, like the combination of a safe, they were a key that would unlock the universe. Only you had to get the order right, and it wasn't all that easy since the right order had nothing to do with the one in which these numbers had first come into your life. The right order was the *right order*, the one that would *work*. If you got it at last the engine would kick over, and powered by the six or eight cylinders of all those Buicks and Chevvies and de Sotos and Fords, it would take you out.

For others it was railway stations. The stations for instance out from Redfern on the Western Line. They went through them slowly, in morning heat sometimes but at others in the chill of smoky winter, on their way to work. The line ran high above the street. Below you could see barefoot men walking greyhounds alongside parks, kids on their way to school with little satchels on their backs, leggy girls, the older ones in checked gingham. Then, after a bit, you took the same journey back. Only at dusk this time and with the names in the reverse order. Factory sirens would be howling over the flat swamplands. You would have a slick of grease on your thumb. The faces along the platform blurring, and the train moving too fast now for you to catch the headlines on the news-boards as you plunged into sleep.

For others again it was the names of all the girls they had done it with. Even if you only got a finger in, it counted. The Muriels and Glorias and Pearls and Isobels going right back to when you were in sixth grade and first could.

The names first, then details. Where each one was: behind the baths, or on a bench under a school somewhere, or in the back of a parked truck. And when: in the Christmas holidays or on a Queen's Birthday long weekend, getting hold of the weather if you could, what she had on – the shoes, if any, the bra and panties, the colour and pattern of her frock, and the sweat-smell, or the soap-smell of what it had been washed in. Or the feel of leather (smooth or with seams) where it stuck to your bare arse in the back of the Vaux, or the splintery floor under the canvas seats at the Elite, and the taste of vanilla malted or popcorn in her mouth, or Wrigley's Spearmint, or the fried fat of chips. Ah, chips! Now that would be something.

On the menu at Maher's Boarding House for Men, the same menu each week over the seven nights, beef stew, shepherd's pie, etcetera. The gravies – lovely! And the picture over the sideboard, a Pears' print of a little girl about two in a sun-bonnet, standing in the nuddy in a galvanised iron tub . . .

Or the words of all the songs in the *Boomerang Songbook* for March 1941: 'I was watching a man paint a fence'. Or the rhymes their sisters and other little girls skipped to in the evenings after school, on the hot concrete under the sleep-out, while they were doing their history homework (Oliver Cromwell and the Civil War), or setting the wing of a balsawood plane with a dob of glue on a matchstick, and might stop a minute to have a quick pull on the bed –

> Over the garden wall
> I let the baby fall
> Me mother come out and give me a clout
> That almost turned me inside out –

cleaning up quickly afterwards with a stiff hanky, the smell of it and of the glue.

Others the no-hoper horses they put good money on, that never came in, and all the winners of the Melbourne Cup back to 1861, Archer.

Others the cows in a dairy herd: Myrtle, Clover, the Gypsy Princess, Angel, Sugarpie, Queenie, Minnie the Moocher.

What Digger remembered, and after a certain time in an official capacity, was the name and number of every man in the unit; including those who had been killed or gone missing and been replaced, then the replacements; and where each man was sent after the surrender; to Sandakan in Borneo, to Blakang Mali Island, the greatest bashing and punching show in Malaya, so they said, or who drew paradise and stayed on in Changi, or who went to Thailand, and in which force and to which camp. Official. All stored that information, safely, permanently, in the last place the Nips would think of looking.

He was so unremarkable, Digger, looked so like all the rest of them, barefoot, filthy, in a lap-lap, all bones, that no one could have guessed what he carried along with the pick over his shoulder or the basket with its weight of rubble and stones.

Once committed to memory these names would be there forever. The whole unit could be called up and paraded in his head, the dead right there with the living, all clean and in good shape again, whether they had drawn a short straw or a long and wherever they were.

Digger remembered *them*, and their names and numbers. And they, each one, remembered whatever it was they needed to keep them halfway in the world or halfway out of it: number-plate numbers, girls, songs, stations, all the flavours of milkshakes and malteds they served at the Mermaid Café, all the shops up and down Elizabeth or Queen or George or Swanston Street, both sides, the names of horses or dairy herds. Put it all together and something, secretly, was being kept alive. What an army marches on when it is no longer marching.

But there were others, Vic was one, who had no time for memories, even sweet ones. What they clung to were the things they could touch, the few bits and pieces they had managed to hang on to, some of it from back before Changi, the rest picked up along the road, at this stopping place or that, and were keeping for the day when it might come in useful: Singer sewing-machine needles, nails, screws, bits of rope or twine, keys, batteries, cards out of a broken pack, folds of newspapers – objects that elsewhere would have been trash, hardly worth stopping for, but were precious relics up here, and useful too, since you could trade them one for another and have something new in hand.

Vic had started off with quite a hoard. Small things mostly, that all went into a single pocket of his shorts, where he could turn them over; not idly, but letting his mind go with them. His fingertips knew every one.

But over the months he had traded some for a fag-end or a bit of something he needed urgently and didn't have; or for things, once or twice, that had taken his fancy in a childish way though there was no point to them. Other things, infuriatingly, had gone lost. Stolen maybe – he had his suspicions; about some things and some men. Or they had fallen through a hole in his shorts that he had found too late. In the end he had only one thing left: two and a half yards of white cotton thread tied in a loop. He had that in the left-hand pocket of his shorts, quite safe, and was keeping it, come what may.

He could have traded it a dozen times and had refused. A length of thread like that would come in handy sooner or later, it was bound to. He'd need it to keep his shorts together, or for some other reason, and if he didn't have it then, where would he be? Besides, he liked the feel of it. Hours he spent just rubbing his thumb and forefinger over it. He got teased for that: 'Watcha doin', Vic? Playin' pocket billiards?' Finally he hung on to it just for itself, whether it was useful or not. Because it was the last thing he possessed.

It had been white at first. Now it was a brownish colour. What worried him was that it might go astray. He kept checking every five minutes or so to see that it was still there. He took precautions. If he lost it he would be done for.

10

'Coolies,' the man behind him whispered, and Digger had time to take a quick look. Just a glance, because one of the Koreans was close, who would knock you down as soon as look at you.

They were working at night now, a real *speedo*. Bamboo fires were blazing all down the lines. They reddened the walls of the cutting and threw weird shadows. Other, more substantial shadows stopped, shovelled, staggered under basketloads of rubble in a din of bellowing and raucous shouts and blows as the guards ranged up and down. There was a haze of dust that the fires turned to hanging flame. Their bodies in it were alight with sweat, but high up, where it thinned out in the dark, the air was bruise-coloured, a sick yellow, then black.

Through the sweat in his eyes, and the hanging dust, Digger saw them on the track: Indians, Tamils probably, half-naked in lap-laps (like us, he thought) and carrying little bundles of next to nothing, a water bottle, sometimes a stove or lamp. For nearly an hour they passed, and every two or three minutes, stretching upright and keeping an eye out for the guard, he dragged his wrists across the sweat of his brow and got a quick look.

Here and there among them were families, women with babies on their hip, but they were men mostly, and mostly young men, though a few of them were old.

He had seen them working along the railroads up country and in road gangs in the towns, camping just off the pavement in orange tents or stretched out on a bedroll in the dirt. Now they were here. They had changed masters, that's all. Another empire to build.

He thought of the look on that fellow's face who had told him once, 'They wanna make coolies of us': the savage indignation of it, at the violation of all that was natural in the world, their unquestionable superiority as white men; but there was also the age-old fear in it of falling back and becoming serfs again.

Whatever indignities that fellow's people might have suffered – mine too, Digger thought – at the hands of bosses or schoolteachers or bank managers or ladies, all those who had the power to humiliate or deny, there was always this last shred of dignity to chew on: I'm not a coolie, I can choose. Whatever you could be deprived of, by bad luck or injustice or the rough contrariety of things, there was this one last thing that could not be taken. That's what they had believed. Only they knew differently now. It could be taken just like that. Easy.

That fellow would be here somewhere, in one of the other camps up or down the line; if he hadn't been clubbed or kicked to death by one of the Koreans, or fallen on one of the murderous night marches that had brought them here from the rail-head at the Thai border, or succumbed to beriberi or dysentery, or to cerebral malaria, or died of blood poisoning or gangrene from an ulcer; or, like so many of the youngest among them, simply from exhaustion and despair. Wearing a lap-lap and filthy shorts, barefoot, covered in sores, he would be stooping to take the basket on his back, pouring with sweat and chewing on the bitterness of it.

'This,' Digger said to no one in particular, to the part of himself that stood apart a little and observed from a distance still, 'is what happened to us in the world. Maybe it wasn't meant to. It was meant for those others, those coolies. It happened to them too, and now it's happened to us. So what do you make of that?'

It was part of an argument he had been having, for weeks now, with Doug; except that it seldom got put into more than a few words. They were too exhausted to argue. But the words went on arguing in their heads, and some of it got across; they got the drift of it. It was an argument, really, that Mac ought to have been making. He would have done it better. Digger was doing it for him, the best he could.

There were fellows now who had begun to take a religious view – that was understandable, Digger could see that – and one of them, astonishingly, after he came through the beriberi, was Doug.

They could hardly believe it at first. They thought he was putting it on and making a mock. But he was dead serious. In the horror of what was happening to them, some teaching had come back to him out of his hellfire youth. Some grim Presbyterian view that had been opened up in his head in the days before he asserted himself and said 'Stuff it' and refused to go to church – half-heard on hot Sunday mornings while he was gazing out a window, his mind a slingshot loosing itself after a sparrow, or his own dick, hard as iron, working its way up a girl's thigh – struck him now, ten years later, as an incontrovertible truth. 'Look about you, lad, and mock if you can. Isn't this what they were trying to make you see? Isn't it?'

'Isn't it *what*?' Digger wanted to know. 'Hell? Is that what you think it is?'

He thought of his father and those Sundays when they had been out on the line. Hell was just a name people had for the worst thing they could think of, the worst thing that could ever happen to them. Well, it happens, that's all. Nobody deserves what they get. You better believe that, son, because every other sort of belief is madness. We don't *deserve* this. Nobody does. We haven't done anything *that* bad, even the worst of us, even you, Douggy, you old bastard! But it's what we've got. Thailand is just a place. Some people spend their whole lives here. It's normal. These coolies, for instance. For them it's normal, it's all they'll ever have — not for any *sin* they've committed. It rains a lot, that's all. The jungle's as thick as a wall. Things rot. Flies breed maggots in everything. Us too, if we get a bit of a nick. We weren't meant to be here, but we are. Eight hours a day and time off for smokos — that's one sort of justice, a pretty rough one; but it's not for everyone, and it's not for us now either, maybe ever again. Oh, it's unfair all right. But who ever said it would be fair? And who can you complain to, anyhow?

'I'm not complaining,' Doug said.

'But you should be,' Digger told him fiercely. He hated to see Doug, of all people, so meek.

Doug just looked at him, half-smiling, and it was true, Digger had hanged himself on his own argument.

But he stuck to it just the same. He had to.

It was so hard to keep your head in all this. It was a kind of madness, but there was a thread of sanity in it, there had to be; in all the twists and turns, a clear straight line into life. He was determined to hang on to it. Sometimes he could.

Later, half-asleep, he sat in the stink of himself and spooned up gruel. He had something fresh to brood over. Coming back from the embankment he had stepped on a thorn. It would fester, blow up and ulcerate. Bound to. That was enough to worry anyone.

Down on the track a new lot were passing, you could hear their feet scuffing the leaves; and a new rumour was being passed among them. 'Cholera. They're Tamils. They'll be carrying cholera!' That whisper on the track.

'As if we didn't have enough on our plate already,' Digger thought bitterly, using a phrase that had lost all meaning up here.

But what really worried him, right now, was his foot. Each time he got up in the dark and trotted to the borehole (four or five times it was, in less than an hour) he could hear them, still passing. Thousands, it must be.

Cholera wasn't just bad, it was the worst. They had seen a bit of it in one of the camps on the way up and had been eager to get out and away. As if they didn't have –

But immediately his foot touched the ground his mind went *there*, to the immediate sore place where the thorn had gone in, and worried and worried.

It was a new eye, this opening in his flesh, and had its own point of view. Darkness was what it was obsessed with. It loved the dark. When he lay down and tried to sleep again he saw nothing but what *it* saw: the road it would take, dragging the rest of him (what was left of him) into bruise-blackness, till his whole body began to drink darkness from the hungry mouth that had opened there – mouth or eye, whichever way you saw it, both hungry for something other than the flesh, but also for the flesh.

The trouble is, he thought, they never tell you anything that's of any real use. Even the books. Even the great ones. You have to learn it for yourself, just as it comes.

Well, he was learning all right; so were they all. Some of it their bellies were teaching them; like how little a man can live on and still drag himself from one day to the next. The history of empires, that lesson was, and what it costs to build them. Top grades he had been getting. Now it was his foot that was beginning to instruct him. God knows what lesson that would be.

It was swelling with the illuminating darkness of an ultimate *wisdom*. First principles. The original chemistry of things. Flashing it throb after throb to the furthest galaxies at the limits of his system. 'This is how it starts,' he thought, 'this is genesis. This is the truth now, spreading fast, beginning as just a pinprick and eating its way through flesh to the very bone. Nothing abstract about this. You can see it if you want, you can scoop it out with a hot spoon. That's real enough surely for any man.'

11

To top it all they gave them the glass-rod test and Digger was discovered, along with about eighty others, to be a cholera carrier. Sent to the isolation ward across the yard, he discovered a little deeper hell inside the larger one. It had been there all the time but he had known nothing of it. New cases were brought in each day, and in the morning, two or three of them, sometimes more, would be dead. Fellows who only hours before had been able to whisper at least, with a fleshy tongue and lips, would be mummies, their skin as dry and yellow on their bones as if they had been laid out like that for centuries. Dried-up twigs, their fingers were. Their feet were wood. You could only tell one man from another by the tag he wore.

A little away from the camp, in a jungle clearing, they had their burning-place. Each day there were new dead to be cremated, and because he was in reasonable shape, except for his ulcer, Digger did it. The wood had to be chopped the day before. The bodies were carried on rice sacks on bamboo poles.

Entering the place Digger felt a sleepiness come over him. It began the moment you stepped off the common path that the work parties used and took this one that led sharply away from it and then a hundred yards or more, in impenetrable gloom, into the forest. Only the dead came this way, except for those who carried them. To enter here you too had to become one of the dead, at least in spirit – the place demanded it. A sleepiness came over you, a torpor of the mind, though your limbs worked well enough.

You were in the antechamber here of the next world – that's what the perpetual blue-grey gloom and the external dampness of the place told you; and the stillness, the suspension of all activity, including the fall of the ever-falling bamboo leaves.

You were at the furthest point now from where you had come from, wherever it was, and could bring no human qualities with you. The place did not recognise them, had never known them from the beginning of time. It was a primeval place of a vegetable dampness where nothing human had yet been conceived.

The air was blueish and so cold that your breath went always before you, as if spirit here had more substance than flesh.

The leaves kept up a slow drizzle, and long streamers of mist floated through just at head level. More breath.

The slowness of the blood that overcame you belonged to lizard life, reptile life. To stand upright and take on the sensations of men might be fatal here; no space had been prepared for it. You preserved yourself by letting a reptile sleepiness come over you and your spirit sink down towards the earth.

There were no ceremonies. The words would have blown back damp against your mouth.

All the more terrifying then that the dead, who after twenty-four hours were no more than the driest sticks, should suddenly, when the teak logs under them roared into flame, sigh and sit upright, start bolt upright in the midst of the flames. This recovery, and the heat that came from it, was too much. You found your limbs and hobbled away as fast as breath would take you. You fled.

12

'Listen mate,' Vic whispered. What was he doing here? 'I heard about something. One of the other blokes tried it and it worked on him. Can you hear me Digger? I'm gunna get you up. Sorry about this.'

The place was full of voices. In the attap roof where rain dripped continuously small lives were on the move, lizards, mice, scorpions, cockroaches – occasionally one of them fell and you would hear a man cry out in alarm and claw at himself to drive it off.

The other hospital inmates, if they could drag themselves to their feet, were never still – that's how it seemed to Digger. They were forever trotting off to the boreholes, five or six times a night some of them, or restlessly wandering up and down between the bunks, in violent conversation with themselves.

Bugs rattled in the folds of his rags, he could hear them. They clattered against one another in the joints of the rack. Sighs, groans, a burst of shouting out of some man's nightmare.

Get up? He would never get up, that's what they had told him. Not on two legs anyway; one maybe. He had begun a light-headed descent towards a place of light, and had decided to go with it. He was letting his body have its own way now. That was the best thing.

'Digger? C'mon. I'm going to get you up, right? It'll hurt, I know. I'm sorry. But it's our only shot. You don't want t' lose ya leg, do you?'

It was Vic's voice but the tone was his mother's. He wondered what Vic had been tuning into that allowed him to get it off so perfectly, but was not surprised. The walls between things had been breaking down for a while now.

'Digger?'

He was being hauled up, away from the light. When his eyes opened it was dark. The hospital hut was all shadows of men moving against the light outside.

'What are you *doing*?' he complained, feeling Vic's arm hooked under his own and hauling him up. He was light enough, but was surprised just the same that Vic could manage it. 'I can't *walk*.'

Vic ignored this. He had him up and hanging. Digger could hear Vic panting and could smell his breath. He began to drag him out under the overlap of the attap roof into starlight. Other men, ghostlike, were wandering about out here but took no notice of them.

'Where are we goin'?' he asked when they had crossed the open space in front of the huts and entered a thicket.

Vic was grunting. He did not reply. 'This is the hard bit now,' he said at last, after they had come some way into the thickening forest. 'Hang on, eh Dig? Digger? Dig?'

They were at the edge of a muddy bank that sloped steeply to a glint of water where blackness swirled. Digger looked out across the wide expanse of it. The river.

'Listen,' Vic was telling him. 'I'm gunna put you down on your backside, right? You gotta slide. It'll hurt, Dig, I know that. I'm sorry. But it's the only way. You ready now?'

He had no power to resist. He felt himself settled with his legs over the edge of the bank, then he was sliding. His bones wrenched. They would break, they must; he was waiting to hear what he had heard often enough in the hospital hut, the unspeakable sound of a legbone snapping, crack! where some bloke turned in the dark. But there was only a shock of pain that he blacked out on, and he was in thick mud. It was oozing all round him. It was in his mouth and eyes, stinking. But he did not have enough weight for it to take him down. No pack, no boots, and there was no meat on him. So in his own case gravity did not function. He floated on top of it, floundering, and the mud was grey-black river-slime with roots in it.

'Digger? Are you OK, Dig?'

That was that Vic again. 'For Christ's sake,' Digger thought, 'doesn' 'e know any other name? Why doesn' 'e torment some other bastard?'

'All right,' Vic said, 'all right, we can rest a bit, no hurry, Dig. You have a rest.'

Vic lay with his face in the mud. It stank, he thought, like an old slate-rag at school. He was sweating. 'No, there's no hurry,' he thought.

He was light-headed. That was the pain. But more than that it was the revulsion he felt that part of him stank worse even than this river-slime, and had the stink of a dead body. He was carrying the beginnings of a dead body along with his live one.

There was no hurry, but he couldn't wait just the same. Another moment of this death touch on him and he'd go crazy now that the cure was so near. But Digger couldn't move again. Not just yet.

'I can wait,' he told himself. 'There's no hurry. The fishes'll wait. If I can just get my ear out of the mud' (he lifted his head) 'I'll be able to hear them.' The tiddlers, he meant, in their shoals at the edge of the river; swishing their tails, waving their gills to breathe, and smelling them: flesh. He reached out and touched the edge of the water. Very gently it tripped over his fingers. It was going somewhere. It would clean them, even if it was itself thick with mud.

'Digger?'

He pulled himself up, put his face close to Digger, who was all mud, and, as if he could by sheer willpower breathe life into him, said, 'Listen, mate, I'm gunna get you up again, right? Digger? Dig?'

Digger rolled his head a little. There were stars, big ones, very close, and so bright that it hurt. They were heavy, he knew that. Tons and tons of gas and luminous minerals burning, rolling, travelling fast but managing to stay up. The weight of them, that light balancing act, was an encouragement.

'Right? *Now*,' the voice said, 'this is it. Right, mate? I'm gunna get you *up*. Upsadaisy! Right?'

Vic was astonished. Digger was just skin and bone but the weight of him was enormous. It must be the mud he was coated in. No, he thought, it's something else. It's the weight of death, heavy as lead in him. So heavy maybe I can't do it. He struggled and the sweat began to stream faster on him.

'That's *good*, that was good, Digger. We're there now. We've made it.' He stood still, supporting Digger who also supported him. He could hear the mad activity there on the surface of the water, where the stars touched it and you could see them beginning to swarm.

'Don't worry, fishies,' he said, in a voice he recognised as his own from when he was maybe three years old, 'we're coming. Only a little while now.'

'Now,' the voice said, and half-supporting, half-dragging him where he hung under the stars (what was supporting *them*?), led him forward.

It was a river. Digger saw the gleaming surface of it, coal-black and churning. 'What *is* this?' he thought. 'What does he think he's doing? This won't help.' The word that had come into his head – it was a word he had never used as far as he could recall – was baptism. But all Vic did was lead him a little way in: one pace, another. He felt the warmth of it rising to just below his knees. It was alive. He could feel the life of it.

'What is it?' he asked, childlike. 'What's happening?'

'It's the fishes,' Vic said. 'Don't worry, they won't hurt.'

'What?'

'Shh, don't scare 'em, you'll scare 'em. They're only tiddlers. They won't hurt.'

Vic too was in a kind of wonder at it. The idea of it had sickened him at first, just the idea: of being fed off by greedy mouths. But in fact it was soothing. The stars high up, so still; and underwater there, in what seemed like silence but wouldn't be, close up, the jaws fighting for their share of the feast. And all you felt from up here, from this distance, was a pleasant *contact*. The touch of their savagery was soft.

'It tickles,' Digger said foolishly.

'Yair, they're just tiddlers,' Vic told him, and he was laughing now. It was so weird, and he had such a sense of the good they were doing him. 'It'll be over in a minute.'

It would be over when they drew blood.

Digger understood at last, but thought it must be a dream. He could hear the fish in a bright wave swarming at the edge of the bank where they stood offering themselves.

There was a smell these last days that had got right into his head. He knew what it was. It was the news of his own corruption, the smell, still as yet a little way off, of his own death. It had sickened him. Now, slowly, he felt the smell recede. All the stink and ooze of it was being taken back into the world, away from him, into the mouths of the living and turned back into life there. He felt the bump bump of gristle as the small fry darted in and their snouts bounced off bone. They were feeding off him, savagely, greedily tearing at the flesh, and what they were giving him back was cleanness.

When he came back into himself and looked about he was standing knee deep in oily water, stars overhead, so close he could hear them grinding, and he could hear the tiny jaws of the fishes grinding too, as starlight touched their backs and they swarmed and fought and churned the blackness to a frenzy round his shins.

'Did any of that happen?' he asked Vic later, when they lay exhausted in the dark.

'Yes, it happened, an' it'll save us. I told you it would. It *works*.'

13

Digger, in the methodical way that was habitual to him, kept track of each day that passed. He could tell you, if you were bothered to know such a thing, what day of the week it was, in which month; how long it was now till Christmas (how many weeks and days), how long since they had left Changi, how many days and nights they had taken on the road up, how many they had been at work on the line. It mattered to Digger that this bit of order should be maintained in his life. In a place where so much had been taken from them, perhaps permanently, this business of time-keeping, which was after all something the Japs had no control over (it was between you and the sun) represented a last area of freedom to him, a last reminder too of what had been essential to the way they had lived back home.

It was no small thing, this capacity to place yourself accurately in time, this bit of science it had taken so many centuries to get right. It was worth holding on to, gave a form to what otherwise might run right through your hands.

So in his monkish way, which Doug teased him over, Digger could be relied on, when any question of times or dates came up, to deliver an answer on the spot.

The surrender? That had been Sunday, 15 February 1942. Not long after, third week in April, they left Changi for the Great World – Mac had died on 7 June. (This was a date in Digger's personal calendar. He did not mention it; but three times now he had kept the anniversary.) In October, the 4th to be exact, they had gone back to Changi, and on 22 April the next year, 1943, had begun the long journey into Thailand: five days and nights on the train, crowded into cattle wagons, then a series of night-marches through jungle camps where cholera was raging, twenty nights in all. From then till the day they started back down the line and crossed the border again into Malaya was a hundred and eighty-nine days. Eighteen months it was since then. Just on.

Other things, big and small, had been happening in the world. Most of it they knew nothing of. The dates Digger recorded, the periods – Changi, the Great World, Thailand, Changi again – that was *their* war. It was three years and six months since they had become prisoners.

He knew well enough how little these measurements told. The days were not equal. Nor were the hours. Nor were the minutes, even.

That minute and a half in the godown, for instance, in which Mac had been killed – there was no way of fitting that into a system that needed sixty minutes to an hour and twenty-four hours to a single revolution of the earth. Some of those days they had worked up there, *speedo*, as the body recorded them, had been centuries, strung out in an agony for which there were no terms of measurement at all. He knew all that.

Their history took place in its own time. But it had to be fitted to the time the rest of the world was moving through or you wouldn't know where you were, outside your own sack of nerves. The two times didn't fit. They never would. Digger knew that as well as the next man. But you kept both just the same and made what you could of it.

So it was three and a half years, just on, as the calendar showed it. August 1945.

14

All the signs now were that it was coming to an end, might even be over already, days, even weeks ago, so that in *fact* (in one version of it) they might already be free. If that was true their watches would be showing the wrong time. They had no certain news, but *something* had happened. You could feel it.

For the past six months they had been at work on a series of tunnels the Japs were digging across the strait in Johore Baahru, a protection for their troops in case of invasion. Vic was with Digger, and Doug had been there too till he got caught in a cave-in and lost an arm. The work was dangerous. They tunnelled into the side of a hill with just picks and shovels, shoring the walls as they went; but the earth was waterlogged after the rains and there were many accidents, the air in the tunnels was foul, and the heat so fierce that they could work for only minutes before they were gasping for breath. If one tunnel collapsed they started in on another just yards away. Now there was this rumour that it was all over anyhow.

Some fellows said no, it couldn't be. It wouldn't end. If it did the Japs had orders to kill the lot of them. They knew too much of what had gone on. They would be herded into the tunnels and machine-gunned or walled up there. That sort of talk, Digger argued, was madness. They couldn't have got this far, come through so much, those hundred and eighty-nine days for instance, to be gunned down like dogs.

He was used to the wild speculations that spread among them. For years now they had been living on them. Like the great sea battle they had got so excited about just after they arrived in Thailand, which had raged for days and days with terrible casualties and would certainly now bring an armistice. Off the north coast of Western Australia, that was supposed to have been, near Broome; the whole Jap navy done for. Only it must have taken place nowhere at all, or in some bloke's head, because nothing more was heard of it.

Sydney was wiped out by incendiary bombs. The Japs were at Coff's Harbour, and Menzies, pig-iron Bob, had flown to Manila to sue for peace. That was another bit of news. What had come of that?

The Japs had set up a puppet government at Townsville. Artie Fadden was at the head of it. Artie Fadden!

The Russians had moved into Manchuria. The Yanks had invaded Japan from mainland China and were in the suburbs of Tokyo. It was a matter of days now – two weeks at the most.

This phantom war, whose triumphs and defeats they clung to because their lives depended on it, would in some ways remain more vivid to them than the real one, when at last they learned of it; or they would go on confusing the two, uncertain which was which.

It was an odd thing to have lived and died a little in a history that had never actually occurred; to have survived, as some of them had, on the bit of hope they had been given by the fall of Yokohama at Christmas 1943, or succumbed, as others did, in the gloom that descended when a few weeks later Churchill died and New Zealand surrendered, both on the same day.

Occasionally, by accident, some fact out of a quite different set of occurrences would get through to them and they would be utterly bamboozled. What were the Japs doing in New Guinea if the Americans were already swarming over the home islands?

They lived off rumour, and rumour, often enough, sprang out of some man's sleep. So what could you believe?

This latest thing, for instance, that it was already over. Best to take it with a grain of salt – that was Digger's view. Let it get your hopes up, if that's what you needed, but don't put money on it.

Still, it affected them as everything did, and in different ways.

Some men who had hung on till now, bad cases of malnutrition or beriberi, just gave up and died. It was good news as often as not that finished a man.

Others seemed dazed. The prospect of going home again scared them. They couldn't imagine how they could ever settle to it. How they could just walk around the streets and pretend to be normal, look women in the eye again after what they had done and seen, ride on trams, sit at a table with a white cloth, and control their hands and just slowly eat. It was the little things that scared them. The big things you could hide in. It was little ones that gave a man away.

Vic was one who thought like this. The more the rumours spread and the closer it got, the more fiercely he rejected the possibility.

'They're fooling themselves,' he told Digger. 'They're mugs.' He was vehement about it. The optimism of some people infuriated him.

'We've heard all this before. It won't *end*. Not like this, it won't. It can't end.'

The truth was he didn't want it to, that's what Digger thought. He's a difficult cuss. You never knew which way he was going to jump – he didn't himself half the time.

They began to draw apart now that they no longer needed one another. Digger shrugged his shoulders. 'Well, if that's what he wants.'

Vic kept away from Doug too, and from all their former mates; turned sulky, drew into himself.

'He's a bastard. I knew that all along,' Digger told himself, but was hurt just the same. He owed a lot to this fellow. His life, maybe. Certainly a leg. These were things that Digger could not easily forget. There were times, up there, when they might have known all there was to know about one another, things you'd never find out about a man, never have to, in the ordinary run of things. It meant something, that. But back here, at the edge of normality, these were matters that could not be alluded to.

'He's ashamed of all that,' Digger thought. 'It's something he doesn't want to know about.'

What surprised him was that Vic seemed closer to breaking down now than in any of their worst moments in Thailand.

It was time that troubled Vic. The opening up of a line into the future would take him back now into the life he left four years ago.

So long as he had been able to hold a view of things in which time was just moments, then days, each one destroying itself in the next; so long, that is, as it was a process without sequence, he could face himself and hang on. Living was vertical. You stood up new in each moment of it, and if you were strong, and luck was with you, you got from one moment to the next. It was all moments and leaps. But now he had to take on again the notion of a self that was continuous, that belonged to the past and was to have a life again in the future. That's what scared him – the need to carry forward into the ordinariness that was coming a view of time, and of your whole life in it, that he had had to suppress in himself simply to stay alive.

He was twenty-two, just turned. Years, he would have, if the vision that had come to him, back there, was a true one, and his body told him it was.

He had done better than some others. Digger had lost all his teeth.

He was gummy. Doug had lost an arm. He himself *looked* whole but felt that he had lost everything.

He had had no word from the Warrenders for more than two years. They had written often in the early days, Pa had anyway, and there was always an added word or two from the girls or Ma, but they had had no mail at all in Thailand, and he had got nothing in the hand-outs since they got to Malaya.

In his years with the Warrenders he had never spoken of the life he had known before he came to them, of his parents and all that world up the coast. He had buried that, kept it to himself.

Of course Pa had got a glimpse of it. But then Pa, amazingly, had known his father, though he couldn't imagine *what* he had known. Pa, understanding by instinct how he might feel about it, and in accordance with his own manly principles, had never alluded to it. So he had kept all that to himself, hoarding it up in the most secret part of him as a thing he would not speak of or let anyone see.

He would not speak of this either, once it was over; since it was pretty certain now that it soon would be. He would push it deep down into himself, face it on his own, and deny, if asked, that he had ever been here: 'No, mate – not *me*.'

That's how it would be for him, and how it had to be. Strange? Is that strange? It's the way I *am*.

Maybe he wouldn't go back at all, that's what he had begun to think. He was too changed. He didn't want them to see (*them* least of all) what had been done to him, and he knew only too well what that was because he could see it in others. It would kill him if he had to see himself through *their* eyes. Lucille's for instance.

He had (he couldn't help it) a kind of contempt for what he had become that was the last resort of his wounded pride. The mere sight of other men sickened him. Their necks all vein and gristle, the tottering walk they had, like old blokes you saw going home just on closing time with a bottle of cheap plonk in a brown-paper bag; the silly, hopeful chatter they went in for, the rumours, the schemes – chicken farms were what they were all for running when they got back; most of all the smell they carried, which wasn't just sweat or shit or green vomit but of what four years of slavery had done to them, sickness of the spirit. It marked you forever, that. There was no way you could get rid of it.

But as the time got closer and the rumours wilder and maybe nearer the mark, old needs and desires began to reappear for no other reason than that they might be capable again of fulfilment; he was racked. And with them, quite unsought, came visions, so real at times that his whole body would be filled with such sensual warmth and yearning, raw need, happiness, and sudden choking emptiness, that he thought he might pass out. Was that what it was to be like?

The visions appeared of their own accord, and in no particular sequence: a stockinged foot, a hairpin, the unbuttoned strap of a suspender. They were the ingredients of spells, his body practising its own form of witchcraft, or they were the symptoms of madness – that's what he thought. But their power was overwhelming. His blood raced and burned, he hardly dared close his eyes. And they came as well when his eyes were open. His mind, or his body, was an infinite storehouse of such vision, of acts and objects he had pushed down into the dark and which were reappearing now to claim connection. Was this madness or some deep healing process? Either way it was a torment to him.

One image especially kept coming back and back, a kind of waking dream. It was of the house at Strathfield, the hallway just inside the front door, with its high white ceiling and pavement of blue, white and brown terracotta tiles.

A radiance as of the westering sun filled it – but that, his reason told him, was impossible: the house faced south. Still, there it was and there he was.

As the light settled out and his heart, which appeared to be the real source of it, slowed at last to normal pace, and since it had been free-floating, came to rest again under his ribs, he saw that Lucille was there, just turning on the second step.

Something had caught her attention. She was looking towards him with a little line of puzzlement between her brows, as if she knew someone was there but was too dazzled by the unaccustomed light to see who it was. He knew he could not call out to her. But his heart was beating so loud he thought she might hear that.

After a moment, still puzzled, she turned and went on up and he was left standing, but quietly now and full of contentment, as if some sort of assurance had been given him.

None had, of course, and with the part of him that was rational and clear-headed he knew it, so what was he doing?

Still, the image, or the dream, or whatever it was, stayed warm in him and kept coming back.

15

Vic, freshly washed and combed, in clean shirt, clean shorts and a new pair of boots, a bit light-headed just with the knowledge that he could go anywhere he pleased, down this alley or that, was out walking in the freed city. They were all out somewhere, rushing here and there like kids in a fairground, not knowing what to try first.

He had come out alone and was in a part of the town he did not know, along a foul canal. He didn't know anywhere in Singapore, not really. He had never had a chance to.

It was a low place, all peeling walls, coal smoke from kerosene tins, and footpaths filthy with squashed fruit and dog-turds and cinders and bloody-looking spit. He had wandered down here looking for he didn't know what. Nothing. Anything. It wasn't any place he had intended to be.

Bicycles passed in droves, all honking. Children sat half-naked on the ground. Salesmen, squatting, had laid out on upturned butter-boxes, or low tables covered with a cloth, the few things, whatever it was, that they had to sell. Suddenly he stopped dead and stood stupidly staring.

What had caught his eye was a pyramid of six cotton-reels on a tray, one of them a sickly green, another royal blue, the rest white, but all dusty and soiled looking. The only other thing on the tray was a packet of needles.

The old woman squatting beside them glanced up under heavy pads of flesh, happy to have attracted his attention. She was preparing to call out to him. But the look he was wearing, or the threatening bulk of him, must have warned her of something. Her hand moved out to cover the single reel at the apex of the pyramid she had made. To save it. She sat staring up at him.

He was in a rage, a kind of madness, and close to tears.

In the left-hand pocket of his new shorts was the length of thread he had kept. His fingers went to it. He hadn't thrown it away – you never know. Its value to him, anyway, was absolute. And here now, in this dirty bit of a place, this old crone of a Chinese woman had six reels of it on her mean little tray, six whole reels – and beyond that, on shelves somewhere in a storehouse, there would be cartons-full. They were common as dirt. He had a vision suddenly of how small it was, all that had happened to him.

The old woman's hand, which was yellow and wrinkled like a duck's foot, kept hold of the reel, expecting this crazy boy to use his boot now and kick the whole tray aside. They were like that, these blond ones. But instead he let out a cry of rage, flung something out of his pocket and ran off.

She watched him go, her hand still protecting her wares. Then she leaned forward over the edge of her tray a little to see what it was. A bit of dirty thread. Nothing.

Minutes later he was back. With his eye crazily upon her, he stooped, snatched up the bit of cotton as if she might be intending to rob him of it, and was gone.

IV

1

On hot nights late in Darlinghurst Road Digger found what he had always been in search of, a crowded place with the atmosphere of a fairground, but one that did not have to be knocked down and set up again night after night. It was simply there, another part of town.

It was a rowdy place, the Cross. It could be violent, sordid too at times, but it had put a spell on Digger just as Mac had told him it would.

Girls, some of them toothless and close to sixty, worked out of mean little rooms up staircases smelling of bacon-fat or sharp with disinfectant. The pubs were blood-buckets.

You would see a couple of fellows come hurtling through the door and in seconds a full-scale brawl would be going on, right there on the pavement, with passers-by ducking aside to get away from it or standing off on the sidelines to watch.

Often it was seamen; but mostly it was young blokes, louts, who had come in on motorbikes to roar about and see what was doing, keen to get a reputation and discover how tough they were.

They wore second-hand air-force jackets, duck-tailed Cornel Wilde haircuts and wanted blood.

They would roam about putting their shoulders into the crowd, waiting to be challenged, with a Friday night ferocity in them that had the pent-up frustration of a week's work behind it, and would only be content at last when the man they were bludgeoning was in the gutter and they heard his ribs crack – 'Ah, that's it, that's the sound' – or when they had gone down themselves and were sitting with their head in their hands, hearing a whole lot of new sounds in there that might be permanent and with their palms wet with blood.

Occasionally it was a woman you saw, still clutching her handbag but with her mouth bloody, one arm like a broken wing, and the man who had done it shouting right into her face, spitting out obscenities but weeping too sometimes, justifying himself. This was peacetime again.

And in between these savage episodes the delivery boys would be out and old people, or women dragging a suitcase in one hand and a reluctant child in the other, would be going about their daily affairs. Well-dressed ladies walked pug dogs. Kids sucking sherbet sticks dawdled back and forth to school. Old fellows slept it off on benches or stood with their sleeve up to the elbow in bins.

There were coffee shops, continental, with mock-cream cakes in the window, and other, darker ones downstairs where it was rumoured that satanic cults were being practised. The paintings on the walls, which were pretty bold, gave you a hint of what they might be: a woman with her legs round a shaggy male figure with horns above his ears, another in which a girl was coupling with a gigantic cat.

Then there were the milk-bars, all fan-shaped mirrors and chrome, spaghetti places where men in business suits lined up for lunch, and barber shops, some with a dozen chairs; always with two or three fellows lathered up for shaving while the barber, razor in hand, harangued them while others, further down the room, would be snipping and chatting or showing a customer the back of his head in a glass, and in the doorway one of the idle assistants hung on a broom.

Barber shops, billiard saloons, dark corners in pubs – this was where the SP bookies followed their trade, using runners and a 'nit' to watch for the cops. But everyone up here had something to sell: petrol, stuff without coupons that had fallen off the back of a truck, nylons, second-hand cars, pre-war of course, and girls.

Towards five, with paperboys shouting the headlines and running out barefoot to cars, working men, still in their singlets, would be strolling home with the *Mirror* under their arm, taking it easy and eating a Have-a-Heart or a Grannie Smith apple; going back to a room in a boarding-house, or up three flights to where a girl was cooking sausages in a two-roomed maisonette, the only place they could get in the housing shortage.

This was the rush hour, the hour before closing. Sailors would be up in mobs from the ships you could see moored at Woolloomooloo, and along with them came fellows, newly demobbed, wearing suits you could pick a mile off (Digger had one) that they had been given to start them off in Civvy Street, but still with their old army haircut, and with the half-expectant, half-lost look of men who were waiting for life to declare a direction to them, now that they were free to go wherever they pleased.

Digger kept away from these fellows. They depressed him. He knew their story. It was his own. They were men who for one reason or another had never gone home – or had done so and come straight back again, one or two of them on the first day. They hung about feeling sorry for themselves and keeping close to one another, looking on at a show they were not part of, not yet, and wondering if they ever would be.

Digger felt that too, on occasions. He hadn't been home either, but not because he was scared of what he might find there. He was putting it off, that's all; enjoying himself, getting back into the stride of things. There was such a sense abroad of streets being swept for a new day, of ties off, sleeves rolled up, girls walking with a new bounce to their heels and their handbags swinging, full of what the world might offer them now and what they could do with it. 'Me too,' Digger thought. 'The war is over and we won!' – Except that it wasn't quite like that.

'We didn't win our war because it wasn't a war we went to. It was something else. It's victories that are all the go now. This is a victory parade. No one wants to know about *us*.'

There were men who were bitter about that, and not just on their own behalf. Digger shared the feeling but would not give in to it.

He wrote to his mother nearly every week and she sent back sharp replies. His father was in Japan now, a hero of the army of occupation. Jenny had run away, she didn't know where. Yes, he assured her, he *would* come back, she knew that. But from week to week he put it off, still dizzied by all that was going on here, all he saw and was trusted with. Once he went back he would be caught. For a little time longer he wanted to be off the hook.

People trusted him. He didn't know why.

A man he hardly knew, though they might have spoken a couple of times, would thrust an envelope into his hand. 'Here, mate, keep this for me, willya? Don't worry, I'll find you. Next week or the week after. Somewhere. Just keep it under ya pillow, eh?'

Digger would sock the thing away behind the mirror of the little room he had at the Pomeroy and forget about it. A week later the man would come up to him in a pub, fool about for a bit, then say casually: 'How's the bank vault? – That envelope I give you, I s'pose you still got it.' With the envelope safe in an inside jacket pocket he would slip Digger a twenty. 'Thanks, mate. I'll do the same f' you some time.'

What had he been part of? He didn't ask. That's why he was trusted.

Someone who had heard that he knew how to look after himself and was handy with his fists put him on to one of the clubs. He got a job as a bouncer at thirty quid a week, working from seven till five in the morning at a place where sly grog was served, and in a room at the back, poker and blackjack were played. He helped clean up afterwards, went out and got himself a cup of tea at an all-nighter, then, in the early-morning coolness, walked home.

He loved the Cross at that hour. Greeks would be setting up fruit stalls, apples and oranges in glossy pyramids. Men in shorts would be unloading fresh flowers, setting them out in buckets on the pavement and sprinkling them from a can against the coming heat. He would buy a paper and scan the morning news.

'Haven' you got any better place to go than this, feller? You don't want to hang around here.'

The man who offered him this advice was a cop, a thick-set fellow with close-cropped straight black hair and freckles. Mid-thirties, a bit flash, with a good overcoat, a soft grey hat, and eyes Digger had taken a liking to. They were very steady and blue. He could offer the advice because he did it lightly. It was a joke between them. His name was Frank McGowan.

Digger had seen him about often enough and they'd got talking. He didn't mind having a drink with him, though he knew he was breaking a code.

'I seen you drinkin' with that dingo McGowan,' one of his acquaintances observed. 'I s'pose you know what 'e is.' There was a little beat of silence. 'Yair, well, 'e's a cunt. An' 'e's crooked as shit, you ast anyone! SP – they're all in on it, you ast anyone!'

Digger listened but did not reply. It was all such tales up here. The Cross was a village, full of intricate alliances and drawn lines. A thing had barely happened, they'd hardly picked the body up off the pavement, before it was in the mouth of every barber's boy and saloon-bar lounger. McGowan was in the Vice Squad. That was enough. It embarrassed Digger sometimes that McGowan should take an interest in him, but he did not believe it was a ploy. He was no use to McGowan.

'So,' McGowan would say each time they ran into one another, 'you're still here. Go an' get lost, why don't you?'

But once, in a darker mood, when they were sitting quietly together, he said: 'I don' understand you, Digger, a feller like you. What are you doin', hangin' about with this sorta rubbish?'

Digger looked up, a shadow of doubt in his eyes. His experience in the camps had given him an ear for the various forms of self-hatred that men go in for, and he thought now that some of the venom in McGowan's voice was directed at himself.

McGowan saw the look. 'Yair, well,' he said, and made a brusque movement with his thumb across the tip of his nose. There was a grossness in it that was deliberate. He had given himself away and was drawing back again. Digger too withdrew.

It was the word he had used, rubbish, that Digger wanted to go back to. What came back to him at times, and too clearly, was that break in the forest and the fires he had tended there. It had given him such an awareness of just what it is that life throws up, and when it has no more use for it, throws off again. Not just ashes and bones, but the immense pile of debris that any one life might make if you were to gather up and look at the whole of it: all that it had worn out, used up, mislaid, pawned, forgotten, and carried out each morning to be tipped into a bin. Think of it. Then think of it multiplied by millions.

What he would have wanted, given the power, was to take it all back again, down to the last razor blade and button off a baby's bootee, and see it restored. Impossible, of course.

He wanted nothing to be forgotten and cast into the flames. Not a soul. Not a pin.

He said none of this to McGowan, but wished later he had done and taken the risk.

'I'm like one of those old blokes you see poking about the bins,' he would have had to say, making a joke of it. But he was serious.

'Not a soul,' he would have said. 'Not a pin.'

2

One Saturday around three o'clock he did something he had been meaning to do for weeks. He got himself ready and took a tram out to Bondi Junction to find Mac's sister-in-law, Iris. He carried with him the letters Mac had given him. It was all he had to pass on to her.

He recognised the house easily enough from the description Mac had given him, but the woman who opened the door was not at all what he expected.

He had seen her often enough. He had stood behind the door in the kitchen and seen her come in, turn on the tap, pour herself a glass of water, and then, with wonderful slowness, drink it, all the time looking out through the window in a dreamy way at the stars.

That woman had worn her hair in a style he remembered from before the war. She was very sober and tall. This one, with the light of the hallway behind her, was shorter, heavier too, and she stepped out of a moment of hilarity that had to do with something that was still going on in the depths of the house. There was a radio playing. He heard thumps from back there and saw the flash of a blue shirt – one of the boys that would be – between the hallway and the back stairs.

'I'm sorry about this,' she said in the midst of her laughter. 'Come on in.'

He stepped into the narrow hallway. He was cleaned up, his hair combed, his feet washed – that was normal now. But he wore a tie as well, feeling the constriction of it, and had the letters, in a clean envelope, in his right-hand breast pocket.

'Here,' she said, 'let me take your hat.'

'Oh – good,' he said. He had been just standing there, staring about.

He had thought he would know the place, and he did in some ways; Mac's sleep-out would be the bottom of the hall to the right. But the whole house was lighter than he had imagined, more airy. More cheerful, too. Mac had described only the things his own plain taste would have put here; the rest he had left out. A lot of what Digger saw now was fanciful: a tall Chinese vase with umbrellas on it, and a little

Alpine house with a man and woman in peasant costume, who came out, the one or the other, according to whether it was fine or would rain.

She settled him in the front room, then went out to turn the wireless down, put a kettle on, and at the same time to shout something through a window into the yard. Digger had a chance to look about.

Above the upright piano, which was covered with a green velvet cloth, was a certificate showing that Elizabeth Iris Ruddick had her letters from the Trinity College of Music in 1921 – the year, as it happened, of his birth. There was a metronome, a bust of Beethoven, a bronze rose bowl with a wirework lid. Another object that took his eye was an ornamental tray in mother-of-pearl. On it was a young fellow in olden-days dress, a satin coat and breeches, who sat with two shepherdesses in a moonlit ruin. In a corner, on a little lacquered stand, was a basket of a kind he had seen before only in the foyers of picture theatres, where it would have been filled with gladiolus spears. This one had half a dozen dolls in it, their spangled skirts fixed to bentwood crooks.

Nothing in her letters suggested any of this. She had subdued her liveliness there, limiting herself maybe to the way Mac saw her. Anyway, it had given him the wrong idea, and when she came back now, bringing in tea and a slice of Napoleon, he observed her with different eyes. She apologised for the Napoleon. It came from a shop.

'Oh,' he said, 'Sargents.'

She was surprised at that, and at his knowing already that she worked there, and he restrained himself from telling her greedily how much more he knew: the sweet-peas, the tomato jam she made that he and Mac had so often talked about and smacked their lips over, the forty-nine piece dinner set Mac had given her and Don as a wedding present, and how upset she had been when she broke the lid of a soup tureen the first time she washed it up. These facts seemed trivial now. He had made too much of them.

Several times, as they drank their tea, he caught her eye on him, a frankly puzzled look, and it was a while before he saw the reason for it. She had no idea really who he was. Mac, he saw, had never mentioned him, or if he had she had forgotten it.

She asked questions of him: where he came from – he gave her a quick sketch of Keen's Crossing – what he was doing in Sydney, where he lived. She came from Queensland herself. Had he been up there? He told her about the boxing. He had never found it so easy to talk about himself.

Once the preliminaries were over they barely mentioned Mac. She simply took it for granted that what he had come for, now that he was here, had to do with her.

The idea alarmed him at first. It took him a little time to get used to it. But once he did he had to admit that it was true, and had been right from the start. How quickly she had seen it! That was a woman for you. She was over forty, he guessed, working backwards from the date on the certificate, but hadn't lost the assurance of her own attractiveness.

She called the boys up to get a piece of Napoleon. They came in barefoot and in their house clothes, shorts and ragged shirts, and were awkward at first but found their tongues at last under her meaningful looks. He knew them already, of course. Ewen, the eldest was. He would be sixteen. The younger boy, Jack, was the high-jumper. They were making something down in the yard and were keen to get back to it. They shifted from foot to foot, and after a decent interval she relented and let them go.

So they came at last to the letters.

He had expected them to provide the climax of his visit and had prepared a speech. But so much had already happened that they seemed like an afterthought now, and when he said what he had to say it was in such a confused, emotional way that it sounded false.

'Goodness,' she said, when he told her what the envelope contained. She looked at it a moment, turned it over in her hands, then lay it, unopened, on the piano stool; and there it sat, very white and clean, for the rest of his visit.

He had expected her to open it and see how soiled the letters were, and from that how many times they had been unfolded and read. When she did not he was disappointed. She would do that later, he guessed, in private, after he left. Or would she? Once they got talking again she seemed simply to have forgotten they were there.

'I make too much of things,' he told himself. He knew how fond she was of Mac because he knew the letters. 'There's a lighter way of handling all this.' It would go, he thought, with the rowdy good humour the house had been filled with – till he stepped in and put a damper on it.

'Thanks for coming,' she said when he was on the doorstep again. 'Really. I appreciate it.'

He swallowed hard. He wanted to say something to her. 'Listen,' he wanted to say, 'You don't know this – how could you? – but I watched you drink a glass of water once and it was amazing. It wasn't you, I see that now. It was a you I made up. But it was amazing just the same. An ordinary glass of water, can you imagine it?'

What he actually said, and he was staggered later by his own temerity, was: 'Would it be all right if I called again?'

If she was surprised she gave no indication of it. 'Of course,' she said. 'Any time. Only not on weekdays. You know, because of the shop. This time Saturday is good.'

'Oh, I saw you coming,' she laughed. 'Saw you a mile off.'

They were lying together on the narrow bed in his room, high up on the third floor of the Pomeroy.

'What d'you mean?' he asked, turning his head so that she wouldn't see his smile. He loved it when she presented him to himself. It was like seeing someone else. He had had no opportunity before this to indulge himself.

'You had messages written all over you,' she told him. 'In nine languages.'

'Did I?'

All this delighted him.

But after a moment he said solemnly: 'It was Mac that I was coming about, that first time.'

She might have questioned this. She did not think so. And the second? But Digger was sensitive on the point. He did not want it to appear that he had used Mac, or the letters, to come to her. He was too scrupulous, she wouldn't have minded; but it was his own integrity he was concerned with. When she saw that, she let him have things his way, and clung to what she knew.

He had gone out the second time on foot. It wasn't much more than a mile and he wanted to take things slowly, no need to rush.

He was going now on his own account. The other business, Mac's, had been settled on the first occasion; so far as it ever would be. He felt light-hearted, youthful. It didn't worry him that he didn't know the right forms for this sort of thing. She would understand that and make allowances. She had an infinite understanding (that's the impression he had taken away) of all sorts of things; things he had no notion of.

He was very conscious of the fact that at twenty-five he was entirely without experience in some matters. Courtship and that – the sort of gallantry that some fellows can manage by instinct, he had none of. But he had a great tenderness in him. Surely if he let that speak it would be enough.

Still, he had armed himself, just in case, with a bunch of flowers, purple and red anemones wrapped in pale tissue. The old girl he bought them from, who looked after six or seven buckets in a laneway, and sat reading the Bible all day on a folding stool, had recommended them as the freshest at this time of the week, and seeing how nervous he was had taken trouble with the wrapping. The flower heads with their strong colours and black furry centres, as if fat bumblebees were at them, just peeped out over the sky-blue tissue, and there was a bit of ribbon, a darker blue.

He felt awkward carrying flowers. He held them downward at arm's length where they were not so noticeable; he wasn't one of those blokes in light suits and polished shoes you saw ringing the doorbell of apartment houses, stepping about impatiently in front of the bronze door and checking how they looked, their parting, their ties, in its diamond panes. Still, he didn't care if he looked foolish. Who was looking, anyway?

He had felt such a warmth of life in her. He was chilled to the bone sometimes, for all the strong sunlight here.

She was dressmaking when he arrived. She came to the door in her stockinged feet, in a frock of some shining material, green, with the pins still in it; and when he followed her into the front room a neighbour, a young newly-married woman, was there. They were drinking beer. Snips of the material like big pointed leaves were in pools all over the floor, and the neighbour, who was a blonde, had a mouthful of pins. She said hullo through them and giggled.

Apologising for the mess, she put the flowers for a moment on the piano stool, just as she had the letters, and promising him a beer in just a moment if he would be patient till they got round the last bit of hem, climbed on to a chair. He saw then that the hem was not quite fixed.

The blonde girl, whose name was Amy, got down on her knees with the pins in her mouth and went on with it, glancing up every now and then to take a look at him. He guessed from this that she already knew about him. So Iris had mentioned him! Her quick little glances were glances of appraisal; she was a second opinion. He laughed at this and did not feel intimidated. Quite the opposite, in fact. He was enjoying himself.

Iris turned in a slow circle above them – Amy kneeling, he in one of the genoa velvet chairs – shifting her stockinged feet very daintily, an inch at a time, with her arms at her side and her head lowered a little to follow the progress of the work.

It was a quiet business and took a bit of time; the quietness imposed by the fact that one of the two parties (he thought of himself as a mere spectator) could not speak because of the pins.

To Digger it was a lovely moment, he had known nothing like it. He was happy just sitting. But the hem was done at last, found satisfactory, and she got down, told him how patient he had been, took the flowers to put them in water, got him a beer, brought the flowers back in a glass vase, and they sat and chatted.

She was a lively girl, Amy. She kept them laughing with tales about her three sisters-in-law, who were called Faith, Hope and Charity – could you believe it? – so that they hardly spoke to one another. Just sat sipping the cold beer and looking. Once or twice Iris turned away in profile and he saw that the hairs on her neck, where she had pinned it up so that Amy could fix the collar of the new frock, were darker, damp with sweat.

'Do you dance, Digger?' Amy asked him in her uninhibited way. 'Ben and I go every Friday night. Do you like Perry Como? Have you seen *The Sign of the Cross*?'

As she fired off her questions, and he answered them, Iris gave him half-amused, apologetic looks that assured him that she was not responsible for this inquisition, and he believed it; she was quite capable of putting her own questions. But she didn't cut Amy short either.

The only thing that worried him was that he might be too old-fashioned for them, for *her*; too out of it. He was embarrassed still by the number of things people took for granted here that he had not yet caught up with. Amy was full of them. He didn't want to be shown up. He bluffed, made a mental note of these puzzles, and wondered who he could go to later and ask.

When the boys arrived they came in a storm, shouting and dumping their boots in the hall. Ewen's team had won, six-three. That was a cause for celebration. With a quick little look that dared her to protest, he took a good swig of his mother's beer. His eyes were on Digger, summing him up, Digger was aware of that, but gave no indication of what they saw.

Jack, the younger boy, was already off out the back and was soon calling.

'I've got to fly,' Amy said, gathering up her things. 'Here,' she told Ewen, 'leave your mother's beer and finish mine. It's only a few drops,' she told Iris. 'I'll get murdered if Ben's tea's not on time.'

She took one last look at the frock, which was hanging now from the picture-rail, to satisfy herself of her own workmanship, took a look at Digger too, actually *winked* at him, and went.

He went himself a minute later; he had to be at the club by six. So that was all there was to it. But it was agreed that he should pick her up after work on Monday and they would do a show.

Lying quietly at his side she got him to tell her stories, and what he had to tell – his mother and father, Jenny, everything about Keen's Crossing – seemed stranger than it had been in the living of it. Why was that? Because he was seeing it through *her* eyes.

One thing he told her shocked him. He hadn't thought about it for nearly twenty years. If his memory were not so good he would have said he had forgotten it. It was the cruellest thing he had ever done.

Once, when she was about eight years old, Jenny had gone up to the highway above the house and somehow or other got herself to the other side. This was forbidden, and she knew it. Why had she done it this time? Anyway, once she was across her courage entirely failed her and she dared not cross back.

It started to get dark and, lost out there, she began to whimper and call. He heard her, crept up under cover of the bushes, and sat there, well hidden on the other side, and watched to see what she would do. She would come up to the edge of the road on her stumpy legs, screw up her courage to cross, then sit down again and weep; then come to the road again and walk up and down the edge of it as if just minutes ago it had ceased to be dirt and gravel and become a deep-flowing stream. He watched for a long time, appalled, but fascinated too by her helplessness. Finally she sank down in the growing dark and in a hopeless way sobbed his name. Over and over, 'Digger, Digger' – it gave him the creeps. At last, pretending he had just arrived, he stepped out into the middle of the road, stood a moment, then went quickly and took her hand.

He was a long time silent after he told this.

'Where is she now?' Iris asked.

'That's just it,' he said, and realised why it was that the occasion had now come back to him. 'She's run off somewhere. My mother thinks Brisbane. She's terrified – mum, I mean. She's scared we'll all do it, go off one after another. Dad did. Now Jenny.'

'What about you?'

'Oh, I haven't gone off. She knows that. I'm different.'

He told her stories of his mother, too, and was surprised to see from her reaction that he had made his mother fearsome, whereas what he had meant her to see was what a fierce grip on life she had – how she had given that to him too at times up there, when it was her presence, her demands on him, that had got him through. She sounded hard, but she wasn't, not by nature. It was circumstances that had made her hard.

'We think the same way,' he explained, partly to himself. 'On'y she doesn' see that. Because the things I've got to hold on to aren't the same as hers. Some of them are. But most of 'em aren't. She can't see it.'

He described the things his mother held on to and told Iris of the room she believed she would sit in one day surrounded by all her worldly possessions; only by then they would be *otherworldly*. Still real and touchable, useable too, but as she too would be then, past all possibility of loss.

'Just ordinary things,' he explained, in case the picture wasn't clear to her. 'She's not grasping, it's not that. She does want the things for what they are now, but what she really wants them for is what they will be then. What they will show about her. Her life.'

Iris looked at him rather hard. 'And what about you?' she asked. She was only indirectly interested in what he had to say of his mother. 'What are the things you need to hold on to?'

He told her a few of them. At last he told her how the two officers had come and asked him to keep a list of the names – the names and what happened in each case, insofar as it was known, to the men: a record, a kind of history. That was one thing.

Billy, James, Leslie, May, Pearl – that was another.

Then he told her, as well as he could, what he hadn't told McGowan, and actually said the words: 'Not a soul. Not a pin.'

187

The flames he was thinking of were the ones that had leapt up round the teak logs in the clearing at Hintock Pass, which was just one fire of the many into which all the cast-offs, all the refuse and broken-down and worn-out rubbish of the world, goes when its newness has worn off, and those who have scrabbled to get and keep it no longer care whether it goes up in flames or down the sewer, or simply gets stamped back into the earth.

You couldn't save it from destruction. And you couldn't make it whole again. Not in fact. But in your head you could.

She listened. She touched his cheek, and lay the tips of her fingers to the place, just above the line of his hair, where a vein beat, feeling its steady throb.

He also told her at last how Mac had died. She listened without looking at him, holding his head against her so that his breath, while he spoke, was on her flesh. After a time she asked quietly: 'Was he buried?'

'What?'

The question surprised him.

'No,' he said at last. 'We never saw him again, the body or that. The Japs would've buried 'im.'

'The word they sent,' she told him, 'was that he was missing. That's all we ever heard.'

'No,' Digger said. 'I saw what happened to him.'

She was silent a while, then sat up a little and told him a story of her own.

'Listen,' she said. 'When I was little, ten or eleven, maybe, we lived up near Gympie in Queensland. My dad had a farm. There were four of us, four girls, I was the second eldest, and my mother's mother, our grannie, lived with us. She was very difficult. She and my mother never really got on. She had asthma and was too weak to get about. She'd sit all day out on the front verandah, and what I remember best is the rug she had. I'd never seen the sea then, but it was sea-colours, all blues and greens and purples in waves. She'd crocheted it herself, so they must have been her favourites.

'They used to tell me I was like her. I mean, I was supposed to be difficult too. My mother would say: "You're just like your grandma," but in fact I didn't like her very much, and if my sisters said it, you know, copying her, I'd pull their hair. Can you see me doing that?

'Anyway, there was a flood. They came out to warn us. Our place was out of town, so we had time to save things. I remember they put a whole lot of furniture, beds and chairs, a sideboard, our sofa with a birdcage on it, on the grass in front of the house waiting for a wagon to take it. I remember how strange it looked. But the river came down quicker than they expected, and in the end there was a real panic. We had to get away in the night, and all the chairs and the sofa and that were swept away. I saw the water take them, it was amazing.

'The thing is, grannie wouldn't go. Or there was a quarrel or something at the last minute and she wouldn't get into the boat. I don't remember exactly, and later the story my mother told was different somehow. When we went back there was no sign of her. But for some reason I kept expecting her to turn up. I'd hear her wheezing in the middle of the night and get up and go to the verandah rails and expect to see her there.

'My mother got furious with me. I was just, you know, at the most difficult, growing-up stage, and we didn't get on either and she was upset by it. Maybe I was being difficult on purpose, I don't know. But I wouldn't accept that she was really dead.

'All our other relations were buried right on the property. We used to go off and play funerals there and pick flowers and put them on the graves. You could read the stones. Being buried was what dead was, and we had never buried grandma. We'd never even seen the body. You can't bury people in water, and water comes back, those floods did. You'd see the light of them off in the trees. I used to go out in the moonlight and look at the light there in the paddocks, under the trees, and the strangeness of it, to me, had somehow to do with my grandmother.'

That was the story. She did not add to it, and he saw after a while that it was her husband she was speaking of, though she did not name him.

What they were doing with the things they told was revealing to one another, in the only way they could, all that was closest to them, but tracing as well the limits of their freedom.

The one or two nights a week that she came to his room were when they had been out to a show and the boys could be left with something cold. Digger could always get someone to cover for him. She never stayed late, nor did she ever invite him to stay at Bondi Junction; and even later, when things were on a settled basis and he came up from Keen's Crossing and stayed overnight, they preserved the fiction of being no more than friends. She made up a bed for him on the sleep-out and came to him there.

It was the boys she was thinking of. 'I'm a middle-aged woman,' she told Digger lightly. 'Forty-three,' and she shook her head in a girlish way, as if in her real self she didn't believe it. 'Oh, you mightn't think of that, but *they* do. I'm supposed to be past all this. That's how young people think.'

The boys wouldn't have worried, even at the beginning, and certainly not later; or so Digger thought. She was observing her own code.

He would lie, still in his singlet, and watch her undress, liking best the moment when, in just her petticoat at last, she would tilt her head first to one side, then to the other, and take off her earrings; then her rings; the pearl-and-diamond engagement ring first, then the wedding band, placing them carefully on the marble top of the wash-stand. This was the real sign of her nakedness. That she kept on her petticoat and he his singlet had nothing to do with it.

Later, when she got up, he would lie and watch her do the whole thing in reverse.

Only when she came to the earrings, then the engagement and wedding ring, was she no longer naked for him.

3

In the afternoon he liked to sit quietly for an hour or so in the bar of the Waratah. Towards five it got crowded, and by half-past fellows would be ordering in half-dozens and lining the glasses up along the sill. He'd slip off then, get a bite to eat and stroll round in a leisurely way to the club.

One afternoon he was holed up in a corner, just enjoying the soft light and the scent of coolness, when he glanced up for no particular reason and Vic was there. He was on a stool at the other end of the bar and had been watching him; goodness knows for how long.

Digger felt a jolt of panic. It was uncanny the capacity this cove had for unsettling him. The once or twice they had run into one another there had been a kind of constraint that had grown at moments to open hostility.

Vic eased himself off the seat, and when he came up it was with a look of surprise and feigned indifference that made Digger furious. Why could he never be open with you? This was no accidental meeting. He had been hearing all week about this bloke who was asking around for him.

'So, what've you been up to?' Digger asked when they were settled over a beer.

Vic looked at him, and there was a little play of light in his eyes. He was preparing some cock-and-bull story, some lie maybe, that he wouldn't even expect you to believe. He would just throw it out in contempt, and defy you to take offence at the effrontery of it. 'Blast 'im,' Digger thought. But when he spoke it sounded like the truth.

'Been out west,' he said. 'Moree.'

'Oh? You don't come from out there, do ya?'

Digger was holding himself in, keeping calm and at a distance. It struck him how little he knew of the bread-and-butter things of Vic's existence. What he did know he wanted to keep away from. It was too intimate for here. He felt a weakness in his gut. He was inwardly trembling. At the mere sight of Vic a shadow of fever had flickered over him and his body was responding to it now with shivers.

'Nah,' Vic said. 'Thought I'd go out an' take a look at what we were supposed to be fighting for.'

Digger looked up enquiringly.

'We might as well 'ave let the bastards have it,' he said, 'if you want my opinion.' He laughed, tipped his head back, opened his throat and poured down the rest of his beer.

'He's been on the booze,' Digger thought. 'Or he's off-colour somehow. Crook.' He felt the pull on him to say something now, as if, for all Vic's offhandedness, what was really being appealed to was an arrangement between them that was still in operation, because there was no way it could not be. Digger was shaken. He had thought, back here, that he might be finished with all that, that this place was to be all beginnings. But once bitten there was no shying away. The medicos had told them that.

'What about you?' Vic was asking. 'How they treatin' ya?'

'Oh, good,' Digger said, and swallowed. 'Pretty good.'

He could barely speak. Suddenly he had seen what it was in Vic that touched him, and it was something he did not want to touch.

They had been prisoners of the Japs up there; anyway, *he* had been; so were Ern and Doug and the rest. It was one of those things that just happened to you, if you were unlucky enough to be in the wrong place. But that wasn't how Vic saw it. The Japs for him were only part of it, so it hadn't ended for him. It was still going on. 'What's more,' Digger thought, 'he wants to drag me into it.' He had even kept the look of a prisoner. And deliberately too, or so Digger thought.

It was a sickness he did not want to get too close to. Maybe you could pick it up just by seeing it in someone, someone you were too close to; or just by realising it could exist.

'Thought I'd try the big smoke again,' Vic was telling him. 'Give it another shot.'

He looked up. There was only one thing Digger could say. 'Got a place?' he asked, and looked quickly away.

'Yair,' Vic said after a moment, and Digger could feel the tension break between them. 'Yair, I'm all right that way. Thanks, mate.'

They sat for a time in silence, Digger all emotion, Vic calmer now. They talked. Digger's mind began to wander. He kept falling through holes in the conversation that were no bigger than single words sometimes, but the distance he fell was hundreds of miles. He began to sweat. All that brutalisation up there had left a weakness in him, a part of his mind that was open on one side to absolute darkness, and the stench that came from that direction was so powerful at times that he gagged on it, not daring to turn his head, even in the clearest sunshine, for fear of having to face again the tattered columns of them, big-boned, filthy, with their muddy eyes and outsized hands and feet.

They went out into the street together, stopped at a pie stall and sat down side by side in the gutter to down a pie.

Digger barely tasted his. Vic offered to finish it. When they parted on the footpath outside the club he was still shaking, and he knew for certain now. It was the malaria. A return bout.

It hit him harder than he expected. He was carried back, not just months, but three or four thousand miles, to a place of jungle heat and wetness that had nothing to do with geography – he knew about geography – but was a condition his body had surrendered to once and could never now be free of. With the physical symptoms came all the troop of events and visions and ghosts he had thought he might be rid of back here. He had thought *she* might rid him of them, but no power on earth could do that.

He was one again among others and could barely make himself out among them, they were all so tattered and thin. They closed in on him, stifling his breath, and when he tried shifting in the ranks to get a glimpse of her, of her sunlit figure through the press, they were too many; thin as they were, mere bones some of them, as if they had just hauled themselves upright out of the mud, they stood between him and even the smallest chink of sunlight, holding their hands up like begging bowls with nothing in them, and each one in a whisper saying the syllables of their own name over and over, as if only in that way could it be kept in mind, in their own mind or anyone's. Anyone's.

Digger tried, against the great hissing sound they made, to speak his own name, but his mouth was dry and he had no breath. He tried to think it, but his head now was filled with *their* names, and he had given his word, officially, and was afraid in his weakened state that he might forget one of them, let it slip. How could he ever face the man, knowing he had let go of him so that he was no longer present and accounted for?

193

But his own name was safe enough. It was buried somewhere. He would dig it up again later.

He had to survive. If he didn't, how could they, since so many of them were now just names anyway, with no existence save as syllables in someone else's head? In *his* head.

His mind went back to that swarm of tiddlers in the river. He felt the touch of the stream, then the tiddlers striking and striking in fury as they tore at his flesh; but with a touch, though it was all selfishness and savagery on one side, that on the other was the gentlest healing. It could also be like that.

His eyes clapped open. The voices now were roaring up from the street. There must be a huge mob down there, all shouting their names and holding their faces up like empty bowls.

A face tilted towards him. Hands brought a coolness to his brow. *She* was here. No, it was a man's hands. Vic's. The whispering rose in a great shuddering wave and he was swept under again, and he battled with it, half-drowning in scald.

He blinked, opened his eyes again, this time on silence, then lapsed a moment, rolling back months into wet heat; then blinked himself back again into the room.

'So. You've decided to come back to the living.'

It was Frank McGowan. He was looking up over a newspaper, with glasses halfway down his nose. He lay the paper aside and took them off.

'How you feeling?'

'I'm all right,' Digger said weakly. 'What are you doing here?'

'Playing nurse. Any complaints?'

'Was that you?' Digger asked.

'Yair. You want to try an' eat something?'

He got up off the cane-bottomed chair and busied himself for a bit at the gas ring with a little saucepan and a tin of soup. He was in shirt-sleeves and braces.

He brought a bowl and spoon and sat on the edge of the bed, preparing to feed Digger with the spoon, but Digger put his hand up. He put the spoon back in the bowl.

'How long have you been here?'

'Not too long. You've been sick for three days.'

He opened his mouth and let McGowan feed him warm pea soup.

'I suppose I've been saying things,' he said after a moment.

'Not much. Here, you should try and get a bit more of this down you.'

'How did you know?' Digger asked. 'That I was crook. The room and that.'

'Oh, I'm a cop, remember?' He met Digger's eyes with his own and there was a flash of humour in them.

'I should be at work – it must be nearly six.'

McGowan took the bowl away. 'It is,' he said. 'Six in the *morning*. Anyway,' he added, 'you're out of a job.' He was fussing about at the gas ring. He turned and faced Digger.

'The club was raided,' he explained. 'Wednesday night. Stroke a' luck, really – f'you. Being crook when it occurred.' He seemed pleased with himself.

Digger frowned. He didn't need anyone to take charge of his life.

'Nah, that was just good luck,' McGowan said, as if he had seen what Digger was thinking. 'Or maybe you'd prefer to have been taken in.'

'I'd be safe enough,' Digger said sharply. 'I've got friends in the force.'

McGowan looked at him and laughed. But Digger was failing. In just seconds he was delirious again. But he saw what McGowan was now. He was an agent for his mother. How on earth had she recruited him?

4

When Digger was in the third grade at primary school, and the teacher allowed them for the first time to take home books, he had for several months been obsessed with atlases and maps of every sort. Kneeling up at the kitchen table to get closer to the lamp, he would screw his eyes up so that he could read even the smallest print, and making himself small, since whole towns in this dimension were no larger than fly-spots, would try to get hold of what it was here that he was dealing with, the immensity of the world he had been born into, but also the relation between the names of things, which were magic to him, and what they stood for, towns, countries, islands, lakes, mountains.

Countries, for instance, the shape of them.

Each one was its own shape entirely, cut out of the whole, out of earth and water, and resembling nothing in nature but itself. The shape was random, determined only by the way a bit of coastline ran or the course of a river, or by the language people spoke, or by battles that had been fought whole centuries ago; but once you were familiar with it you couldn't imagine how it could be otherwise – Spain or Italy or Australia – any more than you could imagine a different shape for the things that nature had evolved or that men had designed to fit a use. A moth, for instance, a sleeve. And the names also fitted. 'Moth' was perfect for the furry thickness and powdery wings of the creature, as 'sleeve' was for what you slipped your arm through. But 'Italy'? 'Australia'? Yet once it was in your head the name perfectly evoked the shape of the country and contained it; the fit was perfect.

Patagonia, the *Pamir Plateau*, the *Great Bear Lake*. You let these names fall into your head and, by some process of magic, real places came into existence, small enough to find a place there with other names and places, as they also fitted on to a page of the atlas, but existing as well in a latitude on the globe that you could actually travel to, where they were immensities of water and rock and sky.

The world was so huge you could barely make your mind stretch to conceive of it. It would take days and nights, months even, for your body to cover in real space what you could spread your fingers across on a page; this is what Magellan and Vasco da Gama and Abel Tasman had had to prove. Yet whole stretches of it could be contained as well in just two or three syllables. You spoke them – it did not have to be out loud – and there they were: *Lake Balaton, Valparaiso, Zanzibar,* the *Bay of Whales.* And among these magic formulations, and no less real because it was familiar and he knew precisely what it represented, *Keen's Crossing.*

It wasn't in any atlas. You could hardly expect it to be. How could you get yourself small enough even to contemplate it, when a city of millions like Sydney was just a dot? But it was there all right, even if they hadn't put it in. He was sitting there. At a table, with the atlas open in front of him under a lamp.

He would fall into a dream. Letting his mind expand till it was as diffused and free-floating as a galaxy off at the limits of space, he would rove about, searching till he had located the world, a pin-point of light, far off and spinning. He would home in on it then, till he could see the exact point on its surface, in New South Wales, where *he* was: Keen's Crossing. He would find Broken Bay first, the mouth of the river; then, moving high up over it in the dark, follow the twists and turns of it till he saw the wharf, the store, the lighted window, his head like another globe bent low over the atlas, and could slip back into it.

His mind would be dazzled, like a moth that had been drawn in out of the dark and was at the centre now, dazed but excitedly fluttering. Around him, in pitch darkness, the Scotch firs soaring sixty feet towards the stars, the pepper tree, the clothes-lines touched with moonlight, the beginnings of an immensity of scrub.

How much of all this was contained by the name he could not determine. There was no visible border. Not enough, clearly, to make a showing in the atlas, but quite a lot if you thought of all the dust you had to wade through to get from the ferry to where the highway crested the ridge; or considered the millions of ants that were scurrying about over the dried-up leaves and twigs of it.

He did see a map at last on which Keen's Crossing was marked. A fellow at the ferry showed it to him, a government surveyor, unfolding the big sheet across the bonnet of his car while they rode across. A dotted line showed the river-crossing, and there was a dot, a red one, to mark the store. Beside it, in italics, *Keen's Crossing.*

So there it was: his own name, Keen, making an appearance in the great world. On a map, along with all those other magic formulations, *Marcaibo, Surabaya, Arkangel.*

There was a tie, a deep one, between the name as he bore it and as the place did; they were linked. And not just by his being there. He could leave it – he would too, one day, he was bound to – but the link would remain. The name contained him, from the soles of his feet to his thatch of roughly scissored hair, wherever he might go, whatever might happen to him, as it contained as well this one particular bit of the globe, the Crossing, the store, all the individual grains of dust and twigs and dead leaves that made up the acres of the place, along with the many varieties of ants and insects and spiders, and the birds that flew in and out of it; all covered. There was a mystery in this that he might spend the whole of his life pondering, beginning at the kitchen table here; except that it was just one of the mysteries, and he knew already that there were others, equally important, that he would have to explore. Still, this one was enough to keep him going for the moment, and he saw, regretfully, that he might have to forgo all those other places, Mont St Michel and Trincomalee, however attractive they might be, if he was to get hold of this one, which he was linked to because he was born here, and because his name was on it, or *its* name on him.

What had Keen's Crossing been, he wondered, before his grandfather stopped here and claimed the crossing and built the store? Did it have any name at all? And, without one, how had anyone known what it was or that it was here at all?

It *had* been here, and pretty much as it was now, if you put back the trees that had been cut down to build the store and the ferry-landing and to make way for the road, and if you took away the clothesline, the three Scotch firs and the rosebushes and gerbera his mother had planted: the same high ridge of sandstone with its forest of flesh-coloured angophoras.

Nameless it would have been; untouched in all time by the heel maybe of even a single black. But here all right. And not even in the dark. You couldn't say that, just because *people* had no knowledge of it.

The same hard sunshine would have beat down on it, the same storms and slow winter rains. The same currawongs and magpies would have been here, blue finches, earthworms, tree snakes, frogs. But it was not Keen's Crossing. It wouldn't have known that there *were* any Keens, to drive their horses across the river and cut down the first tree and make a camp. It hadn't been waiting.

But then the two things met: his grandfather's axe and the hard trunk of one of its trees, and the first letter of a syllable cut into it. Keen meant sharp. The axe's edge was Keen. So the place got a name and he and it had found a connection that was unique in all the world. The shared name proved it.

Years later, in some of their worst times in Thailand, this connection would sustain Digger and help keep him sane, keep him attached to the earth; to the brief stretch of it that was continuous with his name and, through that, with his image of himself. He could be there at will. He had only to dive into himself and look about.

Time after time, in his own shape, or taking on the secret shape of some four-footed creature that could move freely past the guards, he would start running, and, with the air streaming behind him, leap bushes, rivers, over seas at last, and come down through the moonlit trees to where the store stood back from the edge of the river, with the great sandstone ridge behind it, and on the other bank a forested bluff rising sheer to the stars.

He was there now, sweating a little after his run; having come down again from where his fever had dragged him. He stood in the trees at the edge of the clearing and watched while his mother hung out the wash.

She wasn't expecting him, except that he was always on her mind; so she *was*, too. When he stepped out between the trunks he would not alarm her.

In a moment he would do it. But just for a bit he stood panting, letting the big drops of sweat roll off him, and watched her lift up and peg one wing, then another, of a sheet.

V

1

Vic, with the drowse of afternoon sleep still on him, stood in his undershorts, one bare foot on the other, his elbow against the dusty wall. The telephone receiver was loose in his hand. He stood with his head dropped, shaking it hopelessly from side to side. Round the old-fashioned speaking-horn fixed to the wall were scribbles in indelible pencil, numbers, names (some of them horses), an irregular heart doodled in a waiting moment, which was bleeding purple at the tip. Down the hallway a race was being called.

It was a men's boarding house in Surry Hills. He had been summoned to the phone just before tea.

Sprawled on his back in the airless heat, legs spread, mind empty, his body as flat as paper – one of a string of such fellows cut out of a single folded sheet – he had been tempted to call out 'Not in,' but had staggered up, still half in a dream, scratched his head and applied the receiver to his ear. It was Ma. Every Friday night she rang and they had the same three-minute exchange.

She wanted him to come home, of course; but after the first time she had never again tried to persuade or bully him. But she rang each Friday at the same hour, and though he was often tempted not to, he took the call. She was clever, Ma, and had infinite patience. Eventually he would give all this up and come back. She knew that and so did he. In the meantime, as lightly as possible, she hung on.

Sunday dinner – that was the open invitation, a surprise for Pa; no pressure, but the invitation was always there. One Sunday, yes, he promised, but he continued to put her off.

Back in the room he lay on the bed, not thinking, and stared up at the stamped-tin ceiling with its design of circles within squares, and inside the circles, fleurs-de-lis.

In these last years, when the population of the city had very nearly doubled, the big front room of the place, with its long sash-windows and fifteen-foot ceilings, had been partitioned with three-ply to make smaller rooms, he had no idea how many, each with its bare bulb hanging, its wardrobe, washbasin and cot. The long gap between the top of the partition and the ceiling meant there was no privacy here. All night you heard other men coughing, hawking, turning the pages of the Zane Greys they were reading, shifting on the rusty wires and groaning in their sleep. You participated, whether you cared to or not, in their dreams.

He was earning good money now and could easily have had a room of his own. But he couldn't sleep in a room of his own. He wouldn't have admitted it, even to Digger, but he couldn't get through the night. The one time he had taken a room in a hotel and tried it, he had woken in a cold sweat, filled with a panic he could not contain. He had had to go out and sit with the tramps at an all-night pie stall.

The proximities of this place, the indifference, the low-keyed despair of the other men, who were mostly older, were what he wanted; they suited him. So did his job.

For six months he had been out west, moving on from one township to the next and picking up any work he could get; as a greenkeeper in one place, a fencer in another. Out past Bathurst to Orange, then to Moree, Walgett and across the Queensland border. He had done that to lose himself for a while, but in the end had worked his way back. He was employed by the council now as a ganger on the roads, spreading gravel in front of a steamroller, all day in the heat and reek of tar. It was fierce work in the December sun. His hands were calloused and black. There were burn-spots where the hot tar spat. Some nights his arms felt as if they had been torn out of their sockets. But it was what he wanted.

He was home, he accepted that. It was a fact. But some stubbornness in him, a sense of outrage that he would not relinquish, still kept him captive, not to a place but to a condition. He did not *want* to be free of it. To be so would be to accept at last that what had been done to him could be ended and put behind him, and he could never accept that.

He was back, and could have whatever he wanted now, a room of his own, a girl, what Ma called a normal life. But he chose not to. The right to choose, even if the choice was against his own interest, was important to him. By living as he did now he made what had happened to him 'up there' – the deprivations and shame he had suffered, the misuse he had been subject to – that much less of a violation. 'You see, I might have chosen it anyway. Like I'm doing now.'

But he also chose, out of pride, not to let the Warrenders see him like this; however fond they were of him and whatever allowances they might be willing to make. He did not want allowances made. When he saw them again it had to be in his old self as he was before he went away. Those were the conditions he set.

In his last days in the camp, among other letters from Pa and Ma and Ellie, had been one from Lucille. It was written in a style that had immediately enraged him, which pretended to make light of the facts it had to tell and was entirely false. She was married, that's what she had to tell. To a Yank. And had a child.

He accepted these facts. He had a high regard for facts. What he did not accept was their finality. Like the things that had happened to him, they were a result of the extraordinary conditions of war, and were to that extent accidental. He chose himself not to be a victim of accident, in this case or any other. He would in time reverse these facts, but only when he was strong enough to take hold of things with something like his old power. Till then, he would have to wait.

The other men in the house were mostly winos. He met them in the dark hallway or on the steps outside, tottering home with a bottle of port in a brown-paper bag, or stopped halfway up the stairs and lolling. 'G'day, son,' was all they ever said. But one or two of them were old fellows, respectable enough, who had nowhere else to go. No woman any longer, maybe a son or daughter somewhere who had no room for them; or they had never had a family at all. They read the papers, took an interest in the races, exchanged cheap mystery books. To these men all this was normal. They did not look at him and wonder what he was doing here. They assumed he was as they were – only a few years earlier on the road.

He kept away from people he knew, or tried to; but occasionally, in a panic, would need the comfort of a familiar voice. He would go out shakily and ring someone. Douggy mostly, since Douggy was settled; more rarely, but he had done it once or twice, the Warrenders, hoping that he might catch Lucille. It was enough on most occasions just to dial the numbers and hear the phone ring. He could go back to sleep then. Or he would wait for the answering voice and stand listening a moment, too ashamed to speak.

But there were times as well when only one person would do, and that was Digger.

He hung off as long as he could. He hated this dependence and didn't understand it. But sooner or later he would give up fighting and seek Digger out. Once it was up the Cross. The next time he had to hitch-hike all the way up to the Hawkesbury, to Keen's Crossing.

Facing Digger took him right back. He would be shaking so badly at times he thought it must be the malaria coming back; it was *physical*. But it wasn't malaria, and after a little he would be calmer, then a great calmness would settle and spread in him; his spirit would go sleepy with it and it would last for days sometimes, like a laying on of hands.

He did not know why this was. He was moved, and grateful, and wished he had some way of showing it, but Digger needed nothing from him, barely knew, he thought, what had taken place. Digger was patient with him but also held him off. He felt hurt. He was touched at times by a spirit of generosity and affection for the world that broke something in him which needed, he knew, to be broken. He would blunder about empty-handed then, looking to some as if he were drunk, to others crazy, with the light-headed, swollen-hearted sense of being a bearer of gifts that would appear and declare themselves, *must* do, as soon as he found someone who would accept them from him.

2

'Well, he's coming,' Ma said, turning aside from her accounts. 'He's promised this time. But I'm not telling Pa till he's actually here. He'd be too disappointed. Oh,' she added, 'and I think it would be better if we didn't say anything, any of us – you know, about where he's been.'

Ellie did no more than glance up briefly from her book. It was Lucille who said sharply: 'For heaven's sake, why not?'

She was feeding creamed pears to little Alexander. The child, peeved at the interruption, at anything that came between him and the big warmth that shone so continuously upon him, shifted his gaze to his grandmother and his lip dropped. His mother was turned away from him. The spoon was in mid-air, inches from his mouth.

Mrs Warrender did not immediately reply. She understood Lucille's position. It was difficult to be a married woman and a mother, and to have a husband who was thousands of miles off and no household or home of your own. She knew too that where Vic was concerned Lucille was proprietorial. She had no right to be, but all that did was make her touchier.

'Well,' Ma said at last, 'I know Vic and he won't want to talk about it. If he brings it up himself it's a different matter. But he won't, I know he won't.'

Lucille glowered. In these last months she had grown increasingly impatient with Ma, and now that she was about to break free, increasingly critical, scornful even, of the way they lived, the evasions and half-truths they were driven to in being so sensitive always of one another's hurts. She wanted a life now that was robust, and open and honest, even if it hurt, and such a thing was impossible here. She was tired of being a married woman and still a child in her parents' house.

All the months she was pregnant she had felt wonderfully separate and self-contained. She had eaten what she liked, slept till midday, spent her afternoons stretched out in the sun; with none of her usual restlessness, and none of the vexations either that went with her 'difficult' nature. And there was no selfishness in it, because she was no longer thinking only of herself.

Separate, but at the same time connected and in the line of something: real *forces*, by which she meant forces that were outside her will.

Time, for instance.

The clock that had begun ticking in her, which was perfectly synchronised to the sun, was real time, not just clock time, and it synchronised her as well. It could not be stopped or slowed or quickened. She submitted herself to it and felt no violation; in fact the opposite, a kind of release.

Gravity, too.

One afternoon, in the dreamy state she fell into under the blazing sun, she had had a vision of herself as a cloud, so light and transparent that she might have dissolved or risen up and floated. But inside the cloud, far off in a spotlight at the very centre of it, a little figure was performing, not for an audience, not at all, but for himself. In a state of perfect self-absorption he was turning somersaults, and she could see him quite clearly, though in fact he was such a long way off. He wasn't weightless, but he appeared to know enough of the secrets of gravity to play the most astonishing tricks with it. She kept her eye on him; she wanted to learn the secrets of all this – of lightness, but also her own true weight in the world.

For months, with her eyes screwed up against the sun, her feet propped on the arms of a squatter's chair and a jug of Meggsie's lemon drink at her elbow, she had watched him perform. He was very small and far off at first, but the far-offness had to do with time, not space. He grew as he got closer; till he was so close she no longer had to squint to make him out.

Never for a moment in all this did she feel anxious for him, or for herself either. She would not float away and he would not fall. They were held, both of them.

And she did not have to feel impatient either. He was moving in his own time and would not be hurried. *He* was the clock. Somewhere up ahead, at a point they had not yet arrived at, he was already sitting up in his high-chair and banging with a spoon. All she had to do was wait the days out till they were there.

'Well,' she said now, 'I know Vic, too.' She urged the child to open up for a last mouthful. 'You're doing just what he wants. All this carrying on! It's to make us see what a sensitive soul he is and how careful we ought to be with him, that's all. And to make himself the centre of things.'

Ellie looked up again. It was the note of vehemence in Lucille's voice, not the words themselves, that shocked her.

'That's got nothing to do with it,' Ma said, and she too was angry now. 'Honestly, Lucille, there are times when I don't think I know you at all.'

Lucille flushed. It was humiliating to her to come under her mother's criticism and be rebuked. She took up her things, set Alexander on her hip, and stalked from the room.

'Why are you so down on Vic?' Ellie asked later, when they were alone together in Lucille's room, the child on the bed between them. Lucille was sitting up cross-legged threading a needle.

'Am I?' she said.

'Yes, you are. And you haven't even *seen* him. You upset Ma, too. You know how fond she is of him. What's the matter with you?'

Lucille went on with her needle. After a moment she lowered her work and said fiercely: 'He thinks he's the only one in the world that anything's *happened* to. I know Vic. I don't have to *see* him.'

Ellie drew back. She knew these stormy, half-tearful, half-defiant moods in her sister. They were close, and had been even closer in these last months since Lucille was alone.

The three years between them made a difference.

Ellie had been too young to go out with Americans – Pa wouldn't allow it; but she had hung about when they appeared (just as in the movies) with an orchid in a square cellophane box, or chocolates, or nylons, had sized them up in her quick down-to-earth way, and afterwards, when she and Lucille, still in her dancing dress, were rolling about on one of their beds, whispering, laughing, comparing, criticising, could catch just the drawl with which this one said, 'We sure do, ma'am,' or the self-satisfied sprawl or little military stamp and snap of others, or the boiled look of this one, or the muscle-bound, collar-jerking shyness of another, a certain Virgil Farson Jr of Greenwood, Mississippi, who had not been Lucille's favourite at the start, not by any means, then was. In the Virge business she had known at every point what Lucille was up to. To the extent that Ma actually blamed her for not telling and had not spoken to her for a week.

When Vic went away Ellie was fifteen. They were friends and she was fiercely loyal to him. She had taken it for granted that in the end Lucille would choose *him* – there was such a tie between them – and that their other little affairs and flirtations were no more than a kind of teasing play to conceal the inevitability of it.

'No,' Lucille told her gravely, 'that was just kid's stuff. Don't you know the difference?' She was so sure of herself that Ellie wondered what she had missed.

Still, when she got pregnant there was the sense all round, but especially on Ma's part, that a mistake had been made.

Lucille did not think so. She broke the news to Ellie as a sworn secret, and with so much awed excitement and triumph (Ellie had never seen her at once so elated and sober and overwrought) that Ellie had felt a little thump in her own belly at the immensity, the serious adultness of it.

Lucille, she told herself, was right. She was still a schoolgirl and had no grasp of things. Even in the midst of the war, when so much that was terrible had occurred, she had simply gone on in the old way, believing that life, their life, was a story that could end only one way, according to the rules of the films she went to and the romances she read. Lucille had broken through all that, and for all their closeness she had not seen it.

For the two weeks that she had Lucille's secret to keep she had looked on her sister as a being transformed, suddenly endowed with urgency and purpose.

The germ of light that with each passing second was swelling and rounding in her had drawn Lucille into the line of life; and it had been put there, amazingly, in such a precise and effective way, though also no doubt in his usual barging manner and with no clear intent, by Virgil Farson, a big slow boy of less than twenty. At that moment three thousand miles away in the Islands he was lounging about an Air Force base reading his Felix the Cat comics, quite ignorant yet of what he had done.

These facts astonished Ellie. She had gone about the house in a dazed state, aware suddenly of how fragile and important things could be and feeling her bond with Lucille immeasurably deepened. Lucille had crossed a border. Ellie felt that she too had come to the edge of it and was shining now and swelling in sympathy.

It was an exaggeration, of course. She had been stirred by her own possibilities, that's all, had felt the pull in her own nature of the change in Lucille's. She soon came back to earth.

But the little life she had been so aware of then as a mere floating presence, a new, nameless one that had turned towards them and was starting for a point maybe sixty or seventy years away was no longer nameless. It was this odd little Alexander; who filled the house with his squalls and hungers, his smells too, and was at this moment lying on the bed between them, singing to himself, kicking up his heels, and when she put her face down into his naked belly, uttering squeals of ecstasy.

'Do you think he'll be so different, then?' she asked, lifting her head. She was asking on her own account, rather wary now of what it might be that she had not understood.

Lucille was more upset than she would admit. She made a mouth and turned away. It was too difficult. She couldn't put it into words.

He would be, of course he would. He must be. Weren't they all? So much had happened in these last years. But Vic, she knew, had a way of closing himself off from mere happenings. It was a strength; it was also, from another point of view, a weakness. The more he was touched by a thing the more he did it.

He would be changed, sure enough, perhaps horribly, and the possibility of that, however small her own part in it, was painful to her. But he would pretend not to be, and at the same time would want you to see through it and pity him.

So when Sunday came round and he did appear as promised – she heard the bell, then the clamour they were making in the hall, even Meggsie and Aunt James – she did not go down immediately. She took a little extra time, not on herself, she spent no time at all on herself, but on the child. When she came to the door of the front room they were all gathered around him, Ma, Pa, Meggsie, Aunt James (Ellie was still out at her tennis match), in a close family group. He was the lost son come home; they were making a royal fuss of him. She felt shut out. Had she always, secretly, been resentful of his place among them? Was Ellie? But when he turned, and she saw the quick, clenched look of him, she felt ashamed. She went up quickly, holding the child and relying on his warmth and weight to steady her, and kissed him on the cheek. She was shocked. He was no thinner than in the old days but he had a flayed look that went straight to her heart.

The others, Ma, Pa, Aunt James, were watching. She told herself that she had to be careful now of her own emotions. The moment was critical.

His hair, which was brutally short, shaved right up above his ears, gave him the look of a convict. Was that deliberate? She was moved by this but warned herself that she could not trust him. They stood very close, with the child between them, who was crowing and working his fingers in the air.

'How old is he?' Vic asked.

He was staring at the child in a perplexed way, as if he had not expected him to be quite real or had underestimated how much innocent energy and egotism he would possess. The child was laughing and looking from one to another of them with no doubt at all that he was the most important person here.

'Hello, cobber,' Vic said when the child reached out and made a grab for his shirt.

'Alexander,' she told him.

'So you see,' she wanted to add, 'we're no longer the youngest ones – not any more.' She thought this might reconcile him a little, make him see things, as she did, in the longer view.

He put his hands out then and took Alexander from her. She felt the weight go, saw how rough and scarred his hands were, and was surprised by his gentleness, but did not lower her guard. The child had knocked him off balance, that's all. He would be looking now for a way of restoring himself. The child was on his arm and Vic was hefting him up and down as if assessing his weight.

It made her want to laugh, that. He could not enter into rivalry with a fourteen-month-old child. It was too undignified and the odds were too much on the child's side. He was looking for a way round. 'What funny creatures we are,' she thought, and relaxed a little. 'So transparent.'

'He's heavy,' Vic said, and all the time the others were quiet and watching.

'Oh, he's heavy all right,' she thought. '*I* could have told you that.'

She did laugh then. She was filled with such a wave of joy at the weight he added to the world, which she felt even when she herself was not holding him, and in the rush of it felt an affection for *him* too, for his hands that were so scabbed and swollen and for the sureness with which they held the child.

'Listen,' she wanted to say, 'can't we make this easy? There's been a war. Extraordinary things have happened. A boy came all the way from Mississippi to sleep with me; drafted into it by the War Office in Washington. He was nineteen. He had never left home. Now he's gone again, and it may be months before I can go to him, and Alexander is here, and the whole world is different. But it's all right. We're all fine – we're *alive*, aren't we? You can see just by looking at him how easy these things can be.'

He was very quick. She saw from his eyes that he had caught her moment of weakness towards him. He passed the child back, and when he put his hands in his pockets there was a little smile at the corner of his mouth, though he tried to conceal it. He had felt his strength again and was preparing to be difficult. There was a lightness in him and a little buzz, she could hear it, coming off the surface of his skin. She drew away.

She could say none of the things that just a moment ago had come to her lips.

He had felt like a ghost coming back here.

When he got off the train he had walked up and down the platform for a time consulting the timetables, the adverts, and deciphering the graffiti in the glassed-in waiting room; giving a good imitation of a man who had another train to catch.

What he was doing was hanging on to his last moments in limbo.

On a railway platform you can wait without question. You walk up and down with your hands in your pockets; stop to light a cigarette or unwrap a new stick of gum, and that's the limit of it; no obligation to justify yourself, or to greet others or even acknowledge their presence. You stand lifting yourself up and down on your toes and whistling. You stroll to the end of the platform and look down the quarter mile of lumped gravel that serves as a shunting-line. You turn and stroll back. Only when you have passed the boy in the cap and waistcoat who idles at the gate, given up your ticket, gone down the stairs to where taxis are waiting, have you arrived. 'I could stay here all day,' he thought when he had read the timetables twice, and the Bible message, and the ads for Vincent's APC Powders and Bushell's tea, 'or I could catch the next train back.' But suddenly, without thought, he walked to the end of the platform, took the stairs, and before he knew it was in the street.

213

It was a good walk to the house, but he knew every step. Only four years ago he had been a schoolboy here.

He stopped once to peer through the fence of a canning factory where he had gone with other kids to collect metal scrap.

Just beyond it was the ghost house, a verandahed ruin set far back behind beds of cannas and rusty-looking palms. It had been inhabited then by a batty old girl who wheeled a pram with a Pomeranian in it about the streets. The house was empty now and boarded up.

At the corner of Crane Street there was a place where eight or nine years ago, when he was thirteen, he had used his house key to scratch his initials, V.C.C., into the wet cement. They were still there under the prints of a dog's paws.

But there was a quickening in him as well, the re-emergence of a sense of himself that had been there from the moment he first told Ma that he would come.

The familiarity of the walk itself began to work on him, as his body, which had a memory of its own, slipped back into the easy knowledge of how many steps it was from the station to their front door. When he got there, he found himself, out of habit, feeling in his pocket for the key.

Two surprising things occurred when the front door was at last thrown open. Meggsie hugged him and burst into tears, and Aunt James, for the first time, recognised him as himself. 'It's Vic,' she called, just behind Meggsie in the hall.

'My God,' he thought, and felt a bubble of laughter rise in him. 'If *she* knows me I really must be a ghost!'

There were other changes. Pa announced them, a little too quickly, Vic thought, before he could discover them for himself, adopting a humorous tone that gave no indication of what he might really feel.

'I'm retired,' he told Vic. 'Put out to pasture, I reckon. Though officially it's so I can get on with my book.' Ma was making little sounds of disavowal, keeping up the game Pa made of it. 'Meet the new manager.'

'It's true,' she said, rather shy about it. 'I took over three years ago. Now there's a surprise for you!'

'Got rid of *me* first thing she could,' Pa said. 'Sacked for incompetence. For loafing on the job.'

'Rubbish!' she said. 'He couldn't put up with having a woman for a boss, that was the real trouble. Thought it was beneath his dignity.'

'Oh?' said Pa. 'I thought you were always the boss. I thought I was used to it.'

'Anyway,' said Ma, 'we're on top again, that's the main thing.'

'All these years,' Pa said, 'we had this secret weapon an' didn't even know it. We let Ma loose and the buggers fled.'

Behind all this raillery, Vic felt, there were tensions that only humour, their old rough-gentle humour, could deal with.

But it had changed Ma utterly, this move to the centre of their lives. All that had previously been lax in her had come to attention. The vagueness and languor that had seemed constitutional in her, the restless anxiety, had belonged only, it now appeared, to the conditions she had imposed upon herself – against nature, as it were; first to make way for her brother Stevie, then for Pa. When wartime changed the rules, she had simply stepped in and done what she had all along been intended to do; temporarily at first, while Pa was down with dengue fever, then, with scarcely a protest on his part, for good.

War economies had put a premium on local products. Ma, seeing the opportunity it offered, had acted and made a killing.

It astonished Pa that this woman he had lived with for twenty-five years, and known for more like forty, should suddenly reveal herself as a 'buccaneer'. She was a Needham, and her father's daughter, that's what it was. Pa, who had found the old man intimidating, a bit of a ruffian in fact, was amused, but awed too, by the extent to which he reappeared now in female form. He teased Ma and made a joke of it – that was his style – but was disturbed.

Ma too found it easier to present what had happened as a freak of the times. She was pragmatic, Ma. It was one of the qualities she had had no opportunity to reveal till now, but once liberated, she gave it rein, like the rather salty humour that went with it. The agent of her liberation had been, of all things, the Japanese Imperial Army, though that, like so much else that had happened, was by the way. She had not been part of their Co-prosperity Plan.

It was too humorous a view, this, too odd, far-fetched even, to be admitted. She kept it to herself. People, she had discovered, were not very sympathetic to unusual views, however humorous they might be, or to those who expressed them.

Vic had caught the new note in her voice on the telephone. It was partly, he felt now, what had drawn him to come. There was a confederacy between them. It did not have to be evoked. All that had been settled years back in their uneasy consultations, when she had felt his commitment to her and had seen already, as he had not, that they might one day make a team.

She led him off now to see what she had been doing *out there* – in the factory, she meant – and without words, and taking the old relationship between them quite for granted, put it to him: we're partners, eh?

There was no coquettishness in it. She did not play up to the male in him by pretending to be weak or in need. It was an offer between equals. On both sides an opportunity that was too good to miss.

They were standing, dwarfed as you always were here, under the great cross-beamed ceiling of the factory, a place that bore an eerie resemblance, Vic thought, to a godown – but the shadow this threw across his spirit he immediately drove off.

You came in out of strong sunlight into coolness. But it was a coolness of a particular kind, a climate all of its own, and at the touch of it he felt something restored in him. It was like that first waking up into the real temperature of your body after days of fever, the crossing over a line between zones. He felt a goosepimpling all over the surface of him, and what came back, and with an immediacy he was quite unprepared for, was the last occasion he had come here, the eve of his departure.

A self-conscious, self-important eighteen-year-old, he had stood here to take temporary leave of his life, knowing nothing of what lay ahead. Now, five years later, with the knowledge of all that, which was still bitter in him, taken fully into account, he found he could look on his former self with none of the angry disappointment he had been consumed by in the months since he got back. He could face that humourless schoolboy, standing there so full of himself and making so many promises to the world, with detachment and a wary tolerance. There was no shame – or anyway, none so deep that it demanded the penalty of death – in having been eighteen, and so ignorant of what the world could do to you.

It was the place itself that brought this home to him, and he remembered something he had heard when he went down to Keen's Crossing but had dismissed till now as one of Digger's mystifications.

'It's all right for *you*,' he had thought, looking about the clearing and observing how completely Digger fitted in to it; so much so that he had found it difficult to imagine him in any other place – had he really been up *there*? But now he too felt it. Some impression of his presence had remained here and was waiting to be filled. He could, with no difficulty at all, step into it now as if he had never left.

3

At last Ellie arrived, dropped off by a noisy group in a red convertible. She stopped in the doorway a moment to apologise for being late. 'No, don't look at me,' she told Vic when he tried to go to her, 'I'm a mess,' and she ran off to change. When she came down again it was in a cotton dress with little ties at the shoulder and no stockings. 'Ah,' Pa said, 'here's our girl.'

When he left she had been at school; they were mates and had told one another everything. She threw her arms around him now as if nothing had changed between them.

He glanced across to see if Lucille was watching, but she was absorbed with the child, refusing, a little too deliberately he thought, to acknowledge him.

Ellie had a job. She had been drafted at first into a munitions factory, but was working now in a motor pool, driving a six-ton truck and doing all her own maintenance. She showed him her hands. She loved zooming about all over the city, and the long trips up to Lithgow or down the coast to Wollongong. You could tell this from the way she talked about it, and the others, who must have heard her tales a dozen times, seemed delighted to hear them again.

She got up now, still talking, and fetched a bowl of unshelled peanuts that Meggsie had set out. Taking one she cracked it in half, popped one nut into her mouth, then cracked the other half and, just as she would have done in the old days, passed it to him, all the time going on with the story she was telling.

It was as if he had never been away. She had never had for him any of the intimidating glamour of Lucille, so they could fall back now, almost without thinking, or so it seemed, into little unselfconscious habits, like this one with the peanuts.

The story ended, he laughed and she looked up and said, 'Eat your peanut.' He had been sitting with it in his hand.

Food had an almost mystical importance to him; any food, even a crust of bread. He hoarded things, even the most useless scraps and leftovers, but knew how odd it was and hid it.

He looked now at the peanut he was holding. Very slowly, he put it in his mouth and began to chew.

All through Meggsie's long Sunday dinner he did not look once at Lucille. In the front room afterwards he lounged, hands in pockets, in the window and watched her at play with the child.

There were just the three of them in the room. Ellie was on the phone in the hall. He could hear her laughing. The others had gone upstairs to rest. Lucille did not like being alone with him, he knew that, but was unwilling to make an issue of it.

It was a typical summer afternoon in Sydney, muggy, the sky heavy with a threat of storms. He had longed, up there, for the peculiar drowsiness of these long Sunday afternoons, with the luxury they offered of infinite time before afternoon tea, to trail across the golf links and down through the sticky paspalum to Hen and Chicken Bay, then supper, and afterwards, in the dark, their Sunday games. Now here it was.

Lucille had a pile of building-blocks. She would build them up in a pyramid, and the child, with a laugh, would punch out with his little fist and send them down. The same game over and over.

They had not spoken, but her eyes, even as she occupied herself with the child, kept touching him. He could feel it. He smiled to himself and began, very lightly, to whistle.

Lucille was disturbed. They had got through dinner well enough, but she saw that he had accepted nothing. She could feel the little pressure he was exerting on her to make a scene. She could not allow that.

It wasn't true that she had no feeling for what he had been through. But he was too full of his own experience to give any weight to hers, that's what she saw, and it angered her. He really did believe that only he had been touched. It was a way of telling himself that, unless he wanted it, nothing need be changed between them. That's what she was up against. But she didn't want a scene.

He went on whistling, very low and tunelessly. He was keeping his eyes peeled. She was pretending to be absorbed with the child, but that was a bluff; the real game, and she knew it, was with him. 'So,' he told himself, 'I've won *that* round.'

But the advantage was a weak one. She was weaving around herself and the child a circle of magical containment, and kept looking up now to see if he saw this and understood what it meant.

She was a mother. That is, she had become a woman – guaranteed. But there was no guarantee that what he had been through had made him a man. It was a way of putting herself out of reach. By treating him as if he were still a boy – the same one who had gone away.

He was hurt by the unfairness of this. It seemed to him he had earned the right to be treated as a man, but could not demand it. So he was caught all ways.

In this game they were now engaged in he was, for all his swagger, inexperienced. He knew that. But what else could he be? He had lost five years. The unfairness of it choked him, but he kept whistling.

She saw the truculence in him. She knew what it was, too. He was telling himself how hard life had been on him, urging them both towards a scene. She sighed. Then suddenly she saw their situation from outside all this, in the long view, and what she had to tell him was very clear. It's silly, all this. Our being so cross with one another. Don't you see, your unhappiness doesn't depend on me. But neither does your happiness. Don't you see?

She got to her feet and stood with her hands at her side looking at him.

He stopped whistling, his hands still in his pockets. He could not tell for a moment what she was up to, but did see that something had changed in her. The child felt it too. He was sitting on the floor with his face lifted, puzzled by her having got up so suddenly and removed her attention from him.

She came closer. His mouth was a little open. Quickly she bent forward and kissed the corner of it. It was what he had exerted all his powers to make her do; but now, when her lips touched his, his willing had nothing to do with it. He could claim no triumph and he felt none. She had deprived him of it by acting entirely unexpectedly and of her own free will; in a tender way, but one that dismissed the possibility of all passion between them.

She touched his cheek very gently with her hand, then calmly turned away to where the child had his hands up to be taken.

'That's the boy, Alex,' she said lightly, and lifted him, and took him off for his nap.

Vic looked about. He felt let down. Something critical had occurred but his understanding had not caught up with it. He pushed his hands deeper into his pockets and began to whistle again, but his heart failed him and after a bit he dropped it. He stepped from the window and went out to the hall.

There was no one in sight. Treating him as one of the family again, they had simply gone off without ceremony.

He walked up and down on the coloured tiles, feeling the assurance he had built up lapse and drain from him.

He sat down in one of the low-backed cherry-wood chairs that were ranged along the wall. They were ornamental. No one ever sat in them.

He got up quickly and went through the house to the kitchen to see if Meggsie was about. The big tiled room was immaculate, as always, but empty, everything washed up and cleared away.

He came back to the hallway, looked about a little, then went upstairs and tried the door to his room.

It was just as he remembered it. Nothing had changed. It gave him an odd little start, the thought that it had been here, clean, cool, ready, all the time he was *up there*, always in such filth and with nowhere to lay his head. A feeling of anger and self-pity came over him. He rested his brow against the closed door and clenched his fists.

When his passion had passed he turned back into the room and opened a drawer of the dressing table and saw socks there, underpants, too, all neatly folded.

He stood and looked at himself for a time in the mirror, then lay down full-length on the bed.

He did not sleep, but saw himself standing, as he had just a moment ago, at the open door, and the room he was looking into was empty again.

After a supper of cold meat and salad and his favourite pears and junket, Ma insisted on a game of hide and seek. She was apologetic about it – it was to keep Aunt James happy, who loved to sit in the dark and hear them scampering about; but it was really, Vic guessed, for him. It was a hectic affair. They were playing at play, and to make up for their lack of commitment, banged about more than they usually did.

Upstairs, under a net, little Alexander was sleeping, and Lucille, fearful he might be disturbed by the row they were making, kept one ear tuned for his cry. She was barefoot, her hair damp with sweat. Vic too was only half in the game.

At first Pa was It and he found Ma; then Ma found Vic. While the others trooped off to hide he stood with his face to the wall like a dunce in school and counted to a hundred before he was free to go off in his socks and look for them. Once or twice earlier, while they were rushing about seeking places to hide, he had collided with Lucille, but he was shy of her now. He set off to check the pozzies where one or other of them was sure to be squeezed in holding their breath. He knew all the hiding places.

He had let these rooms and their clutter of familiar objects go out of his life. But now, moving through them in the dark, his foot remembered every loose plank, he could judge without fault the precise distance from table-edge to sideboard. He never once bumped into anything. Whatever he felt for was there.

He covered the hallway, all the rooms down one side of it, including the dining room where Aunt James sat laughing, then crossed to the other. A southerly had come up. Each door he opened set the curtains blowing, and from beyond the windows he heard trees in motion. The moon was up, but all this side of the house was dark.

Hidden behind a curtain in what they called the piano room, Ellie saw the door open a crack and a figure appear. 'Damn,' she thought.

There was a time, years back, when she would have been breathless at this point with the wish to fool whoever it was that there was no one here. All she thought now was that if she was found *she* would be It and they would have to begin all over again.

The crack of half-light widened. It was Vic. She could see the shape of him poised there at the threshold, his body so alert that you could feel the energy of it like a new kind of heat in the room. She drew back against the wall. He wasn't so much looking as setting himself like an animal to catch a scent. His body was hard-edged, separate, intent.

She had seen this quality in him, or thought she had, from the very first day Pa introduced him, and he had stepped out, very sturdy and solemn, to shake hands; looking, with his hair chopped off short as it was again now, and his ears sticking out, very tough and little-mannish, but watchful too, as if for all his squareness and solidity he could be hurt. He had been hard-edged even then, aware of the precise point where *he* left off and a world began that might not be entirely well-disposed towards him, and which for that reason he had always to be on his guard against.

He was standing just inside the door, compact, firm, tense with the effort of feeling about for some other presence in the room, his eyes in the darkness taking up the light there was, oily-bright.

'Like a cat,' she thought.

Caught like this, with her heart beating fast, she too felt like some creature, a rabbit perhaps, but was determined not to be mesmerised.

Then something happened. He gave up playing, that's what it was; and having decided there was no one there, simply stood, his body eased, in the belief that he was alone and unobserved.

He stood where the light fell. There wasn't much, but Ellie was accustomed now to the dark. He was looking straight to where she was but did not see her. The curtain rose and fell like a veil, brushing her face. And something in the way the breeze moved and the leaves of the trees clattered gave her the feeling that they were not inside, not any more, but out in the dark somewhere on an unlighted road, and she had come upon him by accident, sleepwalking there. She was looking past his known face to one she had never seen. It was the one he wore when he was too deep in himself to be aware any longer of what he might have to conceal; the face he showed no one, and which even he had not seen.

She heard him sigh. He was very close. Then, thrusting his hands deep into his pockets, he turned on one heel so that he was in profile. He might have been deliberately showing himself to her: first full-face, now this. She was tense, but the little touch of panic she had felt at the beginning was gone. She had given herself up entirely to looking.

She must have made a sound of some kind, just a breath. He turned his head sharply and his face was covered again. He leaned towards her in the dark.

'Who is it?' he said, his voice very low. 'Ellie? Is that you?'

His brow was creased but he was not perturbed, or did not seem to be, that she had seen him. He put his hand out. She froze.

This was the game now. There were rules and they were in operation again. The tips of his fingers came close to her face. He did not touch her but she felt that he had. Her skin tingled.

There was a smile on his mouth. What light there was, which was really no more than a transparency of darkness, was full on him. But what she was seeing still, behind the smile and the clear roundness of his pupils, was the look she had seen earlier, an afterglow as when a bright light has imprinted itself on your eyeball and remains for long seconds after you have looked away.

'Ellie?'

There was a note of amusement in his voice.

In just a moment now, as the game required, he would grasp her wrist, give a shout, 'I've found Ellie,' and bring the others into the room; but he did not want that, not yet.

He brought his fingertips to her cheek, through the light gauze of the curtain, and she flinched. 'Don't,' he said. 'Don't be scared.'

They stood for a moment longer, neither in the game nor quite out of it, very still, with the breeze moving and the curtain lifting and falling with her breath. She had seen him, he knew that, and for some reason it did not bother him. If anything he felt relieved, as if a weight had been taken from him. Only one other person had ever seen him like that, and that was different. It was a man. It put you at risk, of course, but Digger had not let him down.

He took Ellie's wrist, very gently at first, and they stood a little longer without moving. Then he tightened his grip and called.

VI

1

Digger's first days back at the Crossing were spent clearing an infestation of blackberry canes that had invaded the open area between the store and the river and overgrown all that remained now of the ferry, the old wheelhouse and its machinery and the planked approaches to the wharf. Stripped to the waist in the November heat and armed with a machete, he waded into the massed entanglement of it. He used a gloved hand to push aside the barbed shoots, hacking at trunks as thick in places as his own wrist and grubbing out strand after strand of fibrous roots.

It was a single dense growth, its root-system as extensive and as deeply intricate below ground as above. Somewhere at the heart of it was the tap-root, but he never found it. Over and over again he thought he had; he put the machete in and dug out a fleshy tuber. But further in there was always another, tougher stock. At the end of the day his arms, chest and back were criss-crossed with scratches, and despite the gloves he wore his hands were torn, but the work was a pleasure to him. It was a way of getting down to the ground of things. In his sleep that first night he went on with the work, moving with almost no effort now and scarcely feeling the sting of the thorny shoots as they whipped out and clung to him. He saw the bones of small animals that had got trapped in the undergrowth, bandicoots, bush rats, a feral cat; turned up objects he had thought never to see again, that shone out of the over-arching growth with an unnatural luminescence, as if they had managed somehow to preserve the last ray of sunlight they had been touched by, or the last moonlight, before a new shoot launched itself, knitted into the thicket and shut them in.

There was a sun-bonnet of his mother's that had once been blue and was sodden and stained now to a colour he could not name. He tossed it on to the pile he was making, along with a smashed storm-lantern, the crumbling head of a spade, some bald tennis balls, and from deep under, where so little light got in that the undergrowth was hollow, the battered pudding basin that had been Ralphie's water-tin. He saw it glowing like a full moon in the half-darkness, reached in, pulled it out, and sent it clattering on to the heap.

His mother came out to bring him cups of scalding tea or jugfuls of iced water, and would stand there while he drank.

She took no interest in the progress of the work. She would have preferred him to begin on the roof, which leaked in places, or to put in new slumps for her lines, and he would get around to these too, in time; but it was the blackberries that had priority. So when she stood waiting for him to finish drinking it wasn't the work that held her, it was him: the fact that she had him here. Gulping down cold water, he watched her over the rim of the glass, hungrily taking him in.

At the end of the day, casting his gloves aside, he set fire to what he had hacked and torn out and dragged to the bank. The thorny strands crackled and burned fast. The place began to resemble the Keen's Crossing he had left, though there was much that could not be restored. The Crossing now was a dead end. The highway had moved a mile downriver and there was a bridge, a three-spanner, high above the stream.

It surprised him, given this and the war and all, that his mother had been able to hang on so long, but she would, of course, if anyone could. He was struck again by her tenacity, that strength in her that he too had drawn on 'up there' and used to pull him through, and was conscious once again of how alike they were, and how different.

At the table, still shirtless in the heat but with the grime and ash washed off him and peroxide on his cuts, he listened in a numbed way to her talk, which was ceaseless as she went over the list of her grievances: the same bitter anecdotes and illustrations of the hardships she had put up with and his father's many deficiencies. Her war with him had intensified. He was a more powerful presence to her now that he was gone than he had ever been when he was sitting out on a stump somewhere in the dark, sulking and cursing, or when he was traipsing mud from his boots over her floors.

What she could not forgive was his refusal to knuckle down to the hard truth of things: which for her meant marriage, home, family, all she had spent her spirit over the years in amassing and preserving, and which she had expected they would share.

'He's a conquering hero now,' she told Digger. 'Lording it over the Japanese. I *ask* you!'

Digger felt sorry for her. There was no end to the injustice she felt, and since no story she told in illustration could contain the whole of it, no story was ever finished. It opened out at one point or another into a new one, approached some new and deeper injury, and that one led on to the next. The worst of it was, he wasn't even here to face her. He had escaped even that. Digger learned to listen and not to hear.

She told him as well what she knew of Jenny. It wasn't much. She was in Brisbane somewhere.

At the end of the week, when the yard was cleared and he had dealt with the roof, Digger made his own enquiries, took the train to Brisbane and brought her back.

So there they were, all three, united again. Back, Digger thought, despite the seven years and all that had happened, in a life that was barely different in its essentials from the one he had left.

His mother still weighed out and packed orders each Friday night in the room behind the store, and a boy called Cliff Poster came on his bike at eight on Saturday morning and went back and forth, as he had, making deliveries.

She still had her garden, and a war now with the cats. She set Jenny to watch out for them if she couldn't do it herself. A bucket of water was kept ready under the clothes-line to slosh at them.

She still did the washing out in the yard, using a tin tub and a scrubbing-board, and ironed in the kitchen late at night.

She and Jenny shared one room now, and Digger slept in his old bed on the other side of the wall. They could talk right through it if they wanted.

He was surprised, lying on the narrow cot and looking past the windowsill at the same moonlit view, to recall how light-headed and restless he had been in the old days; waiting, fully awake and counting the seconds till the rest of them were asleep, then easing himself off his cot so that the springs didn't squeak, pulling on his pants, and tiptoeing out, his boots in one hand, his shirt in the other, to finish dressing in the dark.

The difference now, he thought, lay in the load of ballast he had taken on; none of which might be measurable in *real* terms. He could still have made the grade as a featherweight, and none of what he was carrying would have registered on his mother's scales, out there in the shop. But it made a difference just the same.

He worked as an odd-job man, and, since it was all word of mouth up here, soon had a reputation as the man to get: 'Get Digger. He'll fix it.'

He had a way with generators, old fridges, every kind of engine, and since the day his father first put a hammer and nail into his hand, and gave him a slab of four-by-two to practise on, had been a dab hand at all sorts of carpentry.

Building restrictions were still on in the early days, so it was repair work mostly, and it remained so, even when the bans were lifted and they moved into a boom. People who wanted new homes got a contractor from Gosford, or brought their pet architect and builder up from Sydney. He worked with other men's blunders, patching and restoring; or with what the weather ruined – they got too much rain up here, too much sunlight too: replacing floorboards, closing in verandahs, hanging doors. He took over the tools his father had left – however careless he may have been in other respects, he was a scrupulous workman and they were in excellent nick. He was happiest when he was straddling the line of a roof with the whole river-country laid out below him; in summer expansive and glittering, on early mornings in winter trailing a line of heaped cloud between its forested bluffs, while up where he was, crouched on the side of a fibro roof and hammering, the sun on his shoulders would be making him sweat.

On Thursdays he went up to town and spent the night at Bondi Junction. He did it without fail, not missing a single Thursday in twenty-six years.

He would walk round to pick Iris up at the cake shop and they would stroll home together, have tea with the boys and maybe go to a show. But more often than not they just sat like a long-married couple and listened to the wireless, while Iris mended socks or did a jigsaw puzzle, and Digger took a toaster to pieces and put it together again. Around eight, Ben and Amy Fielding came in and they would have a game of five hundred or a bit of a sing-song while Iris played.

He began to read his way through Mac's library. There were, he estimated, about seven hundred volumes. Mac had intended them for his retirement, and it pleased Digger that, even if he made not a single addition of his own, there was reading enough on the stacked shelves, and in the unsorted books that were piled under the bed, on top of the wardrobe and round the walls of the little closed-in porch beyond, to keep him going for the rest of his life.

He didn't push himself, there was no need. He read steadily through biographies, travel books, books of history; the collected writings of Wilhelm Stekel, and Adler and Freud; the whole of Havelock Ellis; the novels of H. G. Wells and Arnold Bennett and Conrad and Theodore Dreiser, including the book the Human Torso had given him, novels by Balzac and Stendhal and Tolstoy and Dostoevsky, wondering, as he went, how often he was travelling a path Mac had already been on, and, when he came on something that challenged or shocked him, what Mac might have made of it.

Occasionally, in turning a page, he came on a slip of paper that Mac had put there to mark where he had left off reading – or was it so that *he* could come upon it, five, ten, fifteen years after his death?

Once it was a list of birds.

What was that doing, Digger wondered, in the scene towards the end of *War and Peace* where young Petya Rostov, with his fondness for sweet things and his ten pounds of seedless raisins, does ask after all, in spite of his embarrassment before the older men, about the little French drummer boy, and has him brought muddy-footed into the tent.

Mac's presence, as Digger turned the page and interrupted his reading, imposed itself on the scene. So that for ever after, recalling it, he would think of Mac as having actually been there along with Denisov and Dolghow, and the actual birds, unlikely antipodean angels – the white throated honey-eater, a flock of fire-tails, a Regent bower bird among others – would also be there, flashing about the courtyard where young Petya hangs down from the saddle and Denisov grips the railings of the fence and howls his grief.

At other times it was tram tickets, and Digger would look at the numbers to see if they were in any way significant.

Once, with a dirty mark along the crease where Mac had used a thumb blackened with ink off the tickets he had been pulling, it was an official letter from the tramways office, in reply to a complaint he had made.

These relics moved Digger, and reminded him, if he was ever tempted to forget, of the continuity between Mac's life and his own, which had not been broken after all in the godown that morning. He would look at one of these scraps of soiled paper, taken out of a back pocket or from Mac's wallet when he was called to collect a fare on some late-night run out to Clovelly, and feel the other man's presence as a physical thing, a heat in him that was different from his own, something added. Till it faded in him, the pages he read had a sharper meaning. It was a private thing. Not secret, but he found no reason to speak of it.

He and Iris seldom spoke of Mac. He connected them only lightly. Their life together was made up of things they had discovered in one another, separately and in their own way. Digger never again saw the letters he had brought her, and he did not ask about them. What they had once stood for in his life had been replaced, and filled a hundred times over, by the woman herself, who was quite different, as he now saw her, from the one who had written them. He was not, in that sense, devoted to the past.

He kept the different parts of his life separate from one another, though there was no separation in him; no conflict either.

He told his mother nothing of Bondi Junction, but she knew of course. He was astonished all over again by the extent to which she could get into his head still, and was aware, in a way that disturbed him sometimes, of what he was thinking.

Each Thursday morning she laid out clean clothes for him, shirt, socks, underpants. She did it to show him that however secretive he might have become – and he had been such an open little fellow – he could hide nothing from her.

She would have preferred him to have some local girl, and kept trying to set him up with one. She wanted him married. She wanted grandchildren. But she knew too well his capacity for loyalty, for sticking at things, to challenge him. The laying out of his clothes each Thursday became a ritual, and when she died, Jenny did it, without knowing quite what the ritual meant, except that it was one.

2

'I understand,' Ern Webber said, 'that you an' Douggy got an invite to the weddin'.' There was a good deal of scorn in his voice.

'That's right,' Digger told him.

'I thought you might of been best man,' Ern said. It was what passed, in his mind, as a stroke of wit. 'Considerin'.' When Digger failed to take this up he went back to his own grievance. 'Well, he was never all that shook on me. An' I know why, too. 'Cause I seen through 'im, that's why, 'e never fooled me. Not after that Mac business. I notice 'e never turns up to reunions.'

'No,' Digger said, 'an' neither do I. So what does that prove?'

This sort of talk was painful to him. It raised too many ghosts, put a finger on wounds that were still raw in him. But it was no good saying any of this to Ern. He was a tactless fellow with fixed and emphatic views, and besides, was bitter now at the snub he had received.

'Oh, Vic's all right,' Digger found himself saying to cut off further argument.

In fact Digger had not been entirely happy at the wedding, which was a very grand affair, but he did not intend to tell Ernie this.

Vic had never spoken to him of the Warrenders, not once. He was unprepared for the house at Strathfield, with its turrets and the big hallway laid with blue, white and brown terracotta tiles and lit with a fanlight, and on either side of the door coloured panels of glass. A good deal of renovation had been done for the occasion. All the stonework of the façade had been repainted and the ironwork of the upstairs verandah given a lick of paint. The vision it presented to Digger was of an opulence he had no reference for, outside of books.

He went quiet and felt awkward in his old suit. He had taken it for granted that Vic's people would be like his own, or Mac's or Doug's. That was the impression he had given. Now this! 'All that time,' he thought, 'he was making mugs of us.' He felt himself flush with indignation, though there was shame in it too.

He tried to hide it. He had told Iris a good deal about Vic and of the

233

tie between them. He did not want her to see now how shaken up he was. When Douggy raised his eyebrows and cast a look around the room where they were to leave their things that said, 'Well now, what do you make of this?' he played dumb, and only Douggy's extreme good nature prevented him from taking offence.

A marquee had been set up on the lawn behind the house. It was of a transparent blue stuff, very light and airy, and all round the edges of it alcoves had been created as at a proper ball, each one hung with loops of cornflowers and pink roses and with a medallion above on which the couple's initials, V and E, were very prettily entwined. Iris, who had been at a good many marriages, had never seen anything like it.

There were waiters in Eton jackets with burgundy cummerbunds, stacks of champagne in dry ice, whisky, beer, soft drinks for the children. Waxed planking had been laid to make a dance floor, and there was a three-piece band to play foxtrots, quicksteps, slow waltzes, gypsy taps. They shared their alcove with Doug and his new wife Janet and some younger friends of the bride.

Meanwhile Vic, sometimes with Ellie at his side, sometimes alone, was moving through all this as if he had never known anything else. Not the least sign now, Digger thought, of the close-cropped, half-crazy character who had come to him at the Crossing. When was that – two months ago? No sign in fact of anything Digger had known of him, or of any of the things they had been through. The ease with which he wore his wedding suit, which sat very smooth and square across his shoulders, the big carnation in his lapel, the freshness and youth he suggested as he clapped older men on the back and called them Gus or Jack or Horrie, and made himself agreeable to their wives – all this appeared to make nothing of what he had been, what they had *both* been, just a year ago. It denied that as if it had never been.

Digger felt injured, and not just on his own part, but strangely enough on Vic's part too, the Vic he had once been close to. And on Douggy's and Mac's. He didn't know where to look.

The Warrenders, you could see, doted on him, no doubt of that, and he plumped himself up with it; you could see that too. He glowed. And the assurance of it gave him the power to submit others, the whole world maybe, to his charm.

'What does it mean?' Digger asked himself miserably. 'Is he so shallow? Or is it just that he knows as well how to hide himself among this lot as he did with us?' Either way he didn't want to have anything to do with it. He felt empty and hurt, but sorry too, and if it wasn't for Iris, who had been looking forward to all this, would have gone straight back to the station.

She felt the tightness in him. 'What is it, love?' she whispered. 'Aren't you enjoying yourself?'

She was. The Warrenders were generous people, there was no mistaking that, and some of the warmth of the occasion, and some aspects of the ceremony too, she took as extending to her and Digger: the vows, which she was always moved by, the confetti, the three-tiered wedding cake with its little columned tabernacle on top, and under it a bride and groom, which would be cut up and passed around in slices soon, and eaten, just a mouthful each, by the guests, or sent off in flat tins stamped with wedding-bells to other parts of the country or overseas. When Mr Warrender got to his feet, and instead of making a speech recited a poem he had written, she took Digger's hand, feeling that the words, in a way she had not expected, spoke for her own emotions, which were so full that only poetry perhaps – and she knew nothing about poetry – might contain them.

Some people, she saw, thought it rather queer that what this big man, who looked like an alderman or a Rotarian, should have embarked on was a poem.

The occasion till now had been a mixture of formality and a suppressed but growing rowdiness. Some of the male guests, skylarking about in their restraining collars, and restrained as well, but only with glances, by their wives, had been making rough jokes, hinting broadly at the cruder side of things. The groom had taken this in good part, as he was bound to do, and unmarried girls, caught in a position where they could not help but overhear (which in a good many cases they were meant to), let it appear that they had not caught on; or they drew their mouths down in a disapproving but half-amused and indulgent manner and turned away. Even one or two of the formal speeches had taken advantage of what is allowable and struck a ribald note. So when Mr Warrender started, a group of the noisier fellows took it as a spoof. Only after a good many hard looks were they shamed into silence. They put on expressions of honest bemusement and let themselves be stilled. But others, Iris saw, were, as she was, moved.

As for Mr Warrender, he gave no indication that there was anything out of the way in what he was doing. He spoke as if poetry was his normal manner of address, and after a moment or two it was accepted as such.

He wasn't solemn. There was often a little kick to what he had to say that was quite humorous, and this surprised Iris; she didn't understand it. She had to get Digger, later, who had a gift in that direction, to repeat some of Mr Warrender's lines (he could too, word for word) before she got hold of what she had been so moved by:

'Eternal.' On our lips the extravagant promise
That spirit makes. The animal in us knows
The truth, but lowers its dumb head and permits itself for this
One day to be garlanded and led
Beyond never-death into ever after, being
In love with what is always out of reach:
The all, the ever-immortal and undying
Word beyond word that breathes through mortal speech.

That was one bit of it.

When Digger spoke these lines they lacked some of the ordinariness Mr Warrender had given them. Even under the circumstances of the tent and its decorations, which were unusual enough, and the guests all subdued and with their hands held back a moment from the clatter of knives and forks, and from glasses even, gravely or politely listening, there had been something very natural and straightforward about it; as if, at the moment of his getting up and looking around at them all, the words the occasion demanded had simply come to him of their own accord. It all seemed so fitting to Iris, and so easy too, because the words Mr Warrender came up with might have been her own, even if some of them were a puzzle to her.

But when Digger repeated the lines, they seemed fixed and formal. He might have been reading them off a printed page. And now that it was long past, it was not simply the one occasion they referred to but all such occasions, and this too, Iris thought, she had understood, if only vaguely, at the moment itself. As if there were more of them present, many more, than the guest-list would have shown:

Noon here in this garden, and the daystar
Shakes out instant fire to call up earth, water, air,
Grass, flowers, limbs and the still invisible presences

236

That hold their breath and stand in awe about us.
We are all of us guests at a unique, once only
Occasion – *this* one, *this*, the precarious gift
Alive in our hands again, the mixed blessing
Offered and accepted . . .

'The mixed blessing'. That was one of the things that had puzzled her. It had seemed out of place, suggesting as it did a kind of doubt rather than the easy conviction that is usual to such occasions. But she had come, in time, to see that it said several things at once – that was just the point of it, and she saw then what it was in Mr Warrender that had struck her. He did not take things for granted or just as they appeared. What he said was: 'Yes – but,' in this way allowing for what really was, as well as what you might want life to be.

Vic had sat very attentive through it all, with a single deep crease between his brows, either because he thought he might have at some point to defend Mr Warrender against the rowdy element or because what his father-in-law was saying was important to him and he too was struggling to get hold of it.

Ellie on the other hand was following the poem with her lips, as if she already knew it, word for word.

Later, going over the events of the day, the spring heat that had set their skin prickling and given everything such a fresh glow, then the coolness as shadows began to fall, the music, Mr Warrender's poem, even the magpies sitting humped and patient, waiting for the crowd to thin out so that they could dive after soaked crumbs – going over all this, they came to feel that the occasion had been a special one for them too, and that it was Mr Warrender who had given expression to the various moods of it, and his words, as Digger repeated them, through which they could best recover what they had felt.

But there had been something embarrassing as well. Later in the day Digger had gone up to Mr Warrender to say a few words, and to see if he could find in the man himself some indication of where it came from, the poem, but also his boldness in being able to get up in public like that and deliver it.

Nothing came of the meeting. Mr Warrender was all noise at first, all bluffness and easy affability. Digger was embarrassed. Then Mr Warrender was too and stood ignoring Digger altogether, lifting himself up and down on the toes of his shoes, observing the ground and humming. Digger had had the greatest difficulty in getting away.

Except for a moment outside the church, when he and Iris and Doug and Janet had gone up together to shake his hand, Digger had not spoken to Vic, and Vic, he thought, had gone out of his way afterwards to avoid them. After what he had seen, Digger was not surprised by this, but he did find it uncomfortable. Why had he bothered to invite them? To show himself off? Was that all it was?

Towards the end of the day, while Iris was taking the opportunity offered by bathrooms and such to look over the house, Digger, still chewing on the grievance he felt, went to moon about for a bit under some firs. It was over against a high brick wall where there had till recently, he guessed, been a chicken run; maybe they had got rid of it for the wedding. There were still some feathers about, clinging to the fir branches and caught in the needles underfoot, and resting in a corner were the planks that had made up the perches, all split along the grains, encrusted with droppings and beginning to be overgrown with moss. It was quite secluded in here. He walked up and down and was too deep in himself to see that someone had come up beside him and had been standing, he could not guess for how long, just a few feet away.

'Hullo, Digger,' he said lightly. 'What are you up to?'

He spoke as if there was no constraint between them – not on his part. He had seen nothing, Digger realised, of what *he* was feeling. His mood was entirely calm, joyful even – well, why shouldn't he be? – and Digger felt abashed, as if he was the one who was at fault.

'They looking after you?' he enquired. 'Had a piece of wedding cake?'

He had a piece himself and was holding it, half-eaten, in his palm.

'Enough to drink?'

It pleased him, you could see, to have this opportunity to play host. He did it in a very grave way, but with a kind of shyness too, in case you thought he was being smug, that communicated itself immediately to Digger and made him feel again that he had done him an injustice and was in the wrong. He mumbled something, but could not come up with the light reply that might have made things easy between them.

Vic stood, swaying a little, and looked over his shoulder at the crowd. He had an empty glass in one hand and in the other the remains of his piece of cake. They stood a moment. Then, with a gesture Digger had seen him make a thousand times, but under very different circumstances, he tilted his head back, cupped his palm, and, very careful not to lose any, let the crumbs and mixed fruit roll back into his mouth.

It was utterly characteristic. That, his concern not to let a single crumb get lost, and the way too, when he tilted his head back, that his whole throat was bared, gave so much away to anyone who could feel it that Digger found himself choked. All the resentment he had felt went right out of him.

Vic meanwhile was examining his tie and the front of his suit for crumbs. He picked one off and put it on his tongue; then looked up, half-shy, as if he had been caught at something, and they were back immediately in an intimacy that was so strong, and appealed to something so deep in both of them, that they had to draw back from it.

'What a weird bloke he is,' Digger thought. 'Honestly, I'll never get the hang of him.' One moment he was all smooth impenetrability, and the next he opened up and gave himself away – but only, Digger thought, when he was afraid he might have lost you. How did he manage it? Was it calculated, or were they as guileless as he made them seem, these moments when he put himself entirely in your hands? Digger was inclined to protect himself against his own weakness. 'A man'd be a fool,' he told himself, 'to make anything of this. He'll drop me eventually. He's bound to.' It was so clear to him, from what he had seen, that Vic's was a life he could have no part in. In the normal course of things they would never have met, and they were back now in the normal course of things. Still, something was restored between them, and for the moment he was relieved.

When, soon after, Vic was captured by a woman who wanted her husband to meet him, Digger excused himself. He wanted to think things over. He went off through an open arch into a factory yard. It was mostly in shadow, but the archway, where the sun broke through, cast a skew, truncated reflection of itself across the flags. He dragged a packing case out of a heap of rubbish, set it down in the sun, and rolled himself a smoke.

It was here that Ellie, coming to the archway in search of Vic, found him sitting with his head lowered, his tie loose, his new shoes set far apart on the flags. She knew who he was. Seated on his packing-case in the sun he looked ordinary enough, but there was something too that appealed to her.

He glanced up, startled. He had an odd, thin-faced, rather wooden look, and very deep-set eyes.

'Sorry,' she said. 'I didn't mean to make you jump.' He was getting awkwardly to his feet. 'You're Digger, aren't you?'

'Well,' she added, and laughed, lifting her arms which were sheeted in a shimmering white material, 'you can see who I am,' and any embarrassment there might have been between them immediately vanished. Digger dropped his fag and ground it out. It was a way, for a moment, of not having to look at her.

'I'd have known anyway,' he found himself saying, and blushed because he couldn't think, once it was out, why he had said it or what it meant.

She smiled. 'Well,' she said, 'I'm glad we've met at last. I was wondering what you'd be like.'

'Me?'

'Vic's talked a lot about you – well, not a lot, but – well, you know.'

They were standing just inside the arch. Behind Digger lay the empty yard. Looking at her the sun was in his eyes so that he squinted a little, but he could feel the edge of the archway's shadow on his shoulder, creeping in.

Outside on the lawn the party was beginning to break up. Many of the guests were already gone. Those who remained were scattered in groups, the men all fired up with the last of the day's arguments, sport, politics, business; some of the women now with their high heels kicked off, easing their stockinged feet in the grass. The band still played, but the floor was occupied now entirely by children, little boys in long pants and long-sleeved shirts and ties, some of them bow ties, and girls in party frocks with ribbons. They were pushing one another about on the waxed boards like perfect little adults while one or two real adults looked on. One of them, Digger saw, was Ellie's father, Mr Warrender. He looked rather tipsy, and Digger saw him, over Ellie's shoulder, step on to the dance floor in a top-heavy, deliberate way, as if he feared he might not make it, and begin to weave about among the couples, who looked sideways at him, embarrassed by his dancing alone like that, and steered away from him towards the corners of the floor.

Ellie, seeing Digger's intent look, turned her head, wondering what it was that had caught his eye; but what she saw was not her father making slow circles with his arms raised among the dancing children, but Vic. He was standing just off to the side in a group of older men, all with their heads together. He had turned away from whatever it was they were discussing. With his hands in his pockets, he was watching Digger and her.

He glanced down when her eye caught him and pretended to laugh at something that was being said. But a moment later, when she looked that way again, he was again watching. This time Digger saw it too. And immediately Vic detached himself from the group, one or two of whom turned and looked after him, and came over the lawn towards them.

Ellie looked at Digger, made a face, and smiled.

'Well,' her look said, 'that's that. This is the only moment we'll have. But that's all right, isn't it?'

Digger found that he too was grinning.

'He's scared. You know – that we might get on too well together. I mean, of what we might find out – you know, about *him*, not about one another – if he leaves us alone too long. He's like that.'

'I know,' Digger agreed.

'He can't help it.'

'He's a difficult cuss.'

'Oh, you don't have to tell *me*.'

These were the thoughts that flew between them.

He wondered what it was exactly that Vic had told her; not about him but about the rest of it. Not a lot, he thought. There would be things she would never know. She would wake nights and find him sitting on the edge of the bed (Digger knew these occasions himself) with the sweat pouring off him; stuck in the real heat of a place he had been dreaming about, except that it was never just a dream and there was no way back from it.

'You've found Digger,' he said brightly, coming up and taking her arm. 'That's good.'

He stood looking from one to the other of them, aware of the warmth between them. They were quite easy, gave no sign that anything they had been saying had had to be cut off short by his arrival. But the smiles they wore were conspiratorial, and Digger reddened and looked down. Vic knew him too well to miss it. But Ellie was not intimidated.

'I was just asking Digger to come and see me sometime,' she said, contradicting what Digger thought had been agreed between them. 'You will, won't you, Digger?'

He glanced at Vic. He too was smiling, quite amiably you might have thought, but he said nothing, and he did not want it; Digger saw that quite plainly. Why had she suggested it?

'I should find Iris,' he said quickly. 'She'll be wondering what's happened to me.'

3

A blustery day, late August. High up, flat-bottomed clouds were in flight, sailing fast around the world, but the air was clear and up here on the hill above the Crossing she could see in all directions at last, north, south, eastwards towards the river's mouth and the ocean. The whole landscape was laid out for her.

Downriver, in a dozen little bays and inlets, boats were stuck like bits of paper, white on blue, unmoving at this distance. Upstream the bridge, its traffic silenced by the sound the wind was making, the wrenching of branches, fistfuls of leaves rattling at the ends of twigs and the gulls' crying.

To one side below was the store in its elbow of low land, high and dry and isolated: the ridge of its tin roof, the four posts of her washing-lines, old barrels and kero tins with her bits of shrubs in them, Digger's workbench under the pepper tree. Jenny was there, mooning about in a cotton frock chasing birds.

'She doesn't know yet,' she thought. 'She hasn't realised I'm out of the house.' The panic there would be when she went into their room and found the empty bed! The moaning and flapping! She was sorry about that.

On the high bank opposite, on one of the roofs of the weekenders that dotted the hillside over there and flashed among the trees, Digger would be working, a hammer in his belt, a stub of pencil behind his ear.

She knew it all; where everything was. Only up here was new to her.

And why had she left it thirty-three years to come up here and see it?

Because she didn't want to see things too clearly, that's why.

And why had she done it now?

Because she did.

She had left it till the very last, not to disappoint herself. She could face it now. She was past disappointment.

Far off, forty miles it would be as the crow flies, in a soft haze in which houses, whole streets of them, and trees and harbour water were smudged to the same pastel blue, as if it was a lake not a city, and just the highest towers were visible above the surface of it, was Sydney.

That wasn't what she had come to see. She hadn't even known it would be visible. In her mind it was further off than that. Halfway to England, practically. Thirty-three years off. She had knuckled under and hung on here – somebody had to; kept things together, turned her back on the rest of the world, taken on its name, Keen, and would now be buried under it.

But suddenly, just this afternoon, she couldn't bear to be in the house any longer, in the stuffy little back bedroom, on a day when the wind was up. Everything, every stick of furniture, every inch of the curtains she had ordered and sewn and hung in their three rooms, every teaspoon, and the wedding picture of her husband's parents on the sideboard, and the bags of sugar, rice, salt, and the scales in the back room on which for thirty-three years she had weighed them out in pound and half-pound packets – all that, and her kitchen chairs and saucepans, and the bucket and mop behind the door, and Jenny flopping on the counter, and all the ghosts of the others, squeezed into a corner by the stove and sucking a rusk or pushing ashes into their mouths, Leslie and James and May and Billy – all that and more, weighed on her heart and crushed her. She could have set a match to the lot of it in this high wind and watched it blaze up in a roar of smuts.

So what sort of woman, at last, did that make her?

The very kind she had set out *not* to be.

Tearing off her bedclothes she had rushed out barefoot to the kitchen, snatched up a box of matches and struck one and threw it down, then another, and looking wildly about her said, 'This is the sort of woman I am.'

But the box fell from her hand, the matches spilled. Without looking back she had broken out of the house and, plunging off into the scrub with no thought in her head, only the wind and the high clouds flying, begun to climb.

Once she was actually climbing she was all excitement and haste, as if she had wanted to do this every day of her life and was to see at last what she had for years been held back from. She pushed past ledges of rock where she had to use both hands to haul herself up, and the big, flesh-coloured angophoras with their fat-rolls like naked angels, till she was high enough to get a grip on the dimension of things. She wasn't a coward. No one could have called her that. She could face anything.

When she reached the summit, she looked about, took it all in, then, hunched on an outcrop among scratchy, waist-high grass, and with her arms hugging her breast, chewed on the bitterness of things.

Now that it was about to occur, the thing she had dreamed of, the descent of peace and the gathering around her of all the objects of her life, she did not want it, any of it. She did not want her life – the fifty-four years, so many days and days and the disappointments and defeats and little silent triumphs – to be made visible at last and piled up around her so that she had to say: 'So this is what it comes to.'

That's what she had wanted to get away from, and had, in her head, already burned the evidence of. Not to have, forever, to sit at the centre of it.

Gibbons. That was the name she had been born to.

'My God,' she thought, looking about at the spiky heads of the blockboys, 'where is she? Where's Marge Gibbons? And Bert. Marge and Bert.' It disturbed her that she could no longer actually see them: two hopeless little kids she had let wander off and get lost. They had been so real in the world, and still were, in her mind somewhere, if she could only get back to them past all the things she had accumulated that shut them out.

She began to pluck at the wool of her bedjacket. Little bits of pink fluff blew about in the air and joined the light little seeds and balls of pollen that were streaming and tumbling. The wind could not tell the one from the other of them.

Keen. She had taken that name, and the result was she would be buried under it.

And him? Billy? He was off chasing another war, and had found one too, in Korea this time. He would go on till he found the one that would do for him. She had known for years now that he would not come back.

She plucked at the bedjacket, pecking at it with the hard tips of her fingers. The pink stuff rose up and sailed. But suddenly there was a barging about in the bushes close by, then a wailing, and she was found, which was just how it had been the first time. The big blubbery girl found her and kept clutching and clutching and would not let her be.

*

245

'She won't come in,' Jenny told Digger. 'She says she never wants to. Ever again.'

She was wheeling about in the yard under the clothes-line and wringing her hands. Their mother, wrapped in an eiderdown, was in an old cane chair that had been chucked out as rubbish, her back to the house and shivering.

Digger put his tool-box down. 'Don't worry,' he said, but his calm was pretence. 'You go in an' make us a cuppa tea. I'll talk to 'er.'

He did, but she remained woodenly silent, as if she could no longer hear.

Jenny brought tea. She took a cup, but just sat with it while he drank, and Jenny, who was terrified, kept well away on the kitchen step.

But she would not go back into the house, and though he talked and tried to tempt her with things she had once cared about, she did not hear or would not listen. When it got dark he brought more blankets, wrapped her, put on another sweater himself, and they continued to sit as night deepened and the stars came out, and Jenny, behind a lighted window in the house, looked on.

Jenny brought him something to eat. It wasn't much. She was too upset to make anything proper. Digger sat on an upturned can and ate potatoes with a fork, with bread and a bit of gravy, and their mother continued to sit with her back to the house. It was ashes in her head. The house, the store and all its contents. She had put a match to them, whether or not the flame had taken. Digger could do nothing with her.

He had faced this sort of thing before but had not expected to see it again in his lifetime, and not here. She was willing herself out of the world, and she would do it too.

It was a strange thing, to have the house there, all lighted, and her sitting in the dust in front of it in a broken chair, with the scrub and all its night sounds around them.

Towards dawn he dozed off and she did at last begin to speak to him. The things she told him were terrible. He had not known she was in such despair. Bert, she called him. 'No,' he wanted to say, 'that's not my name. I'm Digger. Remember?' but he was afraid of interrupting her.

But he was wrong, or she did not remember or did not want to. 'Bert,' she called, and he woke, and the conversation they had been having went deep down into him and was gone.

*

'Digger,' Jenny said. 'Would you mind if I ast you something?'

She had come out to where, in an old pair of shorts and with his shirt off, he was at his workbench in the yard. There was a smell of freshly sawn timber.

'Fire away,' he said without looking up. He had thrown himself into work as a way, for a time, of not thinking. He needed a little time always to recover himself, and had settled now for the pleasure of putting a saw into soft wood, the smell of it, very sweet and spicy, and the warmth of the sun on his back.

'What's gunna happen,' she got out at last, painfully twisting her brow, 'to Mumma's *things*?'

'Her clothes, you mean?' He went on working, taking a pencil from behind his ear.

'No. Her *things*. They're *her* things.'

He looked at her now.

'The furniture an' that,' she said hopelessly. 'Saucepans. You know.'

'Nothing's going t' happen to them,' he said gently. 'What did you think? They're yours now. Ours.'

'Are they? Did she leave 'em?'

What had she expected, he wondered. He had no idea, even after so long, how her mind worked. Perhaps she too had taken their mother's vision literally, the one she had herself in the end turned her back on, and expected all the furnishings of the house, right down to the serviette rings and the tea-strainer, to be *taken up* in some way. Maybe literally. If not that, then in essence. Was that it? So that they were no longer, as they had been till now, quite solid and useable.

Or perhaps she thought their mother's spirit had appropriated them and made them dangerous to touch.

The chair she had sat in all night still stood in an awkward place under the lines, but neither of them had thought to move it. It was broken, its canes cracked and bleached by the weather; so much more like a natural thing than a piece of abandoned furniture that after a time, as it sank lower on one leg, they would barely notice it.

'Yes,' he said very quietly, 'she left them to you. They're yours now. You just do whatever you want with 'em.'

'Oh,' she said. 'All right.'

She stood a moment, looking serious, then went off, and he heard her shifting things about in the kitchen, clearing the shelves and rinsing things, instituting little changes that she might have been wanting to make for years – who could know the order her mind followed? – and wouldn't have dared make while their mother was alive.

4

Digger was to discover that he had been wrong on two counts that day of the wedding. Against the odds he did see Ellie again, though not for more than six years, and then only by accident, and Vic did not, as he had put it, 'drop him'. Two or three times a year, sometimes more often, he turned up unannounced at the Crossing and they would pass an hour together. He would sit out under the pepper tree and watch Digger at work at the bench he had there, getting up to steady the other end of a four-by-two Digger was sawing; or Digger would haul out a spare rod and they would go off and fish.

It wasn't always easy. There were times when he was in one of those moods where everything was an irritation to him. He had come for no other reason, Digger thought, than to pick over some old resentment or injury and provoke you into wounding him. Sometimes he succeeded, and Digger would be irritated himself when he saw Vic's satisfaction at having got him to strike out, the odd little smile he wore as he turned his head away. But on other occasions, though Vic went on and on, he would resist. Suddenly, without warning, Vic would be all appeasement, and minutes after in such excellent spirits that Digger could scarcely credit the change in him. It was as if in Digger's refusal to be on bad terms with him he had found the capacity to be on good terms once again with himself.

But there were many occasions when he came only because he had picked up something, some new gadget, that he thought Digger would be interested in and ought to see, or because the mood was on him to do a bit of quiet fishing, or simply because two or three months had gone by and they hadn't seen one another. They never discussed whatever business it was he was involved in. It was only when Doug mentioned it that Digger began to get an idea of what a figure he was cutting out there.

'Ol' Vic's doin' well, isn't 'e?'

'Is 'e?' Digger said. 'What d'ya mean?'

Douggy laughed. 'Don't you read the papers? Needham's –

that's him. He's practically a millionaire. Makin' money hand over fist.'

There was no irony in Douggy's tone. He was, as he had always been, sceptical of what he called the bosses, but he took Vic's rise in the world as reflecting on him as well, on all of them: he did not begrudge it. But who would have guessed it, eh? Who would have thought they would have a mate who was on the way – how old was he? twenty-eight, twenty-nine? – to being a millionaire? Not that he and Vic were all that close any more. But it was a wonder just the same.

'Doesn' 'e talk to you about it?' he asked Digger.

'No. Why should 'e? I don't know anything about business.'

'Well, 'e was never slow to blow 'is own trumpet – not in the ol' days. What's happened to 'im?'

'Nothing,' Digger said. 'I dunno.'

'So what *do* you talk about?' Doug asked after a moment, and his look was humorous.

'Nothing much,' Digger told him. It was the truth. He had to think. 'Cars an' that,' he added at last.

'Oh? So what sort of car does 'e drive?'

'Humber Hawk. Before that a Pontiac.'

Douggy looked impressed. 'Didn' you think from that,' he asked, 'that 'e might be doin' well?'

Digger didn't know what to say. He had seen at the wedding the sort of people Vic came from and the life they led, and had been too absorbed with the vehicles themselves, with raising the bonnet and looking in at the workings of them, to ask himself how much they might represent in the way of 'getting on'.

Vic liked to show them off, but there was nothing show-offish or proprietorial in it. They could have been kids who had come upon the Pontiac or the Riley, the Austin Healey or the Ford Customline, parked in a street somewhere, less concerned with who owned it than with the full panoply of its metal power and the wonderful elegance and achievement of the thing; though it struck Digger as amazing at times (he shivered and went ghostly under his clothes) that they should be here to lay their hands on the sun-warmed gloss, and to feel, when they put their foot down, the full power of these models of 1949, 1952, 1954.

'I believe you're doin' pretty well for yourself,' he said at last, one day when their easiness allowed it. 'So Doug tells me.'

'I'm holding my end up,' he admitted.

Digger was planing a set of planks, three or four of which stood upright against the trunk of the pepper tree. Pale shavings, almost transparent and showing the honey-coloured grain, curled off the blade as he swept his arm through, fell, turned over, and rolled away in the breeze. Vic sat on an upturned kerosene tin.

'I didn' realise,' Digger said.

'Oh – ' Vic passed it off lightly, 'I've had a bit of luck, that's all.'

It was true: things fell into his hand and multiplied. But that wasn't the whole of it. He was smart, he worked hard, never stopped in fact, he was famous for it; he had an eye for the way things were moving and would be on the spot and ready to go before other men, more experienced men too, had seen there was a chance; and he was ruthless – he let nothing and no one get in his path. But he also had luck. It worried him.

Luck, he believed, was a thing you couldn't rely on. It had let him down once, and badly. It could let him down again. It was his opinion that a man who depended on luck was little more than a lounger in the world and had in no way proved himself. What he believed in was character. His achievements, such as they were, all plain and visible, had to be balanced against what was *not* visible because it was within, but which must exist because *they* did, and could therefore be taken on trust.

Sitting out in the dry wind, under the pepper tree, on the upturned tin, what he was worth was not millions but just what Digger might see and reflect back to him, with no need of explanation or proof.

He looked up very frankly to where Digger had stopped still with the plane in his hand, looking at him, and there it was.

It was a moment Digger would remember; when he saw clearly, and for the first time, what Vic wanted of him. He was to be one of the witnesses to his life. Not to his achievements, anyone could see those, which is why he hadn't bothered to draw Digger's attention to them; but to those qualities in him that would tip the balance on the other, the invisible side.

It had taken Digger so long to grasp this because the idea that a man might need *witnesses* to his life was so foreign to him. But once he had seen it, though the role did not please him, he stuck. It was one more of the responsibilities that had been laid upon him. He would not have chosen it, any more than he would have chosen some of the others, but it was there. Chance, life, fate – whatever it was – chose for you, connecting and binding you into the pattern of other people's lives, and making that at last the pattern of your own.

It was Jenny who did the resisting, and this had its comic side. None of Vic's appearances over the years, or the little presents he brought, ever reconciled her to him.

One night they were watching TV when she suddenly turned and asked in astonishment:

'Is that who I *think* it is?'

'Yes,' Digger told her. 'Vic.'

'So what's *he* done?'

Her quick rule of thumb was that anyone who got on to TV, if he wasn't a pop star or a newsreader, must be a crook.

'Nothing. Made a bit of money, that's all, by taking someone over – You know, buying 'em up. There's some trouble with the unions.'

She screwed her eyes up and concentrated. That didn't tell her anything. That wasn't what it was about.

The interviewer was a girl, and after being very nice to her, or pretending to be, calling her by her name, Jane, but showing too that he didn't take any of what she was asking seriously, he suddenly went cold, then lost his temper. Jenny chuckled. This was what it was about.

'*She* doesn't think much of him,' she declared.

'Good on yer, girlie!' she shouted. '*She* thinks he's a crook. Is 'e?'

'No,' Digger told her. He was amused. 'And that girl doesn't think so either.'

'Why's she after 'im then?'

'It's 'er job. She's doing 'er job, that's all. Being aggressive.'

'Mr Smarty Pants!' Jenny shouted, 'Mr Smarty Smarty Pants!'

5

Vic, still in his shirt-sleeves, pushed back the breakfast plates, shifted the pepper and salt shakers and the toast-rack to a new position, poured himself more tea, lit a cigarette, and leaned back in his chair. He had a habit, when he was about to propose a new idea, of clearing a space before him. You could, Ma knew, judge how large or risky the idea was by the extent of cloth he laid bare.

Their consultations together often took place over the remains of breakfast. With Pa already installed in his office and Ellie off delivering the boy to kindergarten, they had a good half-hour to themselves. The domestic setting, the fragments of the meal ('There is something very reassuring,' Ma thought, 'about burnt toast'), gave an unemphatic quality to their talk; the solid grip on things suggested by teacup handles and spoons grounded what might otherwise have seemed fantastic in the ordinary and commonplace.

It astonished Vic, when he recalled the anxieties she had been racked by, that Ma could be so changed. She had never failed him, not once. If he drew back sometimes, and even he had his moments of doubt, though he did his best not to show them, she saw it and would be there to urge him on.

Her mind was sharper than his. He came up with a scheme, presented it to her, and let her knock it down if she could. If *she* couldn't find the crack in a thing it was foolproof.

He relied on her. They were a team. Arguing a deal out with her was like arguing with his other self, the sceptical one he might not otherwise have made contact with, or not so immediately. He accepted criticisms from her that, if a man had made them, he would have felt bound to reject. They knew one another too well for that, and cared too much, both of them, for what they were doing, to be soft with one another.

He was lingering this morning, deliberately holding back. There was a vagueness in him – not quite weakness, it was never that – which she would have in a moment to acknowledge and deal with. She knew him very well by now. But there was also this new space he had opened up. 'First things first,' she thought.

'So,' she said briskly, 'this is it, eh?'

'Yes,' he said. 'Ten-thirty.'

He saw how she was looking at him. He pushed his plate back another inch.

'I find all this a bit difficult,' he said. 'I mean, he can't be *that* innocent. I thought he'd be tougher, a bloke like that.'

'He *is* tough,' Ma told him. 'Don't be fooled by all that soft talk. He's tough in the old way, like my father. You fellows are a different breed.'

She saw the little flicker across his brow. She had not meant it as a criticism.

'He doesn't seem to realise that he'll no longer have control. What does 'e think we are? A charitable institution?'

He was speaking of Jack Creely, an old school friend of Pa's who had an engineering firm with government contracts. Needham's were taking him over.

'He's so full of himself! He thinks he's been clever, pulling the wool over our eyes.' His pride was touched.

What disturbed him, she knew, was the talk it would generate. He had made a good many enemies these last years. People thought he was getting too big for his boots; he was too sure of himself, too successful. They would be only too eager now to use Jack Creely as further evidence against him.

'Look,' she said, 'we're in for forty-six thousand, aren't we? That doesn't look like charity to me. Jack knows the score.'

The sharpness with which she heard herself say this gave her a start. She too had come a long way in these last years.

As for the forty-six thousand, just saying it straight out like that took her breath away. As if it was nothing!

She thought of her father, and saw him raise his eyebrows, half-shocked, but half-admiring too, at the summary way she had dealt with Jack Creely. But what would really have shocked him, as it did her too a little, was the forty-six thousand. Her father's rule had been a strict one. You stayed within limits, you kept out of debt. 'This feller's a lunatic,' her father would have told her, half-admiring of that too, but with a strong suggestion that she ought to look out for herself. 'Can't you see that?' She heard it so clearly in the room that she was surprised Vic didn't jerk his head up, in that aggressive way he had, and answer him.

He had been a buccaneer, her father, but of shallow waters. They were in open waters now.

For more than three years the factory had been abandoned and boarded up. The brickwork was crumbling and weeds had sprouted, not just between the flags of the yard but on the stone windowsills, and even, in places, from the roof. The little boy, Greg, was scared to go there. She had seen him more than once standing in the archway, peering into the yard and daring himself to go on.

The house and the factory, when her father built them, had been a single unit, two halves when she was growing up of a single world. The girls who worked in the packing room were part of the family. They might step across to the kitchen to get a cup of sugar if they were short at morning teatime, and if one of them took sick she would be brought over to lie in one of the rooms off the verandah. As a little girl Ma had often put aside her dolls or her jigsaw, or left off practising with her roller-skates on the long side verandah, to go across and have a chat with her favourites among the packers, Alice Green or Mrs Danby, or to watch a van being unloaded in the yard. Or she would perch on a stool in her father's office and cut out floral patterns from the Needham's labels and advertising placards and paste them into a ledger.

All this had brought the world of manufacturing and business into their daily lives, so that for her there had been no gap between them, the two worlds were interpenetrable. It was this view of things that she meant to re-establish by making the breakfast table the scene of her consultations with Vic, and all the more because what they were engaged with was no longer something you could stroll across to the other side of the garden and *see*.

Margarine. That had been their first move. Astonishing how easily, given a little capital, you could shift from one commodity to another. Soap, margarine – it was all the same, it seemed, though her father mightn't have thought so. He had brought his knowhow about soap-making from the Old Country, and from the Lake District, where he grew up, the recipes for the perfumes he used. It was all very personal to him, and to all of them. The soaps had been named after English flowers, lilac, violet, musk-rose, and the finest and most expensive of them after her mother, Mary Louise. At

Christmas, special packets were made up as presents to clients and friends.

But there was no call these days for things that were hand-made. Hicks had seen the point of the move straight off, and was delighted to be let loose on a new product, with new premises and a real staff, including a dozen trained technicians.

The amount they had had to borrow was terrifying. Hadn't she just got them out of the red? But Vic saw things in a different way.

'Listen,' he told her, 'things have changed. There's nothing to be gained by playing safe and staying out of debt. A millionaire isn't a man who's *got* a million. He's a man who *owes* a million, and if he owes ten million, all the better. That's how we've got to think. If it worries you, Ma, just you leave it to me.'

'My God,' she'd thought. But once she took the idea in she found she could live quite easily with it. That was *him*. He was all energy and unbounded confidence. What's more, the system worked.

His other idea was what he called *spread*. It had nothing to do with margarine – quite the opposite, in fact. Instead of limiting themselves to one commodity, one sort of venture, they took up, in an opportunistic way, whatever offered, using one company to raise credit for another, or they simply let things sit and appreciate.

So he took them into real estate, buying up corner sites all over the suburbs, odd rows of shops, that could be sold off to the petrol companies for service stations. They got into the building trade, financing new-style units, and quite soon owned a demolition company as well. For no other reason than that it was going cheap, he acquired a factory for bicycle parts, but seeing the possibilities in it, switched to specialist parts for the motor industry. Get a hold on just one of those parts, a reputation for being reliable – no strikes, no hold-ups – a good transport side, make yourself indispensable to an assembly-line somewhere, and you were made. Lately he had developed an interest in mining – sand mining up the Queensland coast, bauxite mining in Cape York Peninsula – and had his eye now on several oil-search enterprises, one of them in New Guinea, another in north-west Western Australia. Sooner or later, somewhere on the continent, they would strike oil. The thing was to get in on the ground floor. All this was *spread*.

It seemed a long step to her, from a place on the other side of the yard to sites they had a stake in that were three thousand miles away. But this was precisely what *he* was excited by, the sense of far-flung spaces to be opened up: a map on the wall, and the geography of the whole continent to move in, and not just what was above ground either, but what was below ground as well; and beyond mere *geographical* space, all those decades to come when these provisional ventures and far-sighted risks and hunches would pay off.

He was astonishing. She kept waiting for the moment to come when her father's voice might prevail and she could no longer go with him; but he leapt, and each time she took a good breath and went with him.

Looking now at the area he had opened up among their breakfast things she did not feel anxious. Part of what sustained her, but forced her too, was the need he had to take her with him. What came back to her then was the times she had paced his room, all anxiety, and he had sat so stolidly on his bed – how old was he? thirteen? fourteen? – and she had relied on him. What she had seen in him then was increased now a hundredfold.

She had never told him, but many years before, when she was not long married herself, she had seen his father. She had had no idea then that they would one day be connected.

A good-looking Irish fellow, a coalminer, who ought to have been rough, and was no doubt, but knew how to act soft if it suited him. All that, she had thought, must go over well with the girls, and he tried it out a little with her – having seen that it might be best, if he was to get what he wanted from Pa, to make an impression on her. He knew Pa pretty well, she guessed. That is, he knew how to get round him.

He had been very much then what Vic was now; the same age too, just thirty. Twelve years later, when Vic turned up, the image of the man had come back to her and she saw what he might grow up to be.

It was a type that appealed to her. She could admit that now. The father had seen it and given her the eye, but in a humorous way that said, 'Don't worry, I'm no danger. You'll never see me again. I've got what I wanted here.'

What she had been struck by was the quickness with which he had summed them up. He had been looking them over to see if they would do. The cheek! She could have laughed outright now when she recalled it. 'You'll do, I reckon,' the look said. The effrontery of it!

But he had known better than she had (*something* had known) what was good for them. For all of them.

Vic consulted his watch. Quickly now he outlined the thing to her.
He had needed first to clear the air of that other business, Jack Creely.
He wanted to start off with everything clear between them. So here it
was.

He had, for quite a while, been buying up shares in a margarine
company owned by one of their rivals. He wanted to make a bid now
for the whole show. Of course they would have to sell one or two
things. He laid them out for her. It didn't look like much: an egg cup
with a rabbit on it and the scooped egg turned upside down to fool
someone that it was whole, two slices of dry toast, a honey pot in the
shape of a hive, with a chipped bee on the lid.

Loans? Yes, a few thousand. But interest rates were down and
would go down further, according to his bank manager. Three
hundred thousand, tops. Very little risk. Well, a little, you had to
expect that, but not enough to spoil their sleep. It wouldn't spoil his
sleep, anyway.

That's how he talked.

They went over it. The questions she asked were good ones, and he
had the answers. In another moment he was on his feet, touching a
napkin to his mouth with one hand and with the other reaching for his
jacket.

She sat a moment after he was gone, then put each of the pieces he
had moved, the honey pot, the egg cup, the two bits of toast, back
where they had been, and turned the egg over in the cup to show its
ravaged side. Then she put them all back again as they had been when
he left.

In her own odd fashion she was getting used to the thing, coming
to terms; as when, years back, she used to pick his socks up off the
floor and sniff, then roll them in pairs. It was a form of thinking, all
her own, but in their daily sessions it had become his way too; or
perhaps it always had been, which is why they understood one
another.

An egg cup was just an egg cup, of course; but pick it up, move it,
and you could get hold of that other more abstract thing it stood in for,
which was not so easily graspable. You made it visible, got your hands
on it in its momentary occurrence as egg cup, and a shift took place in
your head. Once that happened you were dealing with the two things
at once.

The men he worked with, who were all very clever, ambitious

258

fellows impressed by his energy and utterly loyal to him (though this did not mean that he trusted them with all he was thinking), assumed that his consultations with Ma were a charade, an act put on to reassure the old girl that she still had a hand in things. They would have smiled indulgently at all this business with egg cups and bits of toast. But they were wrong. Something in the presence of those domestic objects, something in Ma too, was necessary to the release in him not of the insights themselves but of his power to believe in them, and in his power to make them real.

He had two ways of working. The public one, the one he showed and wanted people to see, was all hard edges, assured to the point of arrogance. His reputation was based on it, and if people assumed it was all there was, so much the better. It left his other nature unseen. He was not ashamed of it, but it would have worried him to reveal too clearly what he himself did not fully understand.

This side of him was all dreamy vagueness, a lassitude in which he lost contact with the real world and where the sort of activity of which he was supposed to be a master seemed inconceivable to him. Yet it was in just this state, which if he had perceived it in another he might have despised, that he first got hold of the schemes, mere childish daydreams they were at this point, cloud-doodles, that he would knot out later and present to his more active self as proposals, then hard plans.

He trusted this faculty in himself because it had so often proved itself; but he thought of it as a form of childishness, and everything that had to do with the child in him he feared.

These moods in him belonged to the early morning, and would be on him when he woke. A continuation, he sometimes thought, of his sleep, they grew out of what he had been dreaming, though the dream itself eluded him.

Careful not to wake Ellie, he would pad across the room and go downstairs barefoot in his pyjamas, feeling oddly soft and vulnerable. The day's heat would be coming. As he wandered through the darkened house things took on a new shape, even the most familiar of them. They seemed released of their weight. Or maybe that too was part of his mood. He would sit quietly in a swing on the verandah, and as the trees on the lawn grew out of darkness his thoughts ordered themselves, became clear to him, and birds sang through them, the familiar sounds of this bird or that, very sane and comforting. This was how his thinking got done.

But sometimes, after only a minute or two, he would go through the house to Meggsie's kitchen.

Meggsie, already up and dressed, would be sitting with her plump arms on the table, her hands round a heavy cup. Wordless at this hour, she would swing round to the stove where the teapot sat, haul it across and pour him a steaming cup, the pot so heavy, even in both her hands, that she could barely heft it. He would sit then, his shoulders hunched a little, his hair a mess, and drink.

They were close. As if to make up for all the years when out of loyalty to her girls she had held out on him, she spoiled him these days as she had once spoiled Ellie and Lucille.

She still teased him. He liked the abrasive form her affection took, and would have felt cheated if she had gone soft on him. But the teasing now was no more than the old form of a game through which they could, without embarrassment, explore their affection for one another.

It was a different world out here.

The cups, for instance. They were so thick you could barely get your mouth round them. The handles too.

If it was winter the kitchen would be fuggy warm, the windows still dark. They would sit and watch them turn blue, and after a little she would get up and bring him a bowl of porridge and watch him eat.

In summer she would already have propped the screen door open with a flat-iron, and magpies would be flopping about the dewy lawn. Little points of light on tips of grassblades would be catching the sun a moment before it quenched and dried them up.

They barely spoke. If they did it was in monosyllables and half-finished sentences that to anyone else would have made no sense.

They might have been a quite different pair: she the mother who had just roused him, heavy-headed and unwilling, for the early shift at a factory or in the pit; he a big, loose-shouldered, barefoot fellow, rather lazy and fond of drink, fond of the girls too, but still tied, with only a show of rebellion, to her apron strings.

Often it was Greg who would come out at last to look for him. He would hang there in the doorway, his hair a bird's nest, his stance very like his father's, whom he imitated in everything. He was a timid little fellow, and Meggsie scared him. He wouldn't come in.

'Mummy says,' he would say, 'where are you?'

6

It surprised Vic, as the years went by, that, leaping right over what had been the grimmest period of his life, he so often found himself back in the year before his mother died and the time afterwards when he had lived with his father. He would go itchy under his clothes – the well-cut suit, the shirt Meggsie had starched – and would find himself standing high up on the dunes under a sky that was just on the turn between day and night, waiting for his body to release him into the future and send him hurtling out of himself into a new life. A kind of despair would come over him. The future he yearned for would not appear – and yet here he was right in the midst of it, assured and powerful beyond anything he could have dreamed.

He would stand and watch the wall of sand-grains shift, his mouth agape but unable to cry out as in a vast wave it rose and covered him.

He did not drink, or very little. He saw too clearly the connection between it and a violence he feared was in his nature, and which drink might let loose. It was his son who showed him this. One day, when Vic was especially angry with him, the child suddenly flinched and drew away, as if he had seen the shadow of Vic's hand before he had raised it.

'What are you doing?' His voice was full of shock, but all the boy heard was anger. 'I'm not going to hit you. You know that. Why are you crying? Nobody's going to hurt you.'

This scene, which Vic found so distressing, took place at just the time that Greg was old enough to be a presence in the house, a new focus of energy and will, subtly changing all their lives by exerting pressures this way and that to make room for itself. He was very spoiled, and when he was challenged gave way to tears. His mother, his grandmother, even Meggsie, made excuses for him, and the more they did it, Vic thought, the more the boy whined and the more resourceful he became at getting his way.

He seemed very much, as he developed, a smaller version of the father, with Vic's stance and squareness of frame, his expressions too – everyone noticed it. But the father's qualities had taken their own direction in him, so that what might have appeared as sturdy self-confidence had in the boy become a defensive petulance.

He was sorry for the child, feeling he knew only too well what he was suffering. He was afraid for him. But the likeness was unnerving. It showed up in a naked, even shameless way – though only perhaps because the boy was too young as yet to have learned how to disguise it – all that he, Vic, had taken such pains to conceal.

When Greg was still quite young, not yet seven, he developed the habit of lying. His lies were stupid ones that were bound to be exposed, which was, perhaps, just what he intended. They were lies whose only purpose was to win attention. But what was the point of *that*, Vic demanded, when all it showed was that he was a liar? In low voices, in bed, he and Ellie argued over it.

'Don't be silly,' she told him. 'You're making too much of it. Children grow out of things.'

He tried to talk to the boy man to man. He hated untruth. He found him playing with his Meccano set and made him stand still and listen, but his attention kept wandering and Vic grew angry and did not know how to go on. He was infuriated to see a little smile at the corner of the boy's mouth, as if he was not fearful at all, despite his seeming so timid, and was getting just what he wanted out of him.

By twelve he had found a kind of strength, but it was covert and indirect. On the one occasion when Vic did at last raise his fist the boy's look was of such contempt and triumph, still with that flicker of a smile at the corner of his mouth, and Vic saw himself so clearly reflected in it, that he was appalled.

He tried to pass the thing off with a recognition of fault on both sides, but the boy knew he had won and was defiant. Vic was powerless.

Everything in himself, in his inheritance too, that he had worked to push down and control, had come to independent existence in the boy and acted against him. That's what he saw, and he saw it the more clearly because Greg was just the age that he had been in his last year with his father.

He looked at the boy, saw his contemptuous smile and the likeness between them, and on the other side saw his father; and there was likeness there, too. This was what Ellie and the others could not know. He felt powerless, and at a time when power was just what came to him so easily, and publicly, elsewhere.

7

On one of his usual Thursdays, a bright winter day when there was a little chill to the air but the whole of George Street, all the way to the harbour, was bathed in clear soft sunlight, Digger was just about to cross at the Market Street lights when a woman spoke to him. He recognised her immediately.

'Hullo,' she said. 'It's Digger, isn't it.'

They stood smiling at one another.

'Oh,' he said, 'it's you.'

He did not feel free to call her by her name; but whether it was the unexpectedness of being caught together like this at the lights, forced by something quite outside themselves to come to a halt, or the softness of the day, or simply the pleasure he always had at being briefly in town, among so many people, Digger felt a wave of light-headedness catch him up – as it had, he recalled, the last time they had spoken, as if whenever they came together they were immediately translated to a special place where his awkwardness left him and he was entirely at ease.

They might have been stepping back here into a relationship that went back ages, in which all the usual difficulties had had their edges worn down through long acquaintance and habit. There was no shyness between them.

'I thought you lived – where is it? –'

'Keen's Crossing.'

'Yes. Don't you?'

'I come up to town sometimes. Every Thursday in fact.'

Their eyes met and he thought she might be wondering, in that case, why he had never taken up her invitation and got in touch. But she knew why.

'I've been buying a few things,' he told her, to explain the packages he was carrying. They were outside a hardware store where he liked to potter about for articles he couldn't pick up so easily at home, the new products they had these days, the magic glues and power tools.

264

'It's Vic's birthday Saturday,' she told him as the lights changed and they stepped off the kerb. He did not know that. 'I'm shopping. Why don't you come with me, if you're finished.' They were on the other side now. 'We can have morning tea. I won't be long.'

'All right,' he said.

Downstairs at Farmer's Ellie looked at ties, holding one or two of them up to Digger's shirt-front as she talked. They were wide ones, too colourful for him – for Vic too he would have thought, though no doubt she knew better than he did. When at last she had chosen one she bought two Island cotton shirts, then silk socks, then handkerchiefs.

Digger hung back. It was a slow business and might have been boring, but it made the talk between them so easy, and there was for him so much novelty in it, that he stopped being impatient and found he was enjoying himself. By the time it was all done they had caught up on a good many facts that it might have taken them much longer to uncover if they had not been continually on the move, and if the gaps between one question and the next had not been filled, for him, with the distractions of the store itself, the banks of lights in the ceiling, the escalators, so many women, some of them with children, some with a husband in tow, all happily spending, and turning things over on the open counters while they waited for their parcels to be wrapped; all of which he took in – the dummies too, looking so perfect with their real hair and eyelashes and doll-like eyes – while Ellie was engaged with one of the sales ladies or going through the drawers of hand-sewn handkerchiefs. At last they went upstairs into a big room overlooking the street, found a table away from the mothers and children, and ordered tea. They could relax now. A silence fell and they were forced to look at one another; but they could face that because they had already, in their half-hour of movement and talk, got so far with one another.

Ellie looked at him in a candid, clear-eyed way that sought to see, Digger thought, what there might be beyond his shyness; something she had glimpsed, and been looking for too, he thought now, when she held up to his open shirt-collar one of the expensive ties.

She looked at his hands and he saw her register something – that he worked with them? At his eyes again – What did she see there? (He found he did not mind her scrutiny.) It would be nothing of what really mattered to him. So when he looked at her, and saw the way her hair curled in just at shoulder level, the neatness of her brows, the colour on her lips, he took it for granted that what mattered most to her was also invisible, and would remain so unless she found the words to tell him of it.

She surprised him by speaking almost immediately of her father.

'I remember that poem he read,' Digger told her, 'at your wedding. "The precarious gift alive in our hands again, the mixed blessing".' He did not say, though she might have guessed it from the quality of his voice, that the lines meant something special to him.

'But fancy you remembering it,' she said.

'Oh, I know the whole thing off by heart,' he told her. He didn't mean to show off, and blushed in case she suspected him of it.

'The whole poem?'

'It's a trick,' he said, sorry he had ever let on. 'It's nothing.'

She told him of the work she did. Her father had published two books in the past five years, one a book of poems – Digger could find the Wedding Ode there, if he looked – the other a collection of essays. In the small world of writers, reviewers, university lecturers and other people who cared for these things, he had begun to be well known, but it was a very small world of course; most people didn't even know it existed. She did his secretarial work for him. That, together with the house and her little boy, was enough to keep her going. The next time they met she would bring copies of the books, now that she knew he was a reader.

Digger said nothing, but did observe her assumption that this meeting was not to be their last. He would not have made the suggestion himself but was pleased that she had. They talked on after that, with no hurry to get everything said. There would be time for the rest of it next time.

He told her about his mother, who had been gone for nearly a year now, but whose end, all her bravery and defiance gone down to despair, still haunted him. About Jenny too. At last about Iris. She told him about the little boy, Greg. Some time, she promised, when Vic was going to the Crossing, she would send him along.

'Now,' she said, 'I'd better go. Next time, I promise, the books.'

She was proud of what her father had done. He liked that and wondered what Vic made of it.

It was odd that in all the things they had touched on, they had never once referred directly to *him*. Not deliberately – it wasn't deliberate on his part, and he thought it wasn't on hers either, but to preserve an area between them that was for them alone. If they had tried to include Vic, he would have swallowed up the whole of what they had to say to one another, especially in the beginning, when he might have seemed the only thing they had in common.

She had a particular look, he thought, at moments when the natural thing to do might have been to say 'Vic and I' or 'we', or at moments when, though she did not directly speak of him, he was clearly in her mind. There would be a little change in her then, as if something had come to the surface in her that was secret, not to be spoken of, yet was on the very tip of her tongue. It was, he felt, the thing he had been wondering about that was most important to her. When it came up he could feel the heat of it, as in his case it had been there (had she felt it?) when he spoke the lines of her father's poem, but especially just afterwards, when he had owned up to his trick of recall, which always evoked what was deepest in him.

The meeting, when he thought back over it, was a joyful one. They repeated it over the years, sometimes weekly. At other times, depending on what else was happening in their lives, whole months would pass before they could arrange it.

They would go for tram rides to Watson's Bay, and walk round the path under the coral trees from Camp Cove to where the sea crashes against South Head. They took ferry trips across to Cremorne and Mosman, shopped, went to the art gallery or the city library, or sat in the gardens and watched the crowds. Each time her father published a new book she brought him one.

He did not mention these meetings to Vic, though there was nothing secret about them. He thought it was Ellie's right to tell. If she did, Vic gave no indication of it.

Iris teased him, but only mildly, about his 'lady friend'. She liked to pretend she was jealous. Was she? he wondered. Just a little? She had no need to be.

8

It seemed to Ellie, when she gave thought to the matter, that things could not have fallen out otherwise than they had; and this was strange, because when she looked back ten years and saw them all as they were then, she could find no sign of what was coming – none at all.

A good deal of this had to do with Lucille.

Lucille had been gone for seven years. Her marriage to Virge had broken up almost as soon as she joined him. She was married now to an older man with children of his own, a company lawyer in Denver, Colorado, where she too had a business, in real estate.

These changes dismayed Ellie. They had been very close over the Virge business, which had appeared then to be a culmination and had turned out, for all its intensity and the significance they had put upon it, to be no more than an episode on the way to something else. She wrote to Lucille twice a month, and the letters that came back were racy and full of news, but she could no longer connect them to the girl she had grown up with.

As little things they had fought like tigers. Ellie recalled occasions when they had struggled and torn at one another, red-faced and sweaty in their singlets and pants, both tearful with rage, pulling at one another's hair and spitting.

Meggsie's way of handling this had been to close the door and leave them to it. When they came out, still hot and angry but also ashamed, she would say: 'All right now, you little devils. Go an' wash your faces and take off those filthy clothes' (they had been rolling on the floor) 'an' I won't tell yer Ma what you've been up to. Hurry on now. I've made some nice cold lemonade.'

It had been hard for Ellie. Lucille was just that much older. She had already established her rights in the world, and made some things in the house so much her own that Ellie could not take them up without appearing, as she so often was, an imitator.

She was a latecomer in people's hearts too, they had to make way for her. Lucille didn't mean to be imposing, she couldn't help it. People noticed her and only later, Ellie felt, saw that she too was there, trailing along behind and wondering what it might be in her that was anything more than a reflection of her more brilliant sister.

What puzzled her was that none of this appeared to make Lucille happy. Lucille was by nature restless, difficult, discontented. *She* was the easy one.

Then, just about the time that Vic came to live with them, they had discovered how close they were, how even the animosity they felt, the way they jockeyed against one another, was a bond. It was the element Vic added that made them see this.

He was a boy, and they were astonished, angered too, to observe how this simple fact impressed everyone – Pa, Ma, even Meggsie, though she didn't *quite* give in to him.

Ellie had been pleased at first to see Lucille displaced, but soon understood that if Lucille was harmed she was too.

They teased him. That was easy. He was an awkward boy once you got past his cockiness. But he was a novelty, too; that's what they couldn't resist. Quite soon new affinities had begun to form. A secret one at first between Lucille and him, and once again Ellie found herself on the sidelines, a watcher of the little drama that had begun to unfold. Vic was at a loss in this, because although he and Lucille were the same age, he was still just a boy. So Vic and Ellie had ganged up on Lucille. Lucille thought she was so marvellous, so grown-up. Ellie still belonged, as he half did, to the world of animal spirits and fun.

But in all that she had missed something after all, some other, more important strand; some perversity or quirk in Lucille that had made her fly in the face of all that appeared to have been laid up for her, perhaps for the very reason that it was so fixed and had come so easily. She got pregnant, married Virge. None of this, Ellie knew, had had *her* in view, yet her life too had been changed by it.

The point on which it turned was that moment in the half-dark of the piano room, during what was to be the last of their games. Everything had been quite clear to her at that moment, and to Vic too. They saw in a flash all that had led up to it and all that would lead away from it. But Lucille, she thought, had seen it before them.

So the household was hers. Ma, all her energies taken up with business, was quite happy to hand it over. There was no question of their moving into a place of their own. It was as if the house already contained the forms their life would need. She and Vic had their separate life in it but the household went on as it had always done.

It was for this reason, there being so little visible change, that it took her so long to understand what he and Ma were doing.

Their style of life did not change. She and Meggsie settled up the weekly accounts, and they remained pretty much what they had always been. They took the same amount of bread and milk, and these things cost the same whether you are worth thousands or just sixpence. You use the same number of towels, sleep in the same sheets.

Vic talked a good deal at first of the sums they were dealing in. The figures doubled and trebled, you could grasp that. It was worth boasting about. It pointed to a personal agency you could identify, to foresight, boldness, imagination. But when the momentum increased, as if subject to some law of its own that was purely mathematical, the personal side of it disappeared. There was a scale to it now that was beyond the capacity of the mind to grasp. Keep adding noughts, and although the thing is still there, and in fact occupies more and more space, there develops in it a kind of vacuum, as if the noughts, the nothings, had predominance. The mind loses all trace of it.

Ellie was amazed by him. So was Pa. They looked on in wonder at these powers he had, which like the enterprise itself appeared to double, treble, then move in progressions that were inhuman, magical; though this was only because their imagination could not contain him any more than they could the figures.

Where did it come from, she wondered, this energy and animation that she experienced as such a physical thing? He was so full of it that you wondered how so much force could limit itself, when needed, to the merely commonplace business of manoeuvring a knife or getting peas on to a fork, or as she saw it, to the moments they shared when she would watch him pull a clean shirt over his head and walk round the room in his socks and suspenders, or sit, as he sometimes did, very quiet and abstracted with a towel in his hand, his hair still wet from the shower, on the edge of their bed.

It pained her when she went out to hear him spoken of in a cruel and dismissive way by people who did not know him as she did, from within. He had enough success, she saw, to have become a figure who aroused hostility, envy, also fear, and often this was in men, and women too, to whom he was no more than a name. They had never laid eyes on him.

When she met this impersonal version of him, even if it was only in people's eyes across a dinner table or theatre foyer, she went cold. The certainty with which they were prepared to judge! All the more when she found it in print.

But if he thought himself misunderstood, as she knew he did, he bore it stoically, hiding his hurt behind a show of arrogance. He hid things. The more she knew him, the more she saw that, and understood how extraordinary had been that glimpse of him in the dark of the piano room, how completely she had grasped then what it was in him that she would spend the rest of her life grappling with.

He read the papers with a look on his face that even she could not fathom. It was pain. She could tell that, if others couldn't. But he found a kind of satisfaction in it too. There was, just at the corner of his mouth, the play of a smile. Perhaps he felt flattered that they were making so much of him.

To her these assaults were merely painful. How could she not feel them personally when she had given so much of herself to him, and taken into her custody so much that was vulnerable in him?

She spoke to no one of all this, but it was there often enough, unspoken, between her and Pa, who, looking at things from his own distance, and from a very different centre of power, was as struck as she was by the proximity of so much energy. Some of the capacity Pa himself had discovered over these last years, or so she thought, came as an attempt to understand Vic's kind of power and balance it.

Pa too had surprised them. Who could have predicted that his peculiar nervousness, which had kept the whole household on edge and been so aimless and self-consuming, would find a focus at last in what she dealt with daily now, the individual words and lines that sat, when she typed them, so squarely on the page and spoke with so much authority and had such weight in the world?

The one thing that alarmed her, and increasingly as the years went by, was Vic's attitude to the boy. Nothing else caused her such heartbreak or led to so many quarrels between them.

She was by nature optimistic. She believed people were reasonable. Given time, things solved themselves; all you had to do was be patient. But in this case things got worse, not better. By the time Greg was twelve a coldness had developed between Vic and the boy, a kind of contempt on both sides that she did not know how to deal with.

He was a good-natured boy, full of affection and eager to please, perhaps too much so; but he could not please his father, and after a time, out of disappointment, did not want to, or pretended he didn't.

As for Vic, everything the boy did unsettled or irritated him, especially as he grew out of childishness and became a young man.

The more she argued with him, the more unreasonable Vic grew, and at last she gave up. She had begun to fear the things that were said between them. So long as they were unspoken they had no force. Once they got into the world, and could be gone back to and brooded over, they were real.

'Vic,' she told him wearily, 'they're all like this, all these *young* people. He's no different from the rest.' She named Greg's friends, some of whom were the sons and daughters of men Vic knew and thought well of. 'What does it matter how he wears his hair?'

But he clamped his mouth shut and would not answer. He was angry with her, she knew, because she took the boy's part.

'I would have hoped,' he said at last, like a man repeating something he had already prepared, 'that a son of mine would think for himself, not just go along with what others do.'

'Oh,' she said, but gently, 'a son of yours.'

'He's got no character. No character, no interests, no ambitions. What else can I think?'

It was part of the vision he had of the hardness of things, based on his own life and of the qualities you needed not to go under. She could have no idea how afraid he was of every sort of weakness, how panicky he felt, and when he looked at his son, the vulnerable region that opened in him.

Ellie did know this, and it scared her. But she saw something else, too: that things weren't hard any more, they were easy, and he was one of the men who had made them so. Young people had time now to play. That wasn't a crime, was it?

The issues they fought over were small ones, the length of the boy's hair, the clothes he wore: Ellie thought they were small. But it infuriated Vic to see his son, and all these worthless kids he ran around with, dressed in cast-offs. Old waistcoats and shirts without collars that his father might have worn. Grimy old-fashioned suits like the

272

ones they had been given after the war, still with the sweat stains on them (they did not care about that), and all over both lapels the badges of a war they thought they were waging, gaudy passwords and proclamations of revolt. Sweat-stained felt Akubras (except for these clowns only Digger wore a hat these days), greasy ties and evening scarves, all picked up at street markets or at Tempe Tip, or off the racks of the St Vincent de Paul; the fashionable fancy dress of a misery they knew nothing about, and did not care about either, for all their mouthing of slogans and the rag-tag principles of a revolution they would never have to mount.

He thought bitterly of a wet day when he was maybe nine years old and was taken with a gang of other children to a room at the School of Arts. They were the poorest kids of the district, guaranteed so by the headmaster; though you could have seen it for yourself from the reach-me-down clothes they wore, the sweaters that had to be pushed up at the elbows, the trousers drawn in six inches with a bit of string, the little girls' frocks that came down past their knees.

Herded into the dingy hall, they were presented with a row of smiling, sympathetic ladies and a pile of clothes that had been tipped out of bags onto the floor.

Red-faced and ashamed, they were let loose among them like rag pickers. He had snatched up the first thing he saw, eager to do what they wanted, choose something and get away, and had stuffed what he got, without even looking to see how good it was, down the back of a seat on one of the bus shelters along the shore. The rough wool of it still prickled and rubbed his flesh, as if he had worn it next to his skin for years.

Rags, cast-offs, the stink of other people's sweat – all that was horrible to him. It made his flesh itch. Because for him, and for so many others too, it had been necessity. But to these kids it was just play-acting, in uniforms you could change the moment you were bored with them. Poverty to them was just another rag you could put on, if you were rich enough, to make yourself interesting, or different, or to see how it suited you.

Greg lately had taken to going about without shoes; in a suit with a felt hat, and no shoes. He choked on that. He thought of the lines of men he had seen falling in in the drizzle, to whom the lack of a pair of boots up there had meant death. He was not thinking of himself. He did not mean to refer back to his own suffering, though he felt it again, and with a sense of injustice and anger and weak self-pity that sickened him, but of what others had been through.

It would have shamed him to speak of these things. That a man, even a boy, should not know them already, was incomprehensible to him.

When he and Greg argued there was no common ground between them. Ellie felt helpless. What the boy shouted in his own defence was useless, she knew that and felt sorry for him, and Vic set his jaw and would not speak.

9

Meggsie, who was past seventy, sat down in a chair one day at her kitchen table and found she could not get up. Her legs had gone.

She was very shocked, and frightened too, but did not cry out. She thought of doing so, but it seemed so foolish that when her mouth opened she promptly clamped it shut again and sat frowning, feeling a kind of darkness come over her. She had never felt anything like it. She had her moods, but this one came from outside her, like weather, leaving the windows full of clear sunshine but darkening her mind. She felt weak and increasingly helpless and afraid, but could not bring herself to break the habits of a lifetime and shout. When they found her at last it was because of the smell of burning.

All the time she had sat there a custard had been boiling over on the stove, and she had not noticed it. The mess was awful. She kept apologising for it as they lifted her, and for the trouble she was giving them, and it was this more than anything else that upset Pa. She was the sort of woman, Meggsie, who never apologised.

Her daughters were scattered. One lived outside Rockhampton up in Queensland, another out west. The third, Vera-me-youngest as Meggsie called her, and as she had always been known to them, was married to a lawyer on the North Shore. They phoned her now, and two hours later she drove up in a Mazda.

Ma had known her as a girl and had found her very clever and offensive in those days. She was now a good-looking woman in her fifties, very tastefully dressed. Ma, feeling embarrassed at her own shabbiness, still thought of her as Vera-me-youngest, but she introduced herself as Mrs Moreton.

She was cold at first. For several years now she had wanted Meggsie to give up working and come and live with her. Meggsie was torn but had decided she was too well settled to leave the Warrenders. Mrs Moreton believed they had influenced her, and she looked about now for something that would allow her to feel superior.

She found it at last.

The cars in the drive – there were three of them – were what you might have expected. But the house! The furniture, for example. She knew what these people were worth – who didn't? – but there was no decent furniture in the place, not a thing you could look at. No antiques. Shoddy Thirties veneer, old-fashioned and ugly. They had made no improvements. She remembered coming here once a week, when she was sixteen or seventeen, to collect her pocket money and to be given a box of handkerchiefs or a pair of gloves by Mrs Warrender when her birthday came round. In those days she had thought the place unattainably grand. She was angry with herself for having been so naive. Her own house was a dozen times more impressive.

They left her alone with Meggsie and did not hear what was said.

She wanted Meggsie to go to hospital. Meggsie refused. She was happy where she was: they had a night nurse for her. Mrs Moreton was put out. She was grateful for what they were doing but felt snubbed. 'Don't be silly,' Meggsie told her.

She rang daily after that but did not come again till the end.

She was sick for nine weeks. They had the night nurse. Otherwise it was Ma and Ellie who looked after her and put up with her complaints that everything they did was done badly, that the place was going to ruin, that the new girl they had got hold of might be a dab hand at *foreign* cooking but didn't know the first thing about plain food.

In the afternoon while Ellie rested Pa would drop in for an hour or two, to tease her, taste her medicines and tell her jokes. 'Stop it,' she would yell, 'you're killing me.' Vic too liked to sit with her.

He would go out in the early morning in his dressing-gown, send the nurse to make tea, and when she came back, wave her off. Ellie would find her asleep under a reading lamp in the front room.

In these hours he did all the things the nurse might have done. 'Vic,' Ellie told him, 'you don't have to do these things. That's why we've got the nurse.' She meant to spare him something she thought men shied away from, the intimate business that has to do with bodies. 'Don't worry,' he told her, 'I don't mind. It gives us a chance, you know, to talk a bit.'

'Did you know,' he said one day, 'that Meggsie was a twin? Can you imagine it, *two* Meggsies? The other one died of the Spanish flu. She grew up in Chillagoe, did you know that? When it had a population of 7,000. It's a ghost town now.'

He would be half-asleep on these occasions, very tender and talking half to himself. What he was talking about, she knew, was the mystery of other people's lives, how little we know of one another; lying very close to her, just on the edge of sleep, and almost ready, she thought, because of the softness of his mood, to put into words at last the facts and details of his own life, all that part of it that was still secret in him.

One night Meggsie called to him where he sat half-dozing against the wall.

'Vic, love, are you there? I want to give you something – a present.' She sometimes wandered at this hour, but she did not seem to be wandering now. 'Go to the bottom drawer of me dressing table.'

He got up and went to the cedar chest of drawers where her photographs sat in their celluloid frames. One was of the girls when they were little, the other a composite of half a dozen faded snapshots, her husband Len out west somewhere with a lot of other fellows, all standing in a row in hats.

The drawer was stiff. He had to get down on his knees to shift it. It jerked, came open, and in the half-light from the hallway he saw with a little shock that it was full of leaves. Was he dreaming?

'Take one,' she said behind him.

He put his hand into the drawer in a gingerly way, afraid for some reason of snails, and rustled among the dry leaves. But no, it wasn't leaves. It was lottery tickets, hundreds of them, thousands – every fifth share she had bought, regularly on her afternoon off, from Mr McCann the local newsagent, over more than forty years. He felt among them.

But they were leaves. He had taken them for lottery tickets only in the way one's mind works in dreams, though whether it was his dream or hers he could not tell. It was just about the time that ballots were being drawn to send young men up to Vietnam. Greg was eighteen, and he thought it might be Greg's name he was about to draw. Or was it his own? Again? Could they ask you to go again?

'What are you doing?' she demanded. 'Have you got one?'

He took one of the tickets and went to the bed and showed it to her.

'No,' she said, without even looking at it. 'That's not the one.'

He brought her another.

'No.' She was quite short with him, as if he were being deliberately stupid. He felt like a very young child who could not see the answer to some simple problem in arithmetic.

'Meggsie –' he began.

'Go on,' she told him, 'you're wasting time.'

He dipped again.

'Yes, that's it,' she said with a sigh. 'Good boy! You were always a good boy really.' She smiled. 'Now, don't show it to anyone, eh? Don't tell, or you'll lose your luck. Don't even show it to *me*. Put it in your wallet.'

He obeyed. He put the ticket, which had after all never won anything the first time around, in his wallet.

'No,' she said, catching the feeling of despair that had come over him, 'don't worry. It's a good one. I wouldn't give you anything that wasn't lucky, love, you know that. Don't you know that after all this time? Trust me.'

He did not remember it had happened till the next day when he was in the office and in conference. He broke off for a moment to check his wallet, and there was the ticket.

He told Ellie about it, but wondered later if he had made the point clear, since what it had to do with was what he had *felt*; the odd sensation, when he put his hand into the drawer, that he was moving it among dried leaves, going back years, each with its number. Greg's ballot too had been part of it.

With Meggsie's death a prop went from the house. They all felt it and were surprised how her various forms of tyranny, which they had been inclined to laugh over, had determined the way they lived. Impossible to modernise the kitchen – that was Meggsie's province. Part of her power lay in the fact that only she could manage its many inconveniences. Impossible to suggest that nobody these days ate puddings, a different one each night.

But when she was gone and they were free to make all the changes they wanted, they were at a loss where to begin. For the first time Vic talked seriously to Ma of selling the house and the adjoining factory site and moving. He did it, Ma thought, not because it was a necessary move, or one that any of them wanted, but for reasons of his own that for all their closeness she could not ask about.

For a long time now he had felt a kind of emptiness in him that had to do, he thought, with the way he had closed his heart in the last days before his mother's death, had shut out so completely all the pain and loss he felt that afterwards there was nothing to go back to. Now, in grieving for Meggsie he grieved at last for his mother, in the kind of linking over and back (he was thinking of the way his mother hemmed a skirt) that made up the odd, cross-hatched line he was following.

But there was something else as well. For a time, between eighteen and twenty-one, death had been the closest of all realities to him, a daily thing, more common in that place than the sound of a woman's voice, or a bath running, or a clean shirt. He had thought he would never get used to any other condition of life; that those ordinary things – clean shirts, hot baths, a woman's hand – would go on being so miraculous as to be barely graspable, and only the proximity of death quite real.

The whole of his energy at that time had been engaged in pushing it off; in clinging to his own body and dragging the little bit of life in it from one day to the next. It was huge, that, but also simple. Pure, too. The effort was so pure. You knew what the other was because from time to time, when it was necessary, you held a man whose death was near so close against your ribs that his heart was just a paper thinness from your own, and the beating of it was like your own heart flopping and failing.

For years now no death had come close enough to touch him. Now Meggsie's did, and after so long, his mother's death too. (He was not ready yet to think of his father.) Most of all, he began once again to live with his own, but it seemed mysterious to him now because he was surrounded by so much that obscured even the possibility of it, and because when it came to him here it would, given the odds, be of a kind he had not yet faced, a natural one.

10

For more than twenty years Digger's visits to town had followed the same pattern. Thursday was the day, because in the early years it had been Iris's day off. Later, when the cake shop closed and she retired, they stuck to Thursdays out of habit. Digger went up on an early train, spent the night, and came back on the milk train Friday morning.

If it was one of the days when he was to meet Ellie he would not go to Bondi Junction till after lunch. Otherwise, after a bit of shopping on his own, he went immediately. They would take a picnic to Cooper Park, or eat quietly at home, and in the afternoon he would read a bit or do whatever jobs needed doing. Now that the boys were gone there was always some little thing to be set right. In the evening they took in a show, or went round and had tea at Ewen's or Jack's, who were married now with families of their own.

He got on well with the wives. There had never been any embarrassment about his standing among them. The children called Iris Grannie and Digger was 'Grannie's friend'. They called him Digger because their fathers did – he had baulked at 'Uncle'.

They were freer with him than with any uncle. Their mothers had to step in and prevent them, the moment he appeared, from climbing all over him like some sort of natural phenomenon, an especially co-operative tree or rock. He was fond of children. He showed them old-fashioned tricks even their fathers did not know, with balls made of silver paper out of cigarette packets, that if weighted at one end could be made to dance, and how to weave pyjama-cords on cotton reels. He brought them wooden toys he had made and told them stories, serious ones, that left them struck but which for some reason they could not get enough of. Thursdays he was a family man. He spent a lot of his time during the week thinking up tricks to amuse 'the kids'.

The whole tenor of his life on that one day of the week was different, and had been for so long, given the little changes that had taken place in it, that when he found himself at Central Station on a

Monday morning, same hour but a different day of the week, he felt disorientated.

It wasn't simply that his own routine had been broken. The whole feel of the place was different. The Monday morning crowds wore different faces. The streets had a different pace. It felt less like another day of the week than another city.

He had come up for the funeral of the poet, Hugh Warrender. He was doing it out of affection for Ellie, but also out of respect for a man he had spoken to only once, and then in an unsatisfactory way, but whom he felt he had got to know over the years, and grown close to. Iris went with him.

It was an odd gathering. There were groups of older people who Digger guessed would be friends of the family or business acquaintances of Vic's; but there were others whose presence was so unlikely that he thought they must have mistaken the time and come to the wrong ceremony. A lot of the men were in jeans and high-collared Indian shirts, and some wore washed-out combat jackets with Chairman Mao caps. Most of the girls too wore jeans, but some were got up in full-length cotton like Indian women and had children with them in the same outlandish garb. There was a flock of schoolgirls as well, all in gingham and straw hats.

The presence of so many hippies, he thought, was unfortunate. It did not occur to him till later, when he saw how sober and attentive they were, that some of these people might have the same sort of distant but personal relation to Hugh Warrender that he did and had come in the same spirit. He saw them differently then.

It was February, and hot. Outside in the sunken rose garden where they had milled about waiting, the birds were singing, in a regular, repeatable way but at odd intervals just whenever they pleased, breaking in on the organ music. They were a distraction. Very argumentative and bold they sounded, getting on with their noisy lives while people settled and subdued themselves.

The order of things was impressive. Ellie read one of her father's poems, quite a short one that was unfamiliar to Digger though he knew all the books. If it spoke of death, and he was by no means certain of that, it did so in a light-hearted way, closer to the hubbub the birds were creating than to the solemn music. There was an image of night-smelling jasmine – the flower itself out of sight somewhere, its invisible presence in the room, and of a household, also unseen, all busy voices. One word was repeated and Digger was moved by it. The word was 'returns'.

When the poem was over some overtones of it, of its music, lingered in him, and in the others too, he thought. Iris very lightly touched his hand as on that other occasion, and once again what Mr Warrender had to say drew them together.

There was no sadness in it, none at all. Quite the opposite really. It spoke of presence and completeness, of 'returns'. Much later, Digger would think of the poem and be pleased that he and Iris had heard it together. It would comfort him for his loss. But at the moment it was his mother he was thinking of. It struck him with panic, that image of her sitting in a broken chair out in the yard, with behind her the house and its contents, all she had clung to and held against such odds, turned to ashes in her head.

He had spent so many hours in the consideration of it because the law she had lived by was so like his own. What he was left wondering was how, when the time came, he might let go of things without believing, as she had, that he was not only losing them but had never in any real sense had them.

Mr Warrender's grandsons, Greg and an older boy, Alex, who had come across with his mother from America, were to read the lessons; and strangely enough, it was precisely what Digger had been turning over in his head that Greg now spoke of.

It was many years since Digger had seen him. He had been just a lad then, a neat little fellow in a duffle coat and new boots. He was rather gangling now (he had heard something of him from Ellie, from Vic too once or twice), and was so much, Digger thought, what Vic had been when he first knew him that he decided the differences he saw must have to do with his eyesight. He forked his glasses out of his right-hand breast pocket as the boy read, but saw, when he set them on his nose, that the lack of focus he had been aware of was in the boy himself.

He was less compact than Vic had been. But it wasn't that. What he lacked, and it made all the difference, was cockiness. It brought back to Digger, and vividly, considering the years, just what he had felt about Vic in those early days, his intense antipathy – and what had happened to *that*?

'In the day when the keepers of the house shall tremble,' he read, 'and the strong men bow themselves, and the grinders cease because they are too few, and those that look out of the windows be darkened

. . . Also when they shall be afraid of that which is on high, and fears shall be in the way, and the almond tree shall flourish, and the grasshoppers shall be a burden, and desire shall fail: because man goeth to his long home and the mourners go about the streets . . .'

From his place in the front row Vic looked up. The boy did not read confidently. He stumbled in places and seemed unsure of how the words were connected. Vic's face in profile, as Digger saw it, wore a concerned look, either because he was anxious for the boy on this public occasion, as Ellie was too – Digger could see that – or because of something in the words themselves.

Iris had remarked earlier when they arrived how little changed he was. It was more than twenty years since she had seen him. Digger was surprised. When he turned up at the Crossing it was his immediate mood that Digger looked out for – little signs he had learned to recognise that meant their time together would go easily, others which, however much he disguised them, indicated the opposite. Till Iris mentioned it, he had never considered him in the light of change.

'They go fast,' Iris thought, 'when they do go. That sort.' Digger was of the other kind. He was spare and leathery, and under the hat was very nearly bald. She no longer felt any embarrassment when they were out together. He might have been sixty as she was. (Sixty-seven, in fact.)

The other boy, who spoke with an American accent, was *too* confident, Digger thought. He read as at a performance. It jarred.

There was a third speaker, a man from the university who had written on Hugh Warrender and came here, as a good many of the mourners did, as a sharer in his *public* life, though public, as he pointed out, was the wrong word for something which, in the case of each one of them, and in the poet's case too, was so hidden that if one was to be true to the spirit of it, it could be referred to only in terms that were tentative and indirect.

He was speaking of poetry itself, of the hidden part it played in their lives, especially here in Australia, though it was common enough – that was the whole point of it – and of their embarrassment when it had, as now, to be brought into the light. How it spoke up, not always in the plainest terms, since that wasn't always possible, but in precise ones just the same, for what is deeply felt and might otherwise go unrecorded: all those unique and repeatable events, the little sacraments of daily existence, movements of the heart and intimations of

283

the close but inexpressible grandeur and terror of things, that is our *other* history, the one that goes on, in a quiet way, under the noise and chatter of events and is the major part of what happens each day in the life of the planet, and has been from the very beginning. To find words for *that*; to make glow with significance what is usually unseen, and unspoken too – that, when it occurs, is what binds us all, since it speaks immediately out of the centre of each one of us; giving shape to what we too have experienced and did not till then have words for, though as soon as they are spoken we know them as our own.

This speech made an impression on Digger. That 'other history' meant something to him. When they stepped outside into the strong sunlight, which was thick with bees, he saw a few people go up to the young man who had said so much, shake hands and congratulate him; he looked embarrassed but also pleased with himself.

Digger did not make the mistake this time of approaching him. He settled for the words themselves. They had struck a chord in him, and touched, he felt, on the very thing he had been thinking of earlier: what it is that cannot be held on to but nonetheless is not lost.

11

It was the night of Pa's funeral and still hot. Big storm clouds were building over the flat land towards Hen and Chicken Bay and nervous shudders of lightning touched the edges of them. Vic came away from the table feeling displeased with everyone, and with himself too.

Pa's death, which had come without warning, had hit him hard, and Lucille's arrival with Alex, all adding to the adjustments and changes that had to be made in the household, had made these last days painful to him.

The two boys, despite what had happened, insisted on arguing through every meal, but in a way that was inappropriate and put them all on edge.

Greg's arguments, as even Ellie had to admit, were erratic and one-sided. He was idealistic, full of youthful passion and the assurance of being always in the right, but everything he had to say was second-hand, and for all its predictability was so garbled and incoherent as to be very nearly incomprehensible.

The other one, Alex, who was twenty-four and already a graduate of Harvard, was a stiff fellow, equally one-eyed and insistent, but he hid it with an assumption of coolness that outraged Greg and made him more vehement than ever.

Greg had had great hopes of this cousin of his. An American! In his naive and open-hearted way he had been eager to be impressed and to hear at first-hand all that was happening at the centre of things.

He was bitterly disappointed. He hid it at first; Alex was a guest. Then, when he saw that he was being patronised, he adopted an air of open hostility, but in such a hurt and inarticulate and childish way that Vic found it hard to witness. Tonight he gave Ellie a helpless look and got away. He needed to distance himself.

He went first to sit for a time with Ma, who had gone straight up after the funeral to lie down. She too found these mealtimes exasperating.

He sat beside her bed in the darkened room and they talked a little.

What they talked of was an occasion, years back, when Pa had played a practical joke, a particularly silly one, on a dinner guest, a very pompous fellow who was in line to be a judge. Ma began to laugh, then he did, and they both stopped, not in a guilty way, but thinking, if any stranger heard them, how difficult it would be to explain. When he left her and went downstairs he did something he would not have dreamed of doing a week before. He went to Pa's study. Seating himself at the old-fashioned desk, which was carved in Renaissance style, he sat for a time in the dark watching the lightning flicker, then put his hand out and lit a lamp.

The sense of irritation he had felt at the table was still with him. It was associated somehow with the odd shuddery flashes of the lightning. It made him tense and with no hope of release.

It was the hostility between the two young men he focused on, their foolish tearing this way and that of a dead cat, but he was keeping it in the foreground, he knew, because there was something else that disturbed him more, and it was this he needed to think about.

Lucille at forty-six was not at all the girl who had left them more than twenty years ago. He would hardly have known her. She was very brisk and businesslike, and preoccupied, as was only to be expected, with the family she had left back in the States. She took an interest in all there was to catch up on, but what she saw here fell short, he guessed, of some memory she had kept – of the place, of them – and when he looked at things through her eyes he saw it too.

He had thought what he had done – all he had achieved – was so large a thing. Yet what he was chiefly aware of when they sat down to the table together was how *little* had happened, and how little, in the end, was changed. Pa was gone. They were older. There were these two boys now, slugging away at one another. But the only difference, he felt, was that something he had hung on to, a sense of sweet disillusionment that had to do with Lucille and all he had felt for her, was no longer sweet – and not bitter either – but had dulled and was very nearly gone.

He had loved his disillusionment. It gave him such a sense of his own youth. He saw its going now as the beginning, the first approach, of middle age.

And Pa?

How long was it since they had spoken in a way that touched what was most important to them? They were always close. There was no

286

lack of warmth between them. But they had had little to say to one another in these last years that was new. This shocked him, and all the more because suddenly, now that he was gone, it seemed to Vic that everything he knew about Pa was a puzzle to him. From the moment of their first meeting – and before that, too, the days when his father had been Pa's batman and exacted the promise – everything, Pa's playfulness, his glooms, the life he had had in his head, the poems he had written, was a mystery to him. But what really disturbed him was what he had seen at the funeral today: that there were people who had never even met Pa, who knew him better perhaps than he did. He had the panicky sense of having missed the man entirely, but the source of his panic was the ghostly image this gave him of himself.

'What does it mean to *be*,' he thought, 'except *to be known*?'

He had been delighted, as they all were, by Pa's success, but had never got round to the actual books. He saw now that he ought to have done. He had missed something Pa had to say that others had attended to and he had not, something too that Pa might have meant him to hear. He reached out now and drew the four volumes from the shelf. Opening one, the last as it happened, he set himself to go through it from cover to cover. He read for nearly an hour.

It was like a hard lesson at school. He had forgotten what it was to go over and over something and find that it would not go into your head, because there was some resistance in it, or in you, that would not give.

He had come up against this unpleasant fact before, and each time had suppressed it. Looking now at what Pa had got down, he came upon things that were just beyond his apprehension, eluding him at the very moment of his reaching out for them; but they were things, and he knew this too, that were not strange to him. That was the unpleasant part. They did not belong to some other world at all but to the one he was in, and still he could not grasp them.

What he felt in a quite physical way was the spinning of the earth under him at the very moment when he could also say to himself: 'But the room is still.' And then: 'If the world is like this and I have never properly got hold of it, what *have* I got hold of?'

He sat with the book open on the desk but had stopped reading. What the poems, which he had only vaguely understood, had set off in him was going on now of its own accord.

It is a sobering thing, even when you are a father yourself and have some force in the world, to find, in the childish part of yourself that goes on existing despite the years, that there is no hand you can reach out for.

Almost as soon as his parents died Pa had appeared. Since then it was Pa, for all his weakness, who had stood between him and the knowledge that he was alone in the world. For a time, when he was twenty, that knowledge had been forced on him, but it was premature, it did not last. As soon as he got back it lapsed in him, and once again he had moved back under Pa's protection, relegating to him the father's role, and was shielded. Now, for the first time, he felt orphaned.

When Ellie saw a slit of light under the door she had the odd feeling that what she would see, when she opened it, was Pa. So she approached it very quietly, turned the knob, and paused, afraid to startle herself.

He did not see her for a moment. He was seated with a pool of lamplight on the desk before him, his face half-dark. All round the shelves was the flicker of far-off lightning. He did not look up; he was not aware of her. In the moment before he turned, all that she knew of him was confirmed.

12

It was from Ellie that Digger heard of the break with Greg. Vic would not have told him. In the early days he had been eager enough to talk about the boy. He always had news to tell of what a promising little fellow he was, shy, a bit clinging maybe – that was having so many women in the house – but full of questions and his own odd bright little opinions on the world. Vic was young himself in those days. His pride in the boy ran away with him. He would pull himself up, suddenly embarrassed, and laugh it off. But things changed, and after a time he spoke of the boy only with bitterness. In these last years he had barely mentioned him. Digger, hearing of this latest, this last business, did not know what to say. Ellie did not complain but he saw the grief it caused her.

'He does these things to himself. Why? Why *is* that? The very thing he doesn't want to happen he does himself. It's as if he wanted to save himself, you know, from having it done to him. Is that it? You know him, Digger – is that what it is? So he does it himself. "I did it" – that's what he's saying to himself – "it wasn't just done to me." Then he grits his teeth in that terrible way he's got. "Life is *like* this. We have to put up with it. That's what character is for." And he's brought it all on *himself.*'

They were having a cup of tea together in a timbered booth in a quiet little place in an arcade. It was, Digger thought, one of the few occasions when their talk together was openly of Vic, though a lot of what they had to say to one another had him in mind or as a shadow on the sidelines. It was painful, this.

'You know him, Digger – you tell *me*,' she said. She seemed desperate.

'I don't know him,' Digger found himself saying, and he was sorry the moment after. It was true, it was what he felt at the moment, but it seemed like a betrayal. He saw from her look how surprised she was. He was surprised himself.

*

Vic could not have told Digger of the scene with Greg because there was nothing to tell. It was a quarrel like any other.

Vic blamed Greg for the form their quarrels took. All he could do each time was mouth the slogans he had picked up from his friends, no word of it was personal or his own, and all Vic could say in reaction, he felt, was determined by this, and was equally impersonal and beside the point.

They had never found any way of addressing one another in which the truth could be stated or their real feelings shown. So they fell back each time on what they had said before. Greg shouted his contempt for their whole way of life, all the things they stood for, which he rejected utterly and would have nothing to do with. Vic threw all this back at him, and he too shouted, only half believing in what came out. He knew too well the slipperiness of such terms as self-respect and discipline to use them as crudely as he did, but he did use them that way. He talked of the boy's lack of character, his willingness to live off what he claimed to despise, the contempt even his own friends had for his weak-willed parroting of their every opinion and the way he ran after them, in everything he did imitating this or that one of them, with no will or character of his own. The anger in all this was real, but the arguments were the same ones they had been over on other occasions. There was no reason, no apparent reason, why this should be the last.

What Greg had wanted to say was something quite different, but he could not bring himself, out of perversity, out of the sort of pride too that his father did not credit him with, to put it into words. It would only have increased his father's scorn for him, he thought, if he had asked for love.

Vic too had wanted to say something quite different. What he wanted to speak of were the things in his life that when he stopped and looked at them created panic in him.

To have put this into words might have been a relief, but it would have exposed him, and he believed that in his son's eyes he ought not to appear weak.

Then, too, if he put his fear into words he might, in some magical way, give it a place in the world, where it would grow, increase its power and work against him. The desire to keep it inside, where he alone knew what it was and could control it, was enough to keep him silent, even at the risk, as he saw now, of his losing control of the very thing that lay at the heart of his panic – his vulnerability through Greg.

So nothing new was said. They went over the same accusations and counter-accusations they always used and at the end of it nothing had been said. Only this time Greg took him at his word, or decided out of pride to stick to his own. He quit the house.

One Thursday when Iris was in the front room ironing, with the television on 'just for company', there was a ring at the door. It was after nine, too late for neighbours to be calling.

Digger, reading in the sleep-out, looked up with his glasses on his nose. He saw Iris step out into the hallway; then a moment later she was at the entrance to the sleep-out with Vic. Her eyebrows were raised. It was a look he knew well.

Digger too was surprised. He thought there must be some sort of trouble. But Vic had no explanation to offer. He appeared to be in high spirits, he was a little drunk in fact, and had three bottles of Cooper's Ale with him. When Iris took them, and with another little look in Digger's direction went off to fetch glasses, he stepped into the sleep-out as if dropping in on them like this were the most natural thing in the world. Digger found it took a little getting used to.

He had forgotten till now that when Vic first appeared at the Crossing, and Jenny had come up and pointed to him mooching about there under the she-oaks, he had felt the same little sense of intrusion.

It had faded in time. Vic had come to be as much a part of his life at the Crossing as anything else. Only now did the echo of it come back. Why, after all this time, had he taken it upon himself to break in on them?

But if Vic recognised a coolness on Digger's part he gave no sign of it. When Iris, pleading the excuse of her ironing, left them to it, believing there must be something special he had come for, he cast a glance around the sleep-out and said, 'This is nice. All these books yours?'

'No,' Digger said, and folded his glasses, 'not all of 'em.' And then, because he still felt irritated, he said, 'Most of them were Mac's.'

Was it the first time Mac's name had come up between them? Digger could not be certain. Other names came up from time to time. It would have been unusual if they had avoided that one. But they had, of course.

There was a little beat of silence. Outside in the loquat tree Digger could hear a shuffling. Possums. They had possums that sometimes came right into the house and would take a bite out of some piece of fruit in the bowl on the kitchen table, leaving paw marks all over the floor.

Digger was sorry now that he had said anything. He had done it in a moment of spite. He watched Vic take a book from the shelf, open it and look at the flyleaf as if he needed to see the name there: as proof. Or perhaps it was to feel another twist of the knife. But it wasn't Mac's name he would find. Hardly one of these books had Mac's name in it. Other names, yes, and Digger, being Digger, could have reeled off each one of them. *The Nigger of the 'Narcissus'*, for instance, which was the book he happened to be re-reading, had belonged to Janet Dawkins, Year Twelve, at Randwick Girls' High School in 1936. Mac had picked it up at Tyrrell's. He could have gone on to list dozens, even hundreds, more.

What Vic had in his hand was a tooled leather edition of Tennyson. The flyleaf, Digger knew, would read:

To Mr John Darnell
from
B. J. Checkley
10th May, 1889

all in sepia copperplate, and underneath it:

Kind hearts are more than Coronets
And simple faith than Norman blood.

He watched Vic read it in a sober way, then close the book and put it back.

He looked around the room, frowning a little. Perhaps he felt the oppressiveness of so many volumes set so close on the shelves, or was wondering how many he would have to open before he came to one (he might find one, an old school algebra maybe) with I. R. McAlister in it.

Outside in the front room, he settled on the arm of a lounge chair, one leg thrown easily across the other, a little subdued at first but quickly recovering his spirits. Iris turned off the television, and offered to put her ironing aside as well, but he insisted he didn't mind, in fact he liked it. So with some embarrassment, since she scarcely knew him, she went on damping down pillowslips, handkerchiefs, an apron, one of Digger's shirts, and the smell of heat and damp filled the room.

She was wary of him, he was out to charm her, and she kept shooting little sideways glances at Digger to see if he had noticed it. But she relaxed at last and began to enjoy herself. He was full of light notes and odd, old-fashioned sayings that surprised her. Nothing she knew of him from Digger had suggested this. Digger himself was surprised. There was no sign now of that moment on the sleep-out, or of any of that side of him; and Digger, who had little to say, went even quieter.

What he was doing, Digger thought, was restoring a kind of order in himself, making up for that little reversal out there, when for a moment his image of himself had been disturbed, by winning her approval.

Digger had never seen him playing up to a woman before. It was new to him, the way he paraded his repertoire of charms; this concentration of energy, of interest in him, that made a woman aware of herself. He was all attention, you could feel it. Digger, who knew him so well, was irritated that Iris should be so easily taken in.

She finished her ironing. He leapt up and helped her fold the board. What he wanted her to do now was play.

Lately she found playing difficult. She had arthritis, all the joints of her fingers were swollen; but she sat down, and it was ages, Digger thought, since he had seen her play so easily or with so much heart.

She played Schubert, a great favourite of Digger's, and once or twice as she played she looked aside at him and smiled; but she was playing, he saw, for Vic, and once again he felt a pang of jealousy. Which was foolish, he knew, but he couldn't help it.

Vic sat very silent with his head bowed, and Digger for some reason thought again of Mac, and again of how foolish it was of him to feel hurt, or to feel anything in fact but what the music spoke of – union and peace. Remote, mysterious, yet so full of quiet optimism, it took you right to the heart of things.

'Honestly, Digger,' Iris said later, when she had got out of him what it was that had kept him so quiet. She was half smiling to herself. It did not displease her that he could be jealous. 'All that palaver he goes on with – it doesn't mean anything. Don't you know that? He's a ladies' man. Show him a woman and he can't help flirting with her. Even an old dame like me. There's no harm in it.'

Digger was silent. 'Well, it got my goat,' he said at last, 'him just inviting himself like that. He did it on his own account. I didn't have anything to do with it.'

He waited. He was waiting for some comment from her of what she had felt or seen that would explain it, since he could not; but she lay with her face turned away and did not speak.

Her hair, which had been so rich when he first knew her, was thinning, not quite grey, and he had a particular affection for the freckling of her brow, and the area just below the line of her hair where the skin was almost transparent and the veins showed. He put his fingertips to them, and she turned her head and smiled. It worried her, he knew, that she was no longer beautiful. *She* thought she wasn't.

'He didn't come because he had anything to say, you know. Why do you reckon he *did* come?'

She looked at him. 'Because he was lonely,' she said after a moment. 'He had nowhere to go.' Digger stared. 'Maybe,' she said lightly, 'he fell out with his girlfriend.' She said it carelessly. She saw immediately that she should not have.

'What? What girlfriend?'

'Oh – they say he's on with Susie Stone.'

'Who does?'

'Oh – you know, the newspapers.'

He lay still. He was taking it in.

'Who's Susie Stone?' he said at last. He was amazed by all this, but most of all by her. How did she know these things? It astonished him at times the things that went on in the world that other people took for granted and he knew nothing of. He was surprised, too, how much she accepted now that would once have shocked her. For three years before they got round to marrying, Ewen and his wife Jane had lived together – they even had a little boy. He had been a page at their wedding.

'Susie Stone's a designer,' she told him. 'Sportswear. She's pretty well known – to *young* people.'

'Do you think Ellie knows?' he asked.

'I expect so, yes. I don't suppose she's the first. It's what I said. You can see it right off. Any *woman* could.'

He turned up on odd Thursdays after that, and Digger saw him more often at Bondi Junction in the end than at Keen's Crossing. He began

294

to bring Iris little gifts, as he had Jenny, but Iris, who had none of Jenny's suspicion of him, took the gesture as it was intended and made a fuss over his presents and over him too. He was delighted. The things he gave her he had thought about. You could see that.

Digger never did get used to having him there, but he accepted at last that the flirtations he practised were harmless, at least where Iris was concerned, and that his real reason for coming was the one she had seen on that first occasion: there were times when he had nowhere else to go.

13

Digger was dizzied by the world. He could never, he felt, see it steady enough or at a sufficient distance to comprehend what it was, let alone to act on it. This was a disadvantage; but he had long since come to the conclusion that his perplexity about life, which did not prevent him from living it, was essential to him.

A nailhead. That was clear enough. Round, flanged, with ridges that allowed the hammerhead a grip. The weight of the hammer, too. Driving a nail in, feeling the point go through the soft grain to bite on the last two blows – that was the only action he knew that was simple. Everything else, the moment you really looked at it, developed complications.

Even the least event had lines, all tangled, going back into the past, and beyond that into the *unknown* past, and other lines leading out, also tangled, into the future. Every moment was dense with causes, possibilities, consequences; too many, even in the simplest case, to grasp. Every moment was dense too with lives, all crossing and interconnecting or exerting pressure on one another, and not just human lives either; the narrowest patch of earth at the Crossing, as he had known since he was two years old, was crowded with little centres of activity, visible or invisible, that made up a web so intricate that your mind, if you went into it, was immediately stuck – fierce cannibalistic occasions without number, each one of which could deafen you if you had ears to hear what was going on there. And beyond that were what you could not even call lives or existences: they were mere processes – the slow burning of gases for example in the veins of leaves – that were invisibly and forever changing the state of things; heat, sunlight, electric charges to which everything alive enough responded and held itself erect, hairs and fibres that were very nearly invisible but subtly vibrating, nerve ends touched and stroked.

This was how he saw things unless he deliberately held back and shut himself off.

What staggered him in others, and especially in Vic, was the certainty with which they saw the whole world as a nail to be struck squarely on the head. Yet he suspected at times that Vic did not entirely *believe* in the world. His capacity to deal with it had to do with his conviction that it was there only insofar as he could act on it.

Three or four times a year now Vic went overseas, to Japan, Hong Kong, London. The mineral boom and the listing of Australian shares on the international exchange took his interests out of the country. His nephew Alex had been brought in to run the Australian side. He was a chilly fellow, Alex. Digger heard this from Ellie. He lived on his own in a big old flat at Elizabeth Bay, and Ellie, though she tried, had never got close to him.

Vic came to the Crossing less often now, and when he did come their talk was of a different kind. In recent years their times together had become very easy and sociable, too much so. They had taken one another for granted. But now some of this sociability transferred itself to Bondi Junction, and this allowed their times alone to change. They both felt this, but it was Vic who had managed it, and Digger was surprised yet again, by the talent he had – it was instinctive in him – for getting what he needed.

He had begun to detach himself from things. That was what Digger saw. Or not precisely from things, but from himself. And what this involved was a moving deeper into himself. So when they talked now, it was in a quieter mood. What they were exploring was not the interest of difference, which had allowed them to turn everything they knew of one another into a game of surprises, but what they shared.

A lot of this new style of talk was about the years they had spent *up there*. Three years and a half, to be exact. Thirty years ago.

Vic was all questions; shy ones at times, as if it embarrassed him a little that he should have to ask them. After all, it was his life.

Digger's own memory was exceptional, he knew that; but he was surprised just the same to how large an extent Vic had lost all detailed recollection of that period, or had suppressed it or let it go.

The emotion of it was still strong. There was a bitterness in him that he continued to chew over as Digger did not. For Digger it had been one time of his life among others; a time, simply, that had laid hard responsibilities on him, but ones that were too deeply ingrained in his nature now for regret. He accepted them. He made no complaint.

For Vic the injustice that had been done to him was absolute, a thing he could not forgive. Some possibility had been killed in him then, and though he had found others and made what he could of them – that's how he was; that was his nature, his character – that other possibility, the one that had been starved and beaten out of him, seemed especially precious. It belonged to his youth, to some finer and more innocent self than the one he had been left with when he came back.

He could not forgive that. The hurt of it was still with him. But he had deliberately stamped out all memory of the *details*, and it was these now that he wanted to recollect: little individual moments of his own life that only Digger could lead him to. Events, occasions, men – their names, what they had looked like, what happened to them.

Digger thought some of this talk was dangerous. Not to himself – he had lived with it for thirty years on a daily basis; it was woven into the very fabric of his existence, in the tangled lines of what bound him here and led out into the future. But for Vic they were something else, these details. They were what he had broken contact with. And perhaps the ability to survive, in his case, had depended on it – Digger allowed for this sort of difference between them. Making himself the guide now who would lead him back into the immediate presence of it was not a thing Digger felt easy with.

What disturbed him was the way it took him back too. There was something quite different between going over it all with another and the more ordinary business of going over it in his own head.

Looking up briefly, a kind of pain behind his eyes that half-dazzled him, he would see behind the face of this man of fifty, fifty-one, fifty-three, which he knew so well – behind the lines that were thrown like a net over his features, breaking up the skin, and behind the coarsening skin itself with its net of veins – a look that had been, all those years ago, his first real glimpse into the man, the one that had established for him, whether he wanted it or not, their bond with one another and the beginning of a responsibility he had seen, even then, as extending far into the future, and up to the moment they were in now: that candid, guilty-innocent, animal look of the twenty-year-old he had caught eating his rice, who had shown him a kind of wisdom he might not have come to himself. 'Trust me,' that look had said, in the very act of stealing the food out of his mouth.

It had the power still to shake him. He felt a kind of trembling in himself that might have been the last shadow, after so long, of fever – do you ever, once bitten, get over it? – but was really, he knew, not a physical thing at all but another form of emotion. He had never been much good (it was another of his deficiencies) at telling the one from the other.

14

Digger no longer went up to town. He had no heart for it. Town had been his Thursdays with Iris. To get down off the train at Central and know he was in a city of three million souls and she was not one of them made Sydney an alien place. He couldn't breathe the air of it, or so he felt.

That was in the early days. Later, when his pain lessened, as it did in time, and he saw things more reasonably, what was the point? He could have stayed the night with one of the boys, he would have been welcome enough. He could have gone up for Ellie's sake. But he didn't. He had not seen, till Iris was gone, how his little morning enjoyments had only been such because at the end of them he would be catching the tram (later it had been the bus) to Bondi Junction. Her presence had underwritten everything, even the city itself, all those millions; his own presence too, at least in that place. Only much later, when the children wrote asking why he never came to see them any more, did he begin to go down once in a while 'to see how they were growing up' and to walk out to Cooper Park with them.

At the service in the little chapel, the preacher, who had not known Iris personally, spoke of her easy death (she had died without warning in her sleep); of her long widowhood, and of the husband, the boys' father, whose name she still bore, who had been lost so many years ago in the Islands.

Digger swallowed hard to have all their years together, and so much affection, and so many events, passed over; but death, he knew, is an official thing, so are its ceremonies, and there was no public record of their years together.

She was buried under the name of the man she had in one area of herself remained faithful to, and though it hurt him a little, Digger respected that. It was part of a code they had shared. He knew its rules. A good deal of his affection for her, his admiration too, lay in her commitment to it.

Nine years she had had with the husband. That was official.

Thirty-four without him. Altogether, if you could count them altogether, forty-three. But twenty-six she had had with *him*. And if you counted the years he had shared with her before they met – not her exactly but the shadow of her that she had stepped into – twenty-nine.

What did all these calculations mean? Digger felt strange sitting there in the pew, one of the chief mourners but anonymous and unofficial, totting up figures that were just figures, when the events of any one day or one moment even might have blazed up and made nothing of them.

The boys were very gentle with him. This was in the informal moments, before and after. Ellie and Vic were also there.

So he no longer went up to town, and it was years now since he had seen Ellie. Instead they had begun a correspondence.

At first it was just little notes – a postcard or two from her business trips with Vic, then at last proper letters.

They were, on Digger's side, longer ones than he had ever written before. He put everything he felt into them, and Ellie wrote back of things, he thought, that she would never have told him face to face. He was surprised what words themselves could do when you gave yourself over to them; as if, in containing the expression of what was felt, they knew what you wanted to say before you did, and the very shape of a sentence, once you started on it, held just in itself the shape of what you needed to express; so it got said without embarrassment, and with no fear of falseness or of saying too much and being misunderstood.

After a time it seemed to them that their correspondence was satisfactory just in itself. To meet again might drive them back from intimacy into a politeness they would regret. But he would have liked to see her; to sit, as they used to do, across a table, and watch the way she used her hands.

He sat down once a week and wrote to Ellie as once a week he had gone up to Bondi Junction and stayed with Iris, and if the thing was not quite the same, there was a continuation of a kind in the regularity of it.

He spoke of Iris. Writing was a way of keeping all that part of his life alive in him – it had in most ways been the happiest part; or rather, of finding in it, as the words brought it back, dimensions he had been only dimly aware of in the daily happening. He wrote in a light mood. They had little code-words and quick half-references that came out of the one thing they shared and could draw on, her father's poems. So the poems too took on a new life in their letters. Odd lines and phrases, worked into what they themselves had to say, kept their old meaning, but acquired, as they used them, a new one, coloured and lit up by *their* feelings now.

One of the things Ellie wrote of was Greg. He had used the money Pa left him to go to Europe, overland via India and Afghanistan. He was in Amsterdam, then in Greece, then he was back home again, but in Melbourne. She knew where he was and kept in touch with him.

So six or seven years passed and Digger had a good bundle of letters. He kept them in a drawer, and sometimes, as he had once done with Iris's letters to Mac, he took them out and read them through. It was a pleasant occupation. What he thought of when he lay them aside, full as they were of memories of Iris and of so much else besides, little things he had in mind to tell Ellie, phrases from the poems, was how full his life had been, and that too he wrote to her since she, and all this business of writing to her, was part of it.

So many letters. Seven years.

He did not realise, as he thought this, that there would be so many more. Till it was eleven years. Then twelve, then thirteen.

15

Vic had come by his driver, Brad, in an unlikely manner.

He used to stop occasionally, when he went for a walk out of his office, at a little coffee shop in an arcade, where he could sit and be quiet with his thoughts.

It wasn't a lively place. It had been left just as it was from the days back in the Fifties when espresso coffee first made its appearance, and a Gaggia machine raising a head of steam, a view of the Bay of Naples, and laminated, kidney-shaped counters with high stools offered the promise that somewhere at least there was a *dolce vita*. He liked it because the only people who came here now were tired-looking women shoppers, and a few muddy-eyed older men who wanted a place where they would not be intimidated by too much style.

Tramps half of them looked, or very nearly. They put three or four spoonfuls of sugar into their coffee and sucked it up noisily, with no loss of dignity. He would settle in a corner and feel invisible, though in fact his expensive clothes made him very conspicuous. The invisibility was in his head, but it worked on people and he was seldom approached.

One day the old fellow behind the counter, who emerged every now and then to wipe the tables down with a damp cloth, came across in his shirt-sleeves and apron and spoke to him. He was in his middle sixties, a rough-looking fellow with a shock of snowy hair.

'You don't recognise me, do you?' he said, and there was a smirk on his face that was very youthful. Vic felt then that he did know him, but couldn't put a name or a place to him.

'Felix,' the man told him. 'I used to work for Needham's. In the old days. On the trucks. With Alf Lees. You remember.'

He did too, and the memory was a sweet one. Since their move up to Turramurra, everything that evoked the old house at Strathfield, and the factory, seemed sweet to him. The man, without waiting to be invited, sat down opposite – it was his place, after all – and said quietly: 'I noticed you comin' in here.'

He shifted the two sauce bottles and the pepper and salt shakers, setting them in a row.

'I've got a favour to ask you,' he said. 'I've got a boy, a good lad really – he's honest, I mean – but he's unsettled. Gives 'is mother a lotta worry. I was wondering if – you know, with your contacts, you could maybe do something for 'im. I know it's a big thing to ask.' It was more words, you could see, than he was used to finding all at the one go.

Vic was impressed by the straightness of him. He wasn't at all obsequious. He was speaking as one man to another, taking for granted an equality between them, given a few million dollars, that Vic was glad to accept. He was speaking too as a father, and that also moved him. So he had taken the boy on as a driver.

He did not like him much. He was a young man who thought a great deal of himself. He was always glancing up to take a look at himself in the rear-vision mirror, and what he saw was a pleasure to him. He wasn't very bright either, but did not know it. He talked too much and a lot of it was rot. But Vic liked the father, Felix, very much, and when he went to have his coffee now the man left the counter, brought a cup of his own, and they would sit together for a time and talk.

He was a sad fellow. He had driven for a big trucking company after he left the factory but had done his back in – that's how he had missed the war. After that he had a newspaper run, out Lidcombe way; then, when he retired, had put his money into the coffee shop. He had married late. There was just the one boy.

'I've done pretty well, considering,' he said, and you could see that it did not occur to him that the man he was speaking to had done so much better. They were very easy with one another. Vic felt that in talking to Felix, though the subject was not mentioned, he was relieving himself a little of what he could not say about Greg. The tie between them was always this difficult business of fathers and sons, though it had never come out in fact that he had one.

What Vic had against Brad was that he had none of his father's fineness of feeling. In his empty-headed, egotistical way he took Vic's acquaintance with his father as a feather in his own cap, referring to it sometimes in a way that was quite out of place and which Vic found offensive, though out of affection for the father he did not mention it.

He had very little use for a driver, preferring, except on special occasions, to take a smaller car. Most often it was Alex Brad drove for. Alex liked to work in the car, and Brad, who was very keen on appearances, felt it gave him too a kind of importance – it was like being in a film – to have someone back there making use of a dictaphone and taking calls; though Vic, of course, was the boss.

Vic was using Brad, and the big car, when he found himself one afternoon at the Cross. He had visitors to entertain, two Japanese with whom he had just signed a sizeable contract, and a Swede. They had eaten at a good Italian place in Darlinghurst, drunk well, and these visitors, especially one of the Japanese, having heard of the Cross, wanted to take a look at it – not, Vic warned them, that there would be much to see at three o'clock in the afternoon. He told Brad he could take a bit of a walk – say, half an hour – and, leaving the car in Kellett Street, they strolled in the sunshine to an outdoor café.

He disliked the Cross and never came here except on occasions like this. Its most recent incarnation, as a playground for American servicemen on R and R from Vietnam, was done with now, gone with the war, but the sleaziness and joyless opportunism of that time had set a standard and the Cross was still living up to it. An odour of tropical despair hung over the place, from battlefields that in those days had been just hours away. The boys coming in in their freshly-laundered Hawaiian shirts had still had the smell of battle fear on them.

The mugs were local now, boys in from the suburbs, football teams from interstate; or they were tourists like the Japs who wanted to see what it was the country produced other than wheat, wool, minerals and a few natural phenomena that were sacred sites to one part of the population and to the rest, if they thought of them at all, a kind of geological Disneyland.

The war was over but the Silver Dollar and the Texas Tavern were still there. So were the strip-joints, the skin-flick movie houses, the pinball arcades, the fast-food shops, the fortune tellers with their little velvet-covered tables and Tarot packs; and at every corner the loungers, the lookers, the dealers in this drug and that – and round behind, in an alley full of garbage, only some of it crammed into plastic bags, the bloody syringes and other evidence, with the bodies themselves on occasion. And on the streets here, in broad daylight, the walking wounded, girls in boots and tights, some of whom were no longer girls either, and some of them not *quite* girls, and in the park around the fountain, or in the bar at the Rex, the boys in T-shirts and parachute pants.

It was all more squalid than it used to be. The big men who lived off

305

it were out of sight. They were, if the newspapers were right, some of Vic's business acquaintances – they did not show up here. But their agents were about, moving their shoulders in the sun, and the whole place had a showy half-innocent, half-corrupt air, as if even the corruption might be a fraud, meant only to deceive and titillate, though that too was a deception.

There was corruption all right. Something of what had been in the heads of those boys who had been shipped down here to get free, for a few days, of terror and carnage, had seeped out and infected everything, so that the proximity of death could, if you had a nose for it, be felt more strongly here than in any other part of the city. It was cheap here, commonplace: and that too, whether they knew it or not, drew people.

The crowds came to stare for a bit at a freakshow, to put their hands, just for a moment or two, and at a price, on something forbidden or dangerous; to watch deals being done while pinballs bounced and set small lights flashing and numbers coming up; to listen to the hot-gospellers promising punishment or immediate cleansing and cure, and watch a lamb kebab turn in its own fat on a spit and boys with floury forearms, in dirty white caps behind steamy windows, knead pizza dough.

They settled at an outside table and ordered coffee. The visitors' eyes were everywhere.

A little way down the street there was a commotion. A ragged looking young man with his head shaved up round the ears and peaks of feathery hair, in heavy boots and a T-shirt and braces and with a little black-and-white terrier at his heels, was clod-hopping about on the pavement playing a mouth-organ. The little dog danced round his heels and yipped. His girl, with her legs sprawled out in front of her on the dirty pavement, sat with her head against the wall.

Three young fellows in leather jackets were tormenting them. The little dog snapped at their heels and one after another they kicked at it. The fellow with the mouth-organ, who had fingerless mittens on his hands, was turning his head away like a child, on the principle that if he did not look at his tormentors they could not be there.

On the pavement was a cap with a few coins on it, and one of the louts leaned down now, took a handful of coins from the cap, stood turning them over in his hand, then distributed them, laughing, to his mates.

The girl swore at them, and when the young man with the mouth-organ did nothing, but kept playing, she began to pummel his legs with her fists. The youths, who had begun to walk off, stopped then and turned back to enjoy the scene, the mouth-organ player playing, the girl punching at him. They laughed. The little dog went after them, but stopped when they threatened, and stood there, barking.

The youth and the girl argued for a moment, then she rolled back against the wall again and he began to dance in his heavy boots, playing a jig now, very wild and shrill, and making little nodding and beckoning signs to the passers-by, who shied away. Finally he stopped playing altogether, leaned down, took up the cap, which he emptied into one hand and set anyhow on his head, and gave a call to the dog, which came running. The girl, scrabbling her legs about on the dirty pavement, got herself up and they moved up the street together to where Vic and the others were.

Vic saw then who it was.

He had not seen him for more than seven years. He looked battered. His hair was bleached, he had an earring. The braces and boots, but something too in the nervous set of his shoulders, made him look like a six-year-old who had suffered at the hands of a crazed or brutal adult. When he came up level with their table he stopped dead, and after a moment, grinned in an inane, rather mischievous way, and Vic saw that his front teeth had been knocked out. He came right up to them and thrust out his cap.

The hand in the fingerless mitten was filthy. The flesh of his forearm, which was bare, was like a fish's belly, bluish-white. Behind him the girl weaved about with her head rolling and her eyes closed. The little black-and-white terrier pranced.

The visitors began to feel in their pockets for change. The Swede, who was very aristocratic and fastidious, was trying to ignore this manifestation of local squalor. He was disgusted, you could see that, and a little scared as well. He could not see what the rules were in this place where begging, he had thought, was unknown.

The Japanese were grinning. They were amused. One of them dropped a five-dollar note into the cap, and Greg raised a finger to his temple in scornful salute.

Vic had not moved. He did not feel humiliated or ashamed before these men. They meant nothing to him. What he felt was a blazing anger, and most of all at the Swede. At the clean-fingered distaste with which he dropped a coin into the cap, as if it, and the arm behind it, had materialised out of nowhere, and what might lie beyond was beneath his notice.

The boy was unabashed. He appeared, with his absent-minded grin and the childish little jerking movements he kept making with his head, to accept no responsibility at all for what was happening, and to have no resistance to it either. The moment sat so lightly upon him that he seemed weightless, and Vic had again a vision of him dancing, clod-hopping about on the pavement like a puppet, but one that was not attached to anything.

'But he is attached to *me*,' he thought, and was struck suddenly with the impulse to stand up and say it aloud, to say it right out, just like that, with whatever dignity he could muster, but if there was none to be had, that would not matter either. To say quite openly, with a heart too bewildered any longer to take refuge in pride, what he was saying already to himself: 'This is the thing I was in panic about, that I knew was on the way and knew I had no power to prevent. Now it is here.'

Bright sunlight played on the table-top and round the mouths of glasses, touched the corners of buildings, swam in windows, lit the highest leaves of the surrounding trees. It was three o'clock in the afternoon. It was not a dream.

He said nothing. Without looking up he began to take out his wallet, and the others watched uncomprehending as before he could open it, the beggar or busker or whatever he was reached out and with a silly little laugh plucked it from him: flipped it open, extracted two, three notes – twenties they might have been, no, fifties! – then, with another laugh, tossed it back.

There was a police station not fifty yards away. It was amazing.

Vic did not once look up. What he could not face, but could see clearly enough, was the look on the boy's face. The *boy* – but he was past thirty. Defiant it would be, but in an indeterminate, rabbity way, as if he was himself being dared by a fellow inside there that he had to watch out for – the one who was high on whatever it was that made his eyes so icy-blue but inward-looking and put the smile at the corner of his mouth.

He stood a moment, looking pleased with himself and fingering the notes. Then, losing confidence, he turned, grabbed the girl, who was swaying about on the pavement, and dragged her off.

The others sat staring. They could not see what it meant, what embarrassing intimacy or bit of odd local behaviour had been revealed to them, and Vic did not bother to explain. He did not bother with them at all. Stumbling to his feet, he took the bill, paid it at the counter inside and they had to set off after him.

They found the car. The driver, with an ice-cream cone in his hand, was walking up and down the pavement keeping an eye on it. Up here he liked to keep a good lookout – he was smart that way.

He twigged immediately that something had gone wrong. When they had dropped the Swede off, then the two Japs, he glanced up enquiringly into the rear-vision mirror, past his own reflection this time. Old Trader Vic (as he called him when he was showing off to his mates) was slumped in the corner against the window. He looked like someone had king-hit him. Brad turned his head so that the old fellow would see something more than just the back of his neck. It was a form of question.

He came back to reality then and asked to be driven to a place Brad had never taken him before, way up beyond Ku-ring-gai Chase to the Hawkesbury, and some bit of a store on the river up there where he had to sit around kicking his heels for ages, and a crazy old girl with no hair practically had offered him a cup of tea, then in the middle of it, for no reason he ever discovered, did her block and started to perform and play rough with him.

16

They were the years now of the *real* boom. What had come before was nothing compared to this. What had been measured in millions was to be measured now in hundreds of millions. No one had seen anything like it.

When Jenny saw Vic on the television these days she sat glum and silent.

It wasn't him that worried her – she *knew* him. She didn't know what he *did*, or any more about him than she ever had, but she had been in the same room with him, her own kitchen, and seen the way he sipped his tea with his eyes looking out over the rim of the cup, and ate a pikelet, and the way the skin wrinkled on the back of his hand. She knew the smell of him too. That wasn't what worried her. What she could not fathom was what he was doing in the world of TV, the News and that. How had he got there? She knew how he had got to the Crossing. Through Digger. But the TV was different.

The moment his name came up and his face appeared in the lighted window there, smiling, assured, with his striped shirts and his brushed hair and the face so bronzed and lifelike, the whole thing lost its credibility for her. She couldn't listen to what they were saying or believe any bit of it. The News! She would go glum and start counting in her head – one, two, three, four – till they took him off.

Vic had always played things close to his chest. All his success had come from his willingness to take responsibility for what he was doing, stay quiet, bear the risks, and keep his nerve. Ma had been his only real confidante. She was so still. He would tell her anything she wanted to know, she had only to ask. Alex he told as little as he could get away with.

He had chosen Alex because he was family, and because he had seen, in a hard-nosed way, that the qualities Alex possessed were the ones he lacked. They were qualities he had no time for in fact – they had all to do with caution, consultation, bookkeeping, accountability – but they were what the times, it seemed, demanded. He had chosen Alex as well because he thought, being family, he would have a kind of ascendency over him.

He had been wrong in this. Alex was stubborn. He held to the code he lived by with a fanaticism Vic found he could neither ignore nor negotiate.

Alex was a company man. Accountability was his gospel. When he spoke it was with all the facts at his fingertips and the approval, always, of a board with whom he had gone over every detail. He could not understand Vic. Or rather, he did understand but could not deal with him.

'He's a dinosaur,' he complained to the few men he could trust not to bear tales. 'It was fine in the old days. It was open slather then. This was Hicksville. He could be a one man show and get away with it. He was brilliant, I agree. But we're in a new phase now. Everything's more complicated. That's what he won't accept. I have to watch him like a goddamn hawk. You've got no idea the tricks he gets up to.'

'So what are you griping about?' Vic would argue when some scheme he had been engaged in was in the open at last and his hand revealed. 'We made money on it, didn't we? Have I ever got us into anything that was a loss? What about that Riverdale business? Who got us into that little pile of pooh?'

He knew Alex was watching him, that he was being humoured – patronised, in fact – and that Alex had a core of supporters, fellows full of *his* sort of ideas who were determined to restrain and thwart him and would one day ease him out. He watched them, and after a time he began to watch outside as well. He had a nose for that, for what was not quite right; a sixth sense that warned him when someone was on his tail. He had played that game himself and knew the signs. When he was sure of what was happening he took action but told no one, acting as he always had done, alone. If Alex was in it, he would be caught out and exposed. If he wasn't, he would be delighted, wouldn't he? – astonished too – that the thing had been seen and forestalled.

It was his big gamble. He needed it. He needed the excitement, and the chance it offered to show, once and for all, what he was worth. When all was ready, fixed and about to go, he would lay his hand down and watch their faces.

He had advisers of his own, of course; you needed them these days. But them too he kept in the dark. It would have been good, he thought, to go over it with Ma. He had no wish to deceive her. But Ma was nearly ninety; still clear-headed but racked with anxieties again that he was afraid to catch.

The one person he could be open with was Digger, he owed him that; and the advantage of Digger was that he offered no arguments. He might have done. There were times, certainly, when he looked doubtful enough. But Digger was out of his element. He did not understand the danger, the beauty of the thing.

So though he tried to stay away, he found himself, as the affair reached its crisis, going back and back to the Crossing, eager to have someone to listen while once again he went over the details of it. It was watertight. No doubt of that. He had considered every eventuality. But he needed to talk it into action, to keep it going where he could best control each movement of it: in his head.

Digger had caught on to one or two things that set him thinking. They had come up in passing, but in a way that caught his ear. One of them had to do with the market's being 'nervous'. He was struck by the word because it had already occurred to him in connection with Vic.

He talked a good deal about how cool he was. He prided himself on that. But what Digger saw was that he was overheated, and he could not judge, since he had never seen him till now under circumstances like these, whether it was normal or not, whether it was or was not to be expected as a by-product of what kept him cool. He would have liked to discuss this with someone, with Ellie for instance; she would know. But the secrecy Vic demanded held him back.

This secret side of things was an agony to him. He wondered how necessary it was outside of Vic's need to impose it. Its effect was to bind them even closer now, as fellow conspirators, but in an area where only Vic knew the rules. He swallowed his doubts, afraid, when so much depended on confidence, and trust, that if he spoke them aloud he might bring about the very thing he wanted to prevent – the upsetting of some balance in Vic that would put him off.

'What's going on?' Jenny wailed. 'What's 'e doin', comin' down here all the time? What does 'e *want*? And don't tell me nothin' again, cos I don't believe it.'

17

Vic stirred and woke. The jolt he felt had taken place in his sleep. For just the space of a breath back there he must have been free of gravity. He came to earth now but the sense of strangeness he felt, of estrangement even, was of being in a body that was not his own. His hand when he lifted it seemed further off and had a new weight at the end of his arm. Or maybe it was still, as they say, asleep. He worked it a little to take off the numbness.

He knew clearly enough where he was. It was the bedroom at Turramurra. But what he was chiefly aware of was not the space he was in but the space that was inside him. Echoes were coming up from it, and it was these that gave him a sense of how vast it might be. Something like a stone had fallen a huge distance in there. From where it touched bottom the sound was still travelling upward, having the power, the unusual one, of belonging to a dream but going on past whatever barrier exists between sleep and wakefulness so that he could still hear it.

What *was* all this? On the one hand the feeling of being lifted free of gravity like a bird, and on the other of an even swifter descent in the opposite direction, a long plummeting and the rush of air around a stone.

And if it wasn't a dream but some purely physical occurrence, why all this business of gravity and stones?

He shifted his body on the bed and lay a while with his eyes open and very still in his head, fixed on the ceiling. A moment later he was asleep.

But at moments during the day, which was otherwise normal, his dream, or the sensations surrounding whatever had happened in there, kept coming back to him. He could not shake them off. For whole minutes at a time there was a luminosity round the edge of everything he looked at or touched, even the most ordinary objects, a coffee-machine, a polystyrene cup.

It was the light out of his dream, in which everything, including his body, had been soaked, he saw now, in a phosphorescence whose stickiness accounted for the heaviness he had felt, and still felt, in his limbs, and accounted too for all this shining. It wasn't at all unpleasant, but it was strange and he was changed by it. He felt a tenderness in himself that was childish since it attached itself to things it was foolish for a grown man to feel so much for. The propelling pencil he took up, for example, and the way it fitted his hand, the sun rings thrown on his desk by a water-glass. 'What is happening?' he wondered.

These moments, which came in waves, were states of acute happiness, but of a kind he had scarcely known before, and there was, so far as he could see, no reason for them. They brought with them a lightness of heart that he associated with youthfulness, with some image he had had once of what it was to be young and in love.

Where did *that* come from? It did not seem like a memory of his own. It was new to him. Yet there was a quality of nostalgia in it too, as if he had broken in on the recollections of another man's life and was as moved by them as by his own. The bursts of happiness came and came, and were so unconnected with any cause he knew of that they might have been the after-effects of a drug.

All this surprised him, but he liked the mood and surrendered to it.

He did all the things he usually did: checked the market reports that had come in overnight from New York, then the Hong Kong and Tokyo prices, then the local ones. Everything was fine, couldn't be better: Cavendish was up two cents, Cathedral steady, Randall's up three. It was going fine, better even than predicted.

For a time he had been anxious that the market might be playing them up. But his advisers, who were all very clear-headed, sceptical fellows, statistics freaks, not at all star-gazers or voodoo merchants, had assured him that the upward trend was steady and would continue. They were experts. He was paying them in hundreds of thousands for their opinions. It was crazy to do that and not listen to them.

There was a time, a while back, when he would have followed his own hunches, tuning in to the small hairs at the back of his neck. But the market forces these days were too complex for one man to grasp. Even he had to admit that. What happened here was dependent on what they did in Tokyo and New York. You needed advice at every point. Still, it went against the grain with him.

The good thing was, in three or four days now it would be over. They would be out.

Just on eleven, as always, he called Alex. These consultations were ritual. They made them by telephone since they could gauge better that way the little evasions they practised.

Vic joked today, he was in a buoyant mood, and this put Alex on his guard. He was difficult to talk to, Alex, unless you stuck to figures, but he had no suspicion of what was going on, he was certain of that. 'Watch it, Alex,' he said. It was his routine farewell.

He left the office at two to get a breath of air and was surprised to find, when he stepped into the street, that his mood had translated itself to the whole city, and he wondered if it wasn't this that his body had caught wind of, some meteorological occurrence high up in the atmosphere, the first stirring of an air current that had been gathering there and had only now begun to move in over the edge of the continent.

It was mid-October, and balmy. Girls were out in short-sleeved dresses, young fellows carried their jackets over their shoulders, joggers were about. Lemony sunlight made the edges of buildings and low walls luminous. He had a sense of being not only in deep harmony with all this, but maybe even responsible for it. How good he felt.

He dropped in on Felix. He hadn't done that for quite a while now. They had a coffee and talked. Brad was out on his own these days so it was easy for the old man to brag about him. He did it shyly. Brad was in the car-hire business, and was married and doing well.

When he got back to the office he decided, for no reason, to ring Ellie.

'No, nothing's the matter,' he said when she came to the phone at last from somewhere far off in the garden. He felt foolish. He wanted to tell her simply how happy he was, but she would hear that in his voice. It seemed foolish to make so much of it. 'I was just ringing,' he told her, 'that's all.'

At three he called down and had them bring his car up from the parking lot. He would drive up and spend an hour or two (he was still, he felt, on the track his dream had set him on) with Digger, at Keen's Crossing.

Impossible to say when, but at some point in the fifty-kilometre drive the light changed, his mind darkened, and as on other occasions the high state of elation he was in revealed itself as no more than a mood, some condition of mind or body that passed now as quickly as it had appeared, as inexplicably too. His heart tightened, till the cramp in his chest was so painful and his arm so numbed that he could no longer trust himself to keep hold of the wheel. He pulled over on to the rough verge, rested a moment, then turned into a break in the scrub. He sat hunched over the wheel in almost total darkness. 'I should go back,' he thought, and opened the door of the car and got out.

He must have slept or passed out for a moment. In the lapse of consciousness he found himself back in his dream; except that he saw now that it wasn't a dream at all but an actual moment of his boyhood he had come back to. He was in his own nine-year-old body again, standing barefooted in old serge pants and braces, his whole being drawn taut as a bow, at the edge of the dunes, with the day just on the turn and lights coming on all down the shore. One of those occasions when, in the assurance that he had the power to leap out of himself into an imaginable future, he had stood still, and feeling the animal in him crouched, ready to leap, had let himself go with it.

It took off in a long arc. He went with it, and found himself suspended, outside gravity, at the high point, and with the new moment yet to declare itself. But he must have come down that time, *one* of those times, in the wrong life. That was the only way he could explain now the otherness he felt in himself. *The wrong life.* So that everything that had happened to him, from that moment on, all of it, had occurred in another existence from the one he had till then been moving in and was intended for.

Was that possible? Everything?

It was all real, it had happened all right. It had happened to *him*. It was fact. Part of the real happenings of a world that takes note of such things; that records events and enterprises and makes a life of them, and if they are big enough makes history of them. Only none of it had been intended for him, that's what he saw. What had been intended was something quite different, and he had wrenched himself, by sheer willpower, out of the way of it.

In the deepest part of himself he had always known this. He had felt it in the presence of that boy who had appeared each morning to push his big feet into his shoes, and left dirt marks on the collars of his shirts. Later, hanging about the streets and watching with a bad conscience the lines of men waiting for handouts, he had seen quite clearly the gap in the line where he ought to have been, and had wondered when he would have to pay the price for getting away.

Thailand was different. That *was* intended. At that point the two lives somehow crossed. He had seen so clearly, up ahead, that old, white-headed fellow ('The one I am now,' he thought) who had passed clean through him. He had been in the right line that time.

He thought of all those mornings when, still heavy with sleep, he had sat in Meggsie's kitchen feeling for the contours of an existence, some other one, that his body might fit more neatly (more clumsily that is) than the one he was in. Not an easier life. It wouldn't be easier, he was certain of that. But one that was continuous with something in himself that he was afraid of losing contact with yet could not grasp.

Now, once again, he felt that nine-year-old body prepare to leap in him. He took off. He hung a moment free of gravity, and in the long breath in which he was suspended got a glimpse of what it was he was about to fall back into; which was his own life waiting to reclaim him – that other, harsher life that went back to its beginning in his father's life, in his mother's. But gravity was too strong. He could not stay up there long enough to make out the details of it. Once again he felt the force of things take hold and tug him down. And the life he came back into was the one he was in. He took the weight of it again, against his chest, in his belly and groin, and fell with the full force of his body on stones, little sharp-edged ones, and it stayed with him.

Later, when he came back to consciousness, he was surprised to find himself in deep night, with no light anywhere but where the first stars were showing themselves. 'Where is this?' he thought. He was unsure as yet whether it was a place or another condition.

But when he gathered his senses together he was aware of sharp-edged little stones under him, and there was a great climbing edifice of sound as well, though what the creatures were who were making it he could not guess. Frogs? Night crickets?

He sat up a little and looked about, but there was nothing to be seen.

It occurred to him then that he must have got out here by car, but there was no car in sight, and the light was not strong enough to judge directions.

He recalled, because his body did, a period of sharp pain. He still felt the aura of it, not at this point as a physical thing but as a sense of his

317

limbs being not quite returned to him, or not in their solid form. He had difficulty making judgements about things that ought to have been simple. Like where exactly his fingers were. And along with all this were sensations that were unrelated, so far as he could see, to any fact. A softness of spring weather, delicate breezes blowing about on the bare arms of girls, all of which seemed to have nothing at all to do with the weather but to be a movement of his spirit. He was sitting in the middle of nowhere and had no idea which way to move.

The decision was taken out of his hands. Suddenly a new and terrible anguish gripped his heart, or it was a physical agony, he could not tell which, and he was crushed, his cheek to the hard edge of stones that cut his flesh. He was on his side and writhing, pushing himself into the smothering blackness of the night or some other, deeper darkness, which was all he desired now, a sack that he could crawl into and pull over his head, and where he could kick out to the end of his breath.

He must have been crawling. He had come a long distance, pushing himself deeper and deeper into the grass. He lay now in a nest of it that he had made with the working of his limbs, in an agony of spirit that left him breathless.

The sun was up. Big birds were flopping overhead. He rolled his head a little and saw that he was not awake after all. In the dream he was in, his agony, which was something quite separate from him, had taken the shape of a cat with matted fur that was lying just inches from where his outstretched hand was curled. It had the brutal head and overgrown coarse fur of a feral, gone back, after a generation or more, to wildness, and was lying just beyond arm's length and watching him.

But when he blinked and looked closer, it wasn't a phantom, it was real. Its head had been split by the blade of a shovel, maybe an axe, and half its face was sliced away. It had crawled in here to die. It snarled now, its one fierce eye glaring at him; though the sound it made might not have been hostile after all but a plea for aid. Flies were swarming in the rawness of the open wound and the creature used its paw with the savage claws to keep them off.

Vic lay with his head on his extended arm, watching the cat, and the cat lay two yards away in extreme agony.

'I have seen all this before,' he thought, 'many times. I got out of it then. I survived. I always survived. I know about survival.'

But the cat, he saw, was dying. He looked at it. 'Poor bugger,' he thought, 'I'd help you, if I could. I'd put you out of your misery.'

He and the cat looked at one another, quite close like that, for a long time, and the cat went through agonies but did not die. It was suffering, but in what way, he wondered. What sort of consciousness does a cat have? Does a cat have consciousness?

'I'm sorry for you, mate,' he said out loud, and was surprised to hear his own voice.

The cat did not hear, or did not understand. It made no difference to it, one way or the other. It just watched him with its one eye, and he had no idea what it thought.

18

It was ten in the morning. The range was drawing just right, making a good heat, and Jenny was feeling unusually pleased with herself, which in her case meant pleased with the world, the way it settled around her this morning as if she was, for once, just right for it. She was waiting for a batch of scones to come out of the oven.

It was hot but not too hot. October. The yard was dancing a bit where heat came up in waves off a sheet of corrugated iron that Digger had left out there. The leaves of the pepper tree were also dancing. Half a dozen magpies were under the lines. They were excited. Something, some worm or that, or a smaller bird, was *getting it. Magpies, Magpies! Watch yer eyes!* They would come diving at your head if you passed too close under their nests. *Watch yer eyes!*

She dreamed at the windowsill, her mind on the yard but also on the oven: the big birds at their business, getting it over with, quick, quick now, Geez, heat dancing up off the iron sheet, and further back in her head, but not too far back, the scones on their tray which were for Digger's morning tea, rising nicely now and going crisp on top then browning. They would be ready in about five minutes. She shifted her heavy bulk on the chair.

When she took them out of the oven she couldn't believe it. And just a minute ago she had been feeling so good! She held the hot tray and stared at what she had done. At what *someone* had done. It's what happens, what always happens, when you start getting too sure of yourself. She couldn't believe it. She stared so long that the tray began to burn her fingers through the worn linen of the teacloth. She cursed and dumped the thing down on the sink, then screwed her mouth up, hugged herself a little and counted, using her finger this time. It was still thirteen. How? How had it happened? She was always that careful. Someone – but who? – must have slipped the extra one in while her back was turned.

So who was it *for*? That was the question. Whose bad luck was it?

And which one of them was it? They were all so alike, all nicely raised and browned. She was good at scones. It was her long suit. There was no way of picking it.

But she had to. It was either that or chuck the whole lot to the bloody magpies, and all the philosophy and practice of sixty-nine years went against it. *Waste not, want not*, that was the rule. If you did waste, then one day you would remember these scones and starve for 'em, and serve you right!

Quite fearful now of making a second error (if it was really her that had made the first one), but trusting too in some agency in herself that would work when she needed it, she squeezed her eyes shut, stretched out her blunt fingers, which were freckled and thickly padded round the nails, and let her palm hover over the scones. Then, when her mind was emptied of all thought, she took one.

Well, it had better be it! She had good reason to believe it was. She could work these tricks when she had to. Only where the hell, she wondered, had her mind been – what had her good sense been doing, *sleeping*? – when she made up that lot of dough in the first place and let the one extra in? *If* she had.

So what now? What should she do with it? Throw it back on the coals?

She looked at the scone sitting there on the sink. Innocent, it looked.

With a little sideways slew of her mouth she took it up rather gingerly, put her shoulder to the screen door and stepped out. The magpies were there, big black-and-white buggers the size of cats. They had already caught sight of her looming at the back door, but didn't let on that they were watching. 'Well,' she thought, this'll fix ya!'

'Here I come,' she sang to herself as she crossed the yard, 'here's yer ol' mate Jenny. You don't know what *I've* got in me hand, do yer, eh? Look at this. Which one of yez is it for? Which one of you greedy buggers is gunna swaller *bad luck*?' She tossed the nicely browned, crisp little scone like a soft stone into the midst of them, and the great black-and-white creatures rolled towards it and flapped and scrabbled, beaks going everywhere, wings too, tearing at one another and squawking.

One of them got it and she watched it gobble the thing down and the others go in under its wings for the crumbs.

'So,' she said, feeling a kind of satisfaction now at playing with such powers, bad luck and the possibility of a choking or worse, and of setting things right as well, getting them back into order again, since that extra scone had definitely been a mistake.

It wasn't *her* fault which one got it. Somebody else would be deciding that. All she'd done was throw the bad luck *to* them, she didn't choose. Greed had chosen. The greediest and strongest of them had got it.

She looked at the big bird, which was preening itself, and chuckled. She knew something the bird did not, 'A cat'll get you now,' she thought, watching it strut. 'A feral. Or some kid with a shanghai. Well, good riddance!' She didn't care. The main thing was, she'd got the bad luck off Digger and herself.

She would have liked to keep a watch on that bird and make sure, only she didn't have the time. She slumped back to the kitchen, and when she saw the tray sitting there, on the edge of the sink, had a sick feeling. Maybe she ought to have tossed the lot out anyway. But if you started that sort of caper, tossing good stuff out just because you were scared and couldn't tell good from bad, you'd be lost. You'd end up tossing everything out.

She'd made a choice. That's what you were supposed to do, make a choice and choose right, by instinct. If you started worrying about mistakes, you'd make one, and if you made a *little* mistake, well eventually you'd make a big one.

That's what had alarmed her so much when she saw that one extra. That it might be the beginning of something.

She was pegging out clothes an hour or so later when she saw the birds making a commotion in the scrub. 'Aha!' she thought. She pinned up the other end of the sheet she was hanging, which billowed and filled with light, and, leaving the remainder in the basket, went off through the grass a little to see what was doing. This would be proof now. The big birds were excited.

But what presented itself when she parted the grass on the overgrown track was not a bird at all but a cat, a big feral, black with reddish lights in its fur, and when it turned on her, snarling, she gave a gasp. Half its face was gone. Someone had sliced it away with the edge of a shovel. Some feller who was sick of having his chooks taken, no doubt. It looked up at her with such a dumb, suffering look, in spite of the snarl, that she was stricken. It was in agony, poor creature.

She turned away to find a rock or something to finish it off, and saw something else. A hand coming out of the grass.

'Jesus,' she thought, 'what a day!'

With her heart beating she pushed the grass aside and a man rolled over and looked right up at her.

It was Vic.

She was in real panic now. Was he poisoned? Had *she* done it? But she'd given that scone to the magpies. She'd seen one of them eat it.

She hung over him, very scared and moaning a little, and his eyes rolled, following her movements, his mouth wet and the tongue moving, but no sound coming from him.

She knelt to loosen his collar, which seemed to be choking him, and the hand grabbed hers and tightened on it. She wrenched her hand loose, jabbering, and when she got it free she had hold of a smooth little stone about the size of a kidney, same colour too, which she thought for a moment he might have sicked up. She stared at it.

About the size, too, of a scone. It was warm.

He rolled over now on his side, drew his legs up like a baby, and lay curled up in the grassy nest he had made by rolling about there.

'What is it?' she said.

The thought of a child, a baby, had softened her.

She took his hand. With her other hand she stroked his face. After a moment she squatted, lifted him a little, and took his head in her arms. She began to rock him, and the cat, opposite, watched with its one eye. He yielded in her arms and she forgot now all that she had against him. She forgave him for it, whatever it was, and she did not even *know* what it was. It didn't matter.

He had his face down between her breasts. She could feel a wetness. She began to weep. She could feel his mouth down there and wished, if that's what he wanted, that she could feed him, but she had no milk. She had had no milk now for more than forty years. They had pumped it out of her with a machine. She had begged and begged them, those nuns, not to take it, and all that night had dreamt of mouths pulling at her, and she didn't care in the end *what* they were, babies or poddy calves or little lambs or what, that were feeding off the rich stuff her body had stored up, which had been meant to feed a *creature*, not to be squeezed out with a machine. And all the time, out there somewhere, her own little baby was going hungry; or if it wasn't, it was being fed some other milk, not the one that had been made for it special in all the world; and for the whole of its life, poor thing, it would know that and feel the loss – that the world had stolen something from it that it would never have. She had looked around wherever she went after that, believing she would recognise the face of that little kid she had had the milk for, and who might be looking for it still.

Forty-three years old he would be now, wherever he was. And now, forty-three years late, *this*.

She hugged his head to her breast, but after a little, when her tears stopped, she eased him off and said gently: 'Listen, listen, Mister. I'm not leaving you. On'y I gotta get Digger, right? Right? Two minutes. Right?'

She got up, and there was still the cat, still with its head rolled towards her. She had to step around it. 'Don't worry,' she told it, 'I haven't forgot. I'll get to you later.'

She began calling Digger under her breath all the way to the yard, and when she was in hearing distance she started shouting for him, and right away he appeared round the corner of the store.

19

Digger was walking with Ellie on a terrace of springy turf, the edge of which fell away into a wild little gully, all reddish boulders and giant ironbarks and angophoras growing straight out of the rock. Behind them was the low, ranch-style house that Vic had built. They had come out with tea mugs in their hands to see the birds that filled the garden as they did the gully below, not observing, since it was barely visible, the point where wild nature became nature tended and organised, except that the garden offered the greater variety of green things spiked or spurred or exploding in dark or dazzling showers and was the more crowded. In the space of just seconds Digger identified blue wrens, noisy mynahs, three Eastern Rosellas, two kinds of honey-eater, all as Ellie in her many descriptions of the place had promised. He had never seen it before but knew every corner of this garden as if it was his own.

Ellie walked with a limp. She had never told him of any illness or injury; he was surprised. This little change in her, and it wasn't, as he saw after a time, the only one, alerted him to how many things in her life their correspondence might not have covered. But all that meant was how much more there was to come.

Her smile was the same, and so, almost at once, was the easiness between them.

She was very calm. Her mother was so distressed, she told him, and there had been so much noise and confusion, that she had to be.

In the evening they had been besieged by reporters. They had clambered all over the drive, banging on the doors, front and back, looming up at windows, making camp with their cameras on the lawn. None of them had shown any sort of consideration, or had the least respect for their privacy or grief, or had thought of the event, so far as she could see, as anything more than News. Ellie, who had always hated this public aspect of their lives, and feared it too, was disgusted. They had had to draw the curtains and sit like prisoners in their own house, and still the banging had gone on, the tapping at windows, the shouted appeals. Then suddenly they had all rushed off again, just packed up in great excitement and were gone. An event of world proportions had intervened, and Vic Curran's death, which on any other day would have been headlines, was reduced to a ten-centimetre column on the front page, with a direction to page three.

As for Albert Keen, phantom dealer in millions, whose rise and fall from nothing to nothing had covered just thirty-one days, you had to go to the financial pages and read between the lines to get a hint of that. It was a story that was lost as yet in the clouds of dust in which a whole ghostly edifice had tottered and come crashing down.

The Needham's Group had been hit, and hit badly. That at least was clear, and there were statements, cautious ones, from Alex and from the managers of two major banks.

'Did you see what the papers are saying?' Ellie asked him.

'Yes,' he admitted. 'But you know the papers.'

'No,' she said, 'it's true.' Digger looked to see how much she knew. Was she testing him? 'He was *doing* something, I don't know what. Alex knows. Something crazy. It wasn't illegal – or not quite, he wouldn't have done anything like that. You know what he was like. But it seems –' Her eye moved out over the layered leaves of the garden, all the different kinds of fronds, and heart-shaped and elongated leaves, and sword-shapes and falls of colour and fiery wheels. 'Alex says we're in trouble. He's out of his mind, poor Alex.'

'It was me,' Digger said abruptly. 'I was in on it. Haven't you heard?' It was a confession. He had no reason to boast of it.

'Yes. Alex told me. But Digger – you don't know anything about these things.'

'It was just the name he was using,' he explained, but it sounded unlikely without Vic to expound the thing and make it real. 'It seems,' he said, 'I'm a ruined man.'

She looked at him then. They both saw the humour of it, and he thought he heard Vic laugh. It was the sort of thing that might have appealed to him.

They walked on for a minute or two.

'Can I come and see you?' Digger asked. 'Or do you want to go on with the letters?'

She thought a moment. 'I don't know,' she said quietly. 'Why don't you *write* and ask me?'

326

It was too early to say any of the things they would have at last to get round to. Maybe it would be easier in writing.

They sat holding hands for a time, on a bench under the trees, then she said at last: 'Digger, I must go, I've got to see my mother. Do you want me to get you a car for the station?'

'No,' he said. 'Now that I'm a pauper again I'd better get used to walking, don't you reckon?'

The walk to the station was a warm one. It was hot for October. He had to stop and take his hat off for a bit to let his head breathe. From narrow patches of weeds on either side of the asphalt came the smell of dust and grass-seed, mixed in with an acrid but not at all unpleasant odour that showed there were dogs about. One or two of them came trotting past; out on their own affairs, and leaving at points along their route these sharp-smelling traces of their presence, just a few drops each time, as if it was incumbent upon them to mark their passage in this elemental and entirely personal fashion.

Digger liked the way they trotted about so lightly on their claws, with their ears flopping and their noses to the ground. They knew what they were doing, dogs. You could learn something from them. He walked on.

A list had started up in his head. He let it go on. *Burton, Cable, Carwardine, Cooley, Cooper, Crane* . . . The next one was him.

He let the two syllables out and found himself choked a moment. He could hardly go on: *Curran*.

Curran, Victor Charles, one of a list. But they had, after all and despite all, been as close as any two men could be. How had *that* happened?

He got a flash of him as he had appeared, hovering about behind Doug, in those last days before the surrender, and experienced again, and with a force he wouldn't have thought possible, as if time had no meaning at all, the immediate aversion he had felt. No, it was something more hidden than that. A sense of their being, in their deepest natures, inimical to one another; in some part of themselves that was not accessible to view, or to reasoning either, though they were both aware of it, and would trust it too. Except that they had not, not in the long run. What they had done instead, since they could hardly do otherwise, was let the spirit of accident lead them. First the monstrous accident of Mac's killing, then the stranger one of their

327

physical dependence on one another in the coming and going of their fevers, till what was revealed was something stronger even than their first instinctive hostility; unless that had been, from the start, only the negative sign of a deeper affinity. Which they might have missed, and by a long shot too, forty years, if accident had not imposed itself as the true shaper of their lives.

Accident? But what more mysterious force was that the name for in their inadequate language? . . . *Daley, Dannagher, Deeks, Dewhurst, Dixon.*

He walked on. There were shops now, supermarkets with windows covered with cut-price offers for washing powders or mixed fruit, a café with video games where kids were hunched, utterly absorbed, jerking their shoulders from left to right as they swerved past the asteroids, a newsagent's with the headlines outside on wired boards: the collapse on Wall Street, but also Vic's name, just the last one, Curran, in giant letters. In his case that was enough.

Digger stood and looked at it spelled out there, the six letters. It meant one thing on the newsboard and another thing altogether where its two syllables were tucked away, among so many, in his head. Another thing again as he had actually known the man.

He took up the list again where he had left off. *Doig, Dooley, Doone, Durani, Dwyer* . . . It was a long way yet to the end.

20

The child, his broad feet set firmly in the dust, sits on the bottom one of three steps that lead down from the verandah to their front yard.

It is afternoon, and hot. Across the street are other houses just like theirs, weatherboard with red corrugated-iron roofs and picket fences with numbers on the gate. Their number is six, and he is four. Six Marlin Street, and he is Victor Charles Curran, Vic.

They have lived at number six for as long as he can remember. At night people come to play poker. There is noise, smoke, laughter, and he is allowed to bring in the beer bottles in their straw jackets, and when they are empty he carts them out again and puts them with the others on the back porch. Dead marines, they are called.

His mother gets work to do for ladies. She is sitting now just to his left, on a cane chair she has brought from the kitchen. Her work is in her lap and she is very intent upon it, wearing her glasses. Open at her feet is a little cardboard suitcase where she keeps snips of all different shapes and colours.

Sometimes, to keep him quiet when he has no one to play with, she lets him take the pieces out and sort them into their different colours; but today she has given him something more difficult to do. She has given him a needle, wet the end of a piece of thread, and for the last hour, over and over, he has been trying to do this thing he knows is simple yet finds so difficult.

Now and again, just to reassure himself it can be done, he holds the needle up to see the hole more clearly.

If you bring it up close to your eye you can see the sky through it. It is a big hole and holds a lot of blue. Then if you lower it a little you see a whole house there. Jensens', opposite, where Trudy and Jack live.

It's odd, this. You can see a whole house in it, roof and all, but to get just a bit of cotton through is so difficult. He has been trying for a long time, screwing his eye up and setting his jaw, very determined, and the bit of thread which was white when he started is grubby now and getting grubbier. That's because of his hands. He lays the needle down very carefully, then the thread, and rubs his hands against his shorts. Then he tries again. Then he looks through the eye of the needle again.

He sees a truck parking outside Jock Hale's place. He sees two girls, Milly and Jane Benson, swinging on their gate. They are singing something he can't quite hear, and swinging. He sees a boy in grey shorts learning to ride a bike. The bike keeps wobbling and he puts his bare foot down on the bitumen to steady it, then tries again. The boy is about a year older than he is, maybe six, even. It is himself!

He is puzzled by this and looks across at his mother, but she smiles and does not see anything odd in it.

Men begin coming in from the mine. Soon now it will be dark. When he holds the needle up now the eye of it is smoky. It is close to dark in there.

The boy who was learning to ride the bike is riding easily now, he has got the hang of it. He is hardly wobbling at all. He begins to show off, making figures-of-eight in the road, very pleased with himself and laughing. The light will be gone soon and still the thread has not gone through.

He concentrates and holds his hands just so and draws his whole body together.

Soon it will.

Several accounts of the experience of Australian P.O.W.s in Malaya and Thailand provided general information, hints and details for events and moral inspiration for this piece of fiction, chief among them Stan Arneil's *One Man's War*, Sun Books, 1982, Hank Nelson's *P.O.W. Prisoner of War*, ABC Enterprises, 1985 (from Tim Bowden's radio series 'Australians Under Nippon') and *The War Diaries of Weary Dunlop*, E. E. Dunlop, Nelson, 1986. I should also thank the Yaddo Foundation, Saratoga Springs, NY, and the Literature Board of the Australia Council for generous support, and Susan Chace, Joy Lewis and Brett Johnson for their advice and help.

EGGS OR
ANARCHY

EGGS OR ANARCHY

THE REMARKABLE STORY OF THE MAN TASKED WITH THE IMPOSSIBLE: TO FEED A NATION AT WAR

WILLIAM SITWELL

**SIMON &
SCHUSTER**

London · New York · Sydney · Toronto · New Delhi

A CBS COMPANY

First published in Great Britain by Simon & Schuster UK Ltd, 2016
A CBS COMPANY

Copyright © 2016 by William Sitwell

3 5 7 9 10 8 6 4 2

Simon & Schuster UK Ltd
1st Floor
222 Gray's Inn Road
London WC1X 8HB

www.simonandschuster.co.uk

Simon & Schuster Australia, Sydney
Simon & Schuster India, New Delhi

The author and publishers have made all reasonable efforts
to contact copyright-holders for permission, and apologise
for any omissions or errors in the form of credits given.
Corrections may be made to future printings.

A CIP catalogue record for this book
is available from the British Library

Hardback ISBN: 978-1-4711-5105-7
Ebook ISBN: 978-1-4711-5108-8

Typeset in the UK by M Rules
Printed and bound by CPI Group (UK) Ltd, Croydon, CR0 4YY

Simon & Schuster UK Ltd are committed to sourcing paper
that is made from wood grown in sustainable forests and support the Forest
Stewardship Council, the leading international forest certification organisation.
Our books displaying the FSC logo are printed on FSC certified paper

For Alice and Albert

CONTENTS

AUTHOR'S NOTE

The quotes from Lord Woolton – and other main protagonists such as his wife Maud Woolton or Winston Churchill – are mainly based on Woolton's own writings, from his memoirs, diaries, a long tribute he wrote to his late wife, from his letters and other personal writings and also the diaries of his wife Maud. While his memoirs are more tempered, his private writings are quite extraordinary in both style, tone, temper and sound. So most quotes, dialogue and speech come from those writings – often using multiple sources for individual scenes – which would make the constant referencing of them tiresome. If I have ever paraphrased, elongated or massaged a quote, it is done faithfully and with respect for both the original source material and the reader.

A New Man at the Ministry

Late afternoon, Thursday 3 April 1940. Seven months into the Second World War and, in an office in London's Tothill Street in Westminster, a grey-haired man in his late fifties, dressed in a three-piece pin-striped suit, with a watch chain, was placing the few remaining items left on his desk – a small framed picture and an ink pot – into a box. In an ashtray a pipe smouldered.

Fred Marquis, latterly ennobled as Lord Woolton, was leaving his post, an advisory position with the less-than-exciting title of Director General of Equipment and Stores. His new role had a simpler name and was a touch more glamorous: in a matter of hours he would be Minister of Food.

The previous day, Woolton had received a telephone call from the Prime Minister's office, asking if he would visit Neville Chamberlain at seven o'clock that evening.

'I understand that your department is running so smoothly that you are now unnecessary,' were Chamberlain's opening words when they met.

Woolton, in his memoirs, wrote that it was 'said without a smile, in his rather cold manner, and I realized that for some reason or other he proposed to remove me'.

Woolton assumed that he would then be released to return to his actual day job, as head of the Manchester-based (and country's biggest) department store chain, Lewis's.

'Am I now free to go and look after my own business affairs?' asked Woolton.

Chamberlain replied that this was not his intention, instead he was making some changes in his Cabinet and he wanted Woolton to join the government as Minister of Food.

The task would see Woolton heading a ministry whose job was, in simple terms, to feed Britain and her colonies during the straitened times of the Second World War.

That meant 41 million men, women and children in Britain and Northern Ireland, with an oversight of the 532 million people of the British Empire. He would have to manage the purchase and importation of food, ensure its fair distribution across the country, tackle the very low productivity of home-grown sustenance, and, with the system of rationing that had begun on 8 January of that year, ensure that abuses of the system were kept to a minimum – and a black market thwarted.

Woolton left Downing Street, discussed the proposal with his wife Maud and then accepted the job the following day. At which point he immediately began to feel apprehensive.

'I was embarking on a new life,' he later reflected, 'at the age of fifty-eight, with many fears about my own capacity to succeed in these new and unaccustomed fields of parliamentary responsibility, and with a profound sense of the dire consequences to the country if I failed.'

As he cleared his office he considered the challenges of the coming days. His new offices were just north of Oxford Street, physically some two miles away from the political machine of government in Whitehall.

He would get his feet under the desk and spend the days and nights reading to get on top of the subject. There was a large bureaucracy that supported the ministry and he wondered how immovable a beast it would be.

He pondered on the day he would be presented to the press as the new minister and vowed to be ready for the difficult questions that would be thrown his way.

Those first few days of reading and research would be invaluable; he was a stickler for detail and accuracy. He was also a man of firm mind and steely determination, and remained resolute that no decision, no public comment should ever be made without a very clear understanding of the facts.

There was a knock at the door and the secretary – who had served him well since he had taken up his post at the Ministry of Supply just days after war had been declared – announced a visitor.

'Sir Henry French is here for you, Lord Woolton,' the secretary said.

Woolton looked startled. He had heard about this man; a career civil servant, Sir Henry French was the Ministry of Food's Permanent Secretary, classically implacable and solemn. Sir Henry had joined the Civil Service in 1901 at the age of eighteen as a second-division clerk to the Board of Agriculture; moving slowly but steadily up the ranks, he had built a reputation as a sound, if inflexible, administrator until joining the Ministry of Food at the start of the war. Fifty-six when war broke out, Sir Henry had spent thirty-eight of those years in the same department. He was, according to the *Oxford Dictionary of National Biography*, 'unapproachable and vain. He made up his mind about people and rarely changed it.' He was known to wear the responsibilities of his job in the lines on his face, and there was no known evidence that he had a sense of humour.

Woolton wondered how they would get on. He was a man who liked to get things done, who would often circumvent the traditional channels to implement decisions. Since starting work for the government some six months previously, his battles with the Civil Service had already landed him in hot water. He was keen to start this new job on the front foot. He would be ready for Sir Henry French.

He would settle into his new office, take a puff on his pipe, having spent time studying the machinations of his new ministry. Then he would call upon his Permanent Secretary.

But, it seemed, Sir Henry was already a step ahead of him and had come to stalk Woolton before he had even left his old job.

Sir Henry entered the room, the two men shook hands and, before any platitudes were offered, the civil servant informed Woolton that he had come simply to inform him that the following day he was to address a meeting at the Queen's Hall.

'I was horrified,' Woolton reflected.

This grand building, on Langham Place, was, before the war, a concert hall, but it now served as an ideal place for important political speeches, where the press and public could attend in large numbers (the building would later be destroyed by an incendiary bomb in the blitz of May 1941).

The speech, explained Sir Henry, would bring the press up to date with the Ministry of Food's plans, schemes and tactics.

'But I can't make a speech about something about which I know nothing,' Woolton exclaimed to Sir Henry. The Permanent Secretary looked surprised at this answer and Woolton quickly understood that this was exactly what one did in the upper echelons of politics.

'There was no escape,' he mused in his diary at the prospect of the following day's event, 'The meeting was widely advertised and a wide range of important people had been invited – from press to the Prime Minister's wife, Mrs Chamberlain.'

The occasion had originally been arranged for his predecessor, William Morrison.

'This meeting will be an excellent opportunity for you to make your mark with the public,' said Sir Henry, who then handed him a few sheets of paper, adding 'And here, Minister, is your speech.'

'My trouble was that I had not formulated any policy,' wrote Woolton, 'but Sir Henry told me that there was no difficulty about that, because he had the whole statement most clearly laid out for me.'

It was, explained Sir Henry, officials who decided the

policy and Woolton's job 'to expound the policy, to explain it to the public.' Woolton did not like this. 'That was not my conception of the function of a minister. There was a further difficulty in that I am incapable of making a speech that I have not prepared myself.'

It was now the early evening and, reflected Woolton, 'there was no escape from this meeting. The Press indicated that they were anxious to hear my policy.'

There was nothing he could do. So he cancelled his evening plans, left his old ministry and resolved to work at home until the small hours.

'I sat up all that night studying the papers and getting myself acquainted with the current position of food supplies,' he recalled. 'I felt like a barrister briefed to appear in Court. But what a Court!'

The following day, after just a few hours sleep, he found himself in the Queen's Hall, on a platform alongside Sir Henry French and another ministry official, looking out at a full auditorium and a pack of pressmen flashing their cameras. Questions were shouted, he was asked to pose this way, then that, he felt almost blinded by the ceaseless flashing lights. Then, as the cacophony turned to a murmur and the room began to hush, he heard the whirr of the BBC news cameras, he saw the recording equipment of the radio teams.

As an official introduced the Ministry of Food's new boss to the hall, Woolton considered his resolve that previous night. He would look out at the audience, but in his mind would see far beyond. 'My audience is not the aggregate of the public who are listening but the detail of the individual in front of the domestic receiving set,' he thought to himself, as he recalled in his memoirs. 'In the front of my mind I keep a picture of a man in his cottage, sitting without a collar, with slippers on, at the end of the day's work, with children playing on the rug, with his wife washing up in an adjoining room with the door open.'

If his talk was successful, Woolton allowed himself to imagine an additional moment in that scene. As his voice would come over the radio, 'a visitor arrives in the middle of my broadcast. The man says: "Sit down and shut up; we are listening to Woolton."'

On a table in front of Woolton was the stack of papers that contained the new minister's speech, dutifully presented the previous day. To the right of that were some smaller sheets of writing paper, with notes scrawled across them.

Just before Woolton stood to command the microphone, he conspicuously moved the stack of papers to the left, effectively discarding them, and instead picked up his own notes. He nodded with a faint look of amusement in his eyes to Sir Henry, who could not conceal a look of intense alarm. And then Lord Woolton rose to his feet and uttered the first words of his new career.

2

INTRODUCING FRED

Frederick James Marquis was a particularly treasured child to his parents Thomas and Margaret. He was born on 23 August 1883. Fifteen months earlier, his parents' first born, Ernest, had lived for only eleven days.

His mother Margaret thus cherished this baby, who remained the couple's only child. As she cradled Fred gently as a new-born, so she held him tightly while he grew. She dreaded the day she would have to relinquish him to the care of teachers as school. Then would come the tortuous prospect of his teenage years, giving way to his early twenties, when he might spend nights and even weeks away if he was to satisfy her almost impossible dream that he could attain a university education.

And so as Fred grew up and did escape the nest, Margaret

formed a metaphorical leash, as secure and strong as the force she used to hold him as a baby, except it now came in the form of a constant cavalcade of letters.

Her missives were as frequent as today a worried mother might send an email. The letters came daily – sometimes there were two a day. More often than not, her main subject was laundry. She would sit at home fussing about exactly which clothes he had, which socks he might have on his feet, which shirt on his back. She felt she knew for sure every item of clothing he had in his drawers; each pair of shoes on the floor of his wardrobe, the suit hanging up, the pyjamas under his pillow.

Invariably, the direction of traffic with the letters was one way. It meant Margaret would have to imagine her son's response and so follow it up with another missive that scolded him.

'My Dear Boy,' she started one morning, when Fred was in his late teens, her fraying nerves rendering her just a little cross: 'I told you [sic] would require a clean shirt before the end of the week but you thought not.' Washing had become an obsession. 'I wonder if you have a shirt ready,' she continued, 'you said you are going out to dinner on Thursday.'

Knowing exactly the number of shirts he had, her calculations had raised the dreadful possibility that his evening shirt, if not dirty, was certainly not pressed.

There was further horror in her mind about those items resting under his pillow.

'Bring your pyjamas with you, really they must be awfully dirty, it is ages since you had clean ones,' she implores of him, wondering when his next trip home would be. Indeed, it was vital he bring back home a large bundle of laundry. 'If I were you,' she writes, 'I would put all of them in a bag and then once carrying would get all the dirty things home so that I can see to them and have them ready by the time they are wanted.' Now, anyone casually browsing through the life of Frederick Marquis, first Earl of Woolton, might have been surprised to learn that his mother Margaret didn't just fret about her son's laundry, she actually did it herself.

For when Woolton died at the age of eighty, in 1964, his home was a large pile in Sussex, he had been chairman of the Conservative Party, his son had been at the leading English public school Rugby, and one of his grandsons was down to attend Eton College with two others destined for Harrow School. He spoke with the clipped tones of the elite aristocracy and, as he recorded privately himself, Walberton House, where he lived near Arundel, had 'an adequate staff and a lift'.

Yet Woolton's origins were not just humble, they were emphatically working class. Whereas today the modern politician would barely let an interview pass without eulogising on their near poverty-stricken roots, Woolton never mentioned his very real unassuming origins, indeed he rather buried them.

The house where he was born was on a terrace, long since demolished, in Salford, Manchester. While his mother's letters betray a well-educated woman, his father, Thomas, was an itinerant saddler; his only two surviving letters are written in pencil and reveal just the bare bones of literacy. A note to young Fred (thanking him for a gift of some kind of personal item with his name embossed upon it), reads, free of grammar: 'I am so pleased with it I would not have wished for anything else it is fine and fancy the initials are great.' In another letter, penned on Fred's eighteenth birthday in 1901, his father says: 'it does not seem long since you were only quite a little kid but we must not look back in what you are now one of the rising lights and I hope you may have health to continue to rise with love from Pa.'

Thomas's family had been smallholders, farming in Lancashire. Their small acreage was on the Fylde plain, a flat piece of ground jutting out to the Irish Sea. His father, James, was the second son and had been given none of that modest patch of land to manage; so he found a job as landlord of a pub called the Black Bull Inn in nearby Kirkham. The town was familiar territory for the family, and among the stone tomb chests and monuments in the graveyard of St Michael's Church are several gravestones that bear the family name of Marquis.

James married his barmaid Harriet, apparently to save having to pay her a wage, and, so goes the family story, he threw his newly-wed's bonnet into the fire on returning from their wedding, saying: 'You won't need that for working.'

His son Thomas received the same scant generosity and found a role as a saddler to service the horses and coaches used by those staying at the inn. On his father's death in 1879, the inn fell into new hands and Thomas found himself unemployed. He moved to Liverpool, the big city that was then a magnet for the rural dispossessed; but presumably he was unsuccessful in his quest to find work as, by 1883, he had moved again to Salford, although he had at least found a wife in Margaret Ormerod.

In fact he never did seem to find a constant occupation,

his early skills as a saddler finding diminishing custom as the motorcar began to outsell the horse-driven coach. The impression is of a man more often morose and inactive. 'Our Da is not much better but no worse,' writes Margaret on several occasions. News of him in her letters includes his fixing a wardrobe, visiting the bank and putting down rat poison.

Margaret, meanwhile, clings to Fred. It appears she doesn't enjoy good health, is generally lonely and has few, if any, friends. Any family back in Kirkham are never mentioned with any warmth, and if anyone calls on her they come at the wrong time and then stay too long.

The thrust of her days revolves around Fred and whatever he is doing, and while she keeps a constant watch on him, desperate not to let him go, she also relies on him completely. Once he hits his late teens he looks after all of her finances and he buys her everything, from envelopes to fruit. All the while she continues to scold him; he doesn't write to her often enough – one suspects he couldn't have matched her record even if he'd had the spirit or time for it – he doesn't keep himself out of the rain, his friends are suspect and he works too hard. She dotes on him, desperate that, as she writes to him, he will 'do something proper', imagining fancifully that he could one day attain such status as to be knighted. 'Wouldn't it be great?' she writes, but adds: 'It won't happen if you sit up working until two in the morning. For you will wear all your strength out whilst you are only a young man.' In fact Woolton would spend much of his life working until two in the morning. But at the time his mother was fussing about this particular aspect of his life he was studying at Manchester's College of Technology.

His education had begun in 1897 at Ardwick Higher Grade School. He was there until fourteen when, having won a County Council Exhibition, he went to Manchester Grammar School.

Already he had attained more than any of his family fore-bears. Then came a moment when he achieved something his grandfather, pouring a jug of ale at the Black Bull Inn, would have scoffed at as fantasy. Fred was offered a place at Cambridge.

But he turned it down. Many years later he claimed the reason for this was that his father had told him, on the day he received the telegram with the news from Cambridge, that doctors had recently given him just six months to live. Fred's response was to tear up the telegram and pledge to stay at or near home to help look after his father.

As it transpired, the doctors were a little off the mark. Thomas Marquis lived for a further forty-eight years. Perhaps it was an act of extraordinary selfishness, or maybe it was fear; knowing his wife's possessive obsession with their son, perhaps Thomas dreaded the consequences if Fred moved away to Cambridge.

But there was another reason. Much as Fred would have loved to have gone up to Cambridge, to study and live with the country's best-educated sophisticates, he would not have been able to afford the living costs. He would have strug-gled to pay for accommodation, let alone the high living; the eating, the drinking, the vacations in Europe with new-found friends. His wife Maud would later write in her diary that he wanted to go to Cambridge 'very badly, but he couldn't afford it'.

Frederick Marquis may have been destined to progress

through the class system, but a move to Cambridge aged twenty was a leap far too early.

So he stayed in Manchester, a city that he never ceased to romanticise about. He said of it later that it was 'not so much a city as a state of mind ... Manchester's straight talk, her ferocious contempt for appearances, her unconcealed uninhibited friendliness for people she liked, her gentle cherishing of certain cultural values.' It was a place where the local sport was, he said, 'bubble pricking', a sport that he was to indulge in, although mostly privately in the pages of his diary, many years later when he joined the Second World War government.

The city also had an undercurrent of socialism which Fred actively engaged in, joining the Fabian Society, an organisation that worked to promote such things as equality in life, power, wealth and opportunity. It was an activity that those very government colleagues he would later disparage would cite as evidence that Woolton was a 'pinko'; a not-quite-red but communist sympathiser in the midst of establishment Conservatives. Woolton's early life did indeed see him on the left of the political spectrum; but as he progressed through life he would come to view capitalism as the key solution to poverty. Socialism for him would become a dirty word, an ideology that would not achieve anything. And this man, who at one time worshipped the thinking of Scottish socialist Keir Hardie, would eventually become a passionate Conservative and finally chairman of the establishment Tory party (in 1946, although he would not actually become a paid-up member of the Conservatives until Churchill's party was defeated in the General Election of 1945). Woolton would make a journey from intellectual socialist, to practical businessman to right-of-centre politician.

While the Manchester of the early 1900s certainly had prosperity – it was a town that had grown rich on the cotton trade, had access to the coalfields of the north and had been the beating heart of the Industrial Revolution – it also had its bleak side.

Just half of the homes in the late Victorian era, whose male inhabitants were the cogs of the great revolution from agrarian to machine economy, had running water. Up to thirty families would share the same outdoor privy, rubbish was collected infrequently, and many houses became brick warrens whose dank passages led to tiny rooms devoid of natural light or ventilation.

Fred was more than aware of this standard of living as his parents' home was not exactly on the smart side of town. And he stayed here – to study a mix of chemistry and psychology, followed by an MA in economics – until 1906. The subjects came easily to him.

'I had a natural aptitude for the sciences,' he wrote later in life. He also expressed considerable pride that one teacher was a Professor Samuel Alexander. He was, wrote Woolton, 'One of the greatest of the living philosophers of the time.' Three times a week he would lecture to a select group of just three students. To be chosen for this group was no mean achievement. Woolton delighted in recording the professor's view that 'there was only one person in ten thousand who had the mental capacity to understand what he was talking about.' Their tutorials would start at 4.15 p.m. in Professor Alexander's rooms; the philosopher would usher in his students, pour himself a cup of tea, feed his dog and then talk until eight o'clock. 'He poured out to us his wisdom that was so profound and knowledgeable, that was so exciting, and often disturbing, as to leave us in a state of wonderment as to what we were going to do with it all,' wrote Woolton. But it was this teaching that convinced 20-something Fred that he should become a sociologist; that he should analyse how human society organises itself.

As part of his postgraduate studies, in 1908, he moved for a time to Liverpool, finding lodgings with fellow graduates at 129 Park Street. This was a slum district, near the dock road, in the south of the city, where poverty was even more acute than in his native Manchester. The activities of these graduates were part of what was known as the 'settlement movement', a late nineteenth-century idea which countenanced that poverty could be alleviated by the creation of communities where rich and poor would live close together and share their knowledge and skills. A forerunner of this was Toynbee Hall in the East End of London. Created by a Church of England curate Samuel Barnett, the vision was that future leaders would live and work in such areas and – having been face-to-face with poverty – would later, with their understanding of the real issues involved, be able to enact radical change. Clement Attlee, the Labour Prime Minister between 1945 and 1951, was one such individual who, in 1910, spent a year at Toynbee Hall.

Woolton once reflected on this period of his own life, writing that he was living there, 'in the same spirit as the medical students of the time who were inquiring into the causes of TB'. This was a scientific investigation into the causes and problems of poverty, 'on our very doorstep', he wrote. Yet in spite of the serious subject matter, he was later keen to make it clear that it was not a life of drudgery. He spent a great deal of time, he wrote, 'frankly enjoying myself' and with 'no clear idea of how I proposed to earn a living'.

Fred recalled neighbours whose houses were 'generally vermin-ridden', and with 'human inhabitants [who] were mostly the poverty-ridden victims of sweated labour and casual employment'. These were streets of brick-built houses from the early 1820s, terrace upon terrace of densely packed buildings, the exteriors black from soot, the insides damp and dirty. The streets were filled with raggedy children. On warmer days women sat outside stitching or selling clothes, old shoes or boots, while the men sat on the steps of pubs dressed in thick jackets, worn trousers and rounded felt hats.

Fred and his student pals would not have been the only visitors to this part of Liverpool. The slums drew all kinds of people wishing to study – or correct – its inhabitants. There were housing reformers and temperance advocates, the latter arguing that it was alcohol that created so much of the poverty. Child protectists came, as did photographers hoping to win competitions with their images of people living amid dirt and grime. It wasn't until the late 1950s that the slums were cleared. Almost half of the housing stock was deemed unfit for human habitation, and thousands of homes were then demolished. Families were moved away to towns like Skelmersdale, Kirkby or Widnes.

But with all this evidence laid out before him, right outside his door, student Fred was able to garner data during the day and debate the subject around the coal-fired stove at night.

Fred was made a warden of the settlement and Philip, later Lord, Rea, who became a Liberal politician and merchant banker, recalled meeting him then. 'He had at that time, as I think he always had, a slightly chilling aspect when one first met him, but as soon as he spoke – as soon as his eyes twinkled – one knew that he had a warm heart.'

The consequences of poverty never left Fred. Neither did he ever forget the shock of hearing one day in 1908 that a female neighbour had died, her body lying undiscovered for days. The woman had died of starvation. She had neither asked for help, nor had anyone ever come to her aid.

Those two years on Park Street shaped the mind of Fred Marquis. 'It was an experience that was to fashion much of my thought and actions for the rest of my life,' he recalled.

He had also been joined in what became a passion for social work by Maud Smith, the woman who would become his wife.

Maud was the daughter of a stern man called Thomas Smith. A mechanical engineer, specialising in the construction of boilers and locomotives, he had been married three times and had, Woolton once noted, older brothers the same age as Fred's own father. He was a passionate believer in education and was thus gratified that Maud and her sister would take advantage of it, but he was very wary of young men and had an almost violent dislike of the idea of his daughters becoming romantically attached. Maud never forgot a piece of advice her father once gave her on noting, in her late teens, that she was dressed up and going out to a party. 'Remember this,' he said, 'I would rather see my daughters lying in their coffins than married to any man.'

However independent she might have been, she could not totally cast off her father's views and it made her wary of members of the opposite sex. 'The truth was she was frightened of men,' Woolton later wrote, adding: 'She was always somewhat critical of them and greatly preferred the company of women.'

As students of the same university, their paths crossed occasionally but these were days when women students did not speak to male students in college grounds. It was, wrote Woolton, 'considered very forward, and of course we never used Christian names in speaking to one another either in college or outside'.

Yet one day, for some reason and at a time when Fred and Maud barely knew each other, Maud broke with convention. It was a day of examinations and groups of men and women were nervously anticipating a few hours of intense thinking and writing.

'We both entered the examination hall for the same examination at the same time,' Woolton recalled. 'To my intense surprise, as we entered the hall, Maud stepped out from a group of girls and wished me luck. It was all on the impulse of the moment – we had scarcely met before – and I don't know and I've never known which of us were more surprised.'

The pair got to know each other better eighteen months later in 1906, when, by chance, they found themselves joint secretaries of the University Sociological Society. Woolton recalled that Maud had 'a challenging determination to resist any effort of men to come within any approach to dominating her. At the first it made our relationship a little difficult.'

They had a shared interest in social conditions, political philosophy and current politics and worked together successfully in the society. But, wrote Woolton, 'it was made abundantly clear to me that our relationship was of a strictly unemotional variety.'

And thus their friendship continued for sometime on a purely platonic basis, even though Thomas Smith died, removing one obstacle to marriage. However, Fred was reluctant to move things forward at the time, because he had so little money, later admitting, 'I was frightened of the responsibility of marriage. Not only was I quite unable to see a future for myself which could financially sustain matrimony, but I had the gravest doubts about whether I had the qualities which could make for happiness in my wife.'

Maud meanwhile gave him no encouraging signals. One day a chemist Fred knew approached him, saying that he wanted to propose to Miss Smith. 'I'd like to be sure of your own intentions, Fred,' he said, 'so that I know, so to speak, that she has not already been promised to you.'

This was very noble, thought Fred, and knowing Maud well enough he decided to speak to her about it. 'He has many virtues,' he told her, 'and I advise you to go and see him.'

'But he's so dull,' replied Maud.

'The sky was getting clearer,' Woolton reflected. By this time he had also left university and was earning money as a senior mathematics master at Burnley College. He had also been appointed Warden of the David Lewis Hotel and Club Association in Liverpool – which provided cheap beds in the city's docklands and was promoted by the successful store,

Lewis's – and the University Settlement. He had a salary, a flat, an income of £400 a year, two maids and subsidised food, fire and light.

The pair had another conversation and, in his words, 'we decided we would both like to take the risk.'

Fred proposed properly and, he wrote, 'as soon as we became publicly engaged she changed in her attitude to me and all the defences were withdrawn.' And the tone of her letters to him changed dramatically. Any formality was gone and, like so many engaged couples, she expressed her anxiety at waiting for the wedding day to arrive. 'I do wish we were married,' she wrote in March 1912. She also sent him constant missives urging him to 'rest', joining his mother in telling the workaholic Fred to slow down occasionally – 'gracious you don't seem to know what it means . . . do mind what you are doing.' She was also relieved Thomas Smith hadn't lived to evaluate her beloved: 'I'm glad that you never met my father,' Maud once told Fred, 'I'm sure that if you had you would have been sent summarily on your way.' Her letters were always full of affection ending with the likes of 'Goodbye beloved . . . Here's a kiss . . . I shall miss you . . . I wish you were here . . . Always your sweetheart . . . Please don't overwork . . .'

Finally, on 10 October 1912, in a Unitarian ceremony in Liverpool, the couple were married. Fred's mother Margaret, who approved of Maud, could not resist revealing her fear at the prospect of her son making a final wrench from the nest. The day before their wedding Margaret wrote Maud an emotional letter in which she made no attempt to hide her feelings. 'We don't want you to take our boy away from us,' she pleaded desperately. 'You come to us and we shall be happy and contented seeing you two living for each other.'

Maud possibly did not have in mind that she would spend her married days living with Fred and his parents, but for the time being, that's what happened. In her letter Margaret said she was finding it hard to express herself: 'Excuse this letter for I can't write. If you could read inside me you would be able to understand.' Having finished the missive and signed it 'Mammie' – as she always would to her son – she returned to it later and wrote more on the blank back page, worried, perhaps, that Maud might have got the wrong idea about her.

'I feel sure we shall get on all right why shouldn't we. You are going to make Fred happy which is all I want and of course you to be happy in doing it.' And a last sentence suggests that Maud wasn't altogether comfortable with how her new mother-in-law clung to her son: 'Perhaps as you know me more you will find out all that I would be to you if only you will let me.'

Margaret then wrote a letter to Fred a few days later while the newly-weds were on honeymoon. 'Surely you will not look so tired and worried when you come back,' she clucked and then started panicking about his suitcases, which were, apparently, delayed. 'It is strange that your luggage is so long in getting to you, I hope you have got it by now.' She added that Fred's father had taken a gas stove away to be fixed, that a friend had brought her some rabbits to eat and she asked him if he'd pay the bill for a delivery of tea.

Meanwhile Fred devoted himself to his work and studies. There were the many hours he spent considering the links between ill health and physical incapacity. He learned the importance of providing pregnant women with rounded nutrition, and became almost obsessed with the importance of having good teeth. He grew to understand more than many the importance of nutrition in enabling a fulfilling life.

Thirty years later Lord Woolton found himself running the ration and feeding Britain during a world war. 'It was this experience, in a poverty-ridden district of Liverpool, that gave me the stimulus to use the powers of a war-time Minister of Food,' he wrote.

In preparing for his role as the nation's feeder, Lord Woolton had started far earlier than anyone could have possibly imagined.

3

STEPPING STONES TO GOVERNMENT

Woolton's route to the Ministry of Food took in spells of teaching, lecturing, social work, school management and journalism until, in the 1920s, he found his metier in the retail business.

To his huge frustration, but doubtless his mother's great relief, he had been rejected from military service during the First World War. Exactly why is a slight mystery, but, having been medically examined, he was deemed C3. There is no record of him having 'badly deformed toes or flat feet' (common ailments among those listed as C3s). But in later years, during the subsequent war, he occasionally admits in his diaries to feeling ill and having colitis, a long term inflammatory bowel disease. Indeed in August 1942 he gave an interview with the author J. B. Priestley. Priestley asked him why he had been rejected seven times as an army recruit. 'His reply,' wrote Priestley with delicate diplomacy, 'is indicated by my punctuation:'

(Priestley, incidentally, was at first a little suspicious of Woolton and wrote: 'When I first met him I thought him too urbane to be genuine, that smooth clean shaven face under the grey hair, that perfect careful dress, that precise and cautious speech, that refusal to be hurried about anything, it was all too suave for words.' Yet he ended up being a great admirer.)

So it's likely that throughout his life Woolton suffered from intermittent abdominal pain. Typically, though, he used this to his advantage, taking a constant principled stance against rich, and thus in his view unnecessary, food. In June 1942, for example, he recorded a meal he had with some people who represented the cereals business. 'They gave me lobster for lunch,' he wrote in his diary. 'My constitution wasn't built for dealing with high living, and I was sick at night and have felt queer ever since.'

According to his cook, Mrs Pomford, Woolton had unfussy tastes. 'He is the easiest man in the world to please about his meals,' she told the *Daily Express* in April 1940.

But thus prevented by a delicate constitution from joining many of his friends who had gone to war, aged thirty-one in 1914, he became an economist in the War Office. There he had a range of roles, including managing the provision of blankets for the French and Belgian armies, and providing soap for the Russians.

After the First World War, he dabbled in journalism. In this domain he didn't bring his fevered intellectual brain to the subject of employment for the low-skilled poor or the construction of affordable homes. No, the subject he alighted on was the boot trade, and he wrote articles on the subject for the *Times Trade Supplement*. Spotting a post-war gap in the market, he tried a career in the boot-making world – he had dipped a toe in this field in the War Office, having had some dealings with supplying Russian soldiers with footwear. Of course, Woolton's style of toe-dipping saw him becoming secretary to the Leather Control Board and then being appointed to the role of Civilian Boot Controller.

He had noticed how smart men always stopped to put on galoshes – those rubber over-shoes – before they stepped out in inclement weather, and pondered on there being an opportunity for him: 'I thought that there ought to be in America a market for men's high class shoes that would make it unnecessary for them to wear galoshes whenever they went out in the rain,' he recollected later. So, having first set up a federation to maintain and build on the reputation of Britain's bootmakers, liaising and making allies with the bootmakers' union, he made a business trip to the United States.

It was during that trip he renewed his acquaintance with another passenger, Sir Rex Cohen, managing director of the Lewis's department store. Sir Rex had come across Fred while the younger man was working as a warden of one of the store's social experiments: providing accommodation at the local docks. Sir Rex had offered Fred a job but he refused. Now on the boat, accompanied by their wives, the Cohens and Wooltons became good friends. So impressed was Sir Rex by this assured thirty-something entrepreneur, he decided to accompany Fred as he went on his boot mission around America.

Before leaving England, Fred had been challenged about his boot idea by a cynical colleague he had known from his time in the War Office. 'I am going into business,' he told the man, Harry Bostock. 'I swear to you that I will make a business so successful and profits so large that tears of envy will roll down your cheeks.'

Fred didn't manage to sell his newfangled, high quality boots to the Americans, but his travels with Sir Rex Cohen across the States led the boss of Lewis's to one firm conclusion. Cohen could see a remarkable determination in this young man and renewed his determination to employ him.

The two finally came to an agreement and Woolton joined the firm. 'To go into retail business in 1920 was more of an adventure than I knew,' he wrote. One of his personal challenges was to see if he could merge his business aspirations with his social conscience. Was it possible to make money *and* look after people? He dreamed of social harmony but also had an instinctive knack for business. As he wrote: 'Could the "dream" and the "business" become a work-a-day reality?'

He was joining a sixty-four-year-old family business and he was an outsider. As Rex Cohen himself put it: 'This is the first time that I have ever invited anybody who was not of my family, and not of my [Jewish] faith, to join me.'

The store had been founded in Liverpool in 1856 by David Lewis and had humble beginnings as a small shop selling men's and boys' clothing. It steadily grew in size and merchandising scope, branching into being a 'Universal Provider' and spreading along Ranelagh Street before acquiring a second premises on Bold Street. By the early 1880s it had become a successful department store with branches in Manchester, Birmingham and Sheffield. In 1886, after the founder's death, the store was bought out by Louis Cohen, a senior partner in the firm. It was his son Rex, who ran the business with his brother Harold, who had hired the young man he'd met on the boat to America.

Fred was to experience all aspects of the business – a rollercoaster ride of retail – and it wasn't long before, aged thirty-seven, he was made joint managing director of Lewis's at a time when it was growing to become the biggest retail operator in the UK. Fred, during his forties and fifties – between 1920 and 1939 – was pivotal in growing the business.

By the outbreak of the Second World War there would be Lewis's department stores in Liverpool, Manchester, Glasgow, Leeds, Stoke-on-Trent and Leicester. The company would later open in Oxford, Blackpool, Bristol, Newcastle as well as buying and running Selfridges in London.

His mother Margaret died in 1923, but not before seeing her son's burgeoning career. 'You know it was my one and sole ambition for you to be a parson, never thought of anything higher, did we?' she wrote to him in her old age. 'But fancy what a height you have got to. We often talk about it.'

By the mid 1930s, Frederick Marquis was a successful businessman, a man in a trade that had become respectable, a chap who dressed impeccably, owned a substantial home (Hillfoot House in Liverpool, along with a cook, Elizabeth Pomford and her husband Albert, the butler), as well as a flat in London – and membership of the exclusive gentlemen's club Brooks's on St James's Street – and a holiday home by

Lake Windermere (Fallbarrow, bought in 1931). He had a small family, a daughter Peggy, born in 1917, and a son Roger, born in 1922, and a social life that first dallied on the edge of and then became intrinsic to fashionable London society.

In recognition of his services to the British retail industry, he was knighted in July 1935. F. J. Marquis Esq. was written to from 10 Downing Street and told that the Prime Minister intended to submit his name to the King to confer a knight-hood. The letter was stuck proudly into a private album at home, along with a picture of the new knight in top hat and tails on his way to Buckingham Palace for the investiture.

The newly ennobled Sir Frederick then filled the entire album with the hundreds of telegrams and letters he received from everyone, from friends in London to merchandising managers in Manchester. Although he wasn't political, he had already made his concerns about the rising power of Nazism plain by ending Lewis's trade with Germany after its invasion of Austria in 1938, urging other companies to do the same. But poor health, which had dogged him in private for some time, suddenly interrupted his working life. In the summer of 1938, Maud recorded in her diary that: 'He was in bed for most of August and it left him very depressed. He had got a streptococcal infection and in spite of not making a full recovery he had gone back to work.'

The following January Stanley Cohen, vice chairman of Lewis's, asked to come and meet the couple together. 'Fred has been ill,' he stated frankly to Maud in front of her hus-band, 'he doesn't seem to be getting better properly and he needs a long holiday. Take him away for three months.'

Both Maud and Cohen ignored Woolton's protestations that he couldn't possibly take that sort of time out and the business needed him. And so for three months in early 1939, the couple went to South Africa, accompanied by Peggy.

'The result was that Fred got renewed health, which was providential,' Maud wrote in her diary. She then added: 'As a matter of fact I want to state here now that during both our lives there is marked evidence that a higher power than us has seeded us in most of our actions. All fits in. If Fred hadn't had this holiday, he couldn't have carried on.' And without that return to health and the protection of that higher power Woolton would have been unable to accept a role that would eventually lead him to the Ministry of Food.

The moment they got back a letter arrived from the War Office. On 18 April 1939, Sir Harold Brown, director of munitions production at the War Office, wrote asking Woolton if he would take a position as 'a distinguished industrialist who has a full knowledge of the various branches of the clothing trade, to advise the Department in regard to our plans and problems'.

It was the spring of 1939 and, as the storm clouds of war gathered, the country was reluctantly preparing for the cataclysm to come. Woolton, for whom the army was not an option, believed he should serve his country in another way. He was given the mundane title of Technical Advisor on Textiles in the War Office. As the army quickly expanded in anticipation of war, which would be declared on 3 September of that year, Woolton's job was an ill-defined position between the War Office and the Ministry of Supply.

It transpired that those 'problems' referred to by the

War Office included a lack of communication between the departments, and a wall of bureaucracy which made the actual buying and supplying of clothes for the army almost impossible.

Woolton regretted accepting the job almost immediately. 'In all my life I had never found myself in such a position,' he wrote. 'I saw clearly that war was coming. I had undertaken responsibility. I found nowhere a sense of urgency and I foresaw war breaking out with the army completely unprepared.'

Maud also reflected on the chaos, writing, 'The army clothing was still on a peace time basis. It brought in conscription and it had no uniforms.' She also thought this step of her husband's, into the world of government, was not a good one. 'The whole idea seems the height of folly,' she wrote.

After his first day in the job Woolton reported back to Maud. 'Do you know there are only five firms in this country making uniforms? And no one else seems to want to make them,' he told her.

'For the first month,' wrote Maud, 'he had a very sticky time.'

There was, for example, the issue of trousers and trouser buttons (this being the pre-zip era for flies). Orders had been placed for trousers for soldiers, but because of the system in place, the department that placed the trouser orders was unable to place orders for buttons as these were not deemed actual clothing material. They had to be purchased by another department with a separate budget. But which department and which budget, no one was able to fathom. While the War Office held a budget for trousers, it didn't have one for buttons.

'I asked [the Contracts department of the War Office] what orders had been placed for trouser buttons – and the answer was none,' Woolton wrote. 'Trouser buttons were supplied by the contractors, not by the War Office. I enquired whether the contractors had placed orders for trouser buttons; no one knew. So I pointed out to them the essential nature of the trouser button . . . how the whole morale of any army in the long run might depend upon its trouser buttons.'

Woolton went to see one of Prime Minister Neville Chamberlain's top officials at 10 Downing Street, Sir Horace Wilson, to voice his frustrations about the shambolic system. Whether he voiced his concern that the British army might go to war with its flies undone or, worse, its trousers down is not recorded.

'You are up against the machine of the Civil Service,' Sir Horace told his flustered guest. 'I have myself often been up against it in my forty years of experience. It has beaten me on many occasions, just as it is now beating you.'

This was a red rag to a bull. Woolton was not accustomed to being beaten by faceless institutions or the implacable logic of Whitehall mandarins. He jumped up out of his chair furiously.

'You have landed me in an impossible job,' he bellowed. 'If all you can tell me is that I am being beaten by a machine, I'll go and break its neck!'

Sir Horace replied: 'Well, you'll have to make a success of this as your commercial reputation depends on it.' That remark, noted Maud in her diary, 'made F [Fred] see red.'

'By God,' he stormed, 'my commercial reputation doesn't depend on this. But I'll tell you one thing, your political reputation does, so you'd better see to it that you give me all the help you can.'

Woolton left Downing Street, slamming the famous door as he stepped out. 'I'm not sure whether [I did it] with shame or with gratification,' he later reflected, hinting at a note of embarrassment for having lost his temper in the smart confines of the Prime Minister's office. 'I'm afraid I used some language that was unsuitable for Number Ten Downing Street.'

Galvanised by his anger, Woolton started firing off memos and knocking heads together. He realised that if he approached the various problems as a businessman rather than a politician he might have more luck.

He put a call into Sir Warren Fisher, the head of the Civil Service machine, insisting on a meeting which was granted and during which he outlined the gravity of the situation. 'The army will not be clothed in time unless I am allowed to put aside the peace-time system of contracting and am given a completely free hand to run the clothing of the army as a business organisation,' he told him.

Fisher nodded sagely and indicated that the Treasury would concur. 'You have complete authority,' he said. 'I will give instructions in the Treasury in accordance with this interview.'

Woolton recorded, triumphantly, that 'the way was all clear'. His own civil servants were flabbergasted. 'You know, Sir, it isn't fair,' one told him. 'We have been labouring for months, and you come in, pick up a telephone, and get an interview that none of us could have got, and then get financial authority for which there is no parallel.'

Within four months Woolton had increased the number of firms making uniforms from five to 500. By the summer he had clothed the army and felt his job was done. He had battled against the Civil Service and won, and, as a non-military man, he had served his country at a crucial time. Soldiers were clothed and as they marched to war their trousers would stay up.

'Well, there you are,' he told Maud. 'I've done what they asked me, in fact a great deal more. Now I'll go back to my job.'

But before he had a chance do so much as gather a board meeting of Lewis's, he received a rather pleasant notice from Downing Street. In King George VI's birthday honours list of June 1939 Sir Frederick Marquis was elevated to the peerage 'for public services'. He received the news one May morning while shaving.

Maud was, as was her habit, opening his letters while he got washed and dressed at their London apartment, Whitehall Court. 'Maud was always almost childishly interested in receiving letters,' Woolton reflected years later, when he wrote a long tribute to her for the benefit of his family after she had died.

'Oh, here's a letter from the Prime Minister marked secret,' Maud said from the bedroom as she worked through his usual pile of letters. Woolton professed that he had no curiosity about it so told his wife to go ahead. The last time he had been honoured, he had managed to get to the letter first and had kept his knighthood a secret from her until the announcement was made.

'You can't leave me out this time,' she said. 'The PM wants

to send you to the Lords.' Maud came into the bathroom, found a bit of her husband's cheek that was free of soap, and kissed him. 'I'm glad your services are being recognised in this rather startling way,' she said.

Before agreeing to accept the peerage, Woolton decided to make a journey north from London to Rugby, where the couple's son Roger was studying at the Warwickshire public school. It had been founded in 1567 by a purveyor of spices to Queen Elizabeth I as a free grammar school for the boys of local towns Rugby and Brownsover.

The title being offered was hereditary, so if Fred was to be ennobled he wanted to make sure his son was aware of his future responsibilities. Roger was a shy boy with a stammer that would never leave him. Later in life he would wear his father's celebrity and success heavily. Where his father was self-assured and pragmatic, Roger always lacked confidence and was vulnerable. It was to his boarding school that Woolton made a special journey. While he was to be ennobled for his diligent good works, Roger would be simply saddled with the hereditary title. For a man with a distinctly working-class background, Woolton was very aware of what wearing the ermine meant. He was closing in on a very elite part of society, and Roger needed to be properly informed and have the seriousness of this honour made clear to him. Woolton was becoming increasingly aware of his legacy. There was already a financial one – having made a considerable amount of money at Lewis's – and in due course he would set up a web of trusts for his offspring and their descendants. Now a peerage was being added to the mix.

The conversation with Roger would be formal, not that

this was out of the ordinary. Woolton was not the type to kick a football around with his son. In later life he was known to dutifully pat his grandchildren on the head but it didn't occur to him that he should be anything but stern and forthright with his son. An only child who had long escaped his own semi-literate father, he did not do touchy-feely emotion.

Having fetched Roger from his boarding house, perhaps father and son took a walk and then sat down on a bench that overlooked the school's famous playing fields. According to Maud's diary, Woolton told his seventeen-year-old son the news, and 'pointed out that Roger would inherit'.

'If you don't want the title and the responsibilities that go with it then I will tell the Prime Minister that I do not wish to accept this honour,' Woolton said to his teenage son.

'Roger was very sensible about it,' wrote Maud who believed that 'he realised he was being seriously consulted, and decided that he was willing to shoulder the responsibilities when they arrived.'

Of course the idea that Roger would have suggested otherwise, and then that his father would have told the Prime Minister that his son's ambivalence to the honour meant that he would decline it, is ludicrous.

Roger was then given special permission by his school to attend a dinner in London thrown by Maud to celebrate her husband's elevation to the peerage. Doubtless, seated around the table with Woolton's various business colleagues and friends, the teenage Roger would have again had it impressed upon him what responsibilities lay in the years ahead.

As a result, another private family album was stuffed with newspaper cuttings and messages of congratulations. With

Maud, Fred, in his words, 'had fun choosing a title', finally picking the name of Woolton (the district of his childhood in Liverpool). Using his own name was ruled out at the start, having been informed that to be called Baron Marquis might confuse people that he'd been made a marquess; he wasn't quite ready to make that final leap to aristocracy (he'd need to wait another sixteen years before he would be made an earl). Maud had counselled against one idea that he become Lord Windermere, in honour of the beloved stretch of water where they had a holiday home. She was happy to be Fred's wife, but thought the joke that she was his permanent fan (in reference to Oscar Wilde's play *Lady Windermere's Fan*) would wear thin fairly quickly.

Woolton noted that Maud would enjoy her title of Lady Woolton. 'She was now more than one up on those snobs in Mossley Hill,' he wrote referring to the stuck-up ladies of that district of Liverpool where she had once worked.

Freshly ennobled and just five days after war was declared, on 8 September 1939 Woolton was asked to take on another government job – this time as Director General of Equipment and Stores, working in the newly formed Ministry of Supply. This added the job of equipment to that of clothing – with which he was now familiar – and there were some 16,000 different articles to manage. 'But,' noted Maud, 'having already got the clothing into ship-shape, the task wasn't so difficult.'

Fred and Maud, as Lord and Lady Woolton, now realised that a return to normal life was becoming ever more distant. Maud noted in her diary that the reason for his barony was more than a recognition of his retail work and any other public service. The government 'realising the country was coming to a crisis needed men like F. They knew he wouldn't go in to the House of Commons so this was the best way to use him.'

But these jobs managing supplies seemed almost petty for a man who had run the huge and logistically complicated business of Lewis's. It was therefore of no great surprise when, in April 1940, Neville Chamberlain, casting around to find someone who might be able to run a ministry whose job it was to nourish Britain in time of crisis, landed upon Woolton. The first incumbent, William Morrison, had not been an unqualified success.

Given that Lord Woolton by now had been responsible for clothing much of the nation, it wasn't impossible that he might make a reasonable fist of feeding it, reckoned Chamberlain, so he invited Woolton to Downing Street for a meeting. 'The Prime Minister obviously had not sent for me to give him advice,' he said. 'He told me that I had clearly demonstrated a capacity for organisation on a large scale in an emergency, that he wanted me to do it again on what he regarded as a more important front than clothing the army, now that these supplies were secure.'

Chamberlain asked him to be Minister of Food. Woolton's first reaction was to claim ignorance of the subject: 'I know nothing about food except as a consumer,' he protested. He also insisted that he would only accept the role if he could operate as a businessman would in charge of a critical depart-ment. 'I am anxious not to get mixed up in politics,' he told the PM.

Chamberlain attempted to reassure him on this point. But there was another concern. While Woolton could function as a businessman in government, he would have to cease his real business ventures. 'Do you have any idea of the amount of financial sacrifice that would be involved in my giving up my several and very lucrative business appointments?' he demanded to Chamberlain, a little taken aback. Woolton added that he'd also have to ask his wife what she thought. This rather irritated Chamberlain, who had expected an immediate answer: 'Why do you need to ask your wife?' he said.

Woolton left considering the financial downsides and assuming that Maud would not welcome it. They had, after all, become rather used to the trappings of considerable wealth by now. 'To accept government office meant a complete severance of all business connections and a very heavy loss of income,' he mused privately. His two previous jobs had not been of ministerial level. 'I'll have to give up all of my directorships,' he told Maud. 'There's a financial downside to that, you know.'

'What does it matter?' she replied. 'When you are asked to do something in war time, unless it's peculiarly distasteful or against one's principles, there is only one answer.'

Woolton returned to Downing Street the following day to accept the role. Chamberlain produced a smile more warmly than Woolton had ever thought possible from this dour and serious man. His previous and usual demeanour, according to Woolton, being always 'conducted in a formal and almost frigid manner'.

'They always told me you would make any sacrifice for your country,' the PM told him, 'and they were right.'

So Woolton became a member of the government, and

Chamberlain proposed to ask the King that he be further made a member of the Privy Council, an indication that Woolton would become one of the most senior players and advisors in government.

'He accepted on the Wednesday and it was made public on Thursday,' wrote Maud.

Woolton was taking on the biggest task of his life. Approaching the age of fifty-seven, he was no spring chicken in the vanguard of entrepreneurial youth. This grey-haired, patrician-looking gent who might, in normal circumstances, have been looking forward to a graceful retirement from the rigours of business, was going to be more active than he could ever have imagined. He would need every ounce of energy and acumen in the tough days and months that lay ahead. As he went home that evening, armed with Sir Henry's draft speech, he steeled himself for the task in front of him, not a little nervous at what might happen.

4

The Ministry of Food

Day One

The Ministry of Food was situated in a corner building that overlooked Portman Square. Rented by the government, Portman Court had been chosen to locate the ministry away from Whitehall. His office was an unexciting spacious room with a large estate desk covered with neat stacks of papers. A rust-coloured material covered various chairs and there was a large mahogany conference table.

Woolton would sit at his desk or wander about the room thinking, dressed smartly and formally in one of his three-piece suits. His favourite was charcoal-dark double-breasted and striped, and he was never more comfortable than when clad in its thick and heavy material. Out of the office he wore a trilby and at weekends, a warm day in the country perhaps, he might dress down in a lighter suit or wear tweed and knee-length plus-fours. As a man who had risen from a family where there was never any spare money, this formality was important to him. Although he was known, if out walking in his beloved Lake District, to swap his suit and tie for a hearty costume of longish red shorts, long socks and walking shoes.

In evenings at home with Maud he might remove his jacket as he and his wife sat by the fire and read poetry by the nineteenth-century American writer Henry Longfellow, or the works of the seventeenth-century Baptist preacher John Bunyan. Longfellow's anti-materialistic moral and cultural values appealed to the god-fearing Woolton; likewise the sermons of Bunyan appealed to his Unitarian beliefs, which Maud shared with considerable fervour.

Woolton had no time for lighter pursuits so it suited him to be a workaholic. Once he had finished relishing the contents of his red ministerial box, he could stir his heart with the reading of a religious tract or two. There is little evidence that he enjoyed music, he needed to be dragged to the theatre and his way of letting off steam was to pen his diary in which, so often, he described his acute judgements and analysis of others – and their many weaknesses.

After Woolton's debut at the Queen's Hall, having gone off script and – further against the will of Sir Henry French – given several additional interviews to the large number of pressmen assembled, he headed for the novelty of a ministerial car and went straight to his new offices. As he sat that day at his desk and straightened the pictures that had been moved from his Tothill Street office, he was about to light his pipe when Sir

Henry French knocked and entered. Woolton stood, proffering a hand, and knowing that his off-script speech would not have made Sir Henry a happy man. But he hoped the following day's newspaper coverage might exonerate him.

Sir Henry muttered a greeting without any hint of a smile for his new minister. 'Of course, I must tell you that we are very sorry to lose Mr Morrison,' he said abruptly of Woolton's predecessor.

'Yes I'm sure you must be,' replied Woolton. 'But not as sorry as I am to come.' Sir Henry looked vexed but settled into a chair and then, referring to a typed page on his lap, spoke.

'You will be able to rely on the department to do everything in its power to protect you, Minister,' Sir Henry told him. Woolton looked surprised, partly given that 'this remark to me,' he later wrote, 'was in the nature of an official statement. I did not remember anyone wanting to "protect" me since I was a child.' Yet it was clear that this statement was not made out of some warm benevolence, with one man privately sympathising with a new minister.

'And, Sir Henry,' said Woolton, 'what is it that you are so kindly offering to protect me from? Do tell me what it is that makes you feel that it is necessary to make these pleasant, but I do hope superfluous, remarks?'

Sir Henry breathed deeply, looked down at his papers, then back at Woolton. He may not have actually sighed and may have done everything in his steely civil servant's power not to, but that's exactly what it looked like to the minister. It irritated Woolton considerably to be thought of as a new boy, out of his depth.

'We in the department, Minister,' said Sir Henry, 'are very

conscious of the fact that you have had no parliamentary experience, and that you might not realise that if you make mistakes the House of Commons will blow you out of the water.'

These were dramatic words. Woolton's staff thought he needed protection – 'the protection of the professional for the amateur,' as Sir Henry saw it. 'It revealed the same feeling,' reflected Woolton, 'that I had [later] sensed in Mr Churchill, namely that I was not going to last long in office.'

The officials clearly thought little of Woolton. They would have preferred him not to have been given such an exalted position. Woolton recalled another job offer that had come his way a few months before war had broken out. It had not been a flattering invitation. Woolton thought of it as he listened to Sir Henry. 'It was these officials,' he said angrily in his diary, 'who had thought that my rank should be of an area livestock officer.'

Woolton, ever the optimist, considered that he should show appreciation for this pledge of protection. And so he paused before delivering his response to French.

'Sir Henry, I will never cease to be grateful to you. What you have said will no doubt affect the way I practise my job throughout the whole of the time that I am lucky enough and have the honour to serve in government.' It was a magnanimous and charming Woolton, and for a brief moment French must have thought that he had cowed his man with remarkable speed. But Woolton looked at this long-serving civil servant and decided that he really ought to start as he meant to go on. So he resolved to give the man a small lecture. Woolton was reacting in exactly the opposite way French had hoped.

'Don't you worry about the House of Commons, let's just feed the people,' said Woolton blithely. 'Most businessmen will tell you that if they are right more than six times out of every ten in the judgements they make, they have found the way to commercial success. I shall make plenty of mistakes, and give the House of Commons plenty of targets. When you find I have made mistakes, only be alarmed if you find me sticking to the wrong judgement: that's where the danger lies, and I promise you that when I am wrong I will change direction with a speed that will also alarm you.

'But I do want you to do one thing for me. Whenever I suggest any plan, I want you to oppose it, tell me all the objections to it, all the snags etc. I'm quite strong-minded to stick to my plan if I think it will work. I can then argue my case with others, with peers and with members of Parliament.'

It was, felt Woolton, fear of what the House of Commons would do that was, he later wrote, 'the most dangerously inhibiting force on the creative capacity of ministers'. Yet Woolton would not go blindly into battle. He understood that Sir Henry French was a very experienced civil servant who had seen many talented ministers fall because they had not won over the House of Commons. So he vowed to meet and charm members of both the House of Commons and House of Lords.

In the papers for the first time as Minister of Food

Woolton used his debut at the Queen's Hall to set the tone for his time in office. The subject, avoidance of waste, was one close to his heart; he chose homely phrases to chime with his audience, calling on women to 'mobilise themselves on the Kitchen Front'. He told them that if everybody wasted one slice of bread a day it would take thirty shiploads of wheat a year to make it up.

He asked the nation's cooks to use their skill to make the best use of what was available and to avoid the comfortable habits of peacetime. Addressing the issue of tea rationing he asked that everyone use 'one spoonful for each person and none for the pot'.

Instead of delivering Sir Henry's policy statement of ministry objectives and strategy, he had launched a campaign, likening the nation's housewives to soldiers. 'I want them to go into training for the days which may come when the whole staying power of the nation will depend on their being able to keep up the energy of the industrial workers of this country by feeding them sufficiently when supplies are difficult, when things they have become accustomed to eat and to use are no longer available,' he was reported as saying in the *Liverpool Daily Post* on 6 April 1940. 'The food is stored, enough of it to make Hitler – if he were a sensible and level-headed man – begin to wonder.'

A first thrill at hearing the generous reception of him given by the press was quickly followed by what he described as 'a sense of danger'; the danger to 'either praise or blame to men in public life and I made up my mind that, whilst I remained in office, I would not read what the press said about me unless it was constructive and involved action – and I kept to that.' When his relationship with the press went through stormy waters, as it must for any minister at some point, this adopted wisdom provided a modicum of solace.

But for now the man who soon coined the slogan 'we not only cope, we care' for his ministry was being lauded for his easy style.

The *Evening Express* reported that Woolton 'saw the press for the first time as Minister of Food,' the paper quoting him as saying: 'I suppose I am really going to run the biggest shop in the world.'

He had asked the journalists present at the press conference to treat him gently, 'I have had no experience of ministerial office before,' the *Evening Express* reported. 'I beg of you, as the "new boy", not to be too critical of those people who are now learning this new and difficult job.' He spoke of the 15,000 people who were carrying out the work of the ministry. 'I am responsible for their actions, but how can they all be perfect, when they are just like you and me. They will make mistakes, but don't criticise them too heavily. They are in new jobs. They are learning the ropes.'

Most newspapers reported on the meeting as part of the news of the reshuffle, so fast had the appointment occurred. 'Lord Woolton For Food', heralded *The Times* on 4 April 1940.

The *Manchester Evening News* on the same day wrote, 'Having clothed the army Lord Woolton, now Minister of Food, starts tomorrow to feed the nation.' The headline read: 'Food Hoarders – You Are Warned.' The paper had managed a brief interview with the new minister after his Queen's Hall speech in which Woolton delivered a warning: 'I appeal to housewives not to hoard anything that is in daily use. It is selfish to hoard. I have no doubt about the way to treat hoarders.'

Woolton had also mentioned, rather grandiosely, the business interests he was sacrificing for the role. He said he was 'giving up about ten directorships besides the chairmanship of Lewis's,' adding, somewhat hopefully with regard to his bank balance, 'As soon as the war is over and I am released from office I hope to resume my commercial life.'

The *Liverpool Daily Post* wrote warmly that one of their own had taken up a senior post in government. His appointment was, they wrote, 'peculiarly interesting to Liverpool, and apart from that is a strikingly good one. Hitherto the Food Ministry has been fumbling along in a way that seems inexcusable seeing that there was the experience of the last war to draw upon.' Woolton 'is just the man to do it', the paper continued, adding, 'His experience in business as well as his sociological interests have made him specially sensitive to the feeling of the people, while his gift for organisation should enable him to get the best out of his department.'

The *Daily Mail* also carried an interview with Woolton in which he spoke of his credentials for the post. 'For many years, as managing director of one of the largest chain stores in the country, it was part of my job to feed 40,000 families every day,' he said. 'I know the problems and I understand the difficulties of food distribution. I can assure the housewife that, in my new post, I will have their interests at heart.'

There were frowns, meanwhile, at Woolton's appointment from some of the Tory establishment. 'An obscure business peer, Lord Woolton, has been made Minister of Food,' sniffed the Tory MP Henry 'Chips' Channon in his diary on 3 April.

Even his own wife told the *Daily Mail* on 5 April of his lack of food expertise, stating: 'I would never call him an expert on food' – and then saying of herself: 'I've never cooked anything in my whole life.' (Lady Woolton was soon altering this tune, telling the *Scottish Daily Express* a fortnight later that she liked potatoes ... 'sliced and cooked underneath the joint ... you put an onion in each corner – or a little grated onion – and the potatoes get all the juice from the meat and a little touch of the onion and they're delicious.' She added that: 'My husband is a very easy man to cook for ...')

On day one of his job he was also giving the women of Britain detailed cooking instructions. 'Kitchen food, served straight from the pan or the dish is the tastiest you can get,' Woolton said and the *Express* reported. 'Don't throw away the best part of the potato – the part under the skin. Cook your potatoes in their jackets. Try out unusual dishes. Don't say you can't be bothered with new-fangled ideas.'

It appears to have been the last time that Woolton offered his own cooking tips. Fifteen months later he would give an interview in the *Daily Sketch* – on 22 January 1942. This time he was honest about his own inability to cook. 'There was once a sausage shop at the back of the Bank of England,' he told the paper. 'A man asked the owner to lend him £5. "I'm sorry," answered the sausage maker. "The Bank of England and I have an understanding. I agree not to lend money and the bank agrees not to make sausages." That, says Lord Woolton, is my position. I leave the cooking to the experts – the British housewives.'

But in those early days as Minister of Food Woolton did something that his predecessor and his other government colleagues could not. He brandished his earthy credentials: 'I have lived in working-class houses and have eaten this [simple] sort of food, and enjoyed it much better than most of the elaborate stuff, we, many of us, have to live on in hotels.'

That paper was one of many newspapers that quickly warmed to this side of Woolton; 'this Lancashire business-man,' as it described him, was someone in 'an entirely new line of ministers − "one of us" rather than "one of them"'. In a story run on 1 May, the *Express* reported that Woolton's ministerial car was a twelve horsepower Austin saloon, 'like the one in your garage at home,' the paper commented. It contrasted Oliver Stanley, the War Minister, who drove a 27 horsepower car and Sir Kingsley Wood, at that moment the Lord Privy Seal, who used 28 horsepower: 'more than twice as much as the Food Minister,' said the paper. 'I find it perfectly satisfactory and perfectly comfortable,' Woolton was reported as saying, doubtless to the huge irritation of his gas-guzzling colleagues. The 'Food Minister saves petrol,' said the *Daily Express*. (Family legend, incidentally, has it that Woolton never learned to drive, an early experiment resulting in a collision with a stall of oranges, after which it was chauffeurs all the way.)

Another journalist once noted that Woolton would take the priority label off the windscreen on his car after office hours, so that, unlike most senior government members, he didn't then take advantage of its associated traffic and parking perks.

Meanwhile the unnamed 'agricultural' reporter from the *Daily Express* on 4 April was yet another journalist granted an interview on Woolton's first day in the job. He was impressed with how the minister told his secretary to ignore the telephone when it rang: 'Just take off the receiver and leave it off,' he demanded. Woolton added that this would annoy the exchange but 'it will ensure the comfort of this conference.' The reporter noted how 'a permanent civil servant near him squirmed in horror [presumably Sir Henry French], but the new minister just smiled.'

The journalist went on to describe Woolton as 'brimful of ideas, this good looking man with a broad forehead from which the greyish hair has started to recede. The bushy, sandy eyebrows seem immobile, but there are lines in his fresh face that suggest a smile that's always ready. His voice is soft, tuneful, distinct: his speech is slow and deliberate; Lord Woolton stresses his points by tapping his pencil or waving his spectacles.'

This new minister 'knows the slums', he continued. 'I am going to run the biggest shop the world has ever seen,' Woolton said. 'To supply the nation's food is a stimulating thought: it strikes the imagination. But there are so many places where it could so easily go wrong.'

The *Sheffield Star* reported that Woolton seemed to speak with a refreshing honesty. 'If anything goes wrong,' it reported him as saying on 8 April 1940, 'if the meat is fat or the bacon stringy, or the butter too salty, or the cheese too "asty" – I know for a certainty that the natural instincts of the people will say that if that fellow Woolton conducted his own business like he conducts the nation's, he would be closed down in a week. I won't complain.'

A. J. Cummings in the *News Chronicle* on the same day noted that 'the appointment of Lord Woolton has been received with so remarkable a chorus of public approval that, if he were at all superstitious, the new minister might remember uneasily the warning to beware when men speak well of you.'

While Woolton was pleased at the coverage he was getting during these first few days, Sir Henry did not remark on it. Indeed his office seemed distinctly uninterested. So Woolton, proud at how it was going thus far, sent a message to his office at Lewis's asking that all the press cuttings be saved for his own private collection. If the Ministry of Food didn't wish to collect his press notices for posterity, he certainly would.

Woolton's challenge

Woolton's early press coverage may have been good but it didn't lessen the scale of the task ahead of him. The papers that he'd studied late into the night before his appearance at the Queen's Hall set out the number of mouths that needed feeding; the exact state of Britain's food security; the amount of food grown in the country; and how much it relied on imports.

When the Second World War started, the UK had a population of around 46.5 million. But the British government needed to know exactly how many mouths there were to feed, given how many people were serving overseas or who had emigrated without the knowledge of the authorities. It was also vital to know where they were living, to enable the ministry to distribute food effectively.

It was therefore decided that an identity card system should be imposed which would assist both in food control, and offer a boost to domestic security. So on 29 September

1939 – declared as National Registration Day – everyone in the UK, save servicemen and women, was asked to fill in a form that would reveal their name, address, sex, date of birth, marital status and occupation, at precisely 6.30 p.m. that day.

Some 65,000 enumerators had been employed to distribute forms and help people fill them in. Public service announcements echoed out of wireless sets across the country, during which the broadcaster explained that the forms were 'very simple', adding that servicemen and women on the home front need not be included as they would be fed by their employers.

'I hope nobody will be coy about their date of birth,' said the voice on the radio. But some were coy. A number of women, at first, decided not to admit the existence of their sons, fearful that they would be called up into the armed forces. But many soon relented when they realised that the form would mean the issue of a ration book and access to their share of food.

By nightfall on 29 September, 41 million people had registered, incidentally showing that 9.3 million women said they carried out 'unpaid domestic duties' with 581,000 claiming they worked as live-in, paid servants or cleaners. And of the 6 million children noted in the registration, just 2 per cent lived in London, showing how effective evacuation had been.

Of the servicemen and women who were excused from the register, there were 230,000 men in the regular Army, which with Reservists and Territorials amounted to 684,000 in total. Woolton was not responsible for feeding them. But he did need to ensure that food was secured for the 532 million souls in the British Empire.

Fortunately it was the Empire that fed Britain, rather then the other way around. Yet this was only good fortune in peacetime. Britain was a net importer of food, and when war broke out less than a third of the food on British tables was produced at home. Half of all meat, three-quarters of all cheese, cereals, fats and sugars and four-fifths of fruit came from overseas, forming the 55 million tons of food shipped to Britain each year. It was a major challenge for Woolton. The threat of enemy attacks on shipping, and the inevitable cuts to supply lines would mean that Britain would need to start – and begin in haste – to increase the amount of food it produced at home. Indeed, the German U-boats that prowled the oceans around the UK quickly saw that 55 million ton figure plummet to just 12 million. By 1940, 728,000 tons of food destined for British home ports would be lost to the bottom of the sea.

Having studied the numbers of people that needed feeding, Woolton looked at how they should be fed. The League of Nations – the intergovernmental organisation founded in 1920 as a result of the peace conference that had ended the First World War – had decreed that working men needed 3,000 calories per day.

Woolton's ministry had decided to use this figure for its wartime calculations.

Fortunately the health of the nation seemed rather more robust at the start of the Second World War than some forty years previously, when the army had struggled to recruit healthy men to serve in the Boer War, with service doctors rejecting 60 per cent of those who came forward. Whereas between 8 and 12 of June 1939, when of 17,856 men aged twenty to twenty-one examined for the military, 15,081 were passed as Grade 1 (fit) (84.5 per cent), with 1,583 – or 8.8 per cent – being deemed Grade 2 (fit except for minor disabilities). This figure was encouraging, but it made it even more important that the impending ration did not have a detrimental effect on health.

Moreover a study of working-class families conducted in the London boroughs of Fulham, Bethnal Green and Canning Town reported that in wartime, 'the possibility may arise that some foods normally consumed will no longer be available, and that the diet, although physiologically adequate, may become monotonous to the extent of being a danger to public morale.'

At the time, as the report also revealed, breakfast consisted of 'bread and spread' for most – be they children or adults – and the most widely used drink at that time of day was tea. 96 per cent of those surveyed drank tea, the remainder consuming either 'cocoa or coffee'.

There was then a cooked meal – known to the people of those boroughs as 'dinner' – in the middle of the day, with 'bread and spread' creeping onto many tables. There was little evidence of any pudding being eaten, although many ate a piece of fruit. If there was a pudding, it was a 'milk pudding'; and the richer working-class families might eat a pie or a tart. The only drink that featured at dinner was tea. The obsession with drinking water would not appear for a good fifty years hence.

'Bread and spread' cropped up again at tea, with the wealthier having something cooked; and if 'supper' was served later in those communities, it seemed to comprise of simply bread and cheese – and not a cheese board, a piece of cheddar was quite exuberant enough.

Woolton considered how plain the items were that adorned the tables of the British people, and how it tallied pleasantly with his own dislike for rich food. But it would still be a challenge to fulfil. He made some notes for the Cabinet, writing, quite plainly, that his policy would be 'to feed the people of this country, taking into account their varied requirements and their capacity to pay; and to feed them in such a manner that they can get on with their job of national service'.

It was a simple statement. But delivering it would be an extraordinary challenge.

The Lords and Commons

Three weeks into Woolton's new role, and Sir Henry French informed him that a meeting had been facilitated with key members of Parliament – from both Lords and Commons – in one of the committee rooms. It was surely a daunting prospect, addressing a gathering of people from both the elected house and a chamber of inherited power and influence. The value of the cloth alone that was stitched around the limbs and girths of those men – not to mention the gold signet rings, the heirloom watches and chains, and the silver cigarette cases – could have been exchanged for enough grain to feed a large proportion of the population.

'If you feel I have failed, you must not hesitate to say so,' he told them. 'All I care about is trying to help with the conduct of the war, and if somebody else could be a more effective

Minister of Food than I, then you should know that it is not a position I have sought and I would be willing to give way.' This seemed to go down well with those present. He added: 'But I must warn you that I will not be inhibited in my efforts. I will sometimes fail and you will criticise that. Sir Henry French has already warned me that if I fail, individuals in this room will, to quote him: "blow me out of the water". But I will not let fear of failure prevent me from my job's aim: to feed the people of Britain.'

This gathering of MPs and peers was, Lord Woolton considered later, 'Probably one of the most useful meetings that I ever had.' Members of both houses warmed to him and it would help shield him from some parliamentary criticism, especially while he had battles on his hands within government. But there were men in that room – particularly from the House of Lords – who were not won over, and would remain his nemeses throughout his term in office.

Woolton also had a job to do within his own ministry, and the team of men and women around him. 'The whole place was rather unhappy,' his wife Maud wrote, 'there was resentment about.' Sir Henry, unfortunately, did not add to the gaiety of the place. 'He's an odd man,' she noted. 'He's frustrated, I think I'm right in saying, feeling that everybody is against him [he had been passed over twice for promotion] and not knowing how to manage people.' One person he was having trouble managing was Woolton. The morning after Woolton's meeting with peers, the minister assumed that his Permanent Secretary might cut him some slack, given how well received he appeared to have been by both houses.

But at their morning conference Sir Henry didn't even refer to the meeting the previous day. Instead he sat down in Woolton's office and gave the new minister a lesson in protocol. Woolton recorded his words in his diary that night.

'The way it works, Minister, is thus: If a section head has an issue which they wish to raise with you, then they will report to one of three senior members of the department, those individuals, and myself of course, being the only ones who have access to you. Between us we will then present the problems together with the relevant papers.'

Woolton listened to this protocol and promptly decided to completely ignore it. Maud wrote that he 'began to see all sorts of people, much to Sir H's alarm . . . it was against precedent.'

Even the way in which these meetings took place was also irregular. Woolton didn't summon them to his office, he just turned up at their desks. 'Since every man is more natural when sitting in his own chair, I would like to go round and sit down for a while and hear what problems faced the many heads of sections in the ministry,' he wrote.

Woolton described this informality as 'a new form of shock treatment'. There was a rigidity to the way things happened and, he wrote, 'This was the sort of organisation I wanted to break down.' He was convinced it would improve morale: 'I surmised that they were not a very happy crowd – and certainly they were depressed.'

A few weeks in to his new job Maud wrote: 'Sir Henry French is a bit of a thorn in the flesh to F. He is an odd man and seems to make many enemies. He is on the look out for insults I think, and on the other hand very self-opinionated. He puts his foot in it very easily.'

To improve morale in the ministry, Woolton arranged a visit by King George VI, and wrote afterwards that the event 'did more for the internal morale of the Ministry of Food than anybody else would have done in a year'.

And Woolton soldiered on with Sir Henry, feeling that he had managed tougher assignments than engaging with his senior civil servant. He invited him for dinner on several occasions, and within a matter of months something quite extraordinary happened. In the summer of 1940, Maud wrote of a conversation she had had with a senior official from the Ministry of Food. 'Do you know,' the official told her, 'I actually heard French laugh in the corridor today.'

5

Spring–Summer 1940

On 10 May 1940, Neville Chamberlain resigned as Prime Minister, to be replaced by Winston Churchill. Lord Woolton reckoned his days as Minister of Food were over.

He would look back on his unfeasibly short political tenure with a shrug of the shoulders and get back to his retail business. He had been in the job for only a month, and within that short period felt he had made some headway. But as Woolton was aware of the fragility of political careers, there would be no loss of pride for him. He had been away from Lewis's for over a year and the board would welcome him back.

So he was unique among senior government colleagues in not fearing the chop as Churchill went to Buckingham Palace to seek the commission from the King to form a

63

government. There was, he remembered, 'an atmosphere of intense excitement'. Rather than wait to be summoned and told he would not be needed in the reformed administration, Woolton decided to send a letter to Churchill.

'I have only been in office a few weeks,' he wrote from his study in Flat 110, 4 Whitehall Court, the family's small London apartment. Woolton would write his diary there in the evenings at a desk in the sitting room, with its view out to Horse Guards Parade.

'I have no claims on your consideration and if it is more convenient for you not to include me in government, I shall not only understand but would be glad to return to my business.' To show some well-meaning intention he added that he'd be equally glad, 'to serve the country in any other capacity as I have no desire for ministerial office'.

In fact, he privately rather hoped that Churchill would indeed let go of him, and not just because he didn't relish the politics. He wanted to get back to what he was really good at; running big business, making money. He did not profess to know Churchill personally – the two of them had spoken only a couple of times at political events – but the pair had actually met before, although it was a long time ago. Woolton would recall it, but it would not figure in Churchill's memory.

In 1904, Winston Churchill had ventured upon Fred Marquis's student turf up in Manchester where he had been selected as a prospective parliamentary candidate for Manchester North West, an area known as the Exchange Division. Churchill was fighting to win the seat for the Liberal Party, after he had quit the Conservatives during a row about trading tariffs in the British Empire. He would go on to win the seat and have a short tenure from 1906 to 1908.

The invitation was to address a group of local businessmen in the Memorial Hall, a Venetian Gothic building – all arches and red brick – on Albert Square. Already Mr Churchill had a reputation as a considerable debater, so Fred, then chairman of the university debating society, decided to go along, uninvited, and see what the fuss was about. He arrived early, tucked himself into a seat behind the hall's grand piano and watched the room fill up. Soon the hubbub faded away as Churchill arrived and walked to the stage. Applause spread across the room as he came into view. The speech he made was rousing, of course. Then there were questions.

It just so happened that the first raised hand came from a young man sitting behind a piano. 'What will you, Mr Churchill, or the Liberal government of which doubtless you will be a member, do about unemployment in this country if your new party is returned to power?' asked Fred.

While the businessmen in the room had cheered Churchill's rousing speech, this dose of reality in the room stirred them for different reasons.

'To my great surprise I heard loud cheers and applause,' recalled Woolton. When the noise faded Churchill gave his reply. But whatever he said did not impress twenty-one-year-old Fred Marquis. 'I got a very unsatisfactory answer,' he recalled. His words were 'exasperatingly indefinite, if not evasive.' And while Fred just sat back in his chair disappointed, a contingent of students at the back whose views were, in Woolton's words, 'more violent than mine', started shouting and then moving forwards through the hall. They looked menacing enough for Churchill to be ushered off the stage and out of the hall through a back exit; Fred's question had been the first and last of the evening.

Churchill never recalled the undergraduate who started this minor incident and, despite some brief political dealings, when Woolton was sent for by Churchill as he planned his first government, 'it was quite obvious,' he wrote after the pair finally met at the new bomb-proof Admiralty, off the Mall in London, 'that he did not know me.'

Maud wrote of the feverish atmosphere that abounded around Whitehall after Churchill took office on Friday 10 May. 'Speculation was rife,' she wrote. It wasn't until the Monday that her husband was sent for. 'We had no idea whether he would be asked to stay on,' she continued. 'We thought that Churchill, who had to give office to a lot of his supporters, and also to include several Labour men, and Liberals, would want the MoF for a politician.'

Over the weekend, recorded Maud, there were meetings and lunches and dinners at which MPs and others speculated about who would get jobs in the new Cabinet. She wrote of one MP saying, 'Woolton will have rung up the PM and said, "Do you want me or don't you – because it's all the same to me, only I'd like to know." This finally went round as having happened.'

When they finally met on Monday the two discussed his position, as Woolton recorded in his diary. 'Do you want to stay on?' asked Churchill gravely.

'That is for you to decide, Prime Minister,' he replied, reminding him of the letter he had written to him. 'But I am at your disposal.'

'Do you think you can manage all these civil servants?' the new Prime Minister asked. 'It is a very large staff.'

'I have been accustomed to controlling a staff of 13,500 and don't anticipate any difficulty on that score,' Woolton replied. He added that his only fear was being 'completely ignorant' of parliamentary procedure. Churchill paused and then said that he should continue in the role, but it wasn't exactly a ringing endorsement.

'Well you'd better try for a bit,' was how he put it. Woolton reflected many years later that Churchill 'had very little confidence in me and I heard some time afterwards that he had said to some of his friends, "We shall have to be ready with a rescue squad for Woolton."'

Initially a working relationship looked promising. When Woolton presented his food policy to the new-look government that summer, he knew that Europe would soon be facing food shortages and he thought it would be a wise move if the Chancellor of the Exchequer translated part of the nation's gold reserves into non-perishable food goods to help guard against the nation's hunger.

It was a suggestion that ultimately won the backing of Winston Churchill, who responded: 'The natural Treasury preference for gold or foreign exchange over wheat and whale oil as a capital asset may not be entirely justified in the present exceptional circumstances. Non-perishable foodstuffs will certainly be consumed sooner or later; their possession will set free shipping to bring in munitions should an emergency arise. Gold, on the other hand, and foreign securities, may well prove of perishable quality in the economic world in store.'

But the pair had an early conflict, and it was on a matter than neither could have anticipated.

On Woolton's staff, as parliamentary secretary, was Robert Boothby MP. Elevated to the peerage in the 1950s, Boothby would later gain notoriety for the company he kept with East End gangsters and his affairs with the likes of cat burglar Leslie Holt, whom he met in a gambling club. A few months into Woolton's tenure as Food Minister under Churchill, he discovered that the forty-year-old Member of Parliament for Aberdeen and Kincardine East had received a gift of shares from a company of which he was chairman; one that supplied the vitamins which were being added to the bread available as part of the ration.

This conflict of interest didn't impress the straight businessman in Woolton and he complained about it to civil servants and senior colleagues. Boothby was forced to sell the 5,000 shares he had been given but netted over £8,000 in the process. Woolton then had a meeting – in October of that year – with Churchill in which the matter was discussed.

'I think the Prime Minister was very annoyed with me for having made a fuss about it,' he wrote, 'and we had a rather unpleasant interview.'

'I will enquire into it and see what I think,' Churchill told him, irritated at what he saw as a distraction. Woolton would not let him leave it like that. 'When I know what your opinion is I will be glad if you would consider whether I should remain as minister,' he said. 'I have no intention of having a Marconi scandal association with a department of which I am head.' This was an inflammatory remark; the scandal he referenced took place in 1912, when senior members of

Asquith's Liberal administration had bought shares in the US wireless firm in the knowledge that the British government was about to issue the company with a lucrative contract.

'Unless it is made abundantly clear that Boothby has no sort of financial interest in anything that is being done by the Ministry of Food, then I shall not remain minister,' continued Woolton. Churchill was cross and asked his then Chancellor of the Exchequer, Kingsley Wood, also in the meeting, to deal with it. 'I don't understand these things,' Churchill said, attempting to brush the issue aside.

But Woolton continued to press his point. 'There are standards in good class business and they are very high ones,' he said referring to his life outside of politics, which was bound to infuriate Churchill further. 'Those standards do not include giving the chairman shares in a company instead of an increase in salary,' he said. The matter should not, he thought, be dealt with by the Chancellor but instead by legal minds. 'I insisted on it being handled by Law Officers of the Crown,' he recorded in his diary.

But he left the meeting feeling aggrieved. 'I came out of the whole thing with a sort of conviction that it was I who had the shares and done something wrong,' he wrote. And in the margin of Maud's diary – where she recounts the affair – Woolton added some comments (something he did throughout the diary, on reading it later in life) saying, 'I began to feel in the dock myself.'

While Boothby was made to sell the shares, Woolton was astonished that he was allowed to keep the money: 'whether they decided then to tax him on the proceeds, I don't know,' he wrote, adding a little mournfully, 'I came away with the feeling that my colleagues regarded me as a difficult and angular person.' Word also reached Woolton that Kingsley Wood had been disparaging about him to others, saying, apparently, that at the meeting 'Woolton had been very Wooltonish.'

It later transpired that Churchill did reprimand Boothby on this issue; and over another matter. A select committee was appointed to investigate allegations concerning Boothby's chairmanship of a committee lobbying to get government funds in 1939 over losses they had incurred relating to the Munich agreement, which permitted Nazi Germany to annex parts of Czechoslovakia along its border. Woolton wrote in his diary that the British Secret Service reported that they had found a letter which claimed Boothby had made several hundred thousand pounds from the deal.

Boothby protested his innocence and the claims went away, but not without Churchill giving him a severe dressing down, not that he chose to share this with Woolton. Churchill, he raged in his diary, 'didn't have the grace to tell me anything about it'. Unable to get rid of Boothby he declared simply that he was a 'man with no virtue'.

Woolton bumped into Boothby, socially, one lunchtime in April 1941. He was at L'Escargot, the restaurant in London's Soho. Woolton's lunch companion was his Director of Flour Milling, Norman Vernon; Boothby's lunch companion was Noël Coward.

After lunch, Boothby approached Woolton saying that he was hoping to join the Air Force. 'They're very anxious to have me,' he said. 'I had a commission in the last war, so it looks like I'll be able to get another in this one.'

Woolton wondered why Boothby was telling him this.

Then the MP added, discreetly, 'I'm anxious, of course, that I'm able to defend myself against any unpleasant charges. Anything that might suggest I was ever dishonest . . .'

Woolton looked at the man squarely and said, 'No one thinks that you are dishonest.' This pleased and reassured Boothby. Then Woolton added: 'But many people think you are very foolish.'

It was clear that Churchill had a poor view generally of business people in government; they may have had organisational capacities and some foresight but they always failed to impress the public through the process of parliament. (Woolton had himself some sympathy for this view; 'the training and the atmosphere of doing business in both spheres is widely different,' he commented.) It was not an opinion Churchill only voiced in private. He openly mocked the idea of business people in politics during meetings. 'Whenever men trained in business have come into government it has been disastrous,' he once barked. Woolton recalled challenging the PM on his view, what he called Churchill's 'provoking accusation'. Unfazed, Churchill proceeded to write off a number of senior politicians, but he omitted mentioning his Minister of Food, so the then Secretary of State for the Colonies, Oliver Stanley, piped up. 'Well Winston, how are you going to explain Woolton?'

Churchill replied not to Stanley but looked at his Food Minister – every bit the buffed, polished and confident businessman-cum-politician – with a beaming smile. 'But, my dear Fred, surely you are not suffering from the delusion that the public regard you as a businessman – they think of you as a philanthropist.'

The nation, felt Churchill, saw Woolton as a benevolent figure, a kindly grocer, a Father Christmas for times of austerity, doling out small gifts from his big red sack with even-handed wisdom. He hadn't come into politics the hard way, suffering unpopularity, fighting tough seats in elections, dealing with the chicanery of party politics, coping with vituperative journalists. No greasy pole for Woolton, he had simply been appointed to a senior position in government. But this confident 'Uncle Fred', as he had been nicknamed in the press, would soon find himself coming unstuck, with civil servants, Cabinet colleagues and the press, thought the PM. And then he would be proved right. Woolton would have to be rescued, or, more probably, ditched.

So, just weeks into the job, Woolton realised that he didn't just have an enemy in Hitler and his German machine, calculatingly trying to starve Britain; he didn't just have the brick wall of an insurmountable Civil Service; there wasn't simply the mere problem of food distribution, the extraordinarily complicated procedure of food imports and the effects on public morale if things went wrong – Woolton had a foe right there in government, a battle on his hands with his boss, the most powerful politician in Britain.

But this unexpected new front didn't put him off. Indeed it further steeled him for the fight. 'I was determined not to fail in my part of the war effort,' he wrote. 'And I got a certain amusing stimulation out of the idea that I would show this astute parliamentarian that a businessman also could do a government job and manage both his department and Parliament.'

Rationing

Despite vociferous newspaper campaigns against it run by, among others, Lord Beaverbrook's *Daily Express*, rationing had finally been introduced on 8 January 1940, preceding Woolton's arrival.

It had been branded an attack on civil liberties by many, a view with which Lord Woolton for one had some sympathy. But shortages meant that without rationing there would not be sufficient food to go around.

The *Daily Express* wasn't alone in its condemnation. *Picture Post* magazine described the introduction of rationing as 'the most unpopular Government decision since the war began'. Meanwhile, the *Daily Mail* insisted it was a 'stupid' decision for a country with an extensive empire and said: 'It would be scarcely possible – even if Dr Goebbels were asked to help – to devise a more harmful piece of propaganda for Great Britain.'

However, people who suspected they were always at the back of the queue and wondered if friends, neighbours and local shopkeepers were profiteering, were generally happy to see the introduction of rationing. In a poll, 60 per cent said they thought rationing was necessary. They knew, even if it lacked variety, they would get a square meal.

The government's Ministry of Information was quick to compare the good fortune of the British public with that of Germany, where rationing had begun with hostilities. The British were told they could expect better butter rations and more eggs, bread and meat. 'It would hardly be an exaggeration to say that every other obtainable foodstuff is rationed in Germany while in Great Britain it is officially stated that initially all other foodstuffs may be freely purchased,' the ministry declared.

For the British the first supplies to be restricted that January were those of butter and bacon – both limited to 4oz – and sugar, capped at 12oz per person, per week. That was followed in March by the rationing of meat, dealt with by price rather than weight.

In July, when Woolton was in charge, tea was rationed and that was followed in March 1941 with restrictions on jam, marmalade, syrup and treacle. Two months after that, albeit reluctantly by Lord Woolton (aware of its importance to many manual workers who relied on it in packed lunches), cheese was rationed. Eggs were rationed that year too.

In 1942 rice, dried fruit, condensed milk, breakfast cereals, tinned tomatoes, tinned peas, soap, sweets and chocolates, biscuits and oats were all added to the list. Sausages were the final wartime addition, being rationed during 1943.

Allowances for each food fluctuated during the conflict. For example, the sugar ration tended to increase in the summer months to encourage people to harvest fruits and make jam. After butter was rationed the greatest amount available to adults per week was 8oz, the least amount being 2oz. Sweets that children could look forward to were kept to 16oz a month, an amount that was at times halved.

Rations books were buff-coloured for adults, and green for children. They weren't a replacement for cash, which still had to change hands over the counter. It was a control on the amounts that could be bought each week or month, marked off by the shopkeeper so they could not be used twice. Vegetables and fruit weren't rationed, nor was fish; but they were often in short supply as cargo ships and the fishing fleet were hounded by U-boats. Even before rationing was introduced there were voluntary controls imposed on the purchase of sugar, to prevent people stockpiling.

Rationing was administered by Woolton's ministry where on file, as far as the civil servants could tell as a result of National Registration Day, was the name and address of every citizen of the United Kingdom. With each National Registration Number would come a ration book.

As Katherine Knight commented in her book *Spuds, Spam and Eating for Victory*, 'the ration book was our passport to getting enough to eat.' Ration books, with that individual serial number, were posted out to everyone entitled to receive rations – including members of the Royal Family. While different types of book were sent to those with different needs, such as those with babies or infants, and pregnant mothers, or with extra rations for items such as cheese for registered vegetarians, and with temporary documents for service personnel on leave, the ration was otherwise universal.

By January 1940 everyone should have received their ration book. One's ration book became a very precious commodity. It was a sensible precaution to leave it in a safe and accessible place, so when the siren sounded in the event of an air raid, as you took your gas mask and your identity card, in the words of Katherine Knight, 'you were wise to grab your ration book.' Each individual would then have to register at a chosen shop. On each page of coupons the retailer's name and address would need to be entered.

So one needs to imagine a life in which movement was

pretty limited. No nipping into a store you happened to be passing by to purchase something just because you were hungry, no passing by a butcher and walking in to buy a couple of steaks because they looked nice in the window, no random trips to a store you liked the look of, no weekend supermarket trips grabbing anything you might want or need or indeed filling 'til overspill – in fact, no freedoms whatsoever when it came to food. Today it is almost impossible to conceive of these privations. The only choice that was possible was the freedom to register with a different shop for different items, assuming there was one local to you. So, for example, you could choose to buy sugar in one store and bacon in another.

In the early stages of the war the coupons in the ration book were valid for only one week, but this was soon relaxed so that, for example, you could forgo buying butter one week and then purchase twice as much the next – assuming the store would let you.

Meat, however, had to be bought during the designated week. If you missed the chance, that meant no meat. But you could buy a whole month's worth of tea at one time. Alcohol was also scarce, which made drowning one's sorrows at the lack of gastronomic indulgence rather difficult.

Shopkeepers would keep your coupons and then send them to the local Food Office, who would then allocate them with a buying permit, enabling the shop to buy new stock from regulated wholesalers.

While the food supply to the country's larders stalled, so did the prospect of new kitchen equipment. You could forget the idea of upgrading any of your cooking tools. No new cookers or kitchen appliances were made during the war, as factories were turned over to everything and anything demanded by the war effort.

The administration of the ration was a feat of considerably complicated proportions; all done, of course, without a single computer, just people and paper. At a local level there were Food Offices – some 1,200 of them – whose job it was to administer rationing in towns and villages. It would be to a member of the Food Office that you would report, if, for example, you had lost your ration book in that air raid or you were a pregnant woman seeking a certificate that might entitle you to orange juice. Those Food Offices reported to a Food Control Committee – 1,520 across the country – whose job it was to deal with retailers, hospitals or caterers. The committees in turn took orders from nineteen Divisional Food Offices – in England, Scotland, Wales and Northern Ireland – who reported directly to the Ministry of Food.

The ministry was itself a complex bureaucracy, with its divisions, departments, scientific experts and administrative staff, its buildings managers, as well as code-breakers and other security-related workers. At the top were senior civil servants and leading them, of course, was Lord Woolton, 'the minister for girth control', as someone once joked at a public lunch during the war.

His ministry was not an organisation hastily cobbled together at the outbreak of war. Months before, civil servants had planned and built the department; much of that planning had been done after careful study of the work of the Ministry of Food during the First World War, and the system of rationing that had been put in place then. But, wrote Woolton, 'there was this difference. Rationing and restriction were introduced in the First World War to meet emergencies that had arisen. The planners – wisely with the "Black Book" of the history of the first Ministry of Food ever before them – had built up the conditions for a new ministry to operate at once should war break out.'

So this time the government would not wait until the nation was half-starved before it did something about food; except that what was created was a giant bureaucracy run by civil servants whose instincts, according to Woolton, were to curb enterprise and commercial practice, the exact facets that were needed in order to buy food.

Woolton, free of the political pressures that the elected politicians he sat alongside in the Cabinet faced, was less concerned with the internal machinations of the ministry than the reason it actually existed: to stop Britain from starving. 'The machine, if the bald truth be told,' he commented, 'was unduly concerned with its own meticulous organisation, whilst the major task before it was not to satisfy Parliament that it had made no mistakes, but the more difficult task of feeding over 40 million people,' adding, 'the machine had no common touch with the people.' As he cast his eye around his ministry he pondered on the struggles he had had to clothe the army during his time at the War Office. 'I found myself once again faced with the same circumstances,' he later wrote, 'only now I had learned my lesson.'

It was all very well having a huge and complex food ministry but Woolton felt that it would not achieve its aims, would not deliver actual food to people when they needed it in on-going times of crisis, unless he could rule it with an iron rod.

Woolton felt he needed to run his ministry in the way he ran department stores. 'The man who is head of a business and succeeds – making success and failures – must not be inhibited by the fear of failure,' he wrote. 'The government machinery is completely different from this. I knew that the machinery of government is not there to serve Parliament but to serve the public,' he went on, reflecting that he 'had better waste very little time in applying business methods'.

One radical move Woolton made was to replace some civil servants with businessmen, not unlike himself. For example, Sir John Bodinnar, who came from a Wiltshire sausage-making firm, was made head of one of the supply departments; while John Cadbury, from the famous chocolate-making dynasty, was, of course, put in charge of cocoa. Woolton later reflected that he was lucky to have been able to secure the services of such people, who 'undertook more arduous, and often more dangerous, missions than they were ever called to face in their ordinary business lives'.

However bullish he was at how the department needed to be run he was worried that it would be, in his words, 'onerous'. He would, at the very least, have a battle on his hands with his civil servants. But, he confessed, the feeling was probably mutual. 'Whatever fears I may have had,' he confided, 'they were at least equalled by those that my civil servants had of my methods.' He knew that Sir Henry French was strongly opposed to the beckoning in of businessmen, believing the detailed organisation of the department was the job of civil servants like himself; indeed, so unhappy was Sir Henry about Woolton's changes and methods that he consulted a civil servant higher up the chain of command.

Woolton himself feared one of them would have to resign if their disagreement became further inflated.

However, Sir Henry decided to back down – although he made his reservations known to Woolton in no uncertain terms. Yet a powerful relationship developed between the two and continued to flourish. Only a year after the incident, Sir Henry admitted to Woolton: 'Last Christmas I told you that I had never been – officially – more miserable in my life. This Christmas I would like to tell you that in forty-odd years of Civil Service life I have never been so happy.'

But whatever misgivings Woolton had of the Civil service machine, he was forever grateful for the preliminary work that had been done on rationing. As war broke out, ration books had already been printed, along with a mass of forms. Local Food Offices and committees stuffed with members of civic society had been set up. The machine was ready. So by the time Lord Woolton arrived, 'the problem was not to create machinery,' he wrote, 'but how and when to use it.'

So he took an early and tough decision. He wanted to implement rationing before it was actually needed. 'I planned not to be driven to rationing by realised shortages,' he wrote; instead he would 'put something in the cupboard'. There would be days when supplies would fail, but he wanted to be ready for that. The nation's cartoonists picked up on this and gave him the nickname of 'Squirrel'.

Thus he aimed to get through the hardest part of rationing by the summer of 1940. It would hurt, but it would be essential. So by July, when tea, cooking fats and margarine were officially limited, he commented, 'we had broken the back of rationing'. Of course it had not been popular. The public, for example, 'did not want meat to be rationed – and who can blame them?'

Then that month he went a step further and banned the making and selling of ice cakes. It meant that even on one's wedding day you couldn't have a traditional cake.

And while the British public disliked such limitations, there was no one more disdainful of it than the Prime Minister. Churchill, Woolton commented, was 'benevolently hostile to anything that involved people not being fed like fighting cocks.' He felt that Woolton relished restricting food. The minister, of course, believed he was simply being pragmatic.

Woolton also saw rationing as an opportunity to improve the country's nutrition. He gathered together a professor of biochemistry, the President of the Royal Society, the Minister of Agriculture, among others and, as he commented, 'with this highly skilled advice of widely different approach, we worked out a diet for the nation that would supply all the calories and all the vitamins that were needed for different age groups, for the fighting services, for the heavy manual workers, for the ordinary housewife, for the babies and children, and for the pregnant and nursing mothers.'

The zeal with which he administered the ration, and for which Churchill would relentlessly mock him, came from his earlier life spent working in social service. Having seen the effects of malnutrition, having witnessed the deaths of elderly people from nothing less than starvation, now a unique situation presented itself. It had never happened before and would be unlikely to happen again, as the island nation of Britain became a closed shop. Lord Woolton could pretty much control exactly what and how much every individual in Britain could eat, making him the envy of nutritionists, dieticians, and indeed anyone interested in the health of the nation, before or since. The war presented him an extraordinary opportunity, and he wrote of his 'all-embracing planning . . . I determined to use the powers I possessed to stamp out the diseases that arose from malnutrition,' he wrote, 'especially those among children such as rickets.'

Attached to his diaries were newspaper clippings, touching on the subject of health and body weight; some of those cuttings dated back decades, indicating a lifelong interest in the subject. One such cutting, from Weldon's *Illustrated Dressmaker* from 1900, read: 'There is no doubt that excessive corpulency is a disease, requiring as much careful diagnosis, treatment and attention as any other malady.'

The article went on to talk of a Mr F. C. Russell of London WC1 who was described as 'a most experienced and capable authority as to the best means of reducing superfluous flesh'. The gentleman recommended vegetable-based tonics that had 'most marvellous results in the reduction of fat'.

Another clipping, whose origins are unknown, suggested a form of exercise: 'Going up and down stairs slowly, holding the body erect while doing so is beneficial.'

A clipping from the *Manchester Guardian* of 24 March 1905 was of a letter from T. C. Horsfall. He wrote that the 'physical condition of German is far superior to that of English urban population'. Apparently one reason for this is that 'German people are much under the control of officials.' Perhaps Woolton bore this in mind for the coming days when, rarely in the life of a nation, the English people would be under the control of one official, namely him.

In the late 1950s, five years after the final end of rationing and almost twenty years after he had taken the reins as Britain's food provider, he reflected somewhat gloriously on his achievement. 'The health of the children today is the reward of that policy.'

6

The Secret Life of Colwyn Bay

While Lord Woolton had a good number of staff at his Ministry of Food offices in Portman Square, a canny observer would have noticed that for such an important department it seemed to be a remarkably slim organisation. Indeed civil servants from other ministries communicating between departments began to wonder where exactly the vast number of staff that were surely needed to run the Ministry of Food actually were. In early July 1940 a letter was dispatched from the Burma Office in Whitehall by a civil servant called Johnston writing to a Mr Hutton at the Ministry of Food. He wished to discuss liaison arrangements but was having a problem: 'I am afraid that I find some difficulty in replying to your letter of the 5th of July regarding the liaison between our two departments,' he wrote. 'My difficulty arises partly from the fact that we have no information as to what has happened to the Ministry of Food.'

While there was the office at Portman Court, as far as he was concerned the ministry had all but disappeared. And in fact, this is exactly what had happened. In haste, and in the greatest secrecy, 5,000 civil servants and their accompanying paraphernalia to operate – from pencils to cars – had departed with speed and in such a way that no one seemed to notice and fewer knew.

Orders had gone out as part of an operation called Yellow Move. Under this edict, the most important ministries were to relocate so that their operations could continue free of bombs or sabotage. Lord Woolton's ministry was considered one of those vital to war victory.

So the reality was that Woolton in Portman Square had just a skeleton staff. The rest had moved to a sleepy North Wales seaside town called Colwyn Bay, partway between Anglesey and Liverpool.

During the early stages of the war, the King had sent a telegram to the Ministry of Food. 'The security of the home front is as vital as that of the Fighting Front and I appreciate to the full the work of the ministry staff, both in London and throughout the country, in safeguarding the supply and distribution of the people's food.'

Those words 'throughout the country' disguised the extraordinary secret that the department responsible for the feeding of Britain and her colonies was now in the nicely vulnerable and easy-to-bomb confines of Colwyn Bay. Secrecy was paramount because, had Hitler known, he would have taken great satisfaction in smashing every limb and tentacle, heart and head of this vital asset. Yet even both civil servants and spies in London appeared thwarted.

But as vital as it was for Britain to be fed, it was as inconvenient for the people of Colwyn Bay, as their lives were to be turned upside down.

Miss Constance Smith, for example, was the headmistress of Penrhos College, by Rhos-On-Sea. The school, built in the Victorian era with views out over the Irish sea, was just up the road from Colwyn Bay.

It was a warm summer morning in early July of 1940 and she had, doubtless, sat down and breathed a sigh of relief as the last of her pupils had been waved off as they left for the summer holidays. Miss Smith presided over this all-girls boarding school and after trunks, files of school work, hockey sticks, games kit and toys had been bundled into cars and buses, what seemed to be a perpetual noise of chatter and laughter would finally have ebbed to silence.

The teachers would have been quick to get away and the remaining school staff – cooks and porters – would have cleaned and sorted the kitchens, housemaids would have mopped and polished the floors and emptied bins, the beds and furniture would have been covered with dust sheets, before Miss Smith would do a final walk around the school, locking doors and checking windows.

Life at the school seemed pretty normal. The end of term was just like any other end of term. While there was of course a war on, the population of Penrhos College, indeed most of the people of Colwyn Bay, were living almost blissfully unaware of it. The only chilling reminders – aside from the typical privations of rations and the ever-present worry of loved ones away on war duties – being the low hum of German bombers as they flew home, high over the shores of the Welsh coast, having done their worst to the unfortunate towns and cities of Coventry or Liverpool.

But there was never a bomb dropped near Miss Smith's school, nor over the town. The Germans had bigger fish to fry; Goering had ordered German planes, co-ordinated from occupied Paris, to destroy Liverpool. Miss Smith would have counted her lucky stars that her metier had led her to a life of running Penrhos, with its rambling buildings, large school hall, chapel and hockey fields.

Perhaps with the summer holidays ahead of her, with school reports written by the end of the week and the checking of a few maintenance jobs done – some painting, a few rattling windows replaced – she would retreat to her own family home. Then, ten days before the start of the Michaelmas term, she and key staff would return to the empty school. They would plan for the coming months, everything from organising accommodation for new girls, revisiting dormitory lists, sorting classes, liaising with other schools on sports fixtures and planning menus.

If she was sitting contemplating a relaxing summer, her attention might have been taken by the sight of a Model Y Ford chugging up the drive towards the school. Was this a girl returning – her parents beetling back because something had been left behind? It certainly wasn't a delivery van or the postman.

As the car drew closer, she would have seen two men dressed in identical dark grey suits and looking horribly formal. One can imagine the pang of nerves that could have jangled in the pit of her stomach.

At exactly the same time, a couple of miles away, at the Meadowcroft Hotel on Llannerch Road East, owners Stan and Hester Barlow nervously greeted a man carrying a clipboard who had pinged the bell at the reception desk in the hall. The couple would have come out of the sitting room where they attended to their guests. Their hotel had forty-two rooms; among the guests were several men and women of advanced years who, old and infirm, were permanent residents.

The man with the clipboard would have spoken firmly and without emotion: 'I am requested to requisition this building on behalf of His Majesty's Government,' went the formal announcement. 'I shall hereby serve you formal notice of requisition in order to obtain vacant possession. I, or one of my colleagues, shall then take a schedule of condition of this building and make an inventory of any residual contents – fixtures or fittings.' Perhaps he stopped and went off script at this point. 'So that's things like wall lights, curtains, fitting cupboards and wardrobes.' Then it would have been back to his notes as the ashen-faced Barlows could do nothing but stand there and listen. 'I must inform you that all persons in this building are to vacate in six hours, taking with them all their personal possessions. Actual possession of this building will not be taken until all the visitors have vacated the premises, or at the expiration of six hours. The occupier may remove all perishable food, or other valuables, articles etc which he wishes, providing this is done within the space of a few hours.'

While the Barlows were receiving the news at how their lives were to change within hours, from relative quiet to an uncertain future, the same was happening at Penrhos College. Miss Smith would have been relieved that there were no children in residence. Her job would be to coerce her colleagues into vacating the school before setting about the task of finding and then moving to new premises. She would not let the school simply shut.

Miss Smith would have been informed of the following, according to contemporary notices: 'a schedule of condition will be made of the building as well as an inventory of contents. Before the inventory and schedule of condition is commenced, the occupier, or the manager, shall be requested to see that his staff before they leave, and under their supervision, remove all wines, spirits and imperishable food, linen, silver, crockery, valuables etc, into a room for temporary storage. This room must be locked and sealed in the presence of the manager. Rooms suitable for this purpose, e.g. pantries, linen rooms, cupboards etc, must be selected on account of dryness, etc, but as far as possible, rooms suitable for office accommodation shall not be used. As soon as this is done the staff must vacate the building, and if discharged by the management can seek re-employment by HM Office of Works, in accordance with the notice affixed in the entrance hall.'

Miss Smith was given ten days for herself and her staff to pack their things and go. The situation was rather different at the Meadowcroft Hotel. The establishment, which advertised itself as 'ideally suited in quiet surroundings' could not, surely, be vacated in six hours, as the elderly residents would not have coped. So on this occasion the man from the ministry relented. He gave them forty-eight rather than six hours to leave and find new accommodation.

Across town similar events unfurled. Hotels, hostels, schools and several private residences had visits. Orders were given, lives duly turned upside down. Within days, Colwyn Bay was transformed; the Ministry of Food was coming to town.

But while Woolton's ministry was moving there, he seems to have gone to great pains to spend as little time as possible in the town, preferring to base himself in London and only visit for brief periods. It appears that he tried very hard to ensure that no meetings went on for so long that he needed to spend the night. And this was no doubt fortuitous, because if he had ever needed to stay the night, as his officials had requisitioned all the hotels in the town as offices, finding him a last-minute bed would be difficult.

The closest Woolton stayed to Colwyn Bay was at the Station Hotel at Llandudno Junction, some five miles away. And so that he could avoid the inconvenience of having to take a car from the station, or even walk the short distance, to the ministry's headquarters at the Colwyn Bay Hotel, he organised for a special railway halt to be constructed where the line passed the hotel. It meant that he could alight like the king of some not too insignificantly minor African republic.

As Colwyn Bay-based historian Graham Roberts commented, when Woolton visited the town on official business he would arrive at the hotel and be able to 'alight with great pomp'.

Meanwhile, the ministry's move was as intricately planned as it was brutally implemented. Just a few weeks before those visits to Miss Smith and the Barlows, two civil servants, Bert Fillmore, a senior executive officer, and Tim Deeves, head of branch, came to Colwyn Bay to drive around the town and double-check on the arrangements they had cooked up at their offices of the Ministry of Food in Portman Square.

The Colwyn Bay Information Bureau, in peacetime a useful place for tourists seeking the likes of bed and breakfast accommodation or local insight on the best beaches, had been asked to provide a venue for their meeting. One employee was asked to attend the encounter as a witness. He was wide-eyed as the pair discussed dispersal plans and, referencing maps of the town, identified and then ticked off a list of every hotel and boarding house in Colwyn Bay and the surrounding area. Naturally he was sworn to secrecy, as were local policemen who were required to share the workload of informing individuals about the impending requisitions.

Thus it was a Colwyn Bay copper who arrived at the Edelweiss Hotel on Lawson Road, which advertised itself as an 'AA Approved' guesthouse and 'The most pleasantly situated hotel in Colwyn Bay', to inform the owner that its premises were required by the government. The hotel was to be given a vital role in the coming years as it was used as the Bread Division, the headquarters for the distribution of loaves across the country.

Meanwhile Miss Smith's Penrhos College would house departments for strategy, planning, and a 'Margins Committee', which policed the strict rationing rules.

It was the ingenuity of Constance Smith that saw the Duke of Devonshire agreeing to let the school use his ancestral pile, Chatsworth House in Derbyshire, for the rest of the war. Over the summer months, convoys of lorries ferried beds, blackboards and desks from Wales to Derbyshire. Senior pupils were asked to come back to school a few days early and Michaelmas term, 1940, for Penrhos College began on time and in the particularly refined quarters of one of Britain's finest stately homes. The house librarian gave lessons on subjects such as snuffboxes and miniature portraiture; the girls swam and splashed about in the Sea Horse Fountain in summer and, later, in the early months of 1942, they skated down the iced-over long water at the front of the house.

Back in Colwyn Bay, the Mount Stewart Hotel became the Bacon and Ham Division, Rydal School housed the Meat and Livestock Department, or 'the Black Pudding Department' as it was known, and a detached private house on Pwllycrochan Avenue, Merton Place, became the headquarters for food propaganda. Under Lord Woolton's instruction, the people who worked in this somewhat gloomy and innocuous three-storey house were tasked with selling the message to the British people (via any media possible, from posters to radio) that not only was abiding by the ration one's patriotic duty, but it was in fact good for them. The nation's sparse diet would actually make them feel better and be better. They also let it be known that fighting troops would receive a richer mix of food, which, in turn, was healthier for them.

It was, wrote local historian Graham Roberts, 'a balancing act between maintaining the morale at home and maintaining the strength and morale of the army'.

And so the town, in its schools, private houses, hotels and hostels, housed all the key departments of the Ministry of Food. There were scientific advisors, food experts of every conceivable field, as well as secretaries galore.

Schoolchildren and locals could only gawp opened-mouthed when the train from London began to spill out what a local newspaper at the time described as 'aliens in an alien land of churches, chapels and pubs, [carrying] their brief cases and rolled umbrellas'. They arrived, said a resident, 'wearing their city suits, starched shirts, ties and Anthony Eden hats, with Brylcreemed hair'. Along with them came the furnishings that would be required to convert boarding-house sitting-rooms into offices, and school halls into secretarial hothouses. Trainloads of thick brown linoleum arrived at the station; so much of it, historian Graham Roberts reports that 'some of this stuff still remains to this day'.

Across the town of Colwyn Bay, and stretching out to surrounding villages like Rhos-On-Sea, the Ministry of Food's departments were rehoused from the Edwardian baroque splendour of Whitehall to the rather more quaint, humdrum, and drab semis of this North Wales seaside town. From departments analysing numbers of ships needed to bring food across the Atlantic, to vast pools of typists, from cereal product divisions to animal feed logistics and personnel offices, the town was transformed almost overnight. There was the accommodation too, with men and woman separated, naturally, and offices and spaces set aside for eating and socialising.

Yet in spite of all this activity and disruption, these strangers with their social lives and their actual work, remained discreet, excepting the odd local newspaper report. As Roberts writes: 'Had Hitler bombed Colwyn Bay as comprehensively as he did Coventry, he would have created far more havoc. The British people could have faced starvation.'

The secrecy occurred by no mere chance. Orders were

given to civil servants, logistical staff and many others not to speak about the operation. And once settled in North Wales, information regarding the ministry and its efforts was strictly controlled.

It was a plan effected by the men and women stationed at the Colwyn Bay Hotel. This gothic, turreted building, designed by John Douglas, the Victorian architect of everything from churches to shops, housed the Ministry of Food's headquarters. The hotel, which overlooked the bay itself, contained not just senior ministry officials but officers of the Communication Division. Run by two men, John Jenner and Vic Groves, this department's job was to oversee the coding and decoding of every cable that arrived or left the ministry.

One room in the hotel was known as The Desk. Here, overseen by Jenner and Groves, six executive officers – who resided at St Enoch's Hotel, also on the sea front – sat poring over documents and referring to their government department code books. Every cable that arrived, from any corner of the world, be it about food purchases or shipping, would arrive coded. It would then be decoded and passed to the relevant department. Dispatching clerks ferried these messages around the town, from building to building, careering along the streets and avenues on bicycles. The telephone was not considered secure, nor was it reliable, so uniformed messengers, with small crowns on their lapels, were charged with ferrying round communications. This was disturbing enough during the day for the genteel residents of the town, but the messengers were also busy at night, as cables arrived from Canada and the United States. These needed dispatching and officers would often have to work until the early hours decoding the long messages, some up to 20,000 words in length, so they could be distributed by the morning.

The cyclists were organised into groups led by a 'Supervisory Messenger', one of them a local, John Hughes, who, too old to join the army, was provided with a uniform, a group of young men and some motorbikes. While less urgent missives could be carried on a bicycle, the motorbikes were for messages that needed transferring with speed.

The other communications hub was on the second floor of 5 Penrhyn Buildings, above Bruce's Fruit and Veg shop. Behind the gracefully curved façade of the neo-Georgian block, built in the thirties, was stationed a sound-proofed room, a clandestine news centre; this was a secret BBC studio, linked to transmitters across Britain, which could be operated with others across the country in the event of a German invasion successfully taking over the BBC's London HQ.

But while great efforts were made to maintain operational secrecy of all the communication hubs, there was another government machine whose very *raison d'être* was concealment and security. For also in the town – on the corner of Kenelm Road and Llanerch Road East to be precise – was MI5. The North Wales branch of the British Secret Service was housed in the modestly rambling confines of the Melfort Hotel, its postal address being 'Post Office Box 55, Colwyn Bay'.

The office was run by a Captain Finney, who lodged at a house nearby. The property was requisitioned from owners Mr and Mrs J. M. Clay-Beckitt, who were given just twenty-four hours to vacate. Captain Finney had little sympathy for anyone who got in the way of his plans to find office or living space for his colleagues. 'If I cannot get accommodation for the agents by fair means I shall use foul methods,' he was reported as saying.

As well as responsibilities to the Ministry of Food, they needed to ensure there were no spies in their midst. But MI5 was also there as part of Plan Hegira. This was a top-secret scheme in which double agents would be quickly evacuated from London in the event of an impending German invasion and successful capture of the city. These agents could not be allowed to fall into enemy hands, so rather than shoot them – and their families – they would be given sanctuary in Colwyn Bay. Lists were drawn up of the key agents and Captain Finney earmarked where he could accommodate them. The National Archives records the names of these double agents: there was Snow and Celery, Dragonfly, Gander and Summer, along with Careless, Rainbow and Gelatine. And in 1941, under real threat of invasion, Captain Finney had them all whisked out of London.

Doubtless as Gander and his German wife and children stood at the bar of the White Lion Pub, just outside Colwyn Bay in the village of Llanelian yn Rhos, they might have been joined by a besuited civil servant, a girl from the typing pool, a motorcycle messenger and, perhaps, a sixty-something expert in livestock shipping. None of them would have been able to discuss what it was they were actually doing there, and this mismatch of people – this bizarre immigration – with their cheerily inane remarks about the weather, must have struck any remaining locals of North Wales as extremely curious.

7

Autumn 1940

After a summer of acclimatising to Winston Churchill's style of government, Woolton concluded in his diary – in September 1940, at the height of the Battle of Britain, the air war against the German Luftwaffe raging in the skies above southern England – that the Prime Minister's 'whole interest is in war organisation – hence his lack of interest in the Ministry of Food. Churchill is not really interested, in spite of his long experience, in any of the civil or social problems.'

He also opined generally on politicians, writing: 'I don't think there's much room in the political world for a person who just takes pleasure in getting a job done. That's why so many of them make speeches about things they are going to do, and the press encourages them, because it's news.'

On 13 November 1940, he had lunch with Lord Kemsley –
owner of a newspaper empire that included the *Sunday Times* and
the *Daily Sketch*. The pair were chatting about Woolton's senior
government colleagues. 'How many members of the Cabinet
would you employ at your firm, Lewis's?' asked Kemsley. 'At
the most two,' Woolton replied, 'and one for only a short time.'

Woolton appeared to fight a constant battle to get his patch
of homeland sustenance onto the agenda; so often, in particular, having to make his case to get his hands on ships to
import food – because too often they were commandeered
by his colleagues to use as transport for troops.

Woolton also wrote, on 30 September, that 'the PM and
senior politicians aren't thinking seriously about post-war
problems.' Given the precariousness of Britain's fate at that
time, alone in the world against a Nazi-controlled Europe,
perhaps that's not surprising.

Meanwhile his relationship with Sir Henry French continued to improve. What was once consternation at how
Woolton conducted himself in taxing meetings was turned
into admiration. On 8 October Woolton met a Canadian
delegation to discuss, as he put it, 'how best they could help
us by producing food that we could import from them'.

Prior to the meeting he had met Canadian Major-General
Andrew McNaughton, at lunch, during which the soldier had
outlined his post-war scenario. 'The German nation must be
severely punished,' he told Woolton. 'His "peace" proposal,'
wrote Woolton, 'was the decimation of the German population.'

His afternoon meeting was with James Gardiner, the
Canadian Minister for Agriculture and Defence; a man,
apparently – wrote Woolton – regarded as the future Prime

Minister of Canada. 'He's an entirely undistinguished-looking little man,' he mused. Woolton was a little cross to discover that 'the object of his coming was to enable him to sell so much wheat forward for years to Great Britain that he would be able to increase the amount of money that the Canadians were paying to farmers.'

'Canadian farmers did so well in the last war,' said Gardiner. 'Prices rose so high that they are now becoming a little concerned at the fact that prices are not rising now.'

This, wrote Woolton, was a rather 'naïve' remark. 'Achieving price rises for Canadian farmers is not the object of the war,' barked Woolton witheringly. 'But we will do what we can to help in getting bacon from them.'

However the subject on the table was not bacon but wheat and there was, wrote Woolton, 'a great flurry going on among the civil servants who were sitting behind me'.

Woolton then explained that not only was he not interested in propping up the price of Canadian wheat, but that the price was too high. If Canada could not sell it at the price he was prepared to offer, then he wouldn't buy their bacon either. Of course he needed the bacon, but decided that a little brinkmanship with this 'undistinguished-looking little man' wouldn't do any harm.

The discussion was, he later thought, 'amusing' because he could sense the officials going 'hot and cold'. 'It is customary for ministers to read carefully prepared briefs: I had read the briefs, but had not brought them with me and was conducting the negotiations in my own way.'

'I was told afterwards that the Treasury officials could scarcely contain their horror,' wrote Woolton; one official passed a note to Sir Henry French that simply read: 'Pull your man up.'

Sir Henry scribbled a note back which read, 'Don't worry. It will come out all right.'

Woolton added: 'Apparently I caused some disturbance to the Colonial Office, the Board of Trade and the Treasury, and it speaks well for French when he said afterwards that he thought I had dropped a number of bricks, and was glad of it.'

Twelve days later Woolton met with Gardiner again and he offered to buy all of their surplus production of bacon – 190,000 tons a year at a price of £80 a ton.

'I was almost ashamed of offering the price – it was so low,' he wrote in his diary, 'but we were very short of dollars.' Woolton also offered to buy 124 million bushels of wheat at $85 dollars. Gardiner said he wanted $90, 'to keep his farmers happy,' wrote Woolton, adding: 'I am getting tired of trying to make farmers happy: it seems to me that the higher the price the more they grumble – a bit like spoiled children.' Then he added with a snigger, 'Anyhow, if they accept the bacon price they will really have something to grumble about.'

A few days later a message came back from the Canadians. They agreed to Woolton's price for their wheat and he, happily, bought their bacon.

Sir Henry was impressed. The ministry lifer appeared to be getting the hang of his maverick minister. But Woolton's antics continued to astonish others. The following morning, 9 October, he was running late for a Cabinet meeting and, as he wrote, 'caused a minor sensation'. His chauffeur was nowhere to be found but Woolton decided to go down to the front door and wait for him there. As he stepped out onto the street, a mail van drew up. 'I immediately hopped in,' he wrote, 'told the driver who I was, and asked him to take me to Downing Street.'

Arriving at the Prime Minister's front door he thanked the driver, noticing 'an expression of amazement on the face of the policeman at No 10 at the sight of a Minister of the Crown descending from a mail van'.

While Woolton was able to swat tiresome Canadians or civil servants, there was nothing he could do about Nazi Germany's campaign of bombing London. It started in earnest on 7 September 1940, and a month later the bombs came very close to Lord Woolton's home in Whitehall Court.

On 13 October, just a few days after a bomb had been dropped on the War Office, right in front of Whitehall Court, he recorded 'the worst night of bombing that we have experienced'. The following evening, incendiary bombs had dropped on the actual building and several fires had started; the night after a huge bomb on the War Office shook Whitehall Court 'and us', wrote Woolton, 'and broke nearly all the windows and covered the place with soot, and generally gave us rather a stirring up'. Maude wrote of the incident, 'Suddenly the place shook, we thought we've got a bomb on us,' she wrote. In fact it had hit a neighbouring building. 'The only effect in our flat was that clouds of soot covered everything in the sitting room. I spent the whole of the morning with Pat, the maid, in trying to restore a modicum of cleanliness.' The bomb had fallen some ten yards away from their building, but fortunately the Wooltons were on the second floor. But it was, Woolton wrote, 'very disturbing.'

The German Luftwaffe continued to bomb London through the winter and on into the early summer months of 1941.

As Maud recorded, the couple would vacate their London bedroom during German attacks. 'Since the raids have begun we have been sleeping on cushions in our little hall,' she wrote on 12 October 1940. 'We sleep fully dressed, to be ready to get out in an emergency. When the "all clear" goes we undress, and go to bed. Bed does feel nice then.'

Some days later Woolton – as he recorded later in a memoir he wrote in honour of his late wife – was dining with Churchill at Number 10; guests included the King. 'A very bad air raid started and we were all sent to shelters in the PM's basement,' Woolton recorded.

'There was one small shelter and the King went there with the PM who invited me to join them and a secretary who was there to give us a running commentary relayed from the Air Ministry Roof. Quite out of the blue Churchill suddenly said, "Woolton where is your wife?" I said I had left her in the flat and I hoped she was still there.'

The King pondered on this then said: 'Won't she have gone to your air raid shelter?'

'We don't have one,' replied Woolton, who noted that the King and Churchill were 'horrified' by this answer.

'So what do you do in these raids?' asked the King.

'We stay comfortably in our flat and trust to luck,' replied Woolton.

Churchill suggested to the King that Woolton be allowed access to one of the shelters available to VIPs.

'Certainly,' replied the King. 'Woolton, you and your wife

will go to a fortress [one such secure place]. Prime Minister, you will be good enough to see that such accommodation is prepared tomorrow.'

Woolton was embarrassed that his wife's stoic resolution to stay in their flat, while she could have been in the safety of their house by Lake Windermere, seemed to be reflecting on him as a man who wasn't concerned about his wife's safety.

'It was obvious my stock as a husband was in their eyes at zero,' he wrote. 'The atmosphere was strained until I said: "I am grateful to your Majesty for your consideration of my wife — but, Sire, when your ancestors sent their ministers to fortresses they scarcely came out."' The group laughed and then listened as they received an update on the current bombing raid.

When Woolton got home later he found his wife filling a bath full of water and connecting it to a hand pump to put out a small fire in one corner of the flat.

Maud was less than thrilled at the idea of going to an official 'fortress'. 'Bombs have broken water mains and I've heard of people being drowned,' she protested. Privately, Woolton reflected that her real objection was that 'she had scruples about accepting a protection which others couldn't have.'

But while Maud refused to accept the King's offer, she did have another request. 'Fred,' she said, 'I'd like you to buy me a small revolver which I can carry in my handbag. I beg you not to refuse. I don't suppose I will ever need to use it because I am sure we will win the war. But I know that the Germans have a list of people who will be shot as soon as they are captured and you are on that list — and very near to Churchill who is number one.'

Maud, wrote Woolton, 'was very determined that neither she nor her children should fall into the hands of the
Germans'.

'If you are captured I will shoot all three of us,' she said to
her startled husband.

Woolton reassured her that they would win the war and
none of these measures would be necessary. To his great relief
the matter was dropped and Maud never mentioned her need
for a revolver again.

Days later and there was more bombing; the House of
Commons was hit and, as Woolton recorded: 'Big Ben was
considerably scarred – but still working in spite of a very dirty
face.' His car manoeuvred around the wreckage en route to
Smithfield Market to check on rumours that supplies of meat
there had been hit. The rumours were true. 'On Wednesday
morning meat was still burning,' he recorded miserably. 'A
great waste in these times when the ration is so small.'

And while the ministry was apparently safe in Colwyn
Bay, its local food bureaus were not so protected.

In November 1940 Woolton's London staff took him on
a tour of south-east London to check on the operations of
a local food office; the idea was to return feeling reassured
about the running of this complicated operation. But when
they reached Battersea there wasn't an office to look at.

'In Battersea, the town hall, which contained the food
office and all the records, had just been made into a mass
of twisted iron,' he wrote, having picked his way over the
smoking wreckage of the previous night's bombing raid. He
refused to be driven back to Portman Square, curious to see
the wider area. It was a grim hour. 'We motored through

miles of streets in all of which windows were broken, doors blown off, and there were huge areas in which houses had been completely wrecked,' he noted.

Every survivor of the bombing would be hungry, each would need the reassurance of decent food. The heavy bombing raids, particularly over London, had left thousands of people sitting in air raid shelters and getting hungry. While he tried to open feeding centres near such shelters – and encouraged anyone, Dunkirk-style, to take their mobile canteens or coffee stalls to areas in need – he also utilised a 'Food Train' for the London Underground.

On 14 November 1940, the first such tube train ran through the London Underground, stopping to feed people sheltering on the station platforms. The train then ran, during periods of intense bombing, between seven and nine o'clock in the evenings and five-thirty and seven in the morning.

He then turned his attention to the people who, despite being bombed, were reluctant to leave their homes. In the main, wrote Woolton, they were elderly women. To such streets he sent field kitchens, often just portable stoves – braziers – on which soup could be cooked.

And he then went a step further. Spotting a need to boost morale to those returning to their bombed homes once it was safe to do so, he planned a mission of convoys which would be a combined ambulance and food service. There would be 'food supplies, kitchens, and everything that would produce the hot drinks and food that shocked people needed'.

The service would need funding and there was precious

little budget in his department, although he knew he could count on one particular individual to fund a small part of the outfit.

It was the morning of 20 December 1940 when, sitting in his office pondering what was then 'an ill-formed idea in my head as to how to meet this need', he realised that his next appointment was with one Mr Kruger of the British War Relief Society of America. While he had complained much about the lack of official help for Britain from the United States, this private organisation, which provided non-military aid, was a lifeline to him. Kruger, who represented a cohort of wealthy and socially ambitious Americans, was fishing for ways to assist Woolton; so the timing was perfect.

'I have an idea for which I need your help,' he told Kruger. He then outlined his plan for the convoys and listed what each one would need, having sketched it out on paper that morning.

'Each unit would consist of a mobile water-tanker that can carry up to 350 gallons, there would be two lorries each containing 6,000 meals, two kitchen lorries with soup boilers and fuel, three mobile canteens and five motor-cyclists who will liaise between the area in need and the local authority.'

Woolton explained that the convoys would be mostly staffed by women and that the complete fleet would consist of 144 vehicles.

'I'd like you to consider helping to fund the fleet,' Woolton said to Kruger. Kruger nodded with interest. Woolton continued, in a conspiratorial tone: 'I should add that there is one other individual who has pledged to personally fund eight of those vehicles.' Kruger looked on intently. 'And I should say that it might be indiscreet of me to mention who she might be.'

Woolton paused and his eyes flicked clearly to a framed picture on his desk of himself with Her Majesty the Queen.

Kruger understood exactly and, without hesitation, said with considerable zeal: 'Lord Woolton, we will finance the whole lot.' His compatriots back home would relish the association.

That afternoon Woolton went to Buckingham Palace, where he was due to have an audience with the King; it was a regular catch-up (the King, he wrote, 'sent for me from time to time to hear how the food arrangements were going'), and a chance to complete the deal. He mentioned his idea, adding that this convoy might be called the 'Queen's Messengers', because, he explained, 'the women who will take charge of these convoys will indeed be messengers of mercy.'

According to Woolton: 'The King at once jumped up and said: "Come and ask her."' Maud also, having listened to her husband's report of the encounter, referred to the occasion in her diary. '"Let's go along to see the Queen,"' she reported the King as saying, continuing, 'and the three of them stood in front of the fire and chatted for about ten minutes – all very informal. She is a delightful woman and the country loves her.'

Woolton added that they talked 'in a quite domestic way'. 'Food and kindliness indicate the things that Your Majesty means to the people of this country – practical sympathy,' he told her. 'The vast majority of the people think of you as a person who would speak the kindly word, and, if it fell within your power, would take the cup of soup to the needy person.'

The Queen, wrote Woolton, 'was quite taken aback and said, "Do you really think that people think of me like that, because it is so much what I want them to think. It's what I try to be."'

According to Maud, 'When Fred told her how very, *very* much her presence in bombed areas helped people – she clasped her hands together and, with tears in her eyes, said: "Oh. Do you *really* think so? I do hope it does." She is very humble indeed.' Woolton added: 'It was really quite touching, because there was so much depth in it and such obvious sincerity.'

Woolton and his wife saw the King and Queen on many occasions, and Maud would always relay their meetings with joy in her diary. On 11 October 1940, after Woolton had joined the couple on a tour of some of the Communal Feeding Centres, Maud wrote: 'They are so intelligent and keen. The Queen too is so lovely and interested in everything. The appreciation of the women in the centres was delightful. They were so touched by their Majesties' interest, and they crowded round the carriage when they left one centre – one woman calling out "It is good of you to come." The Queen nearly cried, because most of these women had been bombed out of their houses. When F came home at night, six hours afterwards, he was still thrilled by the success of the morning. "They do do their stuff [he said]".'

The Queen, in due course, paid personally for eight of the convoy vehicles and Kruger's outfit funded the other 136. 'The message which I would entrust to these convoys will not be one of encouragement,' the Queen said, when officially launching the fleet, 'for courage is never lacking in the people of this country. It will rather be one of true sympathy and loving kindness.'

The trucks, vans, mobile kitchens and motor-cycles were all emblazoned with the words: 'QUEEN'S MESSENGERS CONVOY' and Woolton had them strategically placed around the country, in his words, 'ready to set off to whatever town in their sections had been visited by the German bombers'. The first convoy went into action in Coventry and over three days fed 12,000 people. These mobile canteens were manned by the members of the Women's Voluntary Service (an organisation established in 1938 by Home Secretary Sir Samuel Hoare which had 165,000 members by the start of the war, and whose unpaid women ran the rest centres that provided washing facilities and clothes to those bombed out of their homes). A leading figure of the WVS was Pearl Hyde, whose vans often appeared in the streets of Coventry while bombing raids were still in progress. 'You know you feel such a fool standing there in a crater holding a mug of tea,' she later said, 'until a man says "it washed the blood and dust out of my mouth" and you know you have done something useful.'

The new Queen's Messengers convoys would usually enter an area as soon as the 'All Clear' was given, which still put them in considerable danger as no one knew how long an 'All Clear' would last. Woolton recognised this by asking that vehicles had their 'battle honours' inscribed on the side. Chevrons were painted on, similar to those worn by soldiers in the First World War, and each time a convoy went into action its record was marked. The convoys became famous, were cheered on as they ploughed and picked their way to recently bombed areas.

Lord Woolton was gratified at a scheme that was feeding the needy, satisfied his love of an entrepreneurial deal, stirred the hearts of the nation and fostered his personal relationship with the King and Queen.

Private American funding for the Queen's Messengers was, as far as Woolton was concerned, a rare example of actual practical help from the United States.

'American sympathy is an amazing thing: newspapers, broadcasts, American conversations, are all full of it,' he confided to his diary on 14 October 1940, 'but they still won't allow their ships to come into England carrying either food or munitions, and [what] they still don't give is one dollar's worth of goods unless we pay cash for them.'

That day he had been invited to join a group of high-powered American businessmen. Towards the end of lunch, it was mooted that he should say a few words. Casting around the room, well briefed by his team, he was well aware that there were, among the tables, a couple of contenders for future President. As he stood up, he thanked this prestigious group of men for the warm support they had given vocally for Britain. They were murmurs of approval. But, the minister concluded, before sitting down, 'what we need is ships, not sympathy.'

This was not the genial, diplomatic schmooze the Americans had expected and they were clearly surprised and taken aback; Woolton left the lunch with that very slight spring in his step he always felt from having lobbed a few well-targeted missiles at a group of people whose vested interests did not coincide with his own.

A month later Woolton, with his wife, were guests at a lunch at the Carlton Club on London's St James' Street. Woolton was a little uneasy at first, sitting between two well-known society hostesses, Dame Margaret Greville and Lady Simon. Aware of the snobbery that abounded in such echelons, he didn't for a moment doubt that some of those at the table were a little sniffy at this businessman, promoted latterly to the peerage. He 'had very much the feeling of being the unknown factor being submitted to close scrutiny', he wrote privately.

His dining companions spent most of the lunch flattering him. 'You are doing magnificently,' said Dame Margaret, 'really, everything you are doing is so perfect.' Lady Simon was equally effusive: 'The public has the greatest reason to be grateful to you and I wouldn't think that anyone could possibly have any reason to criticise you in any way,' she gushed. 'I thought that was very charming,' wrote Woolton, 'but I didn't believe a word of it.'

So Woolton merely nodded in acknowledgement as another guest, Mr Henshall, First Secretary of the American Embassy, added some platitudes of his own. 'You are indeed doing a fantastic job, Lord Woolton, and I should add that I sympathise considerably with the extremely difficult circumstances in which you and your government are operating,' he ventured.

Woolton quickly ascertained who he was and decided it was a perfect moment to trot out his new favourite line when encountering Americans: 'Thank you for your kind words Mr Henshall,' he said. 'But we want ships, not sympathy, from the United States of America. And until you send us some ships your sympathy is not much use.'

History does not record if the smart ladies and others around the luncheon table recoiled nervously, a few moments of awkward silence striking their end of the table at this lapse in good manners. Perhaps Lord Woolton caught the eye of his ever-supporting and beloved wife a few places away, while the ladies muttered to themselves about the stunning vulgarity of this upstart man from the ministry. Doubtless they had heard of how he was argumentative in Cabinet, and less than respectful of the Prime Minister.

But back at Whitehall Court that night, as he wrote his diary, Woolton was resolute. His talk at lunch was, he admitted with a favourite expression, 'quite bald'. But, he insisted, 'I think there's a great danger of the Americans getting carried away in the belief that all these easy conversations of theirs about "Help for Britain" is what matters, and it isn't. It's help we want, not conversation, and it's precious little we're getting.'

There was precious little help from the Irish either, it seemed. Their policy of neutrality remained intact during the duration of the Second World War. Some historians, notably Max Hastings in *All Hell Let Loose,* believe that the then Irish Prime Minister Eamon de Valera had a 'fanatical loathing . . . of his British neighbours'; whatever the truth of Ireland's stand, even if it appeared to be supported by the vast majority of Irish people, it did not impress Woolton. He posited that Ireland's position had led to a number of shipping losses. German U-boats were able to lurk around the ports of the west coast of Ireland, for example, and attack passing Allied ships. 'They have always been trying to get something from us and they have never given anything,' he grumbled in his diary on 12 December 1940. He recorded his argument made to Cabinet: 'Mr de Valera might keep his neutrality if he wanted to, but if we are losing ships as a consequence there is no reason why we should bother to feed the people of Eire [Ireland] at the cost of the people of the United Kingdom.'

The government then agreed that the UK would restrict the help it gave in securing imports to Ireland. While they would not limit in any way imports to Ireland occurring on their own account, or to Ireland's ships joining Allied convoys, Woolton wrote that: 'we shall have to reduce the amount of goods imported into Eire according to our necessities.' It was harsh, but fair, he believed. 'This, I think, means that Eire will begin to know the meaning of neutrality and doubt the wisdom of keeping German and Italian ambassadors in Dublin.'

In those dark days of war, Lord Woolton had to dig deep to find his rugged reserve. He was reminded particularly of a book he used to read to his children. Written by General Jack Seely – later 1st Baron Mottistone – who led a famous (and possibly the last) great cavalry charge on his horse Warrior at the Battle of Moreuil Wood by the banks of the Arve River in France in 1918, it related his tales of adventure on 'land, sea and air'. He would sit at twilight reading the book aloud and willing his children to sleep with these tales of derring-do, out of which General Jack always emerged glorious and alive. They were stories of bravery – although, according to one critic, not always factually reliable. But they bore the title of *Fear and Be Slain*. As Woolton considered the mammoth task in front of him, to both administer the ration and distribute food, he took comfort from the romanticism of these tales. 'I knew that feeding the nation against the background of submarine warfare and aerial bombardment was so fraught with dangers, that nothing but boldness could succeed; both for the country and for me in my task,' he confided. 'Faint hearts are no use in government office.'

THE BATTLE OF THE ATLANTIC

By the winter of 1940 Britain's providers were in a cascade of stress. Hungry children expected of their mothers, husbands of their wives, to put food on the table in the evening. Those women – and let's face it, it was mostly women – relied on their local butcher, the grocer, or some ingenuity that enabled them to scrounge a rabbit or purloin some roadkill.

Those shopkeepers depended on their local food office, who in turn relied on a variety of suppliers. Wholesalers, particularly those waiting on arrivals of items like bacon or cheese or sugar, relied on the merchant seamen who might be bringing the goods in after a perilous trip across the Atlantic. Those ships then depended on their government and the armed forces to defend them. Whatever Lord Woolton could do both to actually get hold of shipping – which involved some serious tussles in Cabinet – and then have them defended, he, in turn, trusted on a bit of luck.

But, by December, there was considerable worry among senior figures in government. Maud noted her conversations with Woolton in her diary: 'Troubles are looming in the food situation,' she confided to her diary. 'We have had very heavy losses of ships,' she continued, 'some including food ones, by submarines and air attack, many ships have been taken off to become troop ships to take men and materials out to the Mediterranean, and quite an appreciable amount of food has been destroyed by air blitz. One of the major stores full of meat has been destroyed and some ships in harbour have been sunk. All this at the beginning of Christmas is hard.'

As the festive season approached, Woolton was enduring a typical week: haggling, cajoling, persuading, making speeches and broadcasts, travelling, attending Cabinet meetings and tentatively eating his way through working lunches and diplomatic dinners. Sat in his Portman Square office on the Friday afternoon, he wondered if he would be able to fend off the demands of his civil servants before they clocked off and a more peaceful weekend might ensue. At around 3 p.m., though, one of his staff entered his office with a grave look on his face; indeed to Woolton grave expressions from some of his staff never seemed far off. Woolton's thoughts were, as ever, to ponder how bad the news was and how quickly he would be able to resolve things. The man carried a note detailing a signal just received from the Admiralty, the body that commanded the Royal Navy. It was not a cheering message. Neither was the second note, nor the subsequent three.

Fred's father, Thomas, was the son of a Lancashire pub landlord. Barely literate, after work as an itinerant saddler dried up he never found a constant occupation.

A young Fred Woolton looks confidently into the camera. After studying to be a sociologist, he was eager to make his mark in the world of business.

Fred would meet his future wife, Maud, while at university in Manchester. Bound by religious faith, Maud would later claim that a 'higher power' had seeded them in their actions together.

Woolton joined the retail company Lewis's in 1920. He would build the firm, owned by the Cohen family, into a hugely successful national operator.

By the time Woolton entered politics in 1940 he was a wealthy businessman. He had three homes: Hillfoot House in Liverpool, a flat in London and a holiday home by Lake Windermere. Pictured in the formal garb of a member of the Privy Council, with wife Maud and daughter Peggy.

The Woolton family, including Roger in a swimming costume, relaxes in the garden at their home, Fallbarrow, by Lake Windermere, which Fred had bought in 1931.

Woolton poses with his wife, children and the family nanny, along with his beloved pipe, while dressed down in tweed plus-fours.

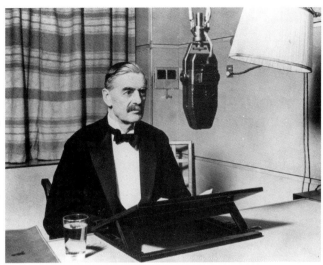

Prime Minister Neville Chamberlain addresses the nation on 3 September 1939 to confirm that a state of war existed between Britain and Germany. Chamberlain appointed Woolton as Minister of Food in April 1940.

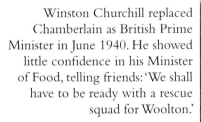

A newspaper seller on the Strand, in London, carries a hoarding pronouncing the declaration of war.

Winston Churchill replaced Chamberlain as British Prime Minister in June 1940. He showed little confidence in his Minister of Food, telling friends: 'We shall have to be ready with a rescue squad for Woolton.'

The German Luftwaffe followed the route of the River Thames in order to target and destroy valuable food and fuel depots.

Warehouses stocking vital supplies of meat burn in the shadow of St Paul's Cathedral in October 1940.

As soon as rationing was implemented in January 1940, queues formed along high streets across Britain.

National Registration Day was declared on 29 September 1939, where everyone – save servicemen and women – filled in forms revealing their personal details and occupation. Ration books and coupons were then assigned to individuals and families, based on age and income.

As the Luftwaffe's bombing campaign of London intensified, the Ministry of Food secretly relocated to the Welsh coastal town of Colwyn Bay. Penrhos College (left) was one of a host of buildings requisitioned by the ministry, in this case used for strategy and planning.

Woolton had a special railway halt constructed so he could alight directly at the Ministry of Food's HQ at the Colwyn Bay Hotel. Here he makes an official inspection of the town's Home Guard.

The Ministry of Food was quick to issue posters as part of a general media campaign to urge households to become self-sufficient in advance of increasing privations.

Woolton's day was often filled with photocalls to drive home the message of efficient cooking. Here he attends the launch of a V (for Victory) Club Lunch in London's Hackney, showcasing the benefits of communal cooking.

The historic lend-lease agreement between the USA and Britain saw aid – from tanks to food – shipped to the UK. Lord Woolton with the US President's special representative (left) greets the first shipment of food to reach British shores.

Woolton poses for the camera while feeding a group of Bevan Boys; these were teenage lads eligible for armed service but ordered instead to go into coal mines to dig for Britain.

Rescue parties relaxing on furniture brought out from bombed houses are fed from a Queen's Messengers Convoy.

King George VI pays a visit to the Ministry of Food – an event, wrote Woolton, that 'did more for the internal morale of the Ministry of Food than anybody else would have done in a year'.

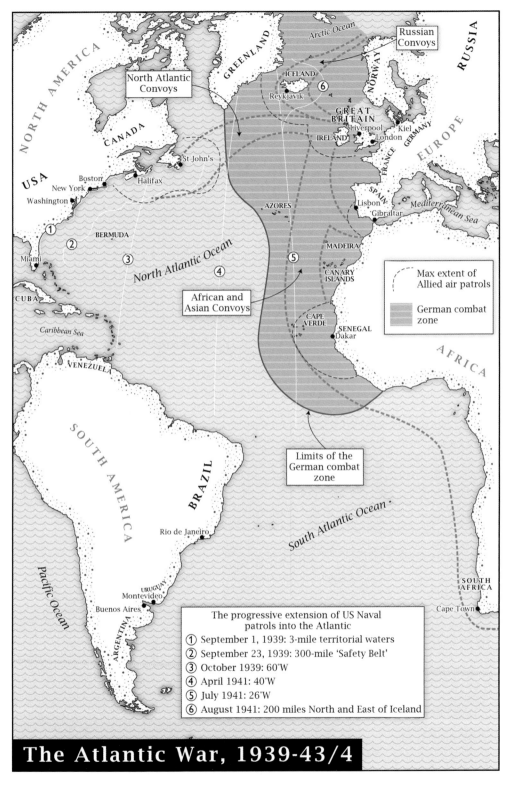

North Atlantic
Convoys

Russian
Convoys

ARCTIC OCEAN
Arctic Ocean

NORTH AMERICA

GREENLAND

ICELAND
Reykjavik

⑥

NORWAY

RUSSIA

GREAT
BRITAIN
Liverpool · Kiel
IRELAND · London

GERMANY
EUROPE

CANADA

St John's

USA

Boston
New York
Halifax

FRANCE

SPAIN
Lisbon
·Gibraltar

Mediterranean Sea

Washington

①

②

BERMUDA

AZORES

③

Miami

④

North Atlantic Ocean

⑤

MADEIRA

CANARY
ISLANDS

AFRICA

CUBA

Caribbean Sea

African and
Asian Convoys

CAPE
VERDE

SENEGAL
Dakar

Max extent of
Allied air patrols

German combat
zone

VENEZUELA

SOUTH AMERICA

BRAZIL

Limits of the
German combat
zone

South Atlantic Ocean

Rio de Janeiro

Pacific Ocean

URUGUAY
Montevideo

Buenos Aires

ARGENTINA

SOUTH
AFRICA

Cape Town

The progressive extension of US Naval
patrols into the Atlantic
① September 1, 1939: 3-mile territorial waters
② September 23, 1939: 300-mile 'Safety Belt'
③ October 1939: 60°W
④ April 1941: 40°W
⑤ July 1941: 26°W
⑥ August 1941: 200 miles North and East of Iceland

The Atlantic War, 1939-43/4

This map emphasises the loss of shipping and their supplies that failed to reach
British shores.

Lady Woolton worked alongside her husband to bolster the war effort and the work his ministry were doing. Here she opens up a food centre in Romford (above) and later that same visit hands over the keys of a mobile canteen to the local authorities (below).

'During the course of two hours that Friday afternoon,' wrote Woolton, 'I received five separate signals from the Admiralty reporting that food ships had been sunk on the Atlantic route.' The sinkings threatened a major British institution: breakfast.

'By some extraordinary misfortune, these five ships were largely stocked with bacon. It was just the luck, or ill-luck, of war,' he wrote. It was never helpful to get this type of news on a Friday, as Woolton liked to think that by the end of each week he would honour the ration. His deal with the British public – that they would abide by the ration and eschew the black market – would collapse if he didn't fulfil his end of the bargain.

So Woolton called in his staff and gave them his usual pep talk. 'We will not fail in the pledge given to the public that the ration will always be honoured,' he said, before adding this time: 'So we need to find some bacon.'

Fortunately such was the meticulous planning of his department over in Colwyn Bay, that his staff identified several warehouses near Liverpool that were housing some large stocks of bacon due to be sent to Lancashire in a few weeks time. Woolton worked out that there was just enough there that, added to the one remaining ship that had not been sunk, he could distribute bacon to the rest of the country.

The only thing was that the bacon needed to be on the counters of the nation's butchers by the morning, as families didn't have the means to store foods in the way we do now. Almost no one had access to domestic refrigeration; by 1948, only 2 per cent of British homes owned a fridge. 'As the one solitary ship that had bacon on board came in to the port of Liverpool, a special squad of men was charged to bring off the bacon with all speed, load it onto lorries and send it straight off into distribution,' recalled Woolton. The system then clicked into place as smaller vans then ferried the rashers out across the country and into the towns and cities. Making such last-minute arrangements often seems tricky enough in peacetime; so it was no mean feat to accomplish it in wartime.

In the early hours of Saturday morning, as the likes of Peter Jennings – the family-run butcher in Twyford (*see* Epilogue) – finished his porridge and thought about firing up the boiler and opening the shutters on the shop, a van from Smithfield market would have pulled up carrying the usual day's approved meat stock. There was the bacon, wrapped in paper. Later in the morning, local housewives would queue up to buy their few rashers to sate the hungry appetites of their family. Little would they know of the midnight drama that only just saved the day.

'We honoured the ration,' mused Woolton that day, whose officials would have been working feverishly to restock the emptying warehouses at the very moment the bacon was being sent out, 'but it was a near thing.'

It would be one of many near things as the war progressed. Both Britain and Germany wanted to be sure that they had learned the lessons of the previous global conflict. As the historian Richard Tames said with regard to the First World War: 'the British Government had given no serious consideration to food policy until the prospect of virtual famine suddenly manifested itself like some malevolent spectre.' Likewise, the scarcity of food that was manifested across Germany during the First World War was cited by many as a major reason for that country's subsequent collapse and defeat.

Like Britain, Germany wanted to secure its own food supplies and deny its enemy's; in addition to competing with Britain to buy food from neutral countries – by whatever devious means possible – Adolf Hitler also vowed to sink as many supply ships to Britain as he could. Britain's proud island status could turn out to be a marvellous weakness, as its food security was remarkably low and every time a submarine sank a ship bearing eggs or grain, Hitler would take another confident stride towards victory.

His order, that German submarines patrolling the world's major trade routes should attack enemy ships without warning, came the moment German troops invaded Poland.

There were fifty-seven submarines under the control of Admiral Karl Dönitz, head of U-boats for the German navy, and his most successful year was 1940. With the help of planes and mines, and the fact that ships had limited radar and submarine-detection technology, the Royal Navy sailed across large areas of sea without any protection at all.

The U-boats were based at a number of French-held ports and their crews returned during what was called 'The Happy Time' triumphant, to be garlanded with flowers and handed champagne for the benefit of German film crews and the beneficial propaganda that would ensue at cinemas across Germany. Meanwhile, survivors who made it back to Britain arrived with horror stories of uncontrollable fires, vessels sinking in the dark, bloodied men and bodies, floating metal and wood, all swilling together in oil-stained seas.

In 1940 some 6,000 British, Indian and African seamen

lost their lives; the death toll between 1939 and 1945 on the Atlantic Ocean of Allied merchant seaman and navy being around 36,000 and 36,200 respectively. As German U-boats became more effective, so the shipping stock became perilously low. Sinkings in 1940 reached 1.8 million tons, and by the middle of the following year, Britain was losing ships three times faster than they were being built.

But Allied attacks on German vessels proved a heavier human cost. Of the 40,000 German officers and men who served in U-boats, just 7,000 came home. The historian David Fairbank White commented that the casualty rate for German U-boat service was 'the highest for any military unit since the time of the Romans'.

For Britain, in addition to submarine attacks on food convoys, 'Air raids added vastly to our troubles,' said Woolton. At the start of the war cold storage facilities had been near all the ports and the Germans, sensibly on their part, had focused on bombing them. 'It made serious in-roads into our refrigerated stocks of meat,' Woolton noted. And so, soon after he took office, he persuaded the Treasury to give his ministry the funds to build a number of cold stores in safer parts of the country and in secrecy. Some were built underground and grain stores were similarly located at suitably inaccessible locations.

Woolton, visiting one such facility during the war, joked to a ministry official that: 'it may well be that people looking at these buildings in a few years' time will wonder why anybody could have been so foolish as to build extensive storages in such inaccessible places and away from the points of either arrival or consumption.'

Once these more secure buildings were constructed, all Woolton had to do was fill them with food. But with shipping being so well targeted, he began to get a little paranoid. 'During this period [the winter of 1940] the shipping position became so dangerous to our food supplies that I created in the Ministry of Food a department which checked the time in port of every ship that carried food,' he wrote.

It meant that if there was any delay in arriving and unloading, an inquiry would be made to the port authorities as to what had happened.

Woolton's food had to travel vast distances over many perilous seas. The Ministry of Food produced a map revealing the miles that foodstuffs had to travel, to drive the point home to householders. It revealed the sardines from Spain had travelled 1,000 miles to the British market – and, in terms of food miles, this was short. The bacon, wheat, eggs, salmon, milk products and dried fruits from America had to travel at least 2,700 miles. Onions were also being imported from the Middle East, some 5,000 miles distant. Coffee and palm oil had a mammoth 9,000 miles trip to Britain while rice, tea, wheat, meat, butter and cheese from the Antipodes were travelling in excess of 11,000 miles.

'In every kitchen there are ways of making these foods go further,' the ministry implored. 'Remember that little economies are multiplied by every home in the land. In this way British housewives can lighten the heavy load of our Merchant Navy.'

For his part, Woolton was in no doubt about 'the unfailing and valorous efforts of the men of the Merchant Navy'. Those who died met a terrible end. For them, wrote Fairbank

White, 'there are no headstones, no markers, no monuments'. Ships would plunge to the bottom of the Atlantic, disappearing often with all hands in a matter of seconds. Others would have perished in that vast, lonely and desolate sea, dying from exposure or starvation in lifeboats or rafts devoid of shelter.

The crews of the cargo ships that made the dangerous journey across that immense sea lived through days and nights of unimaginable stress. One such ship was the *Leise Maersk*, a Copenhagen built vessel completed in 1921. It was 100 metres long, had a diesel engine capable of 10.5 knots and weighed 3,136 tons.

In November 1940, the ship was crossing the Atlantic carrying 4,500 tons of grain and bound for Sharpness, the English port in Gloucestershire on the River Severn.

The shipment had been arranged in part by a group of ladies who sat at the desks and tables in the dining room of the Edelweiss Hotel on Lawson Road in Colwyn Bay; this was the Ministry of Food's bread division. The staff here liaised with the cereal products division run by a Mr Farquherson who, with his team of typists, was located at the Mount Stewart Hotel on the seafront of the town. The ladies in his department had produced a prolific list, hammered out on ancient typing machines, of every flour mill and bakery in Britain. There was considerable pressure from the top to maintain the supply of flour, as Woolton had long insisted that bread should never be rationed. So the departments liaised, hoping desperately they wouldn't fail the minister.

'I was determined to keep free from all rationing, certain food stuffs, notably bread and potatoes, which were energy-giving fillers,' he had said. It meant fending off a great deal of pressure to add it to the ration. To placate a variety of people in his ministry, and around the Cabinet table, he had even gone so far as drafting a bread-rationing scheme – yet he firmly believed the public would not wear it. It would be a ration too far. He said as much to the Prime Minister: 'If the Cabinet feels it necessary to adopt it,' he told Churchill one day, 'then I will not take the responsibility of operating it.' It was a precarious position for the Minister of Food to take, so Woolton had to ensure that it never came to that.

In his favour, he noted, 'there was plenty of wheat in the world; the only question was whether we could get enough ships to bring it.'

It took an average of 16oz of wheat to make a pound of flour, about the right amount to bake a modest loaf. There are 32,000oz of wheat in a ton which meant that, theoretically, the cargo of the *Leise Maersk* could be turned into 9 million loaves of bread.

So quite a few people were hoping it would make it to Sharpness.

On Friday 22 November, the crew of the ship did not have loaves of bread on their minds. They had a vessel to steer and, with hope in their hearts, an end was in sight – in mind if not in vision. There was a wind blowing, the sky was blue and clear to the horizon and the master and crew, numbering twenty-four in total, were not alone. The *Leise Maersk* was part of a large convoy of ships. There were thirty-four in this procession – Convoy SC 11 – and it included the British *Fintra*, a Norwegian ship, the *Brask*, and a Greek vessel named *Panaghis*. Alongside the convoy was HMS *Enchantress*, commanded by Alan K. Scott-Moncrieff, senior officer escort. He was, by one account, 'pleased with the progress of his charges'.

The convoy was heading north-east and, entering the North Channel, finally reaching the last leg of the journey. England was not far off. On board the *Leise Maersk*, third mate H. E. E. Pedersen wondered if they'd almost made it.

Then, as afternoon turned to evening, the clouds gathered. The air turned chilly and rain began to fall. As it lashed the decks, the wilderness of the frothing sea seemed to stretch out to nothingness around them. Then weather conditions went from bad to full gale force. The ships heaved through the growing swell, waves seeping onto the decks, the spray whipping violently against the windows. As darkness fell, so visibility diminished. Worried that in the black of night ships would crash into one another, several made the decision to switch on their navigation lights. So now, across the peaks and troughs of the waves, through the steamed up and rain-lashed windows on the bridge, the crew could just spot the lights of other ships in the convoy.

But as the ships could now monitor each other's progress, so could an enemy lurking amid the stormy seas.

At just after 10.30 p.m., the convoy made an 18-degree left turn to port, cutting through the waves, the rains seemingly more violent. Then suddenly, from out of the distance, came the booming roar of an explosion.

At the back of the convoy, having fallen a little behind, a British freighter, *Bradfyne*, had been torpedoed. Within minutes the smoking hull slipped beneath the waves taking thirty-nine men down with her.

Having scored a first direct hit, U-100, commanded by Kapitänleutnant Joachim Schepke, considered its next target. Commander Scott-Moncrieff was still unaware of the loss of *Bradfyne* and continued to lead the convoy from the front. At 11.45 p.m. there was another explosion; this time, the British freighter *Justitia* was the target. Carrying steel and lumber, she was also well behind the main group of ships and, just six years old, she quickly sank with the loss of thirteen men.

Meanwhile, enjoying his triumph so far, Schepke had radioed to another German submarine, U-93, to say he had found a convoy. The German U-boats then bided their time until some four hours later when, at 3.35 a.m., a smaller Norwegian ship, the *Bruse*, further up the column, just four down from the leader, was struck by a torpedo, which cut through the boat's metal and exploded right in the engine room.

It was Schepke's third triumph of the night. Scott-Moncrieff, now alert to the drama, turned his *Enchantress* round and headed down the convoy. Another explosion thundered as the Norwegian cargo ship *Salonica* took a hit and sank; it was Schepke again. As historian Fairbank White commented: 'He was pumping torpedoes into SC 11 like a sniper with bolt-action reflexes.'

The fifth hit came at ten minutes past seven in the morning. Like all the crews aware of the lurking dangers, seeing with horror ships hit and then sunk, those on board the *Leise Maersk* could do nothing but will their ship on, hoping the next explosion would be someone else's tragic end.

Lying in his cabin, still sleepless in the approaching dawn, was Pedersen. His boat was in the second column on the convoy, third in the line. But suddenly his worst fears came true. There was a slamming shock of a blast. 'I heard a noise like the crack of a gun,' he recalled. Next, he 'felt a terrible shaking and I was thrown from my bunk'.

Pedersen clambered out of his cabin and as the boat began to list he charged up the passage only to find beams and debris from the explosion blocking his path. He finally made it onto the deck where, with other men who had been unable to lower the lifeboats, he jumped into the cold Atlantic water. With seven other men, he spotted a raft which they swam towards and clung to.

The swell of the sea seemed determined to tear the men from their lifeline and succeeded in taking the chief mate who slipped and drifted down into the deep waters.

Two Allied rescue planes sent to find survivors failed to spot the raft. Two ships also passed by, oblivious to the survivors' precarious position in the waves. But after eight hours adrift and marooned, a Dutch tug, *Thames*, found them and picked them out of the water.

While they huddled in the tug for warmth, Schepke was still eyeing up his prey. Now two destroyers in the convoy, *Ottawa* and *Skeena,* were hunting the U-boats, cruising through the waters, dropping depth charges – but Schepke's submarine and U-93 dodged them.

For the rest of the day, as the convoy plugged on, the tension almost unbearable among the crews, there was neither sight nor sound of the German U-boats. But at exactly 8.05 in the evening a huge explosion came from the back of the line. A Dutch ship, *Bussom*, had been torpedoed. This was Schepke's sixth hit. Scott-Moncrieff spotted the submarine and his *Enchantress* surged after it, launching depth charges. But a frustrating hour passed and he gave up his search.

There would be no more torpedoes. Schepke's U-boat disappeared in the darkness of the sea, having sunk six ships in 24 hours. His fellow marauder, U-93, also left but, for some reason, vacated the scene with a tally of zero.

At 4.30 in the morning the convoy was less than 100 miles from Ireland when it came across a final German surprise. The steam-propelled British built *Alma Dawson* hit a German mine. She soon disappeared beneath the waves.

As the convoy reached the Irish sea, the weather calmed and the surviving ships broke off from the line, heading for their prospective ports. Thirty-four ships had joined the convoy; twenty-seven were left. Just after two o'clock on November 25, the *Thames* tug came in to the waterfront of Campbeltown, a fishing port on the Kintyre peninsula, where Pedersen and the other six survivors stepped off the boat and onto dry land. Back there, somewhere in that desolate ocean, were seventeen of his mates, along with 4,500 tons of grain.

News of the sinking was met with grim resignation in Colwyn Bay. Come Monday morning, Lord Woolton looked at the map he had in his office in London. It showed where the main food commodities were being shipped from; if the wheat grain from Canada or the United States went down, at least he could look to India or Australia.

He picked up the telephone to speak with his team in Colwyn Bay. As ever, he was impressed by the contingency plans already put in place, but ships were sinking at an alarming rate. 'The country never realised,' he later reflected, 'how nearly we were brought to disaster by the submarine peril.' The public were protected from the news. Woolton, for example, noted in his diary on 3 December 1940 that, 'We had a Ministers' meeting at which, in great secrecy, Alexander [Earl Alexander of Hillsborough, First Lord of the Admiralty] told us of all the difficulties that the Navy were having in dealing with the U-boats and raiders.'

While his civil servants did what they could logistically, he knew that he needed to get his hands on more ships, and that meant a battle with the Cabinet.

But it was a cold and perfect storm that Woolton faced come the winter of 1940/41. Churchill had ordered that the nation's fastest ships be used to carry troops and arms to North and East Africa, as Italy's entrance into the war that summer had piled the pressure on the Allies as it launched attacks from its colonies in Libya and Ethiopia. With German U-boats effectively closing the Mediterranean to the Allies, Britain had to send troops the long way round, around the African Cape and up the Red Sea. The only ships that could do this quickly were those normally used to carry refriger-ated goods such as dairy products and frozen meat. And while they were converted into troops carriers, fifty escort ships were commandecred from protecting North Atlantic cargo to protecting these troops.

On 28 November Woolton had to explain the situation to a very unhappy group of representatives from the fruit and vegetable trade, the Retail Fruit Trade Federation.

'Sinkings have been so heavy from submarines,' he began, '[while] the position is being made more acute by the fact that we have to feed an army in the near east, both with food and with ammunition. The Admiralty has taken the fast boats for this purpose, so that the convoy can move quickly.'

And so came the bad news for them. 'I'm afraid we have no more shipping space to import any more fruits into this country,' he said, 'and apricots will all have to go.' It was ruinous news for some of those who heard his message. He had rejected a petition signed by the federation – which represented 63,000 fruit and green grocery shops – urging Woolton to review his decision to ban the import of the likes of bananas.

He had a similarly uncomfortable meeting with the British Association of Refrigeration. 'Other than oranges there will be no bananas, apples or other fruits,' he announced, later writing: 'And a chilly crowd they were! I felt that their trade had got into their blood.'

But while he could, privately, muster a sense of humour about it, the lack of shipping was piling on the pressure. 'It's going to make my task very much harder,' he wrote.

'No More Imported Apricots, Apples or Grapes,' was the headline in the *Daily Herald* the next day on 29 November. Woolton had explained how 'the refrigerated ships are required for war work'. And in his message he hinted that he didn't want to be seen as the bad guy, he was just the messenger: 'To me has fallen the task of telling the people of this country that for the rest of the war they must change their habits,' he said. He spoke of how fresh fruits were 'a luxury that we shall have to give up'. He also hinted that there might also be no space 'for all the meat we have imported so freely and cheaply in the past'.

He painted a gloomy picture of what would become an

empty fruit bowl in homes across the country. 'Apples, apricots, grapes, bananas – these things that are not essential to the life of a nation at war – must disappear from our tables, while the ships that used to bring them are used to serve the necessities of our forces overseas.'

After the lunchtime announcement officials from his ministry handed out notes to the journalists in attendance so they could advise their readers about getting alternative nutrition. The *Daily Herald* duly obliged: 'To make up for the loss of vitamins contained in the list of banned foods, you should eat green vegetables, potatoes, carrots, tomatoes, wholemeal bread, and as much protective food – cheese, herring, salmon, liver – as you can get,' the paper advised.

Other papers also carried the story, helpfully using Woolton's line on luxury. It would appeal, he knew, to the people's sense of patriotism. The *Daily Telegraph*, for example, reported that the 'Nation Must Go Without Food Luxuries'. The *Manchester Guardian* in an editorial fleshed out the Woolton line, writing that 'It is pleasure rather than nourishment we shall be losing, for even the famous apple a day is called by dieticians an old wives' tale.'

On the morning of 30 November Woolton read a few more stories in the newspapers and breathed a sigh of relief that having lost his internal battle to get more shipping for food he appeared to be winning the PR battle. Then a secretary handed him a letter from Number 10 Downing Street: 'Why are we getting no bananas?' asked Churchill. Woolton was incredulous.

He bit his tongue and saved his ire for his diary that night. 'The trouble with this government is that it isn't one,' he complained. 'The Prime Minister is the War Lord, and is doing nothing to control or guide or influence the members of his government.'

He wasn't impressed either with the then Minister for Shipping, Ronald Cross (the maternal grandfather of this book's author). He was wasting good ships, he asserted. 'Cross', he said, 'tries to frighten everybody into believing that there isn't going to be enough shipping space to bring goods into this country, and at the same time he carries steel across the Atlantic in the roughest weather, so that it tears the ships to pieces.'

But he had no qualms about battling with Cross's ministry: 'I regard the feeding of the people of this nation as equal in importance to the arming of its soldiers and I have no intention of allowing anybody to take the ships that I regard as essential to maintaining the importing of food.'

At a meeting of the Cabinet he talked of his fears and recorded his words in his diary. 'The loss of our ships has damaged our programme for food distribution so badly that I doubt very much whether we can live up to the ration,' he stated at a full meeting of the Cabinet. 'The ration is already so small that, if we reduce it, it will be absurd. I need to know if my ministry will be able to have use of any further ships?' he asked. In his diary he records that this bald question was met with 'vague remarks about secret happenings in the War Cabinet that could not yet be talked about'.

This clearly irritated Woolton, excluded from the elite gathering of the War Cabinet and made to feel like a pesky outsider with his minor food gripes. 'I got very tired of it,' he commented, his code for being utterly furious. So he let rip at his Cabinet colleagues.

'If we are to send troops abroad in order to fight a war to maintain our existence, as a free country, then that's alright,' he told them. 'But my responsibility is to keep the people – who aren't going to fight, who are making weapons for the soldiers – alive. I can't see the sense of defending our country if the troops are going to come back to find its inhabitants dead of starvation.'

Those running the navy were also, he noted in his diary, acting without proper control. 'The Admiralty takes ships, without consultation with anybody, because it wants them for the near East; as a consequence food supplies have to be curtailed.'

In view of the shipping crisis, Woolton decided it would be a good idea if, in a speech about food he was due to make in Cardiff, he explained that extra hardships were on the horizon. His words were, obviously, aimed at being disseminated to the press.

So, out of courtesy, he wrote to Churchill. 'I will like to tell people that they are likely to have to go without things this winter in order that shipping space for things more vital to the prosecution of war than the import of non-essential foods, might be available for war purposes.' In spite of his private views, he was willing to embrace Cabinet collective responsibility and present reasons why there weren't enough ships for food.

Rather than thank him, Churchill sent a letter back which, recorded Woolton, was 'the sort of letter a headmaster might send to a fifth form boy, telling me I had all the powers and to ration'. It showed, he commented, 'that he had completely failed to understand anything about the food situation'.

Then, as if to rub it in, the following week the Minister of Agriculture, Robert Hudson, and the Minister of Shipping, Ronald Cross, made exactly the same sort of speech he had been planning, but they did so, moaned Woolton, 'without consultation – and apparently without reproof'.

Woolton huffed and puffed about this. 'There is no centralised government in this country and no control,' he fumed privately.

9

THE PR BATTLE

On 21 November Woolton wrote in his diary: 'Food is becoming an article of so much importance to the public that all the newspapers have now engaged food reporters.' While this would give him a useful channel to disseminate his message to the country, he was also wary. 'They are at once a liability as well as an asset,' he wrote. 'Because, being food reporters, they must get news, and unfortunately stories of failure are better than stories of success.'

In an attempt to garner some control over what they wrote, he instigated regular briefings, a press conference each Tuesday at his Portman Square office. The key writers then formed themselves into what they called the Food Reporters Group. Woolton felt he had some understanding of, and empathy with, the reporters, writing, 'I had some advantage in dealing with the Press in that, at one period of my life, I had been a good deal in and out of newspaper offices and earned the major part of my living as a free-lance journalist. I knew how editors and reporters hated being expected to be the organ of government views.'

At his weekly briefings, he began by speaking on the record 'to enable them to give a favourable background to actions that we have to take in the ministry,' he wrote. If a question then came that he could not answer, because replying would not be in the public interest, he would go off the record and explain why. He realised that simply saying that information was not in the public interest would not put off what he called 'the diligent newspaper-man from searching for information because it might well be that the department was trying to hide its mistakes behind that rather pompous barrier of "the public interest"'. This frankness, he hoped, would keep the press onside.

All the leading newspapers had joined the group, he noted, 'except the *Daily Herald* who prefer scoops regardless of whether they are to the national advantage or not'.

The journalists would gather before their meetings at the Bunch of Grapes pub on Wigmore Street, around the corner from Woolton's office. One writer, Charles Graves, an author and journalist, remembered running into what he called 'The First Eleven of England's food correspondents' one Tuesday afternoon. They 'were drinking mild and bitter in the Saloon Bar,' he wrote in a *Sunday Express* supplement, 'preparatory to attending Lord Woolton's somewhat Rooseveltian Tuesday Conference in Portman Square.' The reporters sipped their drinks and chatted about Woolton. 'He can certainly be caustic when he wants to,' said one. Another joked: 'You can never pull the Woolton over his eyes.'

Graves joined the journalists as they trooped along to Woolton's briefing. He described the minister as having 'good hands, no paunch, grey hair, a pink complexion and bluish eyes'. His voice, he said, 'has the slightly flattish quality of the Lancastrian, but is flexible enough. He has probably had lessons in elocution.' His 'mannerisms', meanwhile, 'include the incessant lighting of a pipe or the removal of his spectacles when his alert brain is concentrating on the easy answer to a hard question. He also has the habit of undoing the bottom button and jigger button of his double-breasted jacket and then doing them up again when in thought.'

Graves also wrote that Woolton 'likes a hostile mind . . . He seldom gets angry. If he does, his mood changes to dry humour and then a dangerous quiet. "Really . . ." is a favourite expression of his, "I am not interested" is another. His day begins at 7.45 a.m. when he reluctantly hoists himself out of bed. He then starts work directly after his bath by jotting down notes on a memo-pad kept in his dressing room.'

As for his team, Graves wrote that Woolton 'seems to be almost worshipped by his staff.' Graves suggested this was due to his being always punctual, avuncular, and because he 'dislikes banquets'. He would return home to his flat for lunch, had working lunches at the likes of Claridge's hotel for business – 'but he prefers home cooking of the simple type like Lancashire hot-pot'. Graves also wrote that, 'His practical and unofficial methods of work are shown by his habit of calling out a couple of ordinary typists to give him a snap judgement on a food poster for women.'

Woolton himself recalled meeting one journalist who was regularly hostile towards him. 'My paper is attacking you every day and we are going to continue to attack you until you have gone,' he told the minister. Woolton asked him which paper he represented, although he declined to name it in his memoirs, writing, 'It was a paper with which I could have had some influence in high places if I had so desired.' But the minister looked at the reporter, suspecting that there was something other than a journalist's antipathy towards a government minister.

'Is anything the matter at home?' inquired Woolton, his Uncle Fred persona coming to the fore.

'What has that got to do with you?' spluttered the journalist.

'I'm only wondering because, in addition to what I view as your errors of journalistic judgement, there must be something which would account for your bad manners,' replied Woolton.

The man looked a little wounded and then, recorded Woolton, 'He blurted out that his wife was going to have a baby and she could not get orange juice and the baby would not be healthy.'

Woolton nodded benignly, noting to himself with some amusement that this panic about orange juice was what he called 'a tribute to our propaganda'. He had used a great deal of energy persuading pregnant and new mothers of the importance, in a food shortage, of giving themselves and their babies things of nutritional value and would help maintain good health. Here was a journalist determined to disbelieve everything that Woolton and his department said, without realising he had himself been swallowing the propaganda.

'Do you think your mother had orange juice before you were born?' asked Woolton. 'I can assure you that mine didn't and both you and I seem quite healthy.'

The reporter nodded, a little humbled. 'But let me tell you,' continued Woolton, 'that when the baby is born it should have the orange juice and I shall see to it myself that your wife and baby get it.'

The journalist's wife and child did indeed, in due course, receive orange juice and, recorded Woolton: 'I thought his articles lost a certain amount of their punch after that.'

When he wasn't schmoozing journalists, Woolton made a point of meeting the more powerful newspaper men: the press barons. On 20 December 1940, for example, he had lunch with the owners of national newspapers including the *Daily Mirror* and *The Times,* as well as regional press bosses such as H. M. Heywood who ran the Kemsley Group of northern papers, as well as Lord Southwood of Odhams Press, who published women's magazines. Also at the lunch was Lord Rothermere of the *Daily Mail.* Woolton wrote that he was 'a keen practical fellow – I should have thought a little light on the trigger as regards judgement'.

Woolton addressed them all as they ate, explaining how he hoped that with the deterioration of the food situation their papers would explain that this was due to war, not government failure. 'I was not asking for any commiseration [or] for restraint of their critics. I was merely anxious that they should know all the facts and then do what they thought right in the interests of the nation.'

The meeting proved useful, as the press barons liked Woolton and several told him that they hoped he would stay in politics after his tenure at the ministry. And a few months later, when Woolton was enduring a rough patch with the press, Lord Southwood gathered a meeting of his press contacts and told them that if they knew of a better man to be Minister of Food then they should suggest it. They didn't and – he reported to Woolton – 'I told them they would regret your resignation and I told them to stop attacking you.' Woolton was charmed but privately dismissive. 'I don't suppose for a moment it will have any influence,' he wrote. 'Newspapers can't keep praising because there's no news in that, and the public loves leaders to be attacked.'

Woolton's regular press briefings made him not just one of the most famous men in politics, but something of a national celebrity as well. Sometimes that fame embarrassed him. On 22 November 1940, after a meeting with his officials in Colwyn Bay, he and Maud stopped for the night at Broadway, a village in the Cotswolds, having booked a room at The Lygon Arms. The couple were shown to their room and were surprised at how good it was. Well furnished and homely, it even had a private bath. Then Woolton noticed some framed photographs about the place. 'It was obviously a personal room and it seemed to have been just vacated.' It then dawned on Maud that this room was the private quarters of the proprietors – a Mr and Mrs Russell – so she prompted her husband to seek them out to insist that this was surely a great inconvenience to them.

'We are just very glad indeed to have the opportunity to show you our appreciation for what you have done for the country and also for us as caterers,' Mr Russell told the minister. It was 'embarrassing', wrote Woolton, 'but very nice.'

Then after dinner the couple moved to the lounge, whereupon the owner came in to introduce his mother, and then his niece, and then a large queue of what seemed endless other visitors.

The next day as they left the Russells refused to take Woolton's money. 'It was our private room, we didn't let it so we can't take payment,' said Mr Russell sealing his argument. 'It has given us great pleasure to have given you the room.'

Woolton left feeling a little embarrassed, but admitting to his wife that it 'was very nice'. But, he wrote in his diary that night not wishing to seem ungrateful: 'I sighed for anonymity.'

At the weekends he would often have to wade through endless newspaper features that mentioned him, or profiled him, or commented on him. 'The cheap Sunday papers seem to think I'm news,' he wrote. And he thought little of some of the columnists – often it seemed authors of light literature – who were sent to interview him. On 8 April 1942 Beverley Nichols, a novelist, gardening writer and later a writer of mysteries, had come to write a profile of him. He wasn't impressed by his visitor and complained to his staff for wasting his time. 'It's amazing to see what poor specimens of mankind these popular authors are,' he commented.

He didn't like watching himself on newsreel either. 'I went to see myself on a film,' he wrote on 22 January 1941. It was, he thought, 'a most humiliating experience. These high-speed cameras strip you and reveal all your weaknesses.

I thought I was quite strong, determined etc.: the creature I saw on the film was quite incapable of controlling the food supplies of the country: the actions were weak and feeble, the voice had quality but no smoothness, and seemed to come in nervous jerks, and I came to the conclusion that this was no work for amateurs.'

Woolton thus employed the services of Howard Marshall, a broadcaster who commentated on major sporting events and state occasions for the BBC. Woolton recruited him to both direct PR operations at the Ministry of Food and give him private media training. Marshall 'spent many patient hours, not only teaching me how to use my voice but teaching me how to write the script for broadcasting,' recalled Woolton. It's not unlikely that, as some contemporary journalists noted, Marshall also gave him some elocution lessons, softening his northern tones, making his voice a tad more acceptable as a member of the British political establishment.

It was that establishment that was very much on show at the funeral following the death of Neville Chamberlain on November 9 1940. The event saw a gathering of the most powerful men in Britain and it gave the Minister of Food an opportunity to reflect on his senior government colleagues.

It was a famously arctic November morning during which mourners had sat beneath the bomb-shattered windows of Westminster Abbey.

'I watched it all thinking of this cold unapproachable shy person,' pondered Woolton on the late former Prime Minister. Chamberlain, he said, had 'few of the attributes for a political life of such great eminence except a personal integrity for adhering to his own convictions'.

He looked about at the assembled Cabinet and other powerful men from the newspaper world as they hunkered down under their thick greatcoats.

'I sometimes wish Lloyd George [Prime Minister from 1916 to 1922] were back in the Cabinet. With his vast knowledge he would make most of these other people look like office-boys,' he wrote. 'There's no allegiance to Churchill: there's nobody in the government whom the public would trust. Halifax [Foreign Secretary] belongs to the Old Munich School [appeasement]: Anderson [Lord President] does his best but it's not much, [he] has no imagination and little human sympathy.' Arthur Greenwood, Minister without Portfolio, is 'an economic philanderer' and Ernest Bevin, Minister of Labour and National Service, 'will blow himself out – he's very vain'. (Woolton was outraged to hear Bevin had eaten at a hotel and ordered champagne for lunch.) and '[Clement] Attlee [sometime Deputy Prime Minister and later Prime Minister] does nothing.'

Next he described Lord Beaverbrook, the newspaper proprietor brought into government by Churchill for a number of senior ministerial roles, as 'a complete egotist' and 'a bully' who 'runs his department by "Giving them Hell" all the time.' He noted simply: 'I don't trust Beaverbrook.'

Lord Reith, meanwhile, the founder of the BBC, 'has more egotism than anyone I've come across'. He mocked how at meetings Reith would grandly offer to jump in and tackle things. 'There were signs that he had done some good work some years ago at the BBC,' he wrote somewhat dismissively of the man widely credited for having established the principles of public service broadcasting, before adding that 'he had never accomplished anything since'.

Woolton's wife Maud had also weighed in on the subject of Reith in her own diary. Reith, she said, 'organised the BBC until neither he, nor the staff, could stand him or it any longer!! He is strange, has queer fits of temper, doesn't know how to manage people – is full of his own opinion. He hasn't made a success of anything he has undertaken since the BBC.' Maud notes that, after a 'succession of failed attempts at running ministries, from Information to Reconstruction', he had been promised a barony. 'He is too conceited to see that he is being shelved. But now he thinks he will be the next PM. God help the country!!'

Woolton made the same point on Reith. Reith, wrote Woolton, 'considers he's likely to be Prime Minister within a reasonable time'. But he's not the only one. 'I notice all these people who get tipped as future Prime Ministers, and who imagine they are going to be, fall by the wayside rather quickly.'

Yet Woolton, too, would be tipped as a future Prime Minister, as he grew in stature both as a politician and a famous figure across Britain. Although he was too wise not to caution himself against holding out for such prospects: 'Whenever I come face to face with the rewards of fame,' he wrote some decades before the real age of celebrity, 'I wonder whether they are worth it.'

He also attacked the department of Lord Leathers, the Ministry of War Transport, complaining that 'the internal transport of this country is in such a jam for the lack of wagons that it cannot move stuff away from the ports.'

Woolton had discovered that there had been plenty of wagons available and that they had stood loaded but idle for a year.

'I find it all very depressing,' he concluded. 'I am trying to play in a team. My temptation is either to leave it, or to do what I would like to more than anything else – and that is to take the gloves off.'

The morning after Chamberlain's funeral Woolton travelled to Liverpool where his views of the wasted landscape that was his government colleagues seemed to be reflected in the aftermath of a Germany bombing.

'The whole of the centre of the town had been completely wrecked by a bomb. Rows and rows of houses and shops had just been razed to the ground in a heap of brick, stone and rubble,' he wrote. 'Water mains and gas mains had been broken: great torrents of water were flowing through the streets. It was a desolate mass of destruction.' But, he added, 'the people were not looking too depressed.'

He was further cheered the following day – when he addressed a meeting in Manchester of what he called 'the principal citizens' of that city at the Reform Club.

He talked again about why food was being restricted and was impressed by his audience. 'It was interesting to see the way in which these hard-headed men in Manchester sat and watched and listened without any emotion on their faces,' he wrote. 'It was clear they wanted hard plain speaking, and it was also clear that they were a little curious to know whether this local businessman who had become a inister of the Crown would give them the real ministerial sort of stuff, or whether he was just a plain businessman.'

So Woolton did what came naturally and went off script. 'I

defined the attitude of the government without any consultation with my colleagues or the Prime Minister,' he wrote.
'I felt it was time that somebody came out with a story that
the way to win a war was to attack.'

Woolton finished and the dour men of Manchester got
to their feet and cheered him to the rafters. 'They were
very appreciative,' he wrote modestly, adding that he was
mobbed as he left the hall. 'The police escorted me out of
the town.'

Woolton felt he was doing a good job of slaying those
weak ministers. But then he found another enemy: farmers,
although Woolton had always been clear in his message that,
after the Royal Navy, the Army and the Royal Air Force,
agriculture was the country's fourth line of defence. For
some time they had been gently rocking his cage. In mid
September 1940, one farmer, a Mr F. Ashley from Irlam in
Lancashire – who served on the National Farmers' Union
council – reported to the Lancashire Executive on a recent
meeting with Lord Woolton. 'We gave the minister a sound
dressing down,' he told a room full of tub-thumping farmers
and a journalist from the *Daily Despatch* who reported on
the meeting the following day, 16 September. 'But,' added
Ashley a little sombrely, 'he didn't seem to take a damned bit
of notice of what was said to him.'

But on 9 December 1940, Woolton had to confront a larger
number of them, face to face.

It was a lunchtime meeting, and escorting him into a hall
in Whitehall was Norman Vernon, director of Flour Milling,
who reported both to the Ministry of Food and the Ministry
of Agriculture. Vernon briefed Woolton as they walked along

in the chilly winter air; 'This union is an extraordinary body,' advised Vernon, 'one of the most powerful organisations in the country.'

'Yes,' Woolton nodded. 'But are they a positive force? The union always opposes,' he said. 'And they have a destructive power.'

'Indeed, Lord Woolton. And they can destroy ministers. They have managed to ruin the careers of every Minister of Agriculture I can think of,' said Vernon.

He went on to explain that the current Minister of Agriculture, Robert Hudson, had sworn not to be taken down by this union; he had spent months working for their approval, but it appeared that he was doing it at Woolton's expense. 'He needs to have these men on his side,' explained Vernon. 'It's vital for Hudson, for example, that they under-stand why grain is priced the way it is. Flour has to be universally affordable and as you know only too well the government does not want to add bread to the ration. Of course this means that farmers are not earning as much as they would wish and they resent that.'

Woolton nodded, understanding the challenge. Then as they reached the location for their lunch meeting, Vernon stopped by the stone steps of some faceless government building. 'The farmers seem to be supporting Hudson,' said Vernon gravely. 'But if things go wrong on prices and if they look for a villain, the way things stand, it will not be the Minister for Agriculture who will be to blame – Hudson has seen his predecessors stumble and has vowed they will not have his scalp – it will be the Minister of Food.'

Listening to what Vernon was saying, Woolton took it all

in; then, looking up at the building where the lunch was and wherein lay the next challenge, he breathed deeply. Then he skipped up the steps to the door. 'As far as they are concerned, I am Public Enemy Number 1,' he would write in his diary later that day. Nothing could cheer him quite like a little afternoon tussle with a bunch of farmers.

Inside he found a large number of men standing around and clearly waiting for a fight. Vernon introduced Woolton around and he shook hands with the union president, the chairman and other senior members. He also met the editor of the farming periodical, the *Farmer and Stockbreeder*, in whose pages Woolton was attacked month after month.

'I was right in the enemy's camp,' Woolton reflected. And while he wore an air of confidence, he noticed that the farmers seemed less self-assured. 'They were rather uncomfortable,' he recalled. Doubtless – and having never met Woolton – these men were ready for a bruising fight, prepared to take, head on, yet another aggressive minister. And they knew from past experience that when they met fire with fire the minister soon wilted. They'd get rid of him and then wait around to clobber another.

But Woolton was different. There was no hint of aggression from him. In fact his approach totally disarmed them. 'I treated them with the affability I reserved for my dearest friends,' he said. As they settled down for lunch, Woolton stood and addressed them. 'Gentlemen. In this room are many men with many grievances and there are others who bear me less ill will. But let me make one thing very clear to you all. Whether you choose to attack me or not attack me is a matter of entire indifference to me, so long as the country wins the war. To this end you have a job to do. You must assist in feeding our country and feeding cattle and sheep and tending fields and harvesting crops. That is your job. Your job is not to get exactly the money you believe is owed to you for everything that goes to the market. Your job is not to hustle for every last shilling out of the Treasury. And I will not waver for one second in my duty, which is to keep our nation fed.'

The farmers looked astonished at Woolton. Here was a man not pleading for their support so he could keep his job. And here was a man who talked to them with an honesty that they did not expect from politicians. 'The atmosphere completely altered,' wrote Woolton later. 'These men seemed to like the perfectly bald statement that I made to them.'

As lunch ended the men got up from the table and gathered around Woolton to talk to him personally. 'You're very direct with us,' said one, 'and that means we can just get on and have a business conversation with you.' And what was destined to be a difficult few hours became, according to Woolton, 'a very pleasant afternoon. I think I buried most of the suspicions of the Farmers' organisation.' They no longer suspected him. They knew just what he thought.

Shortly before 4.30 p.m., when Woolton had to leave, several senior union members approached him and engaged, he said, in 'a deliberate breach of confidence on their part'.

'They assured me they would give me their support.' They then explained their irritation at how Robert Hudson, earlier in the year, had 'taken all the credit for getting a big increase in prices for them from the Treasury'. But what he had not told them was that this increased amount was to last for just three or four months during the winter. Furthermore he had then made it clear that any further reductions in prices for their commodities would be the doing of Lord Woolton. 'He left it clear that the Minister of Food was the fellow who was going to adjust downwards.'

The Minister of Agriculture's attempts to curry favour with the farmers at the expense of Woolton had backfired. As Woolton himself wrote: 'Hudson has spent so much time trying to get the Farmers' Union on his side that it is perfectly clear they have no respect from him. They regard him just as a politician out to make a name for himself.'

Woolton returned to his office emboldened about his own principle of plain speaking. Two days later he let rip at what he called 'hoarders'. The *Manchester Guardian* reported on a speech he made in Portsmouth. Woolton had taken Sir Henry with him as the man had hailed from the city. The idea was to launch a 'Food Economy Plan'. Sir Henry appreciated measured speech, and liked to discuss the quotes Woolton was thinking of dispersing to the waiting press. The following day's *Manchester Guardian* included talk from Woolton that was clearly not words chosen by Sir Henry. 'It is against the law to hoard,' said Woolton. 'And if I find any hoarders I will deal with them remorselessly, ruthlessly, and with immense pleasure.'

Despite becoming used to his minister, Sir Henry may have cringed. But Woolton was true to his word – although on one occasion he may have been a tad overzealous. Word reached his ministry that a large house on the banks of the Severn Estuary in Gloucestershire was hoarding vast amounts of food. Woolton was keen to jump on any examples of the privileged classes abusing his ration system, so he approved an aggressive search by his agents.

After the event Woolton was summoned to the House of Lords to listen to a question raised by a Conservative politician, Charles Bathurst, the 1st Viscount Bledisloe.

The property belonged, in Bledisloe's words, to 'Colonel Sir Lionel Darell, D.S.O., Deputy Lieutenant of the County of Gloucester, a county alderman, and for at least twelve years chairman of the local bench of magistrates, a man well known, respected and indeed beloved throughout the county, devoting his energies in his retirement from the Army to unpaid public and philanthropic service of varied descriptions.'

Having ransacked the house – turning over beds and bed clothes, opening every trunk, suitcase and ottoman, looking in every kitchen jar and in old boxes in the dustiest corners of every outhouse – the inspectors had found nothing.

A tip-off had alleged the hoarding of vast amounts of honey, jam and biscuits. The men had also interrogated various members of the Darells' domestic staff, including their chauffeur. 'Have you seen large quantities of honey enter this house,' a ministry agent asked. 'No', was the chauffeur's emphatic reply.

It seemed that a nosy and uncharitable neighbour had watched some lorries moving what were boxes of accumulated piles of paper gathered by the village – and stored by Sir Lionel – for the benefit of the Red Cross. Also spotted were the comings and goings of a van transporting the belongings of a friend of the family's whose London home had been blitzed. Sir Lionel, pillar of the community and his wife Lady

Darell, had offered their house as a refuge for this man and his wife.

The couple's reputation, said Bledisloe, had been besmirched, they had been distressed and humiliated, and he attacked Lord Woolton whose officials had acted without 'a shred of evidence'. He also complained that 'the powers claimed by a certain government department and their mode of execution would appear to be in violent conflict with the traditional sanctity and privacy of the homes of British people.'

Woolton had tried to defend his ministry and wrote in his diary: 'We had had pretty good grounds for making the search but had not been able to find the food that we had been told had been hoarded.' Thus, he added: 'We weren't on a good wicket. I got away with it, but I don't think it left a very good taste in the mouth of my fellow Peers.'

The Lords attack

If he found the senior politicians in the Commons tiresome, he also saved special ire for those in the second chamber. On 19 December 1940 he attended the House of Lords to talk about bread. 'It really was an important speech,' he wrote in his diary. 'There were seven people there, not very heartening.'

It seemed the very building depressed him. 'The House of Lords is the dreariest thing that someone could imagine,' he wrote, 'and its dreariness begets dreariness.' He loathed the place when it was insultingly empty. But he didn't like it much when it was full either.

As thunder and rain poured down onto the London streets

in mid-July the following year, dramatically breaking a short heatwave that saw temperatures reach the low 30s, Woolton took his seat in the Lords.

Viscount Dawson of Penn, who had been doctor to the late King George V, had put down a motion to stress the necessity of providing milk, particularly for children. Dawson had evidence that the production of milk was falling dangerously. It also gave his fellow peers a chance to weigh in on the subject of food and to attack the minister of that department.

'Are the active adult population to be deprived of this essential food?' asked Dawson. 'What folly, at a time when the maximum of health and strength is required.' In a long speech he set out his concerns. 'The production of milk is like a reputation, very easy to lose and very difficult to regain,' he said. 'That is one of the reasons why I am venturing to press your Lordships as I am doing, because it is our one hope at the present time. At this late season of the year, if we are not going to be face to face with great difficulties in the coming winter, we must act here and now to try and prevent that reduction of the production of milk which so seriously threatens. Milk I would rank as a munition of war,' he said, before adding, almost as an afterthought, that 'we must have more eggs.'

Woolton, he admitted, 'has a large and extremely difficult task,' but, he continued: 'He is sometimes let down by the imperfect implementing of his policy. He is at times called upon to make bricks without straw, and I hope that the result of this discussion will be to give him a larger ration of straw.'

If the first peer to speak had a vein of kindness towards

Woolton, the next certainly did not. Lord Davies, a Welsh former Liberal MP, rose to make several general points about food production before addressing the issue of the black market. 'It is very disquieting to know that in regard to this matter there have been and apparently still are so many attempts at evasion,' he said. 'Black market activities were going on in Germany and other countries,' he said, adding that that 'is only natural and just what we might have expected'. But now, 'I venture to suggest that this sort of thing going on in this country must cause us a great deal of disquietude and alarm.' It was, he said 'un-British [and] a sort of disease. It is, moreover, a very infectious disease, because when one section of the community discovers that sums of money have been made by flouting these food restrictions and regulations, it means that others are tempted to do likewise.'

Davies then turned to Lord Woolton, sitting listening. 'One cannot help feeling that this foul growth should have been nipped in the bud by the Minister of Food when he discovered that huge profits were being made in this way. He ought to have put his foot down at once and prevented the disease from spreading.'

Next up was Lord Addison, who had been both a Labour and Liberal MP and a one-time Minister for Health. Addison was a frequent critic of Woolton, often attacking him on subjects like jam, sometimes strawberries, other times fish. The pair once had an altercation on the subject of boiling sugar. Such was Addison's keenness to talk about the availability of sugar and the boiling of it to make jam that Woolton joked that he 'intended to have a private still in his garden'. Addison was furious. 'The noble Lord must not misrepresent me,' he said demanding that Woolton 'repudiate' his statement.

'The Ministry of Food,' Addison asserted, 'for some reason have, I think, been infected with some kind of disorder in the last few weeks.' The ministry issued orders, he argued, without insuring that they could actually be complied with. 'The community has been presented with a succession of quite needless blunders and is being exposed to serious and unnecessary hardship.' Addison talked of the 'propaganda department of the Ministry of Food' being run by people who 'seem to receive very large salaries: I wish they took a bit more trouble to know something about their jobs.'

He then turned to potatoes, which, he argued, had been in such plentiful supply that 'the farmers did not know what in the world they were going to do with them.' But he stated: 'it is due, I am sorry to say, to gross mismanagement that we should now see people standing in queues a hundred yards long outside greengrocers' shops to buy potatoes.'

Next he tackled an issue of bureaucratic management that had affected the distribution of tomatoes. Addison told the story of a shopkeeper who had ordered a box of tomatoes from a wholesaler in Reading. The tomatoes were brought on a van to the shop from Reading – some twenty miles, but, said Addison, 'the shopkeeper was informed that although the tomatoes had been carted twenty miles all he could do, by order of the Ministry of Food, was to look at the box. The driver was not allowed to take the box off the cart and give it to the shopkeeper. He was instructed to take it back to Reading.'

Woolton, listening to the speeches and planning to address

each issue when he was finally able to make his own speech, could not keep quiet at this point. He rose and asked, 'Was that by order of the ministry?' 'He has said so,' replied Lord Addison. 'I do like to be precise,' said Woolton, clearly angry. 'This is a serious matter. Does the noble Lord seriously suggest that somebody should cart a box twenty miles and then take it back again?'

'I do,' retorted Addison. 'I am stating the facts. I am going to urge that the noble Lord should restrain the zeal of his subordinates in these matters and not let himself in for this kind of misfortune.' He then said that there was 'no earthly reason why these things should occur, but I am coming to two which are much worse'.

He then described how a scheme to get villagers to contribute fruit for jam-making had collapsed. 'It is worse than failure,' he said and Lord Woolton had been 'asking for trouble' in launching it. Part of the plan involved village women getting loans to set up jam-preserving centres with equipment such as oil stoves, preserving pans and jars. But, said Addison, 'the scheme has broken down, I do not know of a single village where there is a centre working [and] whoever drew it up had not the faintest idea of what life in an English village is like. The scheme is a failure and masses of fruit will be unused as a consequence.'

Addison then moved on to the subject of eggs, which was where, he said, he needed to 'press the minister to mend his ways'. The egg scheme had been launched in June of that year. Any keeper of poultry who had more than twelve birds had to sell their eggs through packing stations, and needed special permission to retain any for their own consumption.

But, Addison alleged, the scheme had been started before the packing stations were organised and so, he explained, 'there is no channel between the local producer and a packing station of any kind and the result has been that of course you are interrupting the supply between the producer and the consumer.' And where there were packing stations, distribution had not been organised so that thousands of eggs had been left sitting there and going off.

In order to avoid being subject to the scheme, many poultry smallholders simply reduced their flocks by a bird or two – meaning there were less eggs in the system. Thousands of hens, for example, in Devon were slaughtered. Lord Addison spoke of 'three maiden ladies' that he knew personally who kept hens. 'They had been frightened,' he said, 'by the propaganda department of the Ministry of Food. They had got it in their minds that somebody was going to come into their garden and count their hens and they were not going to be left with more than a dozen.' So the maiden ladies rang the necks of thirty-five of their hens. Their actions were foolish and unnecessary, said Addison, 'but it was the exploits of the propaganda department of the noble Lord that made those women kill those hens.'

Lord Woolton, according to Lord Addison, had created unnecessary suffering. He implored Woolton to check the operations of his ministry. 'If there is one thing that is likely to undermine the public morale it is needless hardship in connection with the daily supply of food.' The public, he continued, were willing to participate in any inconvenience which they knew was necessary but, he added gravely, 'what they do and will resent – and I implore the noble Lord to remember it – is any needless hardship, any foolish interference with their habits.'

One can only imagine the frustration Woolton felt; here was a man whose very passion was social service, whose motivation was an understanding of poverty gained from an early age. No one felt the pain suffered by the public at his own administered privations as raw as he did; it was a major motivating factor for him. Yet he had to sit and listen and be lectured to by his peers about the job he was virtually born to do.

But before Addison sat down he had one final anecdote to share. A few days previously he had been driving through a local town where he saw a line of people outside a greengrocer's shop. 'The queue consisted of perhaps eighty or a hundred women, who were marshalled in double rank by a police officer. I suppose that they were waiting for potatoes or tomatoes.'

At which point one lord piped up 'Cigarettes perhaps,' to the delighted chuckles of peers keen for some light relief.

As Addison watched the queue he saw a woman arrive at the shop in a car. 'She was evidently a favoured customer. She got out of the car and went into the shop in front of the queue. Shortly afterwards she came out with a bag of potatoes and a parcel of tomatoes. What happened then was that the women in the queue fell upon her, scattered her potatoes and tomatoes all over the road, and tore her dress. I rather think that she deserved it. I do not think anybody would sympathise with her very much. Undoubtedly she should not have done what she did.'

Having told his anecdote, Addison then twisted the knife

into Woolton with his analysis. 'The point I want to empha-
size to my noble friend is that that kind of thing is very
dangerous and most undesirable. Any step that can be taken
to avoid such happenings should be taken, and should be the
subject of adequate and careful forethought.'

Addison was telling Woolton, the House of Lords, the
press and the public, what the minister knew only too well. It
was what kept him awake at night and the fear of which tore
into the deepest recesses of his soul. If he didn't provide the
nation with the basics, such as eggs, there would be anarchy.

There was a further speech before Woolton would get the
chance to answer these charges. Liberal peer Lord Teviot complained about how new centralised systems, which enabled
the Ministry of Food to quantify provisions of food, meant
that a friend of his who grew tomatoes had to send them to
London, before they were checked and then returned to his
own local town for sale 'employing petrol and transport'.
The consequence, he said, was that local people 'get hardly
any tomatoes. I live very close to the town in question, and
I cannot buy tomatoes at all.' There was, complained Teviot,
'too much control'. Woolton, he said, 'seems to have got into
rather deep water, and I think it is due to over-legislation'.

Finally Woolton was able to get to his feet and speak.
His aim, he said was to 'put these problems into perspec-
tive'. The things that had been discussed, milk aside, were
'jam, tomatoes, new potatoes and eggs'. Yet, he explained,
'how fortunate we are that it is these things that are causing
concern in the country, because it might indeed be, after
twenty-two months of war, that other things were causing
concern.'

He told the Lords that a senior Cabinet colleague had chastised him the previous day, telling him that 'as Minister of Food I was failing in my job because I was not letting the country know how well we were provided with food.' He told him that the morale of the people would be sustained if they knew what the situation really was. He was reluctant to follow that advice, 'because the truth is that if we try to tell the public what we have done, then there immediately comes to some people's minds the charge of complacency, which is, of course, the latest of modern crimes.'

Woolton then referred back to what was his natural territory. 'Before the war,' he said, 'there was no acute consciousness in this country of the fact that so many hundreds of thousands of people were suffering from malnutrition. It was not one of the subjects they read about daily in the newspapers – that there were, before this war broke out, very many thousands of children in the country who had not enough to eat.'

Woolton had heard the charges about over-zealous regulation, problems with petty bureaucracy but, he said, 'I wonder whether they are really sufficiently aware, when we discuss food questions, of the fact that they are largely determined by war conditions.'

He went on to explain that if he could trade with Denmark or Holland there would be no problem with milk, cheese, butter or eggs, that if he had the Channel Islands there would be plenty of potatoes, and that 'if the Battle of the Atlantic had not been raging day by day, noiseless and unseen, for the most part unappreciated by the people of this country, we should have had very few difficulties with our supply of meat.'

Compared with the last war, problems with food supply were of greater complexity and difficulty yet, he said, 'in spite of all the nervous strains of air raids, as a nation we are fit and we are well.'

Indeed, he argued, 'there are fewer people who are suffering from malnutrition now. We have come through the winter, we have had plenty of milk and bread in abundance. Whilst our rations have not been on a generous scale, they have been taken up by the people of this country, thus showing that the food that we have prescribed as a fair share for everybody has been of such amount and at such a price that everybody could get their fair share.'

It was Woolton's passionate belief that 'Before this war started it would not have been possible to say that nobody in the country wanted for food. As a result of the policy of organisation of the distribution of food, and of selling it at a price within the reach of the ordinary housewife, we can say that many people in this country are more adequately fed now than they were before the war started.'

Woolton went on to defend the distribution system while apologising for the occasional local and 'ridiculous error'. 'I am sure there have been many such mistakes made,' he said. There would always be critics, as 'the system arouses all sorts of opposition among people who have been trained in another school of experience.'

As for the tomatoes, he explained that the point of controlling the numbers was 'to secure that a smaller quantity shall disappear down a multitude of throats rather than a comparatively large quantity shall disappear down the throats of fewer people.'

And when it came to eggs, he said that 'all my political instinct warned me to leave eggs alone, but the shortage of eggs represented a serious problem in the nutritional diet of the town dweller.' They also needed to be subsidised as the price producers required was more than most consumers could afford. He batted off criticism about the packing stations, saying that they were in the hands of private companies and 'I do not think they are any less perfect since they accepted instructions from the Ministry of Food, but they are doing a much larger job than they ever did before.' He accepted that there may have been delays in distributing eggs around the country, but more people were getting hold of them than had previously. 'This is not,' he added firmly, 'a story of universal delay all over the country or of universal confusion.'

As to the apparent failure of the jam scheme as highlighted by Lord Addison, Woolton said he was 'unconscious' of it, stating there were 5,667 centres established for dealing with the problem. Lord Addison then intervened and said, 'I am well aware of the number of centres. I say they have not made the jam; that is the trouble.' Woolton countered saying that there had been a very small fruit crop that year and that the scheme had been run by a group of women who oversaw the women's institutes and that 'It is not fair, is it, to say they do not know anything about rural life.'

Lastly he answered the criticism regarding the zeal in which his staff went about ensuring their regulation was administered and adhered to. 'Lord Addison has asked me to curb the zeal of my staff,' he said. 'I do not desire to curb the zeal of people who are doing all they can to try to help in this war effort.' It was a stinging rebuke; his staff were simply being patriotic, the inference being that to criticise them was to be unpatriotic.

As Woolton sat down he hoped that would be the end of the debate. But he was not so fortunate: more peers were lining up to criticise him.

Lord Perry argued that as tomatoes were never a poor man's food, it was unnecessary to curb their availability to some and widen it for others; and the men who policed his eggs policy represented, he said, 'the growing up of this "Gestapo" ... the minister ... has a number who might perhaps be described as "snoopers"; personally I would call them agents provocateurs.'

'No,' cried Woolton, 'I have no agents provocateurs in the employment of the ministry.'

'We will let it pass,' said Perry.

'It is not true,' Woolton cried.

Next the Earl de La Warr, whose full name was Herbrand Edward Dundonald Brassey Sackville and who in the course of his political life served both Labour and Conservative governments, attacked Woolton for 'unnecessary and artificial shortages created by departmental mismanagement'. Woolton had failed to fully answer 'hardly a single question' he said, adding that 'the country as a whole, both consumers and producers, is profoundly disturbed about the present handling of the food supply of this country.'

At home in Whitehall Court that night, Woolton penned his rather more forthright thoughts in the pages of his diary. He cast the lords as wealthy, privileged people out of touch with real life and only able to take an interest when they were personally affected. 'It wasn't a debate,' he wrote. 'The truth is that even the wealthy are now not getting all the things they want to eat, and that rouses them to speech.'

Woolton, for all his titles and ministerial clout, still felt very much the outsider with his fellow peers. 'I think it's pathetic that, at a time when we are in a war on which depends our very existence, the Noble Lords should spend their time calling attention to the fact that tomatoes are in short supply,' he wrote.

The House of Lords was also, according to Woolton, at its worst in the aftermath of the death of the Duke of Kent, the fifth child of King George V and Queen Mary, in August 1942. Prince George, the young brother of Kings Edward VIII and George VI, died with fourteen others when a flying boat he was travelling in, possibly on a military mission to Sweden judging by the currency he was carrying, crashed into a hill in Caithness in Scotland. The death of the thirty-nine-year-old prince saw tributes given by members of both houses. Woolton was not impressed by the lack of sincerity that emanated from all sides: 'It doesn't seem to me that there is really anybody who was very sorry,' he wrote. He noted that the radical, anti-coalition Independent Labour Party, 'which started out with so many ideals, should have descended so completely as to be prepared to make political capital out of a death.'

The former Prime Minister, Herbert Henry Asquith, who became first Earl of Oxford and Asquith, had also contributed some thoughts. But the words washed over Woolton who struggled to pay attention. 'I often wonder whether he speaks at home with such slow deliberation as he speaks in the House,' he wrote, 'If he does it must be very dreary.'

The other House wasn't much better and he was pretty

disparaging about the entirety of MPs, penning his thoughts one evening after some disgruntled members had spent the afternoon attacking his ministry. He had been required to sit in the gallery above and listen to the speeches. 'I thought they were a miserable crowd,' he wrote. 'I wondered how the country could wage a war successfully with a House of Commons like that.'

Woolton was in fact despairing at the whole political class. One afternoon he had a meeting with the Liberal MP Tom Horabin. 'He used to be at Lewis's,' he wrote, referring to his retail business. 'And he wasn't any good. So I sacked him and he went into politics.'

He also recorded with glee an occasion in November 1942 when Labour MP Philip Noel-Baker came to see him on an issue relating to food hygiene. 'I've come to talk to you about rats,' announced Noel-Baker, a serious and rather glum British Quaker and an earnest campaigner for disarmament. Woolton looked at him steadily. 'Do you mean agricultural or political?' he said. Noel-Baker just frowned. 'He didn't like it very much,' Woolton confided to his diary later.

He relished a fight too with the government department that dealt with the colonies of the British Empire. For example, on 28 June 1942, he alerted the Colonial Office that the people of Malta were suffering from food shortages and something needed to be done. It was four o'clock in the afternoon and the message came back that officials would be happy to deal with it in the morning. 'I was furious,' he noted, 'and asked what was the matter with today.' In fact, he added, 'you might have to work all night.' His edict did not go down well, but Woolton couldn't care less, writing in his diary almost happily that 'I don't think the Colonial Office like me.'

Woolton realised of course that all countries were governed by individuals and Britain probably had just as many tiresome officials as the enemy. 'Fortunately Germany is subject to the same personnel difficulties in government,' he wrote on nearing Christmas in 1940. And he remained certain that a great many people of his nation showed the same steel that he had seen among those businessmen in Manchester. 'It isn't the government of this country that's going to win the war – it's the people.'

10

THE BLACK MARKET

Christmas 1940 was, according to Maud, 'very happy . . . the pleasure being increased by having, for three nights, no air raids. Whether it is the weather that has put off the enemy or a spirit of Christmas, we don't know.'

Both daughter Peggy and son Roger were with their parents and the family stayed in London. 'It doesn't matter where we are, so long as we are together,' she wrote, commenting that Roger 'seems to be very happy [down from Cambridge], but we wish he would work more than he seems to.'

But whatever happy conversation the family had over Christmas, Woolton told Maud about his political worries. 'F has been worried lately about the direction from the top,' she wrote. 'There seems to be very little co-ordination between the various ministries, in fact sometimes there is definite antagonism.'

Woolton had written to the PM, because, in his words, 'he really ought to know a little more about the food position,' and was promptly invited to Chequers on Boxing Day. 'I saw a new Winston,' he wrote, 'in the midst of his family, where the relationship was obviously that of the father and not of the Prime Minister.'

Woolton set out a list of grievances and Churchill listened intently. The Home Front 'was not good enough for the job it had to do', the Economic Policy Committee 'under the presidency of [Arthur] Greenwood [a Labour Party politician] came to no decisions and had delayed my shipping programme for weeks', 'the Food Policy Committee under Attlee also came to no decisions, and ... the latter was so weary that he had great difficulty in keeping awake – and didn't always succeed.' He also blamed Churchill because 'he had taken food ships which were bringing meat, to send them to the Near East and that this had caused the trouble that was blowing up regarding the meat ration.'

Woolton was having to reduce the meat ration – discerned by price rather than weight – by a third, from 1s 10d to 1s 2d – hardly the Christmas present the nation might have wanted

In spite of his frankness, Churchill on this occasion, among his family, 'was receptive and helpful', wrote Woolton. The PM sent out an immediate order that a group of ministers convene 'to discuss the food problem'.

Maud gave her own account of the meeting, based on her husband's report. Woolton was 'very pleased', she wrote of the invitation to Chequers, 'because with the PM you never know whether you get snubbed or not.' She described the Chequers scene as 'a very cheery and friendly ... family party. The PM wasn't at all petulant as he often is – he doesn't like being told things aren't going well – but when he has once got over his petulance, he does get things going.'

(While Woolton talked frequently of Churchill to his wife Maud, she did not often find herself in his company, so she made a point of describing an encounter she had with him in April 1942. 'We were invited to lunch with the Prime Minister at 10 Downing Street. It was very interesting for me as I had never met him except to shake hands with, before,' she wrote. 'He is much more benevolent in looks in his own home than one gets the impression of in pictures – but he is difficult to talk to as he hasn't any small talk to get things going.' But his wife was considerably easier: 'Mrs C is delightful – charming – full of fun, and very vivacious,' Maud added.)

A few days later, as a result of the Chequers meeting, a 'Production Executive Committee' was formed under the chairmanship of Bevin. Churchill also moved Greenwood to look after post-war problems. But this committee formation didn't please Maud. She was allergic to committees, writing that 'one of the failings of the Labour Party was its passionate attachment to committees. It's a vice of democracy.'

She felt that her husband's beef was that there were already too many committees and they weren't working together effectively. Politicians always create committees, she said, 'to investigate whatever problem arises ... [but] in practice it wastes an infinite amount of time.'

A week after Woolton's meeting with Churchill, Maud noted that this dreadful new committee had not been 'fully constituted' and 'it does seem awful that still another committee has to be formed.'

Woolton's other problem was to, as he put it, 'check profiteering'. On 6 January 1941 he wrote that 'a large number of people have come into the food trade buying up articles and selling them again at higher prices.' So he issued a 'Standstill Order', so that prices could not be any higher than they were on 2 December. 'People who had been speculating during the interval have had their fingers burned,' he wrote gleefully.

It was a rare reference to the black market, because Lord Woolton liked to think the British food market was a closed shop and, with him as manager, there was little chance of impropriety. In summing up the food situation in early January 1941, Woolton again referenced the black market saying that it irritated the public but the amount of food affected was small and most of the people responsible were, as he put it, 'having a diet at Wormwood Scrubs' (the prison in West London).

It was only many years later, on a summer's morning in 1958, that the Minister for Food finally laid bare his thoughts on the subject of the black market. Woolton, by then the first Earl, was seated in his grand house near Arundel. The library where he worked at Walberton was quiet. A large Persian rug added some colour to the room's conventional cream walls. He was proudly positioned behind a large estate desk, there was a dark leather sofa, and books were set into shelves on three walls. Between each bookcase were arched recesses hung with gentle watercolours. The shelves below were decorated with clocks, small lamps, little figurines and such things as a cigarette box.

On the walls, in this room and all over the house, were the attractive, but safely formal, paintings of mainly landscapes by English watercolourists such as Copley Fielding, John Varley and Peter de Wint. These paintings Woolton had bought (along with antique furniture that he and Maud had gathered) to help confirm the wealthy status he had gained by his middle age.

Walberton served as a place to entertain friends – many of whom were politicians – and such accoutrements were vital for their socialising. And so important was the society that the couple kept, once Woolton had become an established businessman and politician, that Maud recorded some 100 names of those they regularly came into contact with on the first page of her diaries. She writes her 'List of people who have come into our "orbit" since we came to London' and they include businessmen, senior civil servants, politicians, diplomats and aristocrats. There are the names of the wartime American Ambassador, John Winant, one-time head of the Civil Service Sir Warren Fisher, as well as the Dukes and Duchesses of Buccleuch and Devonshire.

High above the fireplace, below the coving, hung proudly the family crest. An ornate mirror was secured above the mantelpiece which itself displayed framed photographs of men such as Churchill. Chintz curtains were gathered by a large window and light flooded the room. On Woolton's desk were positioned more framed photographs. There was a fading wedding photograph of himself with Maud. Another saw him dressed in a dark suit, standing next to King George

VI who was dressed in the khaki uniform of field marshal, the pair examining a map which detailed the country's emergency food storage areas. The King leans over the table, studying the map diligently, while Woolton holds his glasses in his right hand and looks relaxed and confident in the company of the sovereign. Woolton remembered the conversation on 8 May 1940, which had taken place in the Food Ministry's chart room. As the pressman flashed his camera, Woolton was explaining how local food offices were organised and the exact time of day that divisional food offices reported on the local situation.

Another photograph showed him in black tie with the Prime Minister of the late 1950s, Harold Macmillan. There was also a picture, a personal favourite of his, showing him at a lectern at the Conservative Party conference in Bournemouth in 1955. It was three years previously and he was giving his farewell speech as chairman of the party.

Directly in front of Woolton on the desk was a pile of neatly stacked papers. He looked at it contentedly. It contained several hundred sheets of his neat handwriting. This was his current piece of work, his memoirs, and come Monday his secretary would begin to type up the papers.

There would be no clever name, no snazzy title. He had long resolved with his publishers, Cassell & Company, that it would be entitled *The Memoirs of the Rt. Hon. The Earl of Woolton C.H., P.C., D.L., LL.D*; his name, title, awards and doctorates being quite sufficient to herald its contents.

He was almost halfway through writing it; the day before he'd just finished putting in neat order his recollections of how he had managed the internal distribution of food across

Britain. This morning he had just one final bit to add to that chapter; it would merit just three paragraphs and would have a small subtitle – Black Market.

On this subject the first earl was adamant, unequivocal. He set about writing it and within a mere fifteen minutes had concluded all that was needed to be said.

'There was little or no black market in Britain,' he stated. It was, he firmly believed, 'a tribute to the British people which I hope the historians of this period will proudly record.'

He glanced at the image of himself delivering that final speech in Bournemouth and composed the next few sentences as if he were to deliver them forcefully from that same lectern.

'It was, of course, nothing more than the normal operation of the British people, their attitude to the law of the land, and their sense of fair dealing with one another.'

Yet it was not just the resilience and character of the British people that had created this singular absence of a black market; Woolton was resolute that some of the credit should go to himself. He remembered very clearly his thinking at the time. There would always be criminals, there would always be unscrupulous foreigners – both breeds not at one with British values – and so he would have to set up a system of harsh penalties that would deter those most insistent on profiteering illegally from the scarcity of supplies and the rigidity of rationing. He was not worried about small-scale, petty offending; the housewife who got an extra ration from a butcher who had taken a shine to this young woman whose husband was away at war, the boys selling a few apples scrumped from an orchard.

'What mattered,' resolved Woolton, 'was to be sure that there could not be a "market".' And so he would put in place such measures as to prevent that. 'Now and again a combination of people – very often people who had hailed from other countries and [who had] not got accustomed to the British way of life – made such efforts,' he wrote. He would stamp on such villains with punitive legislation, encouraging Home Secretary Herbert Morrison to increase penalties for black market offences. Jail sentences would be dished out and fines paid that amounted to three times the value of the capital involved in the dodgy transaction.

Judges would relish the power Woolton's special legislative orders would give them. 'The penalties for infringement of the food regulations were literally ruinous for the people convicted of breaking the law,' he said, 'and the consequence was that, however great the temptation to make money in this illicit manner might have been, it became so perilous an occupation that few indeed dared to embark on it – and most of those who did so subsequently had plenty of time for reflection, away from temptation.'

If you crossed Woolton you were going down. And alongside his fines and threats of incarceration was a PR plan that, whenever possible, he would front. He would go on the radio, would make speeches, would pen articles, ensuring that the British public would come to understand that his ration system was both fair and correct.

As he wrote, he took great pleasure in recounting the time when an Ambassador to one friendly allied nation had once asked his wife: 'How does your husband account for the fact that there is so little black market in this country?' The man had, reflected Woolton, 'been here a long time, but he had not learned to understand the British character, for the answer to that question was because the British public disapproves of black markets.' And that was that.

But what Woolton failed to mention, either deliberately or through ignorance, was another side to the story.

Take Billy Hill, for example. Hill was a dapper gangster from London's Seven Dials, by Covent Garden, an area police once described as having more pickpockets per square yard than anywhere else in the world. In the late twentieth century it became a fashionable place; but in the 1940s it was an area of destitution, crime and general low life. Hill would become a leading figure of the wartime underworld, and later a notorious gangster operating in everything from smuggling and protection rackets to forgery and ostentatious robberies.

Within weeks of rationing being introduced, Hill, born in 1911, was exploiting the need that rationing threw up. He had spells in prison throughout his life and, after the war, was a prosperous individual. Hill talked proudly of the war years decades later to his biographer, Wensley Clarkson: 'So that big, wide, handsome and, oh, so profitable black market walked into our ever open arms,' he said. 'Some day someone should write a treatise on Britain's wartime black market. It was the most fantastic side of civilian life in wartime. Make no mistake. It cost Britain millions of pounds. I didn't merely make use of the black market. I fed it.'

Convinced his call-up papers would arrive at his home in Camden Town sooner or later, he got busy the moment war broke out to take advantage of a nation's security services focusing on an enemy rather further afield. Amid rumours that he had bribed his way out of the forces, no papers ever arrived, although in his autobiography he insisted he was as baffled as anyone as to why he was never called up.

He quickly realised that storage depots were easy pickings and started stealing and selling whatever he could. 'Four or five smash 'n' grab raids in a week were nothing unusual for Hill's mob,' wrote his biographer Wensley Clarkson in his book, *Billy Hill – Godfather of London*. He also developed a nice line in robbing post offices. When he wasn't selling the likes of fur coats, stolen from warehouses free of alarms or guards and always under the cover of darkness thanks to blackouts, he was selling whisky; with supplies scarce there were numerous small-time illegal distilleries selling dangerously unsavoury spirits. Hill was disdainful of this hooch and realised there was a market for the genuine article. 'I liked to think that if I was crooked, at least I was bent in an honest way,' he reflected many years later. 'I sold only real whisky. Good stuff at that.'

So with his gang he identified and raided facilities that stored whisky, later selling barrels for £500 each. There seemed to be no shortage of people willing to pay a lively price. Similarly he got hold of and sold sausage skins to butchers, and in the early years of the war was making between £300 and £400 a week from his trading. He managed to evade the law even if he did occasionally drink with those seeking to catch him. One night Scotland Yard's chief inspector Peter Beveridge called into Hill's local pub in Camden. 'Make the most of it while you can because when I feel your collar, you're going to stay nicked for a long time,' he told the criminal. 'Well, guv'nor,' replied Hill, 'you can't blame me for everything. I've got to earn, and you've got to catch. What you havin'?'

He was incarcerated in Chelmsford Prison in 1940 after a jewellery heist, but served barely twelve months, returning to his wife Aggie back home in Camden Town who, he noted admiringly, had been pretty diligent herself in his absence. Her kitchen was filled with fresh eggs and butter and a number of other things the ration card wouldn't have permitted.

He quickly returned to what he casually described as his 'bread and butter' – the food and drink black market – and also started hitting sub-post offices again where he stole cash as well as stamps and money orders. Blacked-out windows added to the ease of the jobs, as it meant that passing police patrols couldn't see the criminals working inside with their flashlights. Hill then rented a large barn near a big, yet remote, air base at Bovingdon in Hertfordshire, where he stashed everything that was in short supply during the war years: whisky, clothes, towels, bed sheets, furniture, food, silk, tobacco, jewellery and petrol. It was to the barn that Hill and his gang would ferry unopened safes where they could safely, out of earshot, blow off the doors.

By the time war ended, Hill was in Dartmoor prison having been grabbed by the police while escaping from a botched job knocking a postmaster on the head in Islington. But the end of the war didn't mean the end of the black market. Rationing would continue until 1954 and many goods remained in short supply. It was a time, wrote Clarkson, when 'black marketeers scoured the countryside, buying up broken-down horses which would later be served up as choice rump steak in high-class establishments.'

Of course Billy Hill was not operating alone. The onset of war and implementation of rationing saw a surge of black market operations. In 1939 just twenty people were convicted of black market offences, described technically as 'Persons found guilty of offences against the defence regulations.' In 1941 the figure was 13,580, in 1942 the number leapt to 30,309.

They were figures that caused alarm among those who constantly niggled at Lord Woolton and his ministry, namely peers in the House of Lords. On 15 July 1941 Viscount Dawson of Penn, the King's doctor and regular critic of the minister, accused Woolton of neglecting the issue. Lord Dawson spoke of his disquiet at discovering that so many people engaged in black market activity.

'This sort of thing going on in this country must cause us a great deal of disquietude and alarm, because it is un-British that in a time of crisis anyone should endeavour to evade the regulations and restrictions,' he said. Dawson likened it to a disease and 'moreover, a very infectious disease, because when one section of the community discovers that sums of money have been made by flouting these food restrictions and regulations, it means that others are tempted to do likewise.'

He then socked it to Woolton. 'One cannot help feeling that this foul growth should have been nipped in the bud by the Minister of Food when he discovered that huge profits were being made in this way,' he said. 'He ought to have put his foot down at once and prevented the disease from spreading.' Woolton felt that he had put a stop to such antics with his Standstill Order of 6 January 1941.

Later that year, in May, he wrote of the stern briefing he gave to those officials who were responsible for catching those who profited from rationing. 'I had our Enforcement Officers at a meeting in the ministry and told them we must get this black racketeering stopped.' On 13 June he decided to reprimand the whole nation via BBC radio. 'I broadcast to the people of Britain,' he wrote that evening. 'I told them it wasn't any use them getting all worked up about the newspaper stories of profiteering whilst they themselves helped the profiteer to live by buying his goods.'

In fact the evidence points to there being rather fewer Billy Hills and rather more of what has been termed the grey market. According to historian Ina Zweiniger-Bargielowska, whose book *Austerity in Britain* analysed rationing, controls and consumption during the Second World War, 'There was no large-scale organised black market in Britain.' Instead, she wrote, 'It operated through widespread infringement of the regulations by producers, distributors, and retailers, ultimately sustained by public demand.' Hence Lord Woolton's admonishing of the general populace.

To make it quite clear what he meant by the black market he ordered his ministry to print leaflets defining it. Widely distributed and often visible in shops, the pamphlet described the black market as 'attempts to distribute foods in short supply through abnormal or unauthorised channels with the object of securing profit out of all proportion to the services rendered'. Those who worked the black market were 'unscrupulous men' who worked to obtain 'more than their fair share of goods in short supply'. Those who profited were 'the unscrupulous individual, the trader anxious to build up stocks unfairly'. The language was all about right and wrong and fairness. It was a moral issue.

Working to detect illegal trading were enforcers at the Ministry of Food run by a Director of Enforcement. There were regional teams who collaborated with the police, and local food offices tasked with dealing with minor offences by retailers and the public. The efforts were beefed up in the middle of the war after a report by divisional food officers in April 1943 stated that it 'was obvious that many black market operators worked on a national scale and a co-ordinated effort was needed to defeat them'.

Thus the figures for convictions peaking mid-war can be explained by more rigorous enforcement demanded by politicians such as Woolton, and the fact that recorded crime in general dramatically increased during that period. Some ten years later, criminologists, making a study of the 1940s, pointed to how society erred towards wrongdoing during the war. Family ties were loosened, consumer goods were scarce, bombed-out houses made it simpler for looters, supplies of guns and ammunition were easy to come by and deserters, who lived on the fringes of society without official documents, tended towards criminality. And the general lack of trained police officers and other officials who were abroad fighting meant that law-breakers could often get away with it.

As for the grey market, it was widespread. Katherine Knight recorded some voices for her book *Rationing in the Second World War* which included the following:

'We never had anything extra – except sugar. Don't quite know where it came from, but my mother kept it in the airing cupboard.'

'My father came back from the farm with a big bit of butter about once a fortnight.'

'My father was a Church Warden but we once had a whole side of bacon from his cousin in the country.'

Likewise Lizzie Collingham's *The Taste of War* records a conversation between Vera Hodgson and her grocer in February 1941. 'Went for my bacon ration and while he was cutting it had a word with the man about the Cubic Inch of cheese. He got rid of the other customers and then whispered: "Wait a mo." I found half a pound of cheese being thrust into my bag with great secrecy and speed.' It was nothing more than normal civilian behaviour, it was just that war and rationing had made it an infringement if not actually a crime.

Meanwhile food producers themselves employed a variety of tricks to enable them to keep back food for themselves, or others in their communities, if not for actual illegal profiteering. Farmers could simply fail to register a small fraction of their livestock — an animal here and there — or those at the slaughterhouse could weigh a carcass with its head on, so that the equivalent of the weight of that head could be kept back for an illegal sale.

Yet those members of the public who took a little extra here and there did think that Lord Woolton overstated the case when he denied that a significant black market was operating. In June 1943 a Gallup poll of the British public showed that 72 per cent thought that Woolton was exaggerated in his view that this market was virtually non-existent. Still Woolton claimed there was massive public hostility to the black market – through speeches and via guilt-inducing posters. One advertisement he published, for example, on 14 September 1941 – across the country in national and regional newspapers – featured an illustration of an eyeglass and spoke directly to the readers: 'Ask yourself these 5 questions,' it said in tones of George Orwell's ever-watchful Big Brother. 'Do you ever try to get more than your ration? Or accept more if offered?' It's unlikely that a wave of guilt swept across the nation.

Yet his constant insistence that the public was hostile to the black market was a successful piece of propaganda. And it came hand in hand with very heavy penalties; Woolton relished every time he got legislation through that inflicted harsher punishments on illegal trading. On 17 December 1942 he primed a peer in the House of Lords to ask a question about penalties for those people 'trafficking in the black market', noting in his diary that this enabled him to announce that, 'in addition to the present maximum penalty of £100, people can be fined three times the value of the goods involved in the transaction or three times the price at which they were offered, even if the transaction did not eventually materialise.'

He was pleased with the response to his words. 'The press took up the story very well,' he wrote, 'and it rests with the magistrates to enforce the penalties. The newspapers and the public have consistently blamed me for not making the punishment fit the crime: they forget that I am powerless to enforce the law.'

He was similarly charged up the following February. The harshest month was as grim as it could be, with freezing temperatures and snow on the ground that did not exactly leave the capital looking like a winter wonderland. 'London has had a very heavy snowfall and it is so cold that everybody looks miserable,' Woolton wrote. 'I've never seen a town look so dirty as London does with dirty half-melted snow piled in the streets. There are few men to clean them, and even the shopkeepers seem to be so shorthanded that they do not clean in the front of their shops.'

But Woolton had a tonic that would at least warm his cockles. This time he had the Billy Hills of the black market in his sights, or at any rate those of his ilk who had bank accounts.

He organised a meeting with Sir Eric Gore-Brown, a partner of the banking firm Glyn Mills & Co., a private bank that dated back to the 18th century and had been sold to the Bank of Scotland. Sir Eric was a distinguished soldier and was well respected in the banking industry. 'I want him to persuade the banks to help us in tracing the people who operate the black market,' wrote Woolton.

Sir Eric was, said Woolton, 'a modest and delightful fellow' and the moustachioed, round-spectacled city gent took his seat in Woolton's office.

'The banks must have, in the operation of their business, knowledge of people who are using large amounts of cash, instead of cheques, with which to conduct business,' Woolton asserted. 'The black market is operated on a cash basis, and if we could be supplied with the names of the firms who are handling large amounts of cash and notes, we might get on the track of some of the larger operators.'

This government intrusion into the confidentiality of private bank accounts was met with simply a stalling nod from

Sir Eric. He said he would look into the matter. But there is no record of him making any progress, nor of Woolton having further meetings on the subject.

A fortnight later he had another go, this time pushing through a harsh law that delivered a maximum sentence of fourteen years' penal servitude for black market trading. 'People will think twice about continuing their practice,' he muttered to himself as he penned his diary on the evening of 2 March having announced the measure that day.

Although when he made tough announcements it didn't always please Winston Churchill. Back in February 1941 Woolton had issued new regulations for hotels, culinary establishments and canteens. The *Evening Standard* focused on the penalties Woolton announced with a headline that spoke of 'Imprisonment or fine' and talked of 'Prison if you eat meat or fish, egg or cheese.' 'The PM was furious,' Maud wrote in her diary, 'and sent a "snorter" to F objecting.'

Woolton recorded the details of the 'snorter' in his diary. 'I could have wished that this class of announcement should be referred to the Cabinet before it was made public,' he recorded Churchill as writing.

'F got annoyed,' commented Maud, 'and sent a similar one back indicating that the person to grumble at was the Editor of the ES. The PM cannot bear these food restrictions!!'

Churchill was also irritated at the press coverage Woolton had generated on 18 February, after he had made a speech in the House of Lords 'warning the country that the effects of submarine and air attacks would inevitably mean restrictions on food.' The speech, he noted in his diary, 'had a very good press'. There had been a leader in *The Times* and, wrote

Woolton, 'several members of the government congratulated me on my courage in making it.'

But, just as he was savouring his good PR, 'The Prime Minister sent for me at night, and warned me against the dangers of being drawn into political rationing.'

Then on 2 March Churchill reprimanded him again. 'Perhaps before you have any other important announcements to make, you will consult the Cabinet, and then the Minister for Information who will be able to make sure the right emphasis is put on the orders before the news is given to the newspapers,' he wrote, as Woolton recorded in his diary.

Woolton reflected on such admonishments saying: 'I always felt like a little boy when the Prime Minister used to reprove me for having taken action without consulting either him or the Cabinet, and I had to acknowledge my error and faithfully promise that I would try not to do it again.'

Ten weeks later on 12 March and the pair met again. They discussed food supplies. 'He was in great form,' wrote Woolton, 'and when he had finished making a general attack on me, he said "I have said what I wanted to say: now you go for me" – which I did but in the same mood. I fortunately knew the answers to everything that he had raised, and was able to assure him that everything he had proposed had already been done months ago. It was a good meeting, and it didn't do him any harm to know that his Food Minister neither resented attacks, nor wilted under them.'

Woolton now had in place severe punishments: fines at three times the value of the goods traded, £500 fines for some offences (bear in mind that the average male wage was just over £6 per week) plus incarceration; any non-payment would lead to a bankruptcy order on the culprit's business.

However, Woolton's problem in tackling the bigwigs was that they didn't rely solely on food profiteering. The likes of Billy Hill were into everything from petrol to cigarettes, so they had money to fund fines and could diversify away from food if they guessed their collars were about to be felt. But when it came to controlling the black market in alcohol, Woolton was less concerned. There was a short-age of whisky, for example, not surprisingly and Woolton acknowledged that this enabled those who had it and were selling it to do rather well. 'Large profits are being made by the sale of black market spirits,' he wrote in November 1941. But, he added: 'Personally I am not interested: if people like to be swindled into paying these extortionate prices for spirits, which are totally unnecessary as a luxury, I should let them be swindled.' His department, he felt, had better things to do. 'I see no reason for a government with a war of this nature on its hands spending its time trying to protect people who are foolish enough to pay "through the nose" for liquor.'

Woolton's own tastes and stomach issues meant he was naturally contemptuous of what he saw as luxury foods and alcohol. But he must have ultimately understood that if the housewife was to be thrifty as she sought to care for her family, she might also seek a little extra here or there. And while he liked to claim that it was the British character that lessened the extent of black market trading, it probably has more to do with the fact that Woolton and his ministry held a very tight control over the production and distribution of food. At every stage there was tough enforcement, so criminals actually found it quite hard to get a look in.

Yet Woolton's punitive views were not quite as strong as those of the Paymaster General, Sir William Jowitt. While Woolton was arguing for a maximum fourteen-year term, Sir William announced in a speech he gave at his former constituency Ashton-Under-Lyne, the market town in Greater Manchester, that that those who indulged in black market practices ought to be brought before a war court and then, if found guilty, be sentenced to death before a firing squad.

Sir William's entry into the debate came after a new swindle came to light that month involving the substitution of foods in cans, packages and bottles. The fake food concerned dodgy surrogates for the likes of eggs, onions, oranges and milk. A newswire story on 26 February 1942, revealed that 'egg substitutes were 90 per cent wheat flour with the addition of dye and gum.' It reported a product that described itself as a 'perfect substitute for lemons' and 'contained only citric acid and starch', while 'one common milk substitute was composed of flour, salt and sweetening.' The same thing was happening with other household goods with an item described as mascara being nothing but shoe polish and some rouge-coloured paint powder. The CP cable wire service reported that 'Manufacturers of many of these items have been arrested.'

Sir William's remarks were welcomed by several newspapers who argued that, if sailors had risked their lives in bringing cargo in from overseas, then those who stole it should lose theirs. The same newswire story mentioned the following occurrences: '240 tonnes of molasses stolen from a Thames wharf went into the black market; 144 cartons of tomato puree, stolen from a bombed warehouse, were sold for more than three times the controlled price; 18,000 eggs and 50,000 chickens were sold above the maximum price.'

Yet Sir William's part in the debate was quickly curtailed when a little bit of black market shenanigans was discovered on his own doorstep. Woolton merrily recorded it in his diary: 'it transpired that he had a country estate and has been receiving feedings stuffs above the ration from supplies that had been stolen.' Sir William was prosecuted later that year for buying animal feed without the appropriate coupons for his farm in Kent. He had been zealous in the prosecution of exactly such offences, but in court claimed that he employed a bailiff to run the farm and had no knowledge that the offence was being committed. The court accepted his explanation and he got away with it. And so, by and large, did Billy Hill.

11

REGULATION AND AUSTERITY

On 21 March 1941 Woolton was summoned to Chequers, the Prime Minister's rural retreat in Buckinghamshire.

Chequers, a well as being a haven from bomb-torn London, was a refuge from the ration. Churchill, disparaging of the system, thinking it over-complicated and lacking a bit of common sense, liked to base his views on first-hand experience. He had written to Woolton a few days earlier – on 2 March – complaining about a new system of regulating foodstuffs, whereby consumers had to choose between fish or meat. 'I should have though that an exhortation not to leave anything on the plate, and to take small portions, with, if necessary, a second helping, would be a wise step.'

For Woolton such advice was just Churchillian eccentricity. But clearly that was how Churchill managed his own personal ration. He cleared his plate and then had a second helping if he felt like one. After all there was no lack of food at Chequers or 10 Downing Street. Churchill told his personal staff to write to the Ministry of Food; but not to Woolton. The letters, containing requests for extra ration books, points or whatever was needed, would always be addressed to more junior minions who would not query demands from the Prime Minister.

For example, on 24 June 1940 Churchill's private secretary John Martin wrote to one R. P. Harvey at the ministry to say: 'Both at Chequers and at No 10 Downing Street the rationing restrictions make it very difficult to entertain officially to the extent which the Prime Minister finds necessary. Mr Churchill has asked if an arrangement could be made whereby in both instances extra rations could be supplied to cover official guests.'

Likewise in the same month there was a letter from the Downing Street cook, Georgina Landemere, asking for extra ration books. Other staff, such as Kathleen Hill or Elizabeth Layton – assistant private secretaries – wrote frequently during the course of the war to say they had 'exhausted' their supplies and to ask for extra coupons for meat and cooking fats and tea as well as cheese and butter vouchers. One private secretary wrote to the Army & Navy Store in London asking for extra sugar for 'bottling' at Chequers. Similarly those who had to entertain Churchill – if he was due for a weekend house party, for example, or just coming for lunch – would write to the Ministry of Food.

On 14 November 1940 John Martin put in another request, this time for extra coupons for the chef at Ditchley Park, in Oxfordshire (where Churchill often stayed and sometimes held important meetings).

There is also a record of a telephone conversation between Martin and a ministry official on 20 November 1940, in which the official confirmed that there would be 'no difficulty' in using special diplomatic food coupons at places, other than Chequers, where the Prime Minister might spend his weekends. While Britain had to tighten its belt, it seems Churchill merely loosened his.

But Woolton would not raise his eyebrows at the food on offer at Chequers that evening in March 1941. He had more pressing arguments to make and, not having suffered a bout of illness for some time, rather relished the prospect of a decent dinner. He detailed the events of the night in his diary.

He was told to dress appropriately for it, in black tie and dinner jacket. Churchill himself, who had spent much of the afternoon and evening asleep, shunned that garb, coming downstairs instead in that 1940s equivalent of the onesie, his blue siren suit. Woolton was hungry and they tucked into fish and then cold, rare beef.

Woolton had two helpings. 'Because I actually live on the rations I prescribe for the country I am hungry,' he said to Churchill and his fellow guest Robert Hudson, the Conservative Minister of Agriculture, as he popped another pile of reddish, thinly cut beef onto his plate. 'I think it's important that I get more meat.'

'You're too much like a dictator,' Churchill scoffed, 'you keep wanting to send people to prison.' It had not escaped the Prime Minister's notice that Woolton had administered harsh penalties and threatened prison to those who made minor domestic errors. Just a month earlier, on 25 February, Churchill had written to Woolton saying: 'I must say I do not like all this rather dictatorial publicity. I do not think anyone ought to be sent to prison merely for making mistakes.'

So for the rest of the evening Churchill referred to Woolton as 'General Goering'. After dinner the PM put on some very loud marching music. 'This music does us good,' he yelled above the din of the gramophone record, as he started marching about the room. 'We must have lightness in life as well as food and this music stirs the blood.'

Amid the crashing symbols, drums and bagpipes, Churchill received the news, from a member of staff who seemed quite used to the scene, that two German battleships, the *Scharnhorst* and the *Gneisenau*, were steaming towards the French port of Brest, their guns loaded, ready and threatening. Churchill got on the telephone to Bomber Command and, as the marching tune ploughed on, ordered them to go and bomb the ships. 'We saw the War Lord in action,' wrote Woolton, 'and it was very good action too.'

Come midnight, Churchill suggested they get to work discussing the country's slaughter policy for cattle. Two hours later and they were discussing the issue of ships. 'You have taken my ships that were bringing food into this country and sent them to the Middle East without any reference to the consequences to the food position,' Woolton complained. 'I must have some of them back.'

'It was 2.30 in the morning,' wrote Woolton, and Churchill, having put on another record, 'resumed his parade around the room and told me he would give me 2 million tons of extra shipping.'

'That is only one half of what I need,' Woolton said, almost shouting to be heard above the music.

'So I will give you some refrigerated tonnage to bring in meat,' Churchill shouted back, pausing and standing bolt upright by the fireplace. 'But I want another 2 million tons in addition to that,' said Woolton. 'You're being difficult,' Churchill told him. 'We should go to bed.' Churchill then walked him to his room and told him to look him up before he left in the morning.

'I will,' said Woolton. 'But I shall tell you now that I need 15 million tons of shipping,' and in saying that he presented a formal note of his demand. Churchill, says Woolton, 'was not too pleased, but accepted it and a few days later sent out a directive saying that I was to have what I wanted.'

As Woolton closed the door of his bedroom, he breathed a sigh of relief at the prospect of a few hours of peace, privacy and some sleep. He lay in bed that night pondering on the events of that evening: the marching music, Churchill ordering British planes to rally to the cause and bomb those German ships, his extraordinary suit, those rare cuts of beef. As he drifted to sleep he was sure he could hear the Prime Minister barking out more orders somewhere in the house.

'He works in his own way,' Woolton reflected, 'and consequently it isn't easy to work with him but he continues to be perpetually animating.'

Britain Eats Out

Some five days later, in late March of 1941, *The Times* reported the news of 'British Restaurants In Over 100 Towns.' A banner headline on the same story also announced: 'Emergency Centres Renamed'.

Woolton had been working on a scheme to launch some 10,000 state-run cafes. These were not-for-profit eating centres and Woolton's request to Churchill to approve the plan had not been one he expected to have any difficulty with. The Prime Minister did indeed give Woolton the go-ahead, but in a memo he stipulated one proviso: Woolton must abandon his plan to call them 'Communal Feeding Centres'. 'It is an odious expression, suggestive of Communism and the workhouse', he wrote. 'I suggest you call them British Restaurants. Everybody associates the word "restaurant" with a good meal.'

Woolton didn't argue, made a press announcement and *The Times* duly reported that '"communal feeding centres" is too cold and dreary a name for the new eating houses for all the people which are being started all over the country.'

Woolton also wrote to local authorities around the country, asking that they support his plan for the restaurants. Diners would not have to flash their ration books and, he said, 'If every man, woman and child could be sure of obtaining at least one hot, nourishing meal a day at a price all could afford we should be sure of the nation's health and strength during the war.'

In fact, 79 million meals a week were eaten by civilians outside their homes in May 1941 with the figure rising to 170 million by December 1944, equivalent to an average of some four meals a week for every man, woman and child. These British Restaurants were opened across the country, often officially by Lord Woolton, and frequently in his absence by his wife Maud, something she mentions in her diary. 'I can't speak with authority,' Maud wrote, 'the Ministry of

Food wanted to take responsibility for what I might say and I don't want to talk about F all the time. However, I generally manage to say something fairly innocuous without being too dull.'

The Ministry of Food came across some apathy from boroughs unaffected by air raids, and there was some hostility from commercial caterers worried about the detrimental affects to their business from this subsidised dining. But while Woolton didn't manage his ambition of 10,000 cafes, by 1943 there were 2,160, serving 650,000 midday meals as well as breakfasts and suppers. Most were in areas not served by factory canteens, and often located in town and village halls, serving food consisting of meat, fish, vegetables, soups, puddings, tea and coffee. One such establishment in Liverpool, the Byrom Street Restaurant, sold main courses such as fish pie, beef and dumplings or minced beef with carrots and parsnips, as well as currant or milk pudding. Main courses cost 6d (around £2 in today's money), soup 1d and puddings 3d. Tea, coffee or cocoa was priced at 1d.

There was also a British Restaurant that the Ministry of Food and locals used in Colwyn Bay. The establishment, seating 150 people, opened on 10 January 1942 and was located in the Congregational Church Lecture Theatre on Sea View Road. There, the ministry's civil servants could get a shilling lunch; for that, you could get soup, roast lamb, vegetables, a pudding and a cup of tea of coffee. To ensure no one left carrying any of the cutlery or crockery it was all stamped 'Colwyn Bay British Restaurant'.

Surveys done during the war tended to give these restaurants a reasonable rating although they were not to everyone's taste. One diner, Frances Partridge, a Bloomsbury group writer and more regular habitué of London's The Ivy, wrote of her visit to a British Restaurant in Swindon: 'a huge elephant house, where thousands of human beings were eating, as we did, an enormous all-beige meal, starting with beige soup thickened to the consistency of paste, followed by beige mince full of lumps and garnished with beige beans and a few beige potatoes, thin beige apple stew and a sort of skilly [thin porridge]. Very satisfying and crushing, and calling up a vision of our future Planned World, all beige also ...'

Woolton would, of course, have eagerly dismissed such pompous scribblings. He was happy that these restaurants, in his own words, 'served an urgent need'; people were having their tummies filled, whatever the colour of the food. Not that such places were always above criticism; he often noted, privately, instances of poor cooking, particularly for workers. On 15 October 1942 he had inspected a factory canteen newly opened at the Port of London. 'It is a first class affair from a structural point of view,' he wrote, 'but I thought it shared the usual fault of these places that the food was badly cooked. I'm not a bit convinced that they are as good as they ought to be. To spoil food in the cooking in these days of scarcity is a social crime.'

It was an unusual fact of the Second World War that a very large number of people stopped eating meals in their own homes – and not just because they had been bombed. As John Burnett, author of *England Eats Out*, wrote, 'One of the strange ironies of the Second World War is that more people ate out than ever before and, probably never again, until the most recent years.'

But while the general populace lived with rationing and had regular hot meals in such places as communal halls, it wasn't a picture of unadulterated austerity. Smart independent restaurants or those in halls still operated, albeit with somewhat straitened menus. With Woolton as head of the Ministry of Food however, the world of gastronomy could not count on support from his department; Woolton was not a fan of anything that even nodded to the concept of richness.

On Thursday 15 October 1942, for example, he was found sitting at his desk looking distinctly off colour, feeling in turns sick, guilty, remorseful and cross. And he was tired; he hadn't slept well, his weak constitution having been tested beyond measure. Even his treasured pipe tobacco tasted off.

Lunch the day before, to which he had taken Maud, had been at the Russian Embassy, a grand, gothic building in the smart and exclusive confines of Kensington Palace Gardens. There had been course after course, endless drinks and, as he ploughed his way through the meal, he wondered half-joking if the whole event was some kind of set-up. Perhaps word had gone around diplomatic circles that the current Minister of Food disdained ostentation and a few mischievous individuals determined to make light of it. When he and his wife were finally able to leave the lunch and were putting on their coats, the American Ambassador had turned to Maud and said sarcastically: 'I hope your husband appreciates the austerity under which we ambassadors live.'

The Wooltons were not amused; Maud forever fussed about her husband's delicate constitution, and this lunch was decidedly unhelpful. Indeed, Woolton's groaning stomach had deterred him from returning to the office; he'd gone home instead and straight to bed. He hadn't even had the strength to write his diary.

The following morning at his Portman Square office he, somewhat painfully, recorded the details of the previous day's gastronomic adventure. 'We had lobster and vodka – I tried to pass on both – followed by grouse with potatoes and a salad followed by a soufflé, by cheese straws as a savoury, grapes and coffee: cigars and four different sorts of liqueurs, and of course there had been a choice of two wines.' He called his secretary into his office and demanded he scrutinise the schedule. He didn't want to see the inside of an embassy or a smart restaurant for at least the next forty-eight hours.

The previous day's banquet aside, he was simply not a fan of fancy dining establishments. They served their purpose when it came to entertaining influential newspaper barons, or if he was seeking to persuade a political ally or enemy, but his dislike of large and long lunches or dinners was not a pose for the benefit of the press. He was certainly known by the head waiters of places such as L'Escargot, and the dining rooms of the Savoy or Claridge's, but anything too fussy and rich and he regretted it badly during the subsequent hours, days even. And as Minister of Food he shuddered when he saw anything that came close to waste.

On 22 May 1940, addressing a lunch attended by leading British caterers, he touched on this subject. 'If you knew the amount of time, trouble and anxiety that some of us have gone through to secure the bread supply,' he said, 'you would know what feelings are when I see a waiter, clearing a table, take a roll of bread that has not been eaten and put it in an ash-tray.'

Yet while many might have expected him to put smart restaurants in the firing line – after all he had all but banned ice-cream and jam – he was reluctant to interfere with this field of private enterprise. 'The question was repeatedly raised as to whether hotel and other restaurants should not be closed down during war-time on the grounds that they constituted "luxury feeding". This was not right: people needed relaxation,' he argued. 'I said I did not defend luxurious living, but if I could give to the hard-working people of this country – and those returning for brief periods from overseas – something of happiness, it would be a contribution to national work.'

But Woolton wanted to vanquish any perceptions that smart restaurants continued to operate normally, feeding their customers with whatever they wanted. 'There were the restaurants, and particularly the luxurious ones, which were popularly supposed to have all the food their clientele demanded,' he wrote. 'It was not true: but it was a political issue which, with all the egalitarianism of rationing, could not be ignored.'

There were agitators, for example, such as the Stepney Young Communist League who, on the evening of 14 September 1941, marched down the Embankment towards the Savoy, encouraged by their beloved *Daily Worker* newspaper. 'If you live in the Savoy Hotel you are called by telephone when the sirens sound and then tucked into bed by servants in a luxury bomb-proof shelter,' went one editorial. 'The people must act,' it demanded. So the group trooped to the front door of the hotel and made it inside the lobby, where a strange thing then happened. According to one hotel guest, Constantine Fitz-Gibbon, who witnessed the scene: 'The demonstrators were so awed by the Chaldean splendours of the hotel that they soon forgot to shout their slogans.' The hotel staff breathed a sigh of relief as the gathering was ushered out and dispersed. The establishment did not want untoward publicity; it retained much of its smart clientele and certain pre-rationing standards in the restaurant, and the last thing it needed was any public scrutiny.

As a parry to this threat, the hotel decided to release a set of photographs that showed business as usual in the face of war. Pictures showed sandbags at the front of the hotel, a diminished-looking dining room and off-duty soldiers dining modestly.

Woolton did not want to curtail absolutely the operations of smart restaurants because, while conspicious consumption would not go down well with the British public, the message that one could still eat well in the capital's best dining rooms had its uses in the face of the enemy. As Matthew Sweet wrote in his book, *The West End Front*, 'If Hitler could not disrupt the business of dinner, then what chance did he have against shipping or heavy industry.'

Sweet also mused on the PR tightrope that such establishments walked; normality in London's grand hotels being perceived as 'proof that all were not equal under fire'. If the likes of smart restaurants put out the message that normal service had resumed, 'it represented something less attractive,' he wrote: 'the tenacity of privilege during wartime.'

Woolton though wanted restaurants to behave modestly,

telling the *Daily Express* on 4 July 1940 that he wished to cut out 'ostentatious eating'. At a press conference in Manchester the following day he said, 'We are going to have to be content to live a harder life gastronomically,' but, he added, 'We shall not be the worse off for it.' So Woolton never threated restaurants with closure – instead he hit them with regulations.

Throughout the war there came a stream of orders from the Ministry of Food. Meat allocations to commercial caterers were restricted, restaurants were first encouraged to voluntarily restrict meals to one main course before being ordered to limit it to one main dish of meat, fish, poultry, game, eggs or cheese (soup didn't count). Icing sugar was banned, as was the manufacture of cream, not more than a twelfth of an ounce of butter could be served with a meal, the use of milk in cakes, biscuits and ice cream was banned, as was white flour and white bread, and in September 1942 the manufacture of ice cream itself was prohibited.

It was the limitation on meat and fish, and the disappearance of butter and cream, that most vexed the chefs, although it wasn't just their ingenuity that would be tested. As the home cook used a little creative cunning, so too did regular restaurant-goers, who with a nod and a wink from the manager could get around some of the regulations. At the Savoy, for example, while Crêpe Suzette fell foul of the rules, a diner could order a pancake then ask separately for some brandy and a box of matches, before flambéing the dessert themselves at the table.

Chefs, meanwhile, added a little magic to their meagre offerings by dressing them up in French on the menu. 'Le rable de lièvre à la crème' was a saddle of hare in a cream-less white wine sauce at the Savoy; Madame Prunier's, in St James's, offered 'Moules Chowder' with mussels replacing the American clams and 'Croquettes de Pommes Land Girl', which was simply mashed potato with dried egg powder. The Royal Court Hotel had 'Saumon Florentin' (tinned salmon with spinach), while Simpson's-in-the-Strand played a straight English bat, as ever, offering a 'Simpson's Cream Spam Casserole' (potatoes, tomatoes and Spam) as well as 'Simpson's Spam Pancakes', a dish that merits no explanation. The case was the same for restaurants across Britain. At the Bristol Grill in the centre of that city, for example, the menu offered 'Blancmange Vanois', or jelly as they called it in the kitchen.

Yet many chefs also took advantage of the fact that seem-ingly up-market delicacies such as lobster, shellfish, hare and game were not rationed. The wealthy clientele of the grander hotel restaurants were known to check in with a suitcase in one hand and a brace of pheasant, a whole salmon or a haunch of venison culled from their own estate in the other.

The Grosvenor House restaurant offered game in the form of 'Rabbit Campagnade' and many menus featured wood-cock. The Savoy also served roast kid and pigeon pie, which became so ubiquitous that Nancy Mitford named a novel after it. However, actress Jean Kent recalled a date she had one night with the producer Jack M. Warner – son of the film studio founder – at a West End restaurant, where she ordered a dish called 'Chef's Surprise'. 'I should have known better,' she later said. 'When it came it was a puff pastry case with a turnip inside.'

But it was not just the ration that threatened restaurants. The Blitz, between September 1940 and May 1941, made many diners fearful of venturing out. The Savoy was bombed three times, for example, although its mid-war refurbishment came with added attractions. The River Room's roof was re-enforced and favoured couples were given curtained cubicles where they could dine and then stay the night, a post-dinner late night walk home being deemed too dangerous for favoured customers. The society pages reported the Duke and Duchess of Kent slept one night behind one of these curtained recesses.

The fashionable Regent Palace Hotel in Piccadilly, with its Grill Room and cocktail bar, was bombed twice; the Ritz kitchens attempted to cook on radiators after the gas main was damaged by bombs; both the Langham and Cavendish hotels were attacked; and one night at the Café de Paris, as a large crowd of people danced to 'Snakehips' Johnson and his band, a bomb scored a direct hit and killed eighty people.

Yet Lord Woolton would have been irritated had he made some late night forays to some of London's most famous restaurants. One diner at The Ivy in 1940 recalled that the establishment was full of 'prosperous-looking people as usual, all eating a whacking good meal ... and a delicious creamy pudding'. But while that West End haunt was offering smoked salmon, grouse and chocolate mousse in 1942, its menu was looking a little depleted by 1944 with just oysters, some elderly hens and a distinctly average Algerian wine.

Early in the war Sir Henry Channon, the politician and diarist known as Chips Channon, commented on the fact that not everyone seemed to be struggling. He lunched at the Ritz in September 1939 and said the place had become 'fantastically fashionable. Ritzes always thrive in wartime, as we are all cookless,' he wrote. 'Also in wartime the herd instinct rises.' Twelve months later he recorded that, while dining at the Dorchester, he discovered 'half of London [society] there'. On 5 November 1940 he wrote of the same place: 'London lives well. I've never seen more lavishness, more money spent or food consumed than tonight; and the dance floor was packed. There must have been a thousand people.'

When these places weren't cowering from bomb attacks they were also struggling to maintain good levels of service. Many of their experienced waiters, being Austrian, Italian or German, were interned for the duration of the war. Ferrucio Cochis, for example, was the general manager of Claridge's and had worked at the hotel for twenty-one years when he received a letter on 24 April 1940 ordering him to vacate his quarters. The missive was from his employers, on the advice of the government. It wasn't just that he was Italian, though; the British secret service had been advised by US agents that Cochis was in the pay of Rome and alleged that he had, among other things, once bugged the room of a US Under Secretary of State. He was offered a month's pay and, it seems, few staff protested at his departure on account of his ferocious temper.

It was a similar story for Loreto Santarelli, restaurant manager of the Savoy. On 25 June 1940, as trays of high tea were brought to guests in the lobby, two men from Special Branch arrived. They searched his rooms, confiscated his passport and marched him off to a cell in Brixton Prison.

They took two other Italians as well: the assistant banqueting manager, Fortunato Picchi, and his boss Ettore Zavattoni. They were removed, as were so many others, under Defence Regulation 18B, which allowed internment of people if they were suspected of being: 'of hostile origin ... [or] to have been recently concerned in acts prejudicial to the public safety or the defence of the realm.' 'They came,' wrote author Matthew Sweet, 'for waiters and wine butlers and cooks and restaurateurs across London and delivered them, without criminal charge, from hot kitchens and mirrored dining rooms into police cells and holding camps across the country.' Many so-called aliens remained interned until after the war.

Santarelli attended a hearing on 23 October 1940 in front of a committee which decided to revoke the order and free him, while insisting he attend a local police station each week. He returned to the Savoy but his old panache was gone. His hands trembled as he poured drinks, and before he reached the age of sixty he had a heart attack, collapsing and dying on the soft rich carpet of the hotel one morning before the war was over.

Having defended the private operations of restaurants, Woolton also found himself having to shield another British passion: beer. On 12 May 1942 Woolton had to attend the House of Lords to listen to an assault on the idea of beer consumption.

Lord Arnold, a former Liberal and Labour politician and a pacifist who had supported appeasement towards Germany, got to his feet to express his disbelief that beer was still being sipped across the nation: 'It is indeed almost incredible,' he said, 'at a time when nearly everything of universal consumption is rationed or is going to be rationed, and when we have fervid appeals on the wireless to do with less of almost everything of general consumption, that nevertheless the consumption of beer should remain, and should have remained throughout the war, at about the highest point for the last ten years.

'Now I come to the Minister of Food himself,' continued Lord Arnold who looked down at Woolton, sat on the benches listening diligently while wearing his favourite non-committal and benign expression. 'Only a few weeks ago, he [Woolton] said: "The time has come for a call for great personal austerity, austerity in living, austerity in working, and austerity in thinking." I do not quite know what that means, but that is what he said, and he went on: "I shall have to give you many opportunities for practising austerity." Yes, my Lords, but there is not to be austerity in beer drinking.'

As Lord Arnold sat down Woolton got to his feet and began his reply. 'I was among those – not with such extreme views as, in my opinion, the noble Lord had – who were very anxious to see some reduction in the amount of excessive drunkenness that there was, particularly among the poorer section of the population, in the slums of this country twenty-five years ago. Then the thing for which all of us begged and prayed was a light drink which the working people of the country might have that would give them more pleasure and satisfaction without the bestiality that followed from excessive drinking. We have got that beer now, people are enjoying it, and it is doing them at any rate very little harm.'

Lord Arnold was not satisfied with the reply: 'We have had the usual unsatisfactory and disappointing reply from the noble Lord. It is exactly what I expected,' he said.

Woolton shrugged his shoulders, said nothing more but did commit his thoughts on Lord Arnold that night to his diary. 'He's a bigoted teetotaller of the worst variety and made a speech that was little short of offensive . . . I suggested to the House that at a time when we were calling for the maximum physical effort from the working man it was unfair to deprive him of his glass of beer if he wanted it.'

Whatever Lord Arnold's alcohol-free tipple might have been it was not something that provided him with longevity. Within two years he was dead.

Press difficulties

Lord Woolton was glad that he somehow managed to retain a sense of humour. On 1 May 1941 he spread on his large desk in Portman Square the morning newspapers and some others from that week. 'Mayday, Mayday,' he muttered.

Woolton considered himself rather of a master of PR, a genius in messaging, a man with a knack for judging the public mood and getting favourable press coverage. It was something that doubtless irritated his Cabinet colleagues but it deeply gratified both himself and his wife Maud. Good editorial helped to justify and sustain the minister in his Cabinet battles, those fights with farmers, the doubting public. But on this Thursday morning he was wondering if he'd lost his touch.

He picked up the *Daily Herald*. 'M.P.s attack Ministry for Muddle,' the headline screamed. The paper commented on the previous day's proceedings in the House of Commons, when a report on the state of food in the country had been presented by his parliamentary secretary, the MP Gwilym Lloyd-George, a younger son of the former Prime Minister David Lloyd George.

Lord Woolton had sat in the peers gallery and listened as MP after MP lined up to attack Major Lloyd George as he attempted to outline how the control system had kept prices down, how bombs and population movement had made food distribution difficult, how emergency feeding centres had been set up and how the ministry had by that time opened 299 'British Restaurants.'

The *Daily Herald* talked of 'seething attacks on the Food Ministry'. One MP, Eleanor Rathbone, said she had 'the carking nagging feeling that it was the poor who had to bear the burden'; another, John Clynes, attacked fish prices and claimed the ministry was allowing traders to profiteer and escape punishment.

Woolton then turned to the *Daily Telegraph*. Here there was an assault of a very different tack. 'Lord Woolton & Lewis's – "No Connection"' read the headline. The paper reported on how the MP for Dumbarton, Adam McKinlay, had alleged that Lewis's had been able to sell cooked meats while its rivals had none. 'Where did they get it?' he had asked. 'Supplies of cooked meat were being diverted from working-class districts throughout the west of Scotland. It is strange that in every industrial part of Britain it is common talk that if you want anything in the food line you should go to Lewis's.' The insinuation was clear. 'I cannot explain to all the public outside that it is only a coincidence that the noble lord who presides over the ministry was at one time connected with Lewis's,' he stated, putting the scurrilous idea out there without himself making a firm allegation.

The paper's front page story continued inside and talked of 'startling allegations against the firm of Lewis's, of which Lord Woolton, the Minister of Food, was formerly chairman'. Woolton read the rebuttal that he had agreed the previous evening. An official had stated: 'Lord Woolton has no connection with Lewis's and has had no connection with them since he took office. Any suggestion that Lewis's either in Glasgow or elsewhere have had special treatment is entirely without foundation.' As he scanned through the piece, his eyes picked up the sub-heads with words such as 'Scandal' and 'No Control'.

He pushed the paper aside and looked at another. It was from the day before yesterday. Political commentator Maurice Webb's weekly column, 'Inside Politics', was headed: 'This Woolton Wobble Can't Go On.' Webb was anticipating the publication of the ministry's report. 'Ominous clouds are gathering over the handsome head of Lord Woolton, Commander-in-Chief on the Food Front,' he wrote. 'They are the sort of clouds which, when seen in the vicinity of a Minister, usually signify that his life in Whitehall is moving inexorably to a close. Not long ago Woolton's stock stood high. Today it is on the slide and worth little.' Woolton had read these words several times and could almost recite them. They cut deep.

'On all sides the critics are in full cry,' Webb continued, 'not least in his own department, where responsible administrators make no secret of their dissatisfaction with the way things are handled on top.' This hurt Woolton particularly as he had gone out of his way to make personal connections across the ministry. But with thousands of them in Colwyn Bay, he would never be able to maintain perfect relations and engender a universal understanding of his methods.

'In Parliament powerful voices are to be raised against "Woolton wobbling" over food distribution,' wrote Webb. And of the coming debate: 'The affair will be anything but a love feast. It will leave Lord Woolton in little doubt as to his present standing with the backbenchers. The people most closely in touch with this food business say that the root cause of much of the Food Minister's tenderness is his trading interest. He has a touching faith in the goodwill of big business, which no amount of obvious huckstering seems to disturb.'

Webb's article wounded Woolton on several fronts. He prided himself on the way he conducted himself, that he worked the ministry as a businessman, that it was his 'trading interest' that meant he did deals that others wouldn't, but that he had secured supplies because of it.

He knew he had political enemies but he didn't like the idea of it being written about and discussed in public. And as for the idea that his career in Whitehall was approaching its final chapter, he felt he still had much to do. He resolved to rise above the criticism. Politics was a rollercoaster ride and while these were bad days for his PR he had had much better ones and hoped he would again.

But the many papers that had so warmly welcomed him to the ministry in the spring of 1940 began to play a rather different tune twelve months later. On 9 April 1941 the *Daily Mail* had the headline: 'Woolton gets "ultimatum"' and it told how poultrymen from Lancashire were furious with the minister. Woolton had decided to lower egg prices that month; the men told the *Daily Mail* that this would force small egg producers out of business, and that 'by July there will be a famine in home-produced eggs.' The result, they argued, would be that 'in Lancashire eggs will disappear from the open markets and be sold "back door".'

The egg saga would disturb much of his summer – and he endured torturous attacks on the subject in the House of Lords. 'My press conference today was confined by the subject of eggs, of which I am heartily sick,' he wrote on 17 June. The afternoon had been spent thrashing out a scheme whereby the country's hens got enough food to produce the number of eggs he had undertaken to control and to work out, how, in his words, 'we could tie the producers so that we got the eggs when they were produced by the hens.' The meeting lasted well into the evening after which, he wrote, 'we all felt that although we were hungry we never wanted to see an egg again.' The following day he had to meet a deputation of egg producers. He wrote wearily after: 'I'm very tired of eggs.'

On 26 April the *Daily Herald*'s headline had been a little more strident: 'Woolton Must Go', it said. The paper reported on a delegate at the Scottish Trades Union Conference in Dunoon calling for 'immediate action' to get rid of Woolton because it alleged his ministry did not administer an equitable supply of meat across the country.

Days later, on 30 April, the *Manchester Evening News* reported: 'A move appears to be afoot to oust Lord Woolton from the Ministry of Food.' Within the month it repeated the story, talking of how 'recently the Food Minister has been criticised from many quarters and in Parliament,' and mentioning 'public dissatisfaction with the distribution of non-rationed foodstuffs'.

Woolton attempted to wrest back control of the agenda a few days later on 7 May when he travelled to Colwyn Bay to make a speech to journalists. It was a pleasant day so he decided to speak outside. 'I addressed a meeting on the pier,' he wrote; 'people were standing eight deep all round the place and apparently a large number of people on the pier to whom my speech was relayed. It was very enthusiastic.' He attacked those who tried to play the system and attempted to thwart the ration. Afterwards, returning to his car, he was accosted by a group of women who told him that they thought someone ought to thank him and so they had come to do so. 'I was told that the women of England were against me,' he said jocularly. 'But I see now that I can be assured that the women of Wales will support me.'

The women laughed and chorused back: 'But we come from Lancashire!' The encounter cheered him, but he was more concerned at how his speech would be portrayed in the press. The *Daily Post* duly reported on Woolton's robust message. 'Food Gamblers And Cheats', the paper wrote; 'Lord Woolton's Final Warning.'

The Post told how Woolton had warned people who thought they could make a little extra profit out of gambling in food that he was 'on their tails'. 'They must remember,' Woolton told the assembled throng, 'that he knew something about commercial life, and he recalled the speculation in turkeys last Christmas, when he suddenly dropped the price when they were high and caused the speculators to lose money,' the paper quoted Woolton as saying. 'I am watching some of them now and this is the last and final warning they will get,' he added. The paper also described how Woolton had been asked by a journalist how it was that such people still managed to exist despite the laws he had put in place. 'They are allowed to exist because they are like worms of the earth. They slither along and go underground, and it is not very easy to catch them all the time, but we are digging for them and we are catching them.' Having used his worm analogy he then paused before adding: 'I apologise to the worm, which, I believe is of some use in agriculture, but I have not found use for the people I am talking about.'

Back in London he relished seeing these quotes. He loved it when he was hitting targets hard and he certainly enjoyed seeing his fruity language in print. But while an opinion poll published later that summer in the *Manchester News Chronicle* gave him an almost 60 per cent approval rating ('Fifty-seven per cent of people replied "Yes" when asked "Do you think Lord Woolton is doing a good job of work as Minister of Food?"'), the press were still on the attack.

Woolton despaired as the coverage that summer of 1941 just seemed to get worse and worse. 'The ministry's press has been bad recently,' he admitted in his diary on 28 May. 'We are being attacked on several scores.'

He was also feeling the strain of real attacks. On 16 April he recorded that he and his wife had lain awake as they listened to hundreds of German planes flying overhead and dropping their deadly parcels across the capital: 'It was a terrible night. 500 machines over, and from 9 at night until 4.30 the next morning they dropped bombs and land-mines and did a great deal of damage from blast. The Strand the next day looked as though it had been put out of business. In the Ministry of Food we had not a window left in the place and most of the walls went.'

The bombs were getting uncomfortably close to his flat at Whitehall Court. 'All this, as the crow flies within a few hundred yards of us,' he wrote. Then on 10 May he recorded: 'We had one of the worst air-raids London has had: bombs were dropped indiscriminately over all districts and it looked as if the whole of London was ablaze. We got a direct hit at Whitehall Court, which started a small fire in our flat, but we managed to put it out ourselves.'

It was, wrote Maud in her diary, 'one of the worst blitzes. It was a terrible night and in the morning London was burning so badly that although I believe it was a lovely day, we never saw the sun because of the pall of smoke.'

At the same time bombs had rained down on Liverpool, causing considerable damage to the headquarters of Lewis's. The couple drove there and, wrote Maud, the building 'looked like the Roman Colosseum. It was roped off and F stepped over the rope to get near and a soldier said: "Have you any business here?" and F looked at him and said: "I had."'

On 17 April he went to work. On the way there, he was impressed to note generally that 'I thought Londoners looked as happy this morning as though they had all the excitement of a cup-tie! There was very little feeling of fear about, but everyone passionately hoping that they would get it [retaliatory action] back that night – which they did.' 'The Ministry of Food office was a sight: I decided that I could not do any real work with the office in that state, so I'd better go round and cheer people up, and so I went round every room and had a word with the staff.' But, he added happily: 'They didn't want cheering – they were all very cheerful.' Then he added a sour note: 'The amazing thing to me was that French, as Head of the Department, had not been round. These civil servants never seem to be taught anything about human relationships.'

Of the many newspaper attacks, Woolton recognised that he was on thin ice when the stories were about profiteering. 'They are on a good story in regard to profiteering – because there's no doubt it exists, as does the black market,' he wrote in his diary on 28 May. Yet he continued to believe it was not particularly widespread. The problem was identifying it and prosecuting. 'It is very difficult to put a finger on it. We are prosecuting when we get the evidence, and the number of prosecutions has increased, but governmental machinery grinds slowly, and unless it's very sure it doesn't grind at all.'

That day he had attended a lunch with the Newspaper Society; a group of owners and editors. 'These fellows,' he wrote of them, 'who are short of sensational news in a war that isn't very active at the moment, pick on profiteering incidents and write them up as evidence that the ministry is sitting back and allowing the public to be exploited.'

At the lunch he changed the message he had planned to give. 'I had intended to talk a news speech to these people,' he wrote, as – doubtless – Sir Henry had also intended, 'but I was feeling very sick about them and I got on to my feet and hit them hard.'

'If you have evidence on which you base your stories it is your duty to the nation to give it to us so that we can stop it and protect the public,' he lectured the gathering. 'And if you haven't got that information then you are doing the public a disservice by agitating them about profiteering.' Woolton glared at the assembled throng. 'So either produce your evidence or stop your perpetual sniping.' The lunch over and Woolton considered the effect of his hectoring. 'I think I impressed them,' he noted that night. But it made scant difference to the headlines.

A couple of weeks later, on 13 June, he tackled the public on the subject. As he put it: 'I broadcast to the people of Britain. I told them it wasn't any use them getting all worked up about the newspaper stories of profiteering whilst they themselves helped the profiteer by buying his goods.'

He then decided to toughen his stance with his regular group of food journalists and then meet their bosses, the editors and owners. As they trooped into his office, their pints duly sipped, for their regular Tuesday afternoon briefing on 15 July 1941, he was without his usual affable air. 'It was,' he wrote, 'a period of adverse publicity and I thought I might put them in a better frame of mind.'

With the food reporters sat around his conference table he stood and told them directly: 'You are not representing the view of the average citizen who is satisfied at what he or she can get. This food question always appeals to the man in the street, as there isn't much else to write about. So you work up stories about shortages and queues and bad administration and profiteering. You know that the situation is nothing like as bad as you are making out and that the general situation is very good. But in what you write you are doing no good service to the country.' He finished and then dismissed them.

As they filed out of his office, he retreated to his desk and opened the top drawer. Sitting there was an item he had been sent that day – and it wasn't something he was going to share with the reporters. The post that morning, he reported in his diary, 'brought me a mysterious parcel'. At the time, due to an administrative error, some fruit and vegetables had been wrongly overpriced. 'The result of which,' he noted, 'was that the housewives of this country were being asked to pay up to 1s 6d per pound [7.5p, but, in real terms, some £5 today].

'My parcel contained a large onion with the following note: "I am sending you this onion as a gift. After paying sixpence for it (you will see it weighs half a pound) I had not the heart to cook it. I hope it will bring tears to your eyes, as it did to mine."'

Woolton noted that the 'grim sense of a humour' came from a 'citizen' of his neck of the woods: Manchester. But, he wrote in his diary (with a straight face), 'I had the onion situation in hand.' An Order was effected, and the prices dropped a few days later.

As for the press, that night he complained to his wife that, 'I am suffering from the lack of a good public relations officer. The result is we are being badly put across to the public. It's an annoying situation.'

On 5 June, in the midst of his stormy summer, he was asked to see the Prime Minister. Churchill asked him straight whether, wrote Woolton, 'I was tired of being Minister of Food and asked me if I'd like to take another job.'

Woolton pondered on this because he was not having an easy time. 'Truth to tell, I'm a little tired of it myself,' he wrote, 'but I don't think it's a good thing to take another job just because you're tired of the one you've got, unless the new one is one for which you've a special qualification or desire.'

Churchill raised the idea of Woolton running another ministry but he declined. 'I think it's a good thing to have continuity of control in food supplies during a war,' he told the PM. His job was far from done.

That evening he made one of his occasional visits to Colwyn Bay where he found Sir Henry French. Tired from another day of meetings and the stresses of his work, he told Sir Henry that Churchill had mooted the idea of him leaving the ministry and moving to head up another.

'Although I must have given many headaches to French,' wrote Woolton, 'he said he was delighted that I had decided to stay.'

Woolton pie

On the same day that the *Daily Herald* was reporting demands from the Scottish TUC that 'Woolton Must Go', there was a rather softer piece of PR in *The Times*. 'Lord Woolton Pie', the paper stated on 26 April 1941: 'The Official Recipe'. 'In hotels and restaurants, no less than in communal canteens, many people have taste Lord Woolton pie and pronounced it good,' the piece read, sounding like a public service announcement.

The recipe for the dish had been distributed around the country over the previous month, having been unveiled on

18 March at a lunch at the Savoy hotel. The occasion was organised by the Pilgrims Society, whose raison d'être was to promote goodwill between the United States and Great Britain and who had a tradition of holding a lunch to welcome a new American Ambassador. The latest incumbent was John Winant and, as he was led to his table in the ballroom by Winston Churchill and the Earl of Derby, around him was gathered the most powerful figures in Britain: the elite of the business world, most of the Cabinet, leading military figures as well as newspaper owners and publishers.

For Winston Churchill it was the opportunity to make a great speech. The BBC carried it and he was at his best as he told his ally: 'Mr Winant, you come to us at a grand turning point in the world's history. We rejoice to have you with us in these days of storm and trial because, in you, we have a friend and a faithful comrade who will "report us and our cause aright".'

For the Ministry of Food it was the opportunity to launch a new pie. Or rather dress up an old one and give it a new name. The ministry had tasked Francis Latry, the hotel's chef – a man with short legs and an even shorter temper, by all accounts – to create a pie that made a virtue of vegetables. His recipe was duly printed in *The Times*; it was a mixture of diced and cooked potatoes, cauliflower, swedes and carrots, some spring onions, a little vegetable extract ('if possible') and a tablespoonful of oatmeal. Once cooked and cooled, the mixture was placed into a pie dish, sprinkled with chopped parsley and covered with a crust of potato or wholemeal pastry. Once baked until brown it was served 'hot with a brown gravy'.

If a gathering of the most powerful people in Britain – and the new American Ambassador – could happily dine on Woolton pie at the Savoy, it was surely good enough for men, women and children across Britain. Such initiatives were often launched from smart hotels, so that the public might get the idea that the food of the rich was just as proscribed as that of the poor. Indeed ordering Woolton pie when it was on the menu in restaurants, and then pretending to enjoy it, offered the middle classes the chance to demonstrate their virtue. 'It was the equality of suffering, conjured in root vegetables,' wrote Matthew Sweet who studied in detail the food of London's grand hotels.

But there was one aspect to the pie-launch story that was not reported. While Lord Woolton wrote in his diary that the pie – his first taste of it – 'was extremely good', it fared less well with Churchill. 'When it was offered to the Prime Minister he sent it away, and asked for some cold beef,' Woolton wrote. He further recounted, in an interview with the *Star* newspaper, that when the waiter placed a portion of the pie in front of Churchill, he asked: 'What is this?'

'Woolton pie, Sir,' said the waiter.

'It is what?' barked Churchill.

'Woolton pie, Sir.'

'Bring me some beef,' he said pushing the plate away from him.

Woolton spotted his actions during the lunch but said nothing, not wishing to draw anyone's attention to Churchill's less-than-helpful contribution to his latest PR wheeze. As the lunch ended Woolton quietly cornered the PM. 'I thought you treated my pie with less than respect Prime Minister,' he said. 'Yes,' replied Churchill, 'I thought it was one of your synthetic productions.'

As ever Churchill was keen to prick the Woolton ego bubble whenever possible. Still, Woolton pie became famous and it grew to be a symbol of British resilience as well as a memento of rationing for decades to come. The dish may have been something of a joke but, as Woolton himself wrote in his memoirs: 'The public was either going to laugh or cry about food rationing, it was better for them that they should laugh.'

He did, however, get a little fed up with being offered the dish on rather too many occasions. On opening a British Restaurant in December 1941 in the London borough of Hackney he was given Woolton pie but spotted that it contained sausages, 'which wasn't Woolton pie at all'. He then had his office send the cook, a Mrs Amy, the official recipe so she could get it right next time.

The restaurant opening was not a great success as there was a large group of media in attendance about which Woolton moaned he hadn't been warned. With the 'bevy of pressmen . . . it was impossible for the people to be informal.' He didn't hold out much hope for the ensuing coverage. 'The film they took won't turn out very well,' he said. 'It isn't easy to be informal when you know that pictures of you are going all over the world.'

The trip to the new Hackney restaurant ended at one o'clock and having spurned the Woolton pie it was 'too late to have a proper lunch and too lightly fed for the rest of the day – so I came back to the office and had some sandwiches.' A mundane note in his diary, but comforting, nonetheless, to hear a man in high office, during the Second

World War, uttering a sigh that can resonate with our own twenty-first-century daily moans.

The weight of celebrity was causing him discomfort. He once panicked after a photographer took a picture of him backstage after a trip to the theatre. One of the chorus girls joined him just as the pictures were taken. 'She was dressed in little more than a couple of feather plumes,' he wrote. His office later came to the rescue: 'I believe the ministry bought the copyright of one in order to protect the marble-white reputation of one of its ministers,' he commented.

The Times, doubtless having witnessed him eating his eponymous dish on countless occasions, cruelly noted on 22 September 1944 – as he yet again was faced with his pie – that 'There may have been those who were not convinced by the smile [of Woolton], the look of relish directed at the morsel on the fork.'

But that damn pie kept Woolton's name in the public conscience, even in the decades after his death. Although, frankly, it's a grim and dull pie and, as a famous British dish, a white flag of surrender against any advancing legions of French gastronomy.

The pie also reflected on how Woolton managed to create a warm image of himself to the public. From his radio and television broadcasts (the former, such as the regular broadcast *The Kitchen Front* – often presented by him – sometimes pre-recorded on a gramophone record for occasions such as Christmas Day), he came to be seen as a member of one's family who could be relied upon and trusted, who had everyone's interests at heart and who would treat each person fairly but, if need be, with a firm hand; 'Uncle Fred'. In tandem with his own broadcasts he enlisted the help of Walt Disney himself to create characters to help him urge the nation to Dig for Victory, the campaign to plant vegetables in order to become more self-sufficient. Disney created three carrot characters for the ministry's advertisements and then, as a gesture of good-will, wrote Woolton, 'presented the copyright to us.'

Family matters

Woolton wrote in his diary in early July that his son Roger arrived a day late from a ten-day holiday on a houseboat in Windermere. 'He should have arrived last night, but had succeeded, when leaving the houseboat, in falling into the lake, suitcase and all, and had had to spend the night with friends of his in Windermere so that he could be dried out.'

It was not an episode that seemed uncharacteristic for poor Roger. Perhaps his father gave him one of his haughty lectures on his return. The previous year, when Roger had left Rugby, Woolton decided to give his son a pep-talk on succeeding in business, an episode he recorded in his diary. 'You have concentrated on classics at both your prep school and public school,' he said, 'and if you now go into business you will be able to forget that training. An unbiased mind can concentrate on making money. I have observed that the people who make the most money are the people whose minds are not unduly embarrassed by either education or ideas.'

Roger nodded diligently at this hinted suggestion that he need not therefore go to university, especially if he, as was expected, were to follow his father into Lewis's. Then

Woolton added: 'But I beg you to do one thing for me. When I am dead do not get up in their Lordships' House and seek to guide the nation into its political destiny on the experience of a self-made man.'

His son looked disconcerted. 'The effect of this on Roger was so demoralising that he said if I would like him to go to Cambridge he would be very glad to go.'

So, in order to avoid what seemed endless opportunities to let his father down, Roger duly went to Cambridge. Then, on 16 April 1941, he reported for National Service; Woolton noted the occasion in his diary. His son reported at Acton, in West London, whereupon he was told to go to Waterloo and take a train to Fareham, between Portsmouth and Southampton. Woolton felt they might have saved him his journey in the first place.

But he found time to say goodbye in person. 'I went to see him off. It seemed to me that he was old enough to go and do a job,' he commented, 'but he seemed to me to be ridiculously young to go and fight.' Woolton wrote that he sensed no nerves in his son other than 'feelings . . . that he experienced when going to a new school – rather exciting. He showed no fear at the prospect of a new environment.' Possibly he had no desire to join the Navy but didn't want to disappoint his father, who was clearly so proud of this progression in his life that he had made the journey south to wave him off. And if he felt some trepidation he wasn't going to let his father see it.

But just one day later Roger turned up at the family's London flat. 'The medical test revealed a slight colour-blindness which they said would prevent him from ever having a commission in the Navy,' wrote Woolton. 'The only thing that might happen is that I could become a steward,' Roger told his father. 'The officers have given me four days leave to come home and discuss the matter with you.'

'So do you want to be a steward, Roger?' asked Woolton.

'No,' he replied. 'And I don't want to be a land officer in the Navy either.'

Father and son discussed the issue and, Woolton wrote: 'He has decided that he would like to go to the Air Force.'

Three months later there was a setback with this new plan. On 9 July 1942, Woolton wrote that his son 'has gone to consult a Harley Street man about his stammer'. It is not clear whether this condition was a recent phenomenon or an issue since childhood. But it adds a devastating note to the picture of this hapless young man and the stammer that would stay with him for the rest of his life.

The Royal Air Force were not sympathetic when they came to interview the twenty-year old as he stammered through his answers. He made several attempts to enter the Service; on one occasion, on 8 July, Roger spent a whole day being medically examined. Woolton reported that he 'had a most unpleasant day, being buffeted about from place to place and being described as a "bloody menace" by a medical officer'. Towards the end of the day, 'he eventually came across another medical officer who suggested that his stammer would be a disadvantage to him in the Air Force.'

If he had treatment for it, he was told, he might have a chance. Perhaps Roger endured a tortuous merry-go-round of Harley Street professionals who would have put steel marbles in his mouth and implored him to enunciate his words better.

The situation is never mentioned by Maud in her diaries. But in April of the following year Woolton wrote that he travelled to Manchester to see Roger off, this time on a ship bound for Canada where he was to get training overseas for the Air Force. It seems either his stammer receded or a more understanding officer agreed to accept him.

Almost a month later Woolton recorded news of his son: 'We heard today that Roger had arrived safely in Canada, which was a relief.' With his personal knowledge of how precarious the journey was across the Atlantic, the couple must have been very relieved indeed. His training was a success and he was accepted into the Royal Air Force. His was the most basic aircraftsman rank of A/C2. And he attained a small measure of celebrity in that his friends in the service, with a distinct nod to his father, nicknamed him 'Rations'.

Less problematic was the Wooltons' daughter Peggy. She was a diligent school worker and progressed through the ranks of the Auxiliary Territorial Service – the women's branch of the British Army – during the Second World War. The only time Woolton made a note of any difficulty regarding her was when, on 6 February 1942, he was passed a copy of *Tatler* magazine. Within its pages, charting the social goings on of Britain at war, was a photograph of Peggy. Rather than feel pride as some parents did, and have done ever since, at their daughter appearing in such a magazine, Woolton was cross. 'Nice people don't seek this type of publicity,' he thundered in his diary. It was, he said, 'impertinent that a photographer should supply a portrait that is a private property'.

Autumn

By the end of August, Woolton noted a dramatic change in his press coverage. 'We're having a period now when our publicity is very good,' he wrote, almost surprised. 'We are doing almost everything that's right and indeed are described as a ministry with a vision, doing a difficult job extremely well. Only a few weeks ago, to judge from the press, the ministry was a collection of absolute nit-wits, who didn't even think before they spoke, and who hadn't anything to think anyhow.' He pondered on this turn of events before adding, 'We can't be very much different from what we were two months ago! Popularity's a fickle jade.'

Woolton was more concerned about government policy. He was still arguing with senior ministers about getting his hands on more ships; on 2 October he recorded a frustrating discussion with senior ministers. 'I asked flatly if it was a fact that we could not rely on having the ships: there were vague remarks about secret happenings in the War Cabinet that could not be talked of etc etc. I got very tired of it.'

Government policy was, he then reflected later that day, 'signs of the "war lord" at work. Look after the troops, feed them, transport them, and generally give them first place in every possible way. It's all right, and it's got to be done, but it cannot be done at the total expense of all the other people.' Woolton was irritated at the continuing 'lack of real cooperation in the government'.

'We must win the war,' he wrote, 'we all hope it will be won abroad – but I see no sense in winning it abroad and losing it at home.'

Woolton's grumblings continued into the winter months of 1941. On 10 November he listened to a speech Churchill made at the annual Lord Mayor's lunch at the grand Mansion House, the Lord Mayor's eighteenth-century Palladian official residence in the City of London. 'Winston,' he wrote, 'made an excellent speech about very little: he has an amazing facility for using words and whilst he said nothing . . . that he hasn't said before it went very well.'

Woolton, meanwhile, had been preparing the ground for the next big initiative in rationing: the Points System. It was an adjunct to rationing but he still needed the Prime Minister's general agreement. The problem though, Woolton wrote on 28 November, was that Churchill 'wanted as little rationing as possible. He's not very good in his judgment on these home affairs: he doesn't seem to understand that nobody else wants rationing any more then he does, but that there has to be rationing when there are short supplies.'

The Points System was introduced on 1 December 1941 as a way of limiting the purchase of items like canned meat, fish or beans. Such things were not as sparse as meat or butter, so simple rationing would have been overkill. Yet they still needed to be limited in a way that was measured and practical. Woolton was well aware of the gloom that had been cast across the country when, in July 1940, he had banned the making and selling of iced cakes.

At first every person was given sixteen points a month. The selected range of foods were then given a points value. This could change according to its availability: in the early stages of the system, a can of peas, corn, tomatoes or green beans weighing 1lb 4oz was worth sixteen points. A larger can of

The ration book can be likened to a passport that enabled you to get enough food to eat. With an individual serial number, it was posted to everyone who could receive rations, including members of the Royal Family. It was as vital to grab your ration book as your gas mask when the siren sounded in the event of an air raid.

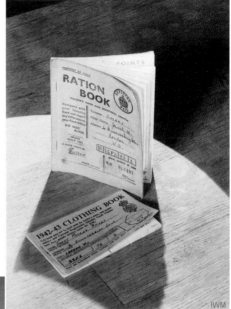

The basic food stuffs two adults in the British Isles would have been entitled to in a weekly ration.

Woolton was keen not to ration bread, although he had drafted a scheme, as he felt the British public would not wear it. Instead he urged people to fill themselves up with 'energy-giving' potatoes.

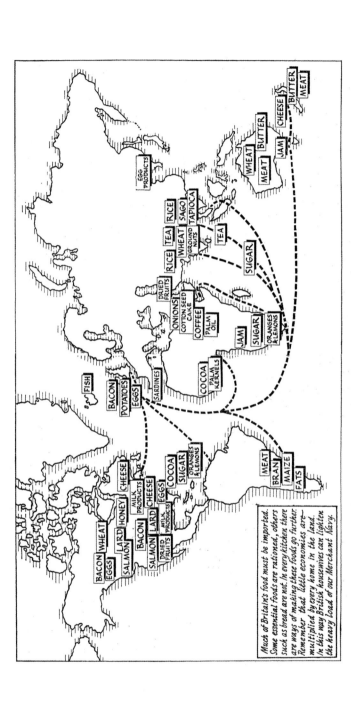

THE FIGURES BELOW GIVE SOME IDEA OF THE GREAT DISTANCES WHICH THESE SUPPLIES MUST TRAVEL BEFORE THEY REACH YOUR TABLE

Bacon	2,700 miles	Egg Products	2,700–13,000 miles
Bran	6,200 miles	Eggs	2,700–2,760 miles
Butter	12,000–13,500 miles	Fats	6,200 miles
Cheese	2,700–13,500 miles	Fish	1,000 miles
Cocoa	3,000–4,000 miles	Ground Nuts	11,000 miles
Coffee	9,000 miles	Honey	2,760 miles
Cotton Seed Cake	9,000 miles	Jam	6,000–12,000 miles
Dried Fruits	2,700–12,000 miles	Lard	2,700–2,760 miles

Maize	6,200 miles	Sago	11,200 miles
Meat	6,000–13,500 miles	Salmon	2,700 miles
Milk Products	2,700–13,500 miles	Sardines	1,000 miles
Onions	5,000 miles	Sugar	4,000–11,200 miles
Oranges & Lemons	1,500–6,000 miles	Tapioca	11,200 miles
Palm Kernels	3,000 miles	Tea	11,500 miles
Rice	11,200 miles	Wheat	2,700–11,000 miles

This chart, distributed by the Ministry of Food, hung in the Portman Square office of Lord Woolton. It was a constant reminder of the distance vital supplies had to travel before reaching Britain.

A typical Allied convoy heading across the Atlantic, their precious cargo and merchant men guarded by the ever-vigilant Royal Navy. Despite chronic losses to German U-boats in the early years of the war, the convoys still managed to bring Britain invaluable supplies.

The merchant navy would lose over 3,500 ships to the U-boat scourge, with over 36,000 seamen and 36,000 sailors of the Allied navies dying in their bid to get supplies to Britain.

Supplying Britain with food was just one of the major tasks
Woolton faced. Equally vital was the job of maintaining a supply
line to British forces overseas, in the Far East, for example. Here an
Allied convoy makes its way through the Suez Canal.

Moving food stuffs around the British Empire was integral to
achieving victory. Above, stores of rice are loaded onto a ship in the
Indian city of Bombay.

Lord Woolton was always keen to showcase the latest Ministry of Food campaign to the nation in order to promote both healthy diets, as well as fostering a community spirit. Here he is seen with the Queen as they warm their hands on a winter's day while viewing the arrangements of a field kitchen.

On leave from the Royal Air Force, Woolton's son Roger relaxes with his parents at their flat, Whitehall Court, in Westminster.

Victory is ours! The crowds come out to celebrate VE Day in central London. Happiness at the end of the fighting in Europe would soon be tinged with frustration for many, as rationing continued to bite for the foreseeable future.

Rationing would continue for the next several years as the country slowly got back on its feet. It would officially end in July 1954, when meat was finally taken off the rationing card. Cheese production would take decades thereafter to recover due to the ministry enforcing only one type of 'Government Cheddar' being made, thus setting back indigenous cheese-making for years.

Lord Woolton would enjoy a successful political career after the war, helping to guide the Conservatives back to government in the 1950s. Here he is seen in 1957 with his old colleague Sir Henry French (centre) at an official government function.

Woolton may have crossed swords with Winston Churchill during the Second World War, but he proved an invaluable ally to him in his post-war political comeback. Here, the two elder statesmen enjoy a quiet word at an official engagement in 1963.

pears weighing 1lb 14oz, was twenty-one points, pineapple twenty-four, grapefruit juice was worth twenty-three points and tomato juice weighing 1lb 7oz was thirty-two points.

The number of points also varied, reaching a high of twenty-four per month in early 1942 and mid 1944.

As time went on, more goods were added to the Points System and they included rice, dried pulses, canned vegetables, condensed milk, breakfast cereals, oatcakes, syrup and treacle. The system did give individuals a touch of liberty because they could be used in any shop that had the goods and were happy to sell them – unlike with ration coupons where you could only shop in premises where you had registered. You could also choose whether to splurge one month on some peaches, or play it safe with some spinach and corn.

Woolton wrote that, ironically, it was 'a system that we borrowed – and, I believe, improved – from the Germans'. He described it as 'a sort of 'Stock Exchange'. The articles that were in the shortest supply cost the largest number of points and vice versa. 'If we found, for example, that we had a considerable quantity of sardines, then we advised the shopkeepers that they were in good supply and presently we reduced the number of points for which they called,' he explained.

But to make it work he had to exercise fierce control over the system. 'The whole scheme depended upon the success of the first two months and on this I took no risks,' he recalled. Several weeks before the scheme came into operation he reduced the supply of all the extra goods to be added to the Points System. Meanwhile shopkeepers were asked to build up heavy stocks of these items but 'on the strict understanding that they were not for sale until released by order of the ministry'.

This required a considerable degree of honesty on the part of the shopkeepers who had to somehow keep the deliveries and storage a secret from their regulars, doubtless among them many beady-eyed and gossipy shoppers. Sometimes gossip and rumour led the public into making rather unusual shopping purchases.

One of the non-food items that Lord Woolton had to control was soap. This became a real scarcity in the war and Woolton did not want to create a soap-related panic. So to avoid any leaks about his impending plans to ration it, the files of papers at the ministry containing soap-related arguments, distribution schemes and much more were given the codename of 'Nutmegs'.

Woolton planned to announce his soap rationing on a Sunday, a practice he used relentlessly with the Points System as, on the Sabbath Day, the shops would be closed and there could be no mad rush to purchase, with people instead thinking things over and planning their points spending. As to the soap plan, he wrote, 'there was no sign of any leakage of information on this subject until the Saturday afternoon.' Then, somehow, word got out. Or, rather, the wrong news did, as reports suddenly came into the ministry that there had been an extraordinary rush in the shops that day on nutmegs. 'I wonder what happened to all the nutmegs [bought by] the credulous people who cleaned up the market on nutmegs on that Saturday afternoon,' he later mused.

As for the real build-up to points items, on the whole the shopkeepers of Britain managed it and, reflected Woolton, 'with great patriotism they legitimately kept these goods "under the counter"'.

'The Points Plan gives you freedom,' he announced after lunch on Sunday 21 November 1941 on the BBC Home Service radio. 'You can buy these new goods where you please in the four-week period. You're free to spend your Points on any foods that you choose on the list and you can go to any shop you like on the list. Everyone doesn't want the same thing every week. We want variety.' Benevolent Woolton was at his affable best selling his scheme to the nation; they, on the most part, cheered him on. His department even issued a new book, available at one's local food office, coloured in a dainty pink. The points came in the form of coupons which were each dated and were only valid on the date printed and, if unused, could not be carried forward to the next month.

The Points System was up and running but Woolton received no thanks from the Prime Minister. He soon discovered that he wasn't the only one disgruntled with Churchill. On 7 December, Woolton and Maud spent the evening with Alan Lennox-Boyd and his wife Florence.

At the time Lennox-Boyd was in the Navy (and would later become a member of Churchill's peacetime government); he had been Woolton's parliamentary secretary when he first became Minister of Food, so he was keen to hear about his career progress and how he was now getting on in his new job in the Navy. But, Woolton admitted, 'I was more interested in the things he told me about the feeling of the House of Commons.' By which he meant the feelings of MPs about Churchill.

'He was very frank about Winston, and told me that the House was beginning to be critical about some of the PM's actions and decisions,' he wrote. It tallied with Woolton's thoughts. 'We are not making headway anywhere except in Africa, and this will be a temporary success,' he commented. 'The German general, Rommel, is clever and we shall have trouble there. The PM is trying to run a one-man show: he has a war Cabinet in which none of the Service Ministers operate, he being Minister for Defence, and accepting responsibility for all the war strategy. This may be all right if the strategy succeeds, but the people won't care whose responsibility it is if we keep on having defeats as a result. They are being urged to work and save for Victory, and soon they'll want to see some.'

On Saturday 13 December 1941 Lord Woolton had set aside some time to write a speech that he was due to give the following Monday when opening a new canteen at a Nottingham colliery. The press had been invited and it was to be a chance for some positive words; this was a new facility for hard-working people; the photographs would show white teeth shining out of the blackened faces of gritty British miners. Woolton would be at his magnanimous best.

But he was struggling to write the speech he wanted to give. 'Japan has declared war on us, and Germany and Japan have declared war on the United States,' he explained, the official declaration of war by the Empire of Japan having been published on 8 December. As the text from Emperor Hirohito read: 'Our Empire, for its existence and self-defence has no other recourse but to appeal to arms and to crush every obstacle in its path.' Woolton felt mournful:

'Practically the whole world is now in the war, and these latest developments are going to make things very difficult,' he wrote.

For Woolton that meant more political difficulties. The supply routes would be further squeezed and that would inevitably mean even less food imports. 'I shall find great difficulty,' he explained, 'because, in the first place, the Pacific will no longer be safe as the Japanese submarines are operating there, and in the second place America will probably need for her own use much of the food that she has been sending us.' Woolton's options were diminishing. 'The closing of the Pacific route will mean a great loss to us, because our meat supplies from Australia and New Zealand have been crossing from those countries to America, and then coming across the Atlantic,' he lamented.

As the press were due to assemble at this Nottingham colliery, he felt it appropriate to make a speech in which he would warn that further privations were coming; that the ration would be squeezed. He had written to Churchill during the week asking him to clear his message. 'I indicated to the Prime Minister that, in my speech on Monday, I wanted to announce the withdrawal of the extra sugar and fat rations that were recently given and to reduce the meat ration. But without the go-ahead from Churchill the hour he had set aside to write the speech was wasted. 'I cannot prepare my speech because I have had no reply from the PM,' he recorded crossly.

The following morning, Sunday, he decided to go to the office and see if he could chase the reply he wanted. Ever the stickler for the best decorum and behaviour, he called at Buckingham Palace on the way to wish the King a happy birthday 'as a good Peer to the Realm to His Majesty'. At the office he saw that a letter had been delivered from Number 10. It was not the answer he wanted. 'The PM's reply had come,' he wrote; 'it was, as I suspected it to be, an unqualified negation to any reductions in the ration.'

Woolton was angry. 'He's not a good home minister,' he ranted. 'In the early days of the war he said that there was no need for any rationing system in this country, the British Navy would keep the seas of the world open to Britain. Fortunately nobody took any notice of him then, or we would now be in a parlous condition.' Woolton firmly believed that he had no option but to make these reductions to the ration – yet here was Churchill vetoing the idea. 'In spite of all the experience we have had he just sets his face against any reductions, regardless of conditions of necessity.'

The public was aware that Japan's entrance into the war would impact their lives so Woolton reckoned that he should take advantage of their being pliant on the issue. 'It's a great pity he has taken this line,' he wrote. 'We shall have to reduce the rations, and that soon, but people are expecting it now and would take kindly an action that they realise is inevitable with a fresh war zone with which to cope. The longer we delay the announcement, the less kindly they will take it.'

So Woolton went to Nottingham that Monday and made his speech. 'It was received well,' he noted, 'although there was really nothing in it.' He cursed the wasted opportunity. 'I had to say that there would be no immediate change in the rations, and this was a pity because we shall have to do it quite soon.'

Within the month Churchill had relented and Woolton announced that as a result of the opening of the war front in the Pacific there would be a reduction in the ration. He made the announcement as a postscript to the BBC news at one o'clock on 11 January 1942. It was a day in which he confided to his diary that 'the war situation is very depressing. The lack of success we are having, and the ever-widening war zone, seems to have little effect on the complacency and lethargy here.'

Yet his words were not just targeted, as they usually were, at the government and Churchill. While Hitler's planes seemed to have paused from their incessant bombing raids a new mood appeared to have crept over the country. 'In this period of freedom from air-raids, life in England seems to have gone back to almost normal,' he wrote incredulously; 'restaurants and theatres crowded; West-end hotels full; nobody seems to care very much about getting the war moving.'

Woolton didn't like it. 'On the continent people are literally dying in their thousands from starvation. The food situation in Greece is desperate: these people, whose heroic resistance to an enemy superior in numbers and equipment delayed the German progress in Europe for many weeks, are starving.

'I've told the Cabinet that I will take the risk of depleting our food stocks in this country so that we shall send them food,' he continued. 'I cannot bear to think of people, at whose expense we've had weeks of respite from attack, dying from lack of food whilst we've had some in the cupboard.'

Doubtless the Cabinet and Churchill sighed wearily at

Woolton's latest pleading. Even when things were looking up, the tiresome Minister of Food seem determined to deliver his gloomy assessments and decrease the ration.

As ever, Woolton was just as dismissive about his colleagues as he was Churchill. 'I wish that in these Cabinet meetings I saw more of the evidence of the will to win the war,' he wrote on 22 December. 'I'm afraid that some of my colleagues are more concerned about their careers than about England.'

12

DEMAND RUNS HIGH

As warring Britain welcomed in 1942, the Minister of Food
saw little signs of optimism about him. With the Japanese
gaining ground in the Pacific, Woolton looked at the map
of the trade routes for food in his office and groaned at the
prospect of fewer items such as cheese, butter and meat arriving in Britain.

'The war situation is very depressing,' he wrote that day
not relishing the task of relaying yet further news of belt-
tightening to the country. Meanwhile Maud was spending
her days at South Africa House, a grand building on Trafalgar
Square which acted as that country's high commission and
consulate. 'I spend most mornings helping to pack parcels
and do all sorts of food jobs,' she wrote. From the packing
room where she worked, were dispatched parcels of food,

clothing and cigarettes. She was, she said, 'the only English person there . . . However they have taken me in and I enjoy the work very much.'

It served as a positive distraction from the realities of the war, about which she ruminated in her diary. 'At the present moment we are almost as much in the depths of woe about the war news as we were at the time of Dunkirk,' she pondered in early February 1942, adding: 'nowhere are we being successful. It is devastating. I don't mean to say that we are down and out – not by any means, but we are sick about these things and dread to think of what is happening in Singapore.'

Maud wrote of her husband's state of mind. 'F is very disturbed,' she noted. But at least the couple could seek some solace in attacking the man in the charge.

'He thinks that the PM is making a muddle of things, because he does see himself in the role of a war lord and strategist,' she wrote, adding that 'rumour says that he wants servicemen about him who are "Yes" men. He can't bear contradiction, and he does insist on keeping everything in his hands. It isn't possible for one man to do all he attempts to do. He really ought to keep an eye on all departments but only in a way of a guiding and co-ordinating hand. Instead he goes into minute details of things he's keen about, and allows some departments to get hopelessly muddled.'

The pair had discussed whether it should be Woolton who should take a stand and publicly criticise the Prime Minister. 'F feels that someone ought to make a protest and wondered whether he ought to be the one to do it as he isn't a politician.' Of course it would mean he would have to quit and so Maud had counselled against it. 'It would be a pity if he'd retire as a protest as his department is talked of as *the* one which is properly run.'

Churchill, sensing grumbles among colleagues, held a three-day debate in the House of Commons on the 'Motion of Confidence in the Government'. He won it of course – on 29 January by 464 votes to 1 – and Woolton was a little cynical when contemplating it in his diary on the day the Prime Minister opened the debate. 'He knows that his personal popularity will secure the vote for him, but it's dangerous and a foolish thing to do, and I think he'll lose reputation through it.'

Woolton didn't hear Churchill's speech, though received word that it had had a 'tremendous reception'. 'But reading it,' he wrote, 'I didn't feel it was that strong.'

February came with a dump of snow and an affliction for Woolton of colitis. He lay in bed for a day but then dragged himself to a meeting to discuss imports. 'It is so important that we import the amount of food that we must have for safety that I dare not risk any decisions being taken in my absence.'

The meeting over, and Woolton looked out of his office window across Portman Square. People, wrapped in their coats and scarves, walked quickly along the pavements, finding paths where the snow had been cleared to stay dry. Cars and buses passed beneath his window and opposite he could see a sentry, who, shivering in the cold, guarded the sandbagged doors to an office on the other side of the street.

Woolton puffed on his pipe – it often seemed the only tonic to his stomach pains – and considered a major problem with rice supplies raised at the meeting of the Import Executive which had just ended. The impending fall of Singapore was affecting imports. Rice may have been a comparatively small part of the diet of the British people, but he had a problem in Ceylon. The Indian population there, which made up a large proportion of the naval base, were refusing to eat wheat and were threatening to leave the colony unless they could get adequate rations of rice. It wasn't just the people in Portman Square who relied on Woolton.

But where on earth was he to find a new supply of rice? His global hunt for this vital commodity was proving fruitless. A shortage of rice in India closed that option, and his contacts in Brazil had assured him they had none. His sources in Egypt told him they had exhausted their exportable supplies, but Woolton had a hunch there was more if he looked hard enough. As he considered these difficulties, there was a knock on his office door and one of his two secretaries announced a visitor. 'I'll be seeing him on his own,' reminded Woolton. This meeting would be private; no notes, no records, no memos. Officially, it wasn't taking place.

The man coming to see the minister was civil servant Harold Sanderson, who, Woolton later wrote, 'seemed to me to have knowledge of all the rice fields of the world at his finger-ends'.

'I have a problem that is more serious than I am able to tell you,' Woolton told his visitor. 'All I can say is that I need rice and I need you to go to Egypt and see what you can find.'

'I'll go without delay,' replied Sanderson.

'Thank you,' said Woolton. 'This will be a difficult job but I know I can rely on you. Whatever you do and however you do it you'll have my support. I know just a little about the Eastern ways of negotiation, so if some issue arises that is beyond your authority do not feel the need to consult me. Using telephonic communication will only involve delay and no assured security. My confidence in your judgement is such that you are at liberty to make any statement or decision that you believe would represent my views.'

Woolton's guest thanked the minister and got up to leave. But as he reached the door, Woolton called out to him: 'Oh by the way Mr Sanderson, don't come back without 200,000 tons, will you?'

A few weeks after Harold Sanderson's brisk meeting with Woolton, the Ministry of Food's Head of Rice was to be found in Cairo, drained and wearied. As he pushed his way through the teeming streets of the city, this Englishman's nose found nothing appealing in the combined smell of exhaust fumes, donkey manure and incense. The road bobbed with fez hats and turbans. But in addition to his own panama there were the berets and khaki caps worn by the variety of allied troops who had now, in their thousands, joined the million-plus Egyptian inhabitants of the city.

As he crossed the street looking for respite at the grand nineteenth-century Continental Hotel, he had to dodge a mismatched chorus of scrawny-looking sheep, tiny Fiat cars and British army motorbikes.

He had had another frustrating morning and it felt like he had exhausted all the usual avenues as he negotiated for rice from a crowded office in the British government's Cairo HQ. What deals he had failed to seal on the telephone were similarly futile as he met his contacts on the hot and dusty back streets.

Passing a small market he mused on how simple it would be if he were only tasked with buying seasonal supplies for a few families. In comparison with cold and dreary war-torn London, Cairo was bursting with produce. There were the stores owned by Greek immigrants, for example, whose shelves heaved with sugar, butter, eggs and soap. Greengrocers were bulging with mounds of every kind of bean as well as maize and cabbages, cauliflowers and tomatoes. Small butcher shops heaved with live poultry and there were other individual stalls selling grapes or eggs. He passed piles of dates and oranges and let out a sigh; his task, his mission for Woolton in which failure was apparently not an option – quite easy to bark out in an office in London, another thing to actually succeed on the ground in Egypt – was overwhelming him with apprehension.

Off the street and into the cooler, more serene confines of the Continental bar, Sanderson ordered a cold glass of South African white wine and moved to a quiet table in the corner. He had no energy to involve himself with the cheery British officers standing at the counter. Their tasks, involving things like blowing up bridges to cut enemy supply lines, seemed a damn sight simpler than his job. And as far as he and Woolton were concerned they were, quite frankly, considerably less vital for the war effort. As he sipped on his drink, he considered what he had secured so far. His contacts had agreed to sell him 100,000 tons of rice; it was a solid order, but only half of what he needed to satisfy Woolton back in London. The white wine cooled his throat, invigorating him a little.

But he had another problem which was a touch more personal. He'd felt some unusual pain in his stomach that morning and, in spite of the heat, he felt a little chilled. He was definitely tired also, an unshakeable malaise which had lingered ever since he disembarked from the overlong and rough journey by ship he had endured some ten days previously. What worried him was the talk of bugs swirling round the city. Sanderson hoped to hell he hadn't caught anything. The next drink he ordered was water.

His night, back at the Services Club on Ezbekieh Gardens, was a terrible one. That slight chill had turned to a fever, the stomach pains into severe vomiting. The next day, pale and ill, the staff called him a doctor. 'I'm afraid you have dysentery, Mr Sanderson,' the doctor told him. 'You should leave Cairo and go back to London.' Sanderson said he couldn't, he had work to do.

Concerned for his wellbeing, some officials from the Egyptian government with whom he'd had some dealings, also came to visit. They told him the same thing. 'Cairo is not a good place to be if you have a sickness like this,' he was told. Furthermore they had a plan to ease his passage home. This time there would be no ship. 'You must go home, Mr Sanderson,' they said. 'We have provided a special plane for you to take you back to England,' they said. 'If you stay here, the doctors say you will die.'

'I'm not leaving until I have another 100,000 tons of rice,' Sanderson replied weakly from his bed. 'My country and her dependents are facing a grave threat and I would rather die in Cairo than face my minister having failed in my mission.'

The next day he dragged himself from his bed and, having made some telephone calls, went out to meet some contacts. Four days later Sanderson took the plane and returned from Cairo. He was very weak and went straight to bed. A few days later he had recovered sufficiently to be able to report to Woolton back in his office on Portman Square. The minister rose from his desk as Sanderson entered the room; noting how ill he looked he eased him into a chair.

'My poor fellow, you didn't need to take my word literally,' said Woolton. 'But I gather that you did get 100,000 tons.'

'I got a damn sight more than that,' replied Sanderson, then, surprised at his own language, added a deferential 'Minister.'

Woolton looked at him, surprised and impressed. 'You did?' he asked.

'I got you the required amount. Yes, and a little more.'

'Well, I thank you in the name of the British government,' Woolton said.

Sanderson nodded appreciatively. But then sat in silence, somewhat awkwardly, for a few seconds. He then breathed in deeply, looked at Woolton and said: 'By the way, Minister, do you remember that you told me before I went that whatever I did that I thought right would have your support?'

'I certainly remember it and I meant it,' replied Woolton.

'Well, as you know, Egyptian standards, both of trading

and respect for government decrees are not quite the same as in this country. So I hope you think it's alright that I bought an extra 130,000 tons of rice on the black market. I hope that you think that was alright.'

'Sanderson,' replied Woolton coolly, 'I shall remain completely ignorant of such things. I do not understand anything about the existence of a black market in Egypt.' He paused before adding: 'And I shall remain so.'

After Sanderson had left the room, Woolton walked over again to his window and looked down at the people in the street below, a smile growing on his face.

'Just how he got the rice out of Egypt was something into which I never thought it necessary to inquire,' he wrote later in his memoirs, noting also that a few years later Sanderson would be awarded with a knighthood for his courage and negotiating skills. 'But they were very grateful for it in Ceylon,' he added. He then considered how some in his team had scoffed at the idea of Sanderson being successful in his mission. 'It showed how unwise it was to believe anything about the "impossible",' he wrote.

While things like rice disturbed Woolton, the political situation was unnerving him. 'I had spent a more or less sleepless night thinking about the state of England,' he wrote on 13 February 1942, 'and I came to the conclusion that it might be my duty to resign from the government in order to break it.'

Churchill, he wrote, 'is not a good strategist: we never seem to have a sufficient force of men or materials to defend ourselves and any efforts we have made to conduct an offensive seem to result in dismal failure. Winston insists that nobody but he can direct our defence policy; from what I hear he treats his Chiefs of Staff with little consideration, sending for them at all hours of the night as well as the day, and, when times of crisis come, issuing orders himself. It isn't reasonable to expect people to work with clear minds when they cannot have a decent night's sleep, and it isn't reasonable to expect clear judgement from anyone who smokes twenty large cigars a day as the Prime Minister does.'

Woolton felt that the Cabinet underestimated the strength of the enemy ('In the East the Japs are just running all over the place') but there was no obvious replacement for Churchill or his colleagues. 'If I were clear that we had personnel to replace the present Cabinet I would myself resign in order to break the current one. There's little talent,' he complained.

Woolton pondered on possible successors. There was the newspaper proprietor Lord Beaverbrook (formerly Max Aitken) who he distrusted and said, 'was always at the Prime Minister's elbow ... and one wonders how much his judgement affects Winston's. I cannot imagine the Beaverbrook judgement having any good influence in the strategical conduct of the war: he's a bully, and you can't be a successful bully when you're smaller than the other fellow and have no weapons.'

As for other senior Cabinet members, 'Attlee [then Lord Privy Seal] does nothing; John Anderson [at the time Lord President of the Council, later to become Chancellor of the Exchequer] does his best but it's not much; Bevin [Minister of Labour] talks all day about mobilisation of labour, whilst people who are willing to work can't get themselves into jobs.' So would Woolton make the bold move? He was in a quandary. 'I am concerned about the situation,' he wrote, flustered, 'and I don't know what to do about it.'

Two days later, and not only was there a row about how a number of German battleships had managed to escape along the English Channel under the noses of the British in an episode later called the 'Channel Dash' – but also Singapore had finally fallen.

Woolton wrote that Churchill made a broadcast that night – 15 February – at nine o'clock. 'He made the most of all the possible excuses,' wrote Woolton. 'Then he went on to say that the only crime would be disunity in the country, and indicated that anybody who dared to criticise him or the government was a Quisling [an enemy collaborator]. It was a foolish and unpleasant speech. He referred to the vote of confidence that had been given to the government, when he must have known his own attitude had made it impossible for the House not to give the vote, but that the giving did not represent a whole-hearted agreement with it. I don't know whether he was deliberately lying, or whether his personal vanity causes him to believe that the House and the country are at one behind him.'

For her part Maud wrote that 'the Sunday newspapers were distinctly critical of the PM yesterday [15 February] but he cannot bear criticism.' She too noted that Churchill's broadcast said 'people who criticised were guilty of spoiling the war effort – and thereby becoming almost quislings. He is most unfair.' She continued that Churchill 'has got this awkward faculty of taking criticism personally.' He had, she also felt, a loyalty to certain colleagues that she called 'schoolboy loyalty; when the country is in danger that sort of loyalty has to go, and your colleagues if they are not competent, must be cut adrift.'

According to Maud, her husband had discussed this lack of constructive criticism with both Lord Kemsley (the owner of the *Sunday Times* and *Daily Sketch*) as well as the senior Labour peer and publisher Lord Southwood. 'They are both worried,' she wrote, 'and feel that criticism is needed.'

Since Woolton was plotting this criticism, he felt the prospect of being accused of disloyalty with anguish. Both Woolton and Maud had been listening to the broadcast at home with some fellow politicians, one of whom was a close colleague of Churchill. 'When he finished speaking there was a complete silence, which I felt was that of courtesy [to the aforementioned guest],' commented Woolton; 'it was a little uncomfortable.' But his wife rescued the situation: 'Maud burst in with a denunciation of Winston's comment about critics being Quislings, and that lightened the atmosphere.'

Woolton was, as they say, considering his position. 'The use of words won't win the war,' he wrote, 'and I'm afraid that feet of clay are being discerned.'

Churchill was looking weak. But what would Woolton do about it? A few days later, he reported a conversation with Lord Rothermere. 'He told me that the press were very worried about the present situation: he told me that my position in the country was second in popularity to that of the PM. He thought that if I resigned from the Ministry of Food and went into private life again it would not be long before I was recalled.'

'You could have any position you liked,' Rothermere told Woolton. 'It's all very flattering,' Woolton reflected in his diary, but, he added, 'I don't want any other job.' Woolton maintained his only ambition was that the war be conducted with more vigour.

Woolton's next meeting with Churchill was in early March. 'When I went into the room the PM was scowling,' he wrote, 'and asked if I'd been flogging anybody that morning. The remark was occasioned because the *Daily Mail* had come out with a headline saying that I had asked for the "cat" [a particularly unpleasant form of whip] for black market racketeers.

'So I said "No",' wrote Woolton, '"we'd had a morning off."'

A few days later, on 19 March, after what Woolton called 'a very bad attack of colitis in the night' he attended a meeting of the Privy Council, 'wondering how I would manage to stand through it [as was the custom]. I managed – but only just.' According to Woolton: 'After the meeting the King took me to his room: he immediately said I didn't look very well, and pulled up an easy chair for me to sit in.' The pair chatted about rationing and the importing of produce. 'He talked very intelligently about the food situation, and very frankly about my colleagues,' he recorded. 'He spoke of Bevin [Ernest Bevin, Minister of Labour and National Service] – and mentioned in passing that when he (Bevin) sat in the chair in which I was sitting he bulged all over the sides. He said that Bevin had no understanding of the mind of the people, adding, "Neither has the Prime Minister".'

Woolton enjoyed this indiscretion, writing that 'The King has been brought up to do the industrial side of the Royal job, and he knows more about working men than the Minister of Labour.'

Later that year Woolton also gleefully recalled a dinner at Buckingham Palace given by the King and Queen on Saturday 24 October 1942 at Buckingham Palace for the

US President's wife Mrs Roosevelt. Woolton noted that Bevin, in his behaviour and conversation with the King, 'was overstepping the limits of courtesy. He then accidentally broke a glass and the King rebuked him saying: "Now what have you done?"', with Woolton commenting: 'I thought [the King treated] him rather like a child who really doesn't know any better.'

The Colwyn Bay Propaganda department

In mid May 1942 Woolton spent two days at Colwyn Bay. There was something about the place that depressed him – the drab seaside town with all those Victorian houses crammed full of civil servants. Usually he would sit in a room in the Colwyn Bay Hotel and delegations from the town would visit him. On this visit he decided to stir things up so, as he wrote, 'instead of sitting in my room and people coming to see me I went in detail through three divisions.'

One of his three stops was the building that housed what Woolton's House of Lords detractors called his 'Propaganda Department', This was at Merton Place on Pwllycrochan Avenue; there a team, having intensively researched the subject of food and gathered evidence from a specially selected band of elite scientific advisors, had the job of convincing the British public that the sparse diet of the ration was in fact good for them.

Those advisors included Lord Horder, physician to the Royal Family (a man whose middle name was Jeeves and whose roles included President of the Cremation Society of Great Britain), Sir Henry Dale, President of the Royal Society (a notorious participant in the 'Brown Dog Affair', a scandal in 1903 involving the vivisection of a terrier) and Professor Jack Drummond, Professor of Biochemistry at University College London and an expert on food contamination (later brutally murdered along with his wife and daughter, apparently without motive, while on holiday in France).

Woolton had explained that however useful the advice of his scientific advisors, what he needed was a small group of women to sell his schemes to the housewives of Britain; at this meeting he would inspect the work of the ministry's latest recruits. Already he had hired Marguerite Patten, who perfectly fitted the mould of what he had in mind. A sensible-looking home economist, she had already proved her salt by working as the face for both the Eastern Electricity Board and Frigidaire. Her job, she once recalled, had been to fulfil the 'thankless task of persuading people to buy fridges when they all thought the pantry was quite good enough'. So convincing British cooks to revel in the prospect of making marmalade with carrots or replacing steak with whale meat, would not, perhaps, be so hard a task.

Woolton recruited her as a regular presenter for *The Kitchen Front* on which he himself sometimes appeared. It was a daily radio broadcast, just five minutes long, during which Patten would teach the arts of thrift and of making food last. After radio came pamphlets, then books (such as *Feeding the Nation*), then short films, including the two-minute *Food Flashes* that aired in the cinema and whose introductory voiceovers sternly preached epithets like: 'Don't waste food. It doesn't grow in the shops you know.'

Patten urged women to plan their menus, and then stick to them when they went shopping. It would be a habit that diligent British housewives would then be reluctant to break for decades after, ignoring any fresh produce that wasn't on their pre-written list. The wartime diet, Patten later reflected, was 'better than I thought it would be . . . Do you think we could have survived all those years if we were producing inedible food?' Although she also once admitted, towards the end of her life: 'People are inclined to make me say I want to go back to the war years. Well, what a load of nonsense. Who wants to go back to six months without a fresh tomato.'

As well as Patten, Lord Woolton had hired Irene Veal, who was only too happy to trot out lines fed to her by the propaganda team. In the preface to her plodding cook book, *Recipes of the 1940s,* with its endless 'Ways with Meat, Ways with Fish, Ways with Potatoes, Ways with Cheese . . .' – ad infinitum – she wrote, 'Never before have the British people been so wisely fed or British women so sensibly interested in cooking. We are acquiring an almost French attitude of mind regarding our food and its preparation . . .'

But on this day, Woolton was presented with a rather more charming little tome, produced by his latest recruit, Doris Grant. Her *'Feeding the Family in War-Time* had an illustration of a bird bringing her hungry nestlings a menu with the words 'Early Worms'; black silhouettes of planes fly above and below there are ships at sea.

The back cover of her book promised to answer questions such as 'Can you make economical, nutritious meals not only palatable but delicious?', 'Do you know how to increase the food value of your rations without added expense?' and the rather stricter: 'Have you learnt how to keep the family up to concert pitch without slackness and lassitude?' Inside she wrote, 'The war has given us all a sense of adventure in cooking. We have had to follow new paths and learn new ways; we have been jolted out of ruts.'

This was just the tone Woolton craved. And he was likewise delighted as he read on: 'We are eating less meat and sugar, and many of us are surprised to find that we are none the worse for this, but feeling better for it; thanks to the Ministry of Food, we are learning the real value of simple foods like potatoes and carrots ... many a sadly overworked liver must be secretly rejoicing at the rationing of fats and enjoying a much-needed holiday.'

Doris Grant also talked of how 'too much sugar' not only disturbed the balance of the diet but 'spoils the appetite for simple natural foods'. She added: 'Too much meat is harmful' but also warned against the danger of – with the lack of both fresh and dried fruit – filling up 'with too much starch'. She encouraged the eating of wholewheat bread: 'Bread made from white flour should have no place in the diet of those who value their health,' she wrote. She advised on adding the likes of Marmite, wheatgerm and 'Horsfield's Health Porridge' ('a splendid food ... which passes for porridge') to your store cupboard, and suggested sprucing up food with a sprig of parsley or a dusting of paprika. She also made suggestions for substituting food that was hard to come by, proposing soya flour as a replacement for meat, rosehip made into syrup instead of oranges and swede juice for any juice ('the juice can be obtained by grating the swede finely and pressing through muslin').

These were at the more palatable end of food substitutes, with stories abounding of rooks in pies instead of grouse. But as real as it was ubiquitous and loathed, was dried egg. Powdered egg, much of it imported from the United States where the eggs were spray-dried, took up less space, was obviously safer to transport, and needed no refrigeration. British households were allowed a grey packet of dried egg, the supposed equivalent to a dozen eggs, every four weeks.

Recalling life in an English boarding school during the Second World War, Jill Beattie wrote: 'The two words which still make my blood run cold, are DRIED EGG. The very worst breakfast ... was a two inch block of hard scrambled eggs oozing with water which saturated the half slice of so-called toast beneath it – and the TASTE – ugh!'

As for Doris Grant, her recipes include cauliflower soup (boiled with mace and half a leek, then sieved), cabbage puree (with evaporated milk, nutmeg and a shaving of margarine), shredded carrot and sultana salad, nettle tops (boiled for twenty minutes), steamed marrow – browned under the grill with grated cheese – liver casserole simmered with grated carrot, baked corned beef finely chopped with mashed parsnips, and baked apple and raisin pudding. Perhaps Lord Woolton licked his lips as he turned the pages, the lack of any hint of richness permeating the dishes appealing to his naturally austere constitution.

The book, with its sensible instructions, would be a useful addition to his other favourite cookery publication, *Food Facts for the Kitchen Front*. This no-nonsense little tome was filled with the likes of artichokes and potatoes in caper sauce (a dash of milk added to artichoke water and a 'few shavings of cooking fat' completing the dish). There were endless dishes of baked vegetables, of soups and broths (spruced up with 'a dash of milk', 'a piece of dripping', 'a pinch of nutmeg'), of rabbits – baked, boiled, jugged, potted and curried (cut, rolled in flour, fried with apple and spring onions and with a spoonful of curry powder) – and handy packed meals like cold kidney pasties.

Woolton expressed satisfaction about these publications before asking for an update on one of his most major publicity campaigns, which he ran in tandem with the Ministry of Agriculture. Some twelve months previously, Woolton and Minister of Agriculture Robert Hudson had launched the 'Dig for Victory' campaign. This was a countrywide campaign, reinforced on film, posters and radio, to deal with the problem that Britain seriously under-performed as a food-producing nation.

According to Woolton, the country's low level of food security, and its huge reliance of imports, arose from an endemic character trait. 'In the poorest homes people were largely ignorant of anything except their appetites and had no knowledge of food values,' he wrote, adding: 'As a nation, it was broadly true to say that we were indifferent to both our agriculture and our horticulture.'

Most wheat, flour and meat, for example, came from Canada, Australia, Argentina, New Zealand or Denmark. Onions had also been imported from France, which presented huge problems when that country fell to Germany in June 1940. In 1939 Britain produced only 40 per cent of its food (and in the 1930s the only food product that Britain was entirely self-sufficient in was liquid milk). 'It was obvious that to reduce the large figure of imports, we had to use every bit of land to the best advantage,' Woolton said.

So, in addition to directives to farmers to make their fields produce as much food as possible, householders were challenged to not just get their allotments productive but to turn parkland, cricket pitches and golf courses into vegetable patches. Famously, the rose gardens at the front of Buckingham Palace that flanked the Mall were turned over for cabbages, the manicured lawns by the Albert Memorial for carrots, and even the grass lawns that lined the moat around the Tower of London became neat strips of sown vegetables.

To front this campaign on film, the Ministry of Information hired the celebrity gardener of the day, C. H. Middleton, who had appeared on BBC radio throughout the 1930s. He gave advice on everything from composting to harvesting carrots, his message being: 'food is just as important a weapon of war as guns.'

The Dig for Victory campaign was hugely effective; by 1944, the nation was producing some 66 per cent of the food it consumed. Cultivated land rose from 12.9 million acres to 19.4 million and the number of tractors rose from 55,000 to 175,000. It was, the British food historian Colin Spencer has commented, a cultural change that occurred across the country: 'What food rationing did was to force everyone to grow their own vegetables; however small a patch people owned, lawns and flower beds were dug up, soil was dug, fertilized and planted with a year round supply of potatoes, vegetables and salads.'

Much of the work to produce all this veg was done by the 80,000 land girls of the Women's Land Army, who, it later transpired, endured a miserable war. They lived on a diet of bread, butter and potatoes and suffered endless sexual harassment from some of the few male farm workers who hadn't gone to war. The land girls' work was supplemented by German and Italian prisoners of war.

Woolton also wanted to encourage the nation to forage through the countryside. For there, among the hedgerows and in the woods, were fruits, berries and fungi which teams of parents and children – often dressed in Brownie or Cub uniforms – could pick until their heart's content. Walnuts could be pickled, chestnuts made into soup, and nettles used as a substitute for sage and onion. Of course, in reality rural scavenging could be less than romantic. Writer Anne Valery recalled her schoolgirl foraging efforts in her memoir *Talking About The War,* in which she wrote: 'I was one of the harvesters. Every autumn weekend, groups from school fanned out over North Devon, ploughing up hill and down dale, drenched or burnt by the sun, and bitten by every insect known to our biology mistress. Stained like Ancient Britons due to steady sampling, we picked for hours, our backs breaking in the search for the tiny bilberries hidden at ground level, and which the school made into jam.'

The foraging, Lord Woolton was told, would be further encouraged by the latest pamphlet to be produced in co-operation with his ministry. He was shown one such title called *Kitchen Front Recipes and Hints* by Ambrose Heath. The author's name was a pseudonym used by Francis Miller, a writer of countless such books and pamphlets. 'A poached egg on a bed of dandelion or nettle puree covered with cheese sauce is an almost perfect meal,' Woolton read out aloud to the assembled throng. It was a perfect recipe for the war effort, great for those country housewives. But it was not a dish that would go down well with Winston Churchill.

Back in London on 22 May, Woolton had a visitor to his office who wanted to discuss Woolton's plan to ensure everyone in the country was able to get their hands on wholemeal bread. If there was going to be just one type of universally available bread, it would be better for morale if it were the more interesting wholemeal than a relentless supply of the white stuff.

His visitor was the Royal physician Thomas, 1st Baron Horder, one of the country's most respected clinicians and an advisor to Woolton's ministry. The pair went for lunch because, wrote Woolton, 'I am anxious to get him to collect evidence from his professional friends who work in hospitals to the effect that the wholemeal bread is not having a bad effect on people's digestions.'

Woolton was aware of a significant number of people who were wary of wholemeal bread. 'There's a section of the public that is convincing itself that wholemeal bread is doing them harm,' he wrote. 'So much so that people write to tell me that they've never suffered from constipation before, but now they have to eat wholemeal bread they do.' Horder reassured Woolton, 'if wholemeal bread has any effect on this distressing complaint it's the opposite one!'

Rumblings about Woolton's rationing policy continued throughout the summer. There were complaints about tomatoes, potatoes, fish, jam, vegetables, fruit, bread and, of course, eggs. Woolton's attempt at controlling the price of tomatoes had led to them disappearing, critics alleged; they had gone underground. Likewise with fish, price controls – to stop profiteering – seem to have limited the supply. Fixed prices for jam had made it simply too expensive for many and there seemed to be a worrying dearth of new potatoes.

'I am assailed by critics,' he told the *Daily Telegraph* on 9 July. 'I am trying in the national interest, he said' – the reporter describing Woolton as exclaiming and 'throwing up his hands'.

He defended his egg scheme, saying he was trying to bring them into towns and within reach of people who had been finding them either out of reach or too expensive. The plan was simply 'in its birth pangs'. But everywhere he looked there were complaints. '"It's going wrong here" and "it's going wrong there",' he described people telling him, saying: 'I am not disputing that people cannot find something wrong with it, but it is a very big scheme ... and it is necessarily an experiment. No nation-wide scheme could be perfect.'

In July Winston Churchill weighed in after hearing complaints. 'The hen has been part and parcel of the country cottager's life since history began. Townsfolk can eke out their rations by a bought meal. What is the need for this tremendous reduction to one hen per person?' The Cabinet should have been informed, groused Churchill.

Woolton proceeded to defend each policy, then said in some desperation: 'I feel like a navvy [labourer] working in the boiling heat surrounded by lots of little flies, and it takes one all one's time to get them away.' So the profiteers were worms, and his critics flies; and the press continued to pile on the pressure.

'Lord Woolton May Leave', reported the *Manchester Evening News* on 17 July. His name was, the paper said, touted as one who faced the chop in an impending reshuffle. 'The Food Minister has been criticised from many quarters, and in Parliament at the beginning of May public dissatisfaction with the distribution of non-rationing foodstuffs was voiced.' Woolton wrote in his diary that evening: 'My press conference today was confined to eggs, of which I am heartily sick. The press were very critical of the scheme we had put in.'

Two days later, on 19 July, the *Daily Herald* yelled: 'Food Folly!' The press appeared to be turning on him again; this time, publishing an open letter by Labour MP Barbara Ayrton Gould. She attacked Woolton for noticing too late that the country had an issue with malnutrition: 'Did it really take twenty-two months of Total War to bring home to you the evils of malnutrition? I have spent twenty years trying to stop this hideous scandal,' she declared. She went on to attack his egg policy, saying, 'Your egg scheme has involved the nation in a serious and easily avoidable wastage of a vital food.'

Ayrton Gould said she had been investigating Woolton's egg policy and reported that 'the net result of the scheme is to provide the consumer with millions of bad eggs.' She alleged that the country's egg collectors 'who have always collected eggs from all the local farms for immediate dispatch to large towns or sales in local markets were instructed by your ministry to hold the eggs for weeks before dispatching them to your depots. How are they expected to keep those eggs in hot weather? They have no cold storage. Most of them have no stock-in-trade except a light van for collection and distribution.' She added that a collector she knew from the West Country had complained that 'weeks on end in a hot barn will finish them.' Furthermore imported eggs from America and Canada had, she alleged, been 'three months old before they reached the consumer. Didn't your advisers tell you that eggs were perishable, and would not keep good for so many weeks on end?'

Next she assaulted Woolton over potatoes. As with eggs, his scheme was to control prices and distribution. 'Were you as ignorant about the wastage of eggs as apparently you were about the shortage of potatoes?' She claimed that thousands of housewives had queued for up to 'twelve days for potatoes and that many had been turned away empty-handed?'

The Labour MP also didn't buy Woolton's class credentials: 'Perhaps you don't know that in millions of working class homes potatoes are the mainstay of the people's diet, and the lack of them causes serious hardship,' she wrote. 'I should like to know what you think about the malnutrition caused by the action of your ministry in mishandling these two vital foodstuffs.'

A month later – on 9 August – the *Perthshire Advertiser* declared: 'Tears for Woolton'. In a savage piece the paper accused Woolton of poking his nose into the kitchens of the housewife, where 'she has hitherto reigned supreme.' He 'has rushed in, with a host of silk-hatted bureaucrats at his heels; and, with the laudable object of making things easy for everybody, has succeeded in converting order into chaos and efficiency into well-nigh hopeless muddle.' Where there had been, the paper argued, a reasonable supply of eggs in many areas, 'there is now an all-over scarcity; where there was pristine freshness, there is now in too many instances a musty look and a disconcerting smell.' The paper also mentioned 'the soft fruit bungle', which, it said, was 'another example of misbegotten ingenuity'.

Attacks continued, coming from every quarter. Sir Ernest Bevin, writing in the August issue of *Truth* magazine, argued that Woolton's control of pricing had taken away the prospect of profit and as a result 'has upset the balance of the market, if not, indeed, destroyed it'. On 30 August novelist Ursula Bloom, in the *Leader* newspaper, accused Woolton of 'gross mismanagement'. His crimes included creating a bureaucracy in which fruit went putrid ('sacrificed to your little forms, to your blue pencil dockets'), eggs went off and 'market-cornering crooks' went scot-free. 'I stood yesterday in a queue for oranges, doled out one at a time for a family,' she wrote. 'I saw seven different members of one family go twice through that queue, and none of your little forms covers that kind of cheating.'

The next day writer Howard Drayton in the *Sunday Sun* also attacked Woolton's penchant for form-filling. 'Growers can't pick their crops because they haven't received their permits,' he wrote, claiming that as a result, 'much of the plum crop will be lost.' On the same day the *Daily Herald* ran a picture story which, it claimed, 'tells the story of millions of schoolchildren in Britain today who are not being properly fed'. The large headline above the story read: 'This isn't good enough Lord Woolton.'

Yet while Woolton was being publicly lashed, he was getting quite a different press behind the political scenes. On 13 July 13 Alexander Erskine-Hill (a Scottish Unionist Party politician), chairman of the Conservative Party's back-bench 1922 committee – an influential group of MPs who liaised with the Prime Minister – came to see Woolton. 'The Conservative Party is becoming uneasy about the value and strength of Winston as PM,' he told Woolton. 'Things are not going well in the war and we are wondering how long he will last. So I've been tasked to come and speak to you to see whether you have any views about succeeding him.'

Woolton reckoned this was because 'the Party wouldn't mind having me if I would take it on, because they know I don't want to hang on after the war.' However, as he wrote in his diary and told Erskine-Hill: 'I don't want to be Prime Minister.' He didn't, however, say that if offered the role, he wouldn't actually take it on.

By midsummer, chatter about Churchill's future seemed to reach fever pitch. A flurry of MPs came to visit Woolton to sound him out on a job outside the Food Ministry. Kingsley Wood, for example, then Chancellor of the Exchequer, arrived to flatter him on 18 August. 'You've managed the food problem very well indeed,' he said. 'I think you've done your job as Minister for Food and it's time you looked for fresh worlds to conquer. My view is that you should hold very high office in the government.' Then Oliver Stanley, at that point Secretary of State for the Colonies, came to have lunch with Woolton. He was 'full of gossip about the Conservative Party and the fact that it thinks Winston has had his day. They are looking for a new leader.'

This talk of Woolton succeeding Churchill continued well into the following spring and summer of 1943. On 2 April 1943 he made the following small note in his diary: 'Incidentally I was told that the editor of one of the national dailies had asked if I had any political ambition and if I had ever thought of myself as the post-war Prime Minister.' He was clearly puffed up to hear such gossip. But while some were touting his name as a possible successor to Churchill, Woolton realised that there were of course others jostling for the position.

He recalled an occasion in the House of Lords on 1 April 1942 when Lord Beaverbook had put down a motion about the costs of milk distribution. 'There was nothing of note in his [Beaverbrook's] speech but he has adopted a technique of putting down a motion about something or other every week to keep himself before the public,' wrote Woolton, who was less than impressed: 'It's a pathetic effort because nobody takes any notice of him and he has completely worn himself out of public favour. But I think that he has an idea that if ever another PM was needed the public might clamour for him.'

Then on 11 June 1943 he recorded a conversation with the Conservative MP Leslie Pym: 'Somebody had told me a week or two ago that at a meeting of very important people in the political world it had been suggested that, in the event of Winston not holding the Premiership, I was the only member of the present government who could take it on. I told this to Leslie Pym, rather by way of a joke, but to my surprise he didn't laugh, but told me that he himself had heard the same proposal discussed seriously in political circles.'

But for all the talk of Woolton attaining the premiership, he could always rely on the newspapers to bring him back down to earth. On 23 November the *Reynold's News* paper put on its steel-capped boots and took aim: 'Lordly Failure', it declared. The paper wrote how, next to maintaining the nation's food supplies, Woolton's job was to maintain the nation's confidence in the Ministry of Food. 'Lord Woolton is falling down on the job.' The paper cited how in early November Woolton had 'announced that no winter milk shortage was in sight. Then he imposed a token cut of 5 per cent. Next he raised the cut to 15 per cent. Tomorrow, he will limit adults to two pints a week.' *Reynold's News* wasn't happy. 'This monkeying with the people's milk must stop,' it continued. 'The public is prepared to go short, to endure inconvenience, even hardship. What the public is not pre-pared to endure is a continuance of mismanagement in everything Lord Woolton touches.'

Maud, his beloved

Woolton read the article, shrugged his shoulders then had it stuck into his cuttings album. He would discuss it with his wife Maud; she never failed to improve his spirits when he was under attack. The couple, well into late middle-age, were as unified and as besotted as ever. Just a few weeks previously – a weekend night before bedtime in London on 9 October 1942 – Lord Woolton had been relaxing in his apartment. 'It's Saturday and the anniversary of our wedding tomorrow, so we've frivolled,' he wrote. 'Maud and I had lunch together, then to a theatre in the afternoon and dined out afterwards. A very satisfactory day.'

Woolton was never more content than when in the company of Maud and years later, five months after her death on 13 September 1961, he sat down to write a long tribute to her. Across fifty-seven sheets of unlined paper, he told her life story. He expressed his gratitude that she had been by his side through every period of difficulty in his adult life and how he had shared all his thoughts with her, from his worries and concerns to the many official secrets that burdened him. He chose to write those words in the library that she had designed for him at their house, Walberton, in Sussex.

He wrote of her strong religious faith – which he shared – and said that 'somehow she had acquired the secret of living, in tune with the infinity.' He sensed her presence: 'I feel that she is "hereabouts".'

'I loved her so deeply that I am impelled to write of her,' he wrote. 'With her encouragement and constant support and loving care, I have been privileged to occupy a prominent position in the service of my country when its people and its future were imperilled.'

As war had approached, and his political rank had risen, so he realised that he would have to spend at least three days a week in London. The happy days he spent relaxing at their holiday home by Lake Windermere would be severely restricted, and he was concerned that his time with his other half would be similarly lessened. London was also a dangerous place, but, he recorded: 'To my delight Maud decided that whilst she couldn't come all the time she was aiming at doing so. We both knew full well that war was coming and that whatever else happened we were going to be separated a great deal. Both our children were at school or college so we resolved that during term time we would move about together and during holidays Maud would live with the children in the Lakes.'

Lady Woolton was more than a dutiful companion; she developed a nice line in public speaking, filling in for her husband if he was unable to open a British Restaurant or attending a lunch to jolly along some community caterers.

'In all this Maud was not only with me,' he wrote, 'but I constantly talked to her about those very secret things and I know I could do so. Not only with benefit, but with security in this speaking of official secrets of the first magnitude. It was all thrilling – and exhausting!'

Maud was similarly devoted to her Fred, often referring to him with the affectionate 'F'. She was pleased and reassured to once record, in February 1941, that after a lunch with Joseph Cohen, one of the directors of Lewis's, 'a medium came in.' Presumably Cohen's idea of post-lunch entertainment. She was left in the room with Maud. 'It was rather thrilling,' she wrote. 'She began by saying that I was psychic – and my husband was, that we were very much "enwrapped", that we had been together in another life.' The medium went on to say that she could see Woolton, surrounded by important men, one of whom was holding a heraldic shield. Maud posited that this could be 'the coat of arms of Manchester University'. One of the men, said the medium, was Neville Chamberlain. 'A third man wore a frock coat,' recorded Maud, 'had a scroll in his hand and was making a proclamation. I may say that she [the medium] hadn't been told who F was, and thus had no means of knowing. She kept saying that F had a great and responsible job, and that he was very tired. He must rest.'

During the school holidays, Woolton missed his wife and wrote to her often. But he also sent her letters while they were both in London. Theirs was a love that endured over many decades and Woolton penned notes to his wife at a similar rate to the letters sent from his mother to his young self. They are indeed as regular as a modern day email exchange between a devoted couple. When Maud was away, his letters talk of how a speech went down, a broadcast delivered or a tricky meeting handled. And every note started with language that makes very clear his devotion to her.

Finding time between meetings to pen quick missives from his desk at the Ministry of Food he would begin: 'Darling', 'Darlingest' or 'Belovedest'. 'Goodbye darling,' he ended one such note, 'I hope you are resting and sleeping and not worrying about anything but the next meal.' In another: 'Goodbye best of wives: I think of you constantly between speeches. Love to the Woolly one.'

One afternoon he wrote simply: 'to tell you what a gloriously happy time you have given me: you have been so sweet and time doesn't wither nor age decay it,' while on one other occasion he told her: 'You know I really am ridiculously dependent on you.'

13

A Spoonful of Sugar

Better news arrived on 24 October: the 1942 crop of potatoes was a good one. 'I want to get people to eat more potatoes instead of bread,' he wrote. Over the coming months he attempted to get this story into the press. In mid-December his ministry launched a campaign and held fairs across the country that demonstrated the marvels of the potato. In due course, in January 1943, stories appeared in both the *Daily Telegraph* and *The Times* of, as the latter put it on 13 January, the 'Urgent Need to Eat More Potatoes'.

The following spring then handed Woolton a further boost when it was predicted, as the *Observer* reported on May 30, that the 'Harvest Will Be A Record.'

Talking that day to 1,600 land girls at Aylesbury in Buckinghamshire, Woolton announced that 'it appears that we are going to have the prospect of the greatest harvest that we have ever had.' He also thanked the nation's dairy farmers saying: 'You have given us milk in quantities that we scarcely even dared hope to get.'

The bumper harvest of 1943 for British farmers saw a transformation: whereas at the start of the war most of the wheat for bread had been imported, in that year one half of the country's bread grain needs were met by home-grown wheat. The biggest increase in food production came in potatoes, which went up 87 per cent. It rather begged the question of what to do with it all, with Woolton's ministry reckoning the best answer was as a substitute for bread.

According to writer Lizzie Collingham in her book *The Taste of War:* 'The end result was that Britain produced too many potatoes ... Those who benefited were the privileged members of society who had the means to keep a pig, as they were provided with a plentiful and cheap food.'

Woolton finished his triumphant speech in Aylesbury heralding what he long saw as one of his greatest achievements: 'When this war is over we shall have an infant and child population which will not have been damaged by the war.'

Lord Boyd Orr, one of Britain's foremost nutrition expert and post-war head of the United Nations Food and Agriculture Organisation, wrote in his memoirs: 'Lord Woolton produced for the first time in modern history a food plan based on the nutritional needs of the people, with priority in rationing for mothers and children ... the rich got less to eat, which did them no harm, and the poor, so far as the supply would allow, got a diet adequate for health, with free orange juice, cod liver oil, extra milk and other things for mothers and children. This was a great achievement for which Britain is indebted to Lord Woolton.'

But while Woolton was publicly talking of great success, he had a problem in his ministry. In early May of 1943 Woolton was in his office talking with Sir William Rook, Director of Sugar at the Ministry of Food.

The two were having some concerned discussions. Woolton stirred his cup of tea, pausing from puffing on his pipe, and noting to himself how well he had retuned his tastes in recent months. He preferred two teaspoons of sugar in his milky tea, but these days, along with everyone else in the country, he was making do with none. Sometimes Rook, given his job title, would bring in a little sugar as a treat for the minister. But today there was no such luck.

'We are getting uncomfortably short of sugar,' Rook told the minister. 'Our usual supplies have either dried up or the passage by ship has become impossible.'

'Well,' replied Woolton, 'we should find new suppliers. Sugar is such an important commodity, there must be other markets.'

'There is another we haven't used,' said Rook.

'Oh yes?' said Woolton, perking up.

'Yes, Minister. It's a supply in Egypt. But there's a big problem. A big expensive problem. And his name is Pasha Abboud.'

Rook explained: there were considerable quantities of sugar in Egypt, but they were all under the control of Pasha Abboud, an Egyptian who had trained as an engineer on the Clyde. He had taken his engineering skills to Turkey where he'd made a great deal of money before returning to Egypt and building ship-repairing yards in Alexandria. He then started purchasing steamships – most of which were involved in the import and export of sugar – before buying control of the reason they used the ports of Alexandria, the location of the country's largest sugar factory. Such was his fortune that he owned a palace larger than the King's, and, with the right infrastructure at his disposal, he was able to control the price of sugar on the Egyptian market, and now in a time of war and of fragmented supply, all across the world. Indeed, he had become the most powerful global figure in the world of this prized and much-needed commodity.

'So there we have it,' concluded Rook. 'We need sugar, households across the country need it. And the only man we can buy it from wants an extortionate price. So either we pay for it, and destroy the ministry's budgets for other goods, or this nation and her colonies have to learn to live without it. But we all know the dangers of not honouring the ration, of damaging national morale.'

Rook was at a loss. But as he finished talking, he noticed a wry smile come over Woolton's face.

'Don't worry, Sir William,' said Woolton. 'I think I can deal with this problem. Just tell me one thing. Where else in the world is there a reasonable quantity of sugar, regardless of how far away it might be, that we could get our hands on?'

Rook paused then answered: 'Well there's sugar in Queensland, Australia. But it's a considerable distance away and the cost of export to Britain would make it financially unviable.'

'OK,' said Woolton. Then he pressed a button on his telephone and one of his private secretaries came on the line.

'Can you get hold of Lloyd's for me?' he asked. 'Tell them the Ministry of Food wishes to charter a ship for us to take sugar from Queensland, Australia to Egypt.'

Rook looked on astonished as Woolton talked. He put down the receiver and then said to his Director of Sugar. 'Once Lloyd's have agreed, can you let your contacts on the Egyptian sugar market know that there's a new sugar supplier in town?'

'I'm confused, Minister,' said a baffled Rook.

'I'm going to sell sugar in Alexandria. And I'm going to sell it for less than this chap Pasha Abboud charges. So he'll have to compete with me and bring down his prices.'

Rook left the room doubtful to say the least about this high-risk strategy. The ministry would be committing millions of pounds to buying and shipping the sugar from Australia to Egypt with all the transport risks that that entailed. And what did Woolton know about the sugar market?

Woolton was rather more bullish, writing later in his memoirs that Abboud 'knew that he had been trying to make us pay an extortionate price for the things he possessed and I think he reasonably expected to be treated a little roughly.' Which was just as Woolton intended. It was not the first time he had brought his business and commercial chutzpah into the department. But it was not without considerable risk.

While Woolton was still exercising his business acumen, he was supposed to have jettisoned his actual business when he accepted the role of Minister of Food. He had made a great play of it, telling newspapers, fellow politicians and his wife of the financial sacrifices he was making to join the government. In fact, he continued to have occasional meetings with the board of Lewis's, having lunch from time to time with directors and he had several meetings – as recorded in his own diaries – with regards to the potential purchase of the London department store Selfridges. For example, on 27 November 1941, he met with a business contact of his, Ivan Spens, who advised him that Selfridges was 'getting no real management and would like us [Lewis's – the firm Woolton no longer worked for . . .] to put somebody in to take hold of the place, in anticipation of our buying it when the war is over'. Woolton recorded his response: 'I told him we had nobody to spare: but the truth is that I have no intention of letting any of Lewis's people go in to tidy up the place and get it making a profit, so that we put up the purchase price for ourselves.'

This talk of 'us' and 'we' with regards to Lewis's was somewhat at odds with the statement put out by the Ministry of Food as reported in the *Daily Telegraph* on 1 May 1941, when rebutting claims made by a Scottish MP (see page 210) that Lewis's had been selling cooked meat when their rivals had none. The Ministry of Food official had been emphatic that Woolton had 'no connection with Lewis's'.

The following year, on 22 December 1942, a distinguished accountant, Sir William McLintock, met Woolton to discuss the negotiations for the store. Woolton recorded, frustratedly, that: 'In spite of restrictions on supply and trade, and shortage of staff they [Selfridges] are doing very well and it's going to cost us more money than it would have done a year or two back.'

On 6 May 1943 Woolton spent an evening with McLintock at Claridge's. The accountant 'brought with him the proposals for the purchase of Selfridges,' recorded Woolton. 'We spent the evening discussing the details and he has gone away to amend them.' (It was another night when Woolton had to endure eating his eponymous Woolton pie. 'It was so poor that I have had to send McLintock the official recipe in order to convince him that it's really all right.')

Yet, most of the time, Woolton engaged his business brain for the legitimate pursuits of his ministry, albeit in ways that often made his officials squirm. Seeking on one occasion to purchase beef from Argentina, he had a meeting with the Argentinian Ambassador. The price he heard was high, far more than he knew was the market rate, 'a grossly advanced price' as he put it. At the meeting, as he recalled, he 'said some rather hard things about the desire of the Argentinian government to make an excessive profit out of the fact that we were at war'.

His moral pronouncements seemed to have had little effect. The Argentinians stuck to their price. As far as they were concerned Britain needed their meat and had no room to manoeuvre. The British could moralise and talk about principles all they liked but they had no choice but to pay up.

'I accept your decision,' Woolton told the Ambassador. The Argentinian assumed he had won this tussle. Then the minister continued. 'And as we cannot trade I will immediately give instructions that our ships will not call at Argentinian ports.'

British ships were not just passing through Argentinian ports to deliver meat to the UK, they were part of that country's vital import and export business. Furthermore, Argentina's cold storage facilities at the time were full to overflowing; processed food needed chilling and, if British ships could not stop at the ports, the country would lose millions of tons of produce. The Argentinians then backed down; they were now desperate to do the deal. At which point Woolton said he was now revising his terms. The Ambassador assumed the price was going to be reduced further, but instead Woolton told him that he wanted Argentina to raise his price, only by a smaller margin than originally proposed. 'One of us is going to win in this battle and one has to lose, he said. 'I prefer you to win.'

Woolton wanted final recognition of the negotiation to belong to the Ambassador so he could claim to his government that Britain was a reasonable country to deal with; a satisfied supplier meant they would continue to sell to him as a customer. He shook hands with the Argentinian and said: 'So you get the victory: we get the meat.'

Woolton may have brought such negotiations to a fruitful conclusion but not all his staff enjoyed the process – some were horrified at seeing what they regarded as low business tactics being employed among diplomatic circles. Vexed by the traditional command structure in his department, Woolton sometimes felt compelled to circumvent the usual routes to making purchases. His view was that by only ever acting with total propriety, opportunities would be missed. Worried, for example, by rumours that the Germans were negotiating to buy whale oil from the Norwegians (which would be used to make margarine), Woolton hastily made contact with the traders, agreed the first price quoted and then bought the entire stock. According to his memoirs, he then had it transported to Britain and hidden in a secret location, well away from any German spies or foreign agents keen to procure or steal whale oil for their own country's desperate needs.

When a row was looking to brew between his department and the Americans over the sale of a million eggs which had arrived rotten, he intervened. Not wishing to upset the Americans with a complaint, however justified, as he wanted to secure a constant trade before a colleague could discover that the consignment had gone bad, he sent in a secret squad of men. Under cover of darkness they removed the eggs from port and then dropped them down a disused mine in Skelmersdale. 'I wonder if, in years to come, some archaeologists will wonder what sort of people would leave this colossal quantity of eggs in such a small area,' he mused on the incident. 'But by then probably both the eggs – and I hope the smell – will have gone.'

When it came to purchasing essential goods such as wheat, there were the formal channels, the official ways of trading and there was the Woolton way; a way determined by him and without recourse to such tedious things as departmental approval or even paperwork.

On 8 September 1942, for example, Woolton attended a ceremony at Canada House. It was a formal occasion, in which Woolton and his senior staff were ushered through the maple-lined passages of this Greek Revivalist building, with its exterior clad in bold whitish–grey Portland stone. In a room filled with a large number of journalists, with photographers on hand to help record this vital moment, lavish documents concerning trade between Canada and Great Britain were laid out for signature.

The formality was a wheat-buying agreement and the result of months of intense negotiating between the British Government and the Canadian High Commission. A quite beautiful set of papers had been crafted; signatures would seal the occasion, before and after speeches that would talk about the spirit of cooperation between key allies; great nations working together to supply food to the common man or woman. Woolton himself, at the appropriate time, signed his autograph on the document, as photographs were taken. All that was missing was a band of trumpeters to play a robust voluntary to muster the soul and stir up a little fervent patriotism. The pleasantries over, he quickly left the building, a mischievous smile breaking across his face, keen to get back to his office where the actual purchasing of wheat took place, Woolton-style.

That night he made a confession to his diary. 'The sum total of the agreement about which there was all this palaver was 10 million bushels of wheat,' he wrote. 'A few weeks ago I had bought 20 million bushels of wheat, certainly without consultation with anyone except the Treasury and without signing an agreement. The whole thing had been done almost entirely on the telephone – which, after all, is the proper way to buy wheat!'

Woolton's other method in securing wheat was to buy options in wheat markets anonymously. He did it without Treasury consent, buying options in every wheat market in the world before terminating those options on the same day. In that way, without his customers knowing he was acting for the British Government, he got a better deal. Usually he was able to fund the deals with the Ministry of Food budget; but one day he had to involve the Chancellor of the Exchequer, Sir Kingsley Wood.

Woolton had telephoned Wood saying he needed to secure funds – £100 million, to be precise. He made the call saying, 'I've been buying some food,' keenly requesting that the money be made available by three o'clock that afternoon.

'You can't treat me in this manner,' said a startled Chancellor, 'you need to write a paper and go through the official channels.' Woolton replied: 'I will not write a paper about a commercial transaction of this magnitude; it would be impossible to keep it secret and the loss to the Treasury would not be less than 20 million if the markets knew what was happening.'

'Is this the way you normally conduct your business affairs?' asked Wood.

'It is,' replied Woolton. He assured him that he would not have to carry any responsibility for the deal as, noted Woolton: 'I was using him as my banker.' Woolton was having trouble completing the last option and needed extra money from the Treasury, but without the Treasury knowing. So it made sense for him to ask Wood, who ran the department. Woolton felt he could trust the Chancellor having, coincidentally, acted as an advisor to him before the war. Wood agreed and, having successfully secured the money, Woolton then managed to buy all the wheat the country would need for the next six months and at a healthy price of 72 cents a bushel. He went to Wood's office to thank him personally and to apologise for the demands he had put on him that morning.

'You will never live to see wheat at 72 cents again,' he told Wood.

'I suppose you have bought it in the name of the British Government,' said Wood.

'I can assure you,' replied Woolton, 'that if anybody had known it was the British Government that was buying we would have had to pay a much higher price. We bought the wheat under every possible sort of disguise.'

Wood was sanguine. 'Well all that I ask is that you can impose some restraint on your activities. I can see that you are difficult to control. But I might add that you are the only minister who has ever come to me to apologise for saving money.'

Woolton was also at his maverick best when working to import ground-nuts from Nigeria, needed to make margarine. Just as with whale oil, nuts could also be used for spreads. Given the large amount needed, 400,000 tons – as Woolton wrote, 'it takes a lot of ground-nuts to make a ton' – he called on an old friend of his, Lord Swinton. Swinton was Minister Resident in West Africa, or, as Woolton put it, 'Ambassador-at-large in Africa' known to the Nigerians as 'the King of Britain'. 'Will you ask the native chiefs if, on the grounds of patriotism, they will provide us with this large quantity of ground-nuts?' requested Woolton.

Swinton, wrote Woolton, arranged a meeting and flew in to a village in his 'white and glittering plane'. 'I, the King of Britain,' he told the tribal chiefs, 'am disturbed that my country is surrounded by enemies who are trying to starve it and my people are in danger.' He explained how the supply or ground-nuts could alleviate the problem. 'This is more than money can buy,' he continued, 'but not more than your patriotism could afford.' According to Woolton, 'the chiefs went and met other chiefs; they had a pow-wow and then came back to Lord Swinton.'

'Please send a message to the British saying that the people of Nigeria do not want the King's people at home going short of fat for the want of ground-nuts,' they told him. 'The whole affair was conducted with the maximum of solemnity,' recorded Woolton. A promise was given and in due course 400,000 tons of ground-nuts came to Britain.

Meanwhile, Woolton still needed to secure that sugar from Egypt. Word reached Abboud that a certain Lord Woolton was considering entering the Alexandrian sugar market and, to Woolton's amusement, in due course, a telegram came to the Department from the Egyptian saying, in Woolton's words: 'that he would like to come over to interview me, with a view to helping our sugar supplies'.

With a meeting arranged with Abboud, Woolton knew he could call off the Queensland shipment. 'We called the Egyptian bluff,' he wrote. 'To the great relief of the Department I therefore decided not to sell sugar in Egypt.'

Once in London Abboud was brought to see Woolton at his office. He had a Scottish wife, the minister discovered, and, apparently, 'a tender spot in his heart for Britain'. The man who came into Woolton's office that day was expecting a stern-faced, cold minister of the British Government, a tough fight and some hard negotiation. Instead Woolton was at his most relaxed and charming. 'Let me tell you how very glad I am to see you. It really gives me such pleasure to welcome you here,' said a warm and effusive Woolton. 'And let me tell you right now, my dear fellow, that I really know absolutely nothing about sugar and I wouldn't venture for one moment to negotiate with you, such a skilled and successful man.'

Instead, Woolton introduced him to Sir William Rook who would, said Woolton, 'be very glad, and at your convenience, to have some discussions with you'.

Abboud by return expressed pleasant views about Britain saying: 'I have merely the desire that Britain should win the war and I am very affectionate for the people of this country.'

'Well, Mr Abboud, these sentiments are very agreeable for me to hear,' replied Woolton. 'So let me just add that I can't disguise the fact that we need sugar and that, in view of your sentiments, I'm sure you would want us to get it at a price that we can afford to pay.'

The two parted, mutual respect having grown between them, agreeing to meet again in a few days. Two nights later they did meet, this time at a dinner party given by the businessman Lord McGowan. It was a discreet occasion with some dozen government people in attendance. As dinner came to an end, and the port was passed around the table, Brendan Bracken, the Conservative Minister of Information, teased the Egyptian guest about his business methods: 'Well Abboud,' he said, 'I suppose you have come to try to take the skin off Woolton's back.'

Woolton recorded that, at this remark, 'I saw a flush rise to the Egyptian's face; I saw that he was deeply offended, so I hastened to say: "You ought not to have said that. His Excellency [Woolton now addressing him with splendid grandeur] has given me every assurance of his deep affection for this country and his desire to help it."'

At this Abboud go to his feet. 'Lord Woolton,' he said,

'Thank you. Now let me tell you gentlemen. These past few days, I have talked with officials from the Ministry of Food who have made it very clear to me the terms on which they wish to buy sugar from me. So let me tell you my decision. I have come to the view that I will not sell you any sugar.'

There was a gasp of dismay around the table.

'No,' continued Abboud, 'I have decided to *give* you the whole of the sugar you need as my contribution to the war effort.'

There was applause across the room. Abboud had agreed to donate a million tons. Woolton picked up his glass and raised it to him, the two men smiling respectfully at one another.

The next day Abboud and Woolton again met at the Ministry of Food office, this time with Sir William Rook who, noted Woolton, 'was most surprised at this turn in the negotiations'.

Woolton, now fearing he knew this Egyptian rather too well, was concerned that his generosity might be later used to demand some kind of payback. So he told Abboud that His Majesty the King would be very grateful, in actual fact, for a loan of the sugar and that he would either be returned the million tons at the end of the war or the value of the sugar in sterling at the time peace was declared. The Egyptian consented.

'We got the sugar and remained very good friends with Abboud,' wrote Woolton. Some years later Abboud contacted the then former minister, saying how fondly he remembered the deal that they did during the war and whether he would like to spend some time during the cold English winter months with Maud at his palace in Alexandria. Also, would the noble Lord be interested in joining his commercial activities in Egypt on, he wrote, 'financially very advantageous terms'? Abboud had finally met his match and could do with a man like Woolton on his board. Woolton, of course, with immense satisfaction, declined.

14

CHURCHILL, MILK AND JOB OFFERS

By the middle of 1943 Woolton was beginning to feel satisfied with the work of his ministry. 'The food organisation was in reasonable shape,' he wrote modestly in his memoirs. He had the right people operating on the purchasing side, and others in his team never ceased to pile on the pressure when it came to shipping. He had oil tankers cleaned out and used to transport grain and he persuaded liners to share their passenger lists so that food, as he wrote, 'could be squeezed into cabin space'.

The UK supply chain also seemed in good order. Woolton had established emergency warehouses across the country, using the likes of closed church halls and disused cinemas for storage, going so far as appointing Voluntary Food Officers in even the tiniest of villages to keep, under their own secret control, emergency food supplies so that their community could be kept alive in the event of a crisis, either because communications had failed or an invasion launched.

Regular exercises were held to test the strength of these reserves. Woolton was determined to know exactly how the country would cope if supplies were disrupted or halted in the event of roads, power stations or bakeries being bombed. 'It became a constant battle of wits against the enemy,' he later wrote, 'with the harrowing certainty that if we failed the people would go hungry.'

By this stage of the war, Woolton was also proud of the work he had done in hospitals in educating people about the importance of good nutrition. 'Food is so important to health,' he wrote, 'and patients in hospital are probably in a more receptive mood than at any period of their lives.' He felt there was an opportunity to implant the knowledge of what he called 'food values' which, he wrote, 'might do a great deal to reduce subsequent ill-health and the necessity for further hospital treatment'.

But, he added, 'the most satisfactory action we took to safeguard the health of nation was among pregnant women and nursing mothers, where the greatest need existed for teaching food values.'

Woolton's scientific advisors had told him that milk, fruit juices, cod liver oil, halibut oil and eggs were the key foods. So, he declared, 'I grasped the opportunity that lay to my hand. On them rested the future health of the nation.'

But these were not easy foods to get hold of, although Woolton felt, with the data stored in Colwyn Bay, he could at least accurately calculate how much he needed.

He then appealed directly to the United States to send fruit juices for babies. And he imported orange juice in bulk and persuaded Boots, the chemist, to bottle it at cost. It was, he wrote, their 'patriotic service'. Woolton reduced the amount of milk that the general adult population could have, in order that expectant and nursing mothers and children under five could have a whole pint of milk a day. He had been worried about this action and was a little trepidatious when it came to informing one of his scientific advisors, the Royal doctor Lord Horder. But his fears were immediately allayed. 'If you continue with this policy you will reduce the attendance of my consulting rooms by half,' Horder told him. Much of the trouble, the physician explained, was that elderly people suffered because they drank too much milk.

Moreover, Woolton later wrote that 'British-like, everyone was prepared to make sacrifices for children, whether they were their own or other people's.' He wrote in the 1950s of the 'reward . . . [of seeing] the children of the post-war period growing up stronger than any previous generation, and to know that now this scientific care of the feeding of nursing mothers and of children has become a part of our national practice'.

There was, in fact, a joke within the Ministry of Food that such was the zeal of Woolton for feeding prospective mothers that officials could get anything out of him if they could convince him that it was for such ladies, who they called 'the preggies'.

Word reached the front line that the wives and children of serving soldiers were being taken care of. Letters poured in to Woolton. Those wives would often send in pictures of their babies to the minister, in his words, 'bursting with food and good health'. His secretaries would often giggle at such a picture on which so often would be written, 'one of Lord Woolton's babies'.

Woolton was also gratified that the Americans had finally come through with help with the arrangement known as Lend-Lease. This had stalled his deep-seated irritation with America. He had been at his most vociferous once on leaving a meeting with a food producer from the United States who seemed only interested in profit. 'I have an insular prejudice against these itinerant Americans,' he wrote, 'telling us how to run our affairs, especially as I suppose it is true to say that there is nothing in which they have not failed – at any rate in point of time – to fulfil their promises to us. It's quite clear that what is happening is that the Americans are in the doldrums, as they put it, being "caught with their pants down" at Pearl Harbor.'

But Lend-Lease calmed his spirit. It was aid in the form of everything from hardware – such as ships – to oil and food, ending any pretence that the US was neutral. Countries such as France, the United Kingdom and China benefited. Some of the aid could be returned – tanks or warplanes – and some was given in return for US use of Allied army or naval bases. The food tended to be free and anyway – as Lord Woolton noted in his memoirs – 'there was a popular idea that the institution of Lend-Lease solved a large number of our food problems. All that it solved was the problem of paying for them when they came from America, for we no longer had the dollars with which to pay.'

So free food donations did indeed solve that problem. The

first consignment of food under the programme had arrived on 31 May 1941 and Lord Woolton and the US President's personal representative, Averell Harriman, went to the docks to welcome the ships for both their own interest and that of the press. 'It was 4 million eggs, 120,000 pounds of cheese, and 1,000 tons of flour,' he recalled. 'To celebrate, I broke my own regulations – and handed over, for division amongst the unloading staff of 240, a 20 pound cheese.'

He later reflected on the benefit of this arrangement from the United States government, saying that 'without their aid we would ultimately have been reduced to almost iron rations.'

Such were Woolton's successes that by June of 1943 Churchill seemed to have tired of arguing with his Minister of Food and when he disagreed with him would merely make a joke of it. On 29 June Woolton attended a Cabinet meeting to argue for his latest cause: that milk should be pasteurised throughout the country and not just, as was the case, in the capital and in major cities. Woolton had seen statistics that showed that, as he wrote, 'the incidence of germs in raw milk are quite frightening and the public must be protected against germ-infected milk.'

Woolton went to see Churchill before the meeting to brief him in the hope that he might get the rest of the Cabinet to agree, and Churchill asked him to join him in his official car so they could chat on the way to the meeting. 'It was interesting to see the way in which he always had his eye on the public whilst we were talking in his car,' wrote Woolton, 'waving his hat and showing the V sign to the people as we passed. I was very surprised that so great a man should have this sense of public showmanship on a journey he must have taken thousands of times.'

As for the meeting, 'he was,' wrote Woolton, 'in a very good mood in the Cabinet.

'"Have you tasted pasteurised milk, Woolton?" Churchill asked.

'"Prime Minister, 98 per cent of milk in London is pasteurised. I have always attributed your own radiant good health to the fact that you drank pasteurised milk."'

The Cabinet burst into laughter and Churchill looked at Woolton and said: 'I've never tasted the stuff.' He sent for a glass so he could see how it tasted. The milk came and he expressed intense displeasure. 'This whole proposal of yours Woolton is part of a move towards modernism of which I disprove,' he said – and then let Woolton have his way.

As Woolton left the meeting, he reflected on how things had changed. He recalled a letter he had received back in July 1940, when Churchill had written to castigate Woolton on the ration he was implementing. 'The way to lose a war is to try to force the British public into a diet of milk, oatmeal, potatoes etc., washed down on gala occasions with a little lime juice,' he wrote. He had traditional views and was disparaging about anything that was not conventional. 'Almost all the food fadists [sic] I have ever known, nut-eaters and the like, have died young after a long period of senile decay.' And as for the advisors Woolton had on his team, Churchill was frank: 'The British soldier is far more likely to be right than the scientists,' he wrote, before adding: 'All he cares about is beer.'

As autumn approached and the gossip about Churchill's

premiership appeared to diminish, some job offers from outside the political sphere began to arrive at Woolton's door,
and then accumulate.

On 25 September 1943 he noted that senior directors at the
Bank of England were lobbying the Governor of the Bank
for Woolton to be made chairman. Woolton, not averse to
this, sent a note to the senior director, Sir Thomas Royden,
thanking him. But there were others on the board who
would prevent a unanimous vote in his favour, notably Sir
Percy Bates with whom he did not appear to get on.

Three days later he was approached to become chairman
of the British Red Cross Society, their current incumbent
being, Woolton wrote, 'too old and ill to be of any use to
them'. He told them he would think about it although he
feared it was not a very well-run organisation and 'there may
be a job to do there,' suggesting that post-war he wanted a
slightly easier number than he'd been given over the past
few years.

Two days later he attended a football match at Wembley;
in the box were several directors of the Midland Bank. They
'were all very pleasant to me', he wrote. He had heard that
his name was in the frame as a possible successor to Reginald
McKenna, then chairman, which added another possible job
to the pile.

A formal offer, rather than postulated ones, was made
on 21 October 1943, for Woolton to become chairman
of Martins Bank. Originally a London-based bank which
had merged with the Bank of Liverpool in 1918, Martins
merged with Barclays in the late 1960s. Woolton knew of
them well as they were his retail firm Lewis's bankers. But

he now dismissed them, talking of their 'lack of guts' as, at the start of the war, they had refused to confirm that they would stand firm if there was a rush to withdraw money as the conflict began. 'I cannot help remembering the anxiety that Martins and its chairman caused me,' he wrote. Now they were lining him up to be chairman. He was telephoned by Lord Colwyn, from the bank's board, who said he hoped Woolton would become chairman as they were concerned about its future.

Woolton had so many people wooing him he wrote: 'In view of certain other representations that have been made to me I felt I could bear this blushing honour with equanimity.' So he told Colwyn that 'life was too uncertain and I couldn't make any commitments for the time being.'

Next, one can only speculate as to whether employment was discussed at a dinner a few days later with the managing director of Baring Brothers & Co., Arthur Villiers. Woolton's diary records that he and Maud then went to stay for the weekend with Ernest Kleinwort at his family house in Haywards Heath in Sussex. Ernest was the chairman of the family banking firm Kleinwort, Sons & Co. but Woolton does not record whether, over a glass of port after dinner, with Maud and Mrs Benson retired to the drawing room, a nice job was offered at their elegant offices in Fenchurch Street.

Then, on 1 November 1943, Churchill asked Woolton to lunch. 'When I arrived he was dressed in his rompers,' wrote Woolton, 'and obviously not looking well.'

The Prime Minister was not in a joking mood and there was no chit-chat, no back-slapping or teasing, no calling Woolton Goering or asking him how many people he'd flogged that morning. 'With the hors d'oeuvres he went straight into the subject on which he had asked me to lunch,' Woolton wrote.

'I want you to become Minister of Reconstruction,' Churchill said. 'Our focus now at this stage of the war must be what I call WHF: work, homes and food. People need jobs, they need a roof over their head and they must not go hungry.'

Well aware of the enormous challenge that creating and building an entirely new ministry would involve prompted Woolton to ask questions. 'How will this ministry work, Prime Minister? Who will staff it? Where will it be located? How will we resource its budget? What precisely will this Ministry of Reconstruction do?' he demanded, while understanding the principles behind the idea. His questions irritated Churchill who brushed them aside.

'So will you take it, Woolton?' he asked. 'You're the perfect man for the job. That you have amply demonstrated these past few years.'

Churchill, Woolton later wrote, 'seemed to be surprised – and a little grumpy – that I didn't jump at his offer.'

'I will go and think it over,' Woolton said coolly. 'Before I take on such a role I will need to be quite sure that I would have the requisite authority needed to carry the responsibility of running such a ministry.'

'You can join the War Cabinet,' said Churchill. This was a tempting offer, as Woolton had so often been thwarted by discussions in the War Cabinet that he was not privy to. 'That will give you all the authority anyone would need for such a job,' the Prime Minister continued. By this point, Churchill was on to a second generous glass of whisky and, recalled Woolton, 'became easier', the alcohol loosening him a little, putting some colour into his cheeks.

'Woolton, you have a reputation for caring for the well-being of your fellow man and this trait of yours will enable you to get the public confidence that will be necessary as we plan for the future of England, a difficult period of transition between war and peace.' Churchill was getting into his stride; uncomfortable on bureaucratic detail, he was happier on grounds such as human character. He took another long sip from his glass. 'In entrusting this task to you I am paying you a very great compliment,' he added. Such flattery would surely do the trick.

But still Woolton stalled. 'I am conscious of what you say and thank you for it. But I am not going to take on a job unless I am quite sure that I will be able to do it.'

'Well go and ask your wife if she thinks you can do it,' Churchill snapped.

'I should also tell you that I have provisionally made a commitment to be chairman of the Midland Bank,' Woolton added, before their meeting and lunch came to an end.

'Well tell the bank that they can wait,' Churchill insisted, raising his voice somewhat.

Woolton left the meeting pleased that he had managed to elicit compliments from Winston Churchill, get a big job offer and infuriate him all at the same time. Yet he was apprehensive about the role. And he would have to ask Maud.

His conversation with her had, he wrote in his diary, 'most extraordinarily revealing results. Instead of being afraid of the job, as I am, she just said: "Well yes, of course, all the experience you have had in life has been just a preparation for this, hasn't it, and so why should you hesitate.'"

Woolton quickly let Churchill know that he would indeed take on the role, and in the same week he also agreed to become chairman of the Red Cross. Churchill then made a speech at the Mansion House, in which he talked of his new mantra: of work, homes and food; according to Woolton, 'obviously preparing the way for the announcement of my appointment'.

It happened just three days later, on 12 November 1943. 'The papers,' he wrote, 'were full of it.' And, more importantly, 'they were all most flattering to me.' Although he sensed a downside to this: 'The more I read about what I'm to do, the more I'm frightened about it. Obviously people are expecting the new heaven and the new earth. It terrifies me to know that I'm to be the provider of it.'

Meanwhile his desk at the ministry's offices in Portman Court was cleared, and the picture of his wife Maud, his personal books, stationery, pens and diaries all boxed up. His successor, Colonel John Llewellyn, who had been Minister of Aircraft Production, was away in Washington and it would be several days before he returned to London and assumed Woolton's old chair. But he thought it best, having officially left the department, to physically do so.

Offices for the brand new Ministry of Reconstruction were yet to be organised, so Woolton suggested that he decamp somewhere suitable for the time being and had rooms prepared at the Carlton Hotel, which had been partly bombed three years previously and then taken over by the government. Designed in the late 1890s by the architect C. J. Phipps as part of a development that included Her Majesty's Theatre, this grand French Renaissance-style building stood on the corner of Pall Mall and Haymarket (it was demolished in the late 1950s).

Woolton's new office would be at Number Four Richmond Terrace, on the east side of Whitehall, opposite Downing Street. It would enable Woolton to stroll to meetings of the War Cabinet and would also, geographically at least, place him closer to the heart of government.

As he sat in the Carlton Hotel contemplating this new phase in his life, he resolved to try to keep things simple. His last two jobs had involved huge bureaucracies and he was determined that this one would not. Woolton grabbed some smart-looking headed paper, bearing a coat of arms – of lions and shields and a crown – designed for the establishment under which it was stated: 'The Leading and Most Fashionable Hotel and Restaurant in London.' Woolton put two thick lines across those words and wrote instead the distinctly less sexy title: 'Ministry of Reconstruction'. Then he began to build his new department. It would last only as long as the war did and devote itself to post-war planning. Knowing how terrible communication could be between ministries and officials, and how systems of government could be built that seemed only to serve the purpose of stopping anything happening, he took pleasure in noting down how his ministry would bring other departments together.

Whether it was food or jobs, homes or well-being, roads and transport, infrastructure or justice, he would ensure department plans were brought into relation with each other. He would fill gaps and eradicate conflicts. He would employ very few staff and the whole ministry would be located almost within his earshot and certainly not in a far-flung Welsh seaside town. He would be able to walk to work from Whitehall Court and, from time to time, he'd be able to have lunch with Maud.

His early plans formulated that morning of 15 November, he then returned to Portman Square for a final meeting with the staff he had worked with since April 1940, three long years and seven months previously.

There was no actual business, instead senior staff came to say goodbye. It would be his last meeting with Sir Henry French. With the staff assembled, Sir Henry thanked his minister and, recalled Woolton, 'was obviously moved'. This was not expected. In fact Woolton had rather assumed that however successful he might have been, these people would have been secretly rather relieved to see the back of him.

And when the patrician, bold and unswerving Woolton himself started to say a few words he surprised himself as he too came close to tears. 'I found myself becoming quite emotional,' he recalled. He spoke of the honour he had had in working for the ministry, of the enormity of the task they had faced and of the extraordinary loyalty, patience and persistence that his staff had shown day in, day out during some of the toughest experiences of their working lives. Yet in the face of terrible odds they had, with him, managed to feed the country. Britain had not starved, it would not now starve and their nation and its allies would now unquestionably succeed in defeating the Third Reich and the corrupt axis of power that propped it up. Woolton would miss his senior staff and the men and women of the ministry.

The meeting broke up and Woolton stood at the door to shake hands with each of them as they walked out. As Woolton said goodbyes and thanks individually to the line of people, he dug as deep as he could to compose himself. 'Many of them were in tears,' he wrote.

As he composed his diary later that night he tried to stop himself from becoming sentimental about the day's events. 'I was sorry to be going,' he wrote, 'I'd had my share of difficulties both with supplies and with staff, but during the past two years things had been working smoothly and I felt I was leaving very good friends behind me.'

He considered how he and Sir Henry French had come to work together so effectively. He recalled how, in due course, he had asked Sir Henry to move his office closer to his and that he had even asked builders to knock a hole in the wall and add a door so the pair could have more constant contact. He had recorded in his diary what he told his senior civil servant after the new door was made: 'Sir Henry, you are welcome at any meeting that I have, whatever is happening.'

Woolton had many reasons to be grateful to Sir Henry. He was a strong administrator, had a great knowledge of food from his long years at the Ministry of Agriculture, and even managed to reach a concordat between Agriculture Minister Robert Hudson and Woolton, which had settled policy between the two ministries for the rest of the war.

The success of the ration owed much to Sir Henry's supervision – that it was fair, efficient and well enforced. His inflexibility had wilted on occasions, such as submitting to Woolton's insistence on hiring businessmen to advise. And his pre-war planning (he was director of the Food (Defence

Plans) department from 1936 to 1939) had enabled the ministry, for all its faults that Woolton tried rectify, to get up-and-running as soon as war had broken out.

Meanwhile Sir Henry's own lack of negotiation skills was ideal as that was Woolton's strong suit, and he learned to focus on administrating while relinquishing the levers of policy to his political boss. While to many people he was unapproachable and vain, this simply amused Woolton who was happy to ignore this aspect of his character. Indeed in later life Woolton enjoyed telling a story of how Sir Henry, in September 1944, made a visit to India. An Indian minister greeted him with the words: 'French, this is the greatest day in the history of India.' Woolton loved the story because Sir Henry often told people about it and appeared to believe it.

Two days later, Woolton had another set of goodbyes to make. He needed to travel to Colwyn Bay for a final time. The train journey, which started at dawn from London, seemed interminable and when he finally arrived in the late afternoon went straight into a series of farewell meetings. The elaborate outfit that was Colwyn Bay never ceased to amaze him and he was rather itching to get going with a simpler organisation. He spent the night in the station hotel exhausted: 'so tired I couldn't sleep,' he wrote.

The next morning he left on the first train which should have got him back to London at 3.30 in the afternoon. But thick fog slowed their progress, outside the air was freezing, while the heating in his carriage was malfunctioning and he spent the long journey 'in intense cold'. Finally the train drew in to London which itself was, he wrote, 'obliterated by fog'. It was, he said, 'a miserable ending to a rather miserable two days.'

Forty-eight hours later he was installed in his new office. Having visited it previously he'd insisted on decorators being employed to give the rooms a fresh lick of paint but it nevertheless had a feeling of gloom about it. 'There's an awful odour of antiquity and decay about the place,' he wrote.

Until Woolton's appointment, the job of reconstruction had been fulfilled by Sir William Jowitt, a grey man in every sense of the word, in his role as Minister without Portfolio. He had been occupying the now refurbished room that Woolton was now sat in. The new minister wondered how on earth anyone could have worked in what had been, Woolton said, 'a dead shade of green'. Given that Woolton was now taking on the role of reconstruction, he was struggling to find out what Jowitt's work had entailed. 'He's a lawyer and not an inspirer,' he noted confidentially. 'I find it difficult to find out what he has been doing. I suspect very little.' Jowitt was still there and had moved to a room next door. Knocking gingerly on the door, recalled Woolton, he 'begged me to give him something to do'.

'I don't think you'll have any difficulty in finding work,' said Woolton, exasperated. He then asked his new assistant to call in for meetings with ministers from other departments with whom he would be dealing. There was William, Lord Portal, Minister of Works, 'a good soul but I'm afraid he's not very adaptable', and Harry Willink, Minister for Health. Woolton liked Willink, a Liverpudlian by birth and 'a very pleasant fellow'. Willink had taken over the department from Ernest Brown who, Woolton noted, had taken months to build a couple of cottages for some workmen, so seemed unlikely to manage building housing on a scale that would be needed at the end of the war.

Then there was William Morrison, Minister for Town and Country Planning (the Minister Woolton replaced back in 1940 as Minister for Food). 'His record is not a good one, he has mishandled every office he has held up to now and I can't see him making a spectacular success of this one,' commented Woolton. 'I'm going to have trouble with [his] department. Morrison is afraid of [facing hostile] political reaction and he's weak.

'These are the main people I am to co-ordinate – and they've never been co-ordinated before. I'm afraid my job is going to be a full time one.' Surrounded, in the main, by ineffectual ministers, seemingly insurmountable problems and an expectant British public, Woolton had a giant task ahead of him – but this was familiar territory, of course. The nation was still at war, the city still under attack and the world a precarious and dangerous place.

He recalled a surprising insight into the unbending Sir Henry. In Woolton's eyes, Sir Henry had at first seemed the epitome of a tricky civil servant with whom he would never strike a chord. Managing the relationship seemed almost as insurmountable as feeding an island nation at war. However, a bond that even Sir Henry might have conceded was a 'warm friendship' had developed. Woolton's mind wandered back to an exchange with Sir Henry that took place near the end of his tenure. It occurred at a press conference when an invited guest was digressing, potentially causing problems with timings further down the line.

Sir Henry said: 'You wrote me a note that read, "How you must suffer when you listen to me, wondering when I am going to say the wrong thing: or does custom dull fear?" Lord Woolton, one of these days we shall have to tell each other what we really think of each other. In the meantime I only say that a wife doesn't love her husband because he's either perfect or colourless. My heart has never gone out to any chief, minister or otherwise, as it goes out to you.'

With this implacable civil servant by his side, Woolton had fed and saved Britain. He had given the nation its food, its eggs, and in return it had not descended into chaos and anarchy.

He lit his pipe, blew out a large puff of smoke and then got to work.

15

THE HEALTH OF BRITAIN

Given the successes of his ministry during the Second World War, did what Lord Woolton set out to do — feeding and improving the nutrition of the people of this country — make him, arguably, this country's most successful minister? For Britain, at the end of the war, was not just in good physical shape, it had — and has never been — so healthy. This wasn't just a healthiness that presented itself in the form of slim adults and rosy-cheeked children; child mortality had never been so low, and far fewer mothers died in childbirth. Fewer babies had been stillborn and children were both taller and sturdier. There was also a markedly lower rate of tooth decay. All of which results were achieved with fewer doctors, dentists, nurses and health visitors, most of whom were deployed overseas with the armed forces.

While the rich ate less, the poorer ate more adequately, while rationing restricted sweet snacks for children, who nibbled on carrots rather than chocolate and crisps between meals. As the cook Marguerite Patten wrote, 'For many poor children the school dinners and milk, free cod liver oil and orange juice provided them with a more nutritious diet than they had ever experienced.'

If there was any doubt in the need for decent food for children in the minds of host families or schools, the Board of Education Circular no. 1571, issued on 12 November 1941, stated: 'On the average the energy value of the food required by a healthy child of elementary school age is estimated at about 2,500 calories a day and therefore the midday meal, which for sound reasons is the main meal of the day for nearly all children, should have an energy value of about 1,000 calories. Moreover most of the necessary first class protein and most of the fat must normally be obtained in this meal. As a general guide therefore, a school dinner should be planned to provide per child.'

Minister of Food Lord Woolton saw the war as a fantastic opportunity to target children with healthy meals. In his diary in October 1941, he wrote: 'To preserve the health of the future nation I wanted to secure that every child, in every school, got at least one good hot meal a day, and I saw no other way of securing this than through the schools.'

That same month *The Times* reported him as saying: 'I want to see elementary school children as well fed as children going to Eton and Harrow. I am determined that we shall organise our food front that at the end of the war . . . we shall have preserved, and even improved, the health and physique of the nation.'

With tremendous foresight he wrote that not to do this would imply 'a very heavy cost to the Exchequer'. 'This is a piece of really constructive work,' he added, of his thinking on school meals. 'I hope, though I'm not terribly sanguine about it, that it will remain after the war is over. Anyhow, I'm very pleased at having got it started.'

However, a report on Stoke's school meals in September 1943 found in all schools, except one, the calorie content of the meals was less than a third of daily requirements. In its summary, it said that although some schools were better than others in providing the necessary calories and fat, all the meals lacked the necessary minerals: 'The vitamin A potency was not unsatisfactory but for safety should be increased. The vitamin C content of meals cooked on the same premises as they were eaten was only about half of the desirable standard while those transported contained less than one third of the desirable standard.'

Even in those schools where the meals were cooked on the premises the vitamin C content of vegetables was lower than of domestic cooked vegetables.

'The calorie content of the meal should be improved by increased helpings, especially of potatoes and other vegetables and of puddings. Second helpings should be provided and all the children should be encouraged to ask for them. Full allowances of cheese and of dried skimmed milk should be provided as they will improve the fat, animal protein and calcium content of the diet. They would also increase the variety of the diets. Vitamin A intake should be improved by an increased consumption of cheese, green vegetables and carrots.'

The report went on to suggest improved ways of cooking to preserve vitamin C:

a) Cook in as small volume of water as possible;
b) Do not overcook. The analyses of cabbages suggest that on some days they must have been either cooked or kept hot too long;
c) Wherever possible avoid use of the 'hot plate';
d) Practise serial cooking – that is, cook successive batches of cabbages in the same water.

Factory workers, meanwhile, were fed nutritious food by their canteens and expectant mothers of all classes were given cod liver oil and orange juice. And as the war effort extended employment across the country, many who had been out of work and now had jobs found that they had more money to spend on food.

But, of course, it wasn't to last. Free meals petered out just as subsidised food did via the government-backed British Restaurants. As rationing ended, the 'nanny state' control of what we put into our mouths diminished. The ensuing decades – but particularly the latter two of the twentieth-century – saw a revolution of choice entering the market via supermarkets and restaurants. And with that choice came the freedom to engage in bad habits, often driven by a combination of price and the feeling of being time-poor.

But what of the control that the government, directed by Woolton, had on the food consumption of the nation? The evidence strongly suggests that society had a good mixed diet, which produced great benefits to the nation's health, although what was offered was not without controversy.

Woolton himself had battles with different factions of scientists, although naturally he agreed with the nutritional advice that came out of the scientists approved by his own ministry. One evening in July 1941 Woolton faced a whole barrage of hostile scientists during a dinner at The Café Royal. Having made a brief speech the floor was open and scientist after scientist got to their feet to attack Woolton and his policies. 'They told me of all the things that were wrong with the food of the nation and the way it was being controlled,' he wrote. Woolton listened and then took the lot of them out with one broad swipe.

'You have all joined the great majority of grumblers,' he said. 'But what I entirely fail to see is that you have made any contribution to the well-being of this country.'

Woolton did, however, have a supporter in *The Times*. A leader on 20 August 1941 entitled 'Tokens of Health' reported that: 'Lord Woolton's assertions that there is no sign of malnutrition in this country is fully borne out by such statistical and other evidence as is now available.' It continued: 'It can therefore be said with satisfaction that the health and strength of the nation have not suffered from any privation due to the war.' It was, noted Woolton, 'a very fair and encouraging leader'.

When it came to the issue of meat consumption, Woolton may have had a rather old-fashioned view of vegetarians but he couldn't help himself having a sneaking admiration. 'I sent for the vegetarians in order to ask them how they were living without meat, and without eggs or cheese,' he wrote in February 1941. 'They were a most healthy-looking crowd of people.' It was not a diet for him, however. 'I found vegetarianism to be a flatulent failure,' he said in his memoirs. But, he added, 'it was clear that with many people it produced life and energy of a very high order.'

While Woolton was focused on the local issues of feeding Britain, he also allowed himself to think more ambitiously, writing of his dream to create, globally, a 'general standard of nutrition', arguing in his diary in August 1942 that the 'world is capable of producing so much food that there is no justification, after the war, for any part of it being hungry.' He talked of establishing 'an international food office', pointing out that 'hungry men are dangerous'.

Indeed he began to lobby foreign politicians and diplomats who always appeared thrilled by his idea. He then, in April 1943, lobbied the Chancellor of the Exchequer to create a fund so that the UK could 'build up a stock of food with which we can help to ease the world's food difficulties at the end of the war. We shall have to send so much to the liberated countries that unless we build up enormous reserve stocks now we shall find ourselves in difficulties. It's no use liberating countries and then keeping them in a state of semi-starvation.'

Woolton's other battle was to convince the Cabinet to introduce legislation to make the pasteurisation of milk compulsory. 'The farmers hate it, the doctors approve,' he wrote after a meeting with the National Farmers Union in February 1942. (According to the *British Medical Journal*, between 1912 and 1937 some 65,000 people died of tuberculosis contracted from consuming milk in England and Wales alone.) He was victorious to some extent, as in July 1942 pasteurisation was introduced to the dairies that supplied major city centres. While Woolton was an early advocate, dairy businesses took it under their own discretion to pasteurise milk during the 1950s, although it was not made compulsory until the 1980s, Scotland being the first to introduce legislation in 1983 and then England and Wales in 1989. It was a UN regulatory drive in 1997 that saw the UK-wide spread of the process.

But what lessons can be learned from rationing today? Lord Woolton was happy to see the rewards of controlling what the nation ate but then he had extraordinary powers for extraordinary times. These days any hint at government tampering with our freedom to choose what we put in our mouths can be condemned as the unnecessary actions of 'the nanny state'.

Danny Alexander, a former Liberal Democrat MP and one-time Chief Secretary to the Treasury, had his hands on the reins of power during his time in coalition government, during which he experienced what it was like to affect the lives of millions through the cuts that he delivered to the UK budget. 'There is a strong case for further positive and negative incentives for people to live healthier lifestyles,' he says. 'Not only is that better in the long run for individuals, it also ensure more healthy years of adult life for people to work and contribute, and would reduce one of the fastest growing areas of cost and pressure in the NHS.'

But for him the big question is, of course, what works? 'Tax measures clearly do have an influence on behaviour,' he says, 'but they have to be pretty hefty to make a difference, as tobacco and fuel duties show. And even then, they work in combination with other levers such as health warnings on cigarette packets.' As for a token tax on sugar, Alexander believes that, while that can send a signal if it were set high enough to make its consumption too expensive, it would be 'politically difficult to impose'. He also feels it would be socially regressive because evidence shows that those on lower incomes spend a higher proportion of their income on food. 'A small tax rise on a heated snack from the south of England created a furore in 2012,' he comments, adding: 'think of the row if a government tried to impose a tax that would fall on a lot of foodstuffs.'

It is thus the view of many experts that the most promising route is regulatory. Governments can set reasonable rules for mass produced foods to ensure that they meet what Alexander calls 'socially agreeable nutritional standards'. It is such efforts that have brought down salt levels in many foods, so possibly the same thing could be done for sugars and saturated fats.

But there is one area where governments and authorities can impose control – aside from in prisons – and that's in schools. The 1870 Education Act made elementary education compulsory for all children and the first free school meals started being served in Manchester. This gave an incentive to poor families to send their children to school as they would be able to spend the day studying rather than earning money to pay for a crust of bread. It also meant that children would not be too hungry to study.

In 1906 a further Education Act authorised local councils to serve free school meals to children who were from the poorest families. But recession and the onset and aftermath of war saw such cuts in government expenditure and the diversion of funds to other areas that, by the start of the Second World War, only half of all local authorities (157) were providing free school meals to children.

The work of Lord Woolton and others saw that during the Second World War nutritional standards were set for school meals. (With a minimum of 1,000 calories and 30g of fat for each meal. Interestingly this compares today to a maximum of 530 calories and 20g of fat in primary school standards today.)

The Education Act of 1944 made it compulsory for local education authorities (LEAs) to provide a free meal for children in state schools. Latterly – during the 1970s and 1980s – children started to turn away from school meals and choose instead a packed lunch prepared at home. A 1980 Education Act then removed the legal requirement for LEAs to provide a meal for every pupil and also abolished the minimum nutritional standards.

In 2013, Henry Dimbleby and John Vincent gathered a panel of experts and produced a School Food Plan for government ministers. 'Only one per cent of packed lunches meet the nutritional standards that currently apply to school food.' The country's serious health crisis, they argue, is 'caused by bad diet'. And the problem needs tackling, 'before the costs (both personal and financial) become too heavy to bear'. Their aim is to have children provided with school dinners and to encourage and enable the people with the power to orchestrate this: namely head teachers.

Dimbleby and Vincent recommend that free school meals be extended to all primary school children, starting in the most deprived areas, and that schools and councils fund universal school meals. Dimbleby has noted that as a result of some free meals 'the pupils whose results improved most markedly were the poorest.' He and Vincent believe their plan can 'improve the academic performance of our children and the health of our nation'. But they recognise that 'it requires a cultural change within each school. It means cooking food that is both appetising and nutritious; making the dining hall a welcoming place; keeping queues down; getting the price right; allowing children to eat with their friends; getting them interested in cooking and growing.'

According to Moira Howie, nutritionist for UK supermarket Waitrose, the key difference between our food related behaviour today and during the war years concerns our physical activity. 'The move towards making everything convenient and easy has conspired to make us a sedentary population,' she says. 'So children are driven rather than walk to school, we sit on mowing machines rather than push them, we press a button on a device to change the TV channel rather than get up and down to do it, we use a washing machine rather than clean clothes by hand and, because our houses are warm, we don't naturally engage in physical activities, such as scrubbing the steps, to keep warm.'

Howie further believes that, while the average calorie intake these days is roughly the same as in the 1940s, in gaining those calories we need to do less. We can, for example, buy a fast food burger rather than go out to snare a rabbit. To rectify this, argues Howie, we do not need to engage in anything of 'a massive magnitude'. As she explains: 'A lot of little things make a big difference: taking the stairs rather than the lift at work, walking rather than using a car for short distances, getting a dog so you walk round the block or park regularly . . .'

The facts confronting us now are startling: Today in Britain 69 per cent of men and 58 per cent of women are classified as overweight or obese. According to a report by consultancy firm McKinsey and Company, the side effects of this problem – from diabetes to heart disease – is now a greater burden on the UK's economy than armed violence, war and terrorism. The cost to the National Health Service of the current rate of obesity and overweight conditions could increase to between £10bn and £12bn by 2030 and, needless to say, this is pushing the NHS to breaking point. The overall healthcare and social costs of an increasingly overweight population has been totalled at £47 billion per year.

Cynics would say that government only starts to take an issue like this seriously when the Treasury begins to panic. But there is also a growing clamour for radical action, as evidenced by the UK-based celebrity chef Jamie Oliver who, in the autumn of 2015, called on the government to impose a tax on sugar to help curb the obesity crisis. Oliver's main target is sugary soft drinks, saying: 'I want to see the introduction of a 20p per litre levy on every soft drink containing added sugar – this equates to 7p per 330ml can.' He has claimed that: 'studies show this could have a significant impact on health in the UK, reducing sugary drink consumption by possibly 15 per cent.'

The Times newspaper argued, in a leader column on 22 October 2015, that the government should, 'give serious consideration to a sugar tax', (which indeed the government decided to do in March 2016 when the Chancellor George

Osborne announced a sugar levy to take effect in 2018.

Drinks over 5g of sugar per 100ml will be taxed at 18 pence per litre and those with 8g per 100ml would be hit with a 24 pence tax. It would mean an extra 8 pence on the current price of a standard can of Coca-Cola. While Jamie Oliver heralded it as 'bold and brave' those in the drinks industry said they would challenge the policy, while lawyers said it could be in breach of European Union laws on competitiveness.) The paper also pointed out that 'the impact of obesity is particularly troubling on the young. By the time they leave primary school one in five children is obese.' The figures it quoted were that obesity-related illness is linked to 53,000 premature deaths each year and costs the NHS more than £5 billion annually to treat.

All of which debate makes a look at the state of Britain's health during the Second World War, when the government really did control what the general public consumed, more than prescient.

THE SHOPKEEPERS' STORY

For all that Lord Woolton did, he and his department, indeed the whole government, relied on the diligence and goodwill of the nation's shopkeepers. They were the people who the country's housewives depended upon immediately and to whom everyday frustrations would be vented. Without their patriotic efforts the battle to keep up morale would have failed.

Two stories, recounted over sixty years later, put a spotlight on how quite how extraordinary the everyday pursuit of supplying a community with fruit, vegetables or meat was.

Cricklewood

On 3 September 1939 nineteen-year-old Harold Gilbert had just finished his tea when his father switched on the radio to listen to the news. He was tired after a long day's work at the family fruit and vegetable store, S Ginsberg, at 89 Cricklewood Broadway in North London. One of four brothers, he seemed to be the one with the muscles so his metier, in his late teens, consisted of lifting, moving, carrying and positioning large sacks, boxes and cartons of fresh produce. He might heave large sacks of potatoes purchased in Covent Garden onto the family truck, or unload huge crates of bananas back at the shop in Cricklewood. There were two other members of staff and his brothers helped too, but his siblings were never quite as majestically strong as he was. Brothers Asher – two years younger – and Arnold – two years older – might have been equipped for the business mentally, but they couldn't swing a sack of carrots quite like Harold. And Dennis, at just twelve, was more adept at running through the store and pinching a hand-full of cherries, or popping strawberries into his pockets.

So Harold was almost dozing when the news crackled over the radio that a state of war existed between Britain and Germany.

'It wasn't very welcome news,' reflected Harold, in understated dour tones some seventy-seven years later. 'We all wondered what exactly would happen. We were very apprehensive.'

In the days that followed, all three elder brothers attended medicals while it was determined which part of the forces they might join. Arnold was the first to be called up, joining an anti-aircraft regiment, while Asher went into the Navy and spent the next two years in a battle cruiser as part of the Arctic convoys; both brothers would survive the war. Arnold returned home eight days after the Dunkirk evacuation. 'We hadn't heard from him and were all terribly worried. Then one morning he just came into the house with a rifle on his back. I was in the bath and he came in and said hello. But he would never talk about what happened,' said Harold. 'No one could ever get it out of him, not even his children. We discovered that he had been rescued by a boat from the St Helier yacht club, but he obviously wanted to forget the war as he never mentioned anything that happened to anyone for the rest of his life.'

But Harold failed the medical. 'I have very little sight in my right eye,' he said at the age of ninety-five, 'so I stayed and worked with my dad. My little brother Dennis was supposed to be evacuated to the countryside, but he didn't want to go and I don't think my mum would have let him anyway. He just left school and never went back. Mind you he went on to have a very successful career and was the managing director of a public company.'

As for the other staff at the greengrocer they also left, seconded to the local ARP, the air-raid protection unit. That left Harold and his dad, Samuel Ginsberg, known to everyone as Sam. Sam steeled himself with his wife Kitty to survive and get through the war. Not a day would pass when Kitty wouldn't worry about her two boys serving overseas. But at least she still had two at home.

'I had mixed feelings about not going to war,' reflected Harold. 'I had feelings of disappointment, feelings of relief and a feeling of worry that I would spend the rest of the war in the shop. It would mean a lot more work. But although I had a problem with one of my eyes, I was as strong as an ox.'

Sam Ginsberg (the family changed their name to Gilbert in the 1950s), whose father Simon had started the business as an immigrant from Latvia – he had literally begun by buying and selling a few oranges and then steadily building up sales – was fastidious about his produce. 'He would go to the old Covent Garden market very early and his strategy was simply to buy the best,' recalled Harold. 'He got to know growers, particularly from Kent and the Thames Valley, but also traders who imported from overseas.' Sam, dressed always in waistcoat, shirt and tie, would return home from the market with a list of what he'd bought and it would be the job of Harold, in his overall and dark tan trousers, to drive back to market and collect the produce.

In peacetime, stalls at the front of the shop and inside would be piled high with potatoes, cabbages, spring greens, sprouts, cauliflower, peas, runner beans, spinach and rhubarb; there were apples, pears, plums, gooseberries, red and black currants, raspberries, loganberries and strawberries – making S Ginsberg the most colourful store on Cricklewood Broadway. The Ginsbergs knew all of their customers by name and knew their own personal preferences, which fruit and veg each member of their family liked. And any children in tow would always be given an apple or a tangerine. 'It was,' said Harold, 'more like a club than a shop.'

But the onset of war changed all of this, and very quickly. 'There were no more imports of fruit, stocks diminished and so did our income,' said Harold. The display on the street, at the front of the shop – generous piles of fruit and veg adorning the pavement which further enticed you to ponder on the glistening wares of S Ginsberg inside – all went.

'Suddenly we could only depend on English produce, so stocks of fruit fell in particular and inside we only used about half of the shop,' he said. Meanwhile a great number of their customers disappeared. Many went to war, others left London to escape the prospect of bombing. But it never occurred to Sam Ginsberg that he should take his family elsewhere; his business and his home were there in Cricklewood. The atmosphere changed among those customers that stayed too. 'Many people were just very, very worried,' said Harold, 'and you could just see it on their faces; while others managed to take it in their stride.'

Which is what Harold appeared to do. 'I got used to the bombings at night,' he said. 'But you had to be wary of the shrapnel which came down from our own guns shooting at enemy planes. At the start of the war I went to the air raid shelter when the siren went off. But after three nights of that I got fed up and decided to stay home in my bed.'

Harold only slept away the family home on one subsequent occasion, when an unexploded bomb landed in the road just outside the local Windmill pub. 'Our whole street was evacuated to a school for two nights until the army defused the bomb.'

S Ginsberg was never hit, but bombs fell within yards of the shop. 'I went to get the truck one morning to drive to the market and found that it was holding up the roof of our neighbours' house,' he remembered. 'We did get quite a lot of bombs because there was a mainline railway at the back of our shop. But they generally missed. The bakery on our street was bombed, though, and I remember four of their bakers were killed.'

While stocks diminished and business got difficult, when rationing was introduced a hard business got even tougher. 'Rationing affected us a lot, although it was worse for a lot of butchers and bakers, as there were no coupons for fruit and veg,' said Harold. 'My days still started after Dad came back from the market and we'd work until it got dark. That could be seven o'clock in the summer or four in the winter. At dusk there would be no one about.'

So Harold worked day in, day out throughout the conflict and, he said, 'I never had a single day's holiday right through the war. Although I did go to Clacton one Saturday. I'd met a girl at a dance so I went to see her. It was nice but I never saw her again. It wasn't meant to be. I found out she had a boyfriend.'

Of course being in the food business also had its advantages. Harold's family would never be short of fruit or vegetables, although he professed that his family 'only took what we needed. Our aim was to sell everything.' But his father was in a position to ask favours of his suppliers. 'My dad was able to get eggs and poultry from the drivers who brought supplies from the country. If he got a chicken, it would be live, so he'd take it up to the Jewish poultry butcher who would kill it for him. My mother was a born cook and she'd roast the chicken and make lovely soup. She'd also pickle things like onions and would pickle herring. And she'd cook fresh fish if my father got some, although I always hated fish.'

Some of their remaining loyal customers would also ask for a little extra. 'We did our best to please them,' said Harold, 'and my dad might keep something in the back for very old customers – who were mainly all working mums with their husbands away at the war. We would help them if we could – but you couldn't call it the black market; even people at the top were doing it [getting a little extra if they could]. My dad was always very careful and never wanted to have any trouble.'

When the war ended and privations eased, and with a fuller staff and the brothers all home, life started to return to normal at S Ginsberg. Tomatoes arrived, then citrus fruits and grapes. 'I remember the first batch of bananas that came into the market,' said Harold. 'I put them out on display at the front and children stopped and wondered what they were. I had to show them how you peeled one.'

Twyford

On the same day that Harold Gilbert heard the news that his country was at war with Germany, eight-year-old Peter Jennings was also listening to the radio with his family in the village of Twyford in Berkshire.

Peter, born in September 1931, was one of six children and they all lived above the family butcher shop, LJ Jennings. The business was started by his father Leonard Joseph and the premises was adorned with the hanging carcasses of pigs, sheep, chickens and turkeys. The shop was on the red-bricked high street of Twyford, a village typically self-sufficient for the time with an abundance of bakeries, grocers, a bread and cake shop, a sweet shop and three other butchers.

While his parents and eldest brother Norman had seemed concerned at the report of war delivered by a sombre Neville

Chamberlain that day, the news sparked little worry in young Peter. He continued to attend the village school, would play football with his friends in the evening or hang around at the back of the shop. There was a slaughterhouse there, and Peter was always fascinated by the sight of animals being delivered, then butchered and prepared for sale.

'We did our own slaughtering every Monday,' he recalled, 'a bloke would shoot them, and then between noon and ten at night they would be butchered.' So the shop was always closed at that time and, if it was school holidays, Peter would stay and watch as his father positioned haunches of meat on the large wooden block, deftly setting about them with his set of knives. He would saw bones, chop parts with a cleaver, or cut strips with a smaller and very sharp looking blade.

At the age of twelve, Peter moved on to Maidenhead Grammar School where he expected to stay until the age of sixteen. His path to a life as a butcher seemed inevitable, but then events conspired to make this journey rather quicker than he or anyone had anticipated.

Just six months into his new school, in 1943, his father fell ill. It was a sausage machine that did him in. Aged forty-eight, a pressure handle on the device flew off and hit him in the mouth. It seemed fine at first, just a broken tooth and a bruised chin. But a large and sinister black blister then appeared in his mouth. It grew into an abscess which poisoned his blood and three weeks later he died.

'It was a big shock of course,' said Peter. 'I was in the house when he died. My eldest brother Norman, who was seventeen, was training at Colchester for the army and a message was sent calling him back.' Norman was needed to run the business alongside his mother Dorothy who looked after the money side. And while the second eldest son Douglas had died of scarlet fever a few years before the war, the family decided that the shop needed another pair of hands.

So at the tender age of twelve-and-a-half, Peter left school and started work at LJ Jennings. His three younger siblings, sister Moran, brother Robert and youngest sister Anne, were spared the labour. But Peter, dressed by his mother in long apron, white shirt and tie, started work and never returned to school.

'Right after my father died, Norman was still on army service. It wasn't until a few months later that he got out of the army on a class B release [a final discharge]', recalled Peter, 'so for a while I had to manage the shop.'

It was a modestly sized butcher. There was the glass front, then a small room behind the shop, a little office and then the fridge; behind was an alley and the slaughterhouse. Before he joined the shop full-time, Peter had delivered small packages around the village and to houses in the surrounding countryside on the company bicycle. With a large wicker basket secured to the front, the cycle's frame bore a smart sign that advertised 'LJ Jennings Purveyor. Twyford Phone 63'.

Now he was progressing from delivery boy to butcher. He had watched his father working so often that he was a natural when it came to cutting the meat himself. And the idea of doing an adult's job before he even reached his teens didn't faze him: 'I don't suppose it worried me at all as I was so young,' he reflected. So he carved up whole ribs of beef, prepared pork into its different parts for sale and plucked, drew and cleaned chickens. 'I could pluck a chicken in three minutes,' he said some sixty years later, 'and I still can.' He was a good salesman too, chatting with the customers, always spirited and smiling. Sometimes he was too efficient.

'I once sold a couple of customers a rather nice few strips of beef that were sitting at the back. My brother was out and when he came back he said to me: "Where's that beef I left back there?" I said I'd sold it. And he went mad and said, "That was my ration."'

And of course wartime meant a little less hard selling and a little more of simply enabling people to buy the amount that rationing allowed. 'I was always cutting out these coupons,' recalled Peter. 'We then had to keep them and pass them to the local Food Office. They then gave us the amount of meat that we were allowed to sell, according to the exact number of registered customers that we had.'

Peter then used his own ingenuity to eke out that ration for the business and their community. 'I could make eighty pounds of sausages out of eight pounds of sausage meat,' he revealed. His trick was to add in, not pork ends, or any dis-carded offal or indeed cardboard, but – to the soaked stale bread he got from the bakery opposite – he added luncheon meat. 'I used to make them every Friday ready for Saturday and I thought they tasted fantastic,' said Peter. 'The Food Office came round the village one week and tested and tasted the sausages made by all the butchers. Ours were the only ones in Twyford that passed the test. I've been making deli-cious sausages ever since.'

Peter and his brother Norman weren't strict when it came to the black market. 'We were always happy and keen to get a bit extra,' he said. 'We were often sold rabbits – which weren't on the ration – by farmers or poachers who came to the back door. I never asked questions; I would just skin them, chop them up and then offer them for sale.'

Peter's youngest brother Bob also showed early entrepreneurial promise. 'He once swapped his school cap for a goat,' said Peter who was more than happy to offer it for sale to his hungry customers. Meanwhile a friend in the village kept pigs at an allotment by Twyford station. 'Every now and then he'd kill one and bring it to us. There was a police station between our butcher and his allotment so he'd have to sneak it past in a van,' recalled Peter. 'One day one of the wheels fell off right outside the station. The police helped fix the van but they never looked inside, thank goodness.

'Another day a lorry from Smithfield pulled up outside. He had four and a quarter sides of beef so I bought them off him and put them in the cellar. If something like that happened then I might say to a customer: "Would you like a bit extra?" We tried to help everybody and if we could get a spare pig then it was very handy. I never thought about getting caught and anyway there weren't that many police about.'

As for his own ration: 'I've always liked every cut of meat and I like vegetables very much. We had roast beef every Sunday – so much so that my mother used to get cross about it. One Sunday she grabbed the beef in a fury and flung it off the table. But I certainly got more than the ration. It's why I've always been fit and healthy.'

Peter's daily routine would start at seven in the morning when his first task was to light the boiler for hot water for the house and shop. Then, after a bowl of porridge, he would open up the butcher and start putting the meat out from the large fridge at the back. He would hang larger pieces up on hooks and place smaller cuts on a marble slab – there were no refrigerated glass cabinets.

'Then I would scrub the benches and cover the floor with a fresh layer of sawdust,' he said. The day would continue with cutting meat and serving customers. Butchery, he felt, was in his veins. 'If I see something in the road I'm after it,' he said. 'It's just my nature.'

With the two brothers serving, their mother Dorothy sat at a desk immaculate in her finest blouse – her hair done, her make up on, her fingers adorned with large glistening rings – and took the money.

After two years of working it occurred to Peter that he ought to be paid. He asked his brother and mother for a weekly wage but they refused – so Peter went on strike. 'I went up the road to a builder's merchants and asked for a job as an electrician.' He returned later to the shop with the news about his new career, at which point they relented and put him on £5 a week.

No bombs fell near LJ Jennings during the war, although Peter recalled hearing the sounds of planes overhead and bombs landing on Reading, some five miles away. Playing football one evening the children saw a plane nose-dive down from the sky. Peter leapt onto his bicycle to the crash site, which happened to be a road bridge nearby. 'I was the first on the scene but there was nothing left of the plane or its occupants.' So he cycled back to the garden at the back of the family shop and resumed his game of football.

Over half a century later Peter could still be found sitting in the same position his mother would have taken in the shop (albeit in a different location – at one point the business had expanded to five shops across the county). He sat at the desk, took the money, did daily deliveries and definitely still took a salary.

The part he had played in the war was just as vital as that of soldiers fighting on the front line. He was one of Lord Woolton's local food heroes; both relied on each other, but did so without being aware of each other's existence.

Postscript

The gravestone of Lord Woolton stands proud in the rustic and grassy cemetery of St Mary's Church, Walberton in West Sussex. Having been born plain Fred Marquis at 163 West Park Street in Ordsall, Salford in Lancashire, on 23 August 1883, he died aged 81 on December 14 1964 as The Right Honourable Frederick James Marquis, First Earl of Woolton at Walberton House, near Arundel. Woolton was given an hereditary earldom in 1956 and the house that demonstrated his ascent up the social ladder would be remembered in the subsidiary title that he took: that of Viscount Walberton.

As newspapers the following day published his obituary, proceedings that afternoon in the House of Lords were altered so that peers could offer their tributes. He was, said the Earl of Longford, 'a many-sided man of far reaching talents and achievements'. The Marquess of Salisbury added that, 'during the war, he never let his fellow countrymen down. He always told them the truth as he understood it, however unpalatable it might be. In this way, I think above all, he gained their trust.'

Collectively the House of Lords sent their sympathy to his surviving son Roger, who inherited the title, and his wife Lady Woolton. This was not of course Maud, for she had died in September 1961. In fact at the age of 79, at noon on Friday 19 October 1962, he married Margaret Thomas, better known as Lyn, the Wooltons' family doctor. Maud had actually died in her arms and out of Woolton's gratitude for her care came affection. Twenty years his junior, she then cared for him as a widower. Woolton installed her in a cottage in the garden, she became his hostess at dinner parties and then he became a little concerned about local gossip. Indeed after their wedding, at the Queen's Chapel at the Savoy in London, he put pen to paper to explain and justify his second marriage. 'What did the village think when they saw my car outside her cottage after I had dined with her?' he wrote.

'I was a lonely old man, in poor health and she twenty years my junior was being very kind to me and there was all there was to it! But was it?' he mused. Woolton had become deeply dependent on her, for her care and for, as he put it, 'the comfort of companionship'.

One sunny afternoon sitting out in the garden at a friend's house, Woolton was feeling a little melancholy. He was there with Lyn and a local friend called Geoffrey. Geoffrey got up to fetch something from the house and when he was out of earshot Woolton said to Lyn: 'I must try to get away from this depression and fear.' Lyn went over to him, put a firm hand on his knee and whispered, 'I will never leave you.'

Back at Walberton, the pair talked. 'Could we go on ignoring the probability of public gossip?' he then reflected, still worrying about his PR and image at that stage of his life. There was one way of dealing with it, of course, but it would break his heart. 'Could we break up this precious friendship?' he said with agony. And so Woolton proposed. He discussed the title she would have to wear and his finances, making the point, as he wrote, 'that it would of course secure her comfort when I died'.

Lyn did not consent at once and was due to go away for a few days with a friend to Wales. 'Think it over,' he said as he waved her off, 'and don't worry, I won't pester you again on the subject.' She did later agree to marry him, or at least gave what he described as 'her reluctant consent' and the couple then waited until after the first anniversary of Maud's death before tying the knot, thus avoiding any accusations of being rather too hasty!

Both Roger and Peggy were very supportive and on the announcement of their forthcoming nuptials the Queen sent a personal telegram. 'I was very surprised at this and very delighted,' he wrote, relieved, no doubt, at not having rocked the establishment with his romantic shenanigans.

On 14 January 1964 he added a final note to the musings on his latest marriage that he had written in October 1962. He wondered if his reader might 'want to know, how it has all turned out,' he wrote, adding: 'I can answer that – as far as I'm concerned. She has made me very happy.'

Woolton liked to have things settled and in order; whether it was family trusts, government departments or his love life. After the Second World War had ended, his desire for stability had focused his mind again on the retail career he had left to join the government. Indeed Churchill's heavy election defeat – which Woolton described as 'shameful' and 'a painful reflection on public gratitude' – meant that he was, as he put it, 'left without occupation'. (His role as Minister of Reconstruction had also been timed to self-destruct the moment peace was declared. And he had tackled the role in reversing Churchill's stated aims for the job; planning for post-war food, homes and jobs.)

But reflecting on a return to Lewis's, he decided that he would better be employed as a less involved chairman of the company (Maud told him: 'You have done all you could do for Lewis's') and that Churchill's defeat in July 1945 had actually galvanised his political instincts. 'I saw that as a consequence the country would be plunged into socialism and much economic disaster.' Lewis's would have to take a back seat while he worked to get what he thought was the sensible party back into power. So he immediately, and for the first time, became a paid-up member of the Conservative Party and joined the Shadow Cabinet.

Churchill now employed Woolton's organisational skills on a matter close to home, he appointed him chairman of the party. This was a perfect task for Woolton because, in his words, 'The organisation of the Conservative Party was the most topsy-like arrangement I had ever come across.'

So he looked at it, dissected and pondered on what to do. He was tempted to venture what he called 'a sound business conclusion and tell the Party that the best thing to do with machinery of this nature was to scrap it and start again'.

But he realised that the organisation was built and run by individuals often working for nothing. So he used a more tender approach and, in working to win the goodwill of members and chairman, build a more effective outfit. From 1946 to 1951 he travelled the country with Maud, both of them making speeches on policy and how a more efficiently run party would have a greater chance at winning the next election. Above all he saw his mission to convince the party, after a heavy defeat, to, as he wrote, 'believe in itself, and in its capacity to convert the electorate to Conservatism'.

The Conservative Party did then win the General Election of 1951 and Woolton was given the added role of Lord President of the Council. It was in this role that he greeted the young Queen – along with Churchill and Attlee – on her return to the UK from Africa following her father George VI's death. He would also play a major role in any Royal succession ceremony.

But then Woolton fell ill and this time not due to his old colonic nemesis. Attending the Conservative Party conference in October 1952 he suffered a perforated appendix and, as he later wrote, was taken to a nursing home where he was attended by '14 doctors and [had] 5 major operations'.

Word reached Churchill that he was dying and with brutal speed he removed Woolton as both chairman of the party and Lord President. Maud heard of this and quickly dispatched a letter of intense anger accusing the Prime Minister of appalling disloyalty to a man who had served his party and country so nobly.

'Churchill had a new experience of having to deal with an infuriated wife who didn't disguise her opinion of him,' wrote Woolton. He reflected that Churchill's actions 'deprived me of any place in the Coronation ceremony'. (King George VI had died on 6 February 1952 and the coronation of Queen Elizabeth II was slated for 2 June 1953)

'I did not die,' wrote Woolton. And Maud's protestations saw him offered the Cabinet post of Chancellor of the Duchy of Lancaster. It was further organised that Woolton was given a role in the subsequent coronation of delivering the Glove to Her Majesty. Not an essential part of the service, it seems that officials conjured up this role as a face-saving gesture. It worked. Woolton sat just behind Prince Philip and travelled just a small distance during the service, presented the Glove to Her Majesty and put it on her hand. The *Manchester Guardian* duly noted that perhaps at future coronations this 'ancient rite will be revived'.

Woolton's restoration to the Cabinet also meant that while weakened from his illness and operation he would be able to retire gracefully from government at a time of his choosing. And this he did some two years later, making a farewell speech as chairman of the party at the Bournemouth conference of 1955.

For his remaining years Woolton continued to serve on various company boards as well as performing his duties as chancellor at Manchester University (one of their halls of residence was renamed Woolton Hall) while spending more time at Walberton where he entertained and set about writing his memoirs.

Now, many years later through the pages of this book,

his diaries, memoirs, notes, letters, essays and private family recollections are brought together the first time to describe and celebrate this monumentally important figure in twentieth-century political and public life.

Paying his own tribute to Woolton the day after he died, post-war Prime Minister Clement (by now Earl) Attlee recalled a conversation he once had about Woolton with an old woman in Devonshire. 'That Lord Woolton,' she said, 'he do sometimes right and sometimes wrong; but we poor folk are beholden to him because he thinks of us.'

Select Bibliography

The Churchill Papers – Churchill College, Cambridge

Hansard (The Official Report) – verbatim reports of proceedings of both the House of Commons and the House of Lords

Food Facts for the Kitchen Front (Collins, 1941)

Papers of Frederick James Marquis, 1st Earl of Woolton (University of Oxford, Department of Special Collections and Western Manuscripts)

Diary of Maud Woolton; 'Really a bit of the life story for her husband Lord Woolton' (Private collection)

Story of Maud Woolton by Lord Woolton – handwritten 1962 (Private collection)

Letters of Lord Woolton and Lady Woolton (Private collection)

Memoirs of The Rt Hon The Earl of Woolton CH, PC, DL, LLD (Cassell, 1959)

The School Food Plan – Henry Dimbleby and John Vincent (July, 2013)

Austerity in Britain; Rationing, Controls and Consumption 1939–1955 – Ina Zweiniger-Bargielowska (Oxford University Press, 2000)

Friends of the People: The Centenary History of Lewis's – Asa Briggs (BT Batsford, 1956)

Nella Last's War: The Second World War Diaries of Housewife, 49 – edited by Richard Broad and Suzie Fleming (Profile Books, 2006)

A Green and Pleasant Land: How England's Gardeners Fought the Second World War – Ursula Buchan (Hutchinson, 2013)

Plenty & Want: A Social History of Food in England from 1815 to the Present Day – John Burnett (Routledge, 1994)

England Eats Out: 1830–Present – John Burnett (Pearson Education, 2004)

The Taste of War; World War Two and the Battle for Food – Lizzie Collingham (Penguin Books, 2012)

Cairo in the War: 1939–45 – Artemis Cooper (Hodder & Stoughton, 2013)

Bitter Ocean: The Battle of the Atlantic, 1939–1945 – David Fairbank White (Simon & Schuster, 2006)

We Are at War – Simon Garfield (Ebury Press, 2005)

Feeding the Enemy in War-Time – Doris Grant (George G Harrap, 1942)

Finest Years; Churchill as Warlord 1940–45 – Max Hastings (Harper Press, 2010)

Rationing in the Second World War: Spuds, Spam and Eating for Victory – Katherine Knight (Tempus Publishing, 2007)

Colwyn Bay Accredited: The Wartime Experience – Cindy Lowe (Bridge Books, 2010)

Wartime Cookbook; Food and Recipes from the Second World War

1939–45 – Anne and Brian Moses (Wayland, 1995)

Colwyn Bay at War; From Old Photographs – Graham Roberts (Amberley Publishing, 2012)

A History of Food in 100 Recipes – William Sitwell (Collins, 2012)

Britain in the Second World War: A Social History – Harold L Smith (Manchester University Press, 1996)

The West End Front: The Wartime Secrets of London's Grand Hotels – Matthew Sweet (Faber & Faber, 2011)

ACKNOWLEDGEMENTS

Firstly I want to thank Iain MacGregor, Publishing Director for Non Fiction at Simon & Schuster in the UK. He commissioned my first book *A History of Food in 100 Recipes* and now has done it again with this one. The idea for *Eggs or Anarchy* sprang from my research for a chapter for that book so it's only appropriate that Iain does this one! But thank you, Iain. I thought this might be a good yarn, was slightly nervous when you became interested in the idea, unsure as to whether I'd be able to stand the story up. But as I delved deeper and deeper I felt I'd got one hell of a scoop. Whether I was right is up to the reader, but I hope you and they are as excited at what I uncovered as I was! Next my thanks go to Humphrey Price who edited the manuscript with such clarity and wisdom. To Karen Farrington for her researching skills. Also to my wonderful agent Caroline Michel for her constant, enthusiastic support and belief and to her editor at PFD, Tim Binding, who gave me such helpful structural comments after I delivered the first draft. The beginning and ending (the latter which makes me cry even though I wrote it!) owes its success to you. Thanks also to Tess and Emily at PFD and to the proofreading team at Heber, to the ever-joyful Em and her uber-cool posse: Tash and Matilda.

I have a particular thank you to make to Simon Woolton, the third earl and my hero's grandson – son of Roger. Your support for the project, your advice, your insight, kindness, hospitality and the loan of family papers and photographs have been invaluable and one of the most rewarding aspects of this project. Thanks to your cousin Charles Sandeman-Allen also, another grandson of Fred, son of Peggy, who helped correct the first draft and who also gave me great advice – as a history lecturer ('Just get writing,' he said as I was flapping around wondering how to tackle the material) as well as the loan of family letters and sight of his own writings on Fred.

Next I need to give thanks to my hero himself, Fred Woolton. He was so fastidious in keeping newspaper cuttings – both friendly and hostile – that his private albums, lent to me by his grandson Simon, were an extraordinary and useful discovery for me. That he wrote his diaries – which remain unpublished – with such honesty and so often with such punchy and modern-sounding language often left me wide-eyed and quietly fist-pumping as I read them in the hushed confines of the Weston Library – part of the Bodleian – at Oxford University (and thanks to the ever-helpful staff there). And to his wife Maud I must offer thanks for her own diary – bolted shut (Simon gave me permission to break it open) – which not even the family had read and which contained amazing stories and comments about such figures as Churchill and the King and Queen and her own takes on events in Woolton's life. Thanks also to Jonathan Weissler who introduced me to his grandfather Harold Gilbert, and to David Jennings – for responding to a plea by me on Twitter – for introducing me to his father, butcher Peter Jennings.

Then I must thank my colleagues at John Brown Media where I have my day job as editor of *Waitrose Food*. My team on that magazine are the most gifted in the business and I would also like to thank our CEO, Andrew Hirsch, who never fails to encourage my work in the food world when I'm not acting as his private restaurant-booking concierge. Thanks also to our MD, Libby Kay. And also thanks to my colleagues at Waitrose – my most esteemed client – for their friendship and support, particularly to Ollie Rice, Alison Oakervee, Rupert Ellwood and Rupert Thomas. Thanks also to the Plumpton posse: to my wonderful children Alice and Albert, to whom this book is dedicated, and to your quite exceptional mother, my wife Laura. Thanks also to my extraordinary and true friends: Toby and Gaby, Jasper and Vanessa and Alastair.

Picture Credits

346

INDEX

347

Index

Index

Index

Index

Index